The Bl
Covenant

Book One in the Medici Warrior Series

by Emily Bex

Foundations Publishing Company
Brandon, MS 39047
www.foundationsbooks.net

The Blood Covenant
Book One in the Medici Warrior Series
By: Emily Bex

Cover by Dawne Dominique
Edited by Laura Ranger

ISBN: 978-1-64583-034-4

Published in the United States of America

"From the power portals of Florence, Italy to Washington, D.C., Emily Bex breathes life into the realm of the undead. Blood Covenant combines the hedonistic jet-setting pleasures of billionaire romance and the dirty little secret thrills of a dead sexy vampire!

"Shade's a gorgeous billionaire immortal, sex-of-your-dreams-lover, warrior-king who owns a slew of quality vineyards. What more do you want? For centuries, he's been a vampiric master among masters and carries royal blood from a golden age when the great Medici family ruled Florence. A passionate lover with a dangerous past, he's since learned patience and knows that what he desires will come to him willingly, and what he desires most is a vivacious redhead. Too bad Shade's true business and existence cannot be publicized... The language is immediate, and the story fast paced. I loved Kate's down to earth sensibility and the way she fostered Shade's protective instincts. This is a slow burn romance that will provide many happy hours of reading."

– Katalina Leon
USA Today Bestselling Author

Dedication

The Medici Warrior book series is dedicated to all the dreamers, the hopeless romantics, and to my partner in crime, Johanna Morisette.

Acknowledgements

This book could not have been written without the help of my collaborator, Johanna Morisette. She dragged me reluctantly into a world of vampires and inspired me to write. She had the initial vision for Shade and was instrumental in the development of his character. Throughout the seven years it took to write this series, she remained my sounding board for the development of the storyline. These characters, and this saga, would not exist if not for her constant support and input which kept me motivated to keep pushing forward.

Table of Reference

Italian words to know:

Amore	Love
Bambino(s)	Baby/babies
Bastardo	Bastard
Bel	Beautiful
Belezza	Beauty
Bellissimo	Very beautiful
Buonasera	Good evening
Cazzo	Fuck
Dipendenza	Addiction
Dolce	Sweet
Fratello	Brother
Grazie	Thank you
Madre	Mother
Mi/mio	My
Moltobella	Very beautiful
Padre	Father
Per favore	Please
Per Sempre	Forever
Rosso	Red
Scusi	Excuse me
Si	Yes
Sorella	Sister
Stupido	Stupid
Ti amo	I love you

Prologue

He knew when he met her how it would end.

Throughout the years, Shade had often wondered if, given the chance, he could have walked away. He was drawn to her like no other, the light in his darkness. From the moment he laid eyes on her, he knew she was the one, but in binding her to him, he had sealed her fate, and his. Maybe, if he had been stronger, turned his back on her, or let her walk away that first night, he could have spared them both.

He has no regrets for himself. He loves her with a passion that burns with the heat of a thousand suns. For him, the risk was always worth the reward. There was no price he was not willing to pay to be with her. When he asks, she says she would change nothing, but still, he can't help but wonder.

1

Alec circulated among his guests at the lavish cocktail party. He called them friends, but they weren't his friends, not really. They knew almost nothing about him, at least not the real him. They knew his name was Alec Canton, and he was a senator from the great state of Connecticut. They knew he had his eyes on the prize, with intentions of ruling as President. But they didn't know he was a vampire, a master.

He lived among mortals, undetected, which wasn't an easy feat. There were many that would try to bring him down. Mortal threats he could manage, it was the immortals he had to pay attention to. He had a legion of warriors who defended him, or who were supposed to defend him. But their skills were lacking. In the past, he hadn't put much effort into hiring his warriors. While he was a master, he wasn't a warrior. He'd learned to survive off his wits, not his brawn. He preferred to leave the physical fights to the vampires who were born with those skills.

He easily assimilated into the mortal realm and as a day-walker, was able to move among them freely. He'd come to recognize his legion of warriors were a rather haphazard bunch who wouldn't serve him well going forward.

That brought him to tonight, and this soiree he'd asked Rissa to host for him. Larissa, his social high-brow mate, had been selected from a pool of mortals for her social standing, her moneyed background, and her connections, all of which would serve him well in his bid for political power. Of course, her beauty was a given, and the fact she was equally as ambitious and manipulative as he, was also a plus. So, he'd turned her, and thankfully, she inherited his gift as a day-walker. Together, they'd rule this town.

Rissa had invited his political cronies, the press, D.C. social climbers, and a few friends, because Shade needed to see them. He needed to see Alec's world, and the people who populated it, if he was going to re-structure his warriors and find someone to lead them.

Shade was standing off to the side, observing, taking in everything, missing nothing. Shade Medici, he was another master and a warrior, but not just any warrior. He was *the* warrior and the whole purpose of this little get together.

He and Shade had known each other for centuries and he'd asked him here from Florence to work with his legion of warriors, check out his lifestyle, and figure out where they needed to go from here.

***

Shade was taking stock of his current surroundings here in the middle of Georgetown. He'd never taken a long-term assignment in the States before. He was the descendent of Medici royalty; the Warrior of Warriors. He was a King and High Master vampire. Not that he went around with a nametag on his chest. In this line of work, it was best not everyone knew who he was.

He administered to his allies in the vampire world and provided masters with warriors for protection, fighting battles for territory, or helping them establish their own legion of warriors. He'd already conquered Europe and had expansion on his mind. He had a wandering warrior's heart and his businesses needed to expand into modern times, blending the old European traditions into the new world.

To the mortals, he was known only for his fine wines and expansive vineyards. More than two thirds of his wine production was shipped to the mortals, but he also made a specific brand exclusively for immortals. They called it Midnight, a secret mixture of blood and wine that took the edge off until a vampire could properly feed.

Alec was the master here, and he took this mortal shit seriously. Shade had never understood why a vampire would have the good fortune to be born immortal, and then wish to live as mortal. Who was he to judge? He was here for money, territory and power. Alec was his pathway to achieving all three. Alec needed his skills if he thought this ragtag bunch of punks were warriors. They were useless, and if Alec sought protection, he'd better figure that out sooner rather than later.

Shade sipped the Midnight and watched the roomful of pompous mortal bastards, inflated with their own sense of self-importance. He listened to their gossip and the ball-breaking deals that always went down outside the office. Some things between the two worlds weren't very different.

He scoped out the women. Hell, he was always up for a good night of feeding and fucking. But none of these women were to his taste. They all had their noses in the air, thinking he was below their means. Little did they know, he could buy and sell all of them many times over. As for the women, he could drop them to their knees with one look, and he never had to chase. They always came to him.

He watched as Alec worked the crowd, the mortals fawning all over him and Shade smiled. The bastard always got what he wanted, but tonight, he was going to change that. He watched Alec walk toward him and knew he wanted to know his assessment of the mercenaries he'd hired. Shade didn't play games when it came to his warriors and his fighting skills. Alec was going to hear the truth. His warriors sucked.

Alec approached him as Shade carefully observed the crowd. "So, what do think? Did you meet my warriors today?"

Shade began, "I met them, but I wouldn't call them warriors. A pack of unorganized punks with no skills is more what I would call them, brother."

Alec creased his brow. "I know they aren't up to the caliber of Medici warriors. I didn't kid myself about that. Can you work with them? Whip them into shape?"

Throwing back the last of the Midnight in his crystal wine glass, Shade gave him a look. "No one is up to Medici caliber, that's why I am here. I can work with them. It's going to take me nine months minimum, more like a year, and that is the low side of my estimate, brother. I don't have much to work with. I can bring in some of my boys, show them how we do it Medici style, and then see if they want to run for the rooftops or stay and play."

Alec ran his hand through his hair, cursing. He was thinking this was going to cost him a fortune. He knew what Shade wanted. He owned every vineyard in Tuscany now, and a few in France and Greece. A money offer wouldn't be nearly as enticing as property with an established vineyard. Even if it did need work, it would get his attention.

"Then how about this," Alec said, "your services for one year and in exchange, I deed over the 3,000-acre property I own in Virginia. It has a house that needs some work and has vineyards on about 800 acres. The plants are established, but not well maintained, and you have room for expansion. The assessed value was coming in around twenty million. That should cover it, and you can live on the property so you won't have additional living expenses while you're here. Teleport into D.C. What do you think? That's a fair offer, Shade."

Shade chuckled. "Fair? You bastard. You think training warriors is easy? Not on your life. No, I am not going to settle for one little piss-ant piece of land in the middle of bum-fuck, Virginia. I want the Medici's to go coast to coast, and you have the means to make it happen.

"I've seen the property, Alec. It will cost me a fortune to renovate the damn place and get the vineyards in working condition. I will need to hire people to get the vineyards up to par, not to mention renovate that house to make it livable—the whole nine yards and then some. But..." Here Shade raised a finger. "You have something else I want, so let's get serious and put your dick back in your pants. I'm done with comparing now."

Alec grimaced. "Yes, it'll take an investment of time and money, I acknowledge that. But it's twenty million, brother. What's it going to take? I mean, you can turn that property around. Produce Midnight here in the States, save on all the import costs. This could be huge for you."

Shade pulled on his tie. He hated wearing suits. He was more comfortable in leathers and boots, but this damn game playing with the mortals was what he had to do.

"First of all, I need good vineyards to produce quality wine and I do nothing but quality. I need a working winery on the property, and I must tell you, that doesn't come cheap. And you forgot one detail. The property sits in the middle of Maximus' territory. It's not a given, Alec. Don't take me for a fool. Max may not sit idly by, while I start expanding my business."

Alec flagged the butler down to bring them another round. This was going to be a long negotiation. "Maximus is an ally, you know that. I've owned the property for years. We have an understanding. I don't tread on his turf, and he doesn't tread on mine. If you want, I'm sure he'll endorse the deal. Will that make you happy?"

The butler handed them both another glass of Midnight. Shade took his time, glanced around at the dandies of D.C. and sipped his Midnight. With every second he stalled, he knew Alec's ass got tighter. Negotiations over territory took time, and Shade had all of eternity.

"That may be, Alec, but when I take this property, you know as well as I do I intend to keep it. Maximus and I will have to figure out a deal, fight it out or whatever it comes to, so don't blow it off like it is nothing. Let's face the facts here, you don't want this place. I know you. What in the hell are you ever going to do with it? Rissa would never step foot in the country, she might break a damn nail. So, I will take it off your hands. Throw in the Napa Valley property with the established vineyards and the new house , and I might take your ass seriously."

Alec looked astounded. "Are you fucking kidding? You want the Napa property too? That piece of land is close to 4,000-acres and sitting in Marin County. It has to be close to fifty million. I grant the property in California is in better shape, the vineyards producing and the house is new. But you'll be here on the east coast, and you still have your coven in Italy to take care of. Spreading yourself a little thin, don't you think?"

Shade slapped him on the back. "It's called expansion, Alec. I have no desire to stay in one spot for long. Just being here for a year takes me away from a lot of my duties. I have Marco, my Second-In-Command, taking care of business in Florence. I have a large coven to take care of, a lot of warriors, they all collect a paycheck that comes out of my pocket."

Shade paused to take a drink from his glass and continued, "You want me, you want my skills... decide. I'm looking where you are right now, where you're going. You will need me and my warriors for a very long time to come. Your investment in me will take you into the future. You think some mortal secret service idiot is going to protect you like a Medici warrior? Think again, because you know when you hit the big time, the Council is going to bust your ass for it. They don't like you mingling with the mortals as it is. Think about it. You know what I want. The deal is on the table, your call."

Alec sighed. He knew there was no way out of this. If he wanted Shade, it was going to cost him the Virginia *and* California properties. If he said no, Shade would be on to the next job before the words were out of his mouth. One thing about the European vampires, they kept with the old traditions. There were no schools for training warriors in the States, and it showed. "You drive a hard bargain, my friend. But for that much money, you damn sure better protect my ass. Otherwise, I'll tell Rissa to be sure to get a refund. You've got a deal. Both pieces of property will be deeded over. I'll have my lawyer draw up the contract."

Shade smiled wickedly. "Deal, Senator. Now, one more thing. There is a place right outside of Georgetown. Run down old house, not sure what in the hell it was used for. Your warriors told me you own the place. The inside is gutted, perfect for creating a command post for the warriors. A central place for them to meet, get their orders and allow me to track their activities. It's a Dead House, brother. Are you up for me using it for my own purposes? I need to have total control of these goons, Alec. No interference. They need to know going in, I don't take bullshit and what I say...goes."

Alec swirled his drink in his glass. "Dead House, that's a good name for it. That place has been vacant for years. I thought I might renovate it, but never got around to it. Was going to sell it, but the realtor said I'd need to do the renovation first. So, it just sat there. Do whatever you want with it. And I'll tell my warriors you're in charge. They all know you, know your reputation. They're all mercenaries. You won't have a problem. We'll set up a meeting with them."

Shade smiled. "Sounds like a plan, brother. I met Tomas, and to be honest, he may be the only one who is going to be of any use to me from the start. He has some skills. I can use him to help train the others. We will go through them all, see where they fall, they either stay or leave. It won't take me long to decide, trust me."

Alec shook his hand. "I'm glad we have a deal. Now, if you'll excuse me, I need to mingle. Politics...it's all about who you know, brother. Everyone here tonight is someone in my circle; other politicians, press, the social climbers, power brokers, lobbyists, and a few of Rissa's clients. Just get a feel for them. There're only mortals here tonight. No other vamps. But these are the people I'm around all the time. I don't sense any danger with this group, but I wanted you to get a sense of the people in my social circle."

Shade emptied his glass and looked around the room. It was a sorry excuse of a social circle.

2

Shaking Alec's hand, Shade watched him work the room. He was one slick politician, but Shade had bested him at his own game. Rule number one when doing business, don't get sucked in by the first offer. Shade knew what he wanted going in and was prepared to walk. It was the ace up his sleeve.

He stood back, watching the people in casual conversations, all mortals, but never harmless. The deadliest enemies Canton had could be right in front of him, and Shade always kept his enemies close. Alec was useless as a warrior, but he was definitely one personable wheel and deal vamp. Alec needed him much more than he needed Alec, but they went back a long way, and each of them had secrets they wished their enemies to never know. He looked around their classic Georgetown home. It was elegant and tastefully decorated.

His eye caught Alec's lovely mate, Rissa. She was a beauty, and not unlike the other women here, had her nose in the air. There was a wild, wicked side to her, just as there was in Alec. They were made for each other. Shade watched her laugh and schmooze with the crowd, the darling of G-town they called her. What a joke. There wasn't a fucking thing *darling* about Rissa, but she could hold her own on the business end of any deal. He saw her smile and wave at someone across the room. His eyes went immediately to her target.

Shade's attention was captured by this petite woman. She couldn't be more than five foot three in her bare feet. He was typically drawn to statuesque women. He preferred strong vampire females who were his equal and this one was clearly mortal. She had a mass of crimson hair that tumbled down her back and swayed when she turned her head. Her bangs framed her face and hung almost to her lashes. Her eyes were large and changed color depending on the light, from a dark brown to deep amber. They peered out from under bright red hair. Her skin was pale. No, not pale. White. She was lily white. Her lips were soft and full. She wore a red lipstick, which only intensified their fullness against her pale, white skin. Her breasts were full, her waist tiny and the curves of her hips and ass had him entranced. She wore a simple, white silk blouse and a tight black skirt that clung to her slender frame.

The black stiletto heels were all straps that wound their way across her feet and around her slender ankles. Her toes were painted bright red, as were the nails on her hands. She looked more elegant in her simple attire, than all the other women in the room who were over-dressed to impress.

He made his way over to Rissa, nodding his head in the direction of the redhead, and asked for her name.

Rissa looked up. "Her? She's no one who could hold your attention for long, warrior. She's not your type. We went to college together."

Shade raised an eyebrow at her response. "I wasn't aware you knew my type, Rissa."

Rissa laughed. "Shade, I've seen some of the women you've been with. I think I have a good idea. And let's just say she's no match for you."

He swirled the Midnight in his glass and looked at her impatiently. "I don't think you told me her name."

Rissa sighed. "What in hell is it about her that has you so worked up? She's nothing. Her name is Kate. Kate Reese. But you're wasting your time. You'll scare the hell out of her. Besides, she's mortal." She laughed and flung her blonde locks back from that highbrow face of hers.

Shade ran the name over his tongue… Kate Reese. He walked across the room to stand closer to her. He picked up the scent of her perfume. Roses, she smelled like roses. He listened to her talking to the other guests. Her voice was soft and breathy…soothing. It calmed and excited him at the same time. Then she laughed. He watched as she threw her head back. Her hair swayed and her laughter sounded like music to his ears. She had a contagious laugh that made the other people around her laugh along. She lit up the room without even trying. She was completely unaware of the stares she drew from the other men. And they *were* watching her. He could read their thoughts and feel their emotions as a few of them wished they had that sweet ass under them, when the night ended. For some reason, the thought bothered him. They were dogs, mortal abusers who wished for nothing but a good lay and to move on. He knew the type. Hell, he was that type. He didn't see one mortal in this fucking room who deserved her. He felt an intense need to protect her. She drew him in. How strange, this small mortal female could bring this out in him. He'd not even spoken to her yet, but that was about to change.

The conversation was breaking up. She was turning away from the group and turned to face him. She stopped short and looked up at him through her red hair. His breath left him. Those dark eyes pulled him in. Their eyes locked for a few seconds before she looked down. Her thick lashes fanned out across her cheeks. When she looked up again, he nodded his head at her.

"Your glass looks almost empty, *mi amore*. May I get you a refill?" He watched as she blushed.

She looked away and stammered a reply, "I, uh...I've probably had too much already, so...no...but, thank you."

She appeared uncomfortable when he stepped so near. He had to know what she was thinking, so he invaded her thoughts. He picked up fleeting impressions. She was wondering who he was, taking note of his height, as he towered over her. She felt intimidated, cornered. He noticed her breath quickened when he spoke, and she found his Italian accent disarming. She thought he was breathtakingly handsome, as she noted he was wearing a suit clearly hand tailored to fit his frame. He watched as her eyes scanned his hair, dark and long, but tastefully tied back in that loose ponytail at his neck. He waited until she locked eyes with him again and was struck by their piercing blue.

"*Scusi,* my manners." He lifted her hand to his lips and bowed slightly. "Allow me to introduce myself. My name is Shade Medici."

He felt her nervousness, but she liked what she saw. The feeling was mutual.

"I'm Kate Reese."

"Kate. What a beautiful name."

He knew she was affected by him, as most women were. She looked away, and he knew she was having a difficult time maintaining eye contact. He felt her pulse quicken and watched as she blushed. "You are friends with Rissa, *si*? She said you went to college together."

"You know Rissa? Are you a client?" She looked around the room for Rissa to avoid looking at him. She felt trapped in his gaze.

He smiled at her discomfort. "Alec and I are old friends, so I have known Rissa for as long as she has been with him."

He knew she was as drawn to him as he was to her, and yet he could tell she sensed there was something different about him. He watched her eyes dart around the room, looking for a way to bolt and run.

Kate stammered. "I...I'm...uh, I hate to rush off, but I was just leaving. I've already stayed longer than I intended."

He watched her look about for a place to set her empty glass when he finally reached out and took the glass from her hand. His hand touched hers and he felt her pull back slightly as they both responded to what felt like a spark of an electric current.

He smiled at her. She was timid and sweet. He liked the look of her soft white skin against the contrast of his dark olive complexion.

"Do you have a wrap, Kate Reese?"

"Wrap? Yes, it's in, uh..."

"I believe your wrap is in the study. Allow me?"

He offered her his arm and watched as she hesitantly placed her small hand around his elbow. She glided in those stilettos. He slid his eyes behind her to watch that beautiful ass swish and sway on the way to the study.

She identified her dark green suede coat from the pile. He noticed the label inside. It was made in Italy...leather from Florence. He smiled. He held the coat for her, as she slipped her arms into the sleeves, then he slid the coat onto her slender shoulders. His hands grazed her hair and neck. He loved the feel of her, touching her. He loved her petite stature to his height and mass. He watched as she pulled those long crimson locks from the collar of her coat and flung them to her back. He was assailed, once again, by the scent of roses. She turned and looked into his eyes again, then quickly looked down. She was unable to maintain eye contact with him for more than a few seconds. "Do I make you nervous, Kate?"

"No, no, no...I, really, I just need to go. Thank you." She scooted past him in the study and back to the formal living room, with all the guests as he followed behind her. Kate approached Rissa to offer her thanks for the invitation, and to let her know she was leaving.

When she turned to leave, she bumped into Shade. "Oh, sorry, I..."

"No apology necessary, *mi amore*." He chuckled at her and the frenzy she'd worked herself into trying to escape him.

She rushed past him to the front door and stepped outside into the crisp air of the fall night. She took a deep breath of cold air. She thought, *What just happened? I've never been tongue-tied in front of a man before. Shade. Even his name sounds mysterious. I'll ask Rissa about him. Or maybe I'll just leave well enough alone and know when I'm out of my league.*

He watched her from the window, as she walked to her car and then she was gone. He couldn't get the image of her out of his head.

He heard Rissa as she stepped up behind him. In her spiteful laugh, she commented, "Like I said, warrior, you'll scare the hell out of her."

He looked at her, hiding his annoyance at her response. "Ah, patience, Rissa. The situation calls for patience."

Rissa shook her head. "Shade, there are at least fifty women in this room who'd climb in your bed tonight. Each one giving you exactly what you crave."

He smiled. "Rissa, if you give up the details I need, I will leave you alone, and you can get back to Alec's cronies, which I am quite sure you cannot wait to do."

Rissa stared at him with her big blue eyes. "I can't imagine how that timid little mouse could please a hot ticket like you, Shade Medici. You're a player. You're the wandering Casanova of vampires. There's no way Kate could keep you entertained. She can't keep a man to save her life. There's a reason they all leave her. She can't hold a mortal's attention, let alone yours. Is it sex, or do you just desperately need to feed? I can't figure it out."

Chuckling, he winked at Rissa. "You do not need to concern yourself with how serious I am. Just tell me where she lives, where she works. That's all I need, trust me."

Shaking her head, she sighed. "Fine, you want details, you can have them. I don't give a fig what the hell you do with her. It makes no difference to me. She lives in Arlington, has a condo around Pentagon City. You should be able to find it. Just don't expect to knock on her door and jump her bones. She's Miss Prim and Proper. You scare the hell out of her, which should be obvious to you after she almost knocked down half my guests getting to the front door. She works for the Brunswick Agency, based here in D.C. They do national magazine ads, commercials, marketing campaigns, and such. Kate refers some of her high-profile clients to me. She's been a good resource. Maybe you could use that as an angle. You need someone to market your wines here in the States."

Downing the last of the Midnight, he set the glass on the table and smiled at her. "Thank you for the information, but let's get one thing clear. I need no angle to get a woman, they usually come to me and so will this one."

Turning on his heels, he headed out the door, and found his journey took him straight to a little condo in Arlington.

3

Shade teleported directly to Pentagon City and had no problem finding her condo. As he checked the listing of residents, he found she was on the seventh floor. He landed directly inside her home, shadowing his presence and blocking any detection; a handy little vampire trick. He could watch her without her ever knowing he was there.

She hadn't arrived home yet. Teleporting these short distances was instantaneous, faster than any mortal human eye could see. He used the time to walk around her condo. It was clean, organized and very feminine. No dog to greet her, no cat to ignore her. No pets here at all. The furniture was comfortable, her style eclectic. She decorated in greys, blacks and white, which sounded harsh, but she had made it soft. She had lots of books; novels, histories, biographies, travel. She was well read, with a diversity of interests. She had interesting art on the walls. He picked up a few pictures she had in frames on the tables; family and friends, at the beach, in the mountains, standing in front of recognizable backdrops like New York, San Francisco, Paris, London, and Hong Kong. For a mortal female, she was well traveled.

He heard the key in the door. He hovered in the corner and watched her as she slammed her back against the door, something had her spooked. He had this overwhelming urge to protect her, watch over her, and he'd be damned if he knew why. He just knew he wouldn't settle, unless he knew she was protected, home, safe and sound.

***

Kate drove home through Washington D.C. traffic to condo. She hoped the traffic would have thinned out by now, but D.C. traffic never stopped. She parked the red Miata in the underground garage and headed for the elevator. As she waited for the elevator doors to open, she thought she heard something behind her and turned suddenly, her keys held in her hand like a weapon, but there was nothing there. She hated this parking garage. It never failed to creep her out.

The elevator doors opened, and she quickly moved inside and pushed number seven. Seven was her lucky number. She lived in unit number 711, doubling her luck. She remembered being so excited to buy this place, giving her a view across the Potomac River and the D.C. skyline. She unlocked the door and stepped inside, closing it behind her, and stood with her back against the door.

The first image in her head, the only image in her head, was of him, those piercing blue eyes, and those long black lashes. "Enough!" She shook her head, trying to rid herself of him.

Tossing the keys on the side table in the entry hall, she walked to her bedroom. The drapes were open, and she stepped to the large picture window, looking out at the lights, and the traffic on the Arlington Memorial Bridge. From here, she could see the Pentagon, the Jefferson Memorial, the Lincoln Memorial, and the Washington Monument. She never got tired of this view. Her family thought she was insane to live this close to D.C. They were always worried about the crime. But she felt safe here...sort of...most of the time.

She unbuttoned her blouse and slipped it off her shoulders, tossing it on the bed. She unzipped the skirt and slid it down her hips, letting it puddle at her feet before stepping out of it. She sat on the bed, crossed her legs and unstraped the black shoes.

She kicked her shoes off and stood. As she started to remove her bra, she felt a shiver down her spine. She turned and looked around the room. Walking back to the window, she drew the drapes, then removed the bra and tossed it on the bed. Sitting back down, she unhooked her stockings from the garter, then slid them down her legs, tossing them aside before unhooking the garter belt. She walked to the closet, wearing only a lace thong. She pulled her robe off the hook, slid it on, and tied the belt at her waist. She turned suddenly. Again, shivers ran down her spine. She couldn't shake the feeling of someone watching her.

That man...Shade...she couldn't get his face out of her head. *Get a grip, Kate Reese! You took a solemn oath in front of Shannon over wine at Happy Hour, one hand on your heart and the other on the wine list...no more men!*

She walked back to her bed and piled her pillows against the headboard, grabbed the remote and turned on the TV, pushing mute. Digging into her purse, she pulled out her cell phone and hit dial for her best friend, Shannon.

Laying her head back on the pillows as the phone rang, she wondered if it would go to voice mail. It was still pretty early on a Saturday night for Shannon, and then she heard her voice. "Hey, you...I thought you were going out tonight?"

Kate laughed. "I did go out. You know, some of us do manage to get home before the sun comes up." She put her phone on speaker and laid the phone on the bed.

"Yeah, well...some of us know how to have more fun than others. Just sayin'! So, what were you up to again?"

"I was at that big cocktail party Rissa was throwing for Alec. A lot of politicians were there, the rich and famous...rubbing elbows."

Shannon responded, "Hmm, sounds boring."

Kate pulled the sheet over her legs. "Well, it was pretty stiff. But I did meet a guy there."

"What? You met someone? Did you get his number?"

Kate sighed. "No, I didn't get his number. I barely got his name. Shan, I was a hot mess. I couldn't even talk. I sounded like a complete idiot. I don't think I'll ever see him again. I practically broke my neck trying to get out of there. Besides, I took a pledge, remember? A sacred oath. Swore on the wine list, so that must be binding. No more men!"

"Yeah, well that pledge was after Ethan cheated on you for the hundredth time, and you finally got a clue. And I think you were on your second bottle of wine, so I'm not sure it counts. Legally, you may not have been 'of sound mind', as they say. So, who is this handsome stranger? He must be handsome if he left you speechless."

Kate was sketching aimless circles on the sheet with her finger. "Okay, could we not talk about Ethan? Anyway, I'm not sure who he is. He's friends with Alec. I mean, seriously, that's all I know about him. Well, I know he's Italian, because he has an accent. His name is Shade. Shade Medici. And that's it. That's all I know. Other than how he looks; tall, dark and dangerous. I mean, really Shannon, I couldn't even talk. He took an empty glass from my hand, his hand touched mine, and it was...electric. He helped me put my coat on and I could barely breathe. I made such a fool of myself. I don't even know how to fix that. And to be honest, I'm not sure I can. If I saw him again, it would happen all over again, me coming undone."

Shannon's laughter rang out in the room. "Oh girl...you've got it bad. Just call Rissa. Get his number. Fuck him and get it over with."

No matter how long they'd been friends, Shannon's brashness always shocked her. "Shannon! Oh my god, I barely know his name. And seriously? Isn't this what gets me in trouble every time? I mean, I fall hard before I know anything about them. You said I extend my trust too easily."

"Hey, I wasn't talking about a relationship, just a hook-up. Get him out of your system and move on. Jeez, Kate, you're so puritanical. Not every guy you meet has to be relationship material."

"I can't do that. If there's nothing there, nothing I think could be long-term, I just can't. And yes, I know it's old fashioned. I'm out of touch with the times. You've told me a million times. And this guy...he's way out of my league, trust me. I mean, you could tell he was wearing an expensive hand-tailored suit. He looked older, sophisticated, not a lot older, late thirties, probably around Alec's age. I don't know. I can't imagine, after my bumbling act tonight, he'd have any interest in me."

Shannon gave her a lecture, "You think too much. Really, Kate, men are men, regardless of how expensive their suits are. Call Rissa tomorrow and get his number. You'll never get him out of your head if you don't. Just meet him for a drink or something."

Kate stood up and walked to the dresser, letting her robe drop to the floor, she pulled a nightie out of the drawer, slipped it over her head, and walked back to the bed.

"Yeah, maybe. I don't know. I'll see if I can get up the nerve. Hey, want to meet me for dinner tomorrow, if you don't have plans?"

"Sure, I can do that. Since you have Italian on your mind, want to meet at that Italian place on H Street?"

Kate laughed at her. "You're relentless. But Italian sounds good. I'm tired, Shan. Going to turn in. See you around seven tomorrow evening then?"

Shannon yawned through her goodbyes. "See ya, and pleasant dreams."

Kate shook her head as she plugged her phone into the charger by her bed, and turned out the light, sliding beneath the cool sheets. She closed her eyes, but all she saw was him.

***

Shade followed her to the bedroom, watching her ass swish and sway in that tight skirt. *Cazzo*, it mesmerized him. He stood back along the wall of windows and crossed his arms over his chest, watching her as she undressed. As she slipped off her blouse, the silk was as white as her skin. He felt his breath catch in his throat at those delicious orbs of smooth, white flesh pouring generously over the edge of the lace bra she wore.

As her garments dropped to the floor, his cock raised and the beast inside him growled.

He watched her every movement, his eyes glued to her. Her motions were so liquid, unaffected and nonchalant. She had no idea what she did to a man—especially this man. She wasn't trying to be sexy or alluring, she was just being herself. He saw a flash of fear across her face, and knew she'd sensed something. She couldn't possibly see him, but it intrigued him that a mortal could occasionally feel his presence. Something about her touched him. She spoke to the beast living in the very core of him, calling out to him on a primal level. He wanted to hold her in his arms, clutch her to his chest and protect her, reassure her nothing would ever touch her again, not if he had anything to do with it.

He told himself to be patient. She'd run like a wild deer, if she knew what he was. She walked right past him and drew the drapes closed. Her nearness made him almost lose control, as the beast struggled for release. He wanted to reach out and run his fingers in that crimson silk. *My bel rosso*. He moved to the opposite side of the room. She climbed onto the bed and he sat down in a delicate French chair to observe her, his big frame barely fitting. He felt uncharacteristically jealous when he saw her pick up her phone. He wondered if there was a male she called to check in with. The very thought of it put his beast on edge, ready to claim her, his fangs aching to punch through.

He heard a female voice on the other end of the call and calmed down. *What the fuck, Shade? She doesn't belong to you. She doesn't even know you.* But he was determined she would. He wasn't letting go of this one, he wanted her and not just sexually, the beast inside him had come alive. He was feeling an emotion he thought was long dead and had his blood rushing through his veins, his beast sitting on his haunches, anxiously waiting. The black bastard hadn't done that for about 100 years. She laughed and it made him smile, his heart lurched at the trilling sound of her happiness. All he could think about was how he could pleasure her, how he could make her laugh like that for him.

She gestured with her hands when she talked. Shade was intrigued, as there was no one there to see the gestures. Well, no one other than him.

He listened to the conversation of the two females and watched her face, her expressions as she talked, and talk she did. It amused him, her facial expressions, the tone of her voice, the way she wrinkled her nose...and those *eyes*, like deep dark pools, *fuck,* he could get lost in them. No, she didn't get his number, but he definitely got hers.

He smiled when she said no more men, no problem there, *bel rosso*. He was no ordinary man. He growled softly when he heard that mortal bastard cheated on her. *What the hell? Was the crazed idiot blind?*

He listened as she described him to her friend. *Oh yes, I am most handsome, but I won't be a stranger for long.*

He loved she remembered his name. He slid his hand through his hair and smiled. Somehow that pleased him, more than he thought it would. The sound of his name rolling off those ruby red lips had, him undone and he adjusted himself in the fucking little chair. *Oh, bel rosso, electric is just the beginning, the next time I touch you, you will light up everywhere. You will see me again, not a problem. I have no intention of leaving here until the sun is up.*

Everything about her intrigued him. He watched the pain roll across her face and how her body stiffened when she mentioned Ethan. He heard her friend suggest a 'hook-up.' His *bel rosso* would not be a hook-up. He'd had enough women in his life to kill dozens of mortal men in sexual bliss. He quickly blocked the images of his darkest days from his mind. They were worse than hook-ups, they were animalistic, barbaric, and he pushed the memories from his head. He listened to her words, her heart spoke deeply, and she described herself as old-fashioned. He wanted her. He loved everything about her. He felt she'd been placed in his path, the perfect woman dropped in front of him from out of nowhere. He knew something special sat right before his eyes.

This would be no walk in the park. She thought he was out of her league, she knew nothing about his world, or who he was, *what* he was, and he'd have a hard road ahead of him. He knew winning a mortal female heart wouldn't be easy. It wasn't looked upon in his world as acceptable, and because of who he was, it could be a disaster. He didn't care, she'd captured him, and he needed more. Besides, his beast was clawing at his insides, demanding her. She called to him like an addiction, his cocaine, and all he could feel and see, was her.

He watched as she sliped into a soft peaceful sleep. He stood beside the bed and looked at her, with those long beautiful lashes against her cheeks. Her crimson locks lay across the white cotton of the pillowcase and spread like a silken sea of red, wave after wave. He couldn't control the need to touch her. His hand slowly slid up her bare arm, soft and white and warm. He lifted her hand and kissed it gently. She wouldn't awaken just yet. He breathed in her rose scent and his cock responded instantly. She smelled so innocent, fresh and sun kissed.

He closed his eyes as his hand slid into her hair, fisting it gently, feeling the silky strands fall between his fingers. She was the most beautiful woman he'd ever laid eyes on, and he watched her move and moan in her sleep. Such a soft, sweet moan, and he wanted desperately to hear it as she writhed beneath him.

He felt her awaken. He covered himself in shadow and watched her sit up straight. She was thinking about her dream of him. As she flopped back down, he waited once more until she was asleep and touched his hand to her head to enter her dreams. Dream-walking was his gift, every vampire had a special talent, and he had his down to a science. He could see what she dreamt, or make her dream whatever he chose, for good or evil. Inside her dream, he stared at her with his icy blue eyes and watched as she looked back at him. *No need to run, mi amore.* He let her see him, without being intimidated, or scared. He showed no emotion and kept his distance. He let her walk closer to him and slid his hand in her hair, kissed her delicate lily-white hand and let her feel no fear from him. He loved how she looked at him with innocent eyes, but there was something more in them, something alluring and sexy. He sensed her vulnerability, and her need to feel protected and he let her feel that in her dream.

***

Kate was carried away in her dream...*He lifted her hand to his lips, a soft kiss on the back of her hand, his eyes peering up through his dark hair. His voice was deep as he repeated her name. His hand was in her hair. Her eyes were closed, and she felt his hand as he ran it through her hair. Goose bumps covered her body with his touch. She moaned softly as his hand slid down her back...*

What the fuck! She sat up abruptly in her bed. Shaking her head, she looked at the clock. 4:00 a.m. This was insane. She touched her hair, calmed her breathing. It had felt so real...his hand in her hair. She flopped back down on the pillow. *Get out of my head tall, dark and dangerous. Now!*

She rolled over on her side, grabbed the other pillow, held it to her chest, and imagined holding him, imagined being held by him. *Stop it!*

Tossing the pillow aside, she sat upright again, sliding her feet to the floor. She stood and walked to the kitchen, flipping on the light. Opening the fridge, she stared. She closed the door and leaned against the counter. Picking up a banana from the bowl of fruit on the counter, she peeled it back and took a bite. *Oh well... that's not too Freudian, is it?*

Shade had stepped back abruptly when she woke and got out of bed. He followed her to the kitchen, standing in the doorway. Watching her was torture. He was captivated by her. He needed to get the hell out of here before he did something he'd regret. She walked so close to him on her way to the window, she almost brushed against him. He could tell she still thought of him, her mind consumed with the dreams he'd given her, and he smiled. Teleporting out without her detection, he sat on the rooftop of a nearby Arlington condo and watched her. "Soon, *mi amore*, you will see me again."

Kate walked into the living room, over to the window and looked out at the view of downtown D.C. She leaned her forehead against the cool glass. *Where are you, Shade Medici? Where did you lay your head tonight? Who am I kidding? A man like that never goes home alone. You will never see this man again, so just get over it.*

She walked back to her bedroom and slipped back between the sheets. The last thought in her head, before she fell back asleep was...*You missed your chance.*

4

Kate woke up late, feeling restless, with vague memories of him. Did she dream of him? Her mind felt fuzzy. Climbing out of bed, she headed to the shower, then dressed for a casual Sunday, binge watching *Scandal* on Netflix. She stopped around five o'clock, to get ready to meet Shannon. After finishing her make-up, she slid on a short skirt and a comfy sweater, then dug through her closet to find a pair of killer Jimmy Choo leopard print heels. She grabbed a black fedora and pulled it down over her red hair, and put on a pair of dark glasses, as she headed to the garage for her car.

Fall was her favorite season, still warm and no humidity. She drove to D.C., fighting the flood of tourists who were all leaving the city after the weekend, and made her way to H Street. Tossing her keys to the valet, she went inside. She stood at the door, and saw Shannon already seated. She waved to her friend, as she moved to join her.

“Hey, Shan! Hope you haven't been waiting long.” Kate gave her a quick hug before she sat down.

“Not at all. I just got here myself. I already ordered white wine for you.”

Kate sipped at the wine, as she picked up the menu. "Yum. Conundrum, you remembered my favorite. You look good. What were you up to today, and more importantly, why were you home when I called last night?"

Shannon picked at the calamari appetizer. “I know, right? Working on a Saturday night? This is what my life has come to? Crap, I had so much work to catch up on. We have that new account, and I'm on a tight deadline for the first presentation. You look rested... Well, to be honest, you don't. Didn’t you sleep well?”

“I...uh...I think I woke up a few times. You know, Shan, I'm really not sure. I kept dreaming stuff, but I can't really remember.”

“Really? Can't remember? You're telling me you didn’t dream of, what did you call him, tall, dark and dangerous?”

“Yeah...no...I mean, I think he was in my dreams. It was just weird, you know? Like I felt him.”

"Oh girl, you have *got* to get his number and get this man out of your system."

"I don't know. I told you...out of my league. Besides, even if I called Rissa for his number, I'm not sure I'd have the nerve to call him. Seriously, if you could have heard me last night, I couldn't finish a sentence I was so tongue tied. I'm sure he found it all very amusing, but I doubt he'd waste five minutes on me."

"Listen to you! Stop putting yourself down, he came up to you, didn't he?"

"True, but I'm pretty sure it didn't take him long to realize his mistake. I wish I had your confidence around men, but sorry, I just don't, and around him especially." Kate picked at what was left of the calamari. Shannon had done a great job of gobbling down the appetizer. "So, what are you ordering? I think I'm having the eggplant parmesan."

***

Shade teleported directly into downtown D.C., dressed casually in jeans and a sports coat. Stepping inside the restaurant he quietly took a seat at the bar. He immediately picked up on the scent of roses. He turned his head, saw her and was instantly mesmerized. She took his breath away. Those crimson locks flowing out from beneath her hat. He let his eyes glide down her long legs, as she sat talking with her female friend and noticed the Jimmy Choo's.

The bartender asked him what he'd like. He knew they carried Medici wine here. It was one of the few places on this side of D.C. that carried his wine for both mortals and immortals.

"Medici Midnight, my man."

The bartender nodded and went for the wine. It took some time before he returned. It must be stored in the rear of the bar, telling Shade not many vampires frequented this establishment.

He sat back and casually looked over at Kate every once in a while, but kept his presence unknown to her for the moment. He listened to their conversation and smiled. *Oh, she had my number all right, straight to my fucking heart and then some.*

As the bartender apologized for the delay, Shade swirled the deep burgundy Midnight around in the glass then took a long sip, keeping his eyes locked on her over the rim of his glass. He was restless to talk to her, touch her. He signaled with two fingers for the bartender to come closer.

"Do you see those two beautiful females sitting at the corner table? Please send them over a bottle of Medici Moonlight, white, 1982 is a good year, with my compliments, of course."

Moonlight, unlike Midnight was his wine made for mortal consumption. The bartender rushed off to grab the bottle, and passed it off to their waiter, he prepared the tray with two fresh wine glasses before delivering it to their table.

Kate looked up as the waiter approached with a tray he sat on their table. "Excuse me, ladies, but the gentleman at the bar asked this be delivered to your table."

He took the corkscrew and removed the cork, pouring the wine into the glasses. Shannon picked up the bottle and looked at the label. "Nice! This is very expensive wine, Kate."

Kate looked at the waiter. "Excuse me, who sent this?"

The waiter pointed in the direction of the bar. "The gentleman seated near the end of the bar, the man with the really dark hair."

Kate looked over her shoulder to see who sent the gift, and gasped out loud. "Oh my god, Shannon, it's him!"

"Who?" She was already sipping the newly poured wine.

"Him! From last night. Tall, dark and dangerous."

Shannon craned her neck to look at him, as Shade leaned against the bar. "Fuck me! Are you kidding?" She held her glass up to him, in acknowledgement of the wine, as Shade returned the gesture.

Kate blushed at her outburst, hoping he hadn't overheard. "Shh, stop that! What do I do now?"

"Well, acknowledging the gift might be appropriate." Shannon poked at Kate's arm. "Kate! Look at him. Do something."

Kate glanced over her shoulder and caught his eye, he was staring at her. She smiled, but immediately felt her face turning a bright red, and quickly turned away.

She turned back to Shannon. "I...see...I told you...*good, lord. He's on the other side of the room and already I can't talk."*

Shannon grabbed the menu and held it up in front of her face. "Get a grip, girl! He's coming over."

Kate gave a startled reply. "He's coming over?" *No! Oh, god...* She felt her mouth go dry.

Shade walked up behind Kate and slid his hand across her shoulder. Taking her hand in his, he kissed it gently, not letting go. "I hope you do not mind the intrusion. I only wished to enhance your meal, and wish you a good evening." He turned to her friend. "*Buonasera.*"

"*Buonasera* indeed, and thank you for the wine. My name is Shannon. Would you like to join us? My friend here seems to have lost her ability to speak, but I'm sure if she could, she'd say she would welcome your company."

Kate kicked Shannon under the table. She couldn't believe she asked him to sit down.

Shannon felt the sharp kick against her shins. "Ouch!" She started laughing. "Really, she'd *love* your company."

Shade smiled and his eyes went back to Kate. "I do not wish to intrude on your dining. I would never do such." He let go of her hand as he flagged down the waiter, and slid a large sum of money into his hand. "Would you please make sure the ladies have whatever they wish to eat or drink with my compliments, and of course, your finest service."

Kate sat perfectly still when he leaned down to her, his lips a mere inch from her ear, his breath hot against her skin, the smell of wine on his breath. Her heart was beating out of her chest, as she realized if she turned her head ever so slightly, his lips would touch hers. She felt the blush creep up her neck and face. Leaning into her, Shade kissed her cheek softly and whispered in her ear, "No need to thank me, and I will decline the meal, for your beauty is feast enough for me to live on for eternity." He straightened and nodded to Shannon. "Enjoy your evening, ladies." He turned and walked away.

Shannon reached across the table and grabbed Kate's hand. "Seriously? Get his number. Go after him. Do something!"

Kate stared back at her with her mouth slightly open. "I can't, Shannon... He just... I can't even think when he gets close to me."

"Men like that don't come around often. You need a game plan. How many chances do you think you're going to get with him?"

Kate shook her head and downed the glass of wine before re-filling it. "I don't expect to have any chance with him. I mean, what a fluke he'd be here tonight. And I blew it...again. It's like my brain shuts down. I can't speak. I can't think. I can barely breathe."

Shannon handed Kate the menu. "Here, drink that down and let's order. He left us more money to spend than we can possibly eat tonight. Don't know about you, but I'm ordering take-out for when we leave."

The waiter took their order and left the table.

"Kate, all kidding aside, I've never seen you come so unglued around a man before. And he's clearly interested. What are you going to do?"

"I don't know. I really don't. I mean, you saw me. Did I even say anything? I don't think I said anything. Last night, at least I could stutter."

Shannon laughed at her. "This better be one patient man is all I can say. I don't know, girl, I think you might have blown it with this one. So, let's just finish this expensive wine, and eat all this food."

As they wrapped up for the evening, the waiter brought Kate another bottle of the wine, to cover the balance of the money the gentleman left behind, and the very generous tip the girls left for him.

Shannon gave her a hug as they stood up from the table. "Go home and drink your wine, Kate. It may be your last memory of tall, dark and dangerous."

The valet brought Kate's car around, she hugged Shannon one last time and climbed in to head back home. She pounded her hand on the steering wheel. *What is wrong with me? Why do I get so dumbstruck around him?* The voice in her head answered, *you mean besides the fact he is so handsome he takes your breath away? Or the fact that every time you see him, you get an ache deep in your belly, a primal ache that is your body screaming for him?*

Pulling into the underground garage, she went up to her condo. Shedding her clothes, she kicked off the shoes, and pulled on her robe. She found a corkscrew in the kitchen, opened the wine, filled a glass, and carried the bottle with the glass back to her bed. She set the bottle on the nightstand, and piled all her pillows against the headboard before flopping down. She sipped at the wine while looking at the D.C. skyline.

"Where are you, Shade Medici? Please don't give up on me."

Kate finished off the glass of wine and picked up the bottle. Shannon said this was expensive wine. She looked at the label...Medici Moonlight. *Wait, what? Medici? Italy? This wine is from Italy? Is this...he owns a vineyard?*

She sighed as she poured more wine into her glass. *And why, exactly, would a rich Italian vintner be interested in you, Kate Reese? He probably doesn't even live in the States. You'd be nothing but another notch on his bedpost.*

She grabbed the remote and turned on the TV. *True Blood...great, I'll watch Eric bang Sookie. That should take my mind off things.*

***

Shade watched her leave the restaurant, then teleported to the rooftop across from her condo. She was different from all the others, she wouldn't chase him. He'd had females play hard to get before, but this one wasn't playing games. She found him intimidating. He was going to have to win her over.

Taking out his cell, he ran through the list of numbers Alec gave him in case Shade needed to contact him. Finding Rissa's number, he dialed her.

"Hello?" she answered.

"Rissa, Shade Medici. Need you to do something for me."

Rissa sounded annoyed. "How did you get this number and what could you possibly want from me? Seriously, I have no time for this."

"Relax, woman. Alec gave me your number in case I couldn't find him. Look, you *will* make time for this. I want Kate Reese to be invited to all these damn events you are having. And I need a schedule of them. All of them, Rissa."

"Have you had too much Midnight? Who in hell do you think you are? I told you to let it go. She's nothing. She'll never be anything. But if that's what you want, fine. I don't have time to argue with you right now. It'll be fun to watch you crush her soppy little heart anyway. I'll send you the list and I'll make sure the skinny ass redhead is invited."

Hearing what he wanted to hear, he smiled and ended the call. *Deed is done. Don't worry your head over my bel rosso, Rissa, she will never be crushed again. Once I work my magic, she will be mine. But damn, I have to get her to talk to me first.*

5

Kate woke to the incessant beeping of her alarm. The TV was still on and she'd slept in her robe. Sitting up in bed, she rubbed her eyes. Him, in her dreams, again. She looked at the bedside table and the wine bottle was half empty. Ugh, no wonder she felt so sluggish. She climbed out of bed, showered and dressed for work.

Walking to the Pentagon City Metro station, she rode the subway into work. D.C. traffic was always insane, but the traffic during rush hour was impossible, so unless it was pouring rain or snow, she'd take the subway. That was just one more thing that freaked her family out. She jumped on the orange line and rode into L'Enfant Plaza, then walked the few blocks to the Brunswick Agency on 7th Street. She and Shannon had taken jobs there after working for Brunswick, as unpaid interns while still students at Georgetown University. She grabbed a coffee at Starbucks on the corner and headed to the office building, scurrying to her cubicle, late again.

Kate could hear Shannon on the other side of the cubicle wall, as she tried unsuccessfully to slip in un-noticed. Shannon stood and peeked over the cubicle at her and asked, "Late night? Anything I should know about?"

Kate looked up and had to stifle a laugh. "You mean something other than the half bottle of wine I drank after I got home, on top of what we drank while we were still at the restaurant?"

Taking off her jacket, she removed her laptop from her bag, and slipped it into the docking station to power up. As she waited, Shannon moved into her cubicle. "Sooo...I guess since you still don't have his number, phone sex is out."

"Shh! We don't exactly have a lot of privacy here."

"You know I'm not going to let this go. That man is interested in you, and you're interested in him. Call your friend Rissa. Get his number."

"Yeah, okay. I will."

"No, I mean call her now, while I'm standing here. Otherwise, you'll just talk yourself out of it. Call!"

Kate fidgeted with organizing papers on her desk. "It's too early, Shan. It's only 8:30."

"Well, actually it's 8:45 because you're late, as always. But Rissa runs her own business. I'm sure she's up by now." Shannon grabbed Kate's cell from her purse and started scrolling through her contacts.

Kate made a grab for the phone, but Shannon turned away. "Wait...Shan...give me my phone!"

Shannon saw Rissa's contact info and hit dial, listening as the phone began to ring, then handed it back to Kate. "Talk! Get a number, or I'll beat you with this phone."

Kate took the phone in time to hear Rissa answering. "Benneteau Beautiful, Larissa speaking."

"Rissa, hi, it's Kate. I'm sorry to bother you so early, I just wanted to call and thank you for a great evening Saturday. That was such an elegant cocktail party. I really had a great time."

Shannon was mouthing to her to 'get his number' and Kate slapped at her arm.

Rissa responded, "Kate? Sorry, I'm just going through some client lists at the moment and my mind is elsewhere. I'm glad you enjoyed it. I have a few more events coming up. I'd love it if you could join us. I love having different classes of people to mix and mingle, keeps things interesting. It's so good for Alec to be seen as a man of the people."

Kate didn't miss the 'different classes of people' dig. She'd never been quite high-brow enough for Rissa.

"Oh! Of course. I'd love that. Just give me a little notice. I travel in my job sometimes, but if I'm in town, I'd love to come. And listen...uh...I was wondering if you might have a phone number for someone, one of your guests."

"Well, I can try, depends who it is. I mean a lot of my guests are Congressmen, Senators, you know the type. I can't give out their private numbers and besides, the way you ran out of there I'd have guessed you didn't have a very enjoyable evening. So exactly whose number did you want? Is this a potential client for Brunswick Agency, perhaps?"

"I...uh...yes, he could be a client. His name was Medici? Shade Medici?" Kate heard Rissa actually laugh out loud.

"Oh, sorry, but I don't think that would be a wise decision. Shade Medici is European aristocracy, and when I tell you he's a player, I do mean player. The man has women at his feet. He picks and chooses who he'll play with. Haven't you learned your lesson from your last player? Shade has them lined up, three a night. And seriously, to be honest, I think he's a bit much for you to handle."

"Oh, I didn't realize."

Kate was aware Shannon could overhear the conversation. She was yanking on Kate's arm and mouthing, 'Get the fucking number!' Kate felt torn between the information Rissa was sharing and Shannon tugging at her arm.

"But...it's not personal...I, uh, thought our agency could benefit him. It's purely business. So, if you don't mind sharing his number..."

"Kate, when it comes to Shade Medici, where there's business, there's fucking, and he's not exactly into safe vanilla stuff. But if you want to step off the ledge and fall flat on your face, who am I to tell you different? Oh, and don't forget, keep your date book open for our annual Halloween Party. I have so much planned for it. Hang on a sec. I have his number here somewhere."

Kate heard the rustling of paper. Rissa finally repeated Shade's number for her and issued a last warning, "Don't get caught up in his bullshit, I'm serious, Kate. Don't let his big blue eyes and charming accent fool you. I'm going to email you the next party invite I'm having. Check your mail."

Rissa had given her Shade's number, and enough bad news about him to make her want to run for the hills. She wrote the number down as she repeated it back, and then signed off.

Shannon grabbed the paper and her phone, and programed the number in right away, then handed it back to her and said, "Call!"

Kate looked at her incredulously. "Did you hear what she said about him? Seriously, I'm setting myself up for a big fall here."

"Look, every guy you date doesn't have to be husband material. Sometimes you can actually just date someone for fun. Get it? You just have to know what you're getting into. This man likes you. He has money. Who cares if it goes anywhere? Go out with him. Have fun, and when it's over, it's over. Now call!"

"Yeah, okay. I'll call." She slipped her phone back into her purse.

"No, call now! I know you." Shannon grabbed the phone from her purse and handed it to her. "Call!"

Kate took the phone from her and hit dial, listening to it ring several times before it went to voicemail. She ended the call without saying anything.

"You didn't leave a message? Oh my god, you didn't leave a message? Kate, you're hopeless."

"I didn't know what to say. What kind of message would I leave? 'Hey...I'm that girl who ran away from you at the party. The girl you bought dinner and wine for who couldn't even talk?' I'll call again later."

"No, you won't." Shannon sighed. "Don't let him get away. Do something!"

"I will. I said I'd call later. Now get back in your cubicle before we get in trouble."

Kate returned to her desk and started working, but he stayed in her head. They got through the work day and she stuck around until about 6:30, trying to get caught up, before catching the metro back home. It was dusk out and she scurried through the few blocks to her condo, getting upstairs and changing clothes. The evening felt cool, so she started a fire in the gas fireplace and curled up with a book. She thought of him, but Shannon was right, she didn't have the nerve to call.

***

Waking from his death slumber, Shade rose and threw his legs over the side of the bed, sitting there waiting for the cobwebs to clear from his head. He checked the clock and knew it was safe for him to venture outside. He decided to shower and teleport over to Kate's humble abode to protect her, unawares of course.

He'd taken a luxury penthouse suite in a complex just across the street, where he could see clearly into the large windows of her bedroom and living room. He had a direct line of sight, and with his exceptional immortal vision, he could see everything. He could be close but not on top of her, watching over her until she fell into her slumber.

He stood up and grabbed his phone and saw he had a few missed calls. He checked them quickly, and recognized them all except for one that came early in the morning hours, shortly after he fell into his death slumber. It was a northern Virginia exchange. Walking to the window, he saw some low lighting in her living room. She sat in front of a fire reading a book. *Could it be? Only one way to find out.* Hitting redial, he watched as she picked up her cell phone... *Cazzo, it was her!* He saw her answer the phone without checking the caller ID. "Hello."

"*Buonasera, mi amore*. You called?"

"I, yes, I did call. I hope that's okay."

"It is more than okay, Kate. I hope there wasn't a problem with your meal or the wine. That would surely break my heart."

He stood at the window and watched her. She looked relaxed and cozy. She was wearing a large sweater that hung off one shoulder. Her legs were bare and curled under her. Her bulky white socks were only a few shades lighter than her lily-white skin. He almost laughed watching her twirl those crimson curls around her finger in nervousness. Even dressed like this, in an oversized sweater, she was beautiful and sexy. *Cazzo, what in the hell is the tiny sexy female doing to me?* He could see her take a deep breath to calm herself.

Kate felt less intimidated by him when talking to him on the phone. "No. The meal was wonderful, thanks to you and the wine. That was quite generous. I wanted to thank you. I should have thanked you then, I apologize. But..." She ran her hand through her hair. "I don't know, Mr. Medici, there's something about you that leaves me... undone. I'm not sure I'm in your league."

Shade picked up on the unspoken thoughts in her head. *Rissa!* That bitch was already trying to ruin her for him. He should have known she'd run her mouth.

"Ah, please Kate, will you call me Shade? Mr. Medici is much too formal, and I do not think we need such formality now that we have met several times, *si*? Please do not let my wealth, or being at the Canton party, give you false impressions of me. I am a simple man. I oversee my family business of producing wine. I am quite harmless. Might I have the pleasure of knowing your occupation? It would interest me greatly."

He could see her relax back in the chair as she answered him. "Oh, nothing as exotic as owning a vineyard in Italy, I assure you. I work for the Brunswick Agency. It's an ad agency. We handle big accounts, luxury cars like Bugatti, some big jewelry houses like Harry Winston. Oh, and Jimmy Choo! Love that one, we get a discount. We create advertising campaigns, arrange for photo shoots, magazine spreads, and do commercials. That type of thing. I was lucky to get on there. I did an unpaid internship with them when I was in college at Georgetown, and it paid off in the long run. How about you? What brings you to the States?"

He listened to her chatter and watched her from his window, seeing her relax. He could sense she was more at ease speaking with him over the phone than in person. He wanted to teleport over there, ring the bell, walk in, and cuddle her on his lap while having this conversation.

"Well, Italy is not exotic, and wine is just grapes. But it is a living that has given me much. It sounds as though you work at a very prestigious agency. I am quite impressed. I own a few Bugatti's myself." He chuckled deep in his throat. "I think this is the longest conversation we have had without you bolting from me. So, tell me Kate Reese, have you ever been to Italy?"

She laughed softly, "Like I said, you made me...nervous, or something. I'm not usually like that, I promise. But yes, I've been to Italy. Shannon, the girl who was with me last night, we went to Italy right after graduation. We went to Rome, of course, and Venice. But Florence was my favorite. I fell in love with Florence. We even rented a little cottage in a vineyard in Tuscany for a few days. Who knows, Mr. Medici...Shade...I could have been staying at one of your vineyards. Now wouldn't that be a coincidence?"

He smiled to himself, he could see her face as she laughed while she spoke, and it melted his heart. The sound of her voice did something to him. It was not sexual; it was something much deeper, deeper than any female had ever touched him. He wondered if she could be the one. Shaking his head, *Get your shit together, Shade!*

"That is quite possible, quite possible indeed. I am from Florence and I do love it there, my family home is there."

Grabbing the schedule from Rissa out of his jeans pocket, he scanned through it and saw there was another event this weekend. "Maybe, someday, you will return to Florence? But while I'm here, perhaps we could arrange to have a coffee? Meet at a local shop, *si*?"

"I...yes, I'd love that. And I promise not to run away this time."

"I will hold you to such a promise, *mi amore*. I will not let you run away the next time."

He stood bare chested, jeans slung low on his hips, in the dark of his condo, watching her. He ached to touch her. He knew the sooner she got to sleep, the sooner he could enter her dreams and be with her. "I shall see you soon then. I will let you go for this evening, I am sure you are quite tired from your work."

"Shade, thank you for calling. It was really nice talking to you, and I look forward to seeing you again. Good night."

"It was my pleasure, very much my pleasure. *Buonasera*."

Hanging up the phone, he stood there motionless and closed his eyes. The sound of her voice flowed through his head. He had to hold himself back from just going the fuck over there and ravishing her. Turning from the window, he went to take one fucking cold ass shower, and then he had a little shopping to do.

Kate laid her head back against the chair. *His pleasure, he said it was his pleasure.* But she realized he hadn't actually made another date. A 'perhaps we could meet for coffee sometime' was not asking for a date. She tried to read her book, but all she could see in her head was him.

She turned off the gas fireplace, and headed to her bedroom. The half empty bottle of wine was still on her bedside table. She climbed into her bed and wondered if she'd ever see him again, or if he was just indulging some foolish girl.

6

Finishing up his shower, Shade dressed quickly before teleporting to Italy and going directly to one of the high-end designer shops. He knew exactly what he was going after, and it wouldn't take him long to find the right pair. Browsing, he asked the assistant for her help in choosing. She brought out some brand-new designs that hadn't hit the American market yet. He knew the exact pair when he saw them.

"Those will do quite nicely." There was nothing like a pair of Jimmy Choo's to woo a woman to your side. He knew, just from looking at Kate, the shoe size she required. He'd been with enough women in his life he could accurately guess the size of any garment she may be wearing. Five hundred years of exploring every aspect of the female anatomy would do that.

He asked the assistant to wrap the shoes for him. She did so with a special gleam in her eye, letting Shade know she was more than available, if he was looking for more than a pair of shoes. He thanked her graciously, leaving a huge tip, then teleported his ass back to his penthouse. Setting the beautifully wrapped package down, he looked out the window and found his *bel rosso* asleep. Taking out a small card, he hand wrote a note for the package. *'Such a beautiful woman should own the newest pair of Choo's. Shade.'*

Attaching the card to the package, he walked back downstairs and asked the concierge to please have the package delivered to Miss Kate Reese at the Brunswick Ad Agency in the morning. "Nine o'clock would be an excellent time."

He tipped him a fifty and headed straight out the door, walking to a dark corner on the street, he teleported inside her condo, wrapping himself in shadow to begin the journey.

He watched her sleep for some time as he sat on the bed, gazing at her. He couldn't help himself. Just looking at her like this brought out his vampire and he felt a need to protect her. Even his beast seemed a bit at ease just watching her sleep. As exciting and entrancing as she was, he was surprised the brute didn't roar up and take over. But the beast stood on the edge of his darkness, waiting his turn.

Shade finally stood and carefully slid his hand along her cheek, letting his thumb glide over her lips. He laid his hand in those crimson locks and walked into her dreams, as if it were normal. As he manipulated her dream, she watched him slowly walk toward her. He could feel she liked this. She was able to look him in the eye and wasn't intimidated. He could tell she felt as though she could trust him to protect her. Now, he wanted her to feel that way when she was awake, not just in her dreams.

He held her in his arms, pulled her close and held her head to his broad chest for some time, feeling her heart beat against his, feeling her blood rush through her veins. He snuggled his head down along her neck, nuzzling and inhaling her scent, the thick, sweet scent of roses calling him. He pulled a red rose from behind his back, and slid it along her cheek, her beautiful, big brown eyes rose up to greet his blue ones. He kissed her gently on the lips, letting the rose fall from his hand as its petals escaped their tightened bud. He watched as she backed away, holding up her hand, palm out as to stop him.

"Please, mi amore, I mean you no harm. Let me kiss you again...come closer." He smiled and held out his hand to her, but she backed away slowly, moving farther from him. Her subconscious was telling him she wasn't ready to give her heart. Something was holding her back, something she feared, but it wasn't him.

He quickly walked from the dream and found her moaning softly in the bed. He stayed seated on the bed by her side until the sun approached and he left her to awaken and go to her employment. Once again, he'd remind her he was here, and he very much wanted her to be his and his only.

***

The sound of the alarm woke her, and she reached from beneath the warm blankets to smack at the clock. She sat up in the bed, the room still dark, rubbed her eyes, and pushed the hair back from her face. She sat quietly, remembering. She'd had the oddest dream, him again. She tried to pull the dream into focus. It was so fuzzy around the edges, but it was definitely him.

He was holding her in his arms, kissing her, and drawing a single rose across her cheek before...*Before what?* She backed away, and the rose petals fell around her...*What did that even mean?* She shook her head and reached to turn on the lamp, while sliding her feet over the side of the bed. A hot shower would clear her head.

As she stood and looked back at the crumpled white sheets, she found several bright red rose petals scattered in the bed. Her heart sped up, as her hand automatically went to her throat. She took a few steps back. *Not possible. Not possible.*

She stared at the rose petals in disbelief. She stepped forward, reached out her hand, extended her finger and touched one petal before withdrawing her hand quickly, like it was burned on a hot stove. *It's real! How can that be?* She reached again and picked up a petal, feeling it between her fingers, and then turned her head quickly from side to side, looking around the room.

She ran to the front door of the condo and checked the door. It was locked. *No sense. This makes no sense.* She leaned with her back against the door, running possible scenarios through her mind, *were there any roses in the house? No. Maybe...maybe...There must have been rose petals stuck to my sweater somehow.* When she climbed in the bed, they became dislodged. She looked down at the over-sized sweater and the socks she wore to bed. This was too confusing for this hour and she was letting her imagination run away with her.

She walked back to her bedroom, pulled the sweater over her head and stripped the socks from her feet, as she headed for the shower. She stepped beneath the hot water, letting it wash away the confusion, as she scrubbed herself with her rose scented body wash, the scent of the roses rising on the hot steam from her shower. The memory slammed into her, the feeling of being held by him. Her heart raced as she fought to control her emotions. She stepped from the shower, wrapped a towel around her hair and began her routine of getting ready for work, letting the memories of that dream tumble around in her head.

She finished getting dressed, grabbed her laptop case and headed out the door for the metro station. *You are losing your mind, Kate Reese.*

***

Shade watched from his window, but he must also watch the time, the sun would approach very quickly, and he'd feel the burn on his skin. He watched her closely when she sat up and stretched. As she shook her head several times, he automatically found his hand over his heart, watching that damn hair, wishing it was being tousled around him. Then he saw the shocked look on her face, her hand to her throat. *What in the hell was wrong?* His eyes went to the bed and the rose petals strewn across the white sheets. *She could be severely freaked out by this or maybe...Nope, she was freaked.* He realized he'd just lost ground. "*Cazzo, stupido bastardo!*"

***

She was late, as always. She was so *not* a morning person. Stopping at Starbucks she grabbed her coffee. The barista had her 'usual' waiting for her, as she ran in and slid the $5 bill across the counter, before running back out the door, and up the street a few buildings. She rushed to her cubicle, trying to slip in un-noticed. As she sat at her desk and started her computer, Shannon rolled her chair into Kate's cubicle.

Shannon gave her a once over. "You're looking a little frazzled this morning. Did you call him? Wait, why am I even asking? Of course you didn't call him."

Kate spun her chair around to face Shannon, and gave her a smug smile. "No, I didn't call him. He called me."

Shannon's eyes bugged out of her head. "What?" She scooted her chair in closer, before whispering in a dramatic voice, "Details!"

"Last night, I was just reading, and my cell rang. I thought it was you, but it was him."

Shannon responded in exasperation. "Okay, when someone says details, they mean *details*, like he said this, and then you said that. What did he say?"

"He was very sweet. His voice sounded very sexy on the phone."

"Kate, his voice sounds sexy in person, so of course he sounds sexy on the phone. What did he say?"

"I thanked him for our dinner and the wine. He asked where I worked. I told him. Said I traveled in my job and that I'd been to Italy. I told him about our trip there, when we stayed in that cottage in the vineyard in Tuscany. He said he was from Florence. That's...about it."

Shannon rolled her eyes. "Okay, that is literally the most boring story I've ever heard. Did he ask you out? What? What happened?"

"Not really. I mean, he said maybe we'd have coffee sometime. Or perhaps, he said perhaps we'd have coffee sometime. Doesn't sound like a date. I don't know. This guy is so out of my league, and then this morning...No, never mind."

Shannon nodded. “It could be a date. He's just probing. He’s trying to gauge your response. See if you're interested, or if he's going to get shot down. But what about this morning? Don't start something and then say never mind.”

Kate was hesitant to share what even she didn’t understand. “I...this is nothing. Just, weird. I had this dream of him, again. He was holding me, and he kissed me and stroked my face with a red rose. And then, this morning, when I woke up...no...It’s nothing. You'll really think I've lost it.”

“Hate to tell you, but I already think you've lost it. So, what? You woke up, and what?”

“I woke up, and...there were rose petals in my bed.”

Shannon looked at her with her mouth open. "Yeah, you're right. I definitely think you've lost it, Kate. That's impossible, you know that, right? What you're thinking? I mean, I'm sure they were there, like I don't think you were hallucinating or anything. But you don't seriously think they dropped out of your dream or something. Or he was there? Do you think he was physically there?”

“I thought maybe he was there. But the door was locked. So no, it couldn’t be. I think the petals may have been stuck to my sweater. Maybe I brushed against someone and they were on my sweater. I don't know, it just freaked me out a little.”

Shannon nodded. “That's got to be it, right? I mean, there’s a logical explanation. Don't go all voodoo on me.”

Drinking her coffee, Kate looked at her over the rim of the cup. She knew Shannon was right. She couldn’t let her imagination run out of control. As they sat there, the guy from the mailroom came up. “Miss Reese? There's a package for you.” He handed her a large gift box, beautifully wrapped.

Shannon's eyes were bulging out of her head again. Kate took the box and noticed the small gift card attached under the bow.

Shannon was bouncing in her chair. “Who's it from? Is there a card? Open the card.”

Kate slipped the small envelope from under the bow, removed the card and read it out loud, “Such a beautiful woman should own the newest pair of Choo’s. Shade.” She looked up at Shannon and their eyes locked.

Shannon shouted, “Well, don’t just sit there. Open it!”

Kate tried to remove the ribbon and the elaborate wrapping paper without tearing it, while she smacked at Shannon's hands to keep her from grabbing at the paper to rip it open. She removed the paper, set it aside, opened the shoe box, and pulled out the shoes. Jimmy Choo heels with a zebra toe box with black straps that laced around the ankles, and a bright red rose on the toe. They were from the upcoming Spring Collection. Their agency just shot the pictures for that ad campaign. These shoes weren't even on the market yet.

Shannon grabbed one of the shoes from the box. "Fuck me! Girl, if you don't hang on to this guy, I'm going for him. Just sayin'. Any man who can get Jimmy Choo's before they even go to market, now that's a man-skill to be envied. Forget taking out the trash, or cooking on the grill."

Kate kicked her own shoes off and slipped on the Jimmy Choo's. They fit perfectly. She wound the straps around her ankles and tied them, then walked outside her cubicle, and they looked...awesome. All she needed was a black sheath dress and these shoes and she'd have the perfect outfit. As she walked around modeling the shoes, she was struck by the fact the shoes had a rose on the toe. The memory of rose petals in her bed came rushing back to her. *Stop it! You are making yourself crazy.*

"Shannon, do you know how much these cost? I can't keep a gift like this."

"Are you crazy? A man gives you next season Jimmy Choo's and you want to return them? No way, there is no way I'm letting that happen."

Kate shook her head. "I don't know. I think a gift like this has expectations."

"Oh. My. God. You did not just say that. I would fuck the pimply-faced kid from the mailroom for a pair of shoes like this. You're not seriously telling me you're going to return these shoes because he may want something in return? Like climbing into bed with that man would be a hardship? Kate! Hello! Twenty-first century."

Kate started to remove the shoes and return them to their box.

"Oh no, girlfriend! You are wearing those shoes today. And tonight, when you get home, you're going to call him and tell him how much you love them. Got it?"

She looked at the shoes on her feet, and they did look fabulous; beyond fabulous. "Okay, against my better judgment. But if this guy breaks my heart— "

"If this guy breaks your heart, you'll still have a great pair of Jimmy Choo's. Get over it."

7

Kate wore the hot shoes around the office. They were a little on the dressy side for work, but every man she walked past took notice, and said, “Nice shoes,” with a sly smile. And every woman said, “Nice shoes,” with a note of jealousy. She took them off at the end of the day, not wanting to wear them on the metro and the few blocks back to her condo. She slipped them back in the box, loaded up her laptop, grabbed her jacket, and headed out.

At seven o’clock, she grabbed a sandwich to go, at Panera Bread and took it home with her for dinner. Once she got home, she put the shoes in the closet, wondering what event she could wear them to. They really were too dressy to wear to work again. She changed into jeans and a soft cashmere sweater and went to the living room. She turned on the gas fireplace and started eating her sandwich, as she opened her laptop to check email. Rissa had sent an invitation to a big charity event this Saturday that required semi-formal cocktail wear. That was unusual to receive two invitations from Rissa in two weeks. Rissa had always been friendly to her, but they weren’t really friends. But hey, who was she to turn down an invitation, and maybe he would be there.

She checked the time, 8:30 already. She finished the sandwich, and drank a green tea. She scrolled through her contacts on her cell phone to find the number Shannon entered for her, *Shade Hot Stuff*. She laughed out loud. It was the first time she’d seen how Shannon programmed him into her phone. She hit dial.

As he picked up the phone, Kate could hear some serious head-banging music in the background. It sounded like “Hail to the King” by Avenged Sevenfold. *Really? The man in the hand-tailored suits listens to heavy metal?* His response was short, abrupt—“Medici.” His voice struck a chord in her, and she started to stumble over her words. She took a deep breath and composed herself.

"Shade? This is Kate. Is this a bad time?” She heard the sudden silence as the music abruptly ended.

"Oh no, *mi amore*, I was just going over some contracts from Alec. Is everything fine with you? I do apologize for my curt response. Please forgive me?"

Feeling braver, Kate began to flirt with him. "Forgive you? And what could you have possibly done that needs forgiving, Mr. Medici?"

"I did not realize it was you, or I would have, most assuredly, answered the call differently, like the gentleman I am, *si*? So please forgive me, and make me feel better?"

Oh my! He has this down to a fine art. Like I should be surprised. "And what do you think it would take to make you feel better, sir?" *Seriously? Did I just say that to him?*

He chuckled. "Ah, now that could lead to an open door. But I shall remain a gentleman, which, I might add, is very hard to do at the moment."

She responded coyly, "An open door? Is that a bad thing?"

"Bad thing? No, it is open for anything. I would like to think good things. Did you have something in mind? Sounds to me as though you may like walking through that door, *si*?"

"That depends. Are you on the other side of that door?"

"I do believe, Kate Reese, you are flirting with me and would very much like that."

"And I do believe, Shade Medici, you can get a girl to walk through any door pretty easily, wearing a pair of Jimmy Choo's. And thank you, by the way, for your most generous gift, too generous."

He walked to the window, and sat on the sill to watch her. He was tempted to just fucking tell her to look out her window, but he knew better. Damn fucking jeans were getting tighter. Opening the button fly, he stretched out and laid his head back, sliding one hand inside his jeans, gripping his cock hard and stroking slowly, just wanting to hear her voice.

"It was my pleasure. I thought you would like them, and I was sure those gorgeous legs of yours would look even better in them. Did they fit, *mi amore*?"

"They fit perfectly. You'd think you had been buying my shoes for years. It does make a girl wonder. And you noticed my legs?"

"Oh *si*, I noticed. A man would have to be blind not to notice you, Kate. You are a beautiful woman, and you make a man take a second, very long gaze."

She is going to kill me here. He stroked harder. Long, slow strokes pulling up the head of his cock, and hoping to all hell fire he got to feel this monster inside her, making love to her slow and sweet. He loved that she was playing with him. "So tell me, did you notice me at all, or could you not get away from me quick enough?"

"Did I notice you? I was undone, completely, utterly undone. But I thought you knew that."

Stroking harder, he watched her as she talked to him, relaxed and in her element, feeling safe from him. "I make you nervous for some reason, *si*? Tell me, why is that? I mean you no harm, the complete opposite. I only wish you pleasure."

"You're a dangerous man, and distractedly handsome. A girl could find herself in over her head before she knew what hit her. I have no fear of harm from you, other than a broken heart. Are you going to break my heart? Am I, as Rissa says, just another notch on your bedpost?"

"*Mi amore*, I ask myself more if you will break mine."

He glanced at her through the window and saw her lifting her cashmere sweater over her head, exposing the red lace bra, spilling over with soft, lily-white orbs, and his mouth watered. He felt like exploding already. His hand gripped his huge cock harder, stroking, as he felt his balls tighten.

"And my bedpost, Rissa has never seen it and never will. She has no idea what it holds. I would never treat a lady as fine as you in that manner. Speaking of Rissa, are you going to this charity event Saturday evening?"

"Yes, I was planning to go. After all, I have a new pair of Jimmy Choo's that need breaking in. So, I take it this means you'll be there?"

He watched her jeans come off and his cock didn't like being held back. This woman was going to kill him.

"I will be there. I am supposed to be there." He tried to keep his voice steady, but his heart was racing, his blood pumping fast, and he could feel his cock throbbing for release. "I will plan on seeing you there, *mi amore*."

He watched as she removed her bra, tossing it on the dresser. She lifted her arms and ran both hands through her hair, shaking out her long locks, before slipping out of her panties and walking to her bed. He could see the rose petals were still on the sheets. She gathered them up in her hand, held them to her nose and inhaled. He saw her pile them in a little stack on the bedside table. She climbed into bed, pulling the sheets up around her. As he watched her disrobe, he reached climax, cum shooting across his chest and he tried not to moan out loud. His fangs punched through and his eyes glowed a deep red as his beast pushed to be set free. He took a few deep breaths and tried to get himself under control.

She responded. "I hope so. I can't imagine a less eventful evening without you."

"Until this weekend then, sweet dreams."

"I seem to only have sweet dreams since meeting you. Good night."

"*Buonasera, mi amore*. Until Saturday."

As he ended the call, he stood, and the beast emerged and growled like the animal he was. *I want her. I want her as my own. She is mine!*

***

Kate turned off her phone, and plugged it in the charger by her bed. Turning off the lamp, she watched as the skyline appeared in the window of her darkened room. The red light on top of the Washington Monument flashed on and off. How many nights did she lie here after the break-up with Ethan, not able to sleep, just watching that light flash on and off? They had been engaged. She had starting to plan a wedding, and then she found him cheating. Never again. Never ever again. That had been the moment she swore off men. It was one broken heart too many. *And now here you are, Kate Reese, playing with fire. And we know what happens to girls who play with fire.*

The little voice inside her head said, *Careful, he's not tall, dark and dangerous for nothing, little girl.*

8

Kate had spent the last two hours getting ready for the charity event. She'd chosen a form-fitting black sheath dress worn off the shoulders. She'd only worn it once before and it drew a little more attention than she wanted, so it ended up in the back of the closet. But Shannon convinced her to pull that dress out again, paired with Shade's gift. She wore her hair down, even though this was a semi-formal event. She knew already Shade was drawn to her hair. It hadn't taken long for her to pick up on that. She checked her make-up one last time before heading to the parking garage to get her car.

She drove instead of taking the metro. She had no desire to walk far in these shoes. Standing on her feet at a cocktail party all evening would be torture enough.

The National Gallery of Art sat right smack in the middle of Constitution Avenue, so there was no parking, but Rissa had arranged for valet service. She pulled up, dropped off her car, and ran inside. There must have been close to two thousand people there. They planned to do a silent art auction of some local artist to raise money, so there were selected galleries set aside to display those works. There was wait staff everywhere, and she was only inside a few minutes before she was approached and had a glass of white wine in her hands. She wandered through the throngs of people, chatting with a few as she went. Looking around the crowd discreetly, she didn't see him. She found a semi-quiet spot to sit down, so she could watch the crowd.

Kate polished off the wine. It was the liquid courage she'd need to face him. Talking to him on the phone was one thing, standing next to him was quite another. She stood and started to walk through the crowd, grabbing another glass of white wine from a passing waiter. There were a lot of recognizable faces in this crowd tonight, the faces she saw on the society pages of the *Washington Post*, but she didn't know them personally. She couldn't imagine the collective wealth of the people in this room. She wondered, and not for the first time, why Rissa invited her to this event. There was no way she could bid on this art.

She looked for him as she walked through the crowd, but if he was here, he was managing to keep his distance. She wondered if he even bothered to show up, or if he'd already moved on to some other female distraction. Rissa's words kept ringing in her ears, and she thought, for the hundredth time, why was she setting herself up for the fall.

***

Teleporting downtown to the National Gallery of Art, Shade had dressed in his finest. A black-tie event with Rissa meant a tuxedo. He looked quite dapper and hoped Kate would like his tux. He was anxious to see her in those Choo's.

As he arrived at the venue he saw Rissa and Alec. Alec threw up his hand in acknowledgment and Shade nodded. No need to talk, Alec thought he knew why he was here, but Shade had a different agenda—her name was Kate Reese.

He'd pulled back on the dream-walking lately. After the incident with the rose petals, he didn't want to scare her off. But he had a few tricks up his sleeve to bring her around. He casually made his way through the crowd, as he looked around the room for her.

He sensed she wasn't there yet, and he hadn't picked up the scent of her rose perfume. He kept himself busy, admiring the art while sipping at his glass of Midnight. He kept a low profile, not engaging with anyone in the crowd as he patiently waited.

Shade recognized her scent as soon as she arrived. He tracked her by the smell of roses, found her sitting quietly, drinking wine, and watching the people. He hung back, hidden from her view, and watched as she scanned the crowd. He didn't want to seem too eager. He kept moving around the small gallery, which held at least a hundred people, never taking his eyes off of her. She sat with her legs crossed, the tight black sheath dress exposing her thighs. She looked amazing. Her crimson hair hung over those white shoulders. He loved her hair down, and his beast came to the surface, licking his chops. *Not yet wicked boy, just hang in there. We have to reel this one in slowly.*

He made sure to stay clear of her line of vision. He'd never wanted a woman more than this one, and he'd been with many women.

He watched her stand and start to move through the throng of people and his eyes were glued to her. Her dress was sleek and off the shoulders. The heels drew his focus to her slender ankles, the curve of her calves, and the plumpness of her ass, accentuating the curves of her luscious body. This woman was made for loving and loving well.

He slowly followed her, slipping in and out of the crowd, staying out of sight. She finally stopped in front of a beautiful piece by Renoir as she stood and stared. He walked up behind her, softly slid his hand around her waist and snuggled into her neck, speaking to her in a low, deep voice, his mouth close to her ear. "Your legs are looking beautiful this evening, *mi amore*."

She gasped and instantly had goosebumps on her skin. She took a deep breath and turned to look at him. "Mr. Medici...and don't you look deliciously handsome tonight."

He felt her trepidation, but she fought it. He knew she wanted to face him, be with him, and he was amused. Most women would have been on top of him by now, inviting him to their place, but not this one. He stared down at beautiful brown eyes that shimmered in the light, shot through with flecks of amber. The backs of his fingers glided slowly up and down her bare arm. He dropped his hand and caught hers in his. Staring deep into her eyes, he lifted her hand to his lips and kissed it gently.

"Almost as delicious as you." He winked and kept hold of her hand. "I do believe you should wear Choo's more often. They suit you, *mi amore*." He looked at the painting. "Renoir, *si*? I am not well acquainted with art, but I do know a bit about the masters."

"Renoir, yes. I spent so many hours in the Musee d'Orsay in Paris, looking at the impressionist period art. It's one of my favorite periods in art, except for the Renaissance period in Florence, of course. It's like walking through history, isn't it?"

He rolled his eyes down to her, smiling. "So tell me, do you like Paris or Florence more?"

"That would be a hard choice to make, they're both beautiful cities. I hope you don't take offense, but I think I'd have to say Paris. I love everything about that city; the art, the architecture, the food. And even the people. I know they say the French hate the Americans, but I've really not had that experience. I found them quite welcoming. Have you traveled to Paris, Shade?"

He felt his heart skip a beat when she said his name. It rolled off her ruby red lips like sweet tempting wine. It took all he had not to lean down and kiss her. *"J'ai voyagé à Paris plusieurs fois ma douce. J'aime l'architecture et le vin. C'est un endroit où les amoureux aiment oui?"*

She laughed out loud. "I'm sorry, but I have no idea what you just said. I love Paris, but I don't speak French, or Italian. Perhaps you could teach me...something."

He chuckled as he slid his finger under her chin and looked deep into her eyes. "I said, I have traveled to Paris several times, my sweet. I loved the architecture and the wine. It is a place for lovers, yes? But, what can I teach you? We shall start simple. Repeat after me. *Vorrei un bacio, per favore*. This is Italian. Now, repeat."

She looked into his eyes as he spoke, she was mesmerized. "*Vorrei un bacio, per favore.* Now please, tell me what I just said."

He smiled down at her. "Well done! I will show you instead, *si*?" Leaning down, he kissed her softly on the lips. They were sweet like sugar and he wanted more.

"Oh...how do you say that again? Maybe you should write it down for me."

He loved the wide-eyed look on her face, almost begging him to kiss her again, and again. And who was he not to oblige. "Let us repeat the phrase in French. *Je voudrais un baiser s'il vous plaît.* Now, repeat."

He could tell she liked this game. He wondered how many kisses he could steal as she repeated the phrase. He slid his hand along her cheek and down her neck before sliding both hands under her hair. He gently lifted her face to his as he kissed her slowly, letting his kiss entrance her. He slid his tongue slowly around hers, letting her know, he liked kissing, and he loved kissing her. She almost melted in his hands. He felt her go weak in the knees and saw the flush on her face. He held her tight a moment longer. Pulling back, he kissed her again, softly and quickly. "I do believe, you would call that a French kiss, *oui*?"

"What? Oh...*oui,* French kiss..."

He chuckled softly. "Careful Kate, you will fall off your stilts. Come along, I think I saw a painting in another room I would like to bid on. Would you oblige me with your worldly opinion?" He bowed slightly to her. "I would be most grateful."

She slipped her arm into his. "Of course, I'd love to see it. I'm no art expert by any means, but I know what I like." She looked up at him through the red bangs that framed her face.

He gave her a crooked smile. "It's always good to know what you like, and go after it."

As they strolled casually through the crowd, he led her through a few galleries until they found the room where the painting hung.

"Ah, here we are. Tell me what you think of this. It reminds me a great deal of the property I just acquired in Virginia."

He stood behind her, his hands resting gently on her hips. It was an oil rendition of the Virginia countryside, painted to reflect the early fall when the leaves were just beginning to change. It depicted a narrow country road, lined with white rail fencing, like so many of the horse farms scattered through Virginia.

"This is beautiful, Shade. I love Virginia and the mountains. I grew up in Charleston, South Carolina. It's called the "low country," and it's flat as a pancake. I was always drawn to the rolling hills and the mountains here. Where did you buy property?"

"I am not familiar with Charleston, but my property is in White Hall, right at the base of the Blue Ridge Mountains. It does have a vineyard, a lot of territory, but it needs a great amount of work. He slid his hand softly against her neck, brushing her hair back and kissing her neck as he whispered, "It is extremely charming when you speak."

As he stood up straight again, she stammered, "White Hall...I'm familiar with it, just outside of Charlottesville, right? I'd love to see it."

She stepped slightly away from him and re-directed her attention to the piece of art on the wall. "Are you going to bid on this piece? I think you should."

"You know, I have enjoyed myself this evening. I do believe it is the first time I have been able to fully enjoy one of these gatherings, and I thank you. Yes, I do believe I shall bid on this piece. What do you think I should bid?"

Kate was glad to redirect the conversation after the unexpected, but not unpleasant kiss on her neck. "Well, here's my strategy at silent auctions. If it's a piece I like, but don't love, then I put down what I'm willing to pay, and hope for the best. If I get out-bid, then...oh well, it wasn't meant to be. But if I see something I want, something I must have, then I'll risk everything. I'll put in some obscene bid. Something way over my budget, and hope the high bid scares off any competitors for the piece. So, I guess my question to you is...how bad do you want it?" She flashed him another look with a sly smile.

He took her in his arms, kissed each cheek, then ran his hand through her hair, and looked down at her, a wicked smile on his face. "Oh I want it very bad, and I am willing to risk it all. But in the end, will it be as rewarding as I had hoped? Now, I think perhaps $2,000 should be a good start, *si*?"

She looked down at the floor and appeared confused by his response. "Oh, I think $2,000 is good. But I'm not sure $2,000 will scare away competitors in this crowd. So I'd say...you like it...you don't love it."

He chuckled, "Perhaps. But you misjudge me. I always get what I want, and I would lose it all for something I feel I deserve. I think I will put in my bid, as is. If I am meant to have it, then it will be. But there are some things worth paying a high price for." He tipped her chin up to his face, locked in the gaze of her soulful brown eyes. "And you can never truly enjoy something so beautiful if you do not have to fight to win it, keep it and truly call it your own. Now, may I escort you home? I would not want you out so late on your own. I would be quite a rogue to let that occur."

"I...uh...I drove here, but you could escort me to the valet, and wait with me until they bring my car around."

"*Si, grazie*! May I?" He took her arm as he led her to the door. "*Mi amore*, your wrap?

"I didn't wear a wrap this evening. I was in such a hurry to get here, it never crossed my mind."

"Please take my jacket." He slipped off his tuxedo jacket and slid it over her, letting his hands glide over her shoulders. Walking with her outside, he handed the valet her ticket. "*Si*. You should be more careful. You could catch a chill in this fall weather. I have enjoyed my evening very much. I hope I was not a bore, and I will let you know if I get the painting. Perhaps you could help me hang it, if I am so lucky to win it."

"I'd like that very much. And thank you for the jacket. I forgot how chilly it gets in the fall once the sun goes down." She turned her head to one side, inhaling deeply his scent on his jacket. This evening had gone by much too fast. She hated leaving him.

"Please take the jacket and wear it home to keep you warm. I am sure we will see each other again soon."

The valet pulled up in a red Miata. Taking her into his arms, Shade pulled her close. "I wish to see you again. I hope the feeling is mutual." Leaning down, he slid his hand to the back of her head, pulled her face to his, and kissed her deeply. His tongue explored her mouth, his hand tangled in her hair. Breaking the kiss, he looked into her eyes. "Be safe, *mi amore*, until we meet again." He walked her around to the driver's side, taking her hand, helping her into the car, and tucked in his jacket sleeves. "Watch those shoes, no breaking a heel." Laughing, he closed the car door and stood back.

She looked at him through the glass, and mouthed the words, 'good night.' As she drove away, she glanced back at him in her rear-view mirror. She knew the scent of her rose perfume would be left on his jacket. She felt like she was marking his territory.

She turned on the radio and Norah Jones was singing "Turn Me On". She sighed as the thought to herself," *no kidding, Norah*. She got back to her Arlington condo, parked the car and headed upstairs. As she stepped inside the door, she removed the shoes and walked barefoot across the living room to the large window. His jacket still around her shoulders, she looked out over the city.

Shade had teleported back to his penthouse and watched her as she stood at her window, looking out into the night, lost in thought. She slid his jacket off her shoulders and carried it to her bedroom. He followed her movements as she walked barefooted to the other room, tossing his jacket on the bed. She reached behind her back and unzipped the dress. Something he'd like to do for her. She lowered the black sheath down her slender body, the knit clinging to every curve. She was wearing a black strapless bra and a black lace thong. He placed both palms against his window, as he watched her move around the room in the barely-there lace undergarments.

He remembered the taste of her tonight, his tongue exploring her mouth. He recalled her scent, the heady fragrance of roses, mixed with her desire for him. He felt his cock turn to steel.

His eyes never left her as he continued to watch from his window. She took off the bra, her breasts freed. He fought the desire to teleport into her room, shadow himself, stand next to her, touch her. He felt his beast rear up inside him, and he heard the low growl. The beast wanted her now and Shade battled hard to push him down, hold him at bay, but the beast would only be held back for so long before he'd demand his due.

He was mesmerized by her as she stood with her back to the window, and raised her arms above her head, running her hands through long red hair that fell around her shoulders. Shade felt his fangs punch through as his eyes glowed red, and the beast roared as he stepped back from the window. He had not fed in a few days, and this cat and mouse play with Kate had pushed the beast too far. He dare not go to her now. He was past the point of being able to control the black soulless bastard inside him.

He paced the floor. He must have an outlet now, but he was still too new to the States to know where to go. He couldn't afford to let the beast loose in a rampage on mortals in Alec's territory. That might draw unwanted attention. Besides, that was not his style. He grabbed his cell and dialed Alec.

"Brother, what's up?"

The beast responded in a hoarse growl, "Need help."

Alec replied, "A feeder?"

The beast growled, "Too late for that."

Alec sighed. "There's a safe house on Q Street, near Logan Circle. The password changes daily. Today it's 'Renegade.' Can you get there in time?" Alec heard the call end and hoped Shade could get there in time.

Shade teleported out to the safe house. There wasn't time for a response. He was running out of time.

A vamp safe house provided a safe environment for any vampire to release the beast to fuck and feed indiscriminately. There were no mortals there, as they'd be devoured, destroyed. A vampire would only find other unattached immortals, seeking violent release for their own beast. Like mortals, vampires had a sexual preference, but unlike mortals, they had no labels for heterosexual or homosexual practices. The beast took what was available, and made no moral judgments. In the safe house, the beast was released to savagely attack, to feed, knowing their partners, and there would be many, would all be healed by daylight.

Shade stood before the heavily fortified door of the building on Q Street. The windows were all darkened and barred. He impatiently rang the bell, and a small portal was opened. He saw the red eyes of another's beast staring back at him. He growled the word, "renegade," and the door was opened. Shade entered the dark rooms and released the energy of his long pent up beast, who immediately succumbed to the hedonistic pleasures that awaited him.

There were vampires who'd release their beast on mortals, knowing it would mean certain death for the mortal, but Shade would not. His Warrior's code prevented him from unleashing such strength and violence on anything so weak and defenseless they posed no immediate threat to him.

In Florence, he had a regular schedule for feeding, mortals who were willing partners, or immortals he could seek out, as well as a compound full of feeders, but he'd not established those relationships here yet. And then he met her, that unexpected redhead who called to him in a completely different way.

Not all vamps had established a permanent bond with a mate, but as a master, it was expected of him. As royalty, it was demanded of him, as he must mate and breed to produce an heir. But in five hundred years, he hadn't found her. There'd been two he'd thought possible, but in the end, he wouldn't seal the blood covenant with either Adriana or Sabine. His relationship with Adriana was centuries ago, and she was long dead, residing now in the spirit realm. His relationship with Sabine was more recent. But with both of these immortal female warriors, he found he couldn't, in the end, give his heart. And while he fed from them, he wouldn't allow them to feed from him, completing the circle that created the eternal bond between master and mate.

In five hundred years of experiencing the sexual jolt that accompanied feeding from others, both mortal and immortal, and watching the pleasure they received as well, he'd never experienced what it felt like to have someone feed from him, that ultimate intimacy of mutual feeding that would bind them for all eternity.

As sunrise neared, the beast was sated and Shade teleported back to the penthouse, stripping away his bloody clothes. Stepping into the shower, he watched as blood flowed down the drain. He leaned his head against the shower wall. His body well-fed, his sexual appetite satisfied, but emptiness in his soul. He hated giving in to the darkness of the beast.

9

Kate slept late after the charity event at the National Gallery of Art and spent a quiet Sunday reading, but her social calendar had kept her from getting any work done. So, now, Sunday evening would be spent trying to get caught up for a client presentation scheduled for Monday morning. She pulled out her laptop, but when she went through her briefcase, she discovered she'd not packed up the client file she needed. *Fuck!* This meant she'd have to go back to the office.

She stuffed her laptop back into the shoulder bag and shoved everything back in her briefcase. She considered taking the car since it was already dark out, but if she took the metro, maybe she could at least get through some email on the trip in. She pulled on a pair of boots with her jeans, grabbed a light jacket, threw the briefcase and computer bag over her shoulder, and headed out to the metro station.

She had only walked a block when she thought there was someone following her. She glanced over her shoulder. The man hung back, looking away, shuffling his feet. She convinced herself it was a coincidence and walked a little faster. She heard his footsteps behind her again, keeping pace with her own. She slipped her cell phone from her pocket and called Shannon, feeling if someone was on the phone with her, she'd somehow feel safer.

She picked up her pace again, as she listened to the phone ring, and roll to voicemail. *Fuck!* She glanced over her shoulder again, and he stopped, turned away from her, acting like he was looking in a shop window. *Okay, this is no coincidence*. Her heart started pounding as she looked around. The streets were empty at this hour. She looked through her phone again, scrolling past out-of-state family members and work associates until she saw his name. Hesitating for a few seconds, she hit dial.

***

Shade was busy at the Dead House, getting ready to call in the gang of so-called warriors. It felt good to get back to what he knew best, being a warrior and taking out the rogues that threaten their kind with exposure to the mortal world. Hearing his cell buzz, he looked and saw it was Kate. "Kate, to what do I owe this most pleasurable call?"

He could hear the tremble in her voice. “I...I'm so sorry to bother you...if you don't mind. Could you stay on the phone with me?”

He stood up from the beat-up office chair and started pacing. “What is wrong, tell me where you are. Talk to me, I am right here.”

“I'm walking to the Metro station near my condo. I need to go to work, but I think someone is following me. So, if you'll just stay on the phone...”

Son of a bitch, if anyone is touching my woman. “I am on my way, *mi amore*, I’m in Georgetown, not far. I’m coming to you, just keep talking to me. It will take me about fifteen minutes. Stay on the phone. Don’t lose sight of him.” *I am going to rip some fuckers head right off if he as much as looks at her*. Teleporting straight out, he had to stall, he couldn’t raise questions by arriving too quickly. He caught sight of her and her predator and stayed close to her on the rooftops. He dropped to the ground and kept hidden, but close enough to nail this scum if he got too close to her.

Kate looked over her shoulder and saw the guy stop again. She spoke a little louder, trying to make sure he knew she was on the phone, and aware of him. "Oh, you don't need to come out...really. I don't want to inconvenience you. I'm sure it is nothing. I just wanted someone to talk to."

As she continued to walk, she could see the metro station ahead, and the platform was deserted. That wasn’t unexpected at this hour on a Sunday night, but she’d been hoping for a few commuters. Now, she’d have to stand alone and wait for the train. Her heartbeat quickened. "Are you still there?"

“*Si*, I am right here, *mi amore*, almost to you. Take a deep breath. Don’t let him see your fear, he will feed on it. I am so close Kate. Stay in the moonlight, out of the shadows and near streetlights. It will deter him, too much light.”

His voice comforted her. “I’m about a block from the Pentagon City Metro platform. He’s still following me. I don't know what to do now. The platform’s deserted. I'll stop walking soon." She could hear the panic in her voice and was kicking herself for not taking the car. "Please don't hang up...but is there someone near you? Someone who could call the police? I don't want to hang up."

“Kate, turn around. Do you see me? I am right here.”

She looked back at the predator and saw Shade walking up fast behind him. She’d never been so relieved to see someone. She turned in his direction and started walking fast, then broke into a run in his direction. The predator looked startled as she ran straight at him, then looked over his shoulder and saw Shade behind him.

As she ran straight into Shade's arms, he picked her up, crushing her to his chest, and felt her shaking. He looked over her head and saw the predator watching them. Shade showed him a bit of fang and watched his eyes bug out of his head. *Now, you fucking bastard, you know what it feels like to scare someone.* He watched as the scumbag almost fell trying to get the hell out of there. Retracting his fangs, he released Kate from the grip against his chest.

"*Mi amore*, shhhh, it's okay now, I'm here. He is gone. You are safe now."

Kate felt herself sobbing she was so relieved. "I don't know how you got to me so quickly, but I'm so glad to see you. Thank you, thank you for coming."

He felt her shaking. This was what he was born to do, protect this woman...his mate? It hit him hard. She was the one. The one he'd been searching for his entire life. This beautiful female with the crimson locks was his. He wanted to throw back his head and howl, letting all the vampires in the night know, 'She is mine!' He slid his hands into her hair. He could feel her heart racing against his chest. Lifting her face to his, he saw her tears and it damn near broke him. He leaned down and kissed the tears from her cheeks. Licking his lips, he tasted the salty sweetness and his beast wanted more. He wanted to taste all of her, her life's blood, which he wanted for his own.

"It is fine now. He is gone, I am here. No more tears. I will never let anything happen to you, I promise you." Tipping up her chin, he kissed her lips gently at first and then intensified the kiss, letting her know he wanted her, he was always here for her, and he'd be hers for all eternity if she'd let him.

He set her back down gently on her feet, as they both reluctantly broke from the kiss. She looked up at him. "Do you mind...if I'm not imposing...could you wait with me until the train comes?"

"Of course I will wait with you, and I am riding there with you as well. No more scary business this night and no argument from you, *si*? It is done. What in the hell are you doing out here at this time of night? What am I going to do with you?" He smiled down at her.

"I was going in to work for a few hours. I had planned to work at home, but I left some of the files I needed at the office. We have a presentation to a client in the morning, so I had to run in. I've lived here in this condo for five years, and I went to college here before that. I've never had a problem before, even though everyone warned me. I guess my good luck ran out. Well, maybe not completely out, you came along."

The subway train arrived. He got on with her, sitting close to her on the bench seat. Snuggling in beside her, he laid his hand softly on her thigh. "So, tell me, how long will it take you to run into the building, grab this file and come back out? I will wait, *si*?"

"Oh, that's not necessary. Please, I've inconvenienced you enough for one night. I was just going to work there for a few hours, and I can take a taxi home. I promise to take a taxi. I'll be safe."

He slid his hand along her thigh and smiled at her. "No inconvenience, I assure you. You call me any time. I worry for you out here at night. I will wait for you to get your files and I'll call for a taxi to take you home. I am not leaving you alone in that building. It is not safe and I will not be comfortable until I know you are home. That is that, *si*?"

She leaned against his shoulder on the small bench seat. She loved how he made her feel protected, and when was the last time someone made her feel like this? To be honest, she hated working alone in that building late at night, it had always creeped her out.

"Thank you." She kissed him on the cheek, a quick kiss, before turning her head and looking down at her hands, clutched together in her lap. "I will take you up on that offer."

The subway pulled into L'Enfant Plaza and they exited. They made their way up the steps to the streets of D.C. He took her shoulder bags and tossed them over his shoulder, holding her hand as he walked her to the building. She grabbed her ID card and swiped it through the card reader to gain access to the building. "I'll just be a minute."

He grabbed the door as it opened, and followed her in. "I will not let you out of my sight this night."

She smiled back at him as they made their way to her cubicle. She quickly found the files she needed, and they left the building together, the taxi already waiting outside.

He walked her to the taxi and grabbed her around the waist, kissing her. "Now, instructions. You get in this taxi, which is paid for. You go straight home. And when you get there, you get inside and lock the door. Are we clear? This is how it is going to be, *si*?"

He pulled her hard against his chest again, and she was aware of his strength and the hardness of his chest. She fought the desire to run her hands up his chest and shoulders, as he kissed her. She was surprised by how much she liked how he took control. She liked that he led the way, looked after her, and commanded her. Normally, she would have bristled at someone giving her orders. But from him, she found it...sexy. Was that just because she'd been so spooked tonight? She thought not.

"Don't worry. Straight home, door locked, and thank you, really. I can't thank you enough."

He handed her the shoulder bags, as she got settled in her seat, then closed the door behind her. She turned and looked back at him standing on the sidewalk, as the taxi pulled away.

The cab dropped her off in front of her condo, and Kate tried to tip him. The driver responded, "No ma'am, everything's been taken care of."

She thanked him and rushed inside, taking the elevator up and hurried to her unit. Once inside, she flipped on the lights, locked the door, and sighed with relief. *What would have happened had he not been so close by?* She shuddered at the thought and brushed it from her head. She dumped the laptop and files down on the table and decided to call him before she started work. Just to let him know she got home safely, or at least, that's what she told herself. She pulled out her phone and hit redial.

***

He watched the taxi drive off with his woman, yeah, *his* woman. He wanted to ride along with her but didn't want to push the issue with her quite yet. He had fallen already, she had him, and she didn't even know it. Now, he just had to make her feel the same about him. He took a deep breath to clear his head. *Shade, old man, you never saw this coming, she is mortal, and this can only mean trouble*. He shook the thought from his head, it no longer mattered what world she came from. She was going to be his.

He teleported immediately back to the penthouse, arriving long before she arrived at her condo, and stood at the window waiting. He needed to know she was home safe. He watched until he saw the lights come on inside her unit and he saw her scrambling around inside. His heart beat faster at the sight of her, his blood pumping and another part of his anatomy coming alive, once again. Damn this woman was like a match to fire. His phone buzzed. He looked down to identify the caller...*that's my woman*! Smiling, he answered. "Tell me you followed my instructions and you are not in trouble again."

He made her laugh. "And if I were in trouble again, would you come to my rescue?"

"I will always come to your rescue. Thank you for letting me know you are safe. It takes a great weight off my mind."

"Thank you again. I don't know how you got to me so fast, I'm just happy you did."

He responded with a single word. "Kate?"

"Yes, Shade."

"If you need me to escort you anytime, just call me. I want you to be careful. I like being able to watch out for you. And...well, never mind. *Buonasera." Cazzo, she leaves me as tongue-tied as I leave her.*

"Thank you. That's a most generous offer."

They were both reluctant to hang up the phone, to end the call, to break the connection to each other. He loved the sound of her voice, but he had run out of excuses for keeping her on the call any longer.

There was a hesitation in her voice when she responded. "So...I guess it's good night then."

"Si." There was silence. Neither of them spoke. Neither of them hung up. He felt inept for the first time in forever with a woman. When had he ever been lost for words with a gorgeous woman? But this was no ordinary woman. She was far more than he could ever dream of. She was his mate. "I miss you already, *mi amore*."

Hanging up, he stared out the window at her and wondered what the future held for both of them. He felt a twinge of guilt. He should leave her alone, walk away. She was mortal and dragging her into his world wouldn't be easy. He shook his head, knowing it was already too late. He couldn't walk away from her now.

***

She heard him end the call. *He missed her?* Kate ran his words over and over in her head. Surely, she misunderstood his meaning. She picked up her shoulder bags and dragged everything into the living room, pulling out her laptop and the damned files that got her in so much trouble tonight. She shook her head. *Okay Kate, get focused!* She tried to clear her head of Mister Tall, Dark and Dangerous and worked on the presentation for the next day.

10

Rushing to get ready for work, Kate piled her hair on her head. She had the presentation to do and thought this would give her a more professional look. After last nights' scare, she forewent her designer shoes for a more practical pair of ballet flats. She gathered all the materials she'd prepared for today and decided it might be safer to drive her car in, even though the streets and subway stations were more crowded during the weekday rush hour. She drove into D.C., parked in an underground garage and walked the two blocks to her job, wondering as she did so how this was any safer than the subway. She grabbed her 'usual' coffee from Starbucks and headed into work, on time, for a change because of the scheduled presentation. The meeting took up the entire morning.

The presentation went well. She got back to her cubicle, ate a sandwich at her desk, and worked to get caught up. Shannon scooted her chair into Kate's cubicle, eager to hear the outcome with the new client. "So how did it go?"

"Oh my God, Shannon, it was horrible."

"The client presentation? What happened?"

"Oh...no...sorry, that went fine. The client was very happy with our proposal. My mind was on something else, entirely. I needed to come back in last night to pick up the client's files, and decided to take the subway. This guy...he was stalking me. Following me! I tried to call you, to just, you know, have someone on the phone in case something happened, but the call went to voicemail. So, I ended up having to call him...Shade. I mean, I couldn't think of anyone else to call. I just wanted him to stay on the phone with me, and he did. He said he was nearby, so he came out and intercepted the guy. I was scared to death. He rode the subway in with me, waited for me to get my files, and then put me in a taxi home."

Shannon smiled back at her. "Your knight in shining armor. How gallant! I'm teasing, you were quite lucky, you know. People get mugged around here all the time."

"Yes, I know. I drove my car in today. Although, I parked in an underground garage two blocks away, so I'm not sure that's any better when I leave here late at night. But, it's not like I have a choice. "

Shannon sighed, "I'm sorry. Call me next time. I'll ride in with you. You really should be more careful."

Kate finished up her lunch at her desk, and then let Shannon know she needed to get focused and back to work since she was now behind schedule after the all-morning meeting. The rest of the day passed uneventfully. Around 6:30, she decided to call it a day. She was feeling tired and hadn't gotten much sleep the night before, and now she knew she'd have to fight the traffic home. She packed up her briefcase and laptop and headed back to Starbucks. She decided to grab another coffee to take with her on the drive.

The streets were solid gridlock, so she made a spur of the moment decision as she walked to the coffee shop to sit it out for a while until the traffic cleared. She grabbed her coffee, turned to find a table, and saw him sitting there alone.

***

He had waited for her to exit the building, picking up on her thoughts to grab a coffee, so he got there ahead of her, sliding into a vacant seat at a table. He knew the minute she arrived. He picked up her scent of roses and it assaulted his nose in the most erotic way. He'd never been affected by the mortal's use of perfumes, but her scent could light him up. He gave her a few minutes to get her coffee and when she turned, he glanced up, locked eyes with her and smiled.

He loved the look on her face. She looked surprised to see him, but happily so. *Cazzo! She is like adding gasoline to a fire.* He beckoned for her to join him. As she walked toward his table he stood and pulled out a chair for her, so she'd be seated next to him.

"So, Mr. Medici, do we chalk this up to coincidence that you just happen to be at *my* Starbucks the day after my near-death experience? Or are you checking on me?"

He leaned down close to her ear as he pushed in her chair. "Perhaps a little of both, and don't think I can't see that glimmer in your eye. You like that I am checking up on you, *si*?"

She tucked her head. "I have to admit, after last night, it feels good to have someone checking up on me. I think I got used to being alone, and I've been lucky. But last night made me feel pretty vulnerable. More than I care to admit."

Sitting back in his chair, he crossed his arms and looked at her. "Kate, you've been very lucky. You need to be more attentive to your surroundings, have your guard up. Anything happens to you, I am not going to like it. So, are we riding the subway back home together?"

"I, uh, drove my car in today. But you can walk me back to my car."

"Oh, you can bank on that, *mi amore*. You will be escorted safely back to your car because if you think, for one moment, I am letting you stroll alone in the dark to wherever in hell you parked, think again."

Leaning in, he tipped up her chin and winked at her. Letting his hand wander into her hair, he gently tugged on the clip holding her crimson locks tight to her head and watched as her hair tumbled to her shoulders, cascading down the side of her face and through his hands. He could get lost in that silk.

"You should never put your silken locks in such a knot. You are so much more stunning with it cascading around that gorgeous face and pooling around those delicate shoulders."

As he slid his hand down her cheek and along her neck, he felt her heart rapidly beating in her veins and his fingers slowly brushed across her collar bone, down her arm and grasped her hand under the table.

"So, tell me, how was your big day you damn near got abducted for?"

His attention to her hair and his fingers brushing against her skin left her addled. He was asking her a question, but her mind struggled to concentrate. All she could focus on was his touch and the path of electric sparks that followed his fingers across her skin. She started to stutter as she answered him.

"It...uh...it went very well...I...think, I think we secured the account." She saw him stifle a laugh as she became more flustered when he laid his hand on her bare thigh.

"So, no Choo's today? Big presentation, maybe if you had worn them you would know if you secured that account. Those legs of yours, in a pair of Choo's, could sell me anything."

Her blush deepened as his hand slid along her bare leg, and he made a remark about her flat shoes. The heat from his hand on her skin sent a shiver through her. Her breath quickened as she slid slightly away from him. She felt rattled. "I'm...I thought...I wore flat shoes because I can walk faster..."

Shade was taken back at her response. Most women would curl closer to him, wanting his attention, this one moved away, but why?

Was he moving too fast for her? Removing his hand from her thigh, he sat back in his chair and wrapped his hands around the coffee he could not drink.

"Well, wearing flat shoes is a smart thing to do, it lets you maneuver faster, run if necessary and does not make you helpless to your enemy. Very wise."

Kate relaxed a little. He'd sensed her unease and removed his hand, and she was glad...and sad. *What? What is wrong with me?* She wanted his touch, but he left her so rattled. She was afraid he'd grow impatient with her and move on. But she was also afraid he'd take what he wanted and move on. *Why does this have to be so hard?* She struggled to find a common ground for conversation.

"So, uh, the land you bought. How's that going?"

"To be honest with you, I have not started developing it. There is much to be done before I can get started. The vineyards need work and the house, well, it is a house." He chuckled softly, "I am pressed for time, at the moment, with a project for Alec. That comes first, once I get that underway, the house can be handled. And what plans do you have this week?"

"I, uh, I actually have some business travel this week. I'll have to fly to New York, meet with a client there."

"I see." He looked down, an expression of concern on his face. "So, you go alone?"

She could tell he wasn't pleased with the idea of her traveling alone. "Oh, I've traveled all over the States, through Asia, and most of Europe on business. I'm always alone. I'm careful, I think. But you get used to it."

He ran his hand through his hair. "How long will you be gone?"

"This is just an overnight trip. I leave on Wednesday, and I'll be home Thursday night. At least I live close to the airport, and it's a very short flight, so no jet lag, right?"

"Well that is good news, *si*? I only have to worry about you for one night. You will call me? Let me know you are all right?"

She smiled at him. "I'd like that. Of course, I'll call you." She finished her coffee and looked around at the thinning crowd. "The traffic looks thinned now, would you mind walking me to my car?"

Standing, he stepped behind her and pulled out her chair, holding out his hand to take hers and lifted her from her seat. He grabbed her bag and laptop. "It would be my pleasure, *mi amore*. And besides, I won't sleep unless I know you made it home safe. Come." He held onto her as they wove their way from the coffeehouse to the street outside, where it was now completely dark.

She led him the two blocks through the busy D.C. streets, now filled with young people looking for bars and restaurants. He followed her to the dimly lit parking garage with many columns where an attacker could hide from view. She pulled out her keys and used the automatic button to unlock the door, the tell-tale beep-beep and the flashing lights indicated the location of her red Miata.

He opened the door for her and shook his head. "Automatic? You bought a sports car with automatic transmission?"

She laughed. "It's not a very practical car. No room for friends, no trunk space, but most of my driving is in the city, and besides, I don't know how to drive a stick shift." She leaned her back against the car and looked up at him. "Maybe you could teach me sometime?"

"You should be punished." He braced his hands on the top of the car and leaned into her, trapping her into the space between his arms. "Who drives a sports car and does not know how to drive a stick-shift. I will think about teaching you, if you make me one promise." He leaned in closer and snuggled into her hair.

She closed her eyes and listened to his voice as his lips were close to her ear. She felt her heartbeat quicken. She had to bite her tongue not to say she'd promise him anything he wanted. "And what is that promise?"

He kissed her softly on the neck, his moan barely audible. "That you go back to taking the subway, this place is far worse and more dangerous. Now," leaning back, he removed his hands from the car and slid them around her waist, pulling her to him. "Let's have a proper kiss goodbye and I will see you on your way home, *si*?"

"Yes...I'll take the subway...and the good-bye kiss."

"Good girl." Leaning down, his tongue slid across her lips and he kissed her, gently at first, before adding more pressure, his tongue glided inside her mouth. She relaxed in his arms and they remained locked in the kiss. She offered no resistance. When he broke the kiss, he locked eyes with her and stared for a few seconds before he spoke. "Let's get you inside the car and keep you warm, *si*? Now, I want you to go straight home. It's late." He helped her inside the car, handing her the briefcase and laptop and shut her door, as she started the engine.

He'd given her another one of those kisses that left her unable to think. She watched as he stepped back from her car and she pulled out of her parking space and drove away. She drew a deep breath, then sighed, and wondered, for the hundredth time, where this was going, and if she was just setting herself up for another fall.

11

Waking from his death slumber, Shade took a shower and decided to look over a few more of the contracts Alec had sent for the California property, but his mind kept wandering. He looked at the clock and knew she was in New York alone. That had him in a ball of nerves to begin with and knowing he couldn't look out the penthouse window to see her, didn't help his attitude.

He lay down on the couch and stared at his cell phone. He should call her. Hell, he should just fucking teleport to New York and find her, but he knew if he did, he wouldn't be able to keep himself away from her. She'd think he was a stalker, which actually, he was, but for a damn good reason. He struggled with that concept and worried he'd scare her off. He knew calling her was less threatening. She felt more confident on the phone. He had to know she was all right, and she was safe.

He threw his feet to the floor and sat up. He needed to feed, and badly. He hadn't fed in a few days, he'd been preoccupied with her, and he could feel himself becoming weaker. He needed to avoid another visit to the safe house, which meant he'd need to address his hunger soon. He sat down in the window, facing her empty condo and saw the lights come on, obviously on a timer. He stared aimlessly at the lit windows without her walking past them and moaned. *Cazzo! She has really gotten to me, who in the hell moans over a female you haven't even fed from or made love to yet?*

***

After spending the day with the client, Kate took a cab back to her hotel. Sometimes she had a co-worker with her on these business trips, and they'd plan an evening out, but since she was alone, she decided to go back to the hotel and order room service. She got back in her hotel, shed her work clothes, and put on a loose sweater, leaving bare feet and bare legs. She took out her laptop and curled up on the bed to check email. She missed her condo. No, that's not true, she missed *him*. She had thought of him a hundred times today. She thought of him on the flight here, in the taxi from LaGuardia into the city, checking into the hotel, all day during the client meeting...but especially now with nothing to distract her.

This man seemed to live on the edges of her life. She thought he was interested, but he hadn't actually ever asked her out. But she knew she sent mixed signals too. Then there were Rissa's warnings, always in the back of her head. She tried to focus on the task at hand, but he pushed all other thoughts from her head. She realized if she was going to get anything done, she needed to just call him, get it over with. She picked up her cell phone and hesitated before hitting dial. Again, she wondered what she was to him, and almost put the phone back down. She could hear Shannon in her head yelling at her to 'just do it,' so she hit dial.

"*Mi amore*? Do you need me to rescue you again?"

Kate laughed. "Rescue me from boredom maybe. Is this a good time? I don't want to intrude."

"I always have time for you. How was business today? Wear those heels?" Chuckling, he couldn't wipe the smile off his face, just hearing her sultry voice.

She leaned back against the headboard. "Do you always have time for me? And yes, I did wear heels today. But I kicked them off as soon as I got back to my room. So, is that your next question? Are you going to ask me what I'm wearing?"

"Let me close my eyes, I see a big sweater that falls off your shoulder, long gorgeous bare legs, no socks, feet that still ache from wearing those shoes all day and beg to be rubbed. Close?"

She was stunned into silence. She looked at the open window of her hotel room, but there was nothing close by that would allow anyone to see into her room. She felt exposed and pulled the sheet over her bare legs.

"I...yes...that's what...that's exactly what I'm wearing. How did...can you see me? Are you here in the city?" *She heard him chuckle.*

"It was a lucky guess. I did not mean to scare you. I can hear in your voice I have upset you. Please, I apologize. Forgive me, *si*?"

Kate shook her head. *Of course he can't see you. Don't be ridiculous!* "Well, then, I think it's only fair. You have to tell me what you're wearing."

"*Si*, that is fair. I am wearing jeans, holes in the knees, a bit worn, black thermal long sleeve, and a light running jacket. No shoes or socks either. Does that help? Can you visualize me?"

Jeans. She usually saw him in a suit, or dress pants. She hadn't seen him in jeans very often. He was in jeans the night he came to her rescue. Even being scared out of her mind, she couldn't help but notice how he filled out those jeans. She got a visual of him in the long sleeve shirt, something that would cling to his broad chest and shoulders, accentuate the muscles in his arms...oh yes...she could visualize him all right. She felt her face flush.

"And why would you need a jacket? Are you getting ready to go out? Did I interrupt you?"

"No, *mi amore*, you did not interrupt anything. Besides, I would stop whatever I was doing to sit and talk to you. I will venture out later, maybe take a run. Get some exercise and fresh air. So, tell me, are you enjoying New York?"

"I'd say normally I enjoy New York. But I think I'd rather be home. I feel...too far away." *What am I doing? If he's a player like Rissa said, am I not offering myself up on a platter? Why does this have to be so hard? Why can't I just be more like Shannon?*

He smiled, he missed her too, more than he cared to admit. "*Si*, I wish you were home as well, I would feel much better knowing you were closer to me. I miss you, Kate."

"Do you? Miss me? This feels...awkward...because I miss you too. I thought about you all day. But I really don't know you. You have my mind in turmoil. What have you done to me?"

"Well, my sweet Kate, I have done nothing yet. But there is one I think we can actually manage. Have you been invited to the Canton's next week, for a cocktail party?"

"Yes, she sent an email invite. I have to say, Rissa doesn't usually include me in this many of her events. She invites me to a few cocktail parties every year, as a courtesy I think, since I refer some of my clients to her. But you know I don't run in her social circles, right? You know I don't have that kind of money, or come from money. I don't want you to think I'm something I'm not."

"Kate, I do not judge anyone by their social standing. Trust me when I tell you, I am not one of those stuffed suits Alec likes to hang out with. All you have seen of me so far is the business side, and I would not normally be with those puffed up penguins either. I am more comfortable in jeans, *si*." He paused and took a deep breath. "May I ask you out for the cocktail party? I will meet you someplace if you feel more comfortable. I could meet you at Alec's house, if you wish to drive separately. But I would very much like to accompany you. Say yes, please."

"I...yes...of course. Is it okay if I meet you there?"

"Ah, perfect. It will just be a bunch of Alec's cronies, old goats who talk politics. It will be nice to have a beautiful face to admire and some good company. I hope you will not be embarrassed to be seen with me?"

"Why would you ever think that? Like I said, I'm the odd one out here. Rissa and I went to college together, we were roommates one year, but it was clear she came from money. I've never been in her league, or Alec's. I remember Rissa's remarks in college when the rich guys would date a middle-class girl. She called it slumming. Are you slumming, Mr. Medici?"

"Well, for Rissa, that would be slumming." He chuckled. "She likes money and power, and Alec gives her that. But she is very successful on her own. I have to give her that much."

There was a knock at her door. "Oh...hold on. There's someone at my door." Keeping the phone on her shoulder, she looked out the peep-hole to see a bellman. She told him she hadn't ordered room service and he said he had a delivery for her, so she opened the door.

"Who is it?" Shade asked.

"It was the bellman. He just delivered a dozen red roses. Wow! They're so beautiful, and I love the smell of roses. Who would send these? I don't see a card. The bellman said the order was anonymous. I can't imagine who'd send these. Who even knows I'm here?"

He chuckled again. "I know one person who knows you are there."

"Really? Who?"

"Someone who loves the smell of you, your scent is of the reddest rose. It inflames the heart. It says when you love, you love deeply without holding back. Perhaps the person who sent them misses you. Perhaps he wishes someone would love him as you would love...giving all."

"What? What are you saying?"

"*Si*, it is me, *mi amore*."

She was overwhelmed by his words. They caught her off guard. He spoke of love. She wasn't sure she was ready for this conversation. She dodged his comments. "You...love that scent? The roses? Shannon says it's too old-fashioned. Do you really like it?"

"You have no idea what it does to me. It is erotic and pure, sexy, and yet innocent. You encompass those qualities without even trying, Kate. I find that extremely attractive. I too am old-fashioned in my way. I only hope the next man who has your heart will earn it and cherish it."

Kate was confused. *The next man?* He said the next man, but not this man. Was he just being kind, a gentleman in town on business who needed a little diversion while he was here? He'd be back in Florence soon, and she'd be a distant memory. *Be careful Kate Reese, and don't get your heart broken...again.*

"That's very flattering. I'll make sure I wear my rose scent whenever you're around. You didn't say how long you expect to be in the States?"

"I am currently working under contract for Alec for the next year, at least. But I prefer to keep things open-ended, besides, I am trying to get these vineyards established here on the Virginia property. Does that please you, Kate?"

She smiled to herself. "Yes, it does please me. And I love the roses. I'll keep them on the table by my bed. I'm not exactly sure how I'll get them through my meeting tomorrow, and carry them with me on the plane, but I'll figure something out."

"Well, if you cannot manage to bring them home, I would be honored if you would allow me to give you more, *si*? You must be exhausted by now, and if I am going to take that run, I need to get moving. I don't want to keep you awake, you need your sleep."

What I need is him! The thought flashed through her head, and her face turned red. She was glad he couldn't see her reaction. "I am tired, and I still have a little work to do. But, if you encounter any stalkers on your run and need help, you know you can call me, right?"

She heard his hearty laugh. "Oh *si*, I know who to call. Be careful, please. Sweet dreams. I miss you, Kate. Let me know when you get back into town. I am sure if we do not see each other before, I will meet you at the cocktail party. *Buonasera, mi amore*. Think of me. I am thinking of you."

12

Shade felt much better after the call, knowing Kate was safe in New York, and she'd be home tomorrow. He sensed she was getting closer to him, trusting him more with each encounter, and he'd definitely have her soon. He knew in his heart, she was already his, now he just needed her to know that. She was still a little skittish, he could feel her pull away from time to time if he moved too boldly, but she flirted with him and he liked that. She was letting her guard down, and he hoped this cocktail party at Alec's would bring them closer still.

In the meantime, he still needed to feed. Deciding to take a long run, he exchanged his jeans for some sweat pants, threw on some running shoes, and pulled the hood on his sweatshirt over his head. He made his way to a small community park where there were some jogging paths and dim lighting. He'd already checked this place out earlier, before sunrise one night, and found it to be a great place. There were mortals walking dogs or running, and most of them were women, offering a good source for feeding. The women runners were easy prey for a vampire, especially a vampire who had a great body and good looks and could talk a woman into anything.

He teleported into the park and began his run. The place was pretty much deserted at this time of night, but he started his run and kept a good pace. He saw a young female running ahead of him. He hung back some distance, watching that beautiful ass. She was no novice at running and working out, her body was firm and toned.

He could sense that the woman could feel his presence behind her and without looking back she picked up her pace.

You can run sweetness, but you will never get away from me. He let his feet hit the path harder, made his breathing more labored, intentionally making his presence known so she'd hear him coming and not be startled. He watched her turn to look back at him and then sped up her own pace once again. He picked up the speed until he was running beside her, throwing back his hood and letting his long black curls fall around his face.

She looked over at him and he smiled, locking her in the gaze of his ice-blue eyes, and began to talk to her. He made small talk, saying he hadn't seen her here before, and how he was just getting in a late workout and enjoying the cool night. Their pace slowed to a more normal jog as they talked more, and she became comfortable with him. She commented on his accent, and he knew he was drawing her in and she no longer feared him. He kept up the conversation about working out, and how good it felt to get out of the office and move, get some fresh air. She was very pleasant and attractive, and she was enjoying his attention.

As the run ended, he walked her back to the small car park. There were several other cars around, but no other people. Perfect. Her body language was telling him a lot, so was her pretty face and inviting smile. She was letting him know she was interested in more than a night run. He made it clear he also had more in mind, and it wasn't long before she asked if he'd like to go for a coffee. As they slid into her car, she carefully maneuvered the car out of the lot but instead of heading to the main street, he suggested she take a side road alongside the park, where it was dark and remote from traffic. She turned to look at his blue eyes, and eagerly complied, following his direction as if entranced, then turned off the engine and turned to him.

"So what do you have in mind?"

He could see the light of the moon reflecting in her eyes as she leaned in closer to him, and he kissed her, as her hand slid between his legs. He heard her gasp as her hand wrapped tight around his cock. He never disappointed the ladies with his length and girth, and she was most delighted. And to help the situation, he was going commando, as always.

His hands went straight into her blonde hair, as he guided her head to his lap, and her mouth consumed him, working her magic. Laying his head back on the seat, he closed his eyes, and all he could see were crimson locks, those gorgeous deep brown eyes, and those red lips he longed to kiss. He felt his beast rise and want his due. He knew before this went too far he needed to feed.

He tugged softly on her hair and lifted her head to face him, kissing her hard. Snuggling into her neck, he could feel her vein pulsing, calling him to take what was his. He felt her hand stroking him, and his fangs punched through as he sank them deep into her neck. He felt her initial struggle, a combination of fear and confusion before she was hit with that lightning bolt of heat between her legs. He drew a deep gulp of her blood and swallowed, feeling the inevitable burst of his own sexual desire.

She quickly stopped struggling as he took more blood. He knew desire would overcome her, allowing him to feed and get his fill, while her own body was wracked in orgasm, the likes of which he knew she'd never experienced before.

He wouldn't drain or kill her, as mortals believed about the vampire myth. Most were careful to cover their tracks and left no evidence of their feeding. Turning a mortal was something vampires did with great reservation, as they must assume responsibility for that mortal. She could only be turned if she was first allowed to drink from him, and in five hundred years, Shade had allowed no one to drink from him.

He held her head gently in his hands, letting her body and his, respond to the waves of sexual pleasure that washed over them. She began to moan and her body relaxed as he felt her heartbeat slow, signaling to him he'd taken enough blood. He retracted his fangs, licked the puncture wounds clean so they'd heal quickly, and then kissed her. Her hand laid limp in his lap, the results of her ministrations, and his peaked desire, his cum dripping through her fingers. She looked at him confused, but not frightened.

He laid his hand across her forehead and wiped her memory clean. She'd remember some of it, but nothing that would endanger him or his kind. He pulled some tissues from a box on the floor and wiped her hand clean of his cum as she stared blankly. Stuffing the soiled tissues in his pocket, he let himself out of the car and teleported high into a tree and waited to make sure she was okay. He watched as she drove off into the night, wondering what in the hell happened. She was unharmed, she'd feel tired, but her body would replenish her blood loss and he left her with the sweet memory of euphoria she felt after that explosive orgasm. It was how he liked leaving them all when he was done feeding. It was his thank you for the meal they provided.

13

Kate was running late as she went through her closet trying to find another cocktail dress. Rissa had said there would be some of Alec's senator friends and their wives in attendance, and she was wondering again, exactly why Rissa invited her? She found the soft mauve colored dress that fit her like a glove. The color looked good against her pale skin and accentuated the color of her hair. It was fairly low cut in front and left her back and shoulders bare, with small spaghetti straps crisscrossing her back. The dress had a ruched center seam that ran straight down the back, conforming to the curve of her rear. Even though she knew Shade loved her hair down, she pinned her hair up as it drew emphasis to the back of the dress.

She spritzed on her rose-scented perfume, grabbed a wrap for her shoulders, and headed to the car. Georgetown was right across the river, so it was a short drive to Alec and Rissa's home. As she pulled up in her car, she saw him, pacing and smoking a cigarette, looking disturbingly handsome in his dark suit and white shirt.

Shade looked up when he saw her car. Unlike Kate, he'd not tied his hair back tonight, and it fell in soft waves around his face. She parked the car and he immediately came to the driver's side, opened her door, and extended his hand. She stepped out of the car to greet him, but before she could utter a word, she found herself in his embrace and in the middle of a passionate kiss.

Ending the kiss, he smiled down at her, taking out his handkerchief he tipped her chin up with one finger, softly but efficiently wiping off the smudged lipstick his kiss had caused.

"I am sorry, *mi amore*, I do believe I smudged your lipstick with that kiss. Tell me, did you miss me?"

She was thinking he should just kiss away all her lipstick and be done with it. But she answered his question, "I did miss you, sir."

Chuckling, he responded, "So formal! You look beautiful tonight. This is a small gathering this evening, more intimate, just a cocktail party. The guests are people from Alec's inner circle of senators. He is obviously schmoozing and buying favor, more than anything this evening. Thank you for allowing me to escort you. I am most honored."

"I'm happy you asked. I was wondering why I even got this invitation from Rissa. I don't really know any of these people. Do you think you're up for the challenge of keeping me entertained for the evening, Mr. Medici?"

"Oh, I assure you, Miss Reese, I am more than up for it."

As they reached the door, Alec's butler, Santos opened it and greeted them, showing them into the formal living room where most of the guests were mingling with drinks in hand. Shade kept his hand on the small of her back, moving her into the room and nodded to Alec, who tipped his glass to him, acknowledging Shade's presence.

"What can I get you as refreshment, Miss Reese?" Shade asked.

"White wine, please. I haven't eaten much today. I should probably take it slow." She looked around the room, recognizing faces from the news, but no one she knew personally. "Wow...this is intimidating."

"Do not be intimidated, no one in this room can compare to your beauty or my money. They are merely power-hungry men who have some evil ways of getting what they want. Let me get your wine. I shall return shortly. I do believe I see Rissa heading your way. Prepare yourself."

He softly kissed her neck and let his hand slide down her back and over her ass, as he walked to the bar.

***

Rissa surveyed the room as most of the guests had already arrived. People were always more than eager to come to their home, hear the latest gossip, and make sure they were included in whatever plans Alec had.

She didn't have to turn to look, she could smell vampire the moment they came close to the house, and since she and Alec were the only immortals in this small party tonight, she knew it had to be Shade Medici. She worked her way around the room, smiling, pouring on the charm before she spotted him and saw he was with Kate. She watched how he moved around her, his hand lying protectively on the small of her back, that signal from the alpha male, mortal or immortal, letting other men in the room know she was spoken for.

Well, well, well, the meek little Kate thinks she is having a vampire, I would think again, sister. I'll need to keep a close eye on this. I thought for sure she'd have taken my advice, but Shade and those damn blue eyes, she couldn't resist.

She saw Shade step away, and decided to approach her. "Kate! So glad you could make it, so lovely to see you." Rissa softly kissed both cheeks with a fake smile on her face. "What a lovely dress, and that color...it's so...unique."

"Thank you for the invitation. You look lovely tonight as well, but then, you always do. I can't imagine your closet and the number of cocktail dresses you must own. If I get many more invites from you, I'll need to go shopping. I heard you were doing some remodeling since I was last here."

Rissa cooed her response "Oh I could never keep count of my dresses. Alec spoils me endlessly. I'd love to show you how I remodeled the kitchen. Good heavens, you have no drink. Oh, I see Shade is bringing you something now and my Alec is making his way over. Have you been formally introduced to Alec? He meets so many people, I am never sure."

Leaning in, whispering through gritted teeth, Rissa hissed at Kate. "What are you doing with Shade Medici? You are in for some severe heartbreak, Kate, I warned you."

Kate felt annoyed but responded to Rissa's whispered remarks. "I know what you told me, Rissa. It's nothing serious. He's just a flirt. This is nothing!"

***

Shade got Kate a white wine and made small talk with a short fat man at the bar in a well-cut suit. Making his way back to Kate, he saw Rissa putting on her usual hostess performance when she began to look a bit agitated and whispered in Kate's ear. *Bitch better watch her step*.

Walking up behind his *bel rosso*, he casually handed her the wine and clinked glasses with her, as he held his glass of Midnight. "To a beautiful night."

Taking a small sip, he smiled at Rissa. "*Buonasera,* you look lovely, as usual, this evening. I see Alec making his way over, no doubt craving your beauty."

Alec joined the threesome. "Rissa darling, would you care to introduce me to your friend?" Alec looked at Kate. "I do apologize, but I've forgotten your name."

Rissa smiled at Alec. "I'm sure you remember Kate Reese, from my college days. She works for Brunswick Ad. Lives in Arlington? Surely, you remember her? She's being escorted by Shade, this evening."

Alec nodded to her. "Of course, I remember now, your old college friend." He gave Kate the once over, sliding his eyes to the floor and back up to her face before he turned to address Shade. "And how good of you, Shade, to make sure she has an *escort* for the evening."

Shade watched his greedy eyes take in every inch of her, and he stepped in closer, putting his arm around her waist and pulling her against him. "*Mi amore*, may I officially introduce you to Senator Alec Canton. I am quite sure you will never forget his name, as he has so conveniently forgotten yours, but of course, you are of no use to him in the Senate. Alec, this is my lovely woman, Kate Reese."

Alec looked annoyed with Shade. "Please, Kate, take no offense. I meet so many people in my job, it's impossible to remember everyone's name." **"Rissa, find out what the fuck is going on with Shade and this mortal."**

Rissa telepathically answered Alec's message. **"Of course, Alec, I was thinking the same thing. She wants a tour of the kitchen. Keep Shade busy while I lead her outside for a tour and some interrogation."**

Alec threw his arm across Shade's shoulder. "Shade, if you don't mind, there are some business issues we need to discuss. Maybe we could let the ladies have some time together, while we talk privately?"

Shade nodded to Alec and said, "*Si,* we can meet now if you want." Leaning down, he kissed Kate's cheek lightly. "I will return shortly, enjoy your time with Rissa, I will not be long, *mi amore*." He followed Alec into his study.

Rissa grabbed Kate's arm and intertwined it around her own, then drug her in the direction of the kitchen. "Come along Kate, we have a tour to take. And you have some explaining to do. Keep smiling and move."

Kate's head was reeling. *Did he just call me 'his'?* His tone with Alec was defensive, and the way he pulled her in close, like he was sending a message. Now Rissa was dragging her off to the kitchen and she was clearly pissed. Kate looked over her shoulder at Shade, as he walked with Alec. He turned his head and winked at her before disappearing down the hallway. *His.* She repeated the word in her head. *His. Am I ready to be his?*

Despite all of Shannon's encouragement, Kate didn't do casual relationships. Her heart only had an on/off switch with no speeds in between. Could she flip that switch to on again and open herself up to heartbreak? She thought it was harmless flirting, and he'd tire of her and move on. But he called her his, and for some reason, the idea of being his made her giddy. She felt the smile spread across her face. *Be careful Kate Reese.*

Rissa snapped at her. "This is the kitchen. And that...is the door out to the pool. Let's go out there and take a nice little tour." Placing her hand on Kate's back, Rissa swung open the French doors and pushed her outside, turning and slamming the doors behind her.

"Start talking! What's going on with you and Shade? He's all over you, it's so obvious, so don't lie or pull that sweet innocent act on me, doesn't work. Talk!"

"Rissa, you're taking this over the top! Seriously, I met him a few weeks ago at the big gala you threw, and since then, I've run into him a few times. We've talked on the phone, and we accidentally met up for coffee. I guess tonight would be our first official date in that he asked to escort me here. I mean, don't get me wrong, I'm very attracted to him, but until he introduced me to Alec as 'his woman'...I guess I'm as caught off guard as you are. But why should you care who I see? It's not like you've been monitoring my dating life in the past. What's the big deal?"

"Do you think he just showed up wherever you happened to be? Come on, grow up!" Walking up to her, Rissa went nose to nose with her. "I care very much who you see when it comes to him. Did he tell you what and who he is?"

Kate felt indignant and resented this inquisition. "Of course he told me. He owns a bunch of vineyards in Italy and apparently has done quite well for himself. Clearly, he comes from money, but you *know* that's not why I like him. Unlike you, the size of a man's checkbook was never high on my list of required criteria when it comes to selecting the men I date."

Rissa laughed in her face. "This has nothing to do with money. Granted, this one has more than enough, not that you'll ever see it. Let me fill you in on a few things. Shade Medici has left out a few key details on his life. Life-altering details, I might add. He and Alec are much more than just business partners. Sit down...we need to have an in-depth conversation, Kate. This is serious."

Kate was steaming at the implications. Rissa had always made sure everyone knew where she came from, and how much money her rich family from Boston had. Even in college, she only went out with the 'right guys'. So what had her so riled up? Was it that she was treading on her turf somehow? "I'll sit down and listen to what you have to say, but really, I think who I date is my business."

Rissa sat down next to her. "When you date Shade Medici it *becomes* my business. What I'm about to disclose to you, if ever repeated, could mean the end of your life, Kate. I take a great risk telling you. I could endanger my own life. Shade isn't human. He's immortal, vampire. Yes, he drinks blood to survive. Did he tell you that? Did he ever take you to dinner? Have you ever seen him eat food? I think you haven't. That deep red wine he drinks, it's a special blend, one he makes himself and is kept in reserve for our kind. It's human blood and alcohol, and no one knows that damn recipe. Alec is vampire as well, and...so am I. He turned me from mortal to immortal to be with him forever. Take it all in, Kate, think about it. Shade came to me, demanding I invite you to all my events. I didn't want to. Seriously, you just don't fit in with our set. I didn't want him to pursue you, but apparently, he has his own ideas. He and Alec are old, very old. Shade is a warrior, a beast who kills mortals and immortals alike. He defends our immortal world. He's vicious and brutal, lopping off heads and ripping out hearts with his bare hands. And he has his eye on you and once you have his attention, he won't be satisfied until he has you...blood and body. And sex with an immortal? I don't have to ask if you've slept with him yet. If you had, you wouldn't be here tonight. Trust me, you're not ready."

Kate was staring at Rissa as if she had escaped from an asylum. *What is she talking about? Vampires? Is she kidding me?* Kate tried to remember if she ever saw Shade eat anything. At the restaurant, he was at the bar, and then coffee, he drank the coffee, didn't he? But that's ridiculous! She's sure she's known a lot of people she'd never seen eat. *This is absurd! What she's saying is absolutely absurd. Shade, vicious and brutal?* He'd been nothing but a gentleman with her.

"Rissa...I'm sorry, but I find all of this just a little hard to believe. I mean...vampires...really? That's the best you can do?"

Rissa looked away from her. "I know it's hard to grasp. But you'll find out for yourself if you don't tell him to get the hell away from you. He wants to have sex with you, drink your blood. It goes hand in hand with them. Many vampires get off on inflicting pain. I know damn well by the way he looks at you, he wants you. Has he ever been at your neck, innocently snuggling? Have you heard him taking you in, inhaling your scent? You need to believe me, Kate. And if you tell one soul...they will come after you, in droves, and rip you apart, sucking you dry...like the savage beasts they are."

Kate backed away from her as she talked, absorbing the images she portrayed. Rissa was scaring her now. He couldn't be this man she described. But why would she make this up? "But Alec...you love him. Do you love him? Does he hold you against your will? What are you saying to me?"

Rissa stood up and stared at her. "I'm telling you to not get involved with him. Let him go. I love Alec, he's my master. He will never love another but me. I'm his mate, his chosen one. He rules my life. He takes my blood to survive. Are you willing to make these changes for Shade? I told you before to be careful. I told *him* to leave you alone. I was looking out for you, trying to protect you from our world. Perhaps, it would be best if you just leave now. You can go out that back gate. It will take you to the side street. Shade will be tied up with business with Alec for a while yet. I'll make your excuses. Think about what I've told you, and remember, you breathe one word, we'll all know where it came from."

Kate allowed Rissa to drag her over to the gate. *Why would she lie? This can't be true.* Vampires weren't real, but Rissa's words scared her. And she had to admit, she'd always seen something dark in him. Didn't she call him 'dangerous' from the first time they met? "Okay...maybe you're right. I feel horrible just leaving, Rissa...he...maybe I should say goodbye first? Let him know I'm leaving?"

Rissa violently shook her head. "No! He'd never let you leave. Not once he realizes you know what he is. You have to go now!" Rissa opened the courtyard gate, and gently pushed Kate out, closing it behind her. "Go! While you still can. This is for your own protection, trust me."

Kate stared back at her, her mouth open, but she had no words. She took the pathway that ran along the side of the house, back to the street and her car. She looked back at the house, her heart breaking. Was she doing the right thing? She got in her car and started the drive back home, feeling fear and confusion, and more than a bit of doubt as the tears fell down her cheeks.

Rissa leaned against the closed gate and laughed. *That will teach you to fucking mess with my world, bitch! You'll never intrude where I rule.* She turned and started walking back toward the house and her guests. **"Alec, she had no idea he was a vampire. He's playing with her. She's a toy to him. I sent her packing. I do believe we won't be seeing her again. I'm back to our guests, don't leave me alone too long, I miss you."**

***

Alec took Shade to his office where he had copies of their contract, along with the deeds for both the California and Virginia properties. "So, I assume you've had time to go over these. It's everything we discussed. Are you ready to sign? I'd like to get started as soon as possible. I know you've already spent some time at the, what did you call it, the Dead House? I'm aware you've met with my warriors already, but the sooner we get started the better."

Browsing over the documents, Shade found them in perfect order and he was also anxious to get the hell out of this office and back to Kate. He felt as though he'd deserted her. "I have gone over them in great detail and everything looks in order. I am more than ready to start getting that ragtag bunch of yours into Medici shape."

Alec shook his hand. "Great. I'll have my lawyer send the originals to you for signature at, uh, the penthouse in Arlington? Are you living there until you can get the Virginia property renovated?"

Alec heard the message from Rissa in his head and knew Kate had left the party. That news was both good and bad. There was no way to predict how Shade would respond.

Shade slowly lifted his eyes to Alec. "Yes, I am staying there for a short period of time until I can arrange to have some work completed on the Virginia property. Problem?"

Alec slapped him on the back. "No problem, brother. I couldn't help but notice how attentive you were to the mortal, is all. Doesn't she live in Arlington as well? Or is that just a coincidence? I just would hate to see you stir up trouble here in D.C. with any mortals. I'm sure I can line up a few immortals for you. I for damn sure understand your needs, and I know your type."

Shade bristled at his remarks. "I can handle my own affairs. You need not be concerned. I have no intentions of causing you or this city any trouble. Speaking of which, I apologize for the late call the other evening."

Alec ran his hand through his dark curls. "Yeah, about that, you sounded on the edge. You make it okay? What set you off anyway?"

Shade shrugged. "I went without feeding for too long. I was so busy checking out the new properties, getting grids and maps organized. You know how it is, brother, busy as hell and you lose track of the time. But I suppose with Rissa and other tempting delights, you have forgotten not having something handy in a strange territory. I made out okay, and *grazie*, I was on the extreme edge and just wasn't paying attention to the hungry black bastard inside me."

Alec looked at him with question, willing to bet anything the redhead had more to do with his beast losing control than he wanted to admit. "Well, all the more reason you need a good, strong immortal female to feed your appetites...all of them. Let me know, brother, as I said, I know who's in the area, who's unattached. You won't be disappointed. Shall we go back to the party?"

He extended his arm out in the direction of the door, not looking forward to Shade's response when he discovered the redhead was gone.

Shade followed his direction and headed to the door. "*Grazie,* brother, I have this under control."

Walking out the office door, they made their way back to the guests. Shade scanned the room for her, didn't see her, and realized he'd lost her scent. *She was gone. Gone?* He got a very bad feeling. Rissa was the last person with Kate and that bitch knew how to stir the pot. Shade spoke through gritted teeth, "Where is she, brother?"

Alec stepped in closer. "Where is who? And I need you to calm down Shade...your temper. Reel it in. You're around mortals here."

Shade growled softly and turned to look at him. "Get your mate over here now, I need to speak with her or you are going to see one pissed off master, mortals or not. I want to know where Kate is."

Alec put his hand on Shade's shoulder, ready to push him from the room if it came to that, and made eye contact with Rissa, signaling she needed to join them. "Let's step back in the office, shall we, brother? I need to be careful around the mortals."

Shade watched Rissa, locked eyes with her for a second and followed Alec back to the office. He was waiting for that bitch to walk in the door. "Someone better explain to me where in the hell Kate is."

Alec tried to soothe him. "Brother...calm down...I'm sure there's an explanation. Rissa, you talked to her. What's going on?"

Rissa entered the study and closed the door behind her. She walked over to Alec and stood close to him. In a defiant voice, she answered, "I wanted to know why, of course, Shade was calling her 'his woman'. That means one thing in our world. She played games with me, claiming nothing was happening. I told her he was immortal. She said she didn't feel well and I offered to let her lie down in one of the spare rooms to wait, but she insisted she go home."

Shade heard nothing beyond hearing Rissa say she told Kate he was a vampire. He growled, and his fangs punched through, he stepped closer to her, towering over her. "How dare you stick your nose in my business. She belongs to me. How could you do this to her? How could you expose all of us like this?" He stared at Alec. "You need to teach her how to control that mouth of hers. *Cazzo*, Alec!"

Alec came to Rissa's defense, trying to end this foolishness with the mortal. "Shade, how can you say she's yours when the woman doesn't even know what you are? Fuck! Unless it's a quick feed, even mortals have a right to know what they're dealing with. No wonder you were out of control the other night. This all makes sense to me now. Do yourself a favor, brother, forget the mortal, and let me hook you up."

Shade felt his breathing hasten and his temper rising. All he could think about was Kate. She was probably scared out of her mind and now he'd lost the chance to explain to her in his own way, who and what he was.

"She is mortal, but if I have my way, she won't be for long. You take care of your own woman. Excuse me, but I have things to attend to." He turned to Rissa, "You should be damn glad your master is standing there to protect you because your ass would be dead if I had you alone." In anger, he teleported out of the house.

Alec was livid as he paced around the study. "Oh, he can't be serious. His mate? He was planning on making her his mate? Is he out of his fucking mind? The vamp lives five hundred years, has fucked everything mortal and immortal across every continent, comes to the States for a few fucking days and thinks he found 'true love'? What kind of fucking bullshit is that? Trust me, I know him, this will blow over. He's been down this road before, just never with a mortal. You did him a big favor, Rissa. The sooner this girl is out of his head the better."

"Alec, relax, she won't have anything to do with him any longer and if she does, I can make sure it doesn't get out of hand. Now come, let's rejoin our guests. I'll get you a fresh Midnight and let's enjoy the rest of the night together." Standing on tiptoe, she kissed his cheek and wrapped her arm around his elbow, leading him back to the party.

***

Kate pulled into the underground garage and rushed to the elevator. She'd been trying unsuccessfully to control her tears all the way home. She just wanted to get inside where she'd feel safe. She got to her unit and unlocked the door. Closing the door behind her, she slid her back down the door until she was sitting on the floor. She released all the pent up tears of hurt and confusion.

Why would Rissa say these things? They can't be true. Did I run away from him for no reason? Did I make a mistake? She shook her head. She'd made an oath to give up men for a reason. Nothing was worth all this drama. She covered her face with her hands and sobbed.

***

Teleporting straight into his penthouse, he saw the lights on in her condo, but she wasn't moving about, and he was frantic to know if she was home. Shade stood at the window but he couldn't see her, and it was killing him. He knew she must be in agony, disappointed in him. *Cazzo, she is probably frightened out of her damn mind.* He was finally breaking through her timidity, bringing her closer, and Rissa went and fucked up any chance he may have had. She'd never come to him now. *Think Shade. Think!*

Going back to his bedroom, he stripped off his suit and threw on a pair of jeans, reached into the pocket of his suit pants and grabbed his phone. She always relaxed when he called her. That was his only damn chance with her now. Walking back to the window, he was so rattled and furious, worried for her. He must win her back, but he needed her to respond to him first.

He saw her stand up from the floor and walk into the bedroom, tossing her things on the bed. She sat on the bed and buried her face in her hands. He hadn't seen her sitting on the floor inside her front door. He saw her face streaked with tears, her make-up a mess. He'd caused her this pain by not telling her sooner, by not leading her slowly into his culture.

Dialing up her number, he ran his fingers through his hair as he heard the cell begin to ring. He watched her look at her phone. *Come on mi amore, pick it up. Answer, please answer!* He listened to the ring until it went to voicemail. *Fuck you, Rissa!* He heard the soft sweetness of her voice in her recorded message, the casual lilt he'd grown to love. He heard the beep to record his message on her phone. "Kate. Please answer and talk to me. We need to talk. Please let me explain. Pleas give me a chance, I want to explain. Rissa is crazy. I have no idea what she may have told you about me, I just know you are upset and confused. I miss you. I just want to hear…" He heard the beep before he could finish his plea and he threw the phone across the room.

Kate heard her cellphone ring and looked at the clutch. With hesitation, she opened it and looked at the ID. She set the phone back on the bed and let the call go to voicemail. She stood and started to remove the dress, letting it drop to the floor. She stepped out of it and reached up releasing her hair from the bun, letting it fall past her shoulders and down her back.

Grabbing a robe from the closet , she pulled off the strappy silver heels, tossing them aside. She walked barefoot back to her bed and heard the beep that let her know he'd left a voice-mail. She picked up the phone and against her better judgment, decided to listen to his message, to hear his voice. She played back the message and heard how frantic he was; begging her, pleading with her, and a fresh flood of tears fell. She felt so broken now, so confused. He was pulling her in one direction, and Rissa was fighting so hard to pull her in another. She didn't have the courage to call him back. She lay across the bed, her face in her pillow and cried.

The phone rang again, and she saw his name. She knew he'd continue to call until she answered. She had no idea what to say to him, she didn't even understand this herself. Before it rolled to voicemail again, she answered, "Hello."

He let out his breath. "Kate. Please talk to me. I'm sorry, I have no idea what Rissa told you, but she said you left and you seemed upset. What is it? Talk to me."

What do I say? She said you were a vampire? I'd sound like a complete idiot. "I...she said...she said I was in danger with you...she just kept saying I needed to get away. Please, I'm not sure I can talk about this right now. I mean, what's going on? Why is she pushing me so hard to break it off with you?"

"I don't know, did she mention anything specific? I have a past Kate, she knows that, but I am not that man any longer. Perhaps she thinks I will play with your heart, but I promise you, I do not want that. I want to be with you, *mi amore*. Please tell me how can I banish those thoughts from your mind?"

Kate wanted to believe him, but she'd been here before. She always wanted to believe them. "She mentioned your past...after the first time I met you when I called for your number. She warned me off then...and again tonight. She was...pretty graphic."

"I have a past Kate, everyone does. Mine is worse, perhaps. Did I ever treat you badly? Was I ever anything but a gentleman to you? Please, I only wish to be given a chance to show you what kind of man I can be. Honest, faithful, and loving."

Kate rolled over on her back. *Faithful and loving, Ha!* How many times had she heard that before? "You know, if I had a dollar for every man who'd promised to be faithful to me, I could retire a rich woman. So what makes you any different?"

"Perhaps, Miss Reese, it is not me but you that has made the difference. I have had sex with many women, but none of them could capture me. You have me spellbound. I can think of nothing but you. And all I want is to prove to you that I am a man worthy of your heart and giving you love as you have never felt, but of which you are so worthy. I am not a man of flowering verses. I am what I am. But I know what I see before me. I dreamt of a beautiful woman with a pure heart, a soul that aches for her mate, a woman with a contagious laugh and beautiful eyes that melt me. Her intelligence and common sense are rare and exceptional. She is the sexiest female I have ever beheld, and she doesn't even try. She is just herself. Then you stepped out of my dreams and walked into my life, and I don't want to lose you or let go of you."

She heard his words and fresh tears fell. She wanted to believe him, but she'd been here before. Broken promises, Ethan was a master of broken promises, and she'd heard them all. "Please...I just need some time. I'm begging you. Give me some space to figure this out."

"It is all I can ask for, *mi amore*. *Grazie*, for giving me a chance to speak to you. I will give you the space and time you need. I understand your pain, Kate. I have been hurt as well. I am not immune to being hurt. The opportunity is yours to give me. I will await your decision."

She listened to the gentleness in his voice and she wondered if she was being unreasonable? His voice held pain as well. How could any of what Rissa said hold an ounce of truth? But then, what did she really know of this man? Nothing!

"I'm sorry...I'm so sorry...I think I was really falling for you, maybe things were moving too fast. I just got out of one relationship...Never mind, you don't need to hear all that. Just...I'm sorry. Please. I need to go now."

He issued his final plea. "Kate, please. Just one more thing, I'm always here for you. You must promise if you need me...you need help, anything, you will call me. *Buonasera*."

She disconnected from the call. His words sent more tears down her cheeks. How could she have listened to Rissa? Her head was clouded in doubt, a part of her saying run away, and another part wanting to call him back and beg him to come to her now. She dropped the phone on the bed, buried her face in the pillow and cried.

14

Kate slept very little, waking often, thinking of him, always him. Now she had to get through the whole weekend with him on her mind, without the distractions of work. She stayed in her robe, not bothering to dress, gorging on junk food. *Okay, this is not as bad as the 'almost at the wedding breakup,' and if I can get through that, I will get through this.* But she kept second-guessing herself because he'd done nothing wrong. Maybe she should call him.

She was sitting mindlessly in front of the TV, not even aware of what was on when her cell rang. Her heart skipped a beat, as she picked up the phone, seeing Shannon on the ID. She answered with some reluctance, hating to tell her best friend the outcome of last night.

"Hey, Shan."

"Uh oh...I don't like the sound of your voice. What's up? Did you go out with him?"

"Yeah, sort of. We went to Alec and Rissa's for the cocktail party I told you about, but I left without him."

"Kate! What happened? What did he do?"

"Nothing. He did nothing. It was Rissa. She pulled me aside and told me a lot of...stuff. You know she warned me off once before, that he was a player, but last night, she just dumped all this other stuff on me. I got kind of panicked and left, at her suggestion now that I think about it."

In a puzzled voice, Shannon answered, "Stuff? She told you stuff? Come on Kate. Is he like a murderer, a rapist, a pedophile? What the heck could she have said to make you bolt?"

Kate replayed in her head all of Rissa's words, and they sounded even more ridiculous in the light of day. She couldn't tell Shannon the part about Shade being a vampire, not even Kate was buying that. And Alec and Rissa were vampires? Get real! She'd seen both of them out in broad daylight. Wasn't that impossible if you're a vampire? But Shannon would push for details. She'd have to tell her something.

"She just told me again what a player he was, implied that he was into rough sex...like, really rough, she practically pushed me out the door."

Shannon laughed. "Is that supposed to be a bad thing? Sorry, I shouldn't make light of this, clearly you were freaked out. But Kate, come on. Has he shown you any indication of this?"

"No, of course not. He's been, if anything, extremely patient with me. But Rissa made some comment about him luring me in. Now I'm just confused."

Shannon continued to probe. "Well, what happened after you left? Did he try to call you?"

"He called. I didn't answer the first time. He left a voicemail, pleading with me. I picked up the second time. His voice...I mean, he sounded as broken as I felt, and he begged me to see him, to let him explain, to give him a chance. I just asked for some time. I needed time. And that's where we left it. So, here I sit, with no clue what to do next. I mean, why would Rissa go to such lengths to warn me off if there wasn't something wrong?"

"Okay Kate, I'm just going to say this. You know me, no filters, right? When has Rissa ever given a fuck about you? I know we were all in college together, but let's get real here. Unless you were New England blue blood, she really didn't want to be too closely associated with you. And you had to come from money, and not just any money, old money. I don't know a lot about Shade, but from what you've shared about him, he's clearly old money. I think Rissa is just jealous, or scared. God forbid you'd end up in her social circles. And maybe if she thinks this guy is really serious about you, she's just trying to break it up, you know?"

"I know you're right about her. She's always kept me at arm's length, and I was well aware of why. But...why would she tell me the sex stuff?"

"Oh hell, Kate, I don't know. Because she knows it would freak you out? Besides, how would she know? Has she slept with him?"

Kate pondered the question. Had he? She hadn't thought of that before. Shade with Rissa. She shook the image out of her head.

"I...she didn't say she had...but he did tell me on the phone he'd been with a lot of women, so it sort of collaborated Rissa's story that he's a player. Maybe he dumped her or something, and she's getting back at him."

"Kate, you don't get to walk around looking like him and not have sex with a lot of women...you get that, right? I mean, the man can have his pick, if you get my drift. But here's the thing. He *can* have his pick, and if he was just a player, he would've moved on. I mean, let's face it, you've been rather high maintenance for him. I doubt seriously the man has had to work this hard to get a woman in bed in his whole life. He's been chasing you for three weeks now, have you slept with him?"

"No! Shannon, you know...you know how I feel about that."

Shannon sighed. "Yes, I do...and you need to get over it. I mean really Kate. I know you're never going to be the girl that puts out on the first date but come on. And besides, don't you want to know? Sex is such an important part of the relationship. I think people need to know how they are together. It's not always great, you know? I mean, all guys think they're good, but you know better. You've at least been with enough men to have figured that out by now. So, why waste all this time exploring your 'relationship', only to discover he's a dud in bed? Let's face it, great sex can make you overlook a lot of other shortcomings in a relationship."

Kate blushed. "I can't believe I'm having this conversation with you."

"Oh, we're having it! So here's my advice. Fuck Rissa, and make your own decisions. You like this guy. I know you do. Give him a chance. Take the time to find out who he is, and where this relationship is going, if anywhere. But you decide. You decide if you want to spend more time with him if he's worth risking your heart. Don't let Rissa dictate how it plays out. Maybe he won't be for you, but that should be something you discover. Come on, Kate. I know you. If you don't follow through, you will question yourself about it forever."

"Yeah...you're right about that part. I'm already questioning myself."

"Right? So get back in the game. And hey, I'm always here for you. If he breaks your heart, we'll just pull another weekend bender getting drunk on wine and you'll get through it. We always do. Okay?"

Kate answered, still unsure. "Yes...I'll think about it. I promise I will."

"Okay, well I have a shit-load of errands to run this weekend, so I have to go. So you 'think', and I'll talk to you later. But I'm not going to let this go, so I'm warning you now!"

Kate laughed. "Shannon, I'd be totally disappointed if you let it go. Now go get your stuff done. I'm fine, we'll talk later."

15

Kate had begged him to give her time, and he'd honored her request. It had been several days now, and he hadn't tried to call, and she hadn't called him. She hadn't had the nerve, despite Shannon's prodding. But he stayed on her mind, always.

She was wondering if maybe he'd just moved on. She was, as Shannon pointed out, 'high maintenance'. There was a part of her that wished he'd ignore her request, a part of her that wished he'd just storm back into her life, with his larger than life persona, and say, 'Enough, Kate!'

One day faded into the next as the week passed by. She looked for him at the metro stops, the Starbucks where they met for coffee, outside her office building, but there had been no more 'accidental' encounters. She feared she'd lost him, and she knew she wouldn't chase him. She'd never have the self-confidence to approach him after this much time had passed. She felt tired, and she knew her emotions played into that as well, as she got ready for bed, slipping on a gown and climbing between the sheets. She turned out the light and watched the red light on the Washington Monument as it blinked on and off before she slipped into another night of troubled sleep.

***

Many nights had passed, and Shade watched her through the window for every single one of them. Her body language and facial expressions told him enough to know she was miserable, and yet, she gave him no sign of wanting him back in her space. She asked for time, and he'd given her a week. How much time did she want? How much thought did she need to know they were meant to be together, she was the one, and she was his?

It felt like the hundredth time since he'd stood at the window watching her, as she climbed into the bed and finally fell to sleep. He'd kept his promise, given her time, while staying close, observing. If nothing else, he'd been a man of his word, but his patience was running thin. She'd had time to think, and still, she hadn't asked to see him, hadn't called him, and there was only one way to hold her and have her, convince her they were meant to be.

He teleported into her condo, shadowing himself from view and waited for her to fall asleep. That crimson hair was tangled about her head and strewn across the pillows. He knew already she was going to be his greatest strength and his biggest weakness, and somehow, he was very comfortable with that.

Sitting on the edge of the bed, he gently brushed the red silk from her face and she didn't move, but there was a slight moan. *That's it, mi amore. Come to the one you need.* He laid his hand upon her head and walked into her dream. This was where he could have her, leave her with a memory she'd never forget, a memory that would drive her to come back to him. It was his gift to dream-walk and he'd never been more grateful for it than right now.

She could see him there among the crowd as she moved through the large room, full of people. She watched him, dapper in his Italian hand-tailored suit, and she loved what she saw. Her gown was red, it flowed to the floor and her heels peeped out from the deep side slits on either side of her gown, those slender ankles flashing with each step.

They circled the room, he on one side, she on the other, and the crowd of people between them. They stalked each other, their eyes locked across the room. There was a sexual tension growing between them, a burning passion building and he could feel it in her body as she moved. Her hips took on a slight sway, the shape of that beautiful ass enhanced with the heels, her gorgeous breasts tightly strapped into the gown, but enough of those lily-white orbs spilling over the top of her dress to keep his eyes glued and his mouth watering.

She knew what she was doing, tempting him, teasing him, but so did he. The music began to play, and couples danced in a blur in the center of the floor. Their eyes did not see the other dancers, they saw only each other. She liked the man she saw across the room, as he slid his hand through his long black curls and smiled at her. He walked straight for her, slowly, sensuously, deliberately taking his time, his ice-blue eyes boring into her dark brown ones. He didn't speak. He took her into his arms and began to dance with her. He danced slowly, holding her tight and close, and the gaze she gave him was one of need and unbridled passion, on the edge, begging him to unleash it and take her.

She came willingly into his embrace as they swayed to the soft sounds of John Mayer singing "I Don't Trust Myself".

Her body melded into his like she was molded perfectly for him and him alone. She was small and delicate compared to his large frame, but somehow, it was perfect, and he could feel her warm and soft against him. Swaying with her to the music as they moved around the large dance floor, they saw no one else. The other people disappeared, and it was just the two of them, bel rosso and her lover. The scent of roses wafted up to him as he twirled her across the dance floor.

Their dance was an erotic play, her closeness, her scent, the feel of her pressed against him, how his hand fit perfectly in the small of her back. Leaning down, he nuzzled her neck, felt the shiver of excitement slide through her delicate frame. He whispered in her ear, his breath hot against her skin, "Enough of this game, bel. No more running from me." Her hands went into his hair, and he softly licked her ear, letting his tongue slide over its shell-like form, and then nibbled the spot on her neck where her vein thumped harder with every heartbeat.

He felt her body give in to him, wanting him. Her body communicated what her mouth refused to speak. She'd missed him, and wanted to experience him and know his words were true. He could love her like no other and she'd be bereft without him. The music changed as The Scorpions sang "Send Me An Angel", and the atmosphere became more heated. He pulled her closer, grinding his hips into her, letting her know he wanted exactly what she wanted. There was no denial from either of them. He danced them to the blurred edges of the room where they broke through, dancing slowly to the rhythm that led them down a long empty hallway. He let her lead him, but stayed close to her and then spun her gently and stopped, pushing her back against the wall, grasping her hands and holding them above her head. He pushed his body into hers, kissing her deeply, passionately, leaving her breathless, her eyes half-closed and begging. His lips were close to her ear, his voice hoarse with passion; his whisper a low growl. "You know you want this. Let me show you what no man can ever make you feel."

Shade let go of her hands, but she kept them above her head. He slid his hands down her arms, down her sides, burying his head between those glorious breasts and licked her cleavage, nipping softly at her skin. He let his hands slide down her hips, grabbing her firmly and slowly gyrated his hardened cock against her.

His hands slid down her thighs, as he slipped them under the slit in her gown that reached almost to her hip. He grabbed the edge of the silken material and ripped it all the way to her breasts, letting it fall in a puddle of bloody red silk at her ankles. Her gasp was soft and breathy as she turned her face to the side, her soft pink tongue licking her lips.

He grabbed her into his arms, her lacy lingerie all that remained on her body.

Her fingers greedily unbuttoned his white shirt and her hands slid onto his chest. Her face was so full of passion, ready to be unleashed for him, and he was ready to take it. He placed his hands on either side of her face and kissed her, as he leaned over her. He slid his arms down her back, releasing her bra and letting it drop away as his hands moved down her back, bending her backward until she dropped to her knees and then sat on the floor. He lowered himself over her, never breaking the kiss, and let her slide gently to the floor. She would be his in this dream he manufactured for her tonight.

***

As he ripped the gown from her body, the sound of the fabric tearing away excited her. He laid her on the floor, wearing only her lacy underwear, as he laid between her legs, his cock like hardened steel pressing into her, pinning her beneath him. He gripped her wrists, holding her down as if she'd leave...as if she'd struggle. He'd find no struggle here. She had imagined this since the moment he caught her eye and made her stumble over her own words.

***

She responded to him just as he knew she would. He felt her desire to be taken, taking what belonged to him. Gripping her hands hard above her head, he lowered his head and nipped at her neck and breasts, suckling each nipple, he teased her with his tongue, and then nipped them hard, pulling at her nipples with his lips. Her hips responded and he pressed his weight down hard to keep her from moving beneath him. Keeping her hands above her head, his tongue explored further down her belly, dipping into the concave of her belly button, swirling it round and round.

Letting go of her hands, she didn't resist but tangled them in her crimson silk, and he stared at the beauty of her lust unleashed. He removed his jacket and ripped off his shirt as buttons flew in every direction. Sliding his body down hers, he could smell her heat, wet and dripping and it belonged to him. He easily ripped away her panties, his eyes traveling to hers and their wide-eyed wanting told him all he needed to know.

He nipped hard on the tender white flesh of her inner thigh. He felt her body jolt and heard the soft moan escape her lips with the gentle erotic pain from his bite and knowledge of what was to come. Lifting his body slightly, he licked the soft bud that peeped out from her sex and felt her body quiver undeniably. Taking that tender bud between his teeth, he rolled it gently, sucking and probing, stoking the passion that lay just below the surface. Feeling her legs wrap around his shoulders, his fingers glide along those swollen, sweet, wet petals as he slid two fingers inside her and felt her muscles pull and tug for more. Thrusting his fingers into her several times, he slowly pulled them free and slid them into his mouth, sucking her glorious honey from his fingers before burying his head between her legs. The desire to be inside her was building and it was killing him with need and passion. She belonged to him, and this was his.

Controlling her dream state, he didn't let her cum for him, but took her to the highest peaks before tumbling and felt her body shake with the need to let go. When she came for him, it would shake her to the very core of her soul, rattle her from her immobilized state, and bring her home to him to have for all eternity. His tongue probed deep into her sex until she was writhing with want. He pulled out and ran his tongue over that sweet nub that was hardened and pulsing.

He stood over her and stripped off his pants. His cock stood at attention and he saw her eyes feast on the monster that now belonged to only her, the steel sword that would claim her as his own. Kicking off his shoes, he towered above her, his chest sweaty and broad. His thighs were thick muscle and he knelt to the floor between her legs. Sliding his hands under her ass and up her back, he lifted her upright against his chest and slide her down just above his cock and felt her body wiggle, aching to be riding him. He kissed her breasts, suckled them, and devoured the white beauty as her crimson hair tangled over his face. He moaned as he lowered her onto his cock. She wanted to be taken, owned, and loved. He read her thoughts. She went in her dreams where she feared to go in reality. Her gasp was music to his ears and then she moaned long and hard as her body adjusted to the sword that had found its target. She threw back her head and he watched as she gave herself up completely to him. He thrusts his hips upwards, gripping her tight sweet ass and began the slow motion ride of passionate love.

Taking her to the highest levels of erotic pleasure and then down again, he was lost in her, lost in the passion she gave in return. Watching her face was the most beautiful thing he'd ever seen as she rode him unabashed, her passion spilling from every pore of her body. Laying her back softly on the floor, his cock buried deep inside her, she wrapped her legs tightly around his narrow hips as he pounded her hard and deep, his body responding fast, but he tapped it back down.

He wanted her to cum in an explosion of sensations unlike anything she'd ever felt before. He thrust deep before he pulled the head of his cock to the edge of her sweet sex then paused, before thrusting again, over and over, until he could feel her body's need for release. She gripped his shoulders and lifted her hips to meet his thrusting and it almost did him in. He watched the small trail of sweat trickle down her brow and he leaned down and licked the salty liquid from her forehead, letting it roll across his tongue.

He felt his heart racing and his breathing increased as he held back the beast inside him and the volcano of passion her body had built. He nuzzled into her neck as he felt her legs tighten around his hips. He stopped moving, still buried deep inside her, and felt her muscles clamping and releasing his cock on their own volition.

He whispered in a deep growl, demanding his due. "Cum for me, mi amore, give me what you crave."

He felt her body ignite one last time, and he went deep and hard, thrusting into her and felt her orgasm, as his own thundered through his body and he called out, "Mine!"

***

He gripped her body, held her firm, and controlled her response to him. He led her where he wanted her, pushing her body's response. He wasn't making love to her. He was claiming her, owning her. When he paused in his relentless pounding to whisper 'cum for me' she was already on the edge, she'd been on the edge because he'd held her there, and she exploded with him. Riding the waves of ecstasy his body gave as she clung to him, clutching and clawing at him, her legs wrapped tight around him, pulling him deeper still, as the orgasm sent her spiraling out of control.

She could hear him scream out 'Mine', and she heard another loud cry, and realized it was her voice she heard. The orgasm didn't stop, but continued to roll through her, heart pounding, gasping for air as her hands gripped his hair, and her hips continued to ride him in this orgasm without end. She felt every cell in her body come alive with him as the sensation gradually faded, and she was left gasping for air.

***

Kate awoke with a start and found her head was thrown back on the pillow, her heart racing, her body covered in sweat as she gripped the sheets in both hands, and the sound of her moans still ringing in her ears. She sat upright, looking around her bed.

That was not a dream. Not a dream! She was still breathing heavily, gulping in air as her body still tingled from his touch. With a shaky hand, she knocked the clock off the bedside table as she turned on the lamp by her bed, and swung her legs over the side of the bed.

She tried to stand, and the muscles in her legs were shaking. She walked on unsteady feet to the bathroom and flipped on the light switch, turned on the cold water and splashed it on her face. She looked at herself in the mirror, her hair was tousled, and her lips were swollen and puffy like they'd been kissed long and hard.

She ran her fingertips across her lips, as she became aware of the tenderness between her legs. Her brain felt scrambled as she tried to sort out what had happened.

It felt real...so real...How could I have a dream that feels more vivid than anything I've experienced in my waking hours? Her hand trembled as she flipped off the light and she walked back to her bed, the sheets wrinkled and tumbled, as she climbed in, and fell back asleep, wanting him again already.

***

When he felt her cum for him, he knew she was his mate, the one he'd never go without, the one he'd die for, breathe for, live for, and kill for. He felt her relax beneath him. He quickly left her dream and teleported back to the penthouse; naked, sated, and watched from the window.

He smiled, like a greedy mongrel, and he did it without regret. She couldn't believe what had happened to her, but all the signs were there on her body. He watched her drift back to sleep and he teleported back into her condo and watched her slumber. She tossed softly, and sweet moans told him she still dreamt of him. He ran his hands through her crimson and kissed her cheek gently.

"You belong to me, *mi amore*. Come back to me now, we are done playing this game. I want you, I need you, and I have only begun to love you."

Feeling the heat of the rising sun, he teleported back to his penthouse. He closed the blackout drapes and barred the door. He flopped onto the bed to await the death slumber that would steal him away from her. He hated this feeling, knowing she was now vulnerable and he couldn't come to her aid in the sunlight hours.

He vowed in their next encounter, he'd reveal all to her, all that he was and that he was capable of loving her as she deserved, for all eternity. "You belong to me, Kate Reese. *Ti amo, mi amore, per sempre*."

16

Kate was reeling from the dream. Everything about it felt real, like the rose petals she'd found in her bed. Yet she knew he hadn't been here. It had been a few days, and she couldn't shake the memory of it and wasn't sure she even wanted to. Still, she hadn't called him.

She had an invitation to Rissa's annual Halloween party. It was the one event Rissa actually did invite her to every year. It was costume-required. She knew if she went, she'd probably see him and she felt torn. There was a part of her that wanted to run back to him, hoping he'd be there. And then there was another part of her brain that said this was a dangerous man, steer clear.

She always felt like a third wheel at this party anyway. Most of the people there would be couples, and not just couples, but high-brow couples from the social elite of Washington. Kate hated going to events where everyone was already paired off, talking about their kids' soccer games, last week's polo match, and carpooling.

She was beginning to lose faith in the whole idea of romantic love and had decided it only existed between the pages of books or on the big screen in the movies. She talked to Shannon, who was pushing her to go. Shan thought she had acted too rashly about Shade, that she should give him another chance. That she should make her own decisions about him and not be influenced by Rissa. And then there was that dream. Her face turned red, and she could feel the heat creeping up her neck.

She decided, at the last minute, she'd go to the party. She told herself she'd just make an appearance and then slip away unnoticed. But now she needed a costume. She'd waited too late to buy anything. Maybe she could just put a costume together from stuff she already owned. Digging through her closet, she found a very short black dress, which she'd worn to rock concerts. The dress was all straps and buckles across the bodice. She had some biker boots that also had a lot of straps and buckles. There was a black wig she'd bought to cover her red hair when she would travel alone in Asia because it helped her blend in. She found some black lace stockings in the lingerie drawer and ripped a few holes in them. This would do, throw on some Goth make-up, and *voila*...a costume.

The entire time she was dressing, he was in her head. Or maybe she should say Rissa was in her head, Rissa's warnings about him, the fact he was a major player, a ladies' man, a heart-breaker, the stuff about the rough sex...and a vampire. Really? A vampire? This was the 21st century!

Kate had no doubts about his past with women. She was sure there'd been many, and he had admitted as much. The rough sex? The memory of the dream flashed through her head again. That wasn't rough sex, but there was a savagery about it, something primal and urgent, but still a dream, her imagination taking over.

She shook her head, trying to remove the pictures in her brain, but they were indelibly etched there. They taunted her, teased her, and lured her. Kate hadn't had enough time with him to know if those claims about him were true, or whether it was just Rissa trying to scare her away. She only knew he was achingly handsome, charming, and very intimidating. She still felt he was completely out of her league. And that whole vampire thing, I mean, come on. It was the one piece of information Rissa threw at her that made her discredit everything else.

She planned to arrive at the party late so there'd already be a lot of people there, and she could blend into the crowd. Rissa had this party every year to promote her event planning business, and there'd be about two to three hundred people in attendance. She arrived at Rissa and Alec's Georgetown house to discover the party was spilling outside, into the courtyard around the pool behind their house.

They had set up a fire pit to take the chill off the late October evening, and they had a DJ with a designated dance floor. The crowds of people were doing red Jell-O shots out of syringes. Kate stopped at the food table and grabbed some cheese and a few crackers. Someone handed her a Jell-O shot syringe and she downed it. They laughed and held up another syringe to her. She opened her mouth and let them inject it, and it went down with ease.

She asked, "What's in this stuff?

The stranger answered, "You don't want to know." He handed her a cocktail and told her she needed to catch up. She took a sip, but he put his hand on the bottom of the glass, tipping it up and said, "Chug it!"

Laughing, she swallowed down the drink, feeling the burn as it hit her empty stomach. She should have eaten something. She could feel her head spinning already.

She headed for the dance floor and grabbed the hand of a werewolf on the way, who handed her another drink. She had no idea who was inside that costume, and she didn't care. She just wanted a dance partner. She sipped from the drink as they walked past the bar on the way to the dance floor and she saw Shade sitting there alone, in all black leather. She defiantly downed the drink in her hand before tossing the cup aside, already losing count of her alcohol consumption.

The memory of that dream flashed through her head, but she wasn't ready to approach him. From the dance floor, she kept surreptitiously casting a glance at him. He carried himself with confidence, or was it cockiness? He carried himself like the guy who always got the girl. His hair was almost black and he wore it down tonight; long, loose, almost to his shoulders. It looked like he might have just climbed out of bed and run his hands through his hair, and it made her want to run her hands through it too. Then there were those eyes, ice blue, electric blue, piercing her soul blue. He caught her glance and locked eyes with her as she danced. His lips were full, sensual, and he sported what looked like a perfect three-day stubble on his strong jaw. He inhaled on a cigarette and then slowly exhaled, and the smoke rose slowly around his face. The skin-tight leather accentuated his body in a way those hand-tailored Italian suits never could. He caught her looking at him and held her gaze until she looked away. She wasn't ready. He still intimidated her, and she turned on the dance floor so she could no longer see him.

She ran through a series of dance partners, first the werewolf, then a Viking, then Freddie Kruger, followed by a guy dressed as Snow White. Someone kept passing her those Jell-O shots, and she downed them quickly. The werewolf laughed and warned, "Be careful with those. That's tequila you're throwing back."

The DJ was great, and the music never stopped, and neither did she. The entire time she was dancing, she was aware, acutely aware, that he was sitting at the bar, and watching her.

Rissa came onto the dance floor and asked the DJ to stop the music. She loudly announced, "Okay everyone, we're going to play a game. I have a bowl filled with cards and you'll be asked to draw a card from the bowl. Your card will describe the character you play in my horror movie. And for the rest of the evening, you must remain in character."

Kate was designated as the third person to draw from the bowl. She walked up, reached in, and pulled out a card. It read 'The first to go'.

She started laughing and said, "Oh great, I'm the stupid chick that gets knocked off in the first ten minutes of the movie." She stepped back, staggering slightly as she felt the alcohol muddle her brain.

Several other party-goers drew their cards, and then Shade stepped up and pulled a card from the bowl. He read the card aloud, and as he did, he locked eyes with Kate, and she felt her knees buckle.

In a deep menacing voice, he read, "Spends the rest of the movie looking for number three."

He started to walk towards her. She couldn't help but notice him. He was wearing a black V-neck t-shirt, a leather jacket, those freakin' leather pants that left nothing to the imagination, and boots that laced up above his ankles. *So what if he has a super-hot vampire costume? Don't get distracted...he's a player, remember?*

As he approached her, he reached out and placed one finger under her chin and lifted her face to him.

Oh, this is so not going how I planned.

He said to her in his thick Italian accent, "Ah, so I see I am looking for the beautiful Kate with the lovely neck."

Nice line, vampire, but a little obvious, don't you think? She was feeling flustered. This was the first time he'd spoken to her since the phone conversation after she ran from the last cocktail party. The tequila had made her brave or stupid, she wasn't sure which, but she'd play along. "Yes, and apparently I'm already dead, so I hope you can help me."

"I would love to do anything you ask, *mi amore*."

Oh I bet you would. No wonder you get all the chicks. But let's see where this goes. She flirted with him, looking up at him through the bangs of her black hair. "Immortality? It sounds tempting. So when do you want to bite me?"

Shade actually licked his lips as his eyes followed the length of her neck.

Kate smiled. *Well, if you're going to role-play, pull out all the stops!*

"Immortality is a very serious journey Kate, but I can assure you, if you wish for a bite, you will enjoy every moment of mine." Then he winked at her and gave her the most deliciously wicked grin.

She was trying to mask the fact she was very turned on by him right now, and she didn't want this little game to end. So she said to him, "Go for it! I've got too much to do to be dead. So if you bite me, does that mean you're my 'maker'? Does that mean I belong to you?"

At that point, another guy in black leather stepped up to Shade. He pulled Shade aside and told him he should back off. *Really? Who is this guy?* Since she could hear his admonishments to Shade, Kate said in a voice loud enough for both of them to hear, "I'm the one who's dead here. Don't I get a say?"

Shade turned back in Kate's direction and locked eyes with her once again. "How can I refuse such a beautiful lady? She is begging?"

Others stepped in, discouraging him. He appeared to know them...*Who are these people?* Kate shouted out loudly, "Please! I'm waiting. Shade! Ignore them, you know you want me."

The look he gave her said he'd eat her alive. He'd have her groveling at his feet. He'd take her body places she'd never dared imagine. Her heart was pounding as she met his stare, and she didn't look away. All of a sudden, she wanted this man. Forget the warnings. Vampire or mortal, not even sure now what the fuck he was, but there was a darkness in him that was pulling her in, and she wanted to dive in headfirst. Was this the tequila talking, or the memories of that dream? She no longer cared.

The others were still pulling at him, trying to drag him away. She wasn't going to let them win. And she knew what she had to do to appeal to his alpha male. Throw down the gauntlet. "Come on, Shade. Man up! Are you going to let them tell you what to do?" And in the blink of an eye, he was at her side.

In a sibilant hiss, he answered her, "No one tells me what to do, *mi amore*, not even you." His words sent a chill up her spine, and she liked it.

She slid her arm into his, her eyes still locked on him, and said, "Are you as bored as I am with these games, lover?" *Lover? Where did that come from? He's not my lover. I've never called anyone lover. You've had way too much alcohol!*

"Si, mi amore, it is time to stop playing games." And again, that deliciously wicked grin, oh the promise of that grin.

"Then perhaps, sir, you'd like to escort me home?"

He placed his hand over hers and said, "The pleasure will be all mine Kate, well perhaps, not *all* mine." His words made her blush and she tucked her head, and she heard him chuckle to himself.

He walked with her to her car, and she handed him her keys, "You'll drive? I think I've had too much to drink. I'll give you the directions."

"Of course, and I need no directions." He helped her into the passenger seat before sliding his large frame into the small red Miata, adjusting the car seat back as far as it would go, starting the car and heading out of Georgetown in the direction of Arlington.

Wait? What? He needs no directions? "What do you mean, you need no directions? Do you know where I live?"

"*Si*, I have known where you live since the first time I saw you."

"Well that's kinda creepy, don't you think?" She was second-guessing her decision to have him drive her to her condo. "Are you like, stalking me, or something?"

"No, and you don't need to worry about my intentions. I was protecting you, and I knew you would eventually find your way to me."

"Wow...really? You're pretty sure of yourself, aren't you? I mean, that was a lot to assume."

"*Si*, maybe, and yet, here we are."

Well, how do you answer that one Miss Smarty-Pants? You not only found your way to him, you just invited him home! "Good point, Mr. Medici."

He looked over at her in the dark interior of the car, the light from the dashboard reflecting off that beautiful face, and smiled. Oh yes, it was definitely the 'I told you so' smile. He didn't need to say it. She shook her head. *Great move, Kate. You're now in the car with a man who took the time to figure out where you live and has been 'protecting' you.*

Alarm bells should be going off in her head, but she found she was still oddly attracted to him.

"And protecting me? From exactly what were you protecting me? I live in the Virginia suburbs outside of Washington. Were you protecting me from soccer moms and runaway school buses?"

"You have attracted some dark elements and I was just keeping an eye on you."

"Dark elements...like vampires."

"*Si*, among other things."

"Really? Come on, I don't believe in vampires. Rissa said you were a vampire, but I'm not buying it."

"Well, here is the thing, it does not matter whether you believe or not."

"Okay then, not."

"*Si*, whatever you say." And the wicked grin returned.

They reached her condo and he pulled the car into the underground garage and parked it in her designated space. Before she could even ask how he knew this was her parking space, he exited the car and came around to her side and opened the door for her, extending his hand to help her out of the car and then walked to the elevator.

As they stepped in and the doors closed, he pushed button 7. She swallowed hard, *how did he know?* They exited the elevator and walked down the corridor. He was still holding her keys, which he used to unlock her door, and then pushed it open to allow her to enter. *Wow, manners and chivalry, when did that go out of style?*

"They never went out of style *mi amore*, and a lady should always be treated like a lady."

She turned and looked at him with a quizzical look as he entered the condo and closed the door behind him. *Did I say that out loud? I must have, surely he didn't read my thoughts. No...reject that.*

He caught her eye, and her expression, and just smiled. He helped her off with her coat, and she looked down at the ridiculous Goth costume.

"If you don't mind Shade, I'm going to go change out of this costume and wash all this crap off my face. Please, have a seat. There's wine in the fridge if you want it. Just help yourself."

"Take your time, I will be waiting." He took a seat on the sofa.

She ran to her bedroom and pulled off the dress and the biker boots and changed into jeans and a soft sweater. She headed to the bathroom, pulled off the black wig, and washed all of the dark black and purple Goth make-up off her face. *Really? Someone came home with me, looking like this?*

She did a light touch-up of her regular make-up, and took her red hair from the tight bun and combed it out. When she walked back into the living room, he'd flipped on the gas fireplace.

"A fire, how...romantic."

He stood up as she entered the room and walked toward her. He reached out his hand and ran it through her red hair. "Ah, *bel rosso*, I have been waiting for you."

"I hope I didn't take too long."

"No, *mi amore*, I was just looking at your home, your books, and the pictures of your travels, your music. The way you have decorated. It tells me a lot about you."

She directed him back to the couch. "So, sit please, because I know very little about you."

"Ah, you know a lot about me, *bel rosso*, and you have already rejected it."

She stood with her hand on her hip, "You mean the vampire thing?"

"The vampire thing, *si*."

She sighed loudly, expressing her exasperation, and turned to walk to the kitchen, returning with the wine and two glasses and sat next to him on the couch. "I only have white, is that okay? I mean I'm sure with you being a vampire and all, you'd much prefer the red."

He chuckled at her and shook his head, and his long hair swayed gently. She really wanted to reach up and touch his hair; grip his hair as she did in the dream, but she restrained herself.

"*Bel*, let me pour you some wine." He took the bottle from her hand and expertly removed the cork and filled her glass. As she took a sip, she noticed he hadn't filled his own glass.

"None for you?" she asked.

"No *mi amore*, vampires do not consume human food."

"Oh right, how could I forget?" she said sarcastically. He just smiled that wickedly delicious smile.

"So other than this vampire thing, here's what I know. You're a lady's man, a player, a heart-breaker. Are you going to break my heart, Shade Medici?"

He reached out and touched her hair, running the back of his fingers softly down her cheek, "I could ask you the same."

And with that, he leaned in and kissed her, softly at first, their lips barely touching. Then he deepened the kiss. He was covering her mouth with his, and she felt his tongue probing against hers. Her pulse was already racing. With his mouth still locked to hers, he removed the wine glass from her hand and sat it on the table. He wrapped his arms around her, enclosing her in his embrace. She slid her hands up his back, and held him to her. Her head was swimming.

She pushed her tongue into his mouth...and she felt...what? No, it was nothing, her imagination. She probed again with her tongue and she felt him respond, but she quickly broke away from the kiss and looked at him; startled, confused. She could feel his fangs with her tongue. She stared back at him, and she had no words.

"*Si, mi amore*. Vampire."

She jumped up from the couch, knocking over his empty wine glass, and started pacing in the room. *This is not real!*

His voice was calm when he spoke. "Are you afraid of me, *bel*?" He hadn't moved from the couch and was quietly watching her, his eyes locked to hers.

"No. Yes. Maybe. I don't know. I really didn't think...I mean I just thought..."

He patted the sofa next to him. "Sit down, Kate."

Her head was saying run, but her heart, or was it another part of her anatomy, was saying sit, so she walked back to the sofa and took the seat next to him.

"So what happens now?"

"Nothing you don't want to happen."

"It's up to me? The outcome is up to me?"

"Of course, *bel rosso*, where we go from here is all up to you. I can leave now, and you will never see me again, although it will break my heart if that is your choice. Or I can stay. "

She couldn't deny her attraction to him. She was mesmerized by him, she felt his darkness, but she didn't feel malice. She wanted him, she really wanted him, but she didn't want to be another notch on his bedpost.

"You think I'd break your heart? My fear, Shade Medici, is you will break mine."

"I have been watching you for some time, *bel*, and something in you calls out to me. I have just been waiting for you to feel the same."

"Well, that doesn't really answer my question, does it? Will you break my heart? Will you make me fall in love with you, and then leave me for the next girl in your long parade of girls? Your reputation precedes you, you know?"

"No, *bel rosso*. I will not break your heart. Can you say the same?"

She stared into his eyes, those ice-blue eyes. It would be so much easier to think if he weren't so beautiful. His answer sounded sincere. It felt sincere. She wanted to believe him. She took a deep breath, and let out a long sigh. Well, so far, her luck with mortal men hadn't been that great, maybe she should try an immortal. And hey, it wouldn't be the first time she'd had the shit kicked out of her by love. Her heart was screaming 'take the plunge.' Her head was screaming 'are you fucking nuts?' Yes, probably, because she had decided to follow her heart.

She reached out and took his hands, and looked at her small hands in his large, strong masculine ones. She loved his hands, the strength in them. She loved the contrast of his dark olive skin against her pale white skin. Then she looked up into that face and those eyes.

"I won't break your heart, Shade Medici. And I'm counting on you to keep your promise to not break mine."

He gave her the softest smile. "A gentleman never breaks a promise to a lady."

He leaned in and kissed her again, followed by another soft kiss, followed by another, and another. She slipped her hands from his and slid them up his arms, and she could feel the power in him. As she reached his shoulders, she wrapped her arms around him, and she felt his hands encircle her waist, and then wrap themselves around her back, pulling her in closer.

She slid one hand into his hair, that hair she'd been aching to touch since the first time she saw him. She felt him deepen the kiss. She wanted him to consume her. His tongue was probing and she could feel her heart racing, again. His hand moved up her back, and she could feel him tangle his hand in her hair, grabbing it by the fistful.

He crushed her to his chest, and she could feel his heartbeat matching her own. His mouth covered hers, and their tongues teased each other. Her head was spinning, again, when he broke the kiss and said, "Breathe, *mi amore*."

Seriously? Who has kisses that make you forget how to breathe? She looked into those eyes and their blue had turned to a red glow. It was both disconcerting and exciting.

"Take me to bed, lover," she whispered to him.

"Are you sure, Kate?"

Was she sure? Oh god yes, like they could turn back now. She reached her hand to his face, she was already falling in love with this man, and she couldn't take her eyes off of him, as his eyes bored into her. "I'm sure. Please take me to bed."

He stood and scooped her up. She was like a feather in his arms, and she loved it. She loved that he was carrying her. He bent his head to her and softly kissed her once again then carried her into her bedroom where he set her down on the bed.

She looked at him unsure, "I'm not sure how this works."

He laughed. "It all works the same, *mi amore*."

He pulled the sweater over her head, and she raised her arms, so he could remove it. She stood so he could remove her jeans, as he knelt in front of her and slid them down her legs. She reached out again and placed her hands in his hair. He leaned in and landed a kiss just below her naval, and she felt her knees buckle. He reached out and grabbed her hips to steady her. He used his mouth to pull the panties away from her hips, and then with a quick bite through the silky fabric, they dropped away. She gasped in surprise, and she saw a flash of the dream in her head.

"Are you all right, *bel rosso*?"

"Yes," she whispered.

"Should I continue?"

"Please, yes," she answered, though her throat felt as if it is closing.

He stood and unhooked the bra and slid the straps down her shoulders, painfully slowly. As the bra dropped to the floor, he cupped each breast in his hands and rubbed his thumbs over each nipple and his touch.... oh god his touch. He was picking her up again and laid her on the bed.

With his eyes locked on her, she watched him as he removed the leather jacket, and then pulled the t-shirt over his head, and stood there a moment, shirtless in those tight, low-slung leather pants.

He sat on the edge of her bed, and pulled off his boots, then stood again to peel off the leather pants. Commando...should have known. He was beyond beautiful, he took her breath away.

She had to take a deep breath, remind herself to 'breathe, *mi amore*.' He slid into her bed next to her, and somewhere in her head, there was a voice saying, 'last chance, last chance, last chance to back out' and she told the voice to 'shut-the-fuck-up'.

He leaned into her, his mouth at her ear, and in a voice as soft as a whisper asked, "Are you sure, Kate?"

"I'm sure."

And with that, his hand was in her hair, his lips on her lips, and his leg across her legs. She slid her hand up his back and relished at the feel of his skin. He enfolded her in his other arm and pulled her to his bare chest. *Skin on skin, does anything feel better?*

"*Si,* there are things that feel better, and I am about to show you."

She was spinning out of control. Was she more taken back by the sudden realization he could read her thoughts? Or by the answer he'd given to her question? She was beyond the point of no return. She could only take this path wherever it led, wherever *he* led.

He covered her mouth with his and began that slow probing with his tongue, and she moaned into his mouth. She felt his grip on her tighten, and his hands started their exploration. He caressed then squeezed her breasts, his hand slid down her waist, over her hip, and across her ass. His touch was lighting a path of fire on her skin. He rolled her over, never letting her go until he was on top of her. She felt pinned down by him, just like in the dream, and she loved the feeling, his weight on her, this feeling of being captured. His hand slid between her legs and his fingers probed to find her already wet and waiting for him. He growled into her mouth, a feral wild animal growl that sent a shiver down her spine. She could feel his engorged cock against her leg, the heat from him, and she wanted him. The truth was, she'd wanted him since the first time she laid eyes on him, but he had intimidated her.

"Relax, I bring you only pleasure."

His touch, his voice, his words, everything he did was adding fuel to the fire.

"Please, lover," she begged.

He looked into her face, with a deliciously wicked grin and said, "Are you begging me, *mi amore*?"

"Yes, yes...I'm begging you!"

He covered her mouth with his and pushed his tongue deep. He slid his hand under her at the waist and lifted her back into an arch as he pushed her legs wide with his own. She felt his cock at the opening of her sex. She was so wet for him. She could feel her juices on her thighs. He pushed the head of his cock inside her and she gasped into his mouth.

She could hear his responding chuckle, and then he thrusts hard and deep. There was savagery to his movements, a forcefulness that took her by surprise. She threw her head back, breaking the kiss. As she cried out with the pleasure of him, her back arched of its own accord. He moved his hips, thrusting into her, and her hips responded to his rhythm. Her hands were gripping his back, clawing, as she wrapped her legs around his hips so she could receive all of him. The dream...this felt like the dream. She could feel his cock throbbing inside her, and she was so undone.

***

In one quick motion, he rolled onto his back so she was now straddling him. She sat upright, her hands resting on his shoulders as her hair swung forward. He placed his hands on her hips and guided her motions as she rode him. He loved the look of lust on her face, and how she had succumbed to him. His hands explored the curve of her hips, and the slender waist, and back down to the firmness of her thighs. He loved looking at her as she took pleasure in his body.

Rarely in his long life had he ever been concerned with the woman's pleasure, although he knew from their response, he left them more than content. Women had been a means to an end, a way to serve the demands of his body, and being skilled in seduction was vital to any vampire's survival. He took what he wanted, and moved on, or had an arrangement for convenience. Watching her now, his *bel rosso*, as she sat atop his cock, grinding her hips, her eyes closed, her lips parted, brought him as much pleasure as the physical sensations that rocked his body. He couldn't take his eyes from her, as the orgasm hit her, and she threw her head back and cried out, before collapsing on his chest.

Before she could catch her breath, he rolled with her again, so he was back on top of her. "Don't stop now, *bel*."

***

Kate was still gasping for air when he flipped her on her back and continued to thrust deep inside her. She wrapped her legs around his hips, as he rode her hard, with the same primal thrust she felt in the dream. He toyed with her, teasing, slowing down the pace of his strokes, almost withdrawing from her. She grabbed at his hips, pulling him toward her, as she tightened the grip with her thighs. Again she heard his low chuckle.

He increased the speed and force of his thrust, and she buried her face in his neck and inhaled his scent. It was heady and erotic as if she needed anything else to make this fire burn hotter.

"Cum with me, *mi amore*," he breathed into her ear, and it was all she needed to hear. She felt herself begin the free-fall into the orgasm to end all orgasms, as spasm after spasm washed over her. She felt like she was spinning out of control...out of body...he owned her body. She sank her nails into his back, and she moaned. She was lost to him. His entire body tensed as he growled in a rumble that came from deep in his chest, and she felt the vibrations of it in the room, as he released into her.

Fill me, fill me...I want you to fill me up. Oh god, oh god, oh god...that did not just happen. That cannot be real. She was gasping for air, her heart racing, and her body covered in a fine sheen of sweat. She felt his body relax on top of hers, as he held his weight on his elbows, and looked down at her. His own breath ragged, his heart beating hard against hers.

With one hand, he reached down and brushed back the fine hair clinging to the sweat on her face, and leaned in and kissed her forehead, her nose, and her lips. Such savagery and gentleness, all rolled up in one man. He kissed her lips softly, followed by another.

"My savage lover," she whispered.

"*Bel rosso*, you have no idea."

Oh really? But I want to. I want to have an idea. I want him to show me. I want to see all the darkness inside of him. And he can take me there. I can feel it.

"Be careful what you wish for, *mi amore*. I can make you feel things no mortal man can."

She was silently processing his words, as they felt hauntingly familiar. *Didn't he say that in my dream? And that mind-reading thing. How do you turn that off?*

She looked up at those blue eyes, "Do you make wishes come true, Shade?"

"*Si*, I can make your wishes come true."

She smiled up at him as he rolled off of her. She already missed the feel of his weight on her. She already felt empty. She wanted him again, and again. *Oh he is so going to break my heart.* She knew his nature. He was a player and she had better get used to it.

"No, a promise is a promise, remember? I will not break your heart. Now the sun is coming up, so I must leave you. But I will come back to you if you want me. Think before you answer because you promised you would not break my heart as well."

"I think I love you, Shade Medici. I don't know how, or when, or why, but I think I love you. So please, come back."

"*Si,* it will be as you wish."

And with that, he was gone, as in gone. He has disappeared right in front of her eyes. *What the fuck?* She looked around the room. *Oh please tell me this was not a hallucination. Please tell me this was not one too many Jell-O shots.*

She slid from the bed, grabbed her robe, and slipped it on. His clothes lay scattered on the floor. Walking back into the living room, the fire was still burning in the fireplace and there were two wine glasses on the table, one with the remnants of her wine, and the empty one tipped on its side. He was here. He was real.

She picked up her laptop and went to Google and keyed '*mi amore*' into the Italian to English translator, 'my love'. He had been calling her 'his love' all this time? She keyed in *bel rosso*; beautiful red. Her heart melted. She didn't think she loved him. She knew she loved him.

17

Shade twirled the cell phone in his hand, smiling to himself. He'd left her last night, sated, and knowing deep in his heart she was his. She'd let down all the barriers and let him in. He still had a lot to prove to her, but he saw no problem in doing that. He wanted to court her for a while, win her heart. He didn't want her to think it was only about the sex, it wasn't. She was the one. The one he'd spent his entire life looking for...his mate. Now he had to convince her beyond a shadow of a doubt because he was already convinced. Hitting speed dial, he waited for that sexy voice to answer.

***

Kate dreamt about him after he left. How could she not? And all day, she'd thought about him, found it hard to concentrate on her work. She didn't tell Shannon she'd slept with him. She wasn't ready to share that information yet. It felt too personal, too private. It felt too 'theirs'.

She was still wrestling with the idea of what he was, even with his fangs, even with his self-admission. She was having a hard time wrapping her head around it. And that disappearing act. What was that? She thought of calling him but didn't want to be one of 'those girls'. She was home now, with no distractions, and beginning to wonder if she'd just imagined the whole thing when her cell phone rang and it was him. She stared at his name on her caller ID and then curled up in the armchair before she answered.

"Hello, lover."

He chuckled softly when he heard her pet name for him, and he rather liked the sound of it rolling off her tongue. "Good evening, *bel*. Miss me yet?"

"I missed you the second you were gone. About that...your leaving. What was that about? I've had men in a hurry to get away from me before, but I believe you set a new record."

He felt a bit uncomfortable, shifting his position, with his feet propped up on the dining room table. Just the sound of her voice made him hard, and he thought about the sensual noises she made beneath him last night.

"I apologize, *bel*. It is just something I can do. There is more to me than what you see. I can only hope you wish to learn more about me, my life, and how I can enhance yours. So tell me, did you enjoy the party last night?"

"The party? I don't think it was the party I enjoyed, Mr. Medici, as much as it was you. And I hope to learn a lot more about you. You're being mysterious already. What do you mean, it's something you can do? What exactly did you do? Your disappearing?"

"I know you have many questions, Kate. Would you allow me to come over, sit with you, and I will gladly answer all of your questions. I am sure this seems quite out of the ordinary, to say the least. But I feel it is important for both of us, that we are together when you ask and I answer. You can see my face, feel me, and I can hold you in my arms, *si*?"

"I, of course, I'd love for you to come over."

He heard her hesitation. "Did I detect a moment of doubt there?"

"No doubt, just surprised, I think. Unexpected."

"I will be there in no time, or do you wish to set a time specifically for me to call on you?"

"No, now is good. I just want to change out of my work clothes and throw on some jeans, so come on over."

"*Si, mi amore*. See you soon."

Shutting off the phone, he laid it on the table, threw his feet to the floor and teleported right in front of her, and watched her startled face, the phone still in her hand. She hadn't even hung up yet.

"*Buonasera*."

She dropped the phone as she stared at him open-mouthed. "What...what is that, Shade? How do you do that?"

He leaned over the chair where she was seated and kissed her softly on the lips. Taking her hand, he lifted her to her feet and snuggled into her neck, inhaling the erotic scent of roses that was hers and hers alone. "Are you complaining, *bel*?"

"No, not complaining. Just confused. How did you get here? Do you fly?"

"Something like that. It is called teleporting. We can teleport to any location we wish. I wish to be here with you, so I think about where it is I want to be and I am there. I can go extremely fast, faster than any mortal can see, or I can slow things down a few notches, check out the area around me. It is very useful."

"So, I guess that whole thing about having to invite a vampire in before he enters your house is a myth. But then, I thought vampires were a myth."

He walked to her couch, sat down, and patted the space next to him. "Come, *mi amore*. Get comfortable. I believe this may be a long night."

She smiled and snuggled next to him, laying her head against his chest as he slipped his arm around her.

"Most of the things you know about my kind are myths, we invented those myths as self-preservation, to keep mortals afraid, and from prying too deeply. Immortals are no myth. I am here to confirm that. Does that scare you?"

"Not anymore. I think I feel more curiosity than fear. So, the night I was in trouble when the guy was following me. Is that what you did? Is that how you got to me so fast?"

"*Si*. I got there even quicker than you knew. I held back as long as possible."

"But this morning, when you left me, why did you leave so suddenly?"

He kissed her gently on the neck and whispered, "Because the sun was rising. I cannot be in direct sunlight. It will kill me, and yes that is one myth that is a truth for some immortals."

She looked up at him. "So, you go to a crypt? Sleep in a coffin? Shade, what about Rissa? She said she was a vampire, but I've seen her in the day."

Did she just say crypt? Squeezing her hips, he chuckled. "Kate, slow down. You are asking a lot of questions. And I will answer them all. First of all, I go into what we call a death slumber. It comes to me when the sun arises. I can fight it off some, but it is never a good idea to fight through the slumber. That is when I rejuvenate my system and heal. It is similar to a mortal sleep only deeper, I do not actually die. My heart still beats and as you can see, I do not have the clammy cold skin as you have been led to believe. I awaken once the night approaches. As for Rissa, she is what we refer to as a day-walker. She can choose when she sleeps, be out in the sun and moon. Alec is a day-walker as well. As for a crypt, I do not own a coffin or a crypt. I sleep in a bed, just like a mortal man, but in a room shielded from daylight."

"So can you become a day-walker?"

Shaking his head, he tried to be careful in his description, so she understood but wasn't frightened by what he was telling her and, of course, some details he'd leave out for now. He wanted to be honest with her, but they were just beginning this journey and he'd never had to explain a damn thing about his life to any mortal, and definitely not one this important to him.

"No, I can never become a day-walker. You are born with your gift. Each immortal is given a gift, a talent, a weapon in some cases. They can use it to their advantage or for wicked purposes. Rissa and Alec's gifts are day-walking."

Kate looked confused. "Born? You mean when you are changed or converted?"

Kissing the top of her head, he found her so fascinating, so intriguing, how she wanted to know so many things, and she was not backing down, not intimidated by his answers.

"Most of us are born immortal. That means two immortals have mated and birthed a child from their union. As for Rissa, she was once mortal like you. Alec chose her as his mate, which required he turn her into an immortal. Does that help you to understand?"

"Born? Vampires have babies? I thought...I thought you had to be bitten or something. So you were born? You were a little boy with parents? I thought you stayed the same. I mean, whatever age you were when you got, what did you call it, turned?"

He kissed the side of her long beautiful neck. "I do believe we are getting in deep here, *mi amore*. I have never truly had to explain my existence to a mortal. But yes, I had a *madre* and *padre*, grew up knowing nothing but immortality as my life. I was given limited exposure to the mortal world as a young boy. That time was spent teaching me skills to survive in the mortal world, as well as how to protect myself against some immortals. Once we begin to mature into adulthood, the aging process slows greatly. Immortality, it is also a word we have adapted to our culture. We can live for thousands of years, but we do eventually age and die."

Kate sat silently next to him, appearing to absorb this information. "So that drinking blood thing, that is a myth as well?"

"No, that is very real."

"So you...bite? Wait, I need to process this. Do you only bite other vampires?"

He turned her around so she was facing him, he wanted to see her face, know that she understood and wasn't frightened.

"Kate," he slowly tucked a stray crimson lock behind her ear and looked into her eyes. "I bite to feed. It is the only nourishment I take into my system. Blood is food for me. I feed from mortal and immortal alike."

She reluctantly asked, "Is that why...is that your interest in me?"

"No, *mi amore*. I do not come here just to feed from you. I am a man of my word. Honesty, respect, and integrity are things I live by, so I must confess to you, your blood calls to me. I do wish to feed from you, but there is much more to feeding. I can feed from anyone, male or female, mortal or immortal, and I do because I must survive. But I would prefer to feed from only one, someone I care deeply for, someone I love. "

He could sense the conversation was making her uncomfortable, but she had to understand this. He heard her tentatively ask, "Is there someone else? Someone you go to now?"

"No one person I go to every time. I hate to use this word, but we call it hunting. It may seem a haunting word and horrible images appear in your mind when I say it. We seek out someone to feed from. I may go on the streets, or a club. I do not harm them, I do not hurt them. I lure them softly, seduce them, take my fill without killing or hurting them, and then I erase their memory of the feeding. They remember the sexual encounter, but not the feeding. They only recall the pleasure that comes with feeding. It is how we survive among mortals, without notice."

She stood up from the sofa and walked a few feet away to the window. He can read her thoughts as she worried about sharing him, how often he'd feed, and whether she could even be his only source for blood. She was questioning her sanity that she was even considering these questions.

"So...you would still go to them...the others?"

"*Bel*, I can answer all those questions you are asking inside your head. You won't share me with anyone, not if you wish for me to feed from you. I feed when I feel my body slowing, when I need energy, just as you need food, I need blood. I do not feed three times a day, but perhaps every other day, depending on the stress I put on my body. If you are not here when I need to feed, I wait for you. I am more mature in my years. I can go longer periods of time without feeding. And if I have my way, you would be my blood source for the rest of my life. You will not experience any symptoms of the blood loss, none. You may experience a bit of dizziness right afterward, but nothing troubling. The more I feed from you, the easier it becomes for you. And for your last question, I would not go to any other but you, if you would grace me with the gift of your blood."

Is this what Rissa meant when she said he was a player? Maybe that's what she was trying to warn me about. He will take from me until...until what? My blood no longer satisfies? Or maybe there's a limit. A limit to how much he can take, and he'll need more? More than I can give him?

She leaned her head against the window. There were a million questions in her head, all pushing to get out, but there was one thing she knew for sure. She could live in his altered world, she could follow this man, but the one thing she wouldn't do was share. Infidelity was her deal-breaker, always had been. She wanted to get that out on the table right now.

"I don't share, lover. Not ever." She turned from the window and faced him, and locked eyes with those piercing blues, she didn't look away. In a stern voice, she repeated, "Not ever."

He heard the struggle in her head and something happened inside her, he wasn't sure what, but once she spoke, he knew her decision was made and she was staking her claim. She wasn't his shy, reticent *bel*, she wasn't playing games, but a woman who meant what she said and in one instant, love slammed into him so hard she could have knocked him over with a feather. *Where in the hell have you been hiding, Kate Reese? You are the mate I have searched the world over for.*

"Your choice is clear, as is mine. As a vampire, I have one that I seek, and will move heaven and earth for. And once she is found, I seek no other, I love no other. She owns my heart and soul and it belongs to her my entire life. She is the light in my darkness. I give my life for her. I drink only from her. She is mine. And I share her with no one, mortal or immortal. I claim her as my own. And if you choose to give me the greatest gift you can bestow upon me, *mi amore*, the source of my life, your blood, then this is what you get in return. I protect my own. I give her no reason to want for anything. She is all to me. All! That choice belongs solely to you."

He sensed she still had questions, but she'd already given her heart. She walked to him as he stood with his arms open, and he enveloped her. She laid her head against his chest. She was his. He knew she hadn't chosen an easy path, and there was much she didn't understand. He knew they'd stumble over the differences in their two worlds, but he also knew that whatever lay ahead, she wanted to face it with him.

"I take that as a yes?"

"Yes, lover. My heart says yes."

Closing his eyes, he'd won her heart and soul, without taking her blood. His heart exploded with love for this woman who now held his world in her hands. "*Grazie,* Kate. *Ti amo*."

"And I love you, Shade Medici."

Picking her up in his arms, he cradled her to his chest. She was light as a feather. Carrying her to the bedroom, he laid her down softly on the bed and they began the night as he hoped they'd begin all the nights to come, together, in each other's arms.

18

For the third night in a row, Shade had spent almost the entire night with these mercenaries Alec called warriors.

He'd taken over control of Alec's warriors and was establishing a command post and central meeting point for the battalion. This abandoned property belonged to Alec, and it hadn't been occupied in years. Alec had boarded up the windows of the old house and let it go. Now it served as the perfect place for Shade to operate. It was on the outskirts of Georgetown, but perfect for them to cover all of D.C. The name Dead House had evolved over the years, as most mortals looked on vampires as the walking dead and any rogues they took down after an unfortunate encounter with them were definitely fucking dead.

The house looked like an old Victorian on the outside, badly in need of major renovation, with boards and bars over all points of entry. Inside, Shade converted the space below ground for use as a temporary barracks for warriors who needed their death slumber or were injured. He also designated space for dungeon holding cells and torture chambers for captured rogues, and an armory for weapons storage. Upstairs, he had set up space for a central command center and meeting room. He wanted his warriors to be heavily armed, and most had a specialty weapon of choice, Shade's was swords. He had this place stocked with every variety of weaponry as was possible.

He still needed to install a high-tech security system in the command center, but currently it was furnished with the old rotting furniture left inside this hell hole. He wasn't looking for comfort. The Dead House needed to be a place for the warrior's to let off steam, and let the beast loose. This was no fucking Hilton Resort, but it was the best location for them to gather, grid out the city, monitor activity, and issue assignments to the warriors for the night. Alec had hired a bunch of stragglers, and by Medici standards, most of them were barely acceptable, useless in Shade's eyes.

But this was what he had to work with, what he was getting paid for. Figure out who he could bring up to speed, who to get rid of, and find some solid replacements. For now, he tried to pair them off, placing a fairly efficient warrior with another who was less so. At least

Alec's warriors knew the city, but after two nights of being out there, Shade could tell already any one of his Medici warriors could do a far better job than six of Alec's warriors.

There were only two from Alec's crew that appeared to have any real skills. One of them was a mercenary named Skelk. He smelled bad, and looked even worse. Shade had seen some street trash that looked in better condition than this one. Skelk was a loner. He preferred to work alone, but the warrior had skills, and he was efficient. He was deadly with a crossbow, had zero social skills, but he did know how to take orders. Skelk liked to work up high on the rooftops. His aim was dead fucking on and convinced Shade he was worth his time.

The top vamp in this group was Tomas. He was another renegade mercenary who'd put in his time as a warrior, taking assignments worldwide. He knew how to handle a city this densely populated, and he was an expert on just about any weapon. He was also sly as a damn fox. He didn't take shit from anyone, but he knew who paid his bills. Shade could already see this one being his Second-in-Command here when he needed a night off.

For the past few nights, Shade assigned Tomas to take half the group and Shade took the other half. They showed them where the key lookout points were, where they had logged rogue activity, and where the hot spots for kills would be. They had logged many hours watching key areas of D.C., especially Georgetown near Alec's home, the night clubs, and anywhere mortals congregated. Crowds of inebriated mortals made prime killing grounds for any rogue who decided they wanted mortal flesh and blood, and D.C. rocked twenty-four hours a day. It was an immortal's playground.

Tonight, they stayed within the confines of the Dead House. He had each warrior show his weapons skills, hand-to-hand fighting skills, and anything else he thought might be useful in fighting a rogue enemy. As he suspected, compared to his world of elite warriors, this crew was strictly amateur. He took a break and let Tomas give them a workout on shuriken's, or throwing stars. That was another one of Shade's preferred weapons, and until tonight, he'd never known a warrior who couldn't handle one.

He needed some cold night air to clear his head. He never cared to be caged up inside any building for too long, and his ass was dragging after three long nights with this fucking lot of losers. He hadn't seen Kate, and as promised, he hadn't fed, and that too had him in knots. His body was screaming for his woman, those soft red lips, flaming crimson silk, and a body that could ride him all night long. *Cazzo*, she probably thought he'd left the damn country since he last saw her. He'd only spoken to her on his cell a few minutes every night. He'd have to make this up to her and make it up in spades, and he was just the vampire to do it.

In addition to establishing the Dead House, he'd been trying to manage the new property in Virginia. He'd thrown a mattress on the floor in the largest bedroom, but the house still needed a lot of work, and staying at the penthouse kept him closer to Kate. Juggling their schedules was a challenge. She worked when he slept, he worked when she slept.

This damn Dead House was busting his ass as he tried to bring some order to this group of apes Alec called warriors. He stepped out into the enclosed courtyard behind the Dead House to take a short break, breathing in the crisp night air. He lit up a smoke as he dialed her up. Maybe, tonight, he could have a little longer conversation with her. *Cazzo*, he missed her!

***

Kate had gotten ready for bed, climbing between the sheets with a book, instead of him. She knew he'd call when he got a break. He always called her. The thought was barely out of her head when she heard the cell phone ring and she made a grab for it.

"Shade. I've missed you. Talk to me, I want to hear your voice."

"I am so sorry, *bel*. I am so busy lately. I have a lot to do and I am trying to wrap up, so I can spend a few evenings with you. Forgive me?"

"Forgiven. But what keeps you so busy? Your vineyards?"

"Some. But I have been working for Alec. It is vital I am here, setting up what is necessary and once that is done, I won't spend so much time away from you. But this is what I do, and it requires me to be available. *Cazzo*, I miss you. How was your day?"

"My day was fine, the usual. You work for Alec? In politics? I don't understand."

He heard her keep the questions coming. She had a right to know what he did, but he was reluctant to tell her he was a warrior; that he killed for a living.

"*Bel*, I am not into politics. I am setting up the tight security and protection Alec needs and will need in his future. I work a lot of nights, training his people on how to protect him out in public."

"Oh, I wasn't aware. I thought the vineyards were how you made a living. So, like a home security system? That kind of thing?"

Shade sighed. His woman wasn't going to make this easy on him. "No, nothing like that. This is more in the line of armed bodyguards. Like the Secret Service? They are usually around the President. That is more in the line of what I do, train them on skills to take down the bad guys. I keep high profile people safe."

He heard the long pause before she answered, and he sensed her concern.

"That sounds...dangerous. I had no idea. I mean, I can understand why Alec would need protection in his job, I get that. But I had no idea that you...that's what you do. You carry a weapon then?"

He looked up in the night sky and closed his eyes. "I do carry weapons. I have extensive training in weaponry, martial arts, and have perfected the art of training others. I know it's very late, but I am asking you, begging you, please, I need to be with you this night. I miss you, *bel*. May I come to you?"

"Shade, you can always come to me. My bed feels empty without you."

"*Si, grazie*. Let me wrap up and I will be there."

Hanging up, he headed back in and told Tomas he was heading out because he needed to feed and do some hunting. Tomas slapped him on the back with a big grin. He understood, there was no explanation necessary.

Shade had decided he wouldn't let anyone know he had a mortal female he was priming for mating. That would stir up way too much shit! Feeding from a mortal was one thing, but choosing a mortal as a mate would bring all kinds of problems he wasn't ready to tackle.

He unloaded all his weapons quickly, leaving them in the Dead House. He'd not fought tonight and knew he had no blood on him since they'd focused only on weapons training. Immediately teleporting into her condo, he walked into her bedroom where she was sitting in bed and he leaned against the doorjamb and smiled. He knew he must look a sight to her; leathers, boots, and a black tee. He looked at her in the soft light of the lamp by her bed, her red hair glowing as the sheets were draped across her legs.

"You are a beautiful sight for these sore, tired eyes."

She looked up from where she was curled up on her bed with a book, startled as always by his sudden appearance. This teleporting was going to take some getting used to. He stood in her bedroom door, leaning against the doorjamb, dressed in those freakin' leather pants. The soft leather conformed to him. He wore heavy black boots that laced up over his ankles and a fitted black tee. His hair hung tangled around his face, and those eyes, always those eyes. He had a slight smirk on his face, but he did look tired, sexy as hell, but tired.

"Come here, lover. Let me make you feel better." She flipped the covers back on the bed, inviting him into the space beside her.

His beast sat up and he had to slam him back down. *Not yet big guy, she is nowhere ready to tackle your ass, she is mortal, remember? And you can be one hideous fucked up animal when let out.*

Shade had never experienced his beast so vibrant and aggressive as he had with Kate. She brought his dark ass right to the surface just looking at her, and he ached to be released. She invited him into her bed and his eyes went straight to that pulsing vein in her neck, beckoning him, calling to him to take what he wanted. His defenses were low. He hadn't fed once since promising her she was his and his only. He wouldn't feed from another ever again, but he had waited, giving her time to change her mind. Now his body was showing the signs of the lack of nourishment, the lifeblood it needed to survive and remain strong. He ached with his body's need to taste her. Sliding the shirt over his head, he threw it to the floor and unzipped his leathers, as he walked to the side of her bed.

She watched him pull the shirt over his head, exposing his bare muscular chest as he started to unzip the leathers. She patted the mattress and he sat on the side of the bed. She slipped to the floor, kneeling between his legs, and slid her hands up the smooth leather that conformed to the muscles in his thighs. His eyes were deadly. How did anyone refuse this man? She untied the laces on one of his boots and tugged until she could pull it free, then unlaced and removed the other boot. She put her hands on each thigh and slid them up to his hips, leaning into him, her lips just inches from his as she whispered, "Tell me what you need, lover."

"I need you, *mi amore*."

He heard the sound of his voice, a deep growling tone, his hunger screaming, and his hands gripping the edge of the bed to steady himself, keeping his beast under control. But the hunger was clawing inside him, and the beast wanted out to ravish and take the beauty that was before him and he trembled, holding back taking her. He needed her to want the feeding, that first experience of him feeding from her was so vital.

She saw him gripping the edge of the bed, restraining himself, holding back. It had been several days since he'd been here and they had the conversation about feeding. He said he usually fed every other day, and yet, he hadn't fed from her. Is that what he fought? Her heart rate picked up, she had no idea what to expect. Would this hurt? There was a savagery in his lovemaking, but he never hurt her. Perhaps the feeding was different, and he feared her reaction. Without the feeding, he wasn't hers. If she didn't let him feed, she knew he'd be forced to go to another, and she didn't want to share him.

"Shade, do you need to feed from me?"

He tipped her chin up and kissed her deeply and passionately, letting his tongue explore, having a small taste of her. "*Bel*, please, I need to feed. It is hard to be around you and not want that from you. I made you a promise and I intend to keep it, but my feeding is necessary. This must be your choice, you must want this. It will only sting for a moment, and I have ways to help you not feel pain, only pleasure, do you trust me?"

She felt the depth of his need. "Of course I trust you, Shade."

He pulled the soft nightgown over her head. As her body was exposed, his hands wandered slowly over her delicate bare skin, as if exploring the map of her soul.

He felt her hands tug at his leathers and watched her slide them down his legs. They were not easy to remove as the soft leather clung to him, but her hands made easy work of their task. She wasn't innocent in the ways of sex, but sensual and soft. She heightened his arousal, yet calmed his inner turmoil at once. Her hand brushed against his cock and he moaned with the warmth of her touch. And tonight, she'd take the next step in becoming his.

He stepped out of the leathers and let his hands slide down her back, cupping her sweet, tight ass in his own large, calloused, and roughened hands. Dropping to his knees, he kissed the inside of her thighs, licking and playing as he went, her scent sweet and alluring. He felt her hands as they slid into his curls and she gripped his hair softly in her fingers and it fired his blood. Nuzzling into the soft patch of crimson that surrounded her honey, he moaned loud and felt his eyes flare into their fiery red, lighting the room in a soft hue. He raised his eyes to hers and flicked his tongue across that sweet nub between her legs and felt her shiver in anticipation.

"Do not be afraid, *mi amore*."

She felt the heat of his tongue between her legs and her knees buckled, his hands steadying her as he stood and lifted her and laid her down on the bed. She watched as he crawled over her, his eyes glowing red. There was a part of her brain that still sent out signals she should fear him, however, it wasn't fear she felt but desire. She wanted him, needed him. She felt safe with him, protected, taken care of. She lay on her back beneath him and watched as he lowered his mouth to hers, his fangs already exposed. His kiss was hard, urgent, demanding, and she wrapped her arms around his shoulders, clinging to him. She slid her tongue into his mouth, across one of those fangs, and felt his body go rigid before he moaned into her mouth.

***

With each movement she made under him, his body felt lit up by flames, she fired his blood and his passion, he ached to take her hard, feed until he had his fill, but he must have patience and lead her to a sexual bliss that would take away the sting of his fangs sinking into her skin. He felt her tongue graze his fangs and his whole body went into overload. Touching or licking a vampire's fangs created the most erotic sensation, it was why the feeding was always accompanied by sex, and she did it without even knowing. How in the hell did she know, how did she push him into this state so fast?

To Shade, it was another sign, bright and clear, that she was his chosen mate. Using his knee, he parted her legs and felt her respond by wrapping her legs around his hips. He drove into her hard and deep and maintained a slow rhythm of riding her, letting her body adjust to him. His tongue explored, sliding over the sweat sheened white skin of her collar bone, leaving a trail of soft light kisses as he went. He slid his tongue over the vein in her neck and could feel her pulse under his tongue and his cock pulsed inside her.

He increased the rhythm of his hips, taking her slowly to heights she couldn't imagine. He felt her body respond, her hips matching his rhythm, lifting to meet him. Her soft gasps and moans and the urgent response of her body told him she wanted release and he intended to make it last as long as he could. No easy task in his position.

Nibbling her ear, he whispered, "What do you want *mi amore*, show me, tell me."

Her hands slid down his back, gripping his hips. She pulled him toward her. "Don't stop, lover...don't stop." She nipped at his shoulder, unaware of how dangerously close she pushed his beast. "I need you!"

He felt his body shake with the restraint of holding the beast at bay and only one thing would satisfy him now. She'd pushed that caged beast too far. He drove into her, thrusting hard. Her body moved with him in perfect rhythm and he nuzzled into her neck.

He wanted to taste her, feel her cum around him. He grazed his fangs along her neck, not breaking the skin but letting her feel their sharpness. His fangs ached, and he was in pain from the aching need of her.

"Cum with me, *mi amore*."

He sank his fangs into the soft flesh of her neck and drew deep, moaning like a wild beast at the taste of her. He held her body down with his own and continued to drive deep, feeling her explode into a glorious orgasm as he drank deep from her vein. Her blood bursts across his tongue and down his throat and he guzzled it like fragrant intoxicating liquor. His head spun, she was his cocaine, his addiction, and he'd never tasted anything so pure and sensual and erotic, and it belonged to only him.

***

She felt his fangs at her neck, and she'd forgotten he was here to feed. She was distracted by the sweet sensations between her legs as he begged her to cum with him. She felt herself letting go just as she felt the sharp but sensuous sting of his teeth sinking into her neck. And with it came an explosion of heat between her legs unlike anything she'd felt before. She cried out as she clawed at him, pulling him deep as he thrust hard into her. They both rode the waves of the orgasm together, and she gave herself up to the sensation of his feeding, the erotic and sensual sounds of his mouth at her neck, the fire released in her blood and between her legs that only he could now quench. *This is feeding? He makes women feel like this when he feeds from them? Oh hell no, I will not be sharing!*

As their bodies united in more ways than one now, he could sense her, feel her flowing in his veins, and he was careful not to take too much, but fuck, she tasted like heaven. He broke from her vein and retracted his fangs, licking the wound so it would heal.

Looking down at her, his eyes had returned to their normal piercing blue color and he kissed her gently. Cradling her head in his hands, he rolled onto his back and pulled her onto his chest, letting his hands caress her softly, tangled in that beautiful tousled mass of crimson.

"I love you. I will love you forever. Are you all right? Talk to me, Kate."

She giggled out loud. “All right? Lover, I passed all right a long time ago.” She rose on her elbows so she could look at him. "So that...that feeling. What happened to me when you fed from me, is that...does that...happen every time?”

"Oh *si*, my sweet *bel rosso*, every time. As I feed more often, you will have a scent that is noticeable to other vampires. They will know a vampire is feeding from you. " He smiled at her. "You have me, *bel*, you have my heart and soul. I am yours. And I will never feed from another. Do you hear me?”

She placed her hands on either side of his face and went nose to nose with him. "So other women...the women you fed from...they felt that?"

He sighed heavily. "They do feel the sexual sensations that come with feeding. It is part of my world. Feeding is sensual to me, it comes with the territory.”

“I understand. Just make sure no one else feels that from you ever again. And I don't understand the scent part. Will you smell different to me? Because, right now, you smell delicious.”

“No, I will smell the same to you, but to other vampires, they will pick up your scent on me as well. The scent will be detectable on both of us. It is meant as a warning and becomes stronger with each feeding. It lets other vampires know you are claimed. But enough of that, I need to apologize to you. I have been gone too many nights and left you alone, unattended, and I do not like that, but sometimes it cannot be helped. I want to make it up to you. What would you wish for *mi amore*? What would make you happy, anything you want. Tell me.”

“What? Make it up to me?”

“*Si*, I have been gone for several days, so I am asking, how might I make it up to you? I can take you anywhere. We can do anything you desire.”

“Anywhere, lover? You can take me anywhere?”

“*Si, bel rosso*, anywhere.”

He could see the mischievousness in her eyes and knew she was teasing when she answered, “Then take me to Paris. You asked what my most favorite city was, and Paris is my most favorite city in the world. I want you to make love to me on a Paris rooftop, overlooking the City of Lights. I want a bed covered in rose petals, and champagne and strawberries. Can you give me that?"

"*Si*, you have made a simple request."

"Simple? Wow, really?"

"Are you ready, *bel*? Are you ready for me to take you to Paris?"

She looked at him with surprise. "Now? We're going now?"

"Is that not what you asked of me? And do not forget, they are six hours ahead of us, so it is well into the night there. If you wish for me to make love to you under the stars in Paris, we must leave now."

She looked down at her naked body. "I need to dress. I need to pack."

He chuckled as he lifted her from the bed, pulling the nightgown back over her head and putting his leathers back on.

"No time for changing and packing, *bel rosso*. Now come here, place your arms around me and hold tight. I will teleport us. You may feel dizzy, but you will be completely safe."

Wait? He's going to teleport me to Paris? Is that even possible? Her heart was racing as she clung to him for dear life. She felt his arms around her when suddenly they were surrounded by the darkness. She felt like they were moving at warp speed, but it was completely dark and very disorienting. She had no concept of time passing, but she could guess only a few minutes had passed and he was setting her down. Still holding her, he gently turned her around so she was facing away from him.

"Tell me what you see."

She looked out across the rooftop and blinked her eyes in amazement. "I see...I see a mattress draped in white satin sheets, and covered in red rose petals and champagne...and strawberries."

"What else, *mi amore*? Tell me everything you see."

"I can see the city spread out below us, and I can hear the traffic and the voices of the people below. I can see the Eiffel Tower, and over there, I can see La Sacra Coeur on the hill in Montmartre."

He took her hand and lead her to the bed. As they stood there together, he slowly undressed her, dropping her gown to the rooftop.

"You are beautiful Kate, your crimson hair and your fair skin. You are my lily-white. Now lay down for me."

He held her hand as she lowered herself to the mattress and stretched out on the satin sheets, feeling the cool silkiness against her skin. She watched him as he disrobed, removing his leathers. He crawled onto the bed, his dark hair hanging forward, his blue eyes locked on hers. He was suspended over her, his weight on his arms, as he leaned down and kissed her; little kisses, teasing kisses, followed by deep kisses. He broke the kiss and sat back on his knees, reaching for the champagne.

"Is this real?"

"*Si*. Quite real."

He popped the cork and poured the cold liquid on her breasts and down her abdomen. She gasped as the cold hit her skin, and she could feel the tingling sensation of the bubbles. She felt his tongue, like fire against the cold of the champagne, as he licked at her breasts, flicked each nipple, and then ran his tongue down to her naval, where he drank the champagne from her skin. She placed her hand in his hair, and moaned with the sensations he was sending through her body.

"Is this the Paris you had in mind for tonight?"

"Yes, lover," she managed in a strangled whisper.

He picked up a strawberry and held it to her mouth, rubbed it across her lips, before slowly running it down her chin, her neck, and between her breasts, across her belly and through her patch of tight red curls.

"Open your legs, *bel*."

Her breathing was ragged, and her heart was racing, she wanted his touch and not this teasing, but she slowly parted her legs for him. He ran the strawberry across her thigh, and then placed the tip of the strawberry inside her wet, swollen sex. She gasped with the sensation and the unexpectedness. The desire to have him inside her was unbearable.

"*Cazzo*!" He jumped to his feet. "My brothers summon me. I must return. I am so sorry, *bel*. There is trouble and I must respond." He was putting his clothes back on as she lifted herself to her elbows.

"What? We just got here." *He's leaving me?*

"Get dressed. I must take you back home."

He reached down and helped her to her feet. She was still reeling from the sensations of champagne and strawberries on her skin, and he was helping her put on her gown and dragging her barefoot across the rooftop.

"Hold on to me, *bel rosso.*"

Before she could even contemplate what was happening, they were once again surrounded by the darkness, and the speed, and then they were back, back in her bedroom. She was looking around like she'd never seen this place before. *What the fuck just happened?*

"I am sorry, *bel*. This is not what I planned for us this night. Now it appears as if I have something else to make up to you. I must leave now. My brothers are in danger. *Ti amo, mi amore*." And with that, he was gone.

She looked at the clock by the bed. Two hours had passed since they teleported from the bedroom. She looked down at her nightgown. *Am I fucking insane? Did this even happen?* She started to undress and felt the sticky champagne on her skin, the tell-tale trail of a light pink stain from the strawberry down her torso, and the taste of the strawberry on her lips.

She looked at herself in the bathroom mirror, her hair was tousled. "What are you doing, Kate Reese?" she asked her reflection. "What path of madness are you following?" But she knew if he showed up again right this minute, she'd go to him.

She reluctantly climbed in the shower and washed away the memories of this night that clung to her skin. She put on a clean gown and slid between her sheets, alone. And all she could think about was him. *I love you, my savage lover*. She knew she'd follow him into the madness.

19

Walking through the empty rooms of his Virginia house, Shade took stock of all the needed repairs. He'd brought in Luciano, his vintner, to survey both the Virginia and California vineyards, and oversee whatever changes necessary to get the properties at full production. He and Luciano had spent the night planning and talking, walking the vineyards, checking out the wineries, looking at production history, and tasting the yield from previous harvests. It was clear that to make both properties fully functional it would take some time.

Luciano oversaw all his vineyards worldwide; Italy, France, Greece, and now in the States, including hiring and managing the vineyard staff. After their assessment of the Virginia property, Luciano had put some things in motion, and moved on to inspect California.

Alone again, Shade casually walked from room to room. He felt such emptiness here. It was a shell of a building, it wasn't a home. He wanted to move here, live here. He felt like he'd found the mate he'd been searching a lifetime for. She'd fill this place with love and laughter, and together, they could reside here.

He hated that she lived in that damn city alone, especially during the daylight hours when he was in his death slumber. He wanted her away from the hustle of the city, away from the dangers there. That lone episode with the mugger at the metro station was enough for him to want her out of that condo, and living here with him.

There were warriors to train and the D.C. area to protect, along with Alec and Rissa. It was his job. But now, he had something much more important to him. It was Kate he wanted to protect and love, and he wanted her here. He already knew deep inside she was his mate. She was the one. There was no doubt. His body craved her in a way he'd not felt before, the taste of her, to feed from her only, and enjoy their eternal life together. The fact she was mortal would be enough to put his ass in one fucking hellish heap of controversy. Immortals of his station were forbidden to mate with mortals. He wasn't just a master, but the Medici King, royal blood. He'd ruled his coven for centuries in Europe, and now, expansion was well within his grasp in the States, and along with it, his mate. To hell with the European Council of Ruling

Vampires, he was the Medici and he'd make them see she was worth her weight in gold to him and his coven.

He'd lived his life by the centuries-old customs established by the Council, with strict rules and old ways, as had his father, and grandfather, and all the Medici before him. But the old values didn't always fit the modern times, and he needed to straddle both cultures, juggling and molding them to meet the changing times.

He could almost see Kate here, taking over this house, making a home for them both. He had staff in Florence, and he could easily transfer some of them here. He wanted her to make this a dream house, something she could only have imagined for herself, a place she loved, felt comfortable and safe in. This house could be something they shared right from the start of their relationship. That damn penthouse was nothing but a torture chamber for him, only able to view her from a distance. He wanted *bel* to come here, plan with him, make a life for them here and his mind went to work on how to pull this off.

He didn't want to push her too fast. So far, she'd been responsive to him. She was no longer frightened of who and what he was, and was willing to explore this life of immortality. There was still much for her to learn, in particular the violence of being a warrior, but that knowledge would come in time. He needed to take this slow, control her exposure to his immortal world. He'd have to turn her into an immortal if she was to be his mate, but that was something far in her future.

He could see the sky lighten as the sun began its slow rise across the landscape that held forests, mountains, and vineyards. It was so beautiful here, so peaceful and isolated from mortal view, yet close enough for him to continue his work for Alec in D.C.

She definitely needed to be here, permanently, and no doubt, she would be. He refused to have it any other way. He wanted to come home to her at the end of every night and have her in his arms, protect her, and feel surrounded by love as he entered his death slumber. He'd have Luciano and some other staff here shortly, they'd be able to protect her during the daylight hours. The house would be a bustle of activity with the remodeling, and the property landscaped, the vineyards fruitful and productive, and Kate at the center of it all, making it home.

There were staff quarters already established on the premises. The building was in fair shape but needed a female's touch. Hell, everything around him needed a female's touch, including him. He could bring her here for a visit, a date, show her the place, tell her his long-term plans for expansion, and ask her to help him. He'd find a way to get her to leave the city and her job and live here while she made this place a home. He had endless funds, he could give her the world, and he needed for her to discover that. All he knew was she belonged here, he belonged here, and the sooner the better for them both.

The death slumber pulled him, trying to take him down, as he quickly teleported back to the penthouse. He walked to the window before the sun started reflecting off the buildings and frying his heart to dust. He could see her preparing for work, dressing, and scurrying around, gathering her papers and laptop. It convinced him, even more, she needed to be the hell away from here and someplace where he could hold her, touch her, love her, and have the comfort of knowing she was safe. He pulled the blackout drapes across the window, and barred the door, then walked to the bed and flopped down, his mind made up. He'd take her to the Virginia house, and it was going to be damn soon.

20

It was early Saturday evening, the sun was sinking on the horizon, and the moon was on the edge of taking her turn in the sky as they moved into shorter days, and longer, colder nights. He decided it was time to take Kate out to the Virginia property. Shade wanted to call her and make it an official date. Hitting speed dial on the phone, he was hoping she had nothing planned for her evening.

Kate had still not shared any news with Shannon about Shade. She'd not told her she'd slept with him, or that he was a vampire, and he fed from her. She and Shade had not discussed it, this small issue of what he was, but she instinctively knew this was a secret she'd be expected to keep, for his own safety. His secret was already isolating her from other mortals.

She laughed out loud. She'd just referred to herself and others like her as "mortals", his word for her world. Besides, who'd believed her? They'd drag her off in a straitjacket if she started talking about being teleported off to Paris by a vampire who showed up in the night to drink her blood and have hot sex with her. Her cell phone rang and she checked the ID, it was him, and her heart soared.

"So, where are you taking me tonight? Somewhere I can enjoy a little longer than Paris, I hope."

"Well now, I do have plans for this evening, if you are willing to take a drive with me. I thought, perhaps, we would go the old-fashioned way if that pleases you?"

"Shade, I threw the rule book out the window after the first night. I'm along for the ride by whatever means you choose. What time would you like me to be ready?"

"How soon can you be ready, *mi amore*? And I will give you a heads up, this is not a very elegant date, so dressing casual is appropriate, jeans and walking shoes may be a good choice as well, a sweater, and a light jacket. Can you handle that?"

Kate looked down at her jeans and sneakers, and the oversized sweater that fell from one shoulder she was already wearing. "Yeah, I think I got that covered." She ran to the bathroom mirror to touch up her make-up while she talked and spritzed on the rose fragrance he loved.

"Good. I will see you in thirty."

He hung up the phone, jamming it into his jeans pocket, and teleported down to the garage. He sat and had a smoke for about ten minutes, stalling for time so she wouldn't be aware of how close he lived. It took him another twenty minutes to drive through Arlington traffic around the block and park inside her garage.

Once parked, took the elevator to the 7th floor and rang her doorbell.

The doorbell? She giggled, he's ringing the doorbell? That was a first. She headed to the door to greet him, wondering what adventure he had in store for her. She opened the door to find him in tight jeans and a hooded jacket. His hair was tousled, and his eyes always dropped her to her knees. "The doorbell? How conventional of you."

He grabbed her up in his arms and kissed her hard and passionately. When he broke the kiss, he smiled at her. "Are you inviting me in? I must warn you, if we step inside, you will not be wearing that sweater much longer."

"Mr. Medici, if that's supposed to be a threat, I must warn you, it's not a very effective one. If removing my clothes is on your agenda for the evening, then by all means, be my guest."

"Be careful what you wish for. Are you ready? We have a bit of a drive."

"You lead, I follow, lover. Where are you taking me? Or is that a secret?"

Grabbing her hand, he led her to the elevator. "Well, it is not a secret. Are you familiar with White Hall?"

As the elevator door opened, he led her in and hit the garage floor button as the doors slid closed. He backed her up against the wall as his hands went straight to her ass and he nuzzled her neck. "I missed you, bel."

She felt his breath on her neck and heard Aerosmith singing "Love in an Elevator", and it made her laugh. *Did he do that?*

"I missed you, Shade," she answered between kisses. The doors opened as they reached the garage level, and the couple getting on the elevator gave them a cold stare as Kate and Shade uncoupled and exited into the garage.

"Prudes," he muttered. He led her to the Hummer, pointing it out to her. "This is me right here."

Walking her to the passenger side, he took her hand and helped her into the monster vehicle, his hand on her backside to give her a boost. "Seatbelt, *mi amore*!"

Slamming the door, he walked around and jumped inside and fired it up. "There are about fifty CDs here in the hatch, choose whatever you want. If you don't find anything you like, tell me what you prefer, and it is yours, *si*?"

She laughed as she rifled through the collection of CDs. "You know you can stream this stuff now, right?"

She pulled out Nickelback, remembering he was listening to heavy rock music over the phone and slid the disc into the player. It seemed like an appropriate CD for a ride in a Hummer. "Where did you say we were going? White Hall? Just outside of Charlottesville, right?"

He wove through the traffic, making his way to Route 29. "White Hall, *si,* it is in wine country. It is where my Virginia home is located."

Placing his hand on her thigh, he hit the highway and kicked it into gear in the fast lane. She best learn right from the start, any vehicle he drove, he drove hard and fast, the faster the better.

"I've been to Charlottesville before, but not White Hall. So I know where Charlottesville is. Right near the mountains. It's beautiful there. When I was at Georgetown University, Shan and I would drive down there. We went to a few football games at UVA, some great tailgate parties, hung out at some of the fraternities on Rugby Road. I'm very familiar. So, White Hall is where your property is?"

"*Si*. I hope you don't mind, but I would really like to show it to you. I need some advice on the place. I want to share with you as much as I can. Are you up for that tonight?"

"I'd love to see it. Shan and I always said we were going to go visit some of the vineyards, but then we never had the time. You have a vineyard there, right?"

He chuckled, "If that is what you want to call it. At present, it needs a lot of attention, but I am told by my vintner Luciano, this can be accomplished with some time and money. I have a house there, some of my cars, a lot of land, mostly just forest land and fields. But some of those fields will be converted into vineyards with what already exists. The property needs some work, so don't expect anything too great. Does that disappoint you?"

"No, it sounds exciting. I can't wait to see it."

He smiled and turned to look at her. "I have a vision for the vineyards. The house, well, I haven't put much thought into it. It is small. But it has a great feel. It reminds me of Tuscany, and I think that is what draws me to it. The land is workable, so there is much that can be added to increase the property value."

"Is that where you're living? You haven't told me where you live, not that you have to. I understand you need to protect yourself. But I want you to know, we haven't talked about this, but I've told no one. I wouldn't tell anyone. I'd never put you in jeopardy."

He looked over at her. "I know you won't tell anyone, *mi amore*. I trust you. It is a good idea to keep what you know of me to yourself, for both of us, at least until I can protect you. But to answer your question, I have been staying here and in D.C., but I would prefer to make this Virginia property my permanent residence."

"You'd live in central Virginia and commute, oh, never mind. I forgot for a moment, you can avoid that whole commute thing. But, you think I need protection?"

"You are safe when you are with me, Kate, but during my death slumber, I cannot protect you. The more I feed from you, the more I can tune into you, feel you, hear your thoughts, detect your locale. It becomes very strong and if you would ever need me, call for me, I would awaken from my death slumber. If I could not come to you, I could send someone to your aid."

She stared at him as he maneuvered the Hummer around the traffic on Rt. 29, driving through Charlottesville to exit onto Rt. 250. He was already able to pick up on some of her thoughts, but this new revelation comforted her. **"Can you hear me now, lover? Do you know how much I love you?"**

Shade smiled as she talked to him telepathically. "*Si*, I can hear you, *mi amore*. I know how much you love me."

Turning his head, he grinned wickedly at her and winked. He took the Hummer off Rt. 250 onto rural Rt. 240, leading her further out into the countryside.

She leaned over and kissed him, restrained by the seat belt, and smiled knowing he could read her thoughts, but then realized the implications. *He can read my thoughts, all of my thoughts!* "Will I ever be able to read your thoughts?"

“Someday, you will be able to do that, but only after you feed from me. You will also learn how to block your thoughts, and your emotions, so others cannot pick up on them.”

He took the Hummer down Rt. 810, a narrow two-lane road barely wide enough for the massive vehicle. “I think the road that leads to the house is just ahead. I am sorry it is dark, but I think you can still see the layout easily enough. Does any of this seem familiar to you?”

He slowed the Hummer down as he looked for the private entrance off the main road. She looked about at the rolling hills of the Virginia countryside, the mountains in the background, silhouetted against the night sky. *What did he say? That she would feed from him? But she’s not vampire. Do mortals feed?* This was too much to take in right now. She’d stick with what she knew, looking at the landscape.

"No...I have never been out here."

"Well, I hope you like it, it’s very quiet, the property edges a park, so there is not much human activity out here, something I rather prefer. Here we are, this is the lane, it’s off the main road a ways."

The private drive was probably a good two miles long and had a fork, one road leading to the vineyards and the other to the house. He rounded a curve as the house came into view. The lights were on inside, and the exterior lighting was lit as well. She sat forward in her seat. It was an old house, built in the style of a Tuscan villa with aged stucco walls and a red-tiled roof. There were large arched windows and wrought iron banisters encircling small patios off the second-floor windows. Old ivy grew up an exterior wall and lush plantings surrounded the base of the house. She felt like she was back in Italy. It was a large house, a winding twisting house, not built like the modern open floor plan structures today. And yes, it needed some work, but oh how beautiful.

"Shade...this is your home?"

“*Si*, this is it. I told you it wasn’t much, small."

Throwing the Hummer in park, he turned off the engine and got out and opened her door, taking her hand to help her out of the vehicle. "Would you like to get a tour inside, I am afraid it is empty but that is the main reason I wanted to bring you here tonight."

Small? Did he say small? If this is his idea of a small house, then what does large look like? She’d already fallen in love with it. She loved its uniqueness, and she couldn’t wait to see inside. "I’d love a tour!" She stood on the running board as he lifted her down to the ground.

He led her to the main entrance of the house while trying to explain some of the area they could see.

"This is the main entrance. There are several entrances and patios off of the first floor rooms. From the main drive, you cannot see the other building that sits around the back. That is where the staff quarters are located. Right now, I only have one staff member residing here and he comes and goes, he is my vintner, Luciano. He oversees all of my vineyards and helps manage that business. He will be here for a while getting the vineyards in shape, hiring workers on the premises. I will give you a small tour outside once we walk through the inside. Please remember, don't expect much. This place needs extensive renovations."

Opening the heavy wooden door, he held out his hand for her to enter and waited for her reaction, praying it was a positive one.

She stepped into a foyer with the original terra cotta tiled floors, the walls were all Venetian plaster. The plaster had chipped away in some places, exposing old handmade bricks beneath. No one built houses like this anymore. He led her through the large foyer and to the left into a large living room with a beautiful European style fireplace, and French doors that led out to the rear of the property. There were dark wood plantation shutters that could be closed over the large arched windows to block out the heat of the mid-day sun, not that he'd ever see that. There were exposed beams on the ceiling, and an old chandelier that had seen better days, easy fix. She was in love with this room.

He could read her thoughts and felt a touch of her excitement. "So, I can tell you like this interior already. Care to keep observing the rooms?"

"Shade! This is...I love this room. I can already see..." She stopped talking suddenly, realizing she was decorating in her head, and this wasn't hers to decorate. She moved forward through an arched doorway and into a connecting corridor that lead past a powder room. She stuck her head in. It needed new everything, but had good bones. She headed through the arched entry into what she assumed was a dining room. She was making mental notes—plaster repair, new lighting—before walking into the kitchen. The kitchen was old, outdated. Like the bathroom, it would need a complete overhaul, but then, why did a vampire need a kitchen.

There was a sunroom attached to the back of the house, with double doors leading out to a patio. She retraced her steps back to the main foyer, Shade on her heels, smiling at her as she ran from room to room, and headed to the other side of the house.

There was an alcove with stairs leading up, and down. She'd explore that later. There was a large room off to her right. A family room perhaps? There were a lot of built-in bookshelves, a library maybe? The room had heavy dark beams on the ceiling, and even unfurnished felt masculine. She stepped back into the hallway and headed to a closed door at the end of the hall. It opened to a small suite of rooms, like a downstairs master suite. Bedroom, sitting room, and a very large bath with a walk-in shower stall.

"Lover, this is amazing. I can't imagine this house was left empty."

Shade followed her as she went from room to room, her mind racing. He loved watching her, seeing her mind working overtime, decorating already, making mental notes. He hoped this was a good sign, and it wouldn't take much to convince her to live here and take over the renovations. He loved this woman more with every second he spent with her.

"This property used to belong to Alec. Who in the hell knows what he planned to do with it, if anything. I can't imagine him here. But I know he received this property through a previous business deal. So I am sure he was just hanging onto it for its land value."

Taking her hand, he led her up the stairs to the second-floor rooms. "Come along, there is still more to see, including my bedroom, or at least where I sleep; nothing fancy, I just need a bed."

Leading her down a hall, he opened the door to his room. "Like I said, not much."

She peered inside to see a sparsely decorated room. Actually, that was being generous. She tried to stifle her laugh but wasn't successful. There was a mattress on the floor. He had leathers hanging from a few hooks on the wall, and boots lined up along the wall underneath.

"Shade, this looks like a prison cell. Please tell me this is not to your taste."

Hanging his head, he leaned against the doorjamb, his arms crossed over his chest. "I have not been here a great deal, just sleeping mostly. It suffices for that purpose, but there is something I want to ask you."

He took her in his arms and looked at her seriously. "*Bel*, I have no time to renovate this place, or make it a home, and without you, I don't need a home. I have deep concerns about your safety living in Arlington. Would you consider doing the renovations, moving in here with me? Living with me? I want to take care of you, protect you, and know in my heart you are safe. There are no limitations on expenses. Anything you want, you can have. You need not work. I want you with me as much as possible. I love you and I cannot take this torture of worrying about you when we are apart. It is a lot to ask of you, but I want you in my life. I am asking you to consider it, think about it, no need to answer immediately. I will set you up with contacts I have here in the States who will do the work you require, help you with whatever you want. Can you make this our home? Make it feel like Italy for me, for us? The house, the landscaping, I leave it all up to you. I plan to bring in house staff from my home in Florence, anything you need. Anything you want. I want us together Kate, *si*?"

She was taken aback by his offer. *Move in? Live here?* She'd have to quit her job. Could she sell her condo? She's known him, what, a month and a half? She stepped back from him, she had to think. She walked from this bedroom and back into a hallway that led to more bedrooms. Could she see a life with him? Actually, she couldn't imagine life without him. He already felt like he was a part of her. But he was vampire and she was mortal. How did that work? Did he plan to make her a vampire too?

He watched her back away from him and it felt like an ax was being driven into his heart. *Cazzo, it was too soon to push this on her.* He tuned into her and could sense her running options through her head..

"*Si, mi amore*, I wish for you to quit your job, the commute would be ridiculous. You won't need money. I have more than you could spend. I hope you can see a life with me, a very long one. *Si*, you are mortal but it can work if we put forth the effort. It won't be easy, but it can be done. At a future date, if it is your will, I wish for you to be immortal as well. That will give you eternal life, to be with me. I know this is a lot to contemplate, I understand that, but I want you here with me, making this our home together. Can you see yourself here with me? Would you like to be given this home to do as you wish? Help me build my empire here in the States, and share in that life with me. I want you as my mate. I want you to be mine, forever."

She stood still and listened to what he had to say. "Can I see myself here? Yes, I can. I can see us building a life together. Honestly, lover, it's hard to imagine otherwise. But how can you be sure? How can you be sure about forever? How can I...how can I be sure? How do you know you won't tire of me?"

"Kate. Come to me."

Holding his arms open, she walked into them and laid her head on his chest and he laid his head on top of hers. "Vampires mate for life. Once chosen, there is never another. I have searched the world over for five hundred years looking for my mate, I have found her, and she is in my arms right now. I crave one thing, to have you feed from me. When that happens, we take the first step toward being mated. No one has ever fed from me before. No one, *mi amore*. That is reserved for one person, my mate, and that right belongs to you. Going forward, I feed from no other, ever. You are the one I have searched for. And I could never tire of you."

No one has fed from him? He feeds from many, but no one feeds from him. Wait...did he just say *five hundred years? He's five hundred years old?* His arms surrounded her, and there was nowhere that felt more like home to her than being wrapped in his embrace. Could she walk away from him? She already knew the answer to that question. With all the other things swirling in her head, all the confusion of his world, and the things she didn't understand, she knew she loved him. And she knew she couldn't walk away.

"Yes, lover, the answer is yes."

"*Si, mi amore*! You have just made me the happiest immortal to walk in this world. I promise to never leave you, to always come home to you. I love you, Kate!"

Lifting her in his arms, he squeezed her tight and swirled her around in circles right in the middle of the hallway. "First thing you need to decorate is our bedroom, *si*?"

"Yes, the bedroom has to go." She laughed with the joy that filled her heart, and the joy she felt from him.

Kissing her, he set her down and grabbed her hand, racing with her down the hall and down the stairs. "Come on, let's walk outside a bit, you game?"

His happiness overwhelmed him as she responded, "Show me everything."

Taking her hand, they walked outside. "I know it's dark, but the mountains and park sit straight ahead of us. Down to the left are the vineyards, and I wish to expand what is already there. There is a great deal of land here, so at some point, I would love to have horses. I breed them in Florence, and I wish to bring some of them here and do the same."

"Shade...that park you refer to, that's the National Park Service, the mountains are part of the National Parks. Are you telling me your land extends all the way to the mountains?"

"Oh *si*, it extends to the base. There are 3,000 acres of land here if you can imagine it." Walking her around the side of the house, he showed her the patios. "I would love to have beautiful gardens here behind the house. I am hoping you can help me with that. Come, let me take you over to the garage. I have a few cars in there, and a few bikes. And beyond that, I think maybe we need to get you a proper sports car with a stick shift."

He held tight to her hand as he led her with pride across the expanse of the lawn and around the back to the garage filled with some of his favorite toys.

"Did you say you were five hundred years old? Are you sure you can keep up with me, lover?"

Throwing back his head, he laughed. "*Mi amore*, I think I can keep up with you. But you can bet I will give it all I've got."

They entered a large garage that was separated from the main house and was clearly built much later, although built in a style that matched the original architecture of the home. The garage was filled with expensive sports cars. Kate was no expert, but she picked out the Lamborghini, a Porsche, a Bugatti, and a Jaguar. There were a few she didn't recognize. There were several custom motorcycles lined against another wall, all Harleys.

"Shade, these are all very impressive, but you know I can't drive a stick shift, I'll keep my Miata."

He howled with laughter as he tossed her a set of keys, which she caught on the fly.

"What are these for?"

"See which car it opens, *bel*."

She walked through the garage, trying to insert the key into the driver's side door of the long line of sports cars, moving from one to another. Kate reached the last car in the line, a silver Jaguar, inserting the key as it slipped in without resistance. She looked back over her shoulder at Shade who was wearing an ear to ear grin. She turned the key and opened the door, slipping into the driver's seat. "Lover, this is too much!"

"Nothing is too much. You will have this and more."

"But...I can't even drive it."

He chuckled, "A small obstacle. I will teach you. Now come. Now that we have taken the grand tour, I think perhaps it is time we head back into the city, or we can spend the night and day here if you wish, but I must be able to escape the sun."

"Sleep in that prison cell?" She laughed. "I didn't pack for an overnight, and besides, I think I'd prefer you in my own bed tonight. I'll make redoing the bedroom my top priority, believe me."

"*Si*, I don't blame you, that thing is not comfortable. But I would sleep anywhere as long as you were in my arms. It is getting late, *bel*, we had best be getting back, I need to get there before sunrise."

Taking her hand, they walked back to the Hummer. He helped her inside and then fired it up and headed down the lane. When they got to the main road, he angled the car so the headlights shone on the sign to the entrance of the property and stopped the Hummer.

"This belongs to you, *bel rosso*, this is yours now. I wanted this to be named after you, our mortal wine brands as well. This will be ours."

She looked at the sign in the headlights of the Hummer, 'Bel Rosso Vineyards.' *He named it after me? The property? The wine? Did he know I'd say yes? Or was he only hoping?*

"Lover, I don't know what to say." It overwhelmed her to think he was already planning their life together.

"You need not say a thing, *mi amore*. And *si*, I knew the moment I laid eyes on you I wanted you for all eternity. I have loved you since the day we met, and I will love you every day for the rest of our lives. This is the beginning of our journey, and it will be a glorious one with love and laughter. I know we have a lot ahead of us. I'm not naïve to all we will face. I know there will be sorrow and pain as well, but I will promise more love than you can ever imagine. Your life is about to change forever, as is mine. We begin here, this night. I have waited for you to come and I had given up hope of ever finding you, and I will never let you go."

21

When Kate woke, it was almost mid-day. She sat up with a start, feeling confused and fuzzy-headed. He'd brought her back home from the Virginia house and stayed with her only a few minutes as the sun was coming up before teleporting out. She had lain down to take a short nap, and now it was noon.

Walking to the bathroom, she washed her face, and let the memories of last night rush over her; his house and her promise. Did she really tell him she'd quit her job, sell her condo, and move in? She walked back into the bedroom and pulled on a pair of jeans and an old shirt. *Kate Reese, have you lost your mind? What if he changes his mind, like the others? You lose more than your heart this time. You will lose everything you've worked to build for yourself.*

There was no one she could talk to about this. Besides, she already knew if she had someone to talk to, exactly what they'd say, the same thing she was saying to herself.

But she wanted this man. She loved this man. And she trusted him, but then, didn't she trust the others too? There was an argument taking place in her head, a tug of war, one side pulling her to him, saying let go of your fears, follow him. And the other side saying, be logical. Protect yourself. But she didn't want to lose him.

The doorbell rang and she looked toward the door with a quizzical look. She wasn't expecting anyone. She went to the door and looked through the peephole to see a man wearing a uniform and carrying a package of some kind. She opened the door leaving the chain on, "Can I help you?"

He looked at her through the slightly open door, "Miss Reese, Miss Kate Reese?"

She looked him up and down. He was from a local courier service, but on a Sunday? "Yes, I'm Kate Reese."

"I have a delivery for you, ma'am. You'll have to sign for it."

"Can you tell me who sent it?" She was still skeptical about opening the door.

He looked down at his notepad, and then read back to her. "Adami and Costa? It's a law firm, ma'am. Look, I can tell you don't want to open your door to me, but all I can say is I was just paid a ton of money to make this Sunday delivery. Our courier service is closed on Sunday's. I was told to make the delivery, to make sure I put it in your hands personally, and you signed for it. Then I'm to immediately return to the law office with the signed receipt. They paid me a thousand bucks, ma'am. I don't make a thousand bucks in a month. So, whatever it is, someone really wants you to have this today."

She looked at him a few seconds longer, then released the chain lock and opened the door. He handed her the thick 10x14-inch brown envelope, along with a pen and the receipt pad for her signature. She signed the pad and handed the pad and pen back to him. She realized she didn't have a tip for him as she slid her hands over her pockets. He laughed. "Really, no need. Not today. Have a good day, ma'am."

She closed and locked the door and carried the large envelope into the living room, sitting down on the sofa as she pulled open the sealed flap. She removed the thick stack of papers from the envelope which contained, among other things, a deed. It was signed and notarized, putting all of the Virginia property in her name.

She took the other document and unfolded it. It was a surveyor's document depicting the plot of land, showing the property boundaries, and indicating the location of the house and other exterior buildings. She sat with the papers strewn about her, stunned. He knew. He knew she'd have second thoughts in the light of day when she was alone to contemplate her decision, when she wasn't mesmerized by those damn blue eyes that could talk her into anything. He knew she'd question the wisdom of her choice. He wanted to eliminate all the fears, all the barriers. His message was clear. Sell your condo Kate Reese, and quit your job. Whatever happened, the property was hers.

She wanted to call him, to let him know, but the sun shone bright through her window and she knew he was deep in his death slumber. Tomorrow, she'd give her two weeks' notice at work, and call a realtor to put her condo on the market. But right now, she'd call her family and start building the web of lies that would remove her from the mortal world.

22

Kate headed straight to Human Resources and submitted her resignation before going to her cubicle. She'd called her family Sunday night, and now it was time to tell Shannon. She slid into her cubicle and waited for the familiar sound of Shan's office chair to come wheeling around the cubicle wall.

Right on schedule, Shan scooted her chair around into Kate's space as Kate was unloading her briefcase.

"So, how was your weekend? I didn't hear from you. Did you see Mr. Tall, Dark and Dangerous? Are you two an item yet?"

Kate kept her back to Shannon, plugging her laptop into the docking station, shuffling papers, anything to not face her as she answered.

"Yes, I saw him. We went out on Saturday night, but he's very busy, you know. I really don't get to spend a lot of time with him. But Shan, on a totally unrelated topic, there's something I need to tell you."

Kate took a deep breath and sat down in the office chair and swiveled in Shannon's direction.

She saw the smile leave Shannon's face. "What is it? Is someone sick? You okay?"

"Oh, nothing like that. Good news, actually. It's just out of the blue and unexpected, but I got this job offer in London. An ad agency there saw my work, liked it, and called to offer me a job."

Shannon's mouth dropped open. "What? When did they call? You're not going, are you? Oh Kate! I'm excited and sad all at the same time. What are you going to do?"

"Well, it's done actually. They called me over a week ago, and I've been talking to them every evening on the phone, and I decided to take it. I mean, I love Europe, and I'll have a flat in London, and I can travel while I'm there. It just seemed too good an opportunity to pass up."

Shannon looked stunned. "Wait. You've already decided? All this was going on and you didn't even tell me?"

"Shannon, it was a hard decision to make. And thinking about leaving people behind was the hardest part. I wasn't sure I could make the decision and think about it rationally if I was dealing with other people's emotions about it. So, I told no one. Please, don't be mad. I'm sure I'll fly home a few times a year, and we'll still see each other."

Shannon asked, "What about your folks? Did you tell them?"

"Yeah, I called them last night. They were concerned, as always. But Shan, they're concerned I live in D.C. I mean, I only see them at Christmas as it is. This won't be a big adjustment for them."

Shannon's disappointment was visible on her face. "Not a big adjustment for them maybe, but what about us? Oh Kate, forget I said that. That was selfish. I'm really happy for you, I am. But I just can't imagine, I mean, we went through college together, and then got this job together. I almost can't remember when you weren't in my life."

Kate gave Shannon a hug, hating that she had lied to her friend. "I know. It was hard to make the split. It's hard for me too, Shannon."

"What about him? Your new international man of mystery? So, I guess that's over too?"

"Shade? He was very supportive. He said he travels a lot in his business and he'd still catch up with me. He said he was in and out of Heathrow Airport several times a month."

"So, he'll still see you and I won't??"

"Shannon, I'm sure I'll still see you. And we can talk. And email. And Skype. And Facebook." Kate feared she was only delaying the inevitable. The day when she'd have to break all ties with Shannon for good.

"You better do more than that, Kate Reese. You better visit! You can come stay with me when you're in the States."

"Actually, Shade has a house in Virginia. He said I could use it anytime I was in the States. Stay there as long as I needed."

Shannon raised her eyebrows, "Move in? You're moving in with him?"

"No. He travels, he's rarely there. The house is empty most of the time. He just offered to let me stay there whenever I'm in the States, that's all."

"So, you're selling your condo then."

"Yes, I'm calling the realtor today. I'll be moving in two weeks."

"Two weeks! I can't believe this is happening. Okay, just be warned. I will officially be spending my vacations with you in London."

"Oh...of course...yes." Now there's a little glitch Kate hadn't thought about.

23

This was it. Moving day! Kate had packed up everything, and Shade had arranged for the movers. He said he'd arrange for that since he wanted vamps to handle the move. The condo sold quickly, but that wasn't unexpected. Any real estate close to D.C. would turn over fast. The movers arrived and loaded up the moving van. She sold off much of her furniture as her more modern style wouldn't work in the old house.

She and Shade both wanted to restore this house and furnish it so it maintained the look and feel of Tuscany. She was taking her bedroom furniture, however. Even if it was only temporary, it would be better than the prison cell mattress Shade had on the floor. Shade told her he'd be there when she arrived but would remain in his death slumber until sunset and he had arranged for Luciano to be on hand to help her with anything she needed.

The movers finished loading the van, and Kate walked through the empty condo one last time, with no reservations about leaving it behind. She made her way to the parking garage and got in the Miata, following the van on the three-hour drive to *Bel Rosso*, and her new life.

As they arrived and the truck lumbered up the private drive to the estate, Kate was taking in the beauty of the place in the daylight. She'd come back here several times with Shade to measure rooms, and windows, and start making plans, but it was always at night. Being here during the day, with the brilliant fall foliage, the clear blue sky, and the crisp fall air was a totally new experience. The property was breathtaking. It was all softly rolling hills and open fields. The vineyards had been harvested, but the vines still clung to the stakes. The trees had all turned shades of yellow and orange for the fall, while the fields remained green, and the mountains provided the perfect backdrop of a dark bluish-green, making it clear why they were named "Blue Ridge." Kate couldn't imagine this would be her view every day.

Luciano came to the door as soon as she pulled up, and directed the movers as to where to place boxes. When she entered the house, all the internal lights had been turned on, and she noticed the windows were all sealed. Luciano pointed out there were electronic blinds, on timers and sensitive to the outside light. The blinds would automatically close and open with the rising and setting of the sun. Luciano showed her the manual over-ride if she was awake during the day and wanted to open them. Kate realized without the internal lighting, the house would be pitch black inside.

All of the things for their bedroom were stacked in a nearby room until he woke. Luciano said he was sleeping and would not disturb him. Kate asked Luciano if the manmade lights would hurt him during the day, and he said "No, only sunlight, although master sleeps in total darkness."

It only took the crew a few hours to unload everything and then they left the property. Luciano informed her that the kitchen had been stocked with food and beverages, and unless there was something else she needed, he had things he must attend to in the vineyards. Kate let him know she was fine and began the process of unpacking.

She started in the kitchen and unpacked the things she brought, checking out the fully stocked fridge and pantry. *Good Lord! How much food do they think one mortal can eat?*

She unloaded her books and placed them on the bookshelves in the room that looked like a library or family room. Maybe this could be space for him, a home office? This room had dark wood beams and one exposed brick wall. It felt masculine. She unpacked the art she had collected in her travels and stacked it against the wall. She was thinking she'd wait until they had furnished the house before she decided where to hang things when she noticed another painting propped against the wall. She walked over to examine it more closely. It was the painting he had bid on at the art auction. She smiled as she lifted it to admire it, astounded at how much it looked like the grounds here. She would hang it here, in this room, which she'd decorate for him.

She had finished unpacking everything except the bedroom, which was put aside until Shade woke. She realized she'd never seen him in his death slumber. Would she be frightened? Did he look dead? Would she be able to sleep beside him? Or was this something he must do alone? She walked to the bedroom door and stood with her hand on the doorknob, and there was only silence.

As she opened the door, ever so slowly, her heart was in her throat. The light from the hallway spilled into the pitch-black room. He lay on his back, unmoving. She tip-toed in quietly and knelt on the floor, leaning in close to him as he slept on the mattress. She saw the rise and fall of his chest, so not really a death slumber. She laid her hand on his chest and felt the beat of his heart, and the warmth of his skin. She leaned over him and gently touched her lips to his. He looked beautiful in his sleep, his dark curls against the white pillow. She slid onto the mattress beside him, laying her head on his shoulder, and putting her hand across his chest, her leg across his thigh.

"I am home, lover."

***

As he lies in his death slumber, the scent of her rose fragrance streamed to him, he couldn't yet wake, but he felt her presence close to him. Her blood now pumped through him, bonding him to her, allowing him to feel her emotions, hear her thoughts more clearly. She gave him life and she grew stronger inside him each time he fed from her. He felt her body slide over his, her hair soft and silken on his naked skin and he slid his arm around her, pulling her close, but the slumber not allowing him full release. He could fight through the grip of the death slumber if she were in harm or needed him, but even that would be a struggle for him now. As he feeds from her more, and she'd eventually feed from him, his ability to arouse from the death slumber to respond to her need would become instantaneous. Her hand lay across his chest. He could feel it over his heart, like a protective cage. He moved to gently cradle her tighter to his body and let his hand slide into her hair, his other arm across the small of her back, protecting her even in his slumber. He could feel her warm breath on him, her heart beating, her blood pumping, and he only hoped she could feel the same in him. He awakened slowly, but gloriously with her in his arms.

"*Ti amo*."

Kate felt him stir, feels his arms encircle her and pull her close just as he spoke, telling her he loved her. She heard the soft whir of the electronic blinds as they automatically opened, letting the last remaining pale light of the evening into the room. She looked up at him, and into those blue eyes.

"Lover, I never asked. It never occurred to me, but will I be able to sleep next to you?"

"It is your choice to make, *bel rosso*, to give up the day and sleep next to me while you are still mortal. But it is the choice I hope you make. Nothing would bring me greater peace than to have you lie at my side in my death slumber. You must be exhausted, how do you feel, *bel*?"

"Excited more than tired. I hadn't realized that I'd never seen the estate during the daytime. It's even more beautiful. It makes me sad that you can't see it."

"*Bel*, I can go out at sundown, especially in the summer, when the sun sets but there is still light. I can also see it on rainy overcast days. It is just the direct sun rays that will burn my skin, so we can enjoy evenings together when I am home and not working. We need to have a little talk about this renovation. Can you handle that at the moment?"

"Yes, I'm eager to get started on this project. I had the movers bring my bedroom furniture. I know it will be only temporary, but it will at least work better than your current prison cell."

He chuckled. "You are in my prison cell, though, are you not, *mi amore*?"

Kate laughed. "Which I hope you see as a true testament of my love, that I would sleep in here to be with you."

"Give you an estate and you get sassy with me. I see how this works, vixen!" He gave her a quick slap across her derriere.

She felt the sharp sting of the slap and curled into him. She slid her arm tighter around his chest, as she ran her foot up his leg, teasing him.

He growled softly and felt his beast rise to the surface, waiting to have her, and Shade must fist his hands to suppress the urgency of the beast. The beast had had a taste of her and he wanted more than she could handle as a mortal.

"Damn *mi amore*, you tempt me. But we need to talk. I need to make sure you have what you need to get this job done. Now come, sit up. Are you hungry? There is food in the kitchen. I can get you something if you wish it, *si*?"

"I saw the kitchen, lover, and I grabbed something earlier. How much food do you think we mortals eat anyway? There was enough stuff in there for an army! But you have my attention. What is it you want to talk about?"

Reaching to the side of the bed, he dug around in his leather jacket on the floor and found the envelope tucked inside a pocket. Positioning himself upright on the mattress, he leaned over and kissed her. "This envelope is for you, for the estate, *si*?"

Kate tore open the envelope to find two credit cards and several business cards. Both credit cards had her name on them. "Shade, I have a credit card. You don't need to give me these."

Tipping her chin up, he stared into her eyes. "Oh *si*, you most certainly do need them. The clear credit card, with the gold trim? You use that on everything you buy for this place, *si*? I mean everything, *mi amore*, nothing is to come from your own pockets. My accountant takes care of paying all the bills, so don't worry about maxing it out. Those business cards are for my immortal business associates, they own shops in D.C., and they will ship anything you wish from Europe; Florence, Milan, Rome, London, Paris...They can get things for you that you cannot find anywhere here in the States. Antiques, textiles, art, are all available through those cards in your hands. They will also arrange for deliveries and any work that needs to be done. You may notice many workers on the grounds. Luciano is busy coordinating those workers for the vineyards, so pay them no mind. You can concentrate on the renovation of this house and our gardens, *si*?"

"You'll love the house when I'm done. I'll make sure it reflects the Tuscany we both love. But what is this other card for?"

"*Mi amore*, you need not worry about money, *si*? I want that understood. Artwork alone can cost great sums of money, and I know you love art. I have it, so spend it. There is something else I wish to talk to you about. I want to take you to the California house, show you that property and have you furnish it as well. It is in much better condition than this property, and the vineyards are already producing. Can I ask something else of you? I know this is a lot for you to accomplish, but I need to concentrate on providing security for Alec and I slumber in the daylight hours."

"Of course, ask me anything."

Pulling her into his arms, she laid her head on his chest. "*Bel*, the staff quarters here are in bad shape, I need you to get that renovated as soon as possible. Luciano is there now with the barest of necessities. But I intend to bring some of my own people here from Florence, my manservant, a housekeeper for you, and a chef, perhaps. We will need the staff quarters renovated and furnished quickly. Could you take that on first?"

"Yes, just let me know your priorities, and I'll coordinate it. I'll start on the staff quarters first. We can set up my stuff here and that will give us a foundation until I can work on our house. No problems. But what is this other card?"

Taking her face into his hands, he softly kissed one cheek, then the other. He kissed her nose and then her forehead and almost kissed her mouth. He could feel her breath on his lips as he whispered softly, "That card is for you; for your personal expenses. Clothes, shoes, whatever you want. You deserve this, you deserve to be pampered and spoiled. Promise me, you will spoil yourself."

"Lover, you already spoil me. I can't imagine what else I could need. But thank you." She kissed him, wrapping her arms around his neck.

"Is this too much for you, you must tell me if it is, *si*?"

"No, I can manage it."

"And so it shall be, *mi amore*. Come, lay with me awhile and let us rest and dream of what our future holds. Is there anything you wish to ask me, talk to me about?"

She cuddled next to him. He was waking up for the night, and she'd been running around all day with the movers. She'd need to begin the process of shifting her schedule so she could sleep when he slept, but for now, she cuddled up next to him, feeling warm and protected in his arms as she listened to the night call of crickets and tree frogs lull her into sleep.

"I can't think of anything. I think we'll just figure it out as we go."

"*Si*, I think that is a wise decision." He could feel the tiredness of her body as her breathing began to slow, and he knew she needed her rest. He rubbed her back gently and kissed the top of her head. He could lie here for the rest of eternity with her, just like this.

"Rest, *bel*, sleep. I will be here, I will not leave you."

24

Kate had been shifting her schedule so she was able to sleep during the day with Shade, climbing into bed with him each morning when he returned from the Dead House. She didn't even want to ask what that meant, or how it got its name. She knew he provided security for Alec, and she didn't probe for details. During the night hours when he was gone, she'd been busy with the renovations. All of the contractor's Shade referred her to were vamps, so they were fine with her scheduling their work at night, and they worked fast.

Kate was amazed at how much work got done. The renovations to the staff quarters were almost completed, and she'd begin furnishing it soon. The workers had gutted the kitchen and all of the bathrooms except the one off the master bedroom in their main house. They'd save the master bathroom and bedroom for last, giving her and Shade a private space to retreat to while the house was being worked on. She'd worked with the contractors to make sure the renovations remained true to the original design of the house and had been delighted with the results so far. She was already working with the interior designers, tracking down furniture and other pieces to move in once the renovations were complete.

She took time every day to walk outside, either early morning or late evening, to enjoy the beauty of this place. Autumn was well advanced, and the leaves were beginning to fall. This morning, she stood in the cool crisp air, a light jacket around her as she watched the sun begin to rise, and the mist that hovered over the ground started to dissipate. He'd be home soon. She saw Luciano is the distance. He had a field of migrant workers, harvesting the last grapes of the season, already hard at work. She turned and went back inside the house. It felt chilly even inside now. She'd have the workers check the heating system, it was probably old and would need replacing, and would need to be moved up on the priority list.

She headed up the stairs to their bedroom, temporarily furnished with all the things from her condo, a room that was far too feminine for Shade. But he'd been good-natured about her removal of the prison cell decor that had been here before as they both worked around the renovations. As she walked into the room, he teleported in, and she wondered if she'd ever get used to that.

***

Shade made a quick night of training the mercenaries as things were beginning to shape up, but they still had a long way to go for this group to be called warriors. As the nights became longer, the cold settled in and he realized he'd need to break out some heavy-duty leathers soon, including his leather trench and gloves. The nights were becoming far colder than he anticipated, and the thought of her warm body in his arms made him want to be home even more. *Bel* had been working on the renovations, and every morning, she'd show him what had been done the previous night. She was excited and pleased with the outcome. She had classic good taste, and an appreciation for beautiful things, and seeing the transformation of the house through her eyes was the greatest pleasure for him. She was happy, and she loved being there and that was all he wanted for her.

Teleporting in, he found her in the bedroom, surrounded by the things she'd brought from her condo. Items he was more familiar with than she'd ever know, but he knew it wouldn't be long before she transformed this room as well into a space that reflected both of them.

"Damn if it's not cold out there! I need to find heavier clothes and something for my head. Is it always this damn cold? Come! I need to be warmed up."

She laughed. "Lover, this isn't cold, this is just chilly. It will get much colder than this. Wait till we have snow. Come, hold me, I'll keep you warm."

Wrapping her in his arms, he pulled her to his chest. He'd never tire of how small she was compared to him, but with such a huge heart. "You are cold as well. Let me change and I will make us a fire, *si*?"

Quickly running into the bathroom that was almost older than he was, he washed up and changed into a bulky sweater with his jeans. Walking back out, he grabbed her hand and led her down to the first floor of the house where they snuggled together on a large rug thrown in front of the fireplace.

"Watch this." With just his thoughts, he ignited a small flame inside the stone fireplace and watched it grow as it licked over the wood stacked there until it was blazing, and the heat was rolling off, warming the room. He turned to her nonchalantly, "So tell me about your adventures today."

Kate looked on in amazement. “How do you do that?”

“I just will it so, *mi amore*.”

He can hear her wondering what other revelations he’d reveal over time. She slid her hands under his sweater, and across his hard-muscled back.

“The workers have almost completed the staff quarters. I'll start furnishing it soon. Once they finish up there, they’ll focus their attention on this house. It’s moving much quicker than I thought. I'm going to have them look at the heating system, it’s probably ancient, and we should go ahead and replace it.”

“I leave those decisions to you. Whatever you do will be fine with me.”

Grinning, he wrapped himself around her and lay back on the rug, feeling the heat roll over them, although he wasn’t so sure all that heat was from the fire burning in the fireplace. Pushing her hair from her face, he stared at her and smiled. "Have I told you how beautiful you are, how much I love what you have done for me? Many women would never do as much."

He laid her back on the rug as he leaned over her.

"Oh, I think there’d be a long line of women waiting to do most anything you want. I can't imagine otherwise." She reached up and ran her fingers through his hair.

“Perhaps, but it would not be for me, only for their gain. A prize to be won, bragging rights, I assure you; gold-diggers, or social climbers. In Italy, catching Shade Medici would mean taking a big step up the social ladder. Even among the mortals, there are those who seek us out as mere curiosities, to say they have been with a vamp. Believe me, I have used it to my advantage, but that is not love. It is not the same when someone you love gives you their heart because they want your life with them to be something special, to build a home together. My home in Florence is my parents’ home. I inherited it, but I’ve never had a true home, a place where I want to come back to every night, where someone is waiting with love and care for me. I do not take this lightly. You understand that, *si*?”

“There are social climbers in the mortal world as well. I’m well aware! I hate to say this about someone I know, but I always felt Rissa was a social climber. In college, she was very much about hanging out with the right people, and the right people being those who came from old money. She was with this Max guy for a while, we didn't see much of him, but he clearly had money. He took her everywhere, bought her things. Then she set her sights on Alec. Of course, I never knew, until recently, that he was a vampire. I mean, I think she really loves him, but I'm pretty sure if he was a poor starving artist, she wouldn't have given him a second glance. I don't know, lover. It seems a pretty high price to pay. I think you have to follow your heart, and the rest will come, you know? I mean, I could live with you anywhere and be happy."

He smiled as she told him about Rissa, and the things she didn't know about Rissa and Alec would remain unsaid for now. She was still mortal and trying to explain Alec and Rissa's lifestyle and how their relationship played out behind closed doors was far more than he wished her to know just yet, or ever for that matter. It made him wonder if he should expose her to more of the reality of immortal life, and what it entailed. It wasn't all money, beauty, and luxury. There was also death and violence and living in a very volatile world.

He liked her as she was with her innocence of such matters. She had no clue of the death he wielded on a daily basis, that he was the master of teaching those around him how to fight and kill, how to protect in the most gruesome fashion, with speed and efficiency.

"*Mi amore*, I know Rissa and Alec love each other, but they are nothing like me, in any fashion. So please never judge me or us by them. They live a lifestyle that is not typical for immortals. As immortal, we must remain hidden and learn to blend into mortal culture, but they appear very publicly in life as mortals and use their immortal skills to climb and get where they need to go. It is a dangerous line to tread, and they risk exposure. But enough about them, I want you to have all the easiness this life can give you. I want you to be happy. I cannot be with you all the time, so you need to love our home here, to feel safe and protected. I also want to ask you something...."

"Anything. You can ask me anything."

"Well, I know you are looking through a lot of decorating options for this home, so I am thinking we should take a visit to the California house soon, perhaps it will help save you time once done here. You may come across things that will suit that house as well, and I want this to be easy for you. That house is larger, has more rooms, and is in much better condition, almost new. So, there is more to decorate. Would you like to go with me one night and see it? Take a tour and tell me if you have a vision of how you wish it to be?"

"Of course! Do you plan on us living there as well? Will you be dividing your time between here and California?"

Leaning over, he kissed her softly. "No, *bel*, I do not wish to live in California, although it is more coastal and warmer, I think. I have vineyards much larger abroad than those in Virginia and California, and Luciano will oversee the vineyards on all my properties. I wish to establish my wines here, broaden my brands in the States. So, the California house is someplace we will visit. I like this place in Virginia, it is us, I believe. I feel at home here. I like this property where our house sits, it reminds me of Tuscany. I like the sounds at night. Tell me, is this too overwhelming for you? Two homes on opposite coasts? I can have decorators brought in to do it."

"No! Let me do it, please. I love the projects, and besides, I need things to do while you're away. I will make sure both homes are perfect for us, I promise. In the spring, I'll work on landscaping the gardens around the house. It will be beautiful. I already love it here. In the city, all I heard was traffic and sirens at night. Here, I listen to tree frogs and crickets, and the sound of the cicada. I love that sound. I haven't heard it since I moved from South Carolina."

He loved the sound of the excitement in her voice, the way her eyes sparkled. She entranced him in every aspect and it confirmed she was the one he'd searched for in his five hundred years of living. She was everything he wasn't, her small frame and delicate features, her pale skin, and dark eyes, her flaming red hair. Her sexuality was subtle. She didn't flaunt it but reserved it for him. She had an innocence and vulnerability about her, and a pureness of heart that was rare. She had such a gentle soul he wasn't sure he could take it to make her immortal, and yet, he couldn't live without her, and never wanted to. So many women in his life, so many and yet, he traveled so far from home and found her here, among this beautiful place and now they would claim it as their own.

He tousled her hair and rolled her to her side, leaning on his elbow as he heard the electric blinds lower for the coming daylight. There were many daybreaks he longed for slumber to take him away, but now, he dreaded them, for they took away precious time from his *bel*. Now he had even more reason to curse the sun.

"It is a big project, *si*? Just take it one day at a time, *bel*. Soon, we will visit California and our home there. I think you will like it, and it can be a place to visit and get away in the long winter that apparently is going to have me shivering in that damn snow."

25

Shade woke in the late evening. It was just past sunset, and *bel* was still sleeping on his chest. He listened to the soft sounds of her breathing as her breath softly caressed his skin. It was time. He wanted her to exhale the scent of his own blood. In five hundred years, no female had been allowed to feed from him and he felt he needed to take her to Castello, his family home in Florence, to have her feed from him for the first time. This was the first step in sealing their bond of mating. The blood covenant would bond her to him, she would be his. If she were already immortal, it would be all that was required to make her his mate, but for her, there'd be a longer journey. At least with the blood covenant, her scent would change, and other vamps would know she was claimed and belonged to him. He'd still have to turn her, but he'd give her more time before that step, for she had much to learn. Slowly moving her off his chest, he heard her soft, enchanting moan as he gently repositioned her in the bed.

He grabbed his cell phone, texting Tomas and letting him know he wouldn't be joining the warriors at the Dead House tonight, giving him instructions on what he wanted to be accomplished in the training exercises, as well as who he wanted assigned on the streets. Just as he hit send, he saw her stretch out on the bed and that pool of crimson spread across the pillow.

He saw her reach her hand out across the empty bed, not feeling him there. She opened her eyes and looked up at him through her tangled mass of hair.

In a voice still heavy with sleep she asked, "You're barely out of my bed and already planning your night? What can I do to get your undivided attention before you leave?"

Shade looked down at her and grinned, pitching his phone to the side table and sliding back in bed beside her. He kissed her deeply, his beast already on edge with just the feel of her against his body.

"*Mi amore*, you are so beautiful when you wake in a tangle of crimson, naked and sleepy-eyed. But, for your information, I have been giving orders so I can spend this autumn evening with you, but there is a small catch, *si*?"

She snuggled against him, putting her nose on his. "And what would that small catch be?"

He licked the tip of her nose and laughed softly, his hands going straight for her ass and squeezing. "Tonight, we journey to Florence, to my ancestral home. I would like to show you where I grew up, where I come from. Are you agreeable to that?”

She sat up in bed. "I...of course! Are you going to need me to decorate that house too?"

He loved how her face lit up, and how her emotions were always visible on her face. He could already see the wheels spinning inside her head and knew a thousand questions were about to shoot out of that kissable mouth.

"No *mi amore*, this house was decorated long ago, and I prefer it to remain the way it is. Now, we will teleport, so you need to move that sweet ass of yours and get dressed, *si*?”

Kate slid out of bed and grabbed a quick shower, put on some make-up, and dried her hair, brushing it to a high sheen. He was dressing in jeans, so she grabbed her jeans and pulled on a pair of brown knee-high boots, slipping a cashmere sweater in a soft peach color over her head. She spritzed on her rose scent and he followed her downstairs to the kitchen where she fixed a cup of coffee and toasted a bagel. He sat at the counter and watched her eat, wiping a crumb from her lip with his finger before he leaned in to kiss her.

"Okay...unless I need a suitcase, I'm ready!"

"No suitcase needed. If we decide to stay there a night or two, I will fit you with a wardrobe. Now come!" Grabbing his leather jacket, sliding it on, he pulled her into his arms and wrapped the jacket around both of them. “Look me in the eyes, *mi amore*. Do you trust me?"

"Lover, I always trust you."

"Good. This journey will take a little more time, similar to Paris, *si*? You may feel dizziness and a bit lightheaded. Do not be frightened. Wrap your legs around my waist, snuggle close, and lay your head on my shoulder. We will be there before you know it. Close your eyes if it makes you feel dizzy, *si*?"

Telepathically letting Gi, his manservant in Florence, know they’d be arriving, he wished for all the servants to not be visible this night. Gi had served him many years and knew Shade, his family, and all of Castello like the back of his hand. Without him, Castello wouldn’t run like clockwork. Still, he knew the staff would be curious. It wasn’t normal for him to arrive with a mortal on his arm, and all would know from her scent before the next sunrise that he was mated to her, and the covenant was sealed.

As her legs wrapped tightly around his waist, he slid his hand into her hair, and pulled her head to his shoulder as they teleported through the night sky, Florence bound.

***

Kate was remembering when he teleported her to Paris, and then back again because there had been some trouble in D.C. She hoped their time together tonight would be uninterrupted. She felt the air getting cooler as it rushed past them, and she kept her eyes closed tight to minimize the sensation of motion.

Shade set her down inside Castello, and brushed the hair from her face, leaning down to kiss her gently. "Open your eyes, *bel*. Welcome to Castello."

Kate opened her eyes and looked around a massive hall of marble, with a wide winding staircase, and a ceiling that looked to be three stories high. Long wide hallways lead off in opposite directions, lined with chandeliers, and frescoes painted on the ceilings, framed in gilded gold leaf. It reminded her of the palace at Versailles, but not quite as large.

"Where are we, Shade? I thought you were taking me to your home?"

He threw back his head and laughed as the sound echoed off the long quiet hallways of his castle. "*Si,* this is my home. This is Medici Castello, where I grew up as a boy, where I was born and raised. This is mine. It will belong to you as well. You are standing in the grand foyer. Ah, and here comes Gi."

Turning his head, he smiled as Gi approached and bowed, welcoming him as Master Shade.

"Gi, may I present my beautiful Kate, *bel rosso*."

Shade turned to Kate. "*Mi amore*, this is my manservant Gi, he has been with my *familia* a very long time, and if there is anything you need, he is the one you go to, *si*?"

Kate knew her mouth was hanging open, even as she was being introduced to this elderly gentleman, dressed very formally in a black waistcoat, starched white shirt, and bowtie. He bowed his head to her, and she started to curtsy, but then realized he was staff, and that was inappropriate. She nodded to him in return and then stammered, "I'm, uh, so glad to meet you, Mr. Gi."

Shade was amused as she stumbled on her words, not sure how to approach Gi and afraid of making a blunder. He wrapped his arms around her waist and smiled at Gi, nodding to let him know he may go for the evening, as Gi informed him all of his requests had been seen too.

"*Mi amore*, you may address him as Gi. Would you allow me to give you a small tour?"

"A small tour? I don't think there's anything small about this place, but please. I would love to see it!"

Shrugging off his leather jacket, he threw it across a velvet brocade chair in the foyer and took her hand, leading her through some of the rooms along the main floor.

"This is the main floor. There is another floor above us, which is used for the privacy of the family, with bedrooms, bathrooms, dressing rooms and my private office, of course. On this floor are the formal living room and dining room, the kitchen, a family room, music room, a library, the ballroom, and many of the ancient paintings that are priceless to me and my *familia*."

She took in everything as he led her through the rooms, her fascination with the castle delighted him. She belonged here with him, he could feel it. It was destiny that he finally found her, and he could feel calmness in his soul as they walked together and there was no longer any doubt in his mind that this night she fed from him, the only one to ever feed on his blood. As they entered a large hallway, known as the hall of ancestors, it was lined with many paintings of the Medici family through the ages, both mortal and immortal. He stopped momentarily and let her browse.

Kate was drawn to a painting of a beautiful woman with blonde hair, braided and wrapped on her head., Her features were delicate, and she was dressed in a heavy brocaded gown from a period long past. The man standing next to her was clearly her husband as indicated by the protective placement of his arm on her shoulder. He looked a lot like Shade, except his eyes were brown. Standing in front of the handsome couple was a boy of maybe ten or twelve.

"Lover? This man looks a lot like you, but obviously, it's not you. Are these your parents? That boy, is that you?"

"*Si*. That is my *padre*, Christofano and the woman is my *madre*, Portia. And that is me, about the age when I went to the warrior camp. This portrait was painted by Michelangelo and originally hung in the upper quarters of Castello. It was painted for my intended mate and her *familia*."

Did he just say Michelangelo? She remembered the history of the mortal Medici's and their patronage of the artist of the Renaissance. "Your what? Your intended mate? I don't understand. You're just a child in this picture. You were engaged to be with someone else?"

He wrapped his arms around her and sat his chin atop her head as they both stared at the ancient canvas.

"In those days, arranged matings were common, especially among royal blood. My *padre* was doing his duty, to ensure the royal bloodline, but I would have none of it. It became a serious sore point between us. I refused to be mated to someone I did not love. My parents' mating was arranged and although they loved one another deeply, that is not always the case with arranged matings. It was my *madre* who stood behind me, supported my decision when I refused to honor the custom. I left Florence once I finished my studies and training as a warrior to travel and live among mortals and learn how to survive on my own as a vampire. Standing up to him was not an easy task for me. My *padre* was powerful and had a strict hand with me. *Madre* was the softness in my life. She also knew how to get around him."

Kate had more thoughts in her head than she could process. She knew arranged marriages were very common in past centuries. Had he not resisted, had he not stood up to his father, she wouldn't be standing here now. He'd belong to someone else. But his parents, she never thought about having to meet his parents! He never mentioned that.

"So, your parents...they live here? Is that why you brought me here? To meet them?"

"No, *mi amore*. They no longer exist on this mortal plane. They reside in the spirit realm."

"So, both of your parents were vampire?"

"Oh *si*, I was born from two immortals, a royal master and warrior vampire and his mate. My *madre* was also royal blood, a descendant of the Lombard family. I am the only child born to them; royal blood. I was born a master and a prince and destined to be a warrior. I became a king only after my *padre*'s death."

"But, if they are both vampires, I thought you were immortal? You said they could live thousands of years. How could they be dead?"

Letting go of her, he slid his hand through his hair and took a deep breath, thinking how to explain their untimely and brutal death. Turning to her, he took her hands in his and for the first time, he gave voice to this event. Everyone at Castello knew of the horror or had lived through it. Those in his coven had learned the legendary tale of the death that befell his parents and how all of this became Shade's, much quicker than he could have dreamed. The few women he'd allowed to get inside his heart were vampire, and warrior, and knew of his history.

But before him stood his mate, the future Queen of Medici, and it was only fair to let her know the legend she'd now become part of. He and his *bel rosso* would make a new beginning, a new legend that was far more powerful and long-lived.

"*Mi amore*, you have heard of the Bonfire of the Vanities, *si*? It was a tumultuous time in Florence, in the late 1490's. There was a Dominican Priest named Savonarola. He preached that all things of opulence could only lead to sin. He led his parishioners in collecting and publicly burning thousands of objects such as art and books, objects of beauty, like jewels, and fine dresses, even mirrors and musical instruments. They were all seen as vanities, the devil's tools.

"The Medici family had long been patrons of the arts, supporting many artists from the Renaissance. Artists like Botticelli, Michelangelo, Da Vinci, and Vasari. If you walk through the halls of Castello, you will find art from all of these artists still here, murals on the walls and ceilings, oil paintings, even sculptures.

"The townspeople turned on the family, raiding all the Medici homes, including Castello. The mortal Medici's were able to flee to the Tuscan countryside and all of our day-walkers here at Castello were also able to flee. I was a young warrior then, fresh out of camp, and my *padre* had sent me out into the world, to learn how to live among the mortals, to hone my skills as a warrior.

"But *Madre* and *Padre*, as well as all the warriors who lived here, were attacked by the hordes of townspeople. They were dragged from their beds in their death slumber and into the sun where they were tossed into the bonfire. The townspeople did not know they were vampire. They would have died in the sunlight anyway. It is a very painful death, *mi amore*, to be burned alive.

"I could feel my *madre's* fear, and my *padre's* anger as he tried to fight back, tried to save them both, but it was no use. Even with his strength, he could not fight off the angry mob under the pain of the sunlight on his skin. I could not respond until my death slumber ended and the sun had set. When I returned, it was all over. There was nothing left of my *madre* and *padre* save for the ashes on the ground in the garden. Many warriors who had trained with me, fought with me, all ashes.

"The day-walkers returned the next day, Gi, Theresa, and a few others. They pledged their loyalty to Medici, but I had to start over, start from scratch to rebuild the Medici legacy. I pledged to make the warrior camp bigger, better, to make the Medici coven the strongest coven, to make sure it could never be destroyed again."

Kate felt how surreal the moment was, listening to this event in ancient history, from someone who lived it. She could feel his pain over his parents' loss even after all this time.

"I remember learning about The Bonfire of the Vanities. I knew the people burned everything that was deemed a vanity, the books, and the art. I had no idea people were killed as well. I'm so sorry! I can't imagine how hard that would be, to lose both of your parents in such a violent way. And the Medici name...I don't know why I never made the association. I've been to Florence before, and I'm aware of its history. It just never occurred to me."

Leaning down, he kissed her. "*Mi amore*, you will be a Medici now as well. Now, enough of this. Let us venture to the upper level and have a browse, *si*? My bedroom is up there."

He took her hand as they walked back to the grand foyer and up the wide marble staircase, with banisters gilded in gold, the sound of their footsteps echoed in the emptiness. As they reached the second floor, there was a wide hallway branching out in both directions, with many closed doors, leading to countless bedrooms. She followed him to his room as he opened the doors for her to enter.

The room was large, like everything else in this castle, and very masculine. There was a massive four-poster bed in dark, hand-carved mahogany, and the room was decorated in a deep burgundy color, much like the wine he produced, with accents of ivory. It suited him. She walked around the room, which included a sitting area with a heavy leather sofa and chairs, a desk, his dresser. There were boots tossed in the corner, and she smiled. It was just like home.

Over the dresser was another oil painting, this one a dark-haired beauty and definitely not his mother. Kate felt a flair of jealousy, even though she could tell from the dress in the portrait this painting was done in another era. But he'd kept her picture hanging in his bedroom. She was important to him.

"Shade...who is this?"

Shade stepped in behind her as she stared at the painting. "Her name was Adriana. *Si*, before you ask, she was a lover. That romance was a long time ago, *mi amore*. Adriana lived here with me at Castello for a time, but our relationship did not survive. She was a warrior like me, we were together a long time, but she wanted to have children and at that time, I could not make the commitment she sought. It is nothing for you to be concerned about. I will have it removed, I assure you."

She could hear the pain in his voice. "She lived here? So...she was mated to you?"

He was shaking his head. "No, *bel*, you must understand something. No one has ever been mated to me. No one has ever taken my blood, fed from me. The blood covenant is only made once, and the bond is eternal. It is why we choose so carefully. *Si*, I did feed from Adriana, as I do you, but we were never mated. I choose you, *bel*!"

"But I've never fed from you. So, we're not mated?"

"Do you not wish to?"

"You've called me your mate. I thought I was your mate. Of course, it's what I want. Does feeding from you seal that bond?"

"*Si*, the blood covenant seals your bond to me, and it becomes known to other vampires. They smell my blood inside you. It will make you stronger. You can use telepathy with me much clearer. I can feel everything you feel, I can read your thoughts with more clarity, and you will be able to do the same with me. Once you take my blood, you will begin to crave it. Until you are turned, you can always make the choice to leave me, *mi amore*, but once you take my blood, I will always feel you for the rest of my life, even if you leave me and are never turned. Make sure you wish for this and understand its permanence. It is not the final step, as you must still be turned, but once you take my blood, my bond to you is eternal, and the covenant can't be broken. Make sure it is what you want. I can tell you already have a craving for my blood when we make love, *si*?"

Kate listened to him talk as she moved through his room, running her hands over his things, walking to the desk, covered in papers, books stacked on the side.

"You know I crave it, lover. I have felt the desire to feed from you for some time. I don't understand how it works, but yes, to answer your question, I want it."

She saw the edge of a photo sticking out from the papers and pulled it free. This was her Shade. He was dressed in a sports jacket and tie, with a woman...always with a woman. She was almost as tall as he was, with coal-black hair, and a slinky black dress. The woman leaned her back against his chest as his arm protectively encircled her waist, and her hand was on his thigh. It was a very intimate pose. She could tell from the dress style, this was a more recent photo, something taken in the last few years. Looking at them together was like a knife through her heart. He'd been honest with her, told her there'd been many women, and explained his need to feed in order to survive. In her head, she understood it, but to see him holding someone else, knowing he held her, kissed her, made love to her was hard to see.

"Lover, and this one? Who is this?"

Cazzo, Sabine! How in the hell does she manage to find things that pertain to every female in my past? "*Mi amore*, I have told you there were many, too many to name. But that is Sabine. I do not want to talk about every damn woman I have been with. I am here with you. Sabine is in the past."

Kate held up the photo to take a closer look when he reached out and took it from her hands. Ripping it into small pieces, he let it float to the floor as the torn paper bursts into flames and turned to ash.

"You see, she is nothing, gone, ash. Dust in the wind to me. There is no one I love more than you, nothing I want more than you. There is only one light in my darkness. I have never seen it with these females, none of them. But I see it with you and what I see is the purest love to ever touch my heart. You give me everything. You care for me. You do not care about who I am, what I am or how much I can give you, how my status will elevate you. You love me for me. Without you, *bel*, I would still be lost, for I have found what I was seeking my whole life, my eternal mate. I sought the world over, had given up ever finding you."

Lifting Kate in his arms, he carried her to the bed and laid her down softly. "*Ti amo, mi amore*!"

As she lay on the bed before him, he got on his knees, straddling her. He slowly unbuttoned his shirt as her hands slid up and spread across his broad, muscular chest, releasing in him a growl. The beast inside him was aching for release, but Shade pushed him down. This night had just begun, and it did not belong to the beast. Her hands slide across his shoulders, pushing his shirt off, before sliding down his rock-hard abs and working the buttons on his jeans, one by one, as his cock grew with each undone button.

The outline of his cock stretched the cloth of the jeans and he could feel the heat of her small delicate hands through the worn and faded material.

"Take what you want, *bel*, I am yours, we belong to each other. Show me you crave what I crave."

Kate ran her hand over the expanding shape of him beneath his jeans. She pulled at his jeans, peeling them down his hips as she freed his cock from the constraints of the denim. She sat up on her elbows and ran her tongue up the length of the shaft and flicked her tongue over the head of his cock as he inhaled sharply. She slid the head of his cock into her mouth, and ran her tongue around him, before dropping back down on the bed.

"Remove those jeans, lover...and then remove mine."

Sliding off the bed, he slowly removed his jeans, as she watched with anticipation. Climbing back on the bed like a beast stalking its prey, his head was low, and he growled as his fangs punched through and his eyes lit up, casting a red glow across her lily-white skin. He slid between her legs and nipped at her inner thighs through her jeans before unsnapping the snap and sliding the zipper down.

Moving his hands up her thighs, he grasped the waistband of her jeans and jerked them off in one quick motion and pitched them behind him. She was left wearing a pair of black lace panties, in stark contrast with her alabaster skin. The thin strip of black silk lay in the crease of her sex. Nuzzling his nose under the silky fabric, the scent of her sex took him places he'd never been. She was the heaven in his hell. He flicked his tongue over the satiny softness of the panties and watched as her hips lifted to meet him. He felt her aching need, his eyes locked with hers.

"What is it you want, *mi amore*?"

She reached her hand into his hair, gripping her fingers in his curls, as his tongue teased between her legs. Her voice was husky with desire as she responded to him. "What I always want. What you always make me want, to feel you inside of me."

"Ah, impatient as always. Perhaps I shall make you wait a bit, you are much too anxious to have your savage lover devour you, *si*?"

Letting out a chuckle, he nipped the silk panties with one bite and they fell away from her shapely hips. He buried his face into her patch of tight crimson curls, dampened by her desire, her scent calling him. Running his tongue through those curls, he teased her more. He felt her body shiver with need, but he refused to give her release just yet, and although it was pleasurable torture, he felt the agonizing need in himself. This woman made him want to devour her every moment he was with her.

She had one hand tangled in his hair and tugged hard as he teased. She shifted her hips under him. "Come to me, lover."

He slid up the length of her body, dragging his cock along her soft skin. It was enough to entice the wildest beast and his needed no tempting. Fisting his hands in her hair, he devoured her mouth, letting his tongue tangle with hers, covering her mouth and taking her breath with it. As she moaned, he released her from his kiss, and slid his hands down her arms, grasping her wrists, pulling them above her head.

His dark, raven curls framed his face as he leaned over her, his mouth was close to hers, but not touching when he drove his cock deep inside her and felt her sex mold around him, pulsing and pulling him deeper inside her.

"Don't move. Just feel me inside you, *mi amore*. Feel how you make me hard as steel. Feel my heart throbbing through my cock. Only you Kate, only you."

He felt her slide her hands down his back, and grip his ass. She wrapped her legs tight around his hips, trying to pull him deeper. She nipped lightly at his shoulder, biting at his skin. He knew she was aware that she was pushing him.

He threw his head back and growled loud enough to rattle the rafters. *Cazzo! I want to feel her taking of me, taking my cock and my blood.* Without another thought, he thrusts into her. Looking deep into her eyes, he felt her sex dripping wet for him, sucking him deep. He could feel the walls of her sex tighten, gripping him harder and making him grow thick and rigid inside her. He plunged to her depths in one stroke and began that glorious dance of two becoming one.

Nuzzling his face to her neck, he licked the length of her vein as her nails dug deep into the hard muscles of his ass and he moaned with anticipation of sinking his fangs deep, sucking that bright red nectar and feeling it caress his tongue and give him life. "*Mi amore*, I am starving for you."

She turned her head to the side, exposing her neck to him, inviting him to feed. Shade sank his fangs deep and drew a long, sweet drink, and felt his body jolt with her blood. The thick sweet nectar was like heroin, never enough to satisfy him, and she was the only female in the world he could never get enough of. He used all of his control to not let the beast loose and have his wicked dark way with her and at the same time, he controlled his own hunger not to drain and kill her. She was a lure like no other, and brought out the darkest and sweetest of him in the same moment. He felt her body orgasm and it would be the first of many this night. Her moans were deep, sexually enticing and he took more of her blood before unlatching with reluctance from her neck, as he claimed her, "Mine!"

***

Kate felt the sweet pain that came with his bite as his lips covered the wound and she felt him sucking at her vein, her blood entering his mouth and the rush of heat that hit her between her legs, driving her release. Her hips thrust into him as her orgasm crests, and he rode her hard, pushing her ever deeper into that chasm of pleasure that rolled over her in waves. She arched her back as her hands clawed at him, clinging to him, and her legs tightened around him as she felt his mouth leave her neck, and the air felt cool against her skin where his hot, wet mouth had been attached to her, and she listened to his familiar claiming cry.

Rolling onto his back, he took her with him, his cock still buried inside her and she looked down at him.

"*Bel*, make sure this is what you want. Do you still crave to taste me?"

Straddling him, she sat up, her hands on his chest. "Tell me what to do."

"You must understand, once you take my blood, you will be bound to me eternally. You belong to me, forever, as I belong to you. Other vampires will know you are mated to a master vampire. Medici blood will run in your veins. It will connect us deeper than anything you have ever felt. I will always feel you. I know your thoughts, unless you block them. Your strength will become greater. You will be able to feel what I feel the more you take of me. There is nothing to fear, you can't hurt me. Are you sure this is what you want?"

She could feel the pull, even as he spoke, to be bonded to him, truly mated to him. He'd called her his mate, but she understood now that was his selection, and only this mutual feeding would make the mating a reality. Feeding from him would complete the circle and would take them both to a new level. She'd feel him more deeply and there was nothing she wanted more.

"I'm sure."

She lay her body down on his chest, his cock still deep inside her, as she nuzzled into his neck, and licked at his pulsing vein, sucking his skin into her mouth, wondering if she could break through his skin. She heard the low moan that rumbled through his chest, and his hands slid to her hips, gripping her tightly. She kissed his strong jaw and his lips, before returning her attention to his neck, kissing the length of his neck as he arched his head back, exposing his neck to her.

Her lips explored, feeling the vein against her tongue as she bit hard into his flesh, and felt the hot rush of his blood in her mouth. It hit her like a sledgehammer and she gripped his hair with both hands, as she sucked his blood into her mouth. She was not expecting the rush, the heat, the intense wave of desire that flooded through her, so much more powerful than what she felt when he drank from her. The intensity was so strong she almost broke away, but his hands held her in a vice grip, her hips grinding into him, moving of their own accord, pulling him in. She'd have all of him, his cock, his cum, his blood. She'd consume him, make him a part of her as she felt the power of his blood surging through her veins.

He had no time to think when her dull mortal teeth clamped hard and he felt his blood flow into her mouth. No one had fed from him and he hadn't anticipated the power of his body's response. Losing his mind to the passion that erupted inside of him, he felt her blood pumping in her heart. Her soul surrounded him, embraced his entire being, and danced with his own, blackened soul. His body stiffened in glorious waves of love and passion, he closed his eyes and his mouth hung open in a silent scream, never wanting it to stop. He gripped her hair and held her there. His cock screamed for release and he felt her body ride him in response to his blood in her veins.

Driving his cock deep, he came much too quickly, but screamed with pleasure. His beast was so close to the edge, clawing to be free and have his way with her, and Shade could barely breathe. She took another deep, intense draw of his blood, and his love for her exploded inside his heart, his soul screaming a song he never thought he'd hear.

Moving his head to her throat again, careful not to dislodge her from her grip on his neck, he sank his fangs into that soft white skin. They drank in unison, and he felt her body shake with her release and he came again, and they were one. She was now all that was his world, there was nothing more. The circle was complete. He had sealed his own fate, as well as hers, as she lay sated and exhausted on his chest. He felt a momentary pang of guilt, for he'd not told her everything, but he shook the thought from his head. He knew more about their future than he'd ever reveal, and he feared telling her would have scared her away. He unlatched carefully and licked the wound clean, watching as it healed slowly. All that remained now was to turn her, but her body would need time to adjust, and he prayed she wouldn't regret her choice.

"Mine. *Ti amo, bel.*"

She collapsed on top of him as they both lay with hearts pounding. She saw the wound her teeth made in his neck healing before her eyes. His lips were red with her blood as she lowered her mouth to his, kissing him deep, their blood mingling in their mouths, as their tongues probed at each other. She moaned into his mouth. Complete. They were complete. And she was his.

"I love you, *bel*. How do you feel, are you all right?" He kissed the top of her head and wrapped his arms around her.

She felt electric, and yet sated. On fire, and yet tamed. She felt things this mortal body had never felt before. She felt things she had no words for.

"I feel...claimed. I feel you inside of me. I feel your energy inside of me. Please tell me you feel the same. I never asked what you felt when you drank from me. Do you feel my blood inside you? Do you feel me inside you? I feel like...like we are one and the same. I don't just hear your words, I feel your words, I feel what you feel."

The power of her emotions overwhelmed her, and she laid her head on his chest, listening to the beat of his heart.

He caressed her back gently. "*Si, mi amore*, we are now one. Nothing can come between us. I have felt you since I fed from you the first time. It is the same for me, but stronger, because I have fed from you longer. The urge to feed will come to you more frequently. You will feel sluggish, something like when you are hungry for mortal food perhaps, but I would think it would be much stronger and harder to control. You will feel my heart always. You will feel my love and protection of you, *sì*?"

Kate issued a deep sigh of contentment as she lay on his chest. His voice was deep and soft, like a lullaby in her ears. He ran his hands through her hair as he spoke to her. His warmth, his strength, they calmed her. She felt him with a new intensity, a new awareness.

Shade continued talking to her. "I never want this moment to end. This is what I have dreamt of for so long. I never thought I would find you. I love you so damn much."

He lay quietly, knowing there was another step for them, the issue of her mortality. As a mortal, she could easily be killed, taken from him, and there would always be those who'd use that against him, but she was nowhere near ready to be turned. He couldn't risk that yet. She must be much stronger before he could take her that final step.

"*Bel*, sit up for me please, and turn your back to me."

She sat up and slid off of him onto the bed and turned with her back to him.

Shade reached to the side table and picked up the blood vial necklace he'd prepared for her and let his hands travel gently up the soft, white skin of her back. His fingers barely brushed against her skin, but she felt so soft against his roughened fingers. Her skin was so white and flawless, against the dark olive tone of his heritage. He brushed aside her crimson locks, kissing her neck softly, giving each side their due. He slid the necklace around her neck and closed the clasp, laying his head on her shoulder. Her skin smelled sweet, of roses and passion.

"This is a special gift I give to you. It is a vial of my blood. I have made it into a necklace for you to wear. I ask that you wear it. If there should come a time when we are separated, and you cannot feed from me, you need to break this vial and drink it empty. It will ease your body and give you strength. Carry it next to your heart. It lays cradled between your breasts. I will feel it there, my blood always warmed by your heart."

"I'll wear it always, but I hope you're never far from me."

Kissing her shoulder blade, his arm surrounded her small frame. He gently turned her to face him, kissing her sweetly, letting his love pour through her.

"*Mi amore*, nothing can take me from you, not even death, and I will fight to my last breath to be with you. I will know if you are in danger, I will always come. If you need me, you call to me, and I will be there before my name leaves your lips."

He tipped her chin up slightly with his finger tip, her dark, beautiful eyes roll up to gaze into his blue ones. "Nothing will touch you. Nothing will hurt you ever again. It is my job to love and protect you with my life. You have all of me. I love you, Kate."

He made a pledge to her he hoped he could keep. The history of the Medici had been instilled in him since birth and kept him from mating for over five hundred years, despite his obligation to continue the bloodline. But from the moment he saw her, he knew there was no turning back.

Pulling her to his chest, they lay back on his bed and he felt her breathing slow its rhythm as she laid there. Her beautiful lashes lay across her delicate cheeks and once again he was overcome with love for this mortal female who'd stolen his heart so swiftly. Together, they'd rule Medici. They'd rise and forge a new Medici legacy on American soil. He'd find a way to overcome the history that had plagued his family. With this female, he finally felt whole, and without her, he was nothing.

26

He held her in a tight embrace through his death slumber as she slept her mortal sleep, her first night and day in Castello. He woke to the sounds of the soft whir of the blinds that sealed the windows from the killing rays of the sun as dusk settled in. They were mated now. After five hundred years of waiting, he'd almost given up hope. He thought he'd found his mate in Adriana, but something always held him back from committing to her, resisting her pleas to allow her to feed from him in this very room. And yet, she held a place in his heart, and he carried the guilt of her still.

Sabine took him on a different path, a dark path that exploited the most savage parts of him. She called it love, and he almost let himself believe it was love. But if he was honest with himself, he knew it was depravity, and it tortured his soul, even though he found it hard to walk away. He knew Sabine resented him still. In between, there were countless others, who served his need for food and sex, until it became hollow and meaningless, but a release his body demanded.

Then there was Kate. So unexpected, but he knew the moment he saw her. The last person he expected to fall in love with was a mortal. But he had no doubts, no reservations. He could no more have turned away from her than he could stop breathing.

He didn't kid himself. He knew he'd chosen a difficult path, for both of them. He had shielded her from much, and in many ways, didn't want to change that. Her innocence and purity were a big part of what drew him to her. He felt such a strong need to protect her, especially from the baser elements of his vampire community. He knew there'd be those who would reject her as his legitimate mate, even after she was turned because he was master and royal blood, and they'd see his choice as a rejection of their kind. But none of that mattered to him. His choice was made, and the bond was sealed. She was his.

He felt her stir beside him as she lifted her head, and looked up at him with those dark eyes, peering through that mass of red crimson, a soft smile on her lips. "Lover," she whispered. He kissed her lightly on the nose, before pulling her from the bed. He wanted to share a little more time with her here before they returned to Bel Rosso.

Shade took her outside into the cool crisp air of the early night and walked with her through the formal gardens of Castello. He took her to a spot where red roses bloomed. Taking her in his arms, he kissed her softly and then turned her in his arms and pointed up to the moon. "It is a full moon. A lover's moon, *si*?"

She looked up into the clear sky. "A lover's moon, yes. Are you giving me the moon, Shade?"

"No, *mi amore*, but I can give you the stars. The moons of Jupiter were named the Medici stars by Galileo, in appreciation of my family's patronage, so now, they too, belong to you. But I have something far more important to your heart."

He stepped in front of her, putting his arms around her waist, staring into her face, the moonlight glinting off her eyes. He dropped down on one knee and took her left hand, placing the massive multi-stone diamond on her finger, kissing the diamond. He looked up at her. "You are the only one, *bel*. We are mated now, *si*?"

"Lover..." She looked down at the ring, so large it caught the moonlight. "This is beautiful."

"You honor me with your acceptance. *Ti amo, mi amore, per sempre*. This ring, it was my *madre's* favorite. Not her ring from my *padre*, but one she held close to her heart, because I gave it to her. It was my first gift to her after I left home and went out into the world as a warrior. I had tried to make something of myself, so she would be proud of me. I had made my fortune, or what I had thought was my fortune at the time. This was my first big purchase, buying this for her.

"She cherished it and wore it always. When they died, and I came back to Castello, I came out here in the gardens, to where their bodies had been left to burn with all the other treasures that were dragged from the castle. All that remained were ashes. I sat in this very garden and wept like a small child. In the pile of ash that was once my parents, I found this ring and I have kept it all these years, hoping another would wear it someday.

"The gardens had been destroyed by the mob as well and the only thing that remained was a single rose vine. It grew and survived through the charred remains. *Madre* had several rose bushes, but they had all been trampled and destroyed under the feet of the angry mob, yet here was this single vine, almost as if she was calling to me to remember her and *padre*. From that single blooming vine, I have made sure the gardeners of Castello have nurtured and cared for it, and all the red roses you see surrounding you are from that single vine that survived their ultimate devastation. They bloom constantly, just as if she tends to them still."

"Oh, Shade, I wish I could have known her. I hope she would be happy with your choice for a mate. I hope to be the kind of mate she would have wanted for you. I want our children to look back and think of us in the way you think of her, and your parents' love for each other. I want our children to see the power of our love and how it carries us through, and to strive for that in their own lives. That's what I want to pass on to our children."

"*Si mi amore*, I want babies with you, many! And *madre* would have loved you. I am the man I am because of the love I saw between my parents, so you can thank them for that. They taught me well the importance of loving your mate, protecting and caring for each other. The only comfort I have from their demise is that they went together. They tried to save each other. One would not survive without the other, and it is the same with us.

"Let us stroll through the gardens and then we must teleport back to Bel Rosso. There is much we need to accomplish."

He hoped that he could make her happy for the rest of eternity. It was a task he felt bound to accomplish for them both. He took her hand and interwove her fingers between his as they walked together in the Florence moonlight.

27

He held her tight as they teleported back to Virginia and lands them back inside their bedroom. He sat her down and she staggered slightly, dizzy from the ride, and he reached out to steady her.

"You okay, *bel*?"

"I'm fine. I'm just not sure I'll ever get used to it...the teleporting."

"*Si*, you will get used to it, and someday, when you are turned, you will learn to teleport on your own, although, I admit, I like taking you with me."

She leaned against the bed and smiled at him. "And I like being taken."

He chuckled at her. "My walking sin, are you tempting me already?"

"I'd like nothing better than to tempt you, but after our trip, I think I need a long, hot bubble bath." She started to undress and drops her clothes to the floor on her way to the bathroom. She looked over her shoulder, "But, of course, you're always welcome to join me."

Shade rushed up behind her and picked her up as he kept walking with her to the bathroom, kicking open the door as he willed the tub to fill with steaming water, and the wicks of every candle flickered and came to life. He kissed her forehead and smiled, "Oh I will join you, *bel rosso*, but not for a bubble bath. My new mate needs something more extravagant, *si*?"

The steam rose above the water, the surface covered in a thick layer of rose petals in varying shades of red and pink, their scent carried on the steam.

She giggled. "I should have known bubbles would be too conventional."

"*Si*, just for my *bel*!"

Sitting her down before him, he slid off her bra and panties and held her hand as she stepped into the tub and sank into the hot water, her face and shoulders surrounded by the rose petals, the candlelight making her pale skin glow. He stood back and winked as he began to strip. He placed his booted foot on the edge of the tub.

"Unlace them with your teeth *mi amore*, take them off your master."

She looked up at him as she grabbed the shoe-strings between her teeth and pulled at the laces, slowly loosening them. As she finished with the one boot, he changed position and placed his other booted foot on the tub for her to loosen.

She gave him a coy look. "There...anything else you want me to do with this mouth tonight?"

He gave her a wicked grin. "You are one impatient imp, and I must teach you patience."

He pulled his t-shirt over his head, baring his broad chest. "Stand up, *bel,* and take off my leathers." He watched as she stood, the water cascading off her body in rivulets, and rose petals sticking to her skin. "You tempt me, *bel*, you tempt your master!"

"Patience, lover. You must learn patience," she said, lightly mocking him.

She grasped the button of his low-slung leathers and released it, and slowly unzipped his pants, which fit him like a second skin. She slid her wet hands inside the waistband on either side of his hips and lowered the leathers. His thick patch of pubic hair was exposed and she nuzzled her nose into him, inhaling his musky scent. As his cock was freed, she ran her tongue over the length of him. Pulling the leathers down his thighs, her tongue followed in their path, until they were below his knees and he could pull them off and step free of them.

"So how was that? Tell me again, I am your walking sin."

"Your mouth aches to fuck my cock, *si*? No, my walking sin, you must learn to have patience. Move forward and stand at the faucet, look straight ahead."

She followed his orders and he was pleased. She understood that the tease only intensified the pleasure. Stepping in behind her, his hands went to her waist and he slid his cock along her ass, snuggling it between her legs. He lowered them both into the steamy water, allowing her to lay back against his chest, her nipples bobbing out of the water, surrounded by the rose petals, their pink almost camouflaged, tempting and teasing him.

"Lay here with me, let me wash your crimson locks, my hands cannot keep to themselves." With her head against his chest, he expertly shampooed her hair, massaging her scalp and shoulders.

"Hmm, I love it when you touch my hair. How can you relax and excite me at the same time? You said you wanted to talk. Are there things you need to share with me? "

"I do want to talk to you. I know you want me to let my beast loose. But you need to feed more from me. I will know when it is time. He could hurt you, drain you. I cannot control him once I unleashed. He is the evil inside me, and you will need to be much stronger to handle him. He wants out. So when I tell you to stop you must listen. I use all my power to restrain him." He slid his soapy hands over her breasts and kissed her neck. "Can you do that for me please?"

"I hear you, Shade, but your words say one thing, and your actions tempt me to push forward. But I'll follow your lead, in all things. It brings me pleasure to bring you pleasure. I can't teleport us to exotic places, or cover you in diamonds, or make rose petals rain down on us, but I can tempt you and bring you pleasure. Guide me...and tell me if I'm pushing too far, too fast."

His hands surrounded her tiny waist and he placed kisses down her spine. "You are my eternity, my walking sin, the beat of my heart, the blood in my veins. I will consume and devour you as my own, for you are mine!"

28

Shade was trying to get back into his routine. Back from Florence, and fresh from having his *bel rosso* feed from him. There was nowhere he'd rather be than home, with the feel of her mouth at his throat. But it was another night at the Dead House, doing what he was getting paid to do. Alec's warriors were performing better, but better wasn't good enough for Shade. Giving them some space tonight, he paired each warrior with a partner, assigning them a quadrant and sent them out into the city. He wanted them to hunt openly. Take out any rogue vampires they encountered, dispose of their bodies, and bring back the numbers and locations of their hits so they could start tracking activity. A rogue was a vampire who had abandoned his master and his coven and frequently traveled with other rogues. They lived outside the boundaries of accepted behavior for the vampire community and risked exposing the carefully crafted façade that protected the species from discovery by the mortals.

He kept tally of the kills and updated the grid activity as the night progressed. It gave them a good indication of where there were pockets of rogue activity. Certain quadrants tended to draw these gangs, because of the clubs and bars where unsuspecting mortals congregated. Shade planned to rotate the warrior's grid assignments so, over time, they'd be exposed to the entire D.C. area.

Each night, as his warriors became more familiar with the territory, they discovered more about the patterns of rogue behavior. Alec's territory, here in Washington, was calm in comparison to some assignments Shade had taken in the past, but he never let his guard down.

He felt restless sitting inside this hell-hole and decided to go out and do a little rogue hunting himself. There was nothing like hunting to keep your edge. He no longer needed to hunt for food, so this night he was hunting for the kill. It was what he did best. Skirting across the rooftops, tuning in his hearing and other senses, he didn't pick up anything. Things were quiet, and it only made Shade more suspicious. When the night was too damn quiet, he began to wonder if something was brewing. Not to mention, he had other things working inside his head.

His mind was preoccupied with his *bel*. Since being with her, he'd had to fight to hold down his beast. His beast reared up every time they had sex, as the beast fought for release to have his way with her. But his sweet, gentle *bel* was mortal, and she had no clue what the hell the beast would do to her. Shade knew the beast could potentially kill her. He'd never met a mortal that brought his beast to the surface as quickly as Kate. A mere look from those dark brown eyes of hers, a flip of her crimson mane or a swish of that tight, sweet ass and the beast was clawing to get out and have his way with her. The darkest evil was his beast. He had let him loose on many immortal women, but they could handle his anger, his strength and, his insatiable appetite for sex and blood. It took all of his concentration to keep him under control and he'd never held him down for so long.

Shade always let the beast loose when there was a fight. He was the demon that struck out and made the kills easy and precision-quick. But Shade's own desire to mate her brought the beast out quickly, anxiously wanting to claim her as his own. He feared if she ever saw him, she'd flee, mated or not. And that was his greatest fear, losing her to the true evil that lived inside him. He'd hidden the beast from her intentionally, but she seduced him with her every move, and he feared losing control.

Dropping down to street level, Shade walked among the clubbers of D.C., shaking his head to clear it of his issues and focus on what was around him. He scanned the streets, watching the mortal couples walking hand in hand, leaving the dance clubs with their throbbing beat, or going for that last drink at the corner bar. Groups of females walked through dark streets, giggling and laughing, young and stupid, with no idea what lay within the shadows.

Shade could feel no intruders, so he hurried along his way. Lighting up a smoke, he made his way closer to G-town. He usually checked Alec's house and surrounding area himself. He took Alec's safety as his personal responsibility, at least while Alec was in his home. Alec's neighborhood was Shade's private grid, more or less. Shade still couldn't figure him out. Why any immortal would seek their power in the mortal realm almost made him laugh out loud. Alec hated that he was vampire. Oh, he loved the immortality, and the strength, which he used to his wicked advantage, but he hated that he was more beast than man.

Before reaching Alec's neighborhood, Shade picked up the scent of a young vampire, but he was no warrior. Letting his nose lead him, he kept his distance and stayed in the shadows. The vamp was with a mortal female and seemed to be quite cozy with her. Shade knew it was a ruse to lure her and that wouldn't be a problem if all the young vamp wanted was to feed, erase her memory, and disappear. This one had no such designs. He was hungry, and he intended to take his fill, leaving the mortal drained and lifeless. As the couple walked under a lamppost, Shade saw the mortal's face and recognized her. No one he knew personally, but someone he'd seen at several of Rissa and Alec's parties. He didn't know her name, but she needed to be rid of this hungry young vamp.

They were near the Canton residence. She probably lived near Alec and Rissa. That's the last thing Alec needed. Some mortal found dead, raped, and ravaged, with suspicious neck wounds right in his neighborhood.

Shade stayed in the shadows, slowly getting closer. His plan was to attack the vamp, but in doing so, he knew the mortal would be terrified. She may even recognize him from the parties. Shade waited for the perfect opportunity as the vampire walked her under a row of large trees that lined the walkway, looking like nothing more than young lovers having a close encounter. Shade saw him nuzzle into her neck, his fangs already bared.

Pulling out his Glock, the silencer already attached, he held the clip in his other hand. His blood raced, his beast ready to rip this little bastard to shreds, but one clean shot was all he needed. Drop him, and let her live. Before he could slam the clip in the gun, the wind shifted, and the vamp picked up Shade's scent, his head spinning in his direction. Shade took a spread-leg stance, ramming the clip into the Glock, watching as the young vampire's hands let go of the mortal, just as Shade took aim. Firing one clean shot between his eyes, the vamp dropped straight to the ground and the mortal took flight, screaming like a banshee.

Rushing forward, he began to see lights switching on in the nearby houses as the mortal ran screaming for her life. Crazy bitch would have the whole of G-town awake soon! He lifted the dead vamp in one arm and teleported after her. She was a mortal female after all, and in those heels, she wasn't likely to get far, no matter how terrified she was.

Catching up with her, he swooped down and easily lifted her with his other arm, but damn she was one fucking little hellcat, kicking and clawing.

"You are safe, relax."

Damn bitch bit into his arm and he decided he had to land, and soon. He couldn't erase her memory with both his hands full. Teleporting into the courtyard behind Alec's residence, Shade dumped the rogue unceremoniously onto the yard by the pool and quickly managed to lay his hand on the mortal's forehead, taking out her memory and relaxing her. He gave her a nice, easy drunk feeling, legless, and sleepy with no memory of the recent events. She'd remember going out for the night, but everything else would be gone. Sitting her down in one of the lawn chairs, ready to pull out his cell and dial-up Alec, he saw him coming to the poolside doors.

Alec walked out and saw Shade standing next to one of his neighbors, slumped in a deck chair, and a lifeless rogue lying on the ground. He gave Shade a 'what the fuck' look.

Shade threw up his hands, "Little present for you, brother. I was making my rounds when I came across the mortal and that rogue snuggling a bit too tight. He was going for the kill." Shade nodded his head in the woman's direction. "I recognized her from some of your events. Erased her memory, she is clean and not harmed. No idea what in the hell to do with her now. Where does she belong?"

Alec stood in the doorway, arms crossed over his chest, looking from the dead vamp to the dazed mortal. *And they wonder why I resent being immortal.* "Yeah, she's a client of Rissa's. I know where she lives, I'll handle her. I'll have my driver teleport her to her front door with her keys in her hand. Good job, brother. How are things at the Dead House?"

Shade joined him at the door, lighting a cigarette. "The warriors are moving forward, making progress, few kills here and there. Things are smooth Alec, no problems. I am taking that piece of shit and disposing of him, and then heading back home. I'll be in California for the next few days. Tomas will be in charge. He can reach me if anything comes up."

Alec nodded as the two bumped fists, and Shade threw the rogue over his shoulder and teleported out. He left the dead vamp in the enclosed courtyard behind the Dead House to sizzle and burn in the morning sun and no one would be the wiser. He teleported back to Bel Rosso. His death slumber called, and when he awoke, he needed to get Kate to California as promised.

29

Landing with Kate in his arms in the driveway of the Napa Valley house, he whispered in her ear, “Open your eyes *mi amore*, welcome to California.”

He set her down in the driveway as the sun was setting and they still had maybe an hour of dusk before nightfall.

“This is a beautiful house, Shade. It looks almost new…and…huge! The property looks beautiful. You can see the vineyards from the house, just like Bel Rosso.”

The house was an expansive, modernized Spanish design, with a reddish-brown tile roof, like the Virginia house, and yet, it had nothing of the old Tuscan feel of their Virginia home. There was a stone foundation, and the exterior, above the stone, was smooth stucco in the palest cream color. The landscape was lush and well-tended.

“This was part of my payment from Alec, for my security services. I was more interested in the vineyards than the house, but if the property is to maintain its value, then it must all be cared for. I did not plan to live here, but now that I have you, it is someplace we can come to get away, *si*? Come, take a look. Tell me what you think.”

They walked together to the front of the house and opened the door. This house was much grander. Vaulted ceilings, floor to ceiling windows, spiral staircases. It would need no renovation, just a decorator’s touch. He sensed Kate was overwhelmed by the size of it as they walked through the rooms. Formal living and dining rooms, a huge kitchen, informal dining and a family room, downstairs powder room, home theater, and a library were all on the first floor. There was a downstairs master suite with a private bath, an arboretum, and another room that looked like it could be used as a home office.

There were eight bedrooms upstairs. Five of the bedrooms had a fireplace, and all of the bedrooms had a dedicated bathroom. The bedrooms were large enough to include a sitting area within each room. There was another master suite that was bigger than her old condo that included the bedroom, a large sitting area, two large his and hers walk-in closets, and a massive private bath. This didn’t feel like a home. It felt like a small hotel.

Kate thought the Bel Rosso house was big, but this house made it pale in comparison. The backyard included a large pool and pool house. Kate walked from room to room, making mental notes. She was learning his taste from her work on Bel Rosso. Shade liked traditional, old-world design, he liked antiques. And she got that. He would have more emotional ties to those pieces. This would be a massive project, but in many ways, easier than Bel Rosso since the house itself was move-in ready.

"I can do this, Shade. Is there anything in particular you want?"

"No, *mi amore*. I have only been here a few times since I acquired the property. Luciano and I surveyed the vineyards and the wine cellars, looked at what we needed to do to expand the operations here, changed our labels, and changed the name of the vineyards to Medici. The house has already been fitted with the electronic blinds, but other than that, I have done nothing. The large master suite upstairs, make that ours. Just follow your own vision."

"How many homes do you have?"

He chuckled as he walked up behind her, sliding his arms around her waist.

"I have my main home in Florence. I have a small villa in the south of France, and another in Santorini, in Greece. They are near the vineyards there, although I do not live in either. I go when Luciano thinks it is important for me to see something there, make decisions about the vineyards. Listen to me, Bel Rosso is my home now. I will always have roots in Florence, but my home is with you now, in Virginia. You can come here with me when Luciano needs my input in the business. It is isolated, like the Virginia house, sits on about 4,000 acres, most of which have been converted to vineyards. So, the vineyards are larger here, occupy more of the property. Over half the production of wine from these vineyards will be used for the Midnight brand, the rest, for the brands sold to mortals."

She walked through the empty rooms. "This is a beautiful space, lover. I'll enjoy turning it into a home away from home for us."

"Oh *si*, I have no doubts. Now there is someplace I'd like to take you tonight. There is a club I used to frequent in San Francisco when I was out here. It is a club for vampires, where they can go and be out in the open. There are mortals there too, the followers, or immortal wannabees. I have kept you from much of my world. But it is time, I think, to start exposing you, little by little."

"I'm ready...I mean, how different could it be?"

"Different. You will see vamps feeding openly from each other. The room is surrounded by booths that are recessed, and darkly lit for privacy, but not so dark you will not recognize what is going on. There will be mortals there as well, hoping to be fed upon. The dance floor is lit but still dim. The music is loud, and the alcohol flows, for both vampire and mortals."

When he referenced feeding, she knew he didn't just mean feeding. She got the inference. There would be people having sex in the club. Before her, this was where he would go.

"Why do you want to take me there?"

"Our community is worldwide, but very small. Vampires make up only about three to four percent of the population. We rely on this network to get news, spread news, about what is happening among our kind. When a vamp feeds from another vamp, it does not change their scent. If a vamp feeds from a mortal, it is immediately detectable to other vamps. I take you there for one reason. My scent has been altered, and yours as well. Every vamp at the club will know we are mated. And by this time tomorrow, every vamp in every coven will know Shade Medici is mated."

Kate processed this information. It was a public claiming, a declaration of sorts. "Lover, the vamps that are there, did you...feed from some of them?"

Shade paused before he responded. He felt her discomfort, but at some point she needed to understand his world. "*Si, mi amore*. There will be vamps there that I have fed from, mortals as well. Do not read more into this than there is. I must feed to survive, I have fed from many. And unlike your mortal world, we make no distinction between feeding from male or female. Although every vamp has a preference, the bloodlust and hunger overwhelm, and we will feed from either."

Kate paced about the room. "And when you say feed...."

Shade followed her with his eyes, giving her space, "*Si*, the sex as well. We seek someone who attracts, we feed, we have sex, we move on. Sometimes there are those we return to, someone we feel more attracted to that we will feed from over a period of time. But the bond is fleeting. It is only when we find our mate that we bond for life."

Kate stood at a window, looking out into the night, seeing her reflection in the glass. Although she knew he'd been with many women, it had never been something she'd had to face head-on. She'd been able to push it out of her mind. But now he was saying he'd been with men too? She'd never considered it before, and to see a woman, or man, who he'd been intimate with, stand face to face with her, she felt jealous despite his explanations.

"So, this appearance, it's basically to say you're off the market, so to speak."

Shade couldn't help but smile at her use of the American expression. "*Si*, off the market. I am permanently off the market."

She turned to him. "Well, in that case, let's go."

Shade took her hand and kissed it softly. "I think you will find a dress and shoes, and everything you need in the closet."

She went to the closet to find a dress definitely deigned for clubwear; short, barely there, and covered in sequins in varying shades of bronze. The color was perfect with her red hair. There was a pair of strappy bronze metallic heels. She put on the dress and shoes and found all her favorite make-up brands in the bathroom, along with her signature fragrance. She finished her make-up and threw the red lipstick and a few other items into the evening clutch, then met him back in the bedroom. He was in black leather pants that left nothing to the imagination, a black t-shirt, and a black leather jacket. His black boots were laced up over his ankles, his hair hanging long and loose around his face. *Seriously? Who wouldn't want to fuck him?*

He gave her a wicked grin as she realized he'd read her thoughts again, extended his hand to her, and pulled her in close. "Ready?"

She nodded her head. She was as ready as she'd ever be.

"Then come dance the night away with me, *mi amore*."

He led her out to a huge garage in the back of the residence, to a red and black sports car. He walked her to the passenger's side and opened the door for her, where she found a single long stem red rose on the seat.

"We are going in traditional style tonight."

She picked up the rose and slid into the seat. "What is this, a Ferrari?"

He walked to the driver's side door and slid behind the wheel. "I have a Ferrari, but this is a Lamborghini. Special edition...and, stick shift."

He gave her a sideways glance as she laughed out loud. He'd never let her live down the fact that she drove a sports car with an automatic transmission.

"I love cars and speed. I have quite a collection."

Kate had seen the collection of cars and motorcycles in the garage at Bel Rosso. She had no idea there would be more to the collection here in California and could only imagine what he kept at Castello.

Shade reached across and grabbed her seat belt, buckling her in, making sure his hands slid across her legs and breasts, taking his sweet time. He pulled on his leather driving gloves and then fired up the engine, ready for action, just like his walking sin.

"Listen, before we get there, you need to know, if there are females there I have fed from, they may approach me. Female vamps will know I am mated...but to a mortal, so they may challenge you. Mortal females will not pick up my scent. You will just be a new female on my arm. It would not be...unusual...for me to have been with more than one at a time. So, they will not be swayed by your presence with me."

Kate was already fuming. So, this wasn't just walking in the door on his arm, so a few vamps could pick up his scent and know he was off the market. This was staking a claim. This was letting every female in the club know, 'back-off bitch, he's mine.'

Shade could feel her blood boil and her heartbeat rise. He knew she had jealous feelings about his past and she struggled to get past it, but this next step was important. She'd be challenged, and even though he desired no other. He knew there'd be a few alpha females who'd try to intimidate her, convince her she wasn't worthy. He'd back them down, but she must also learn to stand her ground, to take her place beside him. In his world, it was truly a matter of survival of the fittest, and he was warrior to the warriors. He was master and royal blood. All the more reason his choice of a mortal mate would be challenged. And all the more reason she must stand strong.

"*Bel*, this is my culture, I cannot escape it. I must feed, and until a male chooses a mate, there is no bond in the feeding. The sex is part of it, it is what it is. But none of them have ever fed from me. That is held by every vampire as sacred, for their mate alone. I waited for you, I chose you. Tonight, the rest of my community will know I chose you. Stand strong with me *bel rosso*, show them I belong to you. Don't back down."

Kate got angrier as he spoke. "Are you throwing down the gauntlet? Do you think I'd stand idly by while some bitch slides her tits across your chest?"

Shade gave her an evil grin, liking how her anger made his cock sit up and take notice. "Would you stand idly by, *mi amore*?"

She shot him a look that could kill. "Don't count on it, Mr. Medici. I'll bring new meaning to the phrase, 'blood on the dance floor.'"

Shade laughed out loud as he shifted into gear and started flying down Highway 101 toward San Francisco, hitting 120 mph. He felt her fear spike with the increasing speed. "Relax and enjoy the ride. I can rock this road like your savage lover rocks your body."

Between the speed, and the challenge that lay ahead of them, his beast was edgy and ready. Her rose scent filled the car and he wanted desperately to get there and claim her to the vampire community. This would bring her one step further into his world, letting her understand their culture more as he prepared her to be turned.

It was a risk, mating her first, and then giving her exposure to their lifestyle. As a mortal, even mated, she could still walk away from him. His bond was eternal at this point, but hers wasn't. Until she was turned, she could always choose to leave. The blood bond made it harder, and he was hoping her love and their blood bond would be strong enough to get her through all she must overcome before she was turned.

He kept glancing over at her as he sped down the highway, aware of her growing sense of unease but captivated by her beauty. "You are such a distraction."

"Me? I'm the innocent one here!"

He chuckled as they crossed the Golden Gate and headed into the bright lights of San Francisco. He headed into the section of the city known as the Tenderloin, to a club that had a long line of people waiting to get inside. A valet rushed to his car, and she realized they knew him here. They were clamoring to be of assistance. He tossed the keys to the valet and opened her car door, reaching in to take her hand.

Once out of the car, he kissed her hard on the lips then smiled at her. "*Bel*, I have messed up your lipstick. Hold still while I fix it."

He took her evening clutch and removed the tube of bright red lipstick and began to apply it expertly to her lips. "There, *bel rosso*, you look beautiful. Are you ready?"

30

As he fixed her lipstick, she was taking in the exterior of the nondescript building, painted black with a Gothic sign that read 'Under the Coffin'. The young people who were waiting to get in were clad in leather and covered in tattoos and facial piercings. This wasn't a club Kate would have ever frequented and her dress made her stand out like a sore thumb.

He smiled into her eyes and grabbed her hand as he led her to the side door. He could feel her nervousness. He was well known here, no need for him to stand in any damn line. "This is the private side entrance. I used to come here a lot, *bel*. They know me."

He rapped out several quick taps on the heavy door as it opened and one of the gorillas that protected the place smiled and beckoned them inside. Shade saw him take a whiff of *bel* as she walked by and then nodded to him. She reeked of his blood to other vampires, but it wouldn't stop many of them from approaching him. She was still mortal and new to feeding from him and wouldn't be seen as a threat.

He sensed her intimidation as the noise level just about knocked them against the walls. The music was deafening, designed to drown the vampire's dark soul, and feed their lusting hunger.

Kate felt the music as the door was opened. The DJ was playing Disturbed's "Down with the Sickness" at ear-blasting levels, producing that loud pulsing beat she could feel inside her chest. The interior was dimly lit in red lights, and the crowd inside seemed to pulse and throb with the music. She was already feeling overwhelmed with the atmosphere. This seemed so unlike anything she'd associate him with, after seeing him at all the cocktail parties and events for the social elite that Rissa threw. There were no men in business suits here. Leather and Goth clubwear were the dress code, and it was unlike anything she'd ever seen. Her heart rate picked up as she backed into him, having second thoughts about entering. This crowd looked like they were one minute away from bedlam.

She gripped his hand. "Don't let go, Shade!"

"*Bel*, you will not be out of my sight. I will lead us to our booth. You need to get some alcohol in you and it will calm your nerves."

As he kissed her neck, he led her through the crowd, weaving his way through the swarm of people, keeping her close. The room was dimly lit, but the activity inside the private booths was plain to see. There were vamps and mortals, all seeking that incredible high of sexual bliss from an immortal feeding. Shade kept moving in the direction of his booth when he saw the female approaching. She had her sights dead set on him and the smile and sway of her hips told him all he needed to know.

Katrina was one of the managers here, an immortal, and before he could steer out of her path, Katrina approached him. She stood almost as tall as Shade, and she completely ignored Kate. She slid her arms around his neck and whispered softly in his ear, “It’s been too long, master.”

Shade disengaged from her and ignored her reference to their past as he introduced her to Kate. "Katrina. Good to see you. Please let me introduce you to my mate, Katherine."

Kate had seen the woman as she laid eyes on Shade and made a beeline for him, sliding up to him and leaning in close. Shade was introducing her, and the woman never took her eyes off him. Kate moved in closer to Shade, forcing the woman to look at her. Kate was bordering on fear and anger; fear at the woman's size and beauty, anger at her aggressiveness with Shade, and her own sense of helplessness as to how to push back against these immortals.

"Perhaps you didn't hear him,” Kate shouted over the music. "He said I was his mate."

Shade wasn’t expecting to have to defend his choice right out of the gate, but he was amused at Kate’s feistiness. Watching as Katrina smiled down at *bel*, his arms went around her like a steel cage. Shade gave Katrina a look and she understood instantly he’d not take her playfulness.

Katrina backed off. “Well Master Medici, a mortal mate isn’t exactly what I expected from you. And you picked a redhead—how precious.” Katrina licked her lips. “You should have given me advance notice you were coming. Luckily, your booth is empty, and I suggest you keep her close. Even though she reeks of you, most will not care.”

Shade watched as she spun on her heels to lead them to his booth. He wrapped his arm around Kate and followed Katrina to the private booths that were held for masters. As he and Kate slipped into the booth, Shade was shaking his head when Katrina blew him a kiss as she returned to her duties.

"Relax please. I know you are overwhelmed, but this is only one aspect of immortal life, Kate. They can openly feed here, not hide who they are. Someone will come for our drink order shortly."

Kate was seething and flashed her eyes at Shade. "Precious? Did that bitch just call me precious?" Her blood was boiling. If this was a preview of the night's events, it was going to be one long night.

He smiled at her. "Is that jealousy I see, *bel*? Made you forget how vulnerable you felt though, *si*? This is no game, Kate. It is dangerous here, but the fastest way to spread the word that we are mated is to come to a place like this. These clubs are all over the world, each culture a little different. Alec told me about this place decades ago, he comes here sometimes, without Rissa, I am sure."

She slid closer to him in the booth, taking note of couples, and threesomes, and foursomes in booths across from them. Some were feeding, and some having sex, making little effort to disguise their activity. Shannon always called her goody-two-shoes, but she had no idea that people would "perform" like this in public and it was clearly a performance. She looked away from the activity in the booths and tried to concentrate on his words.

"Alec...he's not faithful to her, is he?"

"No. But I am not Alec. I brought you here so you would understand the dark side of being an immortal, the lengths I had to go through to feed. This is how I lived previously, but it ends here."

She knew Shade was different, he'd always made her feel like the center of his attention, but then again, when had she had to compete for his attention? She knew tonight wasn't the night to retreat into her shell, even though Shade may have no interest in them, these women, and a few of these men, clearly had an interest in him. She slid her hand up his thigh, her hand gliding over the soft leather that conformed to his shape, leaned into him as she lifted her face to his, kissing him with open mouth, and feeling him respond, their tongues probing slowly and seductively.

Shade could feel she had resolved to make her presence known, to claim him. He could protect her from anyone here, but he wanted her to have a backbone and not cower at this freak show. He felt a hand slide up his back...*Cazzo, Tatiana! Damn, why do women have to appear at the worst times.* Breaking the kiss, he saw Kate's eyes lock with the female standing behind him. Shade shifted in the booth as he looked over at their waitress and another one of his conquest.

"Tatt, took you long enough."

"It's busy as fuck in here, Shade. I have your Midnight. Just need to know if you'll also be ordering your usual."

She sat the glass of Midnight down in front of him and reached to run her hand through his hair. Shade grabbed her wrist before she touched him, lowering her hand. "Tatt, this is my mate, Katherine. Kate, this is Tatiana, she'll be serving us this evening, drinks only. What is your poison, *mi amore*?"

He watched the two cats begin to size each other. What the fucking hell was he thinking bringing *bel* here?

Kate could tell from her intimate touch along Shade's back and the way she made eye contact with him that he'd been with her. *Is there anyone in this fucking club who hasn't fucked my vampire?* She saw him grab her hand before she could run her fingers through his hair. She had long black hair, dressed in leather, a very Goth look with facial piercings. Really? He'd been attracted to her? Shade asked what she'd like to drink. Kate locked eyes with the bitch. She knew this was a contest.

"A shot of Mescal...and be sure to include the worm."

Shade choked on his Midnight as he heard Kate's drink order but composed himself as he addressed Tatt. "You heard my mate. Mescal!" He shook his head as Tatt walked away in a huff. Looking at *bel*, he chuckled. "You never cease to amaze me, *mi amore*. Mescal?"

"I have a confession."

"Is that so? Well, if we are sharing confessions, my ass won't be leaving here for one long fucking time. But tell me yours."

"I've never had Mescal before, and tequila makes me bat-shit crazy. But I wasn't going to order a girly drink in front of that bitch."

Throwing back his head, he laughed loud enough to be heard above the fray. Picking up his glass, he swirled the Midnight around and downed it in one gulp. "In that case, maybe I should order a bottle of Midnight, *si*? I need to keep up with you!"

Tatt whizzed by and slid the drink to Kate and a whole bottle of Midnight to him, without another word.

"Drink up, *bel*. There is a worm just waiting for consumption."

Kate picked up the shot glass and slammed it back before she could think about the fact she was swallowing a worm. It felt like liquid fire as it poured down her throat and hit her empty stomach. She slammed the empty shot glass back on the table and turned it upside down as she saw Tatt watching her from the other side of the room. Kate flashed her a look that would peel paint from the walls. Tequila gave her liquid courage, but as Shannon would always remind her, not in a good way. She felt the alcohol enter her system in three...two...one.

"Tatt!" Kate shouted at her across the room. "Another round here."

Shade knew if she had more than two, he'd be carrying her out of here over his shoulder. "*Bel*, take it easy, my little minx. If you are not used to drinking that stuff, it will make you legless. Since there is no menu, the menu rather walks among the clientele, perhaps you should have something much more filling, *si*?"

Pulling her into his lap and sliding his hands under her tight dress, his thumbs massaged her inner thighs. "Hungry?"

She felt his hand slide under her dress and she wasn't sure which had more heat, the feel of his hand between her legs or the alcohol burning in her stomach. But he was making her an offer to feed in public. Her head was already swimming with the straight shot of alcohol, but even without it, she'd take him up on his offer, hungry or not.

"For you, lover, I am insatiable."

"Claim me here, show them you are my mate and I belong to you."

Straddling him as her skirt slid up to her hips, she ran her hands through his hair, the dim red lights leaving his face in shadows, which only emphasized his bone structure, his high cheekbones and strong jaw, the dark heavy brows over his eyes, which looked pale in this light. She leaned in and licked his lips before sucking his bottom lip into her mouth, nipping at it, drawing blood, and hearing his low growl. She covered his mouth with hers and kissed him deeply, letting their tongues dart and explore.

He laid his head back against the high walls of the booth, and she held nothing back. All those who'd come before her faded in comparison. Her kisses were like fire. He felt her slide her hand between his legs, and through the leather, she gripped his cock. He was lost in her. Laying his head to the side, he gave her free rein to feed, signaling to everyone that he was taken. "Take what you need, *mi amore*..."

She felt the length of his cock as it expanded beneath the soft leather and laid her breasts against his chest as she placed her mouth to his neck and ran her tongue from his ear to his collarbone. She could feel the pulsing in his vein as his heartbeat quickened, and she bit hard into his skin, drinking deep, feeling his blood hit her tongue with more fire than the Mescal she'd swallowed earlier. Its impact on her was immediate, as she felt and tasted the sexual desire in his blood. She slid her hand up and down his steel-hard shaft as she slid her hips forward, the back of her hand now stroking her own sex as well, as she drank from him.

He could feel eyes on them, and he knew word was spreading, he was mated. Everyone wanted to see the mate of Shade Medici, the Warriors' Warrior. Growling loudly, his fangs punched, and he cradled her head against his neck and through his half-closed eyes, watched the parade of freaks walking by, gawking in a slow procession, knowing they'd spread the word that the most eligible bachelor in the immortal world was mated.

Feeling *bel* draw deeper made him wild and he wanted desperately to fuck her long into the night, but he'd never share such intimacy with her in public. He pulled her arm from around his neck and sank his fangs deep into her wrist and drew her nectar into his system, feeling it explode inside him just as his cock did the same inside his leathers. He felt her body jerk as her orgasm shook her, and he held her close. "*Ti amo, mi amore*."

Kate dropped her head back, her scream of ecstasy lost in the pounding rhythm of the music, just as Tatt returned with the second shot of Mescal. She set the drink down on the table and slid it in Kate's direction. Still gasping for breath, Kate looked at her over her shoulder. "Thanks, but I don't need it now. But you look like you could use a drink, so go ahead. This one's on me."

Shade slapped her ass as she got sassy with Tatt and laughed out loud. His hands slid through her shiny crimson hair as it swung softly down her back. "You are such a fiery vixen when you get riled up. I should buy you Mescal more often. Would you like to dance, or are you becoming legless between the worm in the glass and the worm in your hand?"

Still straddling him, Kate leaned her forehead against his as she stroked him through those leather pants. "Forget the worm in the glass, lover. The worm in my hand is about all I can handle. And it seems to me every bitch in this place is in heat, so you better help me keep them at bay. But I'll dance with you. Can you keep up?"

"Only one way to find out, but if you do not remove your hand from my handle, the bitches are going to swarm when they see this monster."

Laughing as she tried to imitate his growl, he lifted her off his lap and onto her feet, watching her shimmy her dress into shape and whip that flowing head of hair of hers.

Tatt had left the shot of tequila on the table despite Kate's offer. Kate grabbed the shot glass and threw it back, downing it all before slamming the glass back down. The tequila took her breath away and she shuddered, feeling the raw alcohol scorch her throat. "Lead the way."

"Woman!" He grabbed her hand, pulling her tight to his side and moved out on the floor. They could feel the floor vibrate as they got closer to the music. A thick haze of smoke hung in the air, reflecting the colorful lights flashing off and on across the ceiling. The steel beams above their heads held even more haunting hell. One bright beam of yellow light scoured across the floor and up and across the ceiling beams to show couples feeding, some danced and leaped from beam to beam, while others engaged in a few choice activities minus their clothing. As the search beam stole across the ceiling again, Kate gazed up and he could feel her raw emotions of shock. Before they could get to the dance floor, he heard someone calling his name. Turning, he saw Colin Vos, Master of Nevada, sitting in a booth with his mate as he beckoned Shade over with a fangy grin. Shade grabbed Kate's hand and headed in their direction.

"Just a short visit, *mi amore*. Another master."

Kate had the giggles now as tequila was making her head swim. He led her to another booth where he was introducing her to some master. It was hard to hear over the pounding music.

Walking into Colin's booth, his mate Elana smiled at Shade and then at Kate as Shade returned the smile. "Damn Colin, should have known you'd be here. This is my mate, Katherine." Shade pulled Kate closer to his side. "Kate, this is Colin Vos and his mate Elana. Colin is Master of Nevada and a regular visitor to the club. They are friends with Alec and Rissa as well, and Colin was gracious enough to show me a bit of California until I learned my way around."

Kate felt flustered as they entered the booth. It looked as if they'd interrupted an intimate moment as Colin seemed to be getting ready to feed from his mate, or perhaps had just finished feeding. She felt like she'd stepped into someone's bedroom at an inopportune time, but clearly in their world, in this club, the intimacy was very publicly displayed. So, what was proper protocol? A handshake? Some secret vampire signal? The tequila made her giggle as she thought up some two-fingered claw sign with her hand that would indicate fangs, but thankfully she hadn't had enough tequila to pull that one off yet, so she just replied with, "So nice to meet you."

Colin looked at Kate as he responded. "Mated? She is...mortal." Colin stood up and gave Shade a fist bump as he cocked his head toward Kate and took her in. "Very beautiful female, but mated. Didn't see that coming, brother. I'm sure you'll hear from Council."

Colin turned to Kate. "May I introduce you to my mate, Elana."

Elana stood and seductively walked around Kate and Shade, stopping in front of Kate as she inhaled her scent then smiled. "So, you're mortal. You probably know Larissa then. Do you want to stay and play?"

Elana reached out to touch Kate's hair and before Shade could respond, Colin grabbed her wrist and yanked her back into his chest as he prepared for Shade's reaction, knowing Elana had overstepped.

Shade growled and bared his fangs at her. "This is not Rissa, and I am not Alec. I do not share my mate."

Kate felt Shade bristle beside her when Elana asked if they wanted to play, and she's pretty sure Elana wasn't referring to a game of cards. Was this couple into mate swapping? She's relieved at Shade's response, as his possessiveness kicked in, and she felt his arm tighten around her as he growled his response. Kate smiled back at Elana as she pulled at Shade's hand, seeking to escape. "We were headed for the dance floor, but enjoy your evening."

Being here had only increased her level of insecurity. Even as they backed away, she realized he was able to teleport here anytime. He could be here in seconds, on any given night, when he said he was at the Dead House. He was everything to her, but how would she ever compete with this smorgasbord of sexual diversity that was clearly no holds barred, anything goes, with anybody at any time?

"Shade, is this what you want? All of...this?"

"No, Kate. This is what I seek to escape. So, rest assured, you are mine and no one is taking you from me or me from you. I do not want this, and I do not share."

Lifting her into his arms, she wrapped her legs around his waist and her arms around his neck.

"*Bel*, when I tell you I love you, I mean it. I love one female for all eternity and I have nothing left to give any others. I would never have mated you if I wasn't ready to leave all this behind."

Setting her back on her feet, he grabbed her hand and led her to the dance floor, the music and crowd around them thick with sexual tension and anticipation. He could smell the blood of the mortals as they offered their gift of life to the immortals here.

Kate could feel the crush of bodies as they gyrated around them. She could see the throngs of people, some dancing, and some in the throes of sexual bliss as they fed; men with women, women with women, and men with men. Their selections seemed indiscriminate, the exchange of a glance and eye contact held for a few seconds was all it took to grant consent, and they were joined, one feeding from the other. She closed her eyes, knowing this was his world. She knew he'd chosen her, she didn't doubt his love, but it was hard to watch this free and easy exchange and know this had been his life. She wasn't sure which was harder to bear. Knowing he'd loved others before her, lived with them for long periods, feeding only from them, or this...this promiscuous, anonymous exchange of intimacy. She turned in his arms, and slid her arms around his waist, laying her head against his chest.

The music of Shinedown was blasting through the room, bouncing off the walls – "Sound of Madness." Good choice, because it was definitely madness. She gave herself up to the music and to him, letting the music move her. She was thrashing to the beat, all hips and hair.

He smiled and growled, grabbing her waist as she leaned back, her hair flowing behind her and he rocked his hips into her as she moved. The music changed and he watched her alter the rhythm of her body to match the music, and he liked it.

The DJ was playing the band Nightwish – "She is My Sin." "Ah, *mi amore*, you are my walking sin!"

He circled her like a predator and she was his prey. When he was in front of her, she ground her hips into him. As he moved behind her, she moved her ass against him. She could feel his cock through those fucking leather pants. Her movements never ceased as she let her body move to the music, hands above her head, and her hair flying.

As the song ended, she had him wound up tight as hell. All eyes began to focus on them as the next song began and he pulled her hard against his body. He lifted her above his head and let her slide slowly down his body, then kissed her passionately. Snuggling into her neck, he nipped her ear softly. The music changed again and Seasons After screamed out "Cry Little Sister."

She wrapped her legs around his hips and squeezed him tight. She threw her head back and exposed her neck to him, letting her hair cascade behind her, knowing full well the effect this had on him. She slowly and seductively pulled herself upright before locking her mouth onto his. Her legs and arms were wrapped around him, her hair covering his face, her mouth sucking at his, biting his lower lip.

Shade broke the kiss and sank his fangs into her neck. His hands were tangled in those crimson locks as the spotlight hit them. He teleported her above the crowd to the beams. He slid one hand up and down her thigh as her legs were locked around his hips, and he drank like she was his ocean. The music that raged through the crowd as he held her was Evanescence – "Wake me up Inside." The spotlight stopped swinging around the room and was now focused in a single beam on Shade and Kate, for all to see. Lowering her back down to the beam, all eyes were on them as the motion ceased on the dance floor. Pulling her close, he kissed her deep and hard, as her blood trickled slowly down the side of his mouth. His claim was loud, and his roar rattled the rafters. "Mine! Medici! *Ti amo per sempre*!"

Kate had felt the rush of heat between her legs that always came when he fed from her, and she clung to him and allowed those sensations to wash over her. She looked down at the upturned faces, some smiled up at him, happy he'd found his mate. Others gave her a cold stare, not bothering to hide their disapproval of his choice. His roar vibrated through her.

Leaving the beams and setting her back down on the floor, the whole place roared and applauded, and he kissed her softly, holding her in his arms. Winking, he wrapped his arm around her waist and headed back toward their booth.

"Had enough?"

"Shade, this isn't me. I make no judgments about how these people live their lives. And I understand this was a part of your past, but I'm ready to leave."

"Then we are done. I promise you, this is the end of all that you see around us. I wanted you to understand none of this has any meaning to me any longer."

Shade felt a hand softly grip his arm and he snapped his head to the right to see one of the young male vampires he'd fed from several times. There had never been any sexual encounters between them, and Shade was damned if he could remember his name. He was a lost boy, on the lowest rung of the ladder among immortals. He had no master and no coven and Shade knew that he'd go to many who'd abuse him profusely in exchange for money. He was extremely young, with long dark hair, and features almost feminine. He'd appeal to many vampires here, happy to exploit him for an evening of deviant play. Shade never took those pleasures, fed from him only, and always gave him a hefty fee, hoping to spare him the agony of letting others abuse him, even if only for one night.

"Master Shade, you're now mated. Congratulations."

Shade watched him nod to Kate and smile softly at her. "*Si*, I am now mated, and I will no longer be returning here. How is life for you?"

Shade saw his sad smile and then read the other emotions in his face: shame, embarrassment, and sadness.

"Life is fine, but I'll miss you, you were always kind to me. I apologize for interrupting, but I just wanted you to know I'm happy for your mating."

As he turned to walk away, Shade grabbed his arm and pulled him back. The young boy's eyes widened and a smile spread across his face, thinking perhaps he'd be asked to join them in feeding. He was wrong. Shade reached into his leathers and pulled out several hundred-dollar bills, shoving them into his hand, hoping it would alleviate some of his pain for the night. The boy hugged him and Shade was startled at first but pounded his back.

"Take care of yourself. Have pride in who you are and do not let them treat you so badly. You do not deserve their wrath."

Reaching back in his pocket, he pulled out one of his calling cards, handing it to him. "Come see me at this location tomorrow evening before I leave. Perhaps I can help guide you out of this lifestyle and into something more appropriate, at least we can discuss it. Now go."

As he turned to leave, the boy understood Shade wouldn't be like some of the other patrons of the club, he didn't share his mate, nor would he ever feed from others again.

Shade watched him as he walked away, sliding the card in his pocket. He hoped he came to see him. Shade thought he could mold him into something. Not a warrior, his frame was far too delicate for that, but perhaps something useful to the Medici coven.

Kate had watched this exchange between the young boy and Shade before he led them through the crowd and back outside. The valet rushed to bring the Lamborghini around, and they climbed back into the car. It was about 4:00 a.m., and if they hurried, they could get out of San Francisco before the commuter traffic picked up. Shade headed back across the Golden Gate, hitting the highway and flooring the gas pedal as he drove back to Napa.

"Shade, I can't get him out of my head. That young boy, he seemed too young to even be in that club. May I ask who he is to you?"

"*Si, mi amore*. He is a lost boy. I don't know his full story, but I know he has no master, no coven. He lives on the streets, he must fend for himself. He hangs out at the club, selling himself. Sexual favors in exchange for money."

Kate was watching his profile as he spoke and was taken aback by what he said. "You...had sex with him?"

"No, not sex, but I fed from him. He is young, and I thought his blood would be strong. His blood...it did not have the energy I expected from a young vamp, but there was something...different that made me return. Not sure. But I never had sex with him. I would always pay him handsomely, much more than the fee he asked for. Hoping he could get himself off the streets."

Kate looked out the window at the landscape flying past them as Shade had the Lamborghini flying full out. "Can you help him?"

"That is up to him, *bel rosso*. I gave him my card. If he wants help, if he is looking for a way out, and he contacts me, then *si*, I will help him."

She laid her hand on top of his as it rested on the gear shift. "I hope he calls you."

He looked over at her as he felt the pain in her heart, her worry over the young boy. He took hold of her hand and lifted it to his lips. His gentle *bel rosso*, she was so innocent in his world of darkness.

31

As they walked through the California house, Kate carried a notebook and pen, along with a tape measure and her cell phone so she could take photos of each room as the two of them took a final tour. They wandered from room to room, Kate making notes as they discussed flooring options, wall textures, furniture, window treatments and the like. He was enjoying this time with her, she was happy, and he loved her enthusiasm and the ideas she had for furnishing this home.

Luciano knocked before entering the room. "Excuse me, Master Shade, but there is a young man by the name of Cory to see you." Shade noted Luciano's tone of disdain when speaking the name.

"Cory? Did he say his purpose here?"

"No, master, but he gave me this."

Watching as Luciano waved Shade's calling card about, Shade remembered the young vampire from the club last night. "Send him in, Luciano." He looked at Kate. "*Bel,* apparently Cory is the young man from the club. Good thing there are a few odd pieces of furniture to at least sit on. Would you mind joining me?"

Kate's face lit up with recognition, "I'm so glad he contacted you. I hope you can help him."

"Perhaps you can help me interview him and get some information. He is no warrior, so let's see what his story is and if we can find a place for him within the coven. He may not be of a mind to join us, but I hope he is willing and ready to change his lifestyle."

Luciano walked in and presented the young man to Shade. Shade signaled for Luciano to bring them all some refreshments. As he appraised the young boy, he looked to be maybe eighteen or nineteen in mortal years. He took in his small frame, and realized in this well-lit room, the boy looked even thinner and more delicate than he did in the darkened club. As they shook hands, his face reminded Shade of someone, but he'd be damned if he could think of whom it might be.

"Cory, good to see you, I am glad you made the decision to come see me. You remember Katherine, my mate. Please take a seat. You will have to excuse the condition of the house. We are in the middle of decorating."

Kate watched the young boy enter. He looked almost frail, like a mortal would look if they hadn't been eating. Was that his problem? He didn't feed enough? Or he let others feed from him too often? He was probably only ten years younger than she was, but he drew out all her maternal instincts.

"Cory. I'm so glad you took Shade up on his offer. Can I get you anything?"

Cory shifted his weight from foot to foot. "Thank you, Miss. I am hungry. A sandwich is good. But I don't want you to go to any trouble. I can pay with my blood."

Shade shook his head, "There is no need to pay, Cory. Our hospitality has no strings attached." Shade was confused by his request for a sandwich. Was he not a vamp?

Cory took a seat, flipping his long dark hair back, and looked around the huge room.

Kate looked at Shade as she addressed Cory, "A sandwich? No trouble at all. But you can eat a sandwich?"

Cory kept his eyes on Shade's face as she asked if he could eat a sandwich. He supposed now was the best time to bust out the truth of what he was. Shade would either pitch him headfirst through the front door, or let him explain, but it wouldn't be the first time he'd been rejected by the vampire community.

"I eat human grub, but I also drink blood. I'm a half-breed—half human and half vampire." Standing up, ready to be tossed, he watched them both stare at each other. "Did you hear me?"

Shade was processing the information. He knew half-breeds existed, but he'd never met one before. *Half-breed? What the fuck? He eats mortal food and he lets immortals feed from him? What in the fuck did I just drop my ass into?*

As Cory stood to leave, Shade stood up as well and held up his hand, wanting him to know there was no judgment. "Cory, sit down. I can feel your edginess, which tells me you have done this before, revealed yourself and it did not go over well. I think I am a bit taken aback. It is not something I have ever encountered, but I am curious."

Luciano returned, bringing in a bottle of Midnight and some glasses and set them down, awaiting Shade's instructions.

Not wanting to reveal anything to Luciano in front of Cory, Shade asked him to open the wine, and to please close the door when he left.

"So, Cory, do you wish for some Midnight? Midnight is a specific mixture of blood and alcohol made strictly for vampires."

"Whiskey, if you have it. Never had Midnight and not sure I want it."

Shade responded in a calm but firm voice. "You will have a glass of wine, no whiskey. And *bel*, would you mind seeing what you can scrounge up in the kitchen something for Cory to eat?"

"Of course, let me see what we have. I'll be right back."

Kate hurried to the kitchen and made him two sandwiches, one turkey and one ham, loading generous amounts of meat on both sandwiches, lots of mayonnaise, lettuce, and tomato. She found some potato salad in the fridge and put a large scoop on the plate, grabbed a fork and a napkin, and hurried back to the living room. There was a whole bag of chocolate chip cookies on the counter and she grabbed them and tucked them under her arm. No telling when he last ate.

***

While Kate was busy doing this, Shade took the time to try and get to know the boy a bit better.

"So, let's begin at the beginning, Cory. While Kate is out of the room, tell me your history. How is it you became a half-breed? And what in the hell are you doing selling yourself at a club? Be honest and I will see where I can help you, lie to me and we are done. I live by a code and I do not tolerate lying or cheating of any sort. Are we clear?"

Cory nodded his head just as Kate came back in and laid a buffet of food in front of him. Picking up a sandwich, he inhaled it. Kate and Shade both stood silent as he quickly consumed the first sandwich, and then picked up the second one. The boy paused long enough to answer his question.

"My mom was human, a vampire fed from her, knocked her up. She met him at a club, kind of like 'Under the Coffin', where humans go to hook up with the vamps. She said they hung together a few weeks before he took off. She never ran into him again after that. Didn't know she was knocked up until after he was long gone. When I was born, I was small, weak. She wasn't sure I'd even make it. She realized after a time that I was vampire too, or something like it. She had me in school, but I never fit in, got bullied. I kept running away, and eventually, I just lived on the streets. Been there ever since. No big deal, I can survive."

Woofing down the sandwich, taking huge bites, he reached for the cookies and ripped open the bag, popping a whole cookie into his mouth, followed by another, and another.

Kate poured a glass of Midnight for Shade and Cory. She took Shade his glass, and then set the glass in front of Cory.

"Cory, I can fix you more if you're still hungry. Just let me know. And, excuse me for asking a personal question, but I'm mortal myself, so I don't understand. Do you also...uh...feed?"

"Yeah, I got fangs, I feed. What is that yellow stuff?" Taking the glass of wine, he downed it in one gulp. "Can I have some more of that Midnight?"

Kate stifled a laugh. "Uh...the yellow stuff is potato salad. Try it. If you don't like it just leave it. And I'll get you more Midnight." Kate took his glass and refilled it. She gave Shade a look that said, *What have we gotten ourselves into?*

Shade had watched him eat like he was starved and wondered where he went to feed and if he must hunt, because he probably didn't have the money or the access to feeders. "Easy, Cory, that shit will kick your ass. So, you have survived being half-breed, selling yourself and hunting. But your lifespan is limited if you keep that shit up. Tell me your skills. What can you do? What can you offer me and my coven?"

Cory picked at the potato salad, pushing it aside on his plate as he picked up the bag of cookies again and downed the wine in his glass.

"I can feed your coven. I won't rob you. I'd just ask for a steady salary. I can keep guard of your house here. I might be little, but I can handle myself good, I've been hanging in the streets my whole life. You got something in mind?"

Shade shook his head. "No Cory, you will not be used as a feeder. I think you have been subjected to that enough."

Kate stepped closer to him, looking at his jacket. For a kid who lived on the street, he was wearing an impressive leather jacket. "Can I ask where you bought your leathers? That jacket...wow, I'd wear something like that myself. It looks like designer quality stuff. Did someone give it to you?"

Cory sat up taller in the chair. "Nope, made it myself. I buy at second-hand shops, stuff is cheap. I take them apart and put together my own designs from the different pieces. I stitch all the designs myself. My mom used to sew my clothes because we were poor, so I learned the basics from her. Taught myself more elaborate stuff. When

I get enough money, I buy good leather and design things to wear. You would buy this?"

"Oh my God, I would totally buy this!" Kate reached out her hand to touch his jacket...."May I?"

He nodded yes, and she ran her hand over some of the seam work and stitching detail. "Shade, this looks as good as the hand-sewn leather I saw in Florence. The jacket is impeccably lined. If he had access to quality leather and other materials, there's no telling what he could make. Why don't you have him make leathers for your warriors? He could custom design pieces for them. And look at the detail on the pants, the reinforced padding in the knee area, like those guys who ride motor-cross. What do you think?"

Shade sat with his hands steepled in front of his mouth, watching and listening. It wasn't a bad idea. The warriors usually purchased their leathers off the rack, paid for through the clothing allowance he provided.

"I like the idea. The warriors just buy whatever is in the stores, but to have someone make their leathers for them, custom-designed to accommodate their specific weapons; I think they would prefer it. I give them an allowance for such but having Cory on premises to measure and design custom warrior gear would be unique and help us tremendously. What do you think, Cory? Can you manage to design and fit them if I provide the tools and materials?"

Cory couldn't believe his ears. He didn't want to act too excited in case Shade changed his mind. "Sure, no problem. I like doing it. And good tools and quality leather would make a difference. I can do better than this with the right shi...stuff. How much does that pay?"

Shade stood up, towering over him. "Let's get one thing straight. If you accept, you belong to me, a member of the Medici coven. You become my responsibility and you follow my command. I do not deal with street living, drugs, or behavior unbecoming. So you better think long and hard. You agree to live in my coven, you live by Medici rules. You represent me, and I do not tolerate any bullshit. No cheating, lying, stealing, and you will never sell yourself for blood. I will draw up a contract with you, as I do my warriors, with salary and living accommodations. There is no negotiating on that. It is what it is. And it will be followed to the letter. If you comply, if you fit into my coven, you become Medici. You prove to me you are worthy of my coven, and life will only get better for you. I provide feeders for all. You no longer need to buy blood nor sell your damn body to anyone. I find out you do, your head leaves your body by my own hand, understood?"

Listened to him, Cory knew he meant business, he was a master, and Medici was world renown for his power and wealth. Imagine him working for this bastard. He knew he could do this, work hard, and earn his keep. He'd have a place to call his own, food, and feeders. Being clean and having a place he belonged to.

"I can be a good worker. I know the Medici name and legend. Who the hell doesn't? Give me a chance. I won't let you down. I'll show you I can do it. I'm tired of living on the streets and having no purpose but to survive. I have nothing here, I can't trust anyone. I know you won't take advantage of me. Thank you, I'll sign and accept whatever your terms."

Shade was glad he made the right choice. He wanted him to realize he expected work, just as he did with his warriors.

"It's done then. The only thing you need to understand is I will need you in Italy at my family home. My warrior camp is there in Florence. I will have Luciano teleport with you to the location, and I will have arrangements made for living, salary, and a place for you to set up your shop. We will provide all the things you need to get started. My warriors are there, that is where I will need you, not in the States. If you agree, I need you to wrap up everything here in California. Do you have family or friends you need to say your farewells to?"

Cory's eyes were as big as saucers. *Italy? Fuck the luck*!

"My mom is alive, but I only see her a couple of times a year, so that's no big thing. I just need to let her know I'm leaving the country so she won't think I'm dead or something. Do they speak English in Italy? I fucking don't know Italian. But I want to go!"

Shade threw back his head and laughed. "I think you are going to fit right in with that pack over there. They speak English, some of them not so damn well. I will have Luca and Marcello keep an eye on you and show you around. Tonight, you sleep here. You no longer belong on the streets. Come sunset tomorrow, I will give you two nights to get yourself together. You come back here. Meet Luciano at 11:00 p.m. If you are not here, this never happened, and you never show your face here again. Understood?"

Cory couldn't believe what just happened. He was now employed by one of the most powerful masters in the world and he was going to live in Italy. This would fucking blow his mom's mind when he told her he was out of this damn place and going to Europe.

"Understood, master. I'll be here. Now can I have another glass of that Midnight?"

"No!" Shade bellowed.

As Luciano entered, Shade told him to show Cory his accommodations for the night. As they left, Shade looked at Kate.

"You are awfully quiet, *bel*."

"Shade, I'm so happy for him. So glad he's taking advantage of this opportunity to do something with his life. He's so young. All he needs is a break. All he's known is people taking advantage of him. He'll need a strong hand. He'll need friends in Italy, but also someone who's going to keep close tabs on him. Make him toe the line, teach him discipline and structure, and where better than a camp that trains warriors?"

He pulled her onto his lap as she snuggled close. "*Bel*, I have seen enough of his kind all over the world, not half-breeds, but vampires without covens. That is how we end up with so many rogue vampires, they have no one. No structure and they turn into killing machines, but this one, not so much. He would be lost to the streets forever, probably even killed before long. Perhaps half-breeds are more accepted here in the States, but not so much in Europe, so I need him protected as well as providing a structured environment and the love of his brothers. No fear, Luca and Marcello will take him in hand, especially Luca. Luca is young and well rounded. This one will be fine, once he is removed from the streets and shown a more productive way. Now, where were we?"

Grabbing her up into his arms, he kissed her passionately. The night was still young.

32

As soon as the sun sets, Shade awoke and dressed, heading out in search of Luciano to let him know he'd hired Cory, and Cory had two days here in the Stares to get his affairs in order and then Luciano was to get him to Florence. Shade popped in on Cory, told him he and Kate were leaving to go back to Virginia, but let the boy know he could contact him on his cell anytime. He gave the fragile boy a hug, welcoming him to the family. He told Cory to eat whatever he wanted, and Luciano would take care of anything he needed.

"And Cory?"

Cory looked up at him. "Yes, master?"

"Lay off the booze. Drink the wine when you must, but with moderation. Understood?"

Cory locked eyes with him. "Understood, master."

Shade ruffled his hand through the boy's hair as he turned and left.

Heading back to their sparsely furnished bedroom, Shade found Kate was dressed and ready to go. She looked up when he came in. "Is he okay? Cory?"

"*Si*, he looks better this morning. I think he spent the night in the kitchen eating."

They both laughed, but Kate came to him as her face turned serious. "I'm glad he came to you. And so glad you are finding a place for him. You've a soft touch for a vampire."

"Shhh, don't ruin my reputation."

He scooped her up in his arms and teleported them back to Bel Rosso, landing in their Virginia bedroom. Kate had her notebook of ideas for the California house clutched to her chest.

The renovations on the Virginia house had been completed, including the renovations to their master bathroom, and knocking out the wall of an adjoining bedroom to convert the space into his and hers walk-in closets for the both of them. The modifications to the staff quarters had also been completed. Now, all Kate had to do was furnish the staff quarters, and Bel Rosso, and that huge California house.

Shade had given her contacts for everything; electricians, plumbers, carpenters, painters, flooring specialists, designers, antiquities dealers, and landscapers– pretty much anything and everything she'd need to complete the project, and all his contacts were vamps. All she did was mention his name and things got done.

They were both pleased with the results so far, as they took a tour of the house to see what work had been completed while they were in California.

"Lover, everything looks like it's done. The Venetian plaster on the walls, repairs to the original tile flooring, and restoration of the hardwood floors. All the plumbing and electrical have been replaced. The kitchen and baths have all been updated. I'll start furnishing and decorating now. It shouldn't take long working with your contacts."

"*Si, mi amore*. It looks very authentic. Feels like Tuscany, *si*?"

"It does. I'll complete everything downstairs and do a few bedrooms upstairs. I don't think I need to furnish all the bedrooms right away. I'll save our bedroom for last since we at least have something in there. This room with the built-in bookshelves, this will be your office. I like this room with the exposed beams and the one stone wall, very masculine. But this suite of rooms at the end of the hall, it looks like it was an addition to the original building. I think the previous owner was adding a downstairs master suite, but I prefer our space upstairs. What do you think?"

"Oh *si*, much prefer the upstairs for us, feels more private to me, *bel*. But I agree, this looks like it was added on to the original structure."

Kate walked through the large space. The sitting area had large windows that would let in a lot of light in the day and more built-in bookshelves. Whoever lived here before shared her love of books. There were French doors that opened onto the patio.

"It's a beautiful space. I'm just not sure what to do with it. So, I'm going to leave it for now. Maybe I'll just get a bed in here, and I'll figure it out later."

Shade smacked her ass as she walked past him. "Whatever makes you happy."

Kate grabbed his hand and dragged him from the rooms, back into the hall. She opened the door that led downstairs to a basement that had been converted into a wine cellar. Shade followed her, having never explored this section of the house before.

"Where are you taking me, *bel*?"

She laughed as she looked back over her shoulder at him. "The dungeon, lover, where else?"

She saw an expression of concern wash over his face as he momentarily slowed his step, or did she only imagine that? As they reached the bottom of the stairs, she opened the heavy oak door, pushing hard against the hinges as they creaked in protest. She flipped on the light switch to a room that was dusty and covered in cobwebs.

Shade stepped around her to look at the wine cellar. Kate was coughing from the dust already, but followed him in.

"It doesn't look like anyone has been down here in...well...forever. I discovered it earlier this week. It will need a lot of work, but it will be perfect, don't you think? Especially as the vineyards are completely restored? I mean, I know you have the large cellar over in the vineyards, but wouldn't you want one here in the house?"

"No, this is perfect! Please add this to your project list. We definitely want this room restored."

Shade walked to the far end of the cellar, and another heavy oak door. "Where does this door lead?"

"I don't know. That door was locked, and I didn't see a key anywhere. I just assumed it was part of the wine cellar."

Shade picked up the heavy black padlock in his hand and willed it open. Kate's face registered her surprise.

"Well, that's a handy trick to have."

He smiled at her as he pushed against the door, opening into a very large, rectangular room that was empty. He willed on the lights as he entered, and she followed behind him.

Kate looked around the empty space. "This is a disappointment. I was hoping for hidden treasure."

Shade took in the space and turned to look at her. "It *is* hidden treasure, *bel*. Well hidden."

"I don't understand, lover."

"Perfect for me, *bel*. Weapons bunker. I will take care of this room. And once done, you will stay out, *si*?"

Kate looked confused. *Weapons bunker? We need a weapons bunker*? "Uh, no problem."

He took her hand and led her from the room, pulling the heavy door closed behind him. "Now I have a surprise for you since you are looking for hidden treasures."

"And where might I find this hidden treasure?"

He swept her up in his arms and carried her up the stairs to the main floor, and up the stairs again to the second floor. "Why, in our bedroom, my sweet *bel*."

She laughed. "Why does that not surprise me?"

He dumped her down on the bed and instructed her to close her eyes while he got her gifts. Kate rolled over on her back and threw her arms over her eyes as she heard him leave the room only to return shortly. He set two wrapped boxes down on the chair and told her she could open her eyes.

"What's this? Is there an occasion I missed?"

"No occasion, *bel*. Other than you have worked hard on the house, and I love giving you beautiful things."

Kate slid off the bed and on her way to the gift-filled chair, stopped to kiss his mouth, and run her hand through his dark curls. She picked up the note, reading it as a smile crossed her lips, 'You are my forever.'

She looked up from the note to see his eyes locked on hers. "And you are mine."

She opened the larger box first to discover a bright red corset with soft satin petals covering the bust.

"Lover! This corset looks delicious...like a cake frosted in roses. Oh, you spoil me. I can't wait to wear this for you."

She looked at him watching her as she held the corset up against her body and his blue eyes sparkled. She ripped into the second box to find a pair of matte black heels trimmed in red, with the trademark red soles.

"And these shoes...Louboutin? I love heels...have you seen my closet? Oh, I can't wait to wear these!"

She slipped her feet into the black heels and walked around the bedroom. "I may never take these off, except to wear red boots, that is. Come to me. Gifts this extravagant deserve a kiss."

He loved how her happiness flooded through him. As she strutted around in her new heels, he chuckled out loud. Her eyes never left the shoes as she pranced around the bedroom. "Oh *si*, I have seen that closet, *bel rosso*. All I can say is, good thing we each have our own, there would be no room for me in yours."

He sat down on the bed, leaning his back against the headboard and slid his hands through his mop of curls, never taking his eyes off of her. "Before I get kisses, you must walk across the floor and model the shoes for me." He crossed his legs at the ankles, his arms over his chest, waiting for her to model the shoes.

"Just the shoes? Let me model both for you. Hold on while I make a quick change."

She stepped into her closet where he couldn't see her change and quickly pulled off her jeans and sweater, dropped her bra and slipped on a red thong. She put on the beautiful confection of a corset. Balanced on the high heels of the shoes, she stepped out of the closet door, and holding the doorjamb like a stripper pole, she did a slow, hip grinding squat to the floor, where she tossed her hair and then began the slow crawl back to a standing position.

"Is this what you had in mind?"

He climbed out of bed and dropped to all fours, crawling slowly across the floor to her, his fangs bared and his growls became louder. Reaching her, he grabbed her ankles and nipped them one at a time, slowly leaving a trail of kisses up her calves. He licked behind each knee and felt her tremble with anticipation. He kissed her thighs then slid his tongue over the soft fabric of the thong, teasing her, pulling the thong with his teeth.

She didn't anticipate the intensity of his response as she grasped the doorjamb for support. It was the only thing holding her upright. As his mouth sought out her sex, she felt her knees go weak, and on cue, he reached out to steady her. She could feel his mouth tug at the thong as a soft moan escaped her lips.

"Lover...the things you do to me."

Biting through the thin strip of fabric, the thong dropped away to the floor. He buried his face between her legs and into those beautiful tight curls, moist with her honey and the scent of her desire. Reaching out, he grabbed her hand and slid it inside his as he guided her hand between her legs. He moved their joined hands over her clit, before inserting their fingers inside her sweet wet sex, slowly sliding in and out of her. He removed her hand, and sucked her fingers, feeling her body completely melt.

"Lean against me, *bel*, and I will take you to heaven."

His fangs were exposed, and she loved it when his passion was so raw he was almost more beast than man. Her knees were like jelly, and she bent over him, hair falling forward. If he were to move away from her, she'd fall like a rag doll to the floor. She loved to tease him, but oh, the sweet retribution.

He felt her body go limp with desire, and he loved that she felt nothing but the pleasure he could give her. He picked her up and carried her back to their bed. He lay her down as he climbed between her legs.

"You are so beautiful like this!"

Bowing his head, he drove his tongue deep and curled it inside her, scooping every drop of her nectar. She arched her back and moaned. Fucking her hard and sweet with his tongue, he pulled out quickly and slid his tongue over her clit and felt her body quiver as she neared her orgasm and he drove his tongue deep inside her again, her sweet honey on his tongue as she rode the waves of pleasure washing over her.

She called out his name when the explosion of pleasure hit her, wave after wave as he continued to lap at her, not allowing the orgasm to subside, but pushing her, over and over. Her head was thrown back, and she was gasping for air. *Too much...too much*. She felt him lick away the juices that run freely from her.

He crawled to the top of the bed and held her in his arms as she laid her head on his shoulder. She was completely spent and he loved that he had the power to give her pleasure beyond her body's limits. No fucking mortal man would ever come close to what he could do to her. He kissed her neck softly, his lips at her ear. "*Mi amore*, come back to your savage lover."

In the softest whisper, she answered him. "The things you do to me."

"The night has just begun, bel."

"Then maybe you'd like to join me in the shower first?"

She rolled out of bed and walked toward the bathroom, still wearing the black heels and the red corset which bared her ass and pushed her breasts up and out. She looked back at him over her shoulder and laughed. "A forest fire out of control, lover. We are a fire out of control."

33

Since getting back from California, Shade was trying to get Alec's warriors back on a schedule. He'd teleport into the Dead House most evenings, shortly after sunset, meeting up with Alec's makeshift crew. He was trying to establish some routine and discipline within these ranks, so he tried to keep their schedule basically the same. They began every night huddled together in the command center, surrounded by maps and grids of downtown D.C. and Georgetown, along with his plans for whipping these misfits into something that resembled warriors. Alec wanted his territory protected, and anything that threatened his rise in the mortal world needed to disappear, without a trace of it ever having been there. Alec's greatest fear was being exposed to the mortal world as a vampire. He'd never be able to step foot in the U.S. again for at least a century, and it would leave their entire vampire community at risk. Most mortals accepted vampires as myth, and the vamps wanted to keep it that way.

As he put the warriors through their paces, he was trying to assess their skill levels. Each of the mercenaries seemed to have one specific weapon they were good at, as opposed to his Medici warriors, who were equally skilled in all methods of fighting. These limited fighting skills weren't going to be good enough on the streets if they ever encountered any real opposition. A true warrior needed to excel in the use of any weapon. In addition, he must be skilled in hand-to-hand, mixed martial arts combat, with the goal of slicing and dicing and bringing home the head of his enemy. This rag-tag group, one way or another, needed to be prepared in all areas. Tonight, Shade had decided he'd teach them the art of fighting with shuriken's and show them what a shuriken could do to an errant rogue. In addition, they needed to learn how to play defense when some rogue sent a shuriken flying right for their throat.

"Listen up you bone heads. Head your sorry asses down to the lower level. I have some targets set up. You will earn your keep this night and I am going to give you a few lessons on shuriken's. It is a vital weapon of choice for my warriors. You need to learn how to carry them in your leathers, how to throw them with precision and speed, and how to aim for the kill. Now move!"

Alec's warriors grumbled under their breath but headed down the stairs to the large open space where three targets had been set up. Two were standard bulls-eye targets and one was a life-size human target. Each target was placed about fifty feet apart. He wanted to see the warriors throw and evaluate their technique. Shuriken's, or throwing stars, came in many shapes and sizes, and some were specifically designed with blades that opened while in the air mid-throw and could do great damage. These were Shade's favorite. When thrown with vampire speed, the enemy never saw them coming. Shade asked Tomas to step forward and demonstrate the proper technique for throwing the stars. Once Tomas had shown them the basics, Shade stepped up and challenged Tomas to a little competition.

"Tomas, let us have a little battle of our own."

Tomas nodded his head and smiled, whipping out his shuriken's as Shade did the same. Asking Tomas if he was ready, he nodded his consent and they both threw their weapons at their respective targets. Shade and Tomas watched the stainless steel, razor-sharp stars fly through the air, knowing both of them were taking it easy so the warriors could see how they held and threw them. Shade shouted, "Again!"

Nodding to Tomas, they both pulled more shuriken's from their leathers and their boots, picking up the speed, holding nothing back this time. The warriors watched in silence. The only sound anyone could hear was the whistling speed of the blades as they flew through the air and the small thud when they hit the target. When they were done with their demonstration, the warriors gave up a cheer and Shade knew this display would pique their interest to learn this skill.

They progressed through the night, he and Tomas working one on one with each warrior, teaching the proper technique in holding and throwing the stars. Shade taught them points to target on the human outline target, emphasizing that when thrown with enough speed and accuracy, a star could sever arteries and kill their opponent.

After working with the group, he split them into two teams, one assigned to Tomas and the other he kept for himself. Shade decided they were going to take it to the streets. This was the ultimate test, a learning exercise in survival and awareness on the highest level. They'd pit one team of warriors against the other, the only instructions, to go for a strike but not a kill shot. Shade knew from his life as a warrior the best way to test a skill was on the streets when your ass was on the line and it was kill or be killed.

He and Tomas took their teams and headed in separate parts of downtown D.C., and then the hunt was on. He and Tomas had agreed there'd be no communication between them. They wanted the hunt to be as real as possible. The war was on and may the best team win. They hunted each other, and the only weapon allowed for the exercise was throwing stars.

Scouring the rooftops and then dropping down to street level, Shade took his group into their assigned grid and worked as a team; watching, stalking, feeling, and smelling anything they could find. Before long, Tomas' team was upon them. Shade's team encircled them, flanking them from both sides until they were cornered in an alley with no outlet but up. The shuriken's began to fly. Shade was impressed with how quickly some of them picked up the skill with just a single night of training. They were nothing but gypsy vampires looking for a buck and a place to be useful, and he had to not only teach them new skills but get them to work as a team.

The battle continued, and Shade had his opponent in sight. He felt him ready to pull his shuriken and aim straight at him, but Shade leaped well above them all and waited for the star to follow. Concentrating on the sound of it spinning, he was able to gauge that he was the ultimate target. He could hear the whistling getting closer, and he had no intention of returning fire, but showing this fucking young pup how to flip and avoid its deadly aim. Watch and learn.

Just as Shade spun into a backflip out of its path, another sound whistled through his brain. It was no shuriken, but something heavier and just as deadly. The arrow sped past his ear from behind him, blowing through his raven hair it was so close, and hit the shuriken midflight, knocking it off course.

Shade turned to see one of the warriors holding a crossbow. It was the mercenary known as Skelk. Skelk hired out wherever and to whoever would take him in. He nodded to Shade as he held up his crossbow. He had no fucking care that in the game they played tonight, shuriken's were supposed to be the only weapon in use. Skelk would play by his own rules and show him the skill at which he already excelled. The precision with which Skelk used the crossbow impressed Shade. He earned his keep here, but he was strange, to say the least.

Skelk hated working ground level and stayed on the rooftops. He was the most anti-social fucker Shade had ever met, but he knew how to survive on the streets. Shade returned the nod and watched him fly over the rooftops and disappear. Shaking his head, Shade knew this was going to be a long road to bring this band of renegades into something he could work with. Each night he assessed their skills, their strengths, and weaknesses, taking into account what he could use them for and what they brought to the table. Tonight, Skelk made sure he was well aware of his value to this legion of Alec's warriors.

Shade's biggest worry with mercenaries was that none of these bastards stayed any place for any amount of time. And if things really blew up, he'd have to pull in Medici Warriors. Alec had paid a high price to have him here, and Shade wasn't going anywhere any time soon. Shade had plans of his own, and they included expansion of his territory here. Medici would roam and protect these streets at some point in the future and he was beginning to see that future much clearer now. It included a vibrant crimson-haired vixen, and her scent suddenly overwhelmed him with just the thought of her. It was time to head back to the Dead House, call it a good night's work and head home, back to her.

34

Shade teleported to Bel Rosso with little time to spare before his death slumber took him. He sought out Kate but heard the familiar buzz of his cell. It was Luciano, saying Cory had returned after only one day and was ready to go to Florence. It was time Shade made a call to his Second-in-Command in Italy, his oldest friend and comrade, and his best warrior, Marco. He and Shade had grown up together in the camp, fought together, and as Shade was an only child, he loved Marco like a brother.

Marco ruled the warrior camp in Florence and was in charge of everything in Shade's absence. They shared the same values and discipline as warriors, and when Shade needed advice, Marco was his go-to man. He wasn't born Medici, but he might as well have been, in Shade's mind. And right now, he needed to give Marco a heads up about Cory. He trusted no one else to get Cory settled into his new life, giving him some protection since he was a half-breed. Dialing up Marco from his cell, he knew Marco would be about ready to rise from his death slumber.

Marco answered. "Old man, your ass is missed here. What the fuck do you need?"

Laughing as he heard Marco's voice, he ran his hand through his hair and then lit up a cigarette, and grinned from ear to ear. "I love you too, you old coot. Damn, it's good to hear your voice. I got some news, so sit your rough ass down. Listen, *fratello*, I got a new one coming in. Luciano is bringing him over. He is American, real young. And he is no warrior."

"Not a warrior? What in the hell am I supposed to do with his ass? Picked up another stray, I see. *Cazzo*, brother, how many times you going to send me strays to bust into shape?"

Shade took a deep breath and lowered his voice, knowing Marco would understand this was serious and must be handled with caution.

"His name is Cory. Frequented a club in California, he was a street-feeder there, sold his body and blood for money. Homeless kid, no coven, but he has talents. He has been abused, in more ways than one, Marco. I have contracted with him to make the leathers for the warriors, all custom design. He has mad skills with leather. Luciano has the complete list of supplies he will need and where I want him to be set up in the camp. And one more thing, *fratello.* He is a half-breed. Father was vamp, mother was mortal. Kid hasn't had it easy. I want him off the streets and into a structured life. He is going to need protection. He has some vamp skills, but he is small and not strong, and you know he will take shit from the purebloods. He eats mortal food and drinks blood. Warriors are going to know soon enough. Hook him up with my boys Luca and Marcello. Get him settled in and acquainted. I want this kid to succeed, Marco."

He heard Marco sigh loudly on the other end of the phone. "I fucking hear you, *fratello*. If Luciano knows what I need to do, it's done, so relax, I got this. But, son of a bitch Shade, a half-breed? The vamps hate the half-breeds! Just once, you could give me an easy assignment. But I will make sure he gets settled, and Luca will look after him as well. You're getting soft in your old age, picking up every stray pup."

"Thanks, Marco. I'll owe you one. And once Cory starts making their leathers, the warriors will accept him into the fold."

Shade heard a long pause before Marco answered. "So, when were you planning on telling me the big news?"

Shade snubbed out his cigarette and sat up straight. Marco had heard the news about *bel*. Word of his mating was moving faster than he expected.

"So, you have heard. It's true brother, I am mated. Don't ask, I will explain as soon as I have some time to get over there, and you will meet her as I get things settled more here in the States. Just know one thing brother, I love her with my heart and soul. From the first glance, there was no going back. How is my boy Luca?"

"She must be some damn female if you fell that fast. Heard she was mortal, that should rile some Council ass, brother! But to answer your question, Luca is doing well. I am thinking of sending Marcello out to Siena to polish his leadership skills. Boy has a knack for it. He can get the warriors to move ass and take command. Thinking of putting him to the test, any ideas?"

Thoughts of Luca rolled through Shade's mind. He had watched him grow into a warrior of merit and it made his heart fill with pride. "Sounds like a plan, keep an eye on him, he has a tendency to get a little wild with the females. Give him a post where he is more remote but has responsibility for a small group of warriors, test him there first and then move him on to bigger things. Don't push him too fast, he will fuck it up, give him a fighting chance. He is going to be useful to us, *fratello.*"

Shade heard his *bel* stirring and needed to get back to her. "Bro, I got business to attend to, so take care of my boy Cory, keep me updated on the situation. Get to your post. I love your fucking old ass."

He heard Marco's laughter ring out loudly in his ear as Shade hung up the phone and went in search of *bel*. He'd only have a short time with her before his death slumber took him.

35

Returning from another night at the Dead House, he got home early. It had been an easy night training the warriors, nothing unusual. But Shade was restless, and it was all about one problem—his beast and Kate. The sex between them was hot and heavy and left him sated beyond comprehension. She filled his every need, but the beast was getting angrier about being held down. The sheer willpower it took to keep the beast under control was exhausting. The tension that hung over Shade was so thick he could cut it with a knife, the smallest thing could set off his temper without provocation, and that was very dangerous. He'd spoken to her many times about the darkness inside the beast and feared she'd be terrified if she ever saw him. He wasn't sure his love for her would be enough to keep her from leaving him before he could get her turned.

Teleporting to Bel Rosso, he wasn't ready to enter the house. She was waiting for him and he knew he had to settle himself in order to keep that black bastard at bay. Walking around the empty fields outside their home, things were always so quiet at this time of the morning. The sun was still below the horizon and he watched the house from a distance. He was thinking of all the things he'd already put her through and so much was still unknown to her. He sat down on a fence rail that was in great need of repair, running his hands through his hair and lit up a smoke. The fence railing gave slightly under his weight, the creaking of wood the only noise interrupting the early morning.

Looking solemnly at Bel Rosso, the outside of the house still needed some work, but the inside was taking great shape. She was fucking amazing, and he was beginning to wonder what in the hell he ever did before he met her. Memories of his dark past were fading fast, and that heinous existence was beginning to feel far behind. A soft light flickered on from their bedroom window and his eyes couldn't stray from the silhouette of her standing there, staring out into the dark. His *bel* was waiting on him, and his beast sat up and growled. Shade stared at the moon and cursed the darkness that lived inside him.

His eyes drifted back to the window. He felt helpless against the demands of the beast, and when she was around, he had less and less control. Yet, she held him like an angel and soothed the demons. He'd never met anyone who could hold him like that. He could feel her blood running through his veins. Her body called to him and he wanted to feel her beneath him. He picked up on her thoughts as she thought of him. She knew he was near. It was close to the time he usually got back every morning. She worried for him, and he'd yet to let her know the full extreme of his life as a warrior. He was aware she had a superficial understanding of what he did, but not the details of the death he dealt. He shielded her from that. She was his to protect and love, and nothing was going to keep him from her, not even the beast.

Jumping down from the fence railing, he knew the only thing that would calm him down and thrill him at the same time was standing in the window, waiting for him. He teleported directly into their bedroom, landing behind her as she still stood looking out the window.

"*Ti amo, mi amore*. Miss me?"

She startled at his voice behind her and quickly turned to greet him. "That was an unexpected entrance."

His restlessness dissipated instantly when he had her in his arms. But the nagging thoughts were still in the back of his mind. If he lost control of the beast, she would surely die. Shade vowed the beast wouldn't take her from him. Her body was soft and warm in his embrace, and her lips tempted him, while the beast fought for release.

"Unexpected, but welcomed apparently!"

She ran her tongue from his collar bone, up his neck, across the course stubble to his jawline, before nipping hard on his chin. "Always welcome, lover. I missed you."

His body responded, and even as the beast fought, he'd never give up these moments with her. She deserved to be loved. Nuzzling into her neck, licking her vein, Shade pulled back. He needed to feed but the beast was so alive.

"Damn woman, I need you, fuck do I need you!"

"And I'm here for you, Shade."

His eyes glowed red and his fangs had punched through when she kissed him, aware of how desperately he needed to feed. He felt her hands in his hair when she slid her tongue across his fangs.

It sent a bolt of erotic pleasure straight to his core. He pushed away from her and was pacing the floor. His growl was deep and low, agitated that his desire for her pulled the beast to the surface, and he couldn't control the beast's beckoning.

He spoke harshly. "*Bel*, never do that again!" He could see the look of hurt and confusion on her face when he pushed away from her.

"I don't understand. What's wrong?"

He didn't mean to hurt her, but she didn't understand what lay beneath his surface, crouched and ready to attack. Standing with his back to her, he stopped the pacing. His voice was low and yet stern.

"I am sorry Kate, but there is darkness in me. I have told you before, and I have struggled to hold it at bay, but you tempt that dark evil beyond anything I have ever felt. You have done nothing wrong, but I can't control it when you lure me with such open need and wanting. Licking my fangs takes me into fucking orbit. Do you understand what I am saying?"

He saw her bow her head, looking at the floor when she spoke.

"You have underestimated me. I've always seen the dark side. From the first time I laid eyes on you. I know you shield me. I'm always aware when you do. But I'm telling you, it's not necessary. I love the darkness. I was drawn to it. Please, don't push me away. You think I need protection from you, and I know better."

He spun on his heels. His eyes burned like flames they glowed so intensely. His fangs were bared, and his growl was fierce. She was mortal and had no knowledge of what she spoke. "You know nothing of what lies inside me, woman. Nothing! He will eat you alive, drain you, kill you. I cannot let that happen! I have no idea how the beast will react. I know from past experience, he rears up inside and plays no games with immortals. I will not take the chance of letting him loose on you, Kate. He would destroy you, have...*Cazzo*! I can't take much more, I can't let him loose on you, please understand this."

Taking deep breaths, he retracted his fangs and his eyes returned to their normal blue. He began to strip off his clothes and walk into the bathroom, his body still clenched like a steel rod, every muscle tense.

"Taking a shower, think about what I have told you. This is no game, no tease, he will be something you have never seen, and it frightens me for you."

She watched as he tossed his clothes aside and walked to the bathroom alone, sending a clear message she wasn't to join him. She heard the water running as she picked up his discarded clothes, then undressed, sliding a gown over her head before climbing in bed. She couldn't imagine there'd be anything about him she wouldn't accept, and his rejection hurt to the core.

***

The water flowed over him, cascading down his muscular form, washing away the night of grit and grime from the Dead House. His body ached and his heart cried out with pain at the words he'd screamed at her. His hunger was still vividly alive. Although he refused to let the beast free, he struggled to keep his inner darkness from touching her. The fucking beast was winning. He was torturing them both, bringing pain to both of them. Shaking the water from his hair, he raised his hands above his head, wanting to strike at something, kill it, rip it apart, but he knew he could never tame his beast.

Could she tame him? He dared not try, but he knew he must go to her now. Finishing his shower, barely running the towel over his body and hair, he flung the towel to the floor and slowly walked back into the bedroom to find her sitting on the bed. She was backlit by the bedside lamp, making her silhouette visible through the gossamer gown, and her crimson looking even redder against the backdrop of her white gown. His breath halted in his throat. She had no idea how the mere sight of her brought him to his knees. Her back was to him, displaying her pain of his hurtful words.

"Kate, look at me."

She looked over her shoulder at him, and then turned in the bed and held her hand out to him. "Come. Whatever haunts you, please, show me, teach me. I'll not turn away."

He gently took her hand and sliding in bed beside her, pulled her to his chest. He felt calmer, the beast pushed down for now, but Shade still felt the gnawing pain of the hunger. His hands stroked her crimson silk, letting the feel of her hair roll through his fingers, calming him.

"*Bel*, I do not mean to reject you. The beast inside me is dangerous. You are not strong enough yet and I have fears of letting him go. Please understand this. I do not know what he will do to you. I have never released him on a mortal before. I could not bear him harming you. I may not be able to control him once he is loose, do you understand? I love you beyond anything I have ever known, and I will not let him take from me what I love most in this world. I promised to protect you with my life, and that includes protecting you from what lies within me. You have my blood flowing in you now, the more you feed, the stronger you will become, and you will feel him rise inside you. I have no choice but to back away when you bring him so close I lose control of him. I love you desperately with all of my being. Forgive me."

"There is nothing to forgive, lover. I fear you worry over nothing. I feel the darkness already. I have always felt it, and I embrace it. It is part of you. This beast is part of you. Teach me what he needs. Let me tame him, let me calm him, as I calm you."

"It will take time, *mi amore*, and more strength. But I will work with you, so you can feel him more rapidly, knowing the signs of his approach within me. You must learn to feel me deep, follow my lead, and listen to my commands, not just for the beast but in all things Kate, for your own safety and protection until you become stronger. It will come with time. Do not rush it, but I need to learn better control myself. I will kill myself if I ever harm you."

Pulling her closer, he nuzzled deep into her neck, nipping her ear and then her shoulder, his fangs punching through.

"Let me taste you, soothe me and the beast, I need you to help me. The blood will help him settle and then I can become stronger to fight him down, *si*?"

She pulled her hair back, tilting her head so the pale skin of her long, slender neck was fully exposed to him, offering herself.

"Lover, in all things, you lead, and I will follow."

Sinking his fangs deep, her words rung loud in his ears and he knew she'd always follow him, even to the depths of hell. He only hoped he could bring them back together. Her blood slid like silk down his throat and his growl rattled the bed, her healing energy filling his veins and he felt the beast settle. Drinking his fill, he felt the intense sexual pull of her body, but he dared not take her tonight.

He slides his hand over her hip, and between her legs. His fingers walked through soft curls and over her clit. Feeling her body grind into his fingers, he growled, his fingers sliding further between that silken cleft, plunging deep inside her.

"Let me take care of you, *mi amore*, cum for your savage lover."

Stroking her deep, he brought her to climax. She was the most beautiful creature when she came for him. He licked the blood from his lips and then licked his fingers clean as her eyes bored into his.

"Relax, *bel*, I am close to my slumber, it is calling me. Tonight, when we awaken, I will stay home. I am not going into the city. I have a request of you, so listen carefully. You will come to me in the evening. You will dress in one thing only. Think about what will please your savage lover. The night will belong to us and us alone, *si*? And I will teach you how to respond to your master."

Feeling the pull of the death slumber, his arms hugged her close to his chest, his hand tangled in her hair, and the words barely audible as the slumber took him from her once again.

"I love you, *bel*."

She watched as his face relaxed in his death slumber, and his pledge of love was still on his lips. His request replayed in her head. *One thing?* He wanted her to come to him wearing the one thing that would please him. She'd have to think about that one. She curled into him, her head on his chest as she felt his arm encircle her, protecting her, even in his sleep.

36

Shade woke before her, slipped from their bed, and pulled on a pair of leather pants before walking barefoot and bare-chested downstairs to call Tomas, leaving him in charge at the Dead House and letting him know he had decided to take a night off. Activity had been light, and there were some things he could monitor from home. He poured himself a Midnight and plopped down in his office.

His beast was getting the upper hand, and there was only so much Shade could do to control him. She teased and seduced, with no idea of how close the beast rose to the surface. If he couldn't control the beast, then he must control her. He must teach her to hear his command, respond to his demands, and restrain her desires when he could no longer restrain his.

***

Kate woke and knew immediately he'd left their bed but could feel he was still in the house. She remembered their conversation from earlier. That he would teach her how to respond to him. She felt confused. Didn't she already respond to him? And the beast, he always worried about the beast.

She got out of bed and still wearing her nightgown, walked barefoot down the stairs, opening herself to him, feeling his presence in the house, and following him into his office, where he sat in the large leather chair. She walked to him in the dimly lit room and climbed onto his lap. He gave her a stern look.

She ran her finger across his lips. "You should have told me your fangs were an erogenous zone."

"Beyond anything you can mortally imagine, *mi amore*. But one day, you shall experience the same."

"But...you told me to never do it again. I don't understand."

He laid his head back against the high-backed chair, closing his eyes. "*Bel*, I have only so much control over the beast. You can only tempt him so much. You do not listen! Must I remind you that you are to follow my lead?"

Kate laid her head on his chest. "I didn't think I was pushing you too far."

A wicked snarl escaped his lips as he gripped her chin in his hand, turning her face up to his, his eyes bored into hers. "Keep it up, my walking sin."

Kate smiled coquettishly at him. "You have much to learn about me, lover."

He raised his eyebrows. "Then you shall teach this old vampire some new tricks?"

"Oh, I am pretty sure you know all the tricks. If you want me to respond differently, you're going to have to think of a different approach."

His blue eyes reflected the dim light. "You will remember there is no pleasure without some pain."

"I remember well. Are *you* tempting me now?"

"You, *mi amore*, are the goddess of temptation! You breathe and you tempt me, you move and I want to kiss every inch of your pure white skin, you look at me and I want to ravish your body. But be careful what you wish for, *bel*, the beast does not understand limits."

She ran her fingers along his strong jaw, "Tempting you is my favorite thing to do, actually, my second favorite thing. What comes after the tempting is always my favorite thing. Last night, you put a rose tipped flogger in my dreams. Do you need to put me across your knee? Or would you prefer to have me kneel at your feet? Is that what you want? Do you want me to obey and kneel at your feet?"

She slid from his lap and knelt on the floor at his feet as he stood up from the chair. "Like this? Is this what you want? Do you want me to wait for your direction...sir?"

His voice was hard, emotionless. "You will not call me sir. I am master, and you will address me as such. Last night, I told you to come to me wearing one thing. I hope you have thought about what will please me. Now, rise and kiss me."

"Yes, master." She stood before him and lifted herself on her tiptoes to kiss his lips, as he didn't bend down to meet her. She placed her arms around his strong shoulders and kissed his beautiful mouth.

He didn't return her touch when she kissed him. He'd never be able to train her as he saw fit if he couldn't control his response, for it would be as much torture to him as it was to her. Inhaling deeply, he could smell her rose scent and he wanted to take her in his arms and hold her, kiss her until she passed out from not breathing.

"Your kiss is sweet. Go now and put on the one item you think will please me. Do you understand?"

"Yes, master. Would you like to give me a hint as to what the one item should be?"

"No. I will give you no hints. You do not ask me questions. You ask permission to speak. I think, my sweet *bel*, you need some rules."

"Master, I think I know what one thing would please you. Would you allow me to go change for you?"

"You will first bathe, cover your skin with the scent that pleases your master. You will choose the one thing to wear that will please me. Show me you understand your master by making the right choice. Make the wrong choice, and the game ends tonight. Understood?"

"Yes, master."

"Now go. And do not return until I call for you." As she turned to flee past him, he swatted her ass hard. "Go, my sweet *bel rosso*."

37

Entering the living room, Shade willed the furniture from the center of the room, leaving a large area in front of the fireplace for his *bel*. Taking the flogger in his hand, he stuffed the handle into the back pocket of his leather pants, letting the soft leather strips hang down, clearly visible. He wore the black leathers and nothing else, bare-chested, and barefoot. He threw a large white satin sheet upon the floor and willed the fire to blaze. He considered bringing the handcuffs, but he didn't want to scare the hell out of her. Tonight, he'd go slowly, teach and guide her, yet be the vampire master he was. She must learn to obey his word and trust his dominion over her. Like a warrior, she must learn to respond to his command without question. The room was ready. He stood facing the fireplace with his back to her entrance.

"*Bel rosso*! Your master calls for your presence. "

Kate had followed his instructions, or at least she hoped she had. She heard him call and hurried down the stairs and into the living room where she could see him silhouetted against the fire, his back to her. "Yes, master. I've given much thought to what you asked of me and I hope I please you." She entered the room completely nude, with the exception of the thigh-high patent-leather red boots. She was second-guessing her choice. Maybe he wanted her to wear something else or carry a single red rose. *What if I'm wrong? Please don't let me be wrong*! She was eager for him to turn but anxious that she may have made the wrong choice.

"I'm ready, master."

Her eyes were glued to him and she quickly noticed the flogger as he stood, legs spread, in those tight leathers with no shirt and no shoes. He flexed his arms and she followed the subtle movement of the muscles in his back, his ass in those tight pants, drinking him in. She was saying a silent prayer over and over in her head, *please like the boots, please like the boots, please like the boots*. She'd hate getting banished to the bed alone this night before this game even got started. As he started to turn, her heart was in her throat, and she continued the mantra in her head. *Please like the boots, please like the boots*.

He stood tall and looked at her, his expression unchanged, but she could see in his eyes she'd made the right choice. She breathed a tiny sigh of relief. He was asking her to turn slowly for him. She felt braver now, knowing she'd chosen the "one thing".

"Turn around for your master, *bel*, let me see you. Turn slowly, so that I may admire your efforts to please me."

She slid her hands down her hips and onto her thighs, and stood with her feet apart, and shifted her weight onto one hip. She glanced up at him and locked eyes but quickly looked down. She started to shift her weight to one foot and turn, slowly, rolling her hips as she did so, like a sensuous dance. When her back was to him, she paused and resumed the spread leg stance with her weight on one hip. She flipped her hair and looked back at him over one shoulder. She wanted to tease him now. Was that in the rules? Could she speak? She didn't think she was supposed to speak. But she was biting her tongue, because she wanted to say to him, "Like this, lover? Is this what you wanted?" But she thought that was breaking the rules, and she wanted to do this right. She wanted to please him. So, the words remained unspoken as she continued her seductive turn until she was back facing him. Once again, she quickly glanced up at his face before looking down. She recognized the metallic taste of blood in her mouth. She realized she'd been biting her lip this whole time in anxious anticipation.

***

Shade watched her move. She was still the temptress and he didn't seriously think he'd ever tame that part of her, nor did he want to. She was all his. He had felt her hesitation, heard her prayers and had kept a stern look on his face, showing her nothing, but she was driving him wild. She tempted his beast, and he needed to control both her and the beast.

He walked to her. Towering over her, her face hit him mid-chest and he reached out and slid his hand through her hair. He felt her intake of breath, but she was learning fast, she didn't speak, and that was exactly what he wanted. Walking around her slowly, he slid his finger down her spine and breathed against her neck. Walking back to the front of her, he whipped the flogger from his back pocket and used the handle to slide it under her chin and tilt her face up towards him.

"You have pleased your master."

***

Kate couldn't believe the tension in her body as he walked toward her. Her attention was laser-focused, and she was trying to second guess his moves. When he snapped the flogger from his back pocket, she stifled the urge to flinch, and thought *"What did I do wrong?"* He told her she'd done well, that she'd pleased him, but then he started the rhythmic slapping of the flogger in his hand, and it both terrified and teased her.

"Tell me, bel, who owns your heart?"

"You do, master, you own my heart."

He felt her every emotion, and it made him want to pick her up and fuck her to hell and back, but he knew that wasn't what she needed. She needed to learn he'd always dominate, for her own protection.

"You have pleased your master with your answer. Drop to your knees."

He watched the subtle movement of her breasts and the flow of those silken crimson locks as she knelt on the floor. Her hair looked like flames in the reflected firelight and her pale skin glowed. His cock turned into hard steel as she knelt.

She felt lightheaded and realized she was holding her breath. She heard the sharp crack of the leather strips of the flogger snapping against his thigh, loud in the quiet room, and she couldn't stifle the flinch.

She wanted him to touch her, and she wanted to reach out and touch him. *Not in the rules, not in the rules!* She remained still, and on her knees, with her head bowed before him.

He felt her hyperventilate and he began to worry. He knew she was nervous, her body language told him she wasn't afraid but aching to please him.

"Look at your master, *bel.*" As she raised her eyes, he locked into them, holding her in his gaze. "Who do you belong to?"

"You, master, I belong to you."

He showed her no emotion as he spoke. "You please your master, *bel*. Get on all fours." Watching as she did so, his heart raced as her love flowed through him. She was so fucking beautiful. "Lower your eyes, *mi amore*. Bend your head and kiss my feet. Let me see your ass rise in the air. Let me see your breasts touch the satin as you lean down. Now!"

She tilted her head down, and her hair fell forward like a curtain around her face. She did as he asked, and was feeling emboldened now, like she'd passed a test. She kissed each foot, and then extended her tongue, and starting at his toes, slowly licked up toward his ankle.

As he looked down at her, she was perfection. She kissed each foot and the simple sensation startled him, sending sparks straight to his cock. Then she began to lick his foot, and he almost moaned as he struggled to gain control. Reaching down, he grabbed a handful of hair and jerked her head up.

"Hold!" Crouching down, he got in her face, nose to nose, "You have misbehaved, *bel rosso*. You did not follow your master's instructions, you became brazen. I am not pleased!"

Releasing his grip on her hair suddenly, she quickly bowed her head, and it almost broke his fucking heart, but he knew she must learn discipline. "Lower your head to the floor in shame, keep your ass in the air. Follow, *bel*, follow!"

***

She was startled when she felt his hand grab her hair and yank her head from his feet. He was in her face, and she wanted to kiss his lips, but he was speaking to her in a stern voice. She had broken the rules. She'd displeased him. He was demanding she lower her head to the floor and she did as she was bidden. This was going to be harder than she thought. She pressed her forehead to the floor, her hands on either side of her face. *I can do this. I want to do this.*

As she did his bidding, he dropped his leathers to the floor. He knew she could see them as they pooled around his ankles before stepping out of them. He slowly walked around her, stood behind her, looking at her ass in the air for him. He crouched down and blew his hot breath across her sex and saw the slight movement of her body. *Oh yes, my bel, you are going to go wild with desire before I ever give you what you want*. Crouching over top her, he slid his hard cock between her beautiful ass cheeks and let the tip of his cock slide along her spine. Putting his wrist to his mouth, he broke the surface of his skin with his teeth, letting the blood rise and pool on his wrist. He slid his finger through his blood and then reached under her breasts and pulled her up against his chest. With his lips against her ear, he whispered in a stern husky voice.

"Your punishment is to taste my essence, something you love, but you will not be allowed to feed." Taking his finger, he slid it across her lips, his blood turning her lips a beautiful red before he slid his finger in her mouth.

Kate felt the wet, hot blood on her lips, and swirled her tongue around his finger before he withdrew it. She licked her lips clean of his blood, but even this small amount hit her like a sledgehammer. She felt the heat between her legs, and she wanted to turn, grab his wrist, and drink from him and feel that electricity through her body. She was consumed with a mindless wanting, and despite her best efforts, the moan escaped her lips.

He smiled wickedly. That's the *bel* he was looking for. He picked up the scent of her sex and knew she was wet for him, aching, and needing him. He grinned, and leaning down, nipped her ear hard and whispered in a deep voice as his fingers teased and pulled on her nipple.

"You let your master know you desire him." Growling into her ear, "You are wet for your master, *si*?"

She felt more than heard the growl, and she wanted to scream 'Fuck me, hard, now!' She could feel her juices between her thighs. Could she talk? Did she risk talking? Her breathing was already labored, and her heart was racing.

"Lover...master...please...may I speak?"

Letting go of her, he stood and walked in front of her. Crouching down, his cock stood straight out, pointing at those full lips of hers, and he wanted desperately to fuck that beautiful mouth, but tonight, he had other things in mind and he restrained himself. Lifting her head with his fingertips, he stared lovingly into her eyes.

"Si, speak, bel rosso."

She took a deep breath and looked up at his face. She locked into his gaze, and he was looking at her with such love, it was crushing. She had to close her eyes against their intensity because the sensations that were assaulting her body had overwhelmed her.

"Master...please...take me now. Fuck me now." Her voice was shaky, her throat constricted, and she waited for his response.

"Open your eyes, *bel*." Looking at her face, and her quivering lips, her body was shaking in need. "You want to be fucked? Are you begging your master for such? Then your master shall give his *bel* her due."

Standing up, he grabbed the flogger in his hand and slowly walked behind her, letting it trail along her spine.

He slid the leather tips of the flogger back and forth over her ass cheeks, as she flinched slightly, her breathing labored, and he heard the most delicious moan.

"You will not cum until you are commanded."

Lifting the flogger, he used a sharp snap of his wrist to let it whip across her ass, leaving beautiful red welts on her lily-white skin. He heard her moan and watched as her muscles tensed. *"Si, mia bel.* You learn well. "

Letting the flogger loose on her cheeks again, the mere sound of the leather strips hitting her skin made him growl and his fangs elongate, and his beast reared hard and fast. Shade gripped the flogger hard, fighting to control the beast. Dropping to his knees, he licked the welts with his tongue, bringing instant relief to the biting pain.

"My sweet *bel*. You are so beautiful. I crave you, and I shall reward you."

Grabbing the flogger, he dangled the leather strips across her sex, teasing her clit, and he could feel her straining to control her orgasm. He slid the rigid handle inside her and stroked her several times as he placed his hand on the small of her back. With each slow, measured stroke of the rigid handle inside her, he knew any moment she would cum and he pushed her limits of restraint. He withdrew the flogger before flipping her over quickly on her back,

He held the rigid end of the flogger up to her mouth. "Lick it clean *mia bel*, taste how sweet your nectar is, taste how much you want me." As her tongue snaked out, he damn near came himself, watching the erotic motion of her mouth around the rigid shaft of the flogger. He lifted her leg and put her booted heel in his mouth before kissing the boots all the way up, past her knee and onto the bare white skin of her inner thigh. He knew both of them were on the edge.

Kate felt his tongue caress her skin and the fire between her legs was unbearable. She was past rules. She couldn't think about rules. She reached for him, hands tangled in his hair, as she pleaded. "Lover...master...I am begging you...please...fuck me now."

His beast reared his head in acknowledgment and Shade was on his knees between her legs. He pushed hard into her as she wrapped her legs around his hips. He growled, looking down into her beautiful face. Leaning over her, he kissed her.

"My beautiful sweet *rosso*, you have pleased your master beyond his imagination." Pulling back, he thrust into her one more time and held again, whispering against her lips.

"Are you asking permission to cum, *bel*? It would please your master to make you cum. Cum hard for me."

He began to ride her hard and fast, and he felt his balls tighten as he pulled her close to his body and kissed her like the moon kissed the stars and they came together like volcanoes erupting, never-ending waves of fire rolling over them. She was crying out, her body shaking and spent, as she convulsed over and over with the pleasure he brought to her. He held her tightly to him as he cradled her and rocked her in his arms.

"My sweet, sweet *bel*, you have done so well. I am your master, and I love you with all my heart. I will always take care of you, protect you, and love you till the end of eternity. *Ti amo per sempre*."

Shade picked her up in his arms and carried her to their bed. He lay with her in his arms, holding her tight. He was her master, and beyond anything else that happened, she must always know he was always her lover and her mate. Feeling her body relax, there were no words between them, for there were none to be said. In his heart and soul, he wanted her to know she was his love for all eternity.

His hands gently slid through her hair, he touched her tenderly, rubbing her back, and holding her against his chest. He wouldn't let go.

"My sweet *bel*, you have brought me so much happiness, so much pleasure. I hope I have taught you well, that in being your master, I will always dominate, but that in no way diminishes you. You are my mate, my partner in all things. Your voice will be heard, and I will honor your opinion, but in all things, I will rule. Contradict me only in private, and I will show you honor and respect in all things. You only make my love grow for you. Every minute, I love you more. You are my weakness when I am strong and my strength when I am weak."

Did he know she would crawl on her hands and knees over broken glass to get to him? Did he know she'd walk across burning coals to get to him? Master was pleased, and that brought her the greatest pleasure of all.

"Hold me, lover...don't let go. You lead, and I will follow."

"I will never let go, *mi amore*. Never! Now you need to rest, this has been an emotional night filled with things you have never experienced. Rest easy knowing I will not leave you. My arms will protect you. I love you, *bel*. You are mine for all eternity. Come to me in your dreams. Let me dance with you there, in the beautiful moonlight, as the stars shine upon us. Our union will never be broken."

Kissing the top of her head, he already felt her asleep on his chest, where she belonged, where he needed her, as he entered her dreams.

38

Shade walked the cold rainy night, his heart was full, but his soul ached for her, to touch her. He patrolled G-town and the neighborhood around Alec's house, making his rounds, as he did every night he was on duty in the Dead House. He hated leaving *bel* after last night, but this was who he was, what he was. He'd grant her much leeway. He understood his vampire culture was a patriarchal one, and females had always been secondary to males, and submissive to their mates. But times had changed, and their culture must change with it. Kate needed to learn he was her master, and he protected her, and he hoped she'd never be exposed to the baser elements of their culture. She needed to feel him, and respond to his commands, just as a warrior would do, as it was for her own safety. And what better way to teach her than last night?

He tuned his senses to her and he could hear her singing to herself as she worked in their home. He could picture her there arranging furniture, hanging art, and opening boxes that contained all the things she had purchased for their home. Every morning when he got home, he saw the transformation and the results of all her efforts to make that house their home. He walked into an alley between a long row of townhouses, leaned against the wall and lit up a smoke, closing his eyes to listen. Her voice in his head only made him ache for her, but the sooner he got done with this watch, the sooner he'd be back in her arms.

The rogue vampire activity remained sporadic and unpredictable, and although he knew these warriors could probably handle it, he still needed to be out there on the streets, setting an example. He stomped out the cigarette with the toe of his boot and took flight across the rooftops of G-town. He sent her a telepathic message from his heart. ***"Ti amo, mi amore, per sempre."***

Moving through the night, the rain started coming down hard and he hated standing watch. He had assigned Alec's neighborhood to himself, so he pulled up his collar as he ducked his head, the rain running down his neck. Suddenly, Tomas was screaming in his head that he had two runners. Sensing his location, Shade was there within seconds, dropping down out of nowhere on the two rogues. He took on one and they stalked each other, waiting to see who made the first move. The rogue came at him fast, but Shade flipped over his head, his beast already out as his fangs were bared and he was ready for attack.

Dropping down behind the rogue, Shade felt the other vamp land on his back. Shade shrugged the vamp free from his shoulders and in one quick stroke, he swung his blade and the first rogue's head rolled across the wet pavement. The rogue's body dropped lifeless to the ground, his head left his body so quickly Shade noticed the surprised look that was frozen on the severed head. *One down, one to go.* He swung around quickly, looking for the vamp that had clung to his shoulders and caught a quick glimpse of Tomas, taking on two rogues at a time. Shade moved to join him, when he was suddenly aware of a burning sensation in his thigh and realized he'd been struck. Whipping around, it was the rogue who'd tried to attack him earlier. The rogue had thrown a shuriken that sliced through his thigh, and he was now approaching with his sword drawn. They circled each other slowly, each looking for an opening when Tomas shouted out something unintelligible, and the rogue looked in Tomas's direction. Shade took advantage of the rogue's momentary distraction, and swung his sword, removing the rogue's arm in a single slice. Arm and sword fell to the ground, as the rogue's blood mingled with the rain. The rogue was scrambling to pull shuriken's from his leathers with his remaining hand when Shade stuck, and again a rogue's head rolled. Without hesitating, he turned back to help Tomas, only to find him standing over two bodies, smiling back at him.

Tomas shouted at him, "Come down off the killer high, *fratello*, we're good."

Sitting down on the pavement, Shade was blood-splattered and on an adrenaline high. Tomas walked up and crouched beside him, advising him to get that wound tended to, as he was losing blood fast. Looking down, Shade's jeans ran red and the gash was deep and long. *Cazzo, bastard cut me good!* It wasn't the first time he'd taken a deep cut, and he knew it wouldn't be the last, but this time was different. He had somewhere to go, and someone to heal him.

Tomas helped Shade up and made sure he could make it back to the Dead House before losing too much blood. Once they were safely inside, Tomas continued to argue that he needed to stay and feed from one of the other warriors, but that wasn't going down with Shade.

He needed *bel rosso*, her blood would heal him. Taking flight, he teleported home and stood outside in the dark. He wondered how in the hell he was going to explain his condition to her. Walking inside, his vision became fuzzy and he prayed he didn't drop before he could clean up.

Making his way into the house from the patio door, he maneuvered around the newly placed furniture. He developed tunnel vision, seeing only a small pinpoint of light as he watched everything fade away. He could feel the blood still oozing from the large gash and his energy and strength draining away with it. He needed her.

He stumbled to his knees and crawled, dragging his injured leg. He felt no pain in his thigh, just the agony of needing her nourishing blood to heal him. He was breathing heavily and knew she was in the house, but where? He tried to call for her, but it was useless, he was losing energy too fast. He crawled slowly up the staircase and into their bedroom where he tried to stand, but was too weak and crashed against the wall and slid down, leaving a bloody streak against the wall as he fell. His breath was raspy, he was bleeding out and she wasn't here. He tried one last time, on the edge of this black abyss, to call for her, his voice barely coming out a whisper as the darkness surrounded him.

"Kate."

***

Kate was working in the kitchen, cleaning and putting things away after the construction had been completed. She had to laugh to herself. She never cooked much for herself, and he ate no human food. This beautiful kitchen wouldn't see much action. She thought she heard a thud from upstairs, and she paused. She felt a momentary panic because she knew she was alone here. She stood still and listened again and then felt more than heard him faintly call her name. She dropped the cookware to the floor where it landed with a loud clatter and she ran barefoot, as fast as she could, through the house and up the stairs, following a trail of blood. She ran to their bedroom where she found him, slumped against the wall, and covered in blood.

She dropped to her knees beside him. "Shade, tell me what to do."

She got no response from him as he lay close to unconsciousness. She applied pressure to the gaping wound in his leg. She didn't understand. She'd watched his wounds heal before her eyes. He'd lost too much blood, and she knew he must feed from her, but he wasn't alert enough, not awake enough to take from her. Panic flew through her as she fought to gain control. She was losing him!

She bit hard into her wrist, ripping at the skin, not the sharp, clean puncture wounds his teeth made. As her blood began to flow, she held it to his lips. "Shade, please!"

Shade could sense her in front of him, smelled her blood, and sank his fangs into her wrist. He felt her other hand glide over him, soft and searching for any other injuries. Slowly, he felt her energy fill his veins. He grabbed her wrist and held it tight against his mouth, gulping down mouthfuls of her essence.

Kate could see his strength and energy return, his wound healing as she watched, the pallor leaving his skin. She was relieved to see him come back to her, and yet, angry that he was injured and wondered what risks he took when he was on the streets.

"Take all you need...I'm here."

His feeding slowed as his body mended. He licked her wrist and watched as it healed. His breathing still ragged, he laid his head back against the wall and told her he'd been injured in a fight, that Tomas wanted him to stay at the Dead House, to give the wound time to heal or to feed from one of the other warriors, but he had refused. He needed her, needing only to get to her.

She helped him stand and stripped from him the bloody clothes. Together, they took a shower. As she washed him, she ran her hands over him, reassuring herself that he was whole and safe. After he was cleaned up, she led him to their bed and climbed in beside him just as she heard the whir of the electronic blinds close out the light of day. He slid into his death slumber, his body healing. She spent the hours sleeping intermittently, waking often to check on him.

***

He had slept soundly in her embrace, but when he awoke he found she was gone. He felt her pain for he'd unintentionally exposed her to that side of his life he'd worked to keep hidden. He now had to face her and deal with the emotions he felt pouring from her. As she walked into the room, he looked at her.

"We need to talk, Kate. I know you have things to say. Will you grant me this time to explain to you why you saw me in such a condition?"

She sat on the bed beside him. "Please, I was angry because I felt like you took an unnecessary risk. Not in the fighting. I understand and accept that part of who you are. But when you tried to ignore the extent of your injury, was that just pride?"

"My injury would heal, as I knew it would." He pulled back the sheet to show her the wound on his thigh, and nothing was there. "Nothing will keep me away from you."

She smacked both hands down flat on the bed in exasperation. "You had lost consciousness on the floor! I didn't even know you were here. I heard your call just before you passed out. What if I hadn't come to this room? You healed because I found you and you fed from me. But what would have happened had I not?"

She went off like a time bomb, and he got rock hard at her beauty, *cazzo, she is feisty as a lioness*. "Do you have any idea of how beautiful you look when you are angry?" He shook his head and held up his hand. "Don't say it. I know I am agitating you even more."

She stood up from the bed with her hands on her hips and that crimson hair flying. "Yes, you are! You asked me to allow you to explain, and I'm waiting for that explanation. Shade, I'm not going anywhere, I'm in this for the long haul. There's nothing you can say that's going to drive me away from you or make me love you less. I just need to understand!"

He slipped from the bed and stood at his full height, nude and powerful as he balled up his fists, puffed out his chest and lowered his eyes to her. "You want an explanation? You shall have it. I am a fucking warrior! I bleed. But above and beyond that simplest of facts, I knew if I made it to you, I would be fine. I told you I would die returning to you. I promised to always come home to you. I could have stayed with Tomas at the Dead House, and would have if not for wanting, more than my life, to be with you, have you to heal me. Your blood will heal me, and it has. My other choice was to feed from one of the other warriors or have someone walk out onto the street and bring me fresh prey inside. I admit, I pushed it too far, but I could think of nothing but getting to you. I wanted you in my arms. I wanted to come home."

She shook her head and took his hands in hers. "You know my anger is rooted in fear, the fear of losing you. I just found you, and I'm bound to you in a way no two mortals can be bound. I can't lose you. I'm struggling to understand. I won't ask you to change who you are. After all, it was the warrior I fell in love with in the first place. But I'd be lying if I said this doesn't frighten me. You don't share details of what you do at night when you go into D.C., and I don't ask. Meet me half-way. I still don't understand where I fit in your world. "

Gripping her hands, his heart slammed against his chest and made him weak, his soul screamed with the memories of another, and how much that ancient event still tortured him. Before him was his second chance, the chance to not allow his pride to dictate, and let love rule instead. He pulled her to his chest.

"I cannot change, *mi amore*. I was born to this life and being a warrior is all I know. You have taught me there is more to life than that. You have humbly shown me I can love, and I am worthy of love. I do not deserve so much from you, I only know I will die for you, and all I ask is you love me through it all. I made a mistake, my pride drove me beyond my limitations, but my love drove me harder to be with you. Because if I am to die, then it will be in your arms, where there is comfort and love. Your arms are my home, for I am a warrior, proud and strong, and only you hold the key to my life. Forgive me? I have...memories, and they drive me...to do right by you."

She looked into the depths of those blue eyes. *Memories?* What memories drove him to risk death to get to her?

"You don't need to ask forgiveness. I've already forgiven, because I know it's your nature, and I know it was in your heart to get home to me. I'm trying so hard to follow your lead. But understand I can't live without you. You carry my heart, and when your heart ceases to beat, mine will as well. So, if you want to keep me alive, you must keep yourself alive. I plan on an eternity of loving you, and I expect you to deliver. You promised me that."

He felt her love, but there was also tension and unasked questions. "*Mi amore*, there is something else bothering you, spit it out. I want no dancing around issues between us. I am going outside to have a smoke, think about what you want to ask, and when I return, I am prepared to answer whatever is still churning in that beautiful redhead of yours."

Sliding on a pair of sweatpants, he walked outside, lit up, and knew he was taking a grave chance, but she needed to know. Looking up at the night sky, his anger ripped through him. He yelled into the dark. "Are you trying to get revenge, Adriana? It's working. But you won't win, *belleza*!" Taking a deep breath, he turned toward the house and decided whatever she wished to ask, he would answer.

Kate looked up at him as he returned to their bedroom. "You said you have memories. There's something that haunts you, pushes you to risk your life getting back to me. There's something I've wanted to ask, something you alluded to when we were at Castello."

He stood before her, preparing himself for her questions. "My heart is open to you, ask."

She looked at the floor as she spoke, "I hesitate to ask because it's in the past, and I have told myself what happened before me is of no concern. But a woman's heart wants to know, and if you decide not to answer, I'll accept that and never bring it up again."

He smiled softly at her. "*Bel rosso*, believe me, I understand jealousy, that is something mortals and immortals share. And although the past is past, it does mold who we are and how we feel, and that is part of my problem. I perceive that you wish to know of Adriana, *si*? You have had questions ever since Florence."

"Yes, you alluded to her when we were in Florence, and you kept her painting in your bedroom for a very long time. So, I am asking, lover. Who is she to you? What is your story? Come lie with me on our bed. I have a feeling this is a long story, and I may not want to be standing when I hear it."

Kate stretched out across the bed and he lay down beside her. "I will begin by telling you, no one truly knows this story, so I am telling it for the first time to you. I wish to get it out of me." He pulled her close to him. "It is a long story, but I can make it brief." Taking her hand, he squeezed it and held it tight.

She locked eyes with him. "Then tell me what you have told no other."

He took a deep breath before he began. "Adriana was immortal. She was beautiful, and a brave warrior. She was from another coven, an ally to Medici. I met her perhaps two hundred years ago. I saw her fight, win, and walk away as if it was an everyday chore and *si*, she took my breath away, I will not lie."

Kate caressed his face. "So she was a warrior, like you."

"*Si*, she was too much like me. She was prideful, brave, scared of nothing, and cocky. I had never met nor seen anyone like her. Later, we ended up together again, as our two covens were working and training together. We began to talk, get to know one another. I had never thought of her as anything other than a warrior. That night, around the campfires, she danced, and she looked like no warrior to me."

Clenching his eyes closed, the vision of her slid across his mind, and he knew she'd haunt him until he released this hell inside him.

Kate swallowed hard, did he love her still? Was she in competition with Adriana? She knew if she showed her jealousy he'd stop talking. "I can understand why you would be drawn to her."

"We knew each other for some time, we battled together, *cazzo*, she was amazing. I began to care deeply for her. Not like with you, though. It was different, like a friend but something more. I cannot think how to explain it. She was my best friend, we had each other's back, we travelled together, fought together, and then one night, it became more."

Kate ran her hand through his hair, brushing it back from his face. "I did not expect a virgin on my doorstep, and certainly not one with your skills. I know you've had many women before me."

"I just need you to understand, she was not like you, nor do I compare you. She was my lover, I hers. She lived with me for many years at Castello, as you know. Did I love her? *Si*, in my own way. But I knew she wasn't my mate. Something held me back, even as she kept luring me on. She wanted us to be mated, to have *bambinos*, but I knew there was something more for me. I could never commit, there was something missing between us, and I refused to let her feed from me. It became a sore point between us, and we argued often. Making a long story short, our pride got in the way, and it kept getting in the way, a battle of wills for control."

Kate rested her head in her hand. "Two head-strong warriors, full of pride, and neither one wants to give in. What could possibly go wrong there? Sorry, tell me your story."

"I am sorry, this must be boring to you, and it must seem childish and ridiculous. I apologize." Sitting up, he swung his legs over the bed and laid his head in his hands.

She ran her hand over the bare skin of his back as he sat beside her in the bed. "Let me assure you, Shade Medici, there is nothing boring about you. Now lie back down beside me and let go of this story that is tormenting you. Do you think I can't see that? Your blood is in my veins now as well, remember?"

Trying to relax, he laid back down. "We had a really big fight, I don't even remember what it was about, but it was bad, and words were said that should not have been. In short, she was delivering an ultimatum. She wanted to be my mate, feed from me, have a child with me, and I refused. She said if I could not commit to her, then she would leave, that I was wasting her time. If you have ever seen two immortals fight, and I assure you, you will, it is ugly, to say the least. But before we could resolve the argument, she was called to battle by her master. At the time, we did not know it was a ruse to flush out some rogue warriors who had infiltrated their ranks. She assumed she would be meeting several of her coven at this location. She asked me to come with her and I refused. I was still angry that she had issued an all or nothing ultimatum. It is a decision I regret immensely to this day."

Kate laid her head on his shoulder and placed her hand on his chest. "All lovers quarrel, and you turned away in anger. We have all made choices we regret, Shade."

Shade closed his eyes as he spoke, letting the memories roll through him. "She left for her assignment from her master. I heard her call once, in my head. I didn't respond. I blocked her thoughts from me. I thought she was playing games with me, to lure me to come help her, and I was angry and did not want to feel her. I blocked her out of anger. But something kept agitating me deep inside, nagging at me that I was ignoring her, and when I unblocked, she was screaming for me, for her life. She needed help, she was surrounded and being attacked and needed me desperately. She was far from me, and the sun was on the horizon. I could not get to her, and they killed her."

His body began to shake, blood tears welled inside his eyes. "She died alone. I never made it to her. I blocked her cries from me. No one was there for her, no one! She died because of me. She died because of my pride. They left her body lying for the sun to turn her to ash. I couldn't get to her, the sun was rising fast, and I could not go and get her, bring her home. It tears me apart to know I left her alone. I left her to die alone. She never heard me, or knew if I heard her cries."

Kate stroked his face. "I'm so sorry! I can't believe you've had to live with this." She covered his face with kisses, wiping away his blood tears. "It sounds like her master set her up, like he used her, knowing full well her fate. And maybe you could have made a difference, or maybe you would've both been killed. That will forever be unknown to you and I understand the pain of not knowing. Oh Shade, I'm so sorry."

Tears streamed down her cheeks as she wept for the depth of his pain, and how long he had carried this burden. "There are no words to ease your burden. I understand that now. But you can't know what's in a woman's heart. Mortal or immortal, women are defined by love, and trust me when I tell you, blocked or not, she knew you loved her. With her dying breath, she knew."

He rolled to her and buried his face into her neck and for the first time since Adriana's death, he wept like a child, letting it all go with someone who loved him, someone he trusted.

"So, you see, *mi amore*, I learned my lesson. I will always come home to you, talk things out, never remaining in anger against one another without finding resolution. I would walk into the flaming sun just to join you. I never wanted to let Adriana down, but she wasn't the one for me. I miss her, but I know her dying was to teach me. I will not die alone on a battlefield. I will always come to you."

She wrapped her arms around her vulnerable warrior and absorbed his pain and tears. "I don't want you to die for me, warrior. I want you to live for me. I want you to fight like all the demons from hell are on your back and you will conquer them one by one with a flash of your sword. I want you to fight as if you have everything to lose, because you do. We make mistakes, and we learn from those mistakes. That's just life, mortal or immortal. Your world is more violent than mine, but the lessons are the same. Thank you for baring your soul to me, and for trusting me with that burden. If you feared I'd turn away from you, then know I only love you more, if that's even possible. Now hold me tight and let me ease this pain in your heart."

Laying his head across her heart, there was strength inside him, a future that looked bright. There would be many more fights for land and blood, but he was ready and willing, nothing would stop him with this woman beside him.

"You have the gentlest caring heart, *mi amore*. It's so gentle and yet, so strong. You love me even though I have shown my downfalls, my inability to move past pride. I hope you understand why I returned last night. Five hundred years I searched, I craved, and bled for a love like yours. And now, I fight for our love, I fight to return to you. I love you, Kate. I will always love you above all others."

She held him in a gentle embrace. "I understand now why you put yourself at risk in that way and I love you above all others as well, but you know that. Deep in your heart, you know that. There can never be anyone else for me. I have placed my fate in your hands, my heart in your hands, so carry me gently, lover."

39

Reviewing his options for the next campaign cycle of Republican Presidential candidates, Alec saw two big obstacles. First, the incumbent President was not sure if he'd run again. If he did decide to run, he'd be a shoo-in as the parties' nominee. So, Alec needed to figure out how to help him decide running for a second term wasn't in his best interest, and he had a few things in the back of his mind to tackle that problem.

His second problem was the very popular senior Senator Ralston. He had a huge backing from the far right, and he'd just written a book. He was pre-campaigning, hitting the book tour circuit, getting on talk shows, and taking the temperature of public opinion. If the President didn't run for a second term, Ralston would be the parties' choice. If Alec could remove Ralston from the picture, then his chances of becoming the parties' nominee were a shoo-in. He happened to know Ralston was a reformed alcoholic, and a reformed alcoholic was always a short step away from falling off the wagon. He just needed a way to break his will, and he thought he had the weapon to do it.

This didn't fall under the terms of his contract for protection services he had with Shade, but he thought Shade would play this game. After all, he got a pretty fucking generous payment for his services, and now he was shacked up with that redhead. He should be one happy ass vampire and ready to return a few favors. Alec pulled out his cell phone and gave Shade a call.

Shade was back in the Dead House now that his injuries had healed. Tomas and the other warriors had been watching him closely but he appeared to be back to normal. He was barking out orders, assigning grids, and getting the warriors' asses out on the streets when he heard his cell phone buzz. Raffling through the papers haphazardly strewn on the table in front of him, he found the cell and saw Alec on the ID.

"*Cazzo*! What in the hell does he want now?" Taking the call, he sighed and flopped down on the chair. "Shade."

"Brother. Streets seem safer with you in town. Tomas has said things are cleaning up nicely. Anything else you need over there? He said the Dead House was working well as a command center, but we can put in some high-end electronic surveillance equipment if you need it. Just let me know."

Shade lit up a cigarette as he gave Alec a recap. "Look *fratello,* things are slowly shaping up.. I'm working this crew and they're showing progress. We've taken out a few rogues here and there, but that's the norm. Nothing to worry about. We are adding a security system, but weapons are my main concern at the moment. I need to increase my stock, bring these boneheads up to speed. Is there something you wanted, because I'm kind of busy here?"

"As a matter of fact, there is something I'd like to talk to you about, but not on the phone. Do you think you can get away from there for a while? Get over here to my place where we can talk in private?"

"Not a problem, brother. Give me fifteen minutes and tell me you got some Midnight over there."

Alec tossed back the remains of the Midnight in his glass. "We never run out of Midnight in the Canton household. I'll be in the study. Santos will show you in."

"On it, brother."

Hanging up the phone, Shade grabbed his leather jacket from the back of the chair, shrugging his muscled arms and shoulders into the soft leather, and feeling the jacket slide into place like a second skin. He let Tomas know he was headed to G-town and the Canton residence and teleported to Alec's front door. Santos, Alec's manservant, answered before Shade could even ring the bell. As Santos led him into the study, Shade's boots hit heavily on the hardwood floors and he could smell Rissa inside the house. He hoped to fucking hell this issue had nothing to do with her.

As Shade entered the study, Santos pulled the door closed behind him, giving them privacy. Alec was pouring them both a glass of Midnight.

"Sit down by the fire, brother. Take a load off. I have a lot to tell you."

He carried the glass of the rich, thick burgundy colored brew to Shade, and sat down in the chair across from him. "I've got a problem. Not a security issue. No threat to my life, but a threat to my ambitions. And you have a little gift I think might be quite useful."

"You refer to my ability to dream-walk. Well, *fratello*, your ambitions can be mighty damn bold, so tell me what in the hell you need, and I will see what I can do."

Alec leaned forward in his chair, his elbows on his knees. "You know my goal is to take the presidency. But this is not medieval Europe. I can't just go in and overthrow the king with an army of warriors like the old days. Unfortunately, I will have to rely on the support of mortals, and the election process. And in order to get there, it will require some serious manipulation. I already have in mind how I can convince President Ashton not to run for office again, but it's too soon to play that card yet, that's a ways down the road. Once I have Ashton out of the way, then I have to get through the whole nomination process for the Republican candidacy. When I look at my contenders, there's only one that's a serious threat. He has the backing of the far right, he has the NRA, and he has a lot of money. Maybe I can beat him...maybe not. Now, if I can get him to drop out of the race, then the candidacy is mine. That's where you come in with your dream-walking. I was thinking you could stalk him, shadow him, and fill his head with dreams of failure. He's a senior Senator now, and his seat is up for re-election. If he runs for President, he can't also run for his Senate seat. So, if he loses his bid for the Presidency, he has no Senate seat to go back to. Politics is all he knows. Being forced back into the private sector would be a death knell to him. He used to have a drinking problem. Been years ago, he did that whole AA thing and carries around the chip. I need you to rattle him. Get inside his head. Find out what his demons are and fill his head with visions of failure. What do you think, brother?"

Shade listened to Alec, realizing he had this plan worked out in his head. Like the master vampire he was, Alec used his wits to get what he needed. Downing the goblet of Midnight in one single swig, Shade sighed and set the glass down delicately on the side table. He stared at Alec as a smile spreads across his face.

"Alcoholics are easy targets. They are weak. Add if this poor bastard has nothing without this prospect of winning then he is easily taken down, brother. But this will take me away from work on the streets, away from renovations in Virginia. Not to mention, training your warriors is a full-time job. Right now, they have limited skills and they only have the weapons they own. I need money for a cache of weaponry, Alec. And what I need, I can't buy at the sporting goods store, which means I need Medici made weapons. So let's bargain here. Get me what I need, it benefits you in the long run. In the meantime, I can take down this mortal with dream-walking. Put a little fear into him. When I am done, he will be cowering in the corner. I need a name and address. Married, *bambinos,* any other relevant information? Deal, *si*?"

Alec ran his hand through his hair. Fuck! He thought he could bundle this deal with everything else he'd already paid out to Shade. He should have known!

"Yeah, okay, whatever you need. Get the weapons in. Of course, you need weapons. I relied on the mercenaries to supply their own in the past. Probably not the smartest move, but hell, I buy mercenaries a weapon and they take it with them when they bolt. So, I want you in charge. You keep tabs on the weapons, and I'll fill the bunker with whatever you want. Just get this fucker off my ass. His name is Senator Ralston. He lives off DuPont Circle near Embassy Row, on Kalorama Road. Big fucking house. He has kids but they're all grown, none live at home, just him and his wife, Helen. His day schedule will mirror mine, and you have that. I think he avoids a lot of big social events, like parties and bars, so he's not tempted to drink. Plays golf with a bunch of business cronies and lobbyists. That should be enough to get you started."

Shade crossed one leg to his opposite knee. "Warriors have a weapon of choice, usually custom made to fit their skill. They rely on that weapon for everything. But Medici warriors are trained on all weapons and are skilled in each. This shit the mercenaries carry for weaponry won't be of much use if we ever have a real battle. I need them to be supplied with custom-designed swords, knives, and shuriken's. We make our own in Florence, *fratello*. This is an investment on your behalf. You wanted me to run this camp, then we run it my way. The weapons belong to the camp, not the warriors."

Reaching into the pocket of his leather jacket, Shade grabbed the Medici-made shuriken and quickly threw it in Alec's direction, watching him move easily to avoid its strike. "That is a Medici shuriken, and it is deadly if used by a trained warrior. Keep it, little gift. I got Ralston. Give me a week or two and he will no longer be a threat to you."

Alec ducked his head to the left as the shuriken came straight at him. He heard the whistle of the throwing star as it whizzed within an inch of his ear. *Fuck! Good thing he was paying attention. Fucking warriors! Always swinging their dicks.*

"I knew I could count on you, brother. Order the weapons you need, and as I said, if you want to put in some surveillance equipment, go ahead. I have it here in the house. I'm sure you have it in yours. If you don't, you probably should. And before you even ask, I won't be paying to put surveillance in your own damn house."

Shade laughed as he stood, fist-bumping Alec. "Done deal, brother. I'll take you up on the surveillance on the Dead House. I'll get that installed. Don't have it at Bel Rosso yet. We're still busy with renovations, but soon. No need to get up. I can see myself out. I will keep you informed of the Ralston situation."

Walking out of the study, Shade saw Larissa coming down the stairs just in time to come face to face with him. He watched the smug look on her face as she glared at him and greeted him with 'Warrior'. He didn't smile but glared back, never completely trusting this female. "Rissa."

He watched her cross her arms over her chest and cock that blonde head of hers to the side with an unpleasant smirk before speaking to him in that bitchy voice.

"Are you done with my vampire now?"

Shade leaned in close to her face and smiled wickedly. "Your vampire's time is his own Rissa, haven't you learned that yet?"

Watching as she huffed and pushed him out of her way, swishing that ass like an angry lioness just robbed of her meal, his laugh was loud as he headed out the door. Shade one, Rissa zero.

40

Shade gathered up a blade and a few shuriken's, tucking them inside his leathers. He had no intention of fighting this Senator, but he never entered any situation unarmed. It was time he got into this Senator Ralston ordeal. The sooner this was done with, the better. Then he could get back to normal, whatever the hell that was. Shade let Tomas know he was making his regular rounds at Alec's house but didn't let anyone know his true intent, dream-walking into Ralston's head. The less people that knew what he was doing, the better off for him and Alec. He wanted to think twice now about what he took on. He couldn't make some of the same impetuous decisions. His life wasn't his own any longer, he had a mate, and she deserved as much of his time as he could give her.

He left the Dead House and teleported along Embassy Row and spotted the Ralston home on Kalorama. The houses here were large and well maintained. Owning a free-standing home in Washington D.C. cost money and lots of it. He checked out the house, making sure Ralston was home, and other than his wife, no one else was inside the residence. He wrapped himself in shadow and teleported inside the main living area.

As Shade walked through the house, he was getting the lay of the land before making his way to the second floor. Every room was decorated in antiques and family heirlooms. He noticed a woman sleeping alone in a very feminine bedroom. She was an older woman, and Shade recognized the Senator's wife Helen from the photos Alec had provided. It appeared she slept in a separate room from her husband. That would make things easier.

He walked inside her room and wandered through it, watching her sleep. One thing was evident, the lady was a lush. She had a large antique dresser, and on it, bottles of alcohol. There was a half-filled glass made of imported crystal, a bowl of lemon and lime slices, and an ice bucket filled with melting ice sitting at her bedside. So, his wife was an alcoholic, and her husband was the reformed one. He wondered how the Senator kept that little secret out of the press. Shade made a mental note to share this information with Alec.

Leaving her room, Shade walked down the long hall of furnished but unoccupied bedrooms that had probably been their children's rooms when they were younger. He slipped quietly into a masculine bedroom, the furniture dark and imposing. In the bed lay an older gentleman, looking older and frailer than he looked in his photos. Something about seeing him sleeping made him look more vulnerable. The Senator lies still, as his loud snoring filled the room. His hair was gray and thinning, and he had a slight paunch to his stomach.

Shade scanned the room and, on the wall, hung several rifles. Elk and deer heads also lined the walls. So, he was a game hunter, and the Senator liked his weapons. Shade stepped inside the large walk-in closet where things were neat and tidy. His closet was compulsively organized with his suits, white shirts, khaki pants, and polo shirts, all hanging together, and organized by color. Expensive brands but designed to not stand out in a crowd. There was a safe tucked into a corner, and Shade laughed to himself. Walking to the bedside table, he pulled open the drawer and found bottles of prescription pills, and a .357 magnum.

Ralston began to moan and awakened with a start. Still shadowed, Shade decided to sit down in a tufted high back leather chair and watch the Senator. Ralston threw his spindly legs over the side of the bed, and wearing only a pair of baggy white boxer shorts, he waddled off for the bathroom and relieved himself. The Senator shuffled back to his bed, opening the drawer of the side table and pulling out a bottle of pills. Shade watched as the Senator shook out several pills into his palm and downed them with a glass of water that sat atop the table. Instead of returning to his bed, the Senator stumbled across the room to a large desk. He flipped through a datebook and a few newspapers and then went back to the bed, grabbing the remote and turning on the large screen television to CNN. *Cazzo, bastard is boring as hell.* After approximately forty minutes with the TV still blaring, he fell asleep and began to snore. Shade stood up, walked to the bed, and placed his hand across Ralston's forehead and walked into his dream-state.

He wandered into his dreams, staying to the edges, unseen and unknown and watched the mishmash of thoughts flowing in and out of Ralston's mind. He hated his wife's drinking and hated that he still craved the relaxing feel of alcohol. He knew he'd driven his wife to drink through their life in politics and living in the public eye, not to mention a few of his own escapades. Shade pulled hard on the

Senator's memories, feeling fear and pain and shame. The good Senator was not so good after all, and as Shade already knew, mortal or immortal, politics were strewn with corruption. Shade pulled out a very interesting scene that played heavily on Ralston's mind; he dreamt of it often, it plagued him still.

Ralston had used his old money connections and his family name to climb the political ladder, and married into money as well. But he liked his booze, his women, and expensive toys. As Shade watched the scene unfold, the Senator had been handsome in his youth and easily went through a long list of beautiful young women. The Senator's tastes were more deviant, however, and he preferred whores. Not the expensive girls from the escort services who lived in a penthouse paid for by their sugar daddy, but street whores who did nasty little deeds for cheap. The Senator's memory unfolded his ugly past as Shade saw the young blonde whore as the Senator plied her with booze. They were skimming at a high rate of speed in a Cigarette Rough Rider race boat across a huge lake. The only light supplied by the moonbeams streaking across the waves created by the boat he was piloting. He hit something huge in the water, perhaps a log hidden below the surface and the boat flipped up in the air, tossing both of them overboard. They flailed and struggled in the dark abyss, the Senator unable to swim, but finally getting back to the overturned boat. Ralston watched as the young girl floundered, calling for help, and eventually slipped beneath the surface, never to be seen again. As the dream unfolded, bits and pieces were missing, but Shade knew Ralston had paid a lot of money to cover up the accident, and no one was the wiser of a dead whore lying at the bottom of the lake.

The Senator had continued to drink heavily after this, but still remained in the public eye and climbed the political ladder, his wife beside him. Children followed, but his sexual preferences never changed, and his wife knew all about them, and her own drinking increased as well. *What a fucking happy ass life he had.* The incident of the young girl drowning as he helplessly watched repeated itself over and over in his head. Shade knew that once he put the images of the Senator failing to win his election into his dreams, it would never leave, and the mission would be accomplished. Shade felt the pull of sunrise coming and quickly teleported out. He had enough background information on the Senator to create fear and doubt for a failing career path. For Shade, this would be a walk in the park, and he'd get some damn fine weapons out of the deal as well, all for a few nights of well-placed terror inside an elderly politician's head.

41

Checking in with Alec, Shade gave him a recap of what he'd learned about Ralston. On the second night, he teleported directly inside Ralston's home, shadowed from view, and headed straight for the second floor. As Shade walked past the wife's bedroom, the door was ajar. Looking in, she was sprawled across the bed, still dressed, and passed out, the empty bottle of vodka clutched in her diamond-studded hand. Shade shook his head, been there, done that. He'd had enough of his own nights when he drowned his misery in alcohol, and it sure looked like alcohol was the poison of choice in this residence.

Shade made his way to the Senator's room to find him sleeping. He was late arriving tonight, a few problems with two stray rogues kept him working in the Dead House longer than anticipated. Walking quietly to the side of the bed, he laid his hand over Ralston's forehead, stepping into his dreams like a man on a mission. The vision Shade created was clear, precise, and frightening to a man with nothing to rely on but his political career. The vision let him know he had nowhere to go but down. If he chose the presidency, then losing the nomination would unseat him in the bid for the Senate seat. Shade made the dream more specific, showing him a clear vision of Alec unseating him for the parties' nomination. Shade painted a picture of Alec as being more powerful, the people loved him, drawn to his youth and energy, his intelligence, his charmed life with his beautiful bride to be. He showed Alec capturing the youth vote, as well as the women voters, and making this country strong and proud again. Shade showed Ralston's campaign as weak and failing. He'd start to lose favor in the polls, and as the campaign progressed, Canton would run him over by a landslide. Shade hinted at scandal, the exposure of that long-ago accident finally uncovered and put the dream loop on replay. His long-suffering wife's drinking would be exposed, and he'd fall off the wagon himself. Over and over, the cascading images kept repeating like a broken record and Ralston was the broken man trapped inside.

Shade took his seat in the leather-bound chair and watched the nightmarish images replay over and over in the Senator's head. Ralston began to break out in a cold sweat. He rolled from side to side and then sat bolt upright in his bed, his hands shaking. The Senator opened the bedside table drawer, grabbed several sleeping pills, and started to reach for the glass of water. He paused briefly before sliding from the bed and walking to his wife's bedroom, returning with a bottle of Grey Goose. He poured the clear vodka into the glass, tossed down the pills and gulped down the alcohol. Shade watched as the Senator collapsed back on the bed, surprised he'd caved so early. This assignment was going to be over in no time.

Shade left him lying there, the Senator's mind filled with failure and the impending, overwhelming victory of Senator Canton. Shade understood the allure of the addiction and had no doubt the Senator's fall from sobriety would be full-blown before he knew what hit him. Combined with the nightmares that would rob him of his sleep and the return of his alcohol addiction, the good Senator would become a bumbling, blithering idiot on the hill. He'd need no help from Shade or Alec to lose it all. A week or two was all it would take to land the Senator right where he wanted him. But until then, the never-ending hell of that nightmare would replay over and over in his head and no amount of alcohol would diminish it.

Shade kept up his routine of checking on Ralston every other night and found him progressively turning to the bottle for relief. He knew the Senator was weak, but it only took a few weeks for the man to unravel. Shade had seen the man's eyes become more bloodshot and had viewed several Fox News and CNN clips where the Senator was seen at a few campaign fundraising events and in every single one, a drink graced his hand, his face was reddened, and he looked completely unsteady on his feet. The press was starting to make subtle comments about his drinking.

Tonight, he found the Senator awake in his bedroom. Wrapping himself in shadows, Shade walked in to see him sitting as his desk, his face in his hands, a half-empty bottle of vodka sitting beside him. Watching this man slowly disintegrate was a sorry sight. Shade watched as Ralston slid right off his chair and plopped limp on the floor, passing out. Shade walked to him, lifted him in his arms, and laid him out on the bed.

Walking back to the desk, he looked through the Senator's itinerary for the week. Ralston had an exclusive interview about his Presidential campaign bid scheduled with Anderson Cooper that would be shot live and seen nationwide. *Well, isn't this just the perfect ticket for the old boy?* Shade grinned and walked to the bedside of the passed-out Senator as he lay in his drunken stupor, and placed his hand upon his forehead, projecting an image of a nervous and fidgeting Senator responding in terror at the questions being fired at him. Shade left him with the distinct impression in his mind that with enough drink right before the televised interview, his nerves would be calmed, and he'd appear in control. Shade let the dreams repeat over and over, adding how important it was for the Senator to nail this interview to keep public opinion on his side. Shade exited the room, leaving the Senator tossing in a restless sleep, waking constantly in a cold sweat. That should give him a head start on looking worse for wear at his interview.

The following night, in the Dead House, Shade gathered the warriors together for a briefing, letting them share what they were seeing out on the streets, hearing suggestions before he barked out grid assignments and instructions, and sent them into D.C. for the night. Tomas was on patrol as well tonight, as Shade stayed at the command center. Checking his watch, it was almost time for the live interview. Shade flipped the widescreen monitor from the surveillance feed over to TV and watched the Senator unravel on national television.

The Senator's face was blotchy and red, his speech was slightly slurred. He spoke in that slow, controlled, deliberate manner of so many drunks, trying to maintain control. Anderson asked him about his history with alcohol, and the Senator admitted he'd had a problem in the past, but he had been sober for years. When Anderson moved on to the specific issues of the Senator's campaign, Ralston stumbled over his answers, forgetting key points, performing badly. And then Anderson asked him about the rumors of the boating accident that had occurred years ago. In a panic, the Senator pulled the microphone from his lapel, mumbling that he wouldn't be subjected to this, and stormed off the set.

Shade flipped the monitor back to surveillance mode and smiled to himself. He was pretty sure Alec would have been watching this performance as well. He smiled down at the list of Medici weaponry that he was ordering to be hand made in Florence and shipped here for their use. Alec's bill was beside it and that made him grin. There was something deeply satisfying about emptying Alec's coffers. Hell, Shade didn't need money, but he did need the vamps of his coven to be employed and making a fair living to take care of their families.

Teleporting out, he made his rounds over the Canton residence. He was making sure the area was safe when he heard Tomas in his head.

Two of his warriors had come upon a small group of rogues inside a club. They were preparing to move out onto the streets and were within a few miles of the Canton residence. Tomas and the others were gathering to take them out as they left the club and Shade knew he had to be there. It would take several of them if the rogues split up, and between him and his crew, they'd follow them until they could take them out. He much preferred killing rogues to dream-walking any day.

At sunrise, he was teleporting home to Bel Rosso, and landed in the bathroom, stripping away the bloodied leathers before stepping in the shower. He could hear Kate in the bedroom. As he walked to her, wearing only a towel, his hair still damp, his beast calmed by the night of kills, he told her there was something he needed to check before he came to bed. He headed downstairs to his office and turned on the TV for the morning news. The talking heads were all in a buzz over last night's interview with Senator Ralston, and his early morning announcement that he was pulling himself from the campaign race.

42

It had been several days since the dream-walking assignment, and Shade was back into his routine at the Dead house. As day approached, he teleported home, and his sweet *bel* teased him. He felt the beast push to the surface, and he pulled away from her, watching the disappointment in her face.

It was the discussion that never went away, the one hurdle they couldn't get past, and the wedge that remained between them--the beast. Shade still hid his true nature from her, still warned her about the beast that resided in him and pushed her away. She played him the song by Kelly Clarkson, "Dark Side."

He listened but feared she didn't understand the depths of the darkness. "Can you say that, *mi amore*, can you truly say that? You have not seen the darkest of me and I am not sure you will stay afterward. But *si*, this makes me fear that once you see the beast you will never love me again and I will lose you. I will lose all if that happens, for I cannot go on without you."

She ran her hand over his chest. "Shade, there's no way back for me. I'm committed to you, heart and soul. Your darkness is the first thing I saw, and it's what drew me to you. I do understand that you've shielded and protected me, but I promise you, the only thing that can break this mortal girl is for you to leave me, stop loving me. I can bare all else. How can I ever convince you? Until I do, I won't fully have your heart. You won't be able to love without reservation if you still have doubt, and I want all of you, lover. All of you, including the dark side."

It had become their eternal struggle. What he hid from her. He feared she'd leave him once she saw the beast and understood his true nature. He feared the beast would hurt her or kill her and pushed her away when the beast was too close to the surface. He felt frustration and anger, she felt hurt and rejection. There was no resolution and she fell asleep beside him as he slipped into his death slumber.

He woke at sunset, getting dressed and leaving their bed before *bel* awoke. The night was slowly creeping in and he was restless as hell. This divide between them was eating him alive, the fucking reality of what he was, and the struggle to keep the beast under control never left him. Slipping out quietly onto the patio, he leaned against the side of the house, lit up a smoke and inhaled deeply, his mind screaming. She was his, she loved him. But she hadn't seen the beast and that thought made his heart go dark and black. She said she'd stay, but she couldn't possibly know, neither of them would until the beast was exposed.

The beast ruled his soul and she'd never understand that until they faced each other head-on. Would the beast walk away the winner? He could love her with everything he had, but she didn't know how twisted and sick he was inside when the beast took over, and it was getting harder to hold him back. She tempted him, lured him with her body, her words, and the way she loved him. She saw Shade the man, but she had yet to see Shade the beast. And her strength to tackle the beast was not near enough at this point, but Shade was losing control and the devil laughed every time she pushed him further to the brink.

He teleported back to D.C., into a crowded part of the district. He stalked and paced inside the alleyway. He had no intention of hunting or killing, but his restless heart refused to let him stay still for long. The night called to him and he felt better out here under the moon, the cold air clearing his head. This was where he could release the beast without hurting her. Maybe he did need a fight, someone to rip apart, someone to hunt.

Suddenly, he felt the air change and he picked up a scent...vampire. Crouching down, his senses went into overdrive as the sounds got closer. That scent, it was familiar, and it was definitely a warrior. His blood began to rush. This wasn't a vampire from the D.C. territory and it wasn't one of his Medici. Whoever it was, they were deadly and meant business. The scent was strong, and it was getting closer.

Female! Slowly pulling out a blade from the sheath at his waist, his whole body was tense and warrior mode kicked in. He saw her as she strolled toward him like a fucking member of the devil's own brigade. Her raven black hair cut short from the last time he'd seen her. Her eyes shone, the stars above reflected in their beauty. She stood tall, sleek, and trim, just as he remembered her. She filled out that leather with her every honed, hard-muscled curve. Her boots were noiseless. She was all warrior. The moon graced her moves like a halo. She walked without fear...Sabine.

Standing tall, his legs were spread as he asserted his alpha male position over her. He could feel her and knew she meant him no harm, but his mind began to wonder what in the hell she was doing here. "Sabine."

He never took his eyes off of her as she stood like a hellcat only inches in front of him. Her height almost equaled his as his eyes locked with hers and her voice was like pure fire burning through his veins.

She purred out her greeting. "Shade, did you think you could defend yourself with that weapon? You're losing your touch. Tell me you miss your pussy-cat."

Same smart mouth, nothing had changed about Sabine. Sheathing his knife, he stepped back away from her and tilted his head. "Well, you haven't changed, except your locks, you cut them. What in the hell are you doing here, Sabine? This is far from your territory."

She moved in fast and slid her hand down his cheek, her lips close to his. "Shade, my deviant lover...what is that stench? Mated?"

He watched as the look of shock flashed across her face. She quickly pulled her hand away from him. She stepped back, looking at him as if he was some creature from another planet and heard her begin to laugh and pace around him.

"Shade, you have mated? Well, well, well, haven't we come a long way? I'd heard rumors you had mated but dismissed them. When I heard your sweet ass was based in D.C., I thought maybe you'd want a little company. But mated? Who is she? I can't imagine she quenches your beast better than me?"

Growling, he stalked toward her, his beast angered and fired up from her words. "You damn hellcat, she is my mate! And it is none of your business who I mate or why I am here. You and I go back a long way Sabine, but you no longer have rein over me or my soul. You do not tempt me, and I am no longer interested. What we shared is in the past. You dragged me to the depths of hell. You found the darkest parts of me. I discovered more evil in myself than I even care to acknowledge, then or now. I finally found the strength to break free, and you moved on to other warriors to tend to your unending appetite for depravity. It took me a long time to climb out of that dark hole. So, do not come here and judge where my heart has gone. This is none of your business, Sabine. Go home and tell all the covens in Europe all is well in D.C., report back to whoever has sent you."

Turning his back on her, he strolled angrily from the alley, her words ringing through him.

"Shade, wait." He stopped and stood still, waiting to hear whatever was coming, when he felt her lay her head against his back.

"You love her deeply, she's given you something, changed you inside. Something I couldn't. But there's turmoil. I feel it rolling off you. Talk to me Shade, as a warrior, not a lover. I didn't come here on anyone's order, but for my peace of mind, to find you, check on you."

Turning, he looked at her. He no longer found her attractive, he knew her darkness. She had no damn heart for him, nor did she care, she only wanted to play with him, as she had from day one. Looking at Sabine, she was now just a bad memory of a female who never cared nor understood him. The darkness consumed her as it once had him, but his eternal love had given him light and that was something Sabine would never understand.

"You know Sabine, my mate is mortal, and you could never understand the love she has shown me. I will love her until my dying day. She is mine for all eternity and you, just a speck in a dark and tortured part of my past."

As she slowly backed away from him, Sabine's eyes were filled with jealousy and hatred. He doubted Sabine would ever touch her, she knew his strength was much greater than hers, and he'd kill her without provocation if she started any trouble.

"Go, Sabine! And take a message with you. She is mine! You and yours come anywhere near her, I will kill you where you stand. I taught you all you know hellcat, and I know where you are weakest. I will take you down, without a backward fucking glance, and let you burn in the sun. Never let me see you again!"

Watching as she teleported from the alley, he saw her crouched above him on the tower across the street. She shouted to him, her words rang clear in his head.

"She will never tame your beast as I did, she is a mere mortal and she'll be terrified of the beast. She'll run from you Shade, if the beast doesn't kill her first."

As she teleported away, he stood stock-still, his worst fear spoken out loud from his former immortal lover. She knew him too well, for she could feel the fear that still lingered inside him, his greatest weakness. He fell to his knees and covered his face with his hands. *You are my strength Kate, and my greatest weakness.*

He had no idea how long he knelt there before he finally came to his senses, still struggling with all that had happened so fast with *bel*, and teleported back home. It had been a night of self-revelation, cleansing of the old, and fear of the future. He only knew he loved *bel*, and he was nothing without her and somehow, he must trust that her love for him was enough for her to stay.

***

Kate woke with a start and knew the bed is empty. She could feel his absence. "Lover?" He didn't respond, and the house was still and dark. "Shade?"

There was still no answer as she slipped from their bed and wandered from room to room, making sure the house was empty. She checked outside on the rear patio for that tell-tail glow of his cigarette, but she saw nothing. She walked back upstairs to their bedroom and stood in the middle of the floor as panic rushed through her. This wasn't like him, to leave her with no explanation. They'd argued again this evening, him pushing her away. What was their last conversation before she fell asleep?

The song, she played him the song about loving his dark side. But he had doubts that she'd stay once she saw the full extent of his darkness. What if he'd left for good? What if his doubts about her were so strong, he felt like the pain of ending their relationship now would be easier than waiting until they were even closer? *Oh please, lover! Please give me the chance to show you. How do I reach you? You said you'd always be here!* Tears flowed down her cheeks as sobs wracked her body. *I'm losing him.*

She wiped the tears from her face and took a deep breath. *How do I fight for him? How do I get through?* She stood still and cleared her head, allowed herself to reach out to him as he'd instructed her, tap into him, feel him, and find him. When she was able to quiet her mind, she could sense him. He was troubled. But he wasn't alone. She heard him talking to someone, but she couldn't hear their words. *Vampire*. He was talking to another vampire, she was about to sigh with relief when she was hit with another image. *Female!* He was with another female. Is that what he wanted? How did she compete with an immortal, when his biggest fear was to show her that side of himself? How did she reach him?

She moved from fear to anger in sixty seconds. *Beast? You want to see a beast?*

***

Teleporting back to the house, Shade was hit full force with her pain, and he wanted to rip something to pieces knowing he'd hurt her. This was his fault, she could feel him, and then his heart felt her jealousy and anger. *Damn it, Sabine!* He was shocked that she could feel things so clearly. It was a reminder to him that she'd taken his blood more than he realized, and her strength was quickly coming to her.

Going inside, he quietly walked upstairs to her, letting her feel him there, knowing she was working through a lot, and it was overwhelming to her. She turned as he entered their bedroom, and it just about broke him to see the look on her face, one that he never wanted to put there. He knew they were about to go ten rounds and he only prayed when it was done, they were still together.

"*Bel rosso*, I am here."

She jerked around to see him standing there and charged at him, slamming both fists into his chest. "Who is she? You leave our bed in the middle of the night? You leave our bed for her?"

He slid his hands around her slender waist, holding her in place. "Stop it, Kate! Stop this damn nonsense."

Slowly releasing his grip on her, he tried to get his emotions under control. He took deep breaths as he shook his head. "Please, give me a chance to explain, I did not seek her out. Do you doubt my love? What have I ever done to make you doubt me? What do I need to do to make you trust me? Damn it woman, tell me!"

"I'll stop when I understand why you left our bed in the middle of the night. I'll stop when I know who she is, and what she means to you. And what would you do, Shade Medici, if you woke to find me gone...and with another man? Something tells me that man would be dead by now, so don't tell me to stop! I don't doubt your love for me. I've never doubted your love for me. But I think you have doubts about mine, and those doubts are driving you away from me."

Pacing the floor, he ran his hand through his hair, feeling trapped. He couldn't find the words he needed to make her understand the fear that lay inside him. He lowered his head.

"I come to you broken, with fear of something so deep inside me that I can't breathe. I have no way to describe how I feel when I bring you pain, jealousy, anything to make you doubt any part of me. I am scared, so scared of something that could take you from me, make you too frightened to ever love me ever again. Please, let me explain her, and why I left here. I need to have a chance to explain calmly."

He watched her take a deep breath and relax her shoulders, releasing some of her anger.

"Then tell me why you left. I'll listen to what you have to say."

"Thank you. I am sorry, please forgive me, I never meant for things to play out as they did

They were not of my own accord. I...Sabine is..." Stopping suddenly, he knew he had to choose his words with care.

She pulled back from him slightly at the mention of her name, and she could feel her own back stiffen involuntarily. *Sabine?* She'd seen the photo of them together when he took her to Florence. The tall, exotic beauty he held in his arms, the intimacy displayed in that photo apparent to even the blindest eye. She knew this man had been with many women before her, both mortal and immortal, and that, in itself, brought insecurity. But even though she knew he loved her, it was still hard not to have a visceral reaction to the women she knew he'd been intimate with. After all, she knew what was in his heart, she had no idea what was in Sabine's, and this one came looking for him.

"I'm listening."

She allowed him to lead her to the chair by the bedroom window, where he sat down and pulled her into his lap.

"Sabine is from Florence. She came seeking me out. She had heard rumors of our mating. She came to..." He ran his hands over his face, "Hell, I don't honestly know what she came for."

He sighed heavily. "I was restless, and I went for air, that's all. I just needed to deal with things inside my head. She came looking for me. She is a just another warrior."

Kate looked at the anguish in his face. "She's a woman first and a warrior second. And she's not just another warrior. I saw the photo of the two of you together in Florence before you tore it up. And I have no doubts about what she came for. You don't think Sabine feels your restlessness? It breaks my heart. There's this void in you that you won't let me fill, and as long as that exists, I'll always be threatened by every immortal female who feels she can step in and take my place. Hear my words, Shade. I don't doubt your love. You doubt mine."

"I understand that now, *mi amore*, but do you understand if my beast lets go, he could kill you? I can't always control what happens, the beast is wicked, and it takes strength to calm him. I don't know what will happen, and it frightens me because I love you more than my own life. He might be fine when unleashed, and then again... You tempt him out of his mind. You drive me over the edge with wanting you, I can't stop thinking about you, and it's a constant. When he is released, I could not bear if anything happened to you at my own hand! The beast is evil, *bel rosso*, he is my wickedness, and you have seen nothing of him, nothing!"

"But is he not you? At his core, is the beast not you? Wouldn't the beast recognize me? Couldn't I call you back? How do I fight? This battle with the beast is pulling you away from me, Shade. Do you think I fear to stand before him? Because I don't! I embrace him, for the beast is you. I will lie at the feet of the beast."

"*Si*, I am the beast. And fighting him and taming him will be something I cannot teach you. I do not know what will curb his hunger for you. I have little control of him while he is out, but if you push him, I cannot honestly say how much I can control him. You are mortal. It takes much for him to come to the surface and you seem to have called to him immediately. He wants you, *mi amore*, he wants to claim you, to calm himself. I do not know how to explain this, I go into a different realm, and I become true evil, true vampire when he comes out. Blood will be his top priority. He will seek it like nothing you have seen. Please, you must wait longer, until you have taken more of my blood. It will help you with whatever he deems to do to you...*cazzo*! I sound like a raving lunatic and I am frightened for you."

"So where are we, lover? Am I supposed to get used to your restless wandering in the night, while your legion of female followers seeks you out to comfort you?"

Slamming his hand down on the arm of the chair, he rolled her off his lap and stood, pacing the floor.

"You know I love you. I did not ask for this or for her. Sabine is a warrior. She is a mercenary and came to the camp for training. She is a fucking hellcat, and one bitch to take in hand, but I did it. She did not stay with Medici. She was happier working solo, and she knows how to fight, and how to kill. She is at the top of her game right now. I also know her weakness and what will take her down. Yes, I fucked her, is that what you want to know? We stayed together for some time, she lived at Castello. She was my lover, but not like Adriana. Sabine brought out all that was dark and evil in me. She came here I am sure because she felt great changes in me. And you can bet she thought she could strut her hell back into my life and make you go away. That didn't happen, now, did it? Because I love you, you are my mate. Not her! So, if you think this will be a problem, yeah, it's going to be because I don't know what I am going to do. I could either lose you to the beast or lose you when I walk out of here because you can't deal with who I am and what I am. I just want to love you, I want you happy. You are the one who has my heart and soul."

Kate stood from where she's tumbled to the floor, her voice filled with exasperation. "Let's get one thing clear, Shade, because it's the thought that's in your head. It's the thought that drives you from our bed in the middle of the night. I'm not leaving. The doubt that nags at you is yours, not mine. I'm not leaving. Whatever this path reveals, I'll deal with, because I've chosen you, I love you. So, fuck the beast, and fuck your legion of females. You underestimate me, you underestimate my willfulness, my stubbornness, and my determination, but most of all you are underestimating my love for you."

He hung his head, "You think I underestimate your love for me?" He turned and left their bedroom, walking down the stairs and outside, to light up a smoke.

Her anger flared as he walked away, and she followed him outside and stormed up behind him like she'd unleashed all the demons of hell. "Seriously, did you not hear one word of what I just said? Don't walk away from me. Don't you dare walk away from me! Tell me what you want. Tell me what to do to get through to you. I love you, I'll never leave you. What is it you want from me? Tell me, and I will do it!

"Lover, if you think I'm the one who'll leave because of your darkness, then yes, you're underestimating me." She stabbed at his chest with her finger. "You're the one wandering in the night...not me. You're the one with doubt." She grabbed his shirt in both fists, shaking him. "Don't turn the tables, and don't run away from this. You're driving a wedge between us, and I won't let it end this way."

He remained silent as he leaned against the house smoking, his calmness only feeding her anger.

"Don't ignore me, Shade...This isn't going away. And I won't let you throw us away, do you understand?"

"*Si*, I heard every word you said. *Si*, I do wander the night and *si*, I think you might just take one look at my beast and the darkness and leave me."

Taking her hands in his, he looked deep into her eyes. "I need time to think about the beast and his capacity to kill and my capacity to control him. Tonight, I need to be alone and so do you, before we both say things we regret."

Kissing her hand, he disappeared, teleporting to the Dead House.

Her mouth is open as she stared at the empty space he'd just occupied. She was too numb to scream, too numb to cry. She turned and stumbled back across the yard and into the house. She closed the door and leaned her back against it because her knees felt weak and she was not sure she could walk much farther. *I'm losing him. I'm really losing him! How did this go so wrong?*

The tears started to fall down her cheeks, and she was wracked with sobs. She slid to the floor, where she wrapped her hands around her knees and let the tears flow freely. *Why is he making this so hard? Why can't he trust me to love him?* A million questions in her head and no answers, not one.

She pulled herself up from the floor, the house was deathly quiet. There were no songs playing for her tonight. No fire in the fireplace. What if he never came back? The very thought of it sent a wave of panic through her, and a fresh set of tears. She stumbled up the stairs, blinded by her own tears and looked at their bed. Was it only a few days ago they were playing in this room, him showering her with gifts, her teasing, him responding, teleporting her to California to see that house, and the progress she'd made? *How can we fall so far so fast? How do we fix this? How can he not know I'd do anything he asked?*

She felt so broken. She stepped into the bathroom to wash her tear-stained face and stared at her red eyes in the mirror. *I look like hell.* She left the bathroom and dropped her clothes behind her. She picked up his shirt, thrown casually across the bed, held it to her face and inhaled. Him...she could smell him. She put his shirt on, as this was as close as she'd get to him tonight, and a fresh wave of pain washed over her.

She pulled down the blankets from their bed and climbed under the cold sheets and blankets, and a big empty space beside her. The pain in her heart felt unbearable. *Can he even feel that? Can he feel what he's done? Lover, please!*

But there was no response from him tonight, not this night. She grabbed the pillow where he laid his head and hugged it to her, burying her face there and letting the tears flow again. She'd slept beside him all day, so sleep wouldn't come to her now, but she craved the escape that sleep would bring so she opened the drawer of the bedside table. She pushed aside the weird collection of weapons he'd left there, knives and something he calls shuriken's. She fumbled through pens and bookmarks, and assorted rubble to find that one bottle. Ah, there it was--Ambien. She rarely took them and hadn't touched one since Shade had come into her life, but she wanted that unconscious release from her pain. She needed to escape, so she took two, and swallowed them down before she could second guess her decision. She'd not eaten, and it didn't take long for the drug to hit her system. Within minutes, she was groggy, and she turned out the light and slid down in the bed, their bed, holding the pillow to her chest as she fell asleep.

***

She was awakened by a sound and she sat up in the bed. It was dead quiet. Did she hear something? Or dream something? She looked at the clock, she'd been sleeping for about two hours, and still felt the groggy pull of the drug. She was about to lay her head back down on the pillow when she heard it again. *Yes, footsteps!* Her heart was racing because she thought he had come home. He'd had time to cool off, and he was as miserable as she was. He wanted to climb back in their bed and hold her...kiss her...fix this mess they'd created.

"Lover, Is that you?"

She waited in silence, but he didn't answer her.

"Shade, please, I know we can fix this...."

She reached for the lamp on the bedside table and turned on the light as she swung her feet out of bed and started to stand, feeling a rush of dizziness from the pills. She steadied herself and turned to search for him and stopped dead in her tracks. Standing in the middle of the bedroom was Sabine, clad in leather, eyes red, fangs bared. Kate stumbled backward...was she really seeing this?

"Not who you were expecting?" Sabine stood with her legs spread, one hip out, and a wicked smile on her face.

Kate steadied herself on the bedside table, adrenaline flowing, her head clear now. "What do you want here?"

"Shade didn't tell you? He didn't tell you about me? We have a long history, Shade and me. And I just thought I'd stop in and see his latest mortal plaything."

Sabine was staring at Kate with such evil intent it sent a cold chill down her spine. Kate moved to the wall, and placed her back against it so, at least, Sabine couldn't get behind her.

Sabine laughed. "Clever move...pointless, but clever."

"I know who you are...you're Sabine. He told me about you." Kate kept her back pressed against the wall.

Sabine was laughing still, toying with her.

"Well, I doubt he told you *all* about me. Did he tell you how we fucked? Did he give you the dark and dirty details? How many times? How often? He's one nasty boy who plays with nasty toys. He loves delivering pain almost as much as he likes giving pleasure. You can't seriously think a mortal can satisfy the appetites of someone like Shade Medici, do you?"

Sabine was very slowly stepping closer to her, like a cat stalking a bird, as Kate slid along the wall, keeping her back plastered against the surface, working her way in the direction of the closet. She struggled to stay calm and keep a clear head. She was no match for Sabine. She'd seen Shade move so fast she couldn't see him, and she knew this vamp was capable of the same.

Kate snapped back at her, "I am not his plaything. We are mated."

Sabine hissed at her when she uttered the word mated and released a deep growl that made Kate want to drop to the floor. The look Sabine gave her was pure evil as she spit out her words.

"That is an abomination and a trick. He's royalty. Do you think you are deserving of royalty? He's a warrior, and look at you, cowering against the wall. A warrior needs a warrior, someone worthy to be his mate. You are a temporary distraction at best."

Kate's mouth was dry, and her throat felt like it was closing on itself. *How the fuck do I get myself out of this?* She continued to inch her way to the closet door, and Sabine stalked her like prey, moving ever closer to her.

"He loves me. He is mated to me!"

Sabine chuckled, "Really? Vampires do not love. They claim. They possess, and then they move on. So where is he then, if he loves you so much? Did he leave you a protector outside? I don't think so, my poor naïve mortal. He left you here alone, for me. I clean up his messes. I get rid of his playthings when he's had his fun."

Kate felt the cold panic in her veins. *Oh God...that can't be true. No, not true, he loves me. I know he loves me, oh please Shade...please.*

Just as Kate reached the doorway of the closet, Sabine crouched as if to launch herself at her, mouth open, fangs bared, eyes glowing and releasing a bone-shattering growl from her throat. Kate reached inside the closet door and grabbed the only weapon she knew how to use, the only weapon with no skill level required, a shotgun. As she pointed the gun in her direction, Sabine leaped at her. She fired the gun and felt the recoil as it knocked her to the floor, and she screamed for him at the top of her lungs.

"Shade!"

She'd closed her eyes with the jolt of landing hard on the floor and the anticipation of this she-beast ripping her throat out. She wasn't even sure if her shot hit the mark. Before she could open her eyes, she heard a different roar, louder, more guttural...more familiar. Her heart was beating out of her chest, and she was holding her breath as she looked from her position half in and half out of the closet door. She saw him, his back was to her. It was Shade, only not Shade. He was larger, more menacing. He had positioned himself between Kate and the she-beast, protecting her. He was screaming something at her in Italian, and they circled each other like boxers in a ring, both ready to spring.

As Shade turned, she saw that even his face was changed, the eyes brighter, the fangs longer. And she was in awe of him. *Kill her, Shade...please kill her!*

When the attack came, their actions were so swift Kate couldn't follow them; she could only listen as she heard wood splinter and glass break. But what she could see was the constant and never-ending splattering of blood...so much blood. *Kill her, Shade!*

Then Kate saw her, the she-beast. She'd broken away from him and was ready to pounce on her. Kate started to push herself back into the closet with her feet, but she was cornered here, and then there was another flurry of fighting that was so fast her eyes couldn't follow, until the headless body of the she-beast dropped across her legs, and Kate felt her face and chest spattered in Sabine's blood.

She felt the hot blood dripping from her face as she absorbed the reality. Dead, Sabine was dead. Kate looked up to see him standing before her...her beast, her master. He stood majestic, completely nude before her, covered in blood, hair matted, eyes blazing, and fangs dripping thick saliva, holding the head of the she-beast in his hand. She locked eyes with the beast. She dared not look away. He had to know she honored him, she respected him, but even more than that, she loved him.

She ran her hand down her face and chest until it was covered in the blood of the she-beast, and she held it out for him to see, palm out, facing him, and then held her hand to her mouth and licked Sabine's blood from her hand.

The beast roared and lifted the bitch's head in the air before grabbing her lifeless body and tossing both out the window to burn in the rising sun. Then he came to her, this man-beast, crouching before her as he pulled her into a protective embrace.

"I love you Shade," she whispered into his chest. "I'll love you forever."

His beast, now soothed, embraced her with honor. He was accepting her as she showed him no fear but only gratitude and love, taking the blood of his kill. As he cradled her, his beast refused to leave her alone, her words whispered softly against his bloodied chest as he lifted her in his arms. Walking to the shower, he willed on the candles and the warm water and stepped inside. Sitting her on her feet, he never let his hands leave her. He pulled her into his chest, as he wrapped his arms around her waist and the beast spoke to her, his voice raspy and low.

"Lift your head to the water, wash away her stench. Let her very existence run down the drains to hell. She will never touch you again, you belong to me. You are mine!"

As the water ran red, it rinsed away all the pain and confusion between them as well, and he leaned down into her neck and licked her vein, the sound of her blood pumping and encouraging him. Shade could no longer rein in the beast, and he didn't want to, this was who he was, and he trusted her, loved her, and knew she'd never turn from him now. Sliding his tongue into her ear, his breath hot, he whispered, "I need you."

His cock ached to have her, his body screamed for her blood, he was weak from the fight, and all he wanted was *bel*. "Feed me."

She tilted her head back and freely exposed her neck to him.

"Drink...And feel my love flow through your veins."

Before the words left her mouth, he struck the vein and took her blood, feeling it fill him. His heart began to beat normally, his body relaxed, and he drew deeper, swallowing her love and how much she gave to him unconditionally. Shade felt the beast was tamed, and knew for now, he needed no more. He was satisfied and wouldn't push her beyond her already shattered state this night. Taking one last draw of her blood, he licked the wound clean and held her close in his arms. He was loved, his beast was loved, and the fear was gone from him.

As the beast retreated, Shade picked her up and carried her downstairs to the living room and willed a blazing fire. Snuggling her to his chest, he pulled the heavy throw from the sofa and lay them down on the rug in front of the fireplace, and then pulled the throw over them. He laid his head on top of hers. He had no words.

Kate was exhausted from the fear, from that nightmare that appeared in their bedroom, from the arguments that had kept them both on edge and unable to connect, from the worry about whether she'd lost him. She sighed with relief and nuzzled her face into his chest.

"One thing, lover...Life with you will never be boring."

Shade felt her relax into him. "Kate, before I can even begin to say all the things I want to say, I need to know if you are hurt."

"I'm fine, really. I fell hard on my ass when I pulled the trigger on that shotgun, but other than that, I'm fine. She never touched me, thanks to you."

He shook his head, "Speaking of that shotgun, where in the hell did you learn to shoot a shotgun? I thought you knew nothing of weapons. Granted, you did not kill her, but it bought you time. *Cazzo, bel rosso*, a shotgun?" He chuckled as he rubbed her back.

"When I was living in the condo, everyone said I should have a gun in the house for protection since I lived alone. I didn't know how to shoot a gun. I'd never shot a gun before. But I figured my aim wouldn't have to be that great with a shotgun, so that's what I bought. I just stuck it in the closet when I moved here and forgot about it, until tonight. I had no idea it would knock me on my ass!"

"*Bel*, a shotgun is much too big for you. We need to find something a bit smaller with less recoil. I will help you." He kissed the top of her head. "I am sorry. I am sorry for my words, leaving you alone, letting you suffer through what you have. You did not deserve this treatment, I hope you know this. Tell me what I can do to make this up to you. There is nothing in this world I won't do for you Kate, name it and it is yours."

"Lover...you're here, that's all I need. You were here when I needed you most. We were locked in a struggle, you and I, and neither of us could get through to each other. We're both stubborn, so we should probably prepare ourselves for the fact this won't be the last time we butt heads. But please, don't leave me in anger again. I was certain I'd lost you, and that is a pain I cannot bear."

"The beast came out, you saw him, faced him. He loves you, my fears were for nothing. You were right all along, and I will never doubt you again. How did you know? I saw the way you looked at him, you charmed him immediately. He will return again, *mi amore*. I cannot put him away. His lives inside me and you tempt him beyond anything I ever felt. But I no longer fear when he comes out, and I will let him come. I think now I can control him much better because I know in my soul, you love him as you do me."

He willed music for her, for them, and Eva Cassidy sang *"Songbird"*.

"I love the beast, Shade, because the beast is you. I saw the darkness the first time I saw you and I was drawn to it. I saw the pain, and the loneliness, it was like looking into a bottomless black hole filled with pain and hurt. Instead of being afraid of you, I was drawn to you. My heart called out to you, and I knew to love you meant I'd have to look into that bottomless black pit, and face whatever was there. I was intimidated by you in the beginning, not your darkness, lover...never the darkness, but by your worldliness, your experience. I felt out of my league with you, and sometimes still do. I worry if I'll be enough. Because I want nothing more than to please you, so be patient with me. Show me, teach me, and lead me."

"My sweet *bel*, you fill that loneliness, you make me whole. No one has ever been able to do that. You need never worry *mi amore*, you feed my appetites in all areas, you constantly distract me, I will never stop wanting and needing you. I will love you for eternity, you are my addiction."

Pulling her up to his lips, he kissed her softly at first, and then deepened his kiss. Breaking the kiss, he threw his head back. "Ah, you see, addiction!"

He felt her hand slide up his chest and along his neck, and he trembled from the mere touch of her. "*Mi more*, take my vein, take my strength, my love, my power. Let me love you as only I can."

"Addiction, good word, for I'm also addicted to you. Will this fire ever burn out, or will it just consume us both on some night of wild passion. I'm hoping for option two."

He closed his eyes and cringed. She was closer to the truth than she knew.

She pushed his hair aside and ran her finger along the vein. She could feel his body respond to her touch, and he invited her to take his vein. She leaned into him, her hair falling across his face, and ran her tongue along the length of the vein. She kissed his neck and gently sucked his skin into her mouth before she bit down hard. She was balanced over him with her hands on the floor on either side of his head, her mouth locked to him. As soon as his blood hit her, she felt the heat building between her legs, that delicious rush that only came when she fed from him. She pushed her hips into him and felt the rigid hardness of his cock pushing back as she felt his arms encircle her and pull her closer. She continued to draw his blood into her mouth, and she could hear his moans over her own.

She dropped her weight to her elbows, so her hands were free to grab his hair, and she gripped his head in her hands as she sucked harder and felt him arch his neck to her. What started as foreplay for her–the biting and feeding–had now become a need. She needed his blood inside her almost as much as he needed hers. She made herself pull away from him because the taste of him filled her with a pleasure this mortal girl had never known. She looked at him, his eyes half-closed and lost in his own world of pleasure, and lowered her mouth onto his lips, sharing the blood in her mouth with him.

Lying on top of him, she positioned her hips to slide onto his cock, aching to have him buried deep inside her.

With his eyes locked on hers, he gripped her hair in both hands, and her body began that sweet rhythm. She felt him arch his hips up, penetrating deeper and his moans joined with hers in their own lullaby to each other. She sat upright and straddled him, leaned back, stretching her arms out behind her, and grabbing his thighs. He rose up on his elbows and watched as his cock slid in and out of her. It was so beautiful to see their bodies joined in passion. This was what she wanted. Him, she wanted him, to feel him inside of her. She was staring into his eyes and could feel his love for her, his burning desire for her. She moved her hips in unison with his. She loved riding him like this, on top, where she could move freely and control him. She grinded her hips on him even harder, and could feel his cock throbbing inside of her and knew he was close.

"Lover!" she screamed out as she felt him cum, gripping his legs with her nails digging deep, and felt her own release. Their mutual pleasure came in wave after wave, spasm after spasm, until they were both gasping for air. He reached for her, and pulled her upright, and she fell forward in his arms and onto his chest, where both their hearts were pounding furiously against each other. Covered in their own sweat, they laid in silence as their breathing and hearts resumed a normal pace.

"Addiction," Kate whispered, "sweet addiction."

"*Si, mi amore*," he answered, "*dolce dipendenza*."

43

Waking from his death slumber, Shade took a moment to orient himself. His sweet *bel* lay curled up next to him, her arm across his chest. He remembered picking her up and carrying her to one of the guest bedrooms after they made love in front of the fire. Their own bedroom had been destroyed by the battle between his beast and Sabine. He closed his eyes as the memories flooded through his brain. He could have lost her. He realized in his desire to protect her from his world he left her more vulnerable. He knew what he had to do, and he's hoping she's ready for the adjustment to her lifestyle, again. He looked at Kate with her head on his shoulder, her red hair falling across her face, her soft breath on his chest. He reached down and brushed back her hair, and gently caressed her cheek. Her eyelids fluttered before they opened, and she looked up at him and smiled.

"*Mi amore*, we must talk."

She ran her hand over his chest. "About last night?"

"*Si*, last night. I was foolish to think I could protect you from my world by keeping you here in this house. Because you are not vampire I thought I could keep the darkness that makes up much of my world from entering the house. But I misjudged. I will not make that mistake again."

Kate rose up on her elbow. "You're not sending me away!"

"No, *bel*. My love for you, my bond with you, I am afraid your loss would be more than I could bear, although you would be safer without me in your world. We are going back to Florence. You will pick from my warriors a protector."

Kate furrowed her eyebrows. "A protector? I don't understand. You're my protector."

"*Si*, when I am with you, *bel rosso*. But look at how often I am away. I will always feel you, hear you, as you are bonded to me. And while I am able to teleport to you, the further I am away, the longer it takes. I cannot take the risk. Most masters who are warriors will have protectors for their mates. It is a high honor for a warrior to be selected to protect what is most precious to his master."

Kate sat upright in the bed, pulling the sheet around her shoulders to ward off the chill. "But, what does he do, this protector?"

"He will live here, in this house. If I am away, his job is to be with you. It does not limit you. He can be as visible or invisible as you want. If you need to go somewhere, he goes along. After last night...well, I cannot leave you unguarded again. I am not asking you, I am telling you, this is something I must do, and I need you to accept this."

Kate shrugged. "So, he's like a bodyguard then."

"*Si*. In your mortal world, you would call him a bodyguard. I think you will find he is more. That is why you must choose. We will go to Castello. I will select from my best warriors, and you will choose among them. A protector will stay with you for life. He will be an extension of our *familia*. Understand?"

Kate remembered the ice-cold fear in her veins as she turned on the light and saw Sabine standing in their bedroom. Their estate was isolated, and the idea of a protector didn't seem like a bad idea.

"I understand."

"Good, then let's get this done. Get dressed, and get something to eat, and then we will leave for Florence. I will call Alec and let him know I have to go back for a few days and tell Tomas to manage things at the Dead House while I'm gone."

Kate slid from the bed in the guest bedroom and walked back into their bedroom and stopped abruptly. The furniture was destroyed, the window shattered where the beast tossed Sabine to burn in the sun, the carpet and walls were splattered in blood. She stepped over the wreckage and headed to the walk-in closet. The shotgun was still lying on the floor. She pulled the nightgown over her head and dressed in jeans, a sweater, and knee-high boots as a shiver ran up her spine. She left the bedroom and closed the door behind her. She'd deal with this mess later. Heading down the stairs to the kitchen, she heard Shade in his office, making calls.

Kate grabbed a pear as she waited for the coffee to brew, the aroma from the freshly ground beans wafting through the room. She was pouring the hot brew into a mug when Shade walked in. "Will we be gone long?"

"No, two, three days, maybe. You will select a protector, and since we have the staff quarters completed, I can also bring back staff to help run the house."

She sipped at the hot coffee. "Do you think we need staff?"

"*Si*, I will bring Gi with me, my man-servant. You recall meeting him, *si*? And Reynaldo, he is the chef at Castello. When I lived at Castello we would entertain, we invited mortals there, and Reynaldo prepares all the food. And a housemaid, I think. Theresa has been with our family the longest. It would be a promotion for her to go from being one of many to being in charge of Bel Rosso."

Kate was silent as he shared this new information. "Lover, I thought I was in charge of Bel Rosso?"

"Oh *si*! You are in charge. The staff works for you. What is wrong, *bel*? I can read your face that you are not pleased?"

"I don't want to sound ungrateful, but I'm wondering what I'll do? I mean, if we have staff, what's left for me to do?"

"*Bel*, there is much to do. You have the renovations to complete, the gardens in the spring, the staff is here to help you. It is how I grew up. They are discreet. They will live in the staff quarters, they are not underfoot. Did you see them when you were at Castello? No. And yet there are about fifty people working at Castello. Please, do not worry." He pulled her into his arms. "It will be fine. And you will not be alone here. You will come to love them as I love them, *si*?"

"And what if I don't...love them."

"*Bel*, will you give this some time? Will you give them one year? If you are not happy with things in a year, then I will keep Gi and your protector here, and send the others back to Florence. Vampires are safer living within their coven. The numbers will be small compared to my coven in Florence, but as the estate grows, and the vineyards expand, we will need the help and protection of a coven. Will you give me that, *mi amore*?"

"That's fair."

"Good, now come. Hold onto me. There is much to do."

He held her close as she laid her head on his chest and they teleported inside Castello. He sat her down inside his bedroom. "You remember my room?"

"I'll never forget this room, lover. It is where I first fed from you."

"I need to arrange a few things for the interview process with the warriors, check in with my staff, and let them know we have arrived. Will you be fine here?"

"Yes, I'll be okay. I'll just stretch out on the bed and rest while you're gone...jet lag...or teleport lag. It makes me a little dizzy."

She sat on the bed and looked around this room, and noticed the large oil painting of Adriana had been removed.

He chuckled as he kissed the top of her head. "You will get used to it, I promise. Don't wander, please. I don't want you to get lost. Now listen to me. There is a walk-in closet over there. It has been filled with clothes, shoes, jewelry, everything in your size. You can use my bathroom. The top drawer on the left is filled with your favorite things...perfumes, bath salts, and make-up. You are now lady to the master, and you will need to present yourself as such. My warriors will definitely be checking you out."

Kate walked to the closet which looked like he emptied every designer shop in Italy. "How should I dress? What should I wear to meet your staff, and for the interview?"

"Not formal. Not casual. Something in between, perhaps." He kissed her softly. "I must go. There are things to arrange. I will be back shortly. Just call, I will come if you need me."

Kate was looking through the closet at the seemingly unlimited options, "Take your time, lover. This dress selection may take a while."

"One other thing, *bel*, the staff here, the warriors, they will all address you as 'my lady.' That is your correct and respectful title. If anyone refers to you as Kate, they will lose their head, for that is disrespectful to you and me."

"My lady? Seriously?"

He chuckled at her response. "You will get used to it. Now I must go. Enjoy your new luxuries."

He kissed each cheek before turning and walking out of the room and downstairs to find Gi and Marco to get this show on the road.

After setting up the meetings, Shade had met with Marco, his Second-In-Command inside the warrior camp to help select the five warriors who were candidates for the role of protector. He had reviewed their performance history with Marco, as well as their skill levels, and selected only his best warriors. All of them were raised in the Medici camp and were loyal to Medici. He had given the five warriors their instructions, and he knew Gi had the conference room prepared. All was ready to go, he just hoped *bel* was up to this and could choose from the five he'd selected for her protector. Before he headed back to Castello to begin the interviews, he had one more piece of business to attend to.

"Marco, tell me about Cory. He is fitting in, *si*?"

Marco beamed at him. "Shade, I have to admit, I had my doubts about this one. You have sent me some straggly pups over the years, and this one was one sad specimen when he arrived. Never seen such a scrawny vampire before. But he took to the feeders, and Reynaldo made sure he was eating human food as well, and he looks like a healthy mortal now. He has been working hard. The warriors were skeptical at first, but I expected that. He made custom leathers for Luca and Marcello, which made all the others get in line. And Raven? Not sure giving Raven the option for custom leathers is a good idea, *fratello*. He looks like a fucking magician instead of a warrior." Marco shook his head.

Shade laughed out loud as an image of Raven flashed through his head. That vampire always had a flare for the dramatic. "Little fucker is fast though, got to give him that. Hell, I don't care what he wears as long as he gets the job done. And where is Cory now? Where did you set him up?"

Marco pointed in the direction of the barracks. "He bunks with the warriors, but he has his own workshop in that room on the end. Easy to find, it's the building with the warriors standing in line, waiting for him to take their measurements."

Shade slapped Marco on the back and headed out to check on Cory. The warriors standing outside Cory's workshop saw Shade approach and all stood at attention. He nodded at them, telling them at ease, and entered the crowded workspace. Cory had stacks of quality leather, purchased from the best shops in Florence, mostly in black and brown, but he saw a few stacks of bright colors. Cory was busy taking measurements on one of the warriors and recording everything in a book. He had an industrial sewing machine and a large work table with handmade patterns stacked to the side, and the instruments of his trade scattered about. Cory looked up in surprise when Shade entered, and the warrior stood at attention. Shade dismissed the warrior, asking to have some privacy with Cory. The warrior quickly exited, and Shade took a chair, kicking another chair out for Cory.

"Take a seat, son. Tell me how things are going for you."

"Master, I can't even tell you how much I love it here. I stay busy all night. Every warrior here wants custom leathers. And I do repairs for them as well. I have a feeder. I could never afford a feeder at home, and most of the street kids were as malnourished as I was, so feeding from them did little to sustain me. I would hunt, but I was never really trained to hunt, so that was not always successful. No one feeds from me now. I did as you commanded."

Shade reached out and put his hand on Cory's shoulder. "I am proud of you, son. Marco says you are doing well, and the warriors accept you here. You have any problems, you call me, understood?"

Cory beamed at him, glowing in his praise. "Yes, master. I don't know how I'll ever repay you. For the first time, I feel like I'm part of a family."

Shade smiled at him. "You repay me by working hard, changing your life, upholding Medici values. You look good Cory, healthier, stronger. Now, I have other business to take care of."

The boy was still frail by vampire standards, but he'd clearly put on weight, his color not so pallid and the dark circles were gone from beneath his brown eyes. His dark hair still hung long and shaggy, but not unkempt. His face was still boyish and slightly feminine in appearance, making him more pretty than handsome.

Shade stood, giving him a bear hug and a couple of hard pounds on his back with his closed fist before turning to leave.

Cory stood in the doorway of his workshop as he watched his benefactor stride back across the training field in the direction of Castello, feeling affection for the man that picked him off the street and most likely saved his life.

Shade headed back to Castello. He needed to go over a few things with Kate before they began these interviews. Heading into the bedroom, he called out for her and laughed to himself. Clothes were strewn everywhere, and it looked as though a tornado had gone through.

"*Bel*, where the hell are you?"

Kate called out from the closet. "I'm almost ready! I think I tried on every dress. I'm so nervous, I hope this is appropriate. I was unsure of what you wanted."

She had chosen a simple but classic red sheath dress with a scalloped hemline, black patent leather heels, and a pair of ruby and diamond earrings.

"Just come out, *mi amore*, I am sure you will be fine."

Kate stepped from the closet, her hair down, her make-up done, wearing his favorite red. "Is this okay? I can change if you don't like it."

"*Bel*, you look beautiful!"

Kate sighed in relief. "Now please, tell me what to do. I'm so nervous."

He walked to her, sliding his hands around her waist and kissing her softly. "I am going to give you some instruction. I have chosen five warriors to meet with you, like an interview more or less. I have already drilled them on their responsibilities. You need not worry about such. I wish for you to get to know them. Get a feel for them. You will meet them one at a time and then make a decision. It is a very high honor for them. I am not only master here, but one of the few remaining royal bloodlines in the vampire community. To be selected as your protector is the highest honor that can be bestowed upon a warrior, but also, you must be able to get along with him, trust him. Go with your instinct, I will approve any of the five you chose. It is important to me you like him. I think if you go with your gut, you will make a great choice. Understand?"

Kate bit at her lip. "What do I ask them? I don't know anything about warrior skills."

He smiled down at her. "Has nothing to do with their skills. I have all of that covered. I have selected only my best warriors as candidates. Ask them about themselves, if they have family, what they like to do, if they like music. Find out who they are, you will be spending much time with whoever you select. Relax, please. They will be much more intimidated by you than vice versa."

Kate looked surprised. "Intimidated by me? I doubt that. But I think I know what you're asking of me. You'll stay with me, of course?"

"*Si*, at least until one of them is appointed. Now come, we must go, they wait for us."

Taking her arm, he led her down the long marble hallways and felt all eyes on them. None of the staff was visible, but he felt them watching from their hidden perches to get their first glimpse of his mate. He puffed out his chest, his stride was strong, and he felt like he would burst with pride at the beauty on his arm.

Kate's heart was beating fast as she allowed him to lead her through these hallways. She felt like the one being interviewed. Thank goodness he was with her. She drew strength from him. He was confident, in his element, and it showed. She'd try and mirror his confidence. She held her head up high and tried to keep up with his bold stride through this palace.

As they approached the conference room, Gi was standing by. Kate remembered his kind face from her first visit.

"Good Evening Gi, you, of course, remember my mate, Katherine?" Shade released her arm and placed his hand lightly on the small of her back, watching as Gi bowed low and smiled at her.

"It is a great honor, my lady, to have you back within the walls of Castello. We are all pleased to see our master so happy and we wish to be of the utmost service to you while you are here. Please call upon me personally if there is anything you need."

"Kate, Gi is the majordomo here, head of my house and the entire working staff. He served my *padre* in his younger days and has seen me grow to be the vampire I am today. I have already spoken to Gi today to inform him that he will be coming back to Virginia with us, and he is to select from the house staff someone to take over his position here."

Kate smiled warmly at him. "Gi, may I call you Gi? I only saw you briefly when we were here before. I look forward to hearing more about your time with Shade growing up. Something tells me you will have more than a few stories to tell."

Shade observed her as she took his manservant in stride, he could feel her relax. He could tell she liked Gi. They'd get along fine, and he'd make her life much easier and more comfortable when he returned with them to Bel Rosso. Gi opened the conference room door for the both of them, and Shade led her inside.

Kate stepped into the massive room, turning her head in all directions to take it in. "This is your conference room? This room is huge!"

The long room was filled with a massive oval conference table polished to a high sheen that would easily seat fifty people. But most impressive of all were the walls. Each of the four walls had been painted in frescoes depicting Florence or the Tuscan countryside. She walked over to the walls and saw a signature in the corner. She squatted down for a closer look...Vasari. A painter from the Renaissance period and he was here, in this room, painting these walls. Kate realized that even among art historians, this work existed here unknown and unseen by the mortal world. She stood and turned to look at him.

Shade smiled widely, knowing she recognized the artist. "The murals are very old, and many historic things have been decided in this room. Now, I have young warriors ready to meet you. So, come, let me settle you down, and I will call in the pups."

He took her hand and led her to a chair at the head of the huge table, pulling it out for her and making sure she was comfortable. Leaning down, he kissed her softly.

"Relax. They are just vampires, like me. Are you ready?"

She looked into those blue eyes. "Vampires like you? Hardly like you, lover. But I'm ready, nervous but ready."

As they went through the interviews, four of his warriors had passed through, and he was impressed with Kate. She'd made him proud and he loved her elegant and composed demeanor. She had relaxed a little and he let her take the lead after the introductions. He had yet to get a feel from her that she'd connected in a positive way with any of the candidates and there was one she clearly didn't like at all. He had to hold back his laugh. He'd saved Luca, his personal choice for her, for last.

Calling in Luca, Shade watched as he strolled in and nodded his head to his master. Then he went to Kate, knelt at her side, took her hand, and kissed it lightly. Luca told her he was most honored to meet her before standing, waiting for Shade's command.

"Luca, my beautiful mate has some questions she wishes to ask of you. As always, I expect you to answer them honestly. " Shade smiled at Kate. "You have the floor, *bel rosso*."

Kate took a deep breath. This process had been exhausting. She wasn't sure what she was supposed to be looking for. She wondered what she was supposed to see in these men to make her think they were the best choice for serving as her protector. Shade knew these men. He could just choose someone for her. She really didn't feel a connection to any of them, if that was what was supposed to be happening. There was only one left, and she'd be glad to get through it. The last warrior entered the room and Shade introduced him as Luca.

Kate sensed something in him immediately. This warrior was different. She could see that he felt more at ease with Shade. He deferred to Shade, as was proper, but held his own. He came to her side, knelt, and took her hand. She wasn't used to all the formal greetings and thought this would take some time to get used to. There was something in his eyes. Kate sensed warmth in him and a real affection for Shade, but there was something else in his eyes, something that said, 'Don't fuck with me.' This was a warrior who relished in being a warrior, just like Shade. This was a warrior who never backed away from a fight, and while she knew he had no real sense of loyalty to her yet, she felt the depth of his loyalty to Shade and knew he'd do anything for Shade, including protecting her.

"Luca, please, take a seat. You make me quite nervous looming over me." She smiled as he nodded and took a seat at the table. "*Si*, my lady."

"Luca, do you live here in Florence? Do you have a family? A wife, or mate?"

"*Si*, my lady, I was born just outside Florence in a small town called Empoli, but I have lived in the warrior camp since I was a boy of ten and have been here my entire life, although, as you know, warriors travel extensively. We go where we are ordered. As for family my lady, I have one cousin who is here in the camp, and no, I am not mated."

His voice was soft, and his accent was thick. "I only ask, because as I'm sure Shade has explained, we're living in the U.S. currently, in Virginia. So, you'd be away from Florence for much of the time. I was concerned you'd feel isolated being away from your family."

"No, my lady, I'm quite used to living where I'm assigned. It's a warrior's life."

"I, uh, I hesitate to ask, Luca. But you know I'm mortal? I've been led to understand that mortal mates are not seen as appropriate choices for a master. Does that...bother you at all?"

"No, my lady. You are my master's mate. He trained me. I have studied under him since I was ten, all my skills as a warrior, I attribute to him. It would be my honor to serve him, and you."

"Oh, I had no idea Shade had trained you. Well, that makes a difference, doesn't it?"

"It does to me, my lady. He is my family. I was born to be a warrior, but not all warriors can get into the Medici camp. It was my father's dream for me, to be a Medici warrior. Shade took me in when my father died."

Kate now understood the bond between these two men and knew it would never be broken.

"Luca, I'll be honest with you, I'm new to this world, your world of vampires. Shade is teaching me, but I still have much to learn. Shade has explained you're a day-walker. I try to coordinate my schedule to Shade's as much as possible, including sleeping during the day when he's at home. We're in the process of furnishing two homes, one in

Virginia, and one in California and that takes a lot of coordination. As I understand it, you'd be required to go with me whenever I leave the house."

"Yes, my lady. I assure you, my presence will be as visible or as invisible as you require it as you go through your day. There are times when my physical presence can act as a deterrent in itself, and other times when I know you will want your privacy. I'll be close at hand, and aware of everything taking place around you, but you won't see me unless I'm called upon."

"Luca, this is a very serious question."

"Yes, my lady?"

"Can you drive a stick shift?"

"Excuse me, my lady?"

"Well, it seems Shade has bestowed upon me a Jaguar I can't drive, so I was wondering, can you drive a stick shift?"

Luca bit his lip to suppress a laugh. "Yes, my lady, I assure you, I can drive a stick shift. I'll be happy to take you wherever you need to go, we can teleport, or I can teach you how to drive a stick shift if you prefer."

Kate placed both hands palm down on the table. "Well good, that's one problem solved."

Shade laughed loudly as he shook his head. "*Bel bosso*, you continue to surprise me." Leaning in, he kissed her softly, and she felt her cheeks burn, knowing her blush was visible.

Luca was startled by his master's sudden outburst of laughter. He'd never heard his master laugh before, and he watched the exchange between his master and his mate, and the love they held for each other in their eyes, his kiss, and her blush. He'd been aware his master was holding her hand beneath the table. This was a side of his master he'd never seen before. He sensed his master's protectiveness over her and understood how important this role of protector would be to his master.

"My last question Luca, since I understand you'll be living inside our home, do you like music?"

"Yes, my lady, I love music."

"But Luca, do you like music twenty-four hours a day? Because we play music all the time, sometimes it even plays when we sleep."

"That should not be a problem for me, my lady."

"But Luca, it's not always soft and soothing music. It turns into the head-bangers ball in that house."

Luca had heard Shade's playlist before. "You mean like Shinedown, Foo Fighters, Skillet, and classic AC/DC, my lady?"

For the first time, he dared to smile during the interview. She smiled back at him and turned to Shade. "I think I have asked all the questions I need to ask."

Standing, Shade reached his hand out to Luca. "Thank you, Luca. We shall make a decision and I will let you know as soon as I have had time to share my *bel rosso*'s thoughts. Anything you wish to ask or add?"

Luca shook his hand and turned to Kate. "My lady, I am honored to be asked to have this opportunity to serve you. I wish to thank you, even if I'm not chosen. And my best wishes to you and master for a loving eternity together."

As Luca bowed and retreated, Shade pulled out *bel*'s chair and took her into his arms, hugging her tight. "You did fine, Kate."

"I'm glad that's behind us. I was nervous. So, what are your thoughts?"

"Kate, my thoughts are not of importance at this moment. It is your choice to make. If you do choose one of them, and they do not work out, it will look bad upon them. I can wiggle them out of it, but the sting and failure will remain with them for the rest of their lives, so do not take this lightly. If you do not like any of them, we will begin with another round until you feel a connection. *Si*?"

"If you're asking me which warrior I was most impressed with, and the warrior I feel will fit into our lives and best serve us, then I'd have to say that is clearly Luca. His loyalty to you is evident. I saw it as soon as he entered the room."

Cocking his head, he looked at her. "*Bel*, Luca is close to me. He was trained by me personally. His loyalty to me and this family is like none other. But I needed you to see that, I needed you to make this choice, the two of you must get along, must trust each other."

He paced back and forth, "He has earned this honor, and if you do not choose him, you will not hurt me, so please do not pick him because he is close to me. I will find something for him suitable here in Florence. His *padre* served my own. And when his *padre* was killed, I promised him before his death I would look after Luca. He has worked hard and steadfast to be a good warrior and he is damn good, he will serve you well, he is loyal, and I have no doubts he will give his life for either of us."

"Lover, I already trust him. He has such deep respect for you, he looks up to you, it shows in his face. It's clear he's already extended that umbrella of loyalty to those you love."

"Speak the words, *mi amore*. Is Luca your choice?"

"Yes, Luca is my choice."

Picking her up, he hugged her and spun her around. *"Ti amo! Grazie!"* Kissing her face all over, he was overjoyed. "Let us go change and then we shall go tell Luca the good news, *si*?"

"Change? What do you want me to wear now? I left all my clothes strewn on the floor."

"Well, where we will find Luca, you will not make it far in those heels. They are on the training field, a place inside the warrior camp that is designed for the warriors to train. They will be at sword practice at the moment. They have their barracks there, and most live there if they do not have mates. I believe you may want to change, perhaps into some jeans?"

"Jeans! That I can manage. And some flat shoes. Can you help me find our bedroom? If you send me back unescorted, I have no idea where I'll end up."

"Oh *si*! I will take you there. And I think I should change into some leathers and boots." Picking her up, he teleported them right into the bedroom.

Shade had Gi bring a small snack for Kate to eat while they were changing, and he convinced her to wear some boots instead of flats, before they headed out for the training field. He was conscious that she'd not seen much of the place, and he led her through some of the formal gardens as they walked along outside. He watched as her eyes grew large at the size of the place, and how much land it covered. The Medici Castello was well known in Florence. Holding her hand, he felt happy here, something he hadn't felt in a very long time.

"So, what do you think, *mi amore*? Do you like it here in Florence? I know it is not Paris, but I hope you can think of this as your home now as well."

"Shade, this...palace. I had no idea it was so large. It's beautiful, and you know I love Italian architecture. I've visited Italy, and I loved it. Florence is my favorite city in Italy. I'd seen this castle from a distance on the Arno before. I could never have imagined that, someday, it would be my home. But my home is wherever you are, Shade."

He squeezed her hand. "And my heart is wherever you are, *bel*. You shall have whatever you wish here. The house, the gardens, they are all yours."

As they got closer to the field, the clanging of swords became louder, and it sounded like music to his ears. The cheers and cursing were also loud and cut through the sound of the swordplay. Looking over at her, he smiled and stopped.

"*Bel*, my warriors are a bit gruff but respectful, so I ask that you excuse whatever you hear before we get there since they do not know we are coming."

She laughed softly. "I'm sure I've heard it all before. I think I'll be fine."

Taking her hand, he led her around the blockade of towers that housed his warriors and onto a huge field. They stood at its edges, viewing the activities. There were about fifty warriors fighting with swords, sparing, and working out, some doing acrobatics in the air as vampires do when fighting. Shade stood with his arms crossed and said nothing, letting her take it all in. One by one, the warriors became aware of his presence and laid down their swords, standing at attention.

"You have trained all these warriors?"

"*Si*, I trained them, along with my Second-In-Command, Marco, since I travel all over the world. But in my youth, I spent my days and nights as they do now, living as a warrior in training. Now come, we have a task at hand, and a very important one."

Taking her hand, he led her onto the field. Positioning her in front of him, he stood behind her, his hands upon her shoulders, his pride bursting.

"My brothers in arms, at ease! You are looking well this night. Your master is pleased with your progress. I wish to present to you my mate, Katherine. You will show her the respect that is her due. You will show her what Medici warriors are made of, not only strength and honor, but integrity."

As each warrior went down on one knee and bowed their head before her, his heart roared with pride, for these were his legion, this was his destiny and they accepted her as their own.

"Kate, my warriors are honoring you with this gesture. You may ask them to rise and they will, and then I will call forth those we saw today, *si*? Speak loud and clear. This is what you should say...*Sorgere guerrieri di* Medici!"

She did her best to imitate the words he spoke, and called out to the warriors, "*Sorgere guerrieri di* Medici!" She had no idea what she had said...Charge the barracks, for all she knew.

He smiled at her thoughts. **"You just said, 'Arise warriors of Medici!"** He watched as they each stood, legs spread and hands behind their backs, and it pleased him. He'd done what he'd been taught to do, bring forth the Medici warriors into the new century. "You did well, *mi amore*, but we do need to work on your Italian."

Calling out each of the candidates for her protector by name, he asked them to step forward. "I thank each of you for your loyal service. You were hand-selected by me for consideration as my lady's protector because you represent the highest standards of a Medici warrior. I have asked my lady to choose a protector from amongst you this night and she has made her decision. Luca step forward!"

As he approached, Shade noticed Luca caught her eye and smiled softly. Luca stood before her in his leather garb and went down on one knee, took her hand and kissed it lightly. ***"Mi amore*, your protector is before you, you are required to do nothing at this moment. Just watch what happens and I will instruct you."**

Taking her hand, Shade led her to the block containing many swords. "*Bel*, you must pick one of these swords, we must honor Luca in front of the others as is his due. I know you are nervous, but you must carry it back to him. I will then proceed with the ceremony and help you. It is not difficult, bear with me."

She looked at the block that contained numerous swords of different lengths and designs,
and removed one from the pile.

Taking her hand, he led her back to Luca where he remained kneeling. Shade stood behind her and wrapped his arms around her as they gripped the sword together, his hands on top of hers. Luca bowed his head. **"Just watch and move your hands with mine."**

"Luca, warrior of Medici, as your master, I honor you with the title of protector to my mate. You shall, from this night forward, give your life to her as if she were your own, honoring me and my mate."

Taking the sword, he raised it above their heads and then lowered it slowly, tapping Luca first on the left shoulder. "Your heart belongs to her."

Raising the sword again, they lowered it together and tapped his right shoulder. "Your soul belongs to her. Arise!"

As he stood, Luca kissed each of her cheeks and took two steps back.

"*Bel*, release your hands from the sword and just watch, do not move an inch!" Taking the sword from her hands, he raised the sword to the sky and tossed it high in the air behind her. As he did so, the warriors raised their swords in the air and shouted in unison, 'Medici, *per sempre*!'

Luca leaped into the air and did a flip over her head, retrieving the sword in midair, then performed a mid-air backflip, landing in front of her, standing at attention, the sword pointing to the ground between his legs.

"Go forward and take the sword from him and place it across his heart, he will hold it there for you."

She stepped forward and reached for the handgrip on the sword as Luca released it to her hands. She raised the sword and placed it at an angle across his chest and heart. Luca raised his hand and held the sword in place.

Shade hoped she understood this ceremony was important to Luca. He stepped up closely behind her and placed her hand over Luca's as he held the sword, as she was now sandwiched between him and Luca.

He spoke to Luca, "I give you my sword Luca, to protect my heart and soul, for she is all I have in this world. We form the wall of protection that no other can break through."

Nodding to him, Shade watched as Luca's eyes bored into hers and he spoke to her and her alone. The night air was still, and no one moved for this was a solemn moment, one of greatest honor, one a warrior worked his entire life for.

"I am Luca of Medici, and I am now your protector, my lady. I honor you with my heart, my soul, and my life."

As he finished, there was a moment of silence, and Shade could feel his parents around him, he could feel *Madre's* hands on his shoulders in approval of his choice and he looked at Luca, his face solemn and honored. He was master here, but this moment was overwhelming even for him. **"You may say something to Luca, *mi amore*. You may also hug him or kiss him on the cheek and the ceremony will then end."**

She reached up to place one hand on each of Luca's shoulders. "It is my honor, Luca of Medici, to be under your protection." She must stand on tip-toe to kiss each cheek, before stepping back. She felt Shade behind her and leaned her back against him, letting her head rest back on his chest, as she felt his arm encircle her.

In unison, the warriors dropped to their knees, swords in hand and raised their heads, fangs elongated, eyes blazing and the growl that roared through the night shook the earth under them. All of the vampires of Tuscany knew the master had taken a mate and they were now stronger with their bond.

The warriors called out in unison, "*Per sempre* Medici!" As they dropped their swords and turned to slap each other on the back, Shade took her hand and led her away from the camp.

The warriors cheered and exchanged fist bumps before returning to their practice. Luca walked from the field, heading to the barracks to begin packing his stuff. He passed Cory on the way as he watched from the doorway of his workshop, and nodded to him.

"Good thing you made me new leathers. Looks like I'll be leaving with master to live in the States." Cory smiled back at him. "So, what was all that about, Luca?"

Luca beamed back at him. "I've been selected as protector to our master's mate. I'll remain with him now, and her, for all of their lives."

***

As the night progressed and Shade held her in his arms, the travel and the night's events took her into her dreams. Once she was soundly sleeping, he crawled silently from the bed and made his way outside of the castle in need of a smoke. He could hear the crackling of a fire and he grinned. Someone else was also up and he turned the corner to find Luca sitting in one of the portico alcoves staring into the fire.

"Luca, you should be preparing to head to the States, why are you out here alone?" Shade plopped down in one of the chairs opposite him and lit up, wondering what was going through his head.

"I'm ready, master, but you think I could relax after this night?"

Shade watched as Luca smiled and twisted the ring on his finger. "Well, I suppose you cannot, but you have earned this honor Luca. I needed Kate to make her own decision. I had hoped she would choose you and she did."

"I'm more than honored, master. I can tell you love her with all of your heart. You are fortunate to find your mate." Luca stood up and paced in front of the fire.

Shade frowned as Luca continued to twist at the ring. "Damn it, Luca, what is it? You can't hide it from me." Shade recognized that nervous habit of twisting the ring on his hand, and almost laughed out loud.

Luca stopped his pacing and looked up at him. "I hope she likes me. This will be a great change for her, being mortal and coming into our world. And even though I have left Florence before, it was not a permanent move, and now I'll be leaving, alone."

Shade felt his melancholy. He understood that leaving home was never easy. "Luca, you will not be alone, you will have me with you, and Kate. I will also be bringing Gi back with me, as well as Theresa to help Kate with the house, and Reynaldo to cook for her. I need Luciano to oversee the vineyards. We live in the countryside, in a vineyard on about 3,000 acres, and it will be a culture change, living in the States. You are warrior. It is a lonely life, you are still young, and you have much time to find a mate that suits you. Besides, Kate likes you. She will come to love you as do I. You need to feed, build your energy, the States is one hell of a teleport and it sucks the energy from you. Do you have a feeder?"

Luca turned toward him. "Of course, I have a feeder. I am worried for her, she knows I am leaving. She's in my quarters now. Will you make sure she's well cared for? Will I be able to find another where we're going?"

Standing up, Shade threw the cigarette butt into the flames, turned to Luca, and put his arm around his shoulders. "Luca, I will arrange everything for her. I cannot have you worried about such things. Your head needs to be clear and concentrating on Kate. Do not let me down. As for a feeder, there are feeders in the States, very different from our feeders, but do not worry. You will have no problem with feeders. Now get to your quarters, be prepared to leave at sunset. I need to get back to *bel*."

As Luca turned and gave him a brotherly hug and slapped him on the back, Shade knew he'd be fine. Being a young warrior and leaving home for good was never easy, he'd done it himself once.

44

Teleporting inside the Virginia house, Shade set *bel* down and stretched. "It feels good to come home, *mi amore*. Fuck, it's cold in here."

Walking to the fireplace, he raised his hands and watched the flames roar up, the wood already stacked there. He turned on his heels. "Luca! Damn, where the hell is he?"

Kate looked about. "Did we lose him? I don't know how teleporting works. And what about Gi and the others? "

"No, we teleport separately. But that trip takes energy, it sucks it from you, and they may not be used to it, the house staff especially. It is a long trip." Hearing a rustling, he saw Luca coming from the kitchen.

Luca walked in, looking around the living room. "Is there is a place you wish for me to stay, master?"

"*Bel*, will you show Luca where you wish him to stay and perhaps give him a tour? Get the others settled in the staff quarters once they arrive, please."

Kate stepped forward. "Of course. Luca, I apologize. We haven't lived here long, and I wasn't expecting you, so I haven't had time to really finish all the work here. But you'll have your own space in the house." As she spoke, Gi, Theresa, and Reynaldo all entered.

"I am sure Luca will be very comfortable here, *bel*. I must go into D.C., check in with Alec and the warriors and make sure there were no problems while I was gone. I will return as soon as I can. Take Gi and the staff to the staff quarters and take Luca with you so he can see the property before you get him settled."

Looking at Luca, he nodded, indicating he wanted Luca to stay with her, not leaving her for any reason. Pulling *bel* into his arms, he whispered softly into her ear, "You will be fine here with Luca."

She responded to his embrace, laying her head on his chest. "I miss you already, but yes, I'll be fine. Just be safe and come back to me as soon as you can."

Hugging her tightly to his chest, he sighed, hating to leave her for any amount of time, but feeling better knowing Luca was with her. "I always come back, Kate. You know that."

Tipping her chin up, he ran his thumb over her lips and leaned in, kissing her like it was the last moment he'd ever have with her, and then whispered softly. "I love you so much. It pains me now to have to leave you. I won't be gone all night. Please get the staff settled, start getting to know Luca, help him acclimate, *si*?" He slapped her ass lightly. "Now I must go, you minx, before you do something to keep me here."

Kate watched him leave, and her heart broke a little. She hated when he had to leave her. But it was comforting to know he'd be back before sunrise. She sighed and turned to Luca and the rest of the staff.

"Well, I guess I should show you around. Compared to the castle in Florence, this house is very small. Well, compared to the castle in Florence, all houses are small....and again, we haven't completed all the work on these rooms. Tomorrow, if Shade is busy, there are some things that will need my immediate attention, and I may require your help."

Luca nodded. "Yes, my lady, it would be our honor."

She stifled the urge to cringe at his use of 'my lady'. She knew it was important to Shade, and it was customary, but it felt so unearned.

"Okay, well the staff quarters are behind the house. If you'll follow me, please."

Kate led Gi, Theresa, and Reynaldo out the back entrance of the house and through a garden path to the large stone staff quarters, as Luca walked along beside her. The Tuscan style house had a very large central great room with high beamed ceilings. The large open room included living, dining, and kitchen space with a huge stone fireplace, and four bedrooms with dedicated bathrooms and individual sitting rooms off from the main great room. The house had been decorated in the same style as the main house and was lavishly appointed with beautiful pieces that reflect their Tuscan homeland.

As they walked into the great room, Kate explained, "I thought everyone could use this space, and Gi, Shade said you might need a space for the staff to gather, so I thought this room could be used for that purpose as well."

They all looked around the space but remained silent. Kate felt uncomfortable, thinking this was a big step down from Castello and they were probably all disappointed. She led them to the largest bedroom, which she had assigned to Gi as he was the senior staff member and would be in charge of the rest of the staff.

Gi entered the space as the others looked on from the doorway. "My lady, this is quite..."

Kate frowned, fearing she hadn't lived up to the living conditions to which they'd all become accustomed. "If this is not to your liking, please, we can change anything."

Gi turned to her and bowed his head slightly. "Quite the contrary, my lady. Our accommodations at Castello were quite modest. I was the only staff that lived inside Castello, and my room met all my needs but was quite modest. The others, including Theresa, and Reynaldo, resided in separate staff quarters designed to be functional. This is...opulent. This looks like a home for a master."

Kate hadn't seen any of the staff living quarters at Castello. She had decorated this building as she would a guesthouse.

"It is a home, Gi. It's your home, and Theresa's, and Reynaldo's. I hope you'll be happy here. And feel free to change things to your personal taste. I didn't know when I was working on it who would be living here. So, shall we keep going? Reynaldo, your room is here."

Kate led him to another room that had a very masculine feel. Reynaldo nodded approvingly as he entered the room, taking stock, walking through the bedroom, sitting room, and his private bath, a large smile on his face.

"I hope you like this. Get some rest, and tomorrow, I'll show all of you the main house. And Reynaldo, I'll turn the kitchen over to you. It is quite large and has just been remodeled. But I'm the only one that eats, so I'm not sure how busy you'll be."

"This is perfect, my lady. And don't worry. At Castello, with master away, there were no events scheduled, so there was no one to cook for. I will look forward to shopping for you and preparing only the best." He nodded his head as Kate started to think about her waistline.

Kate turned to Theresa. Like all vampires, Theresa was very tall. She was quite slender but lacked the hard-toned body like Sabine. She wore her brown hair pulled back in a tight bun at the nape of her neck. Her face was pleasant, but she wore no make-up, no jewelry. Kate had only seen her wearing her uniform, a black dress and white apron, and the small white cap sitting atop her head. Kate led her to the one room decorated with a feminine touch. These rooms had large windows, letting in lots of light. Kate had used light colors in the sitting room, and a beautiful old iron bed in the bedroom. Theresa seemed delighted with her space.

"Shade said you were all day-walkers. Theresa, I thought you'd like this room with all the natural light, and a view of the gardens, although there isn't much growing this time of year."

Kate pointed out the fourth room. "This one is Luciano's. He comes and goes, but you probably know that already. I never know when to expect him, but he's here sometimes, overseeing the vineyards, and then he leaves for the California vineyards. I think Shade said he still oversees the vineyards in Europe as well. He hires migrant farmworkers, who are mortal, but I think most of the people who actually produce the wine are vampires. He moves people around, so I can't say I know them very well. You may recognize them, though. There is a patio out back, with a beautiful view of the vineyards and the mountains. So, that's it. Just make yourself at home. Add what you want. Change what you want. I hope you'll like it here and let me know if there is anything I can do for you."

Gi stepped forward. "My lady, we are here to see if there is anything we can do for you, not the other way around."

Kate looked at Gi with his kind face and his white hair, always impeccable in his black waistcoat and bowtie.

"Well, I'm not used to being waited on, so can we just figure this out as we go? Do you have any personal belongings? No luggage?"

Gi nodded. "Our personal belongings are being flown over on master's private jet. They will be arriving tomorrow."

"Well then, take your time. Get settled here, get some rest, and explore the grounds. Whenever you're ready, just come to the main house tomorrow and I'll give you a tour and we'll figure everything out." Kate said her goodbyes to them, and she and Luca walked back to the main house.

Luca had remained quiet during their tour of the staff quarters. He turned to her as they walked back along the garden path. "That house is quite lavish compared to what they are used to, my lady. You need not worry. They were all honored to be selected to come to Virginia to serve master and his new mate."

She gave him a sideways glance. "I hope so, Luca. I know it's important to Shade they're here."

Luca opened the rear entrance door that led into the back hallway and allowed her to enter. He closed and locked the door behind them, checking the style of lock as he did so. Kate looked at him inspecting the door.

"Is everything okay?"

"I will have these changed, my lady. All of the locks will be changed to eliminate keys and will open on fingerprint recognition only. Is there a security system installed? I don't see anything."

Kate shrugged. "Uh, no. You mean like alarms and stuff?"

Luca smiled. "Yes, my lady. Alarms and stuff. Surveillance cameras. Laser motion detectors. We should have them around the perimeter."

Kate smiled to herself. *The perimeter?* "Yeah, well, you can discuss that with Shade. I'm out of my league here. Do you want to see the house?"

He nodded and held his arm out for her to lead the way. She headed down the hall back to the front of the house.

"Right, so let me show you the first floor, we have the living room, or living quarters, as I think Shade calls it. And if you'll follow me?" She felt a bit awkward showing him around, especially since he seemed so quiet. She reached into her jeans pocket and pulled out her phone.

"Any musical preference, Luca?"

"No, my lady, whatever you choose will be fine."

"Okay then, I'm more of a potluck kind of girl. I like to just hit shuffle and listen to whatever comes up."

She hits shuffle and The Hollies started singing, "The Air That I Breathe". She smiled, as she listened to the lyrics and her heart ached for him. **"Do you feel me, lover? I am missing you already."**

"*Si, mi amore*. I feel you, and I feel what is in your heart. I will be in your bed before you know it."

Kate realized she was just standing still, staring at the phone, and listening to Shade in her head as Luca stood by patiently. *Jeez, he must think I am a complete ditz. Get moving!* She led Luca down the hallway, pointing out the rooms.

"Okay, here's the downstairs powder room, and there's a dining room over here, where we never dine." She started laughing and noticed that he cracked a smile. "And here is the kitchen, with a personal chef for one." She was laughing harder, and Luca had started to chuckle. "There's a sunroom on the back of the house, and there are exits from the living room, sunroom, and your private suite that lead out to the patio and rear gardens." She led him into a hallway and back to the front of the house to another room.

“This room is a study for Shade. And then down this hall, you will have your private quarters. Your quarters will be close to Shade’s study. That way when he’s here working, you’ll be close by.”

She opened the door that led into his suite of rooms.

“This will be your bedroom. Right now, all we have is the bed, but I’ll get furniture for you. If there’s something in particular you need, just let me know. Over here is your private bathroom, there’s a huge shower stall as you can see. It has multiple showerheads. Shade said as a warrior, you’d appreciate that.”

She led him out of the bathroom and into a living room. “And this is your sitting room. It’s a pretty large space, so we can modify it to accommodate whatever your needs are. It has a lot of built-in bookcases. Shade said you loved to read, so plenty of room for your books. And the light is really nice in here during the day. Shade explained you were a day-walker. The rest of the house has been modified with electronic blinds that are on timers, and are also sensitive to light, so they automatically close at sunrise and open at sunset, but you can modify the timer to your own needs. You have these French doors that lead out onto the patio. You can come and go as you please when Shade is home. If you smoke, you can slip outside onto the patio...That’s what Shade does. There’s a fireplace on the patio if you like sitting out here at night when the weather is cool.”

She turned to look at him as she finished showing him his space and he had a slight frown on his face. “Is there a problem, Luca?”

"No, my lady, this is so much more than what I was expecting. As a warrior, I lived in a barracks with other warriors. I’ve never had my own space. I’m an artist. I love to paint. I may use some of this sitting room as an art studio. There is more than enough room for it.”

She was standing in amazement. It was almost beyond her comprehension that he’d never had his own private space. But then, so much about Shade's world was beyond her comprehension. A warrior with an artist’s soul, you don’t see that every day.

“Do you need to see the upstairs, Luca?”

"Yes, my lady, I need to be familiar with your surroundings as that is how I will best be able to protect you."

“Okay then, follow me upstairs, but I need to warn you, the last night we were here...there was an...uh...altercation.”

"An altercation, my lady?"

They walked into the master suite with demolished furniture, shattered glass, the broken window, and blood-spattered walls. Luca stepped into the debris field and put one hand on a dagger sheathed at his waist.

Kate looked around the destruction. "Let's just say one of Shade's ex-girlfriends was less than pleased with his choice for a mate."

"Sabine," he said under his breath.

"You knew her?" Kate asked.

"Yes, my lady, and we heard rumor of the 'altercation' as you call it."

"Yeah well, things ended badly for Sabine."

"Clearly," he answered.

"So," she said and looked at him. "Now you know why you're here."

"Yes, my lady, master has made it very clear, and you have nothing to fear. I will lay down my own life in protecting you."

Kate kicked at the pieces of broken furniture under her feet. "Wow, that seems really heavy, doesn't it?"

"Heavy, my lady?"

"Heavy? Like a big freakin' deal? I mean, you don't even know me, Luca."

"My lady, this is what I have spent my life training for. It is the highest honor to be chosen."

She looked over at him. "I understand that. I mean, I'm trying to understand that, Luca. This is all just a little overwhelming for me. I'm a mortal girl who fell head over heels in love with a vampire, and not just any vampire. Oh no, I have to fall in love with royalty! At least I have good taste, huh?"

He smiled and shook his head. Kate continued talking, "I mean three months, Luca. Three months ago, I was a normal mortal girl living in a normal mortal house and I didn't even believe in vampires, and now I'm being teleported all over the world, have houses too big to furnish, and cars I don't know how to drive, some vampire bitch who tried to kill me in the middle of the night, and a protector who calls me 'my lady' and has taken a vow to protect my life with his own. That's heavy, Luca. That's the definition of heavy."

"I understand, my lady."

"Really? Because I'm still struggling here. I mean, I love this man. I really love this man, and I have no regrets about my choice to move forward with him. I wouldn't change anything. But I realize, with every passing day, there's more that I don't know than what I do know. He's teaching me, guiding me, but it's a long road and I have a long way to go. And so much of this...including you, feels unearned."

"Then you are just like me, my lady."

"Just like you? How so?"

"You were chosen, my lady, by my master, to be his mate. And from what I have observed...if I may speak openly?"

Kate threw up both hands. "Please! Please speak openly. And don't ask for my permission."

"From what I have observed, my lady, your devotion and love for my master is quite evident, as is his for you. The act of choosing makes you deserving, just as I was chosen as your protector."

"You make it sound so simple, Luca."

"Because it is, my lady. I can assure you that my master doesn't feel you haven't earned the right to these things and much more."

"No, you're right about that. He'd give me the world if it was his to give. And maybe it is." She laughed as she asked, "He already gave me the stars. Can he give me the world, Luca?"

"No, my lady, I don't think even master can give you the world, but he can show you all that's in it," as he cracked a smile once again.

"Yes...I'm sure he can. Okay, let's finish up this tour, shall we? Over there used to be walk-in closets, and over there used to be a master bath. Clearly, I won't sleep in this room tonight. I guess it's a good thing we were renovating anyway. If you'll come with me, we have many other bedrooms on this floor. I haven't furnished all of them yet, but I'll show you where I'll stay tonight."

They stepped over the broken pieces of furniture, leaving the destroyed room, and walked down the hall and into each bedroom. She pointed out the room where she and Shade last slept. "We'll stay here until the master bedroom is cleaned up. And that's it. Do you need anything else from me?"

"Yes, my lady, I need to walk through the entire house again, check all entrances to the facility, as well as scout the outside perimeter."

"Outside perimeter?" She was laughing again. "You mean the yard, Luca?"

He laughed. "Yes, my lady, the yard, and all of the property here. Also, master mentioned a bunker?"

"A bunker? Oh...that room behind the wine cellar. Follow me."

She led him down the stairs to the main floor, and down the second flight of stairs into the wine cellar. She went to the door to open it but saw the large black padlock.

"Oh. I don't have the key."

Luca stepped forward and took the large padlock in his hand and willed it open, pushing the huge oak door inward.

Kate laughed. "Well, so much for security. Exactly how do you keep out other vampires?"

"The key is to never let them get close enough, my lady. Nothing keeps them out if they want in. We have laws in our culture, just as you have in yours. Since we can teleport anywhere, it is against our laws to teleport into the home of another vampire uninvited. To do so means certain death as dictated by Council."

"So, I guess the whole garlic defense is out then, huh?"

He laughed as he walked around the room, checking the walls in this windowless space. "I understand garlic is great on Italian food, but it has no impact on us, my lady. I've heard when we drink from mortals who've eaten garlic we can taste it in their blood. But I haven't experienced that for myself."

Kate was thinking this might be the strangest conversation she'd ever had. "Okay, Luca, you can scout away. I'm feeling rather tired, so I'm going to go to lay down now."

She turned and left the bunker and he followed her back up the stairs.

"Yes, my lady. I'll remind you I cannot hear your thoughts as clearly as master, but if you call out to me, I'll hear you." He stopped in the hallway as she headed up the second flight of stairs to the bedroom.

"Thank you, Luca...and Luca?" He paused and turned to look at her. "Thanks for listening to me."

He bowed his head and said, "It is an honor and a privilege, my lady."

She gave him an exaggerated bow in return. "Yeah, yeah...now get out of here." He smiled as she turned and continued up the stairs.

45

Waking before the sunset, it was still light outside. Shade rolled over to find *bel* snuggled deep under the blankets, naked, with her crimson waves tangled across the pillow. Kissing her softly on the forehead, he made sure the covers were tucked in around her. Pulling on a pair of jeans, he padded barefoot down to his new office. He loved the heavy leather sofa and chairs and the massive desk she'd placed in this room for him, and he didn't fail to notice she'd hung the painting he won at the art auction. It made him smile.

He dug out the boxes that contained the security system for the house, all the cameras and motion detectors, internal monitors as well as the central monitoring station, along with the plans to assemble it. This was the same brand of equipment he'd installed at the Dead House, and it would be added security for *bel*. Even with Luca here, he liked the idea of having the house and grounds constantly monitored.

Reading through the instruction manual, he propped his feet up on the desk and decided he needed to wake Luca, so they could get this installed. No more did the thought cross his mind than he saw him leaning against the stone arch to the study.

"Luca, did Kate get you settled in last night?"

"Yes, master, she did. We went through the staff quarters as well as a tour of this house. I'm glad to see the security system. I was going to suggest it, along with a few other measures."

"Other measures? What do you have on your mind?"

"Master, I noticed all the windows have the electronic blinds that close on timers and light sensors, but I'd suggest all the windows be replaced with bulletproof glass. And the standard key locks should be removed and replaced with the locks that use fingerprint technology."

"Good idea, Luca. I will have Kate work with the contractors who have been doing the renovations to do both."

"My lady showed me the bunker. It's an excellent location, couldn't have asked for better. Do you wish for me to start ordering weapons from our Florence inventory, and supplementing where necessary?"

"*Si*. I have sent a weapons order for Alec's warriors as well, such as they are. But if you could start working on a list for here, let me see what you come up with, and then we will get the bunker supplied. Talk with Gi about a conference table and chairs. I don't want Kate bothered with this part."

"Of course, master."

"Make sure the electrical is up to code in that room. We will want a security monitor inside, and internet connections, cell connections, so we may need to run some cables."

"I will take care of it, master."

"Now, come help me install this system, all the feed we get on the monitors is recorded, so it can be played back, and we can hook this up to our cell phones. That way I can check on things here when I am away at night. You will be able to check in as well when you have a night off. I think this will make *bel* feel safer."

"Master, she mentioned an altercation with Sabine."

"*Si*. I was foolish to think I could isolate her here and keep her from being exposed to our world. I left her unguarded. I knew Sabine was in the States. She confronted me in D.C., but I had no idea she would try to attack *bel*. What I had with Sabine...I am not sure you can even call it love. More like a dark sickness. I thought I had ended that relationship. I had not seen or heard from her since. I had no reason to think she would show up here, which just goes to show you I don't know when something from my past will play a role in my future, and I cannot let Kate suffer for it. So...Sabine is no more."

Luca absorbed this information. The outcome of the battle was pretty clear from the evidence displayed on the walls of their bedroom, but Shade was confirming what he thought to be true.

"So, my lady knows how to handle a weapon, *si*?"

Shade shook his head. "*Bel* has no knowledge of weaponry. Hell, even Italian mortal women will whip off a heel and take your eye out if necessary."

Luca responded, "She's not familiar with weapons of any sort? She doesn't seem timid. Perhaps you'd wish me to train her on methods of defense and some basic weapon skills? I'd be willing to train her, with your permission, of course."

Shade stood up quickly and backed Luca's ass across the room, as his fangs elongated and he got in his face. Luca didn't back down but growled his warning back at him. Shade didn't raise his voice but spoke through his tight jaw.

"You take great liberties with my mate, Luca! Do not ever presume you can just handle her in any fashion you wish. You are her protector, not her teacher. That is *my* job and when I feel she is ready, I will handle it. *Si*?"

"Understood, master."

Shade watched as Luca lowered his head, and Shade nodded. "Now, get your ass in gear and help me install all these cameras. I need you to get on the roof. We need to figure out the best placement to view the property. We need cameras on the staff quarters and winery as well, and a camera at the entrance of the private road. We will put motion detectors around the perimeter of the property and at several points along the private drive. I do not want any alarms sounding outside. We will wire it so the alarms are quieter and only heard inside the house, your private suite, of course, and the bunker, also inside the staff quarters. We live among mortals. I do not want alarms going off. Let's go."

***

Kate woke up in their bed and knew without looking he was already up. She could feel the emptiness beside her. She rolled over and grabbed his pillow, pulled it to her, and inhaled his scent. She felt him when he came back from the Dead House at sunrise and slid into bed beside her. She lifted her left hand and looked at the huge ring, loaded with diamonds that had belonged to his mother.

There was a part of her that feared his mother would have been disappointed in his choice of a mortal girl. He'd already implied as much about his father. And then there was the matter of her family and friends. She'd managed to hide this relationship from all of them with her story of living abroad. But how did you hide a whole lifetime? And children? He talked about children. Would their children be vampire or mortal, or something in between, like Cory? The ramifications of her choices were slamming home. She sat up in the bed, still holding his pillow, with her knees drawn up to her chest.

She had woven this elaborate story about living and working in London as the excuse for her absence, speaking to her friends and family by phone or on Skype, but she realized, at some point, she'd have to completely separate from them. Just "disappear" somehow. Because how did you hide a whole life? How did you hide the fact you had a husband? Okay, not a husband, a mate, a vampire mate...and children? She'd already made her choice when she decided to feed from him, but the loss of the people she'd known all her life was sobering. How long could she continue this façade of living abroad?

She knew she couldn't share with them the reality of Shade. That wasn't possible without putting him at risk. She laid her head back against the headboard. To follow her chosen path, to follow him, she must let go of all that came before him. She said a silent good-bye to them, at least in the way she'd lived with all of them in the past, because a life without Shade would be no life.

She slipped out of bed and got dressed in jeans and a sweater. Her mortal body was hungry, and she was wondering what Shade was up to. She could feel him in the house, so she left this temporary bedroom and headed downstairs. She stopped in the kitchen and was startled to find Reynaldo already at work. He had the coffee brewing and a bowl of freshly sliced fruit, fresh from the market, ready for her while he prepared an omelet and a toasted bagel.

"Good morning...I mean, evening, Reynaldo."

She looked around at the elaborate kitchen space and had to smile. The toaster, the microwave and the coffee-maker were the only things she'd even used in this room. Reynaldo seemed in his element and was so happy to be preparing food.

"And what would my lady like for lunch today?"

"I don't usually eat lunch." She saw the disappointment in his face. "I do eat dinner. But Reynaldo...keep it light."

He smiled at her. "Understood, my lady."

She quickly polished off the omelet and bagel and savored the freshly brewed coffee, and then went wandering in search of Shade. They should probably talk about this whole marriage/mating/baby thing. After the 'warrior picking ceremony', she was wondering what a vampire wedding looked like? And when should she extricate herself from her family? And children? Good Lord, she was beginning to understand why his parents didn't want him to choose a mortal girl. Oh well, too late for that now. She loved him, and she felt his love for her, so no turning back.

Kate walked into the living room to find it empty. She looked out onto the patio and it was also empty. She headed down the corridor to his study and could hear voices. She had to smile. She knew Luca was here as her protector, but she could sense Shade's joy in having him here as well. She hated to disturb him in his study if he was working, but the door was open, so she stepped into the doorway. He had electronics spread across the floor. It took a moment to recognize what it was, a bunch of security cameras, and motion sensors, tons of cable and several small monitors, one large monitor, and a massive console that controlled everything. He was talking about getting on the roof.

She'd live in a fortress surrounded by security cameras and under the protection of not one, but two vampire warriors. The memory of the night Sabine appeared in their bedroom flashed through her head. She knew he had downplayed it, but he was a warrior who fought against opposing vampire forces. Would their children be safe? Would her children be sent away, to be raised in a warrior training camp like Luca? The depth of what she didn't know overwhelmed her.

"Shade? We need to talk..." Shade sensed her turmoil, and he nodded to Luca as he stepped out.

"Kate? What is wrong? Has something happened? " Walking to her, he took her hand and looked into those dark eyes and he could see her mind was racing with millions of questions and he knew he needed to sit with her and talk.

"Okay, this is serious. I can feel your turmoil. Let's go and talk this out, I can feel your doubts, and your fear."

She laid her head on his shoulder. "Is this a bad time? You're busy here with Luca. I can come back later."

He squeezed her to him and said, "No, *mi amore,* I can feel you are upset. We will talk now. Luca can wait."

"Well, first of all, I'm fine. I just woke up with a million questions in my head. Things I need to understand. I try so hard to live inside this bubble, where only the two of us exist. But the reality is, there's still so much I don't know. Please, I can feel your concern for me, and I can read it on your face." She placed her hand on his cheek. "Before we start talking, you need to know I'm not going anywhere. I can't imagine a life for myself that doesn't include you. Let's go in the living room, sit in front of the fire, and talk."

He led *bel* into the living room and lit the fire, settling down beside her on the sofa as she looked at him. "So tell me what is on your mind."

She curled up next to him on the sofa and pulled a throw across her legs against the chill.

"I woke up with so many things in my head. I don't even know where to start. I was thinking about my family and how I should manage things going forward. I've kept our lives together secret. I don't know how I can continue to do that for a lifetime. And if we have children, I mean, how do I hide the fact I have children? I hate to disappear from them. I told them about the new job in Europe, and I can always say that I'll be living there permanently. I don't know, lover. What have other mortals done?"

Shade raised his eyebrows, watching her spill out question after question. "Let us address one issue at a time, *si*? As for your family and friends, it is true, there will come a point in time where you must pull away. Once you become immortal, if that is your wish, you will age, but very slowly. You see me at five hundred. Alec does not look much older than me, and he is seven hundred and fifty. Gi has been with my family for many generations, he is two thousand, maybe older. You can see his age now. He looks like a mortal of about seventy or so. You are an only child. Your parents are almost sixty. Perhaps, if you are careful, you can maintain a relationship with them, by phone until their mortal death. But it is true, *mi amore*. If you become immortal, the deception must continue. Do you not wish it so? I will not force this decision on you. It is yours to make. We are bonded now. You drank my blood, and for the rest of my life, I will feel you. But if you chose to leave..."

"No! I don't choose to leave. I've made peace with my choice. I think I just needed to say it out loud. Acknowledge that I have to find a way to marginalize the people in my life, and I'll do that because I can't move forward without you."

His sigh was audible. He couldn't imagine his life without her. "Ask me another, one at a time please."

"I guess my next question, after witnessing the ceremony in Florence for Luca, is there a special ceremony for a vampire mating? Or will there be something expected of us, because you're royalty?"

"There is much ceremony in my immortal world, and it is extremely ritualistic, and you need not worry about such at this time. Because you are mortal, the Council will not officially recognize you as my mate until you are turned. When you become immortal, you are also royal blood. You will rule with me over my coven. We will discuss that later, much later, for it is very involved and you will need coaching beforehand. Does any of this scare you? Or confuse you?"

Kate pulled the throw around her shoulders. "Actually, becoming immortal was on the list of questions in my head. So, we are only partially mated? Do I need to be immortal before we're completely mated? Also, I assumed I'd need to be immortal before we could have children. I mean, at first, I didn't think vampires were born, only turned. And then only born to immortals, but then I met Cory. I am confused, lover." *Also, a little freaked out because I haven't been on any birth control since I've been with him, but I'll leave that discussion for another day.*

"Kate, there have been extremely rare incidents of mortal/immortal pregnancies. It is very difficult for a mortal to be impregnated by an immortal. But when it does occur, those children are half-breeds. Like Cory. They have many attributes of a vampire, but will never be as strong, or live as long. The vampire community rejects them, and, of course, they do not fit into their mortal community either. So that is the reason I wish for you to be immortal before we have children. It is crucial my children be born as vampires, to ensure their royal blood. There must be no questions about their royal lineage. My males must carry forth the Medici legacy, born full-blooded warriors, taking over the warrior camp, and assuming responsibility for the coven. They will have every privilege given to them without question if they are born of two immortals."

She had an internal sigh of relief as he stated how rare mortal/immortal pregnancies were.

"Shade, you're assuming our children will be all boys. There's the possibility we'd have a daughter, yes? But, our children, Luca mentioned he'd been under study as a warrior since he was ten. Will our children be sent away? Would our boys be sent to a warrior training camp? And Sabine was a warrior, and you said Adriana was a warrior, will our girls also be sent away? Will I be allowed to raise our own children?"

Shade stood up and paced, his hand over his mouth. *How in the hell do I break this to her*?

"Kate, because I am warrior born, our male children are more likely to be born warrior. It is more common for males than females. We will not know their fate until they are born, but the first-born son is almost always warrior. He is the heir to the coven. I was born warrior, as was my *padre*. It is in the blood. For any of our children born warrior, their training begins at ten, and I will see they are trained at Castello. We can live there if you wish. I am sorry Kate, I will have it no different, and my children will be ruled by me, the sons especially."

Kate was stunned by his revelation. "I...I don't...we can live at Castello, I understand...but will I see them? Will they live with us? What do you mean ruled by you? Are you saying I have no say?"

Shade flopped down on the sofa and laid his head back, closing his eyes. "Kate, we live in such different worlds. They will need to learn to be in my world, they will be vampire and royal, my sons will grow to be masters, my daughters will mate with masters. They will need every skill they can manage to survive, to protect their coven. They will have to be able to hunt for food, find a mate, and survive in both the immortal and mortal world. A boy is sent to the camps when he is ten to develop his skills as a warrior. When he reaches eighteen, he is sent out in the world and left to his own devices to travel and learn how to apply all that he has learned. He will need to have these skills to survive. If our daughters are not warrior born, they will be kept at home until they mate. The children will have private tutors who come to our home, as the children cannot attend school with mortals. The tutors will teach them everything a mortal child would learn in school, in addition to learning our vampire history and culture. Whatever gift our child is born with, they will need to learn to hone that skill. Even our daughters must be taught skills for survival among mortals. This is why I want you to make sure this is what you want, *mi amore*. Their mother is most important. Your children are not taken away from you and you will be involved in every part of their life. Before they are teens, they see very little of the outside world. They are cloistered and sheltered, for their own safety. They will rely on you as every child relies on their *madre*. If they are not born as day-walkers, they will sleep as I do, in their death slumber, and need protection. Newborns feed only from their *madre*. Within a few weeks, the baby will be weaned from you to feed from their nanny and their wet feeder. The wet feeder remains dedicated to that one child until the child is between sixteen or eighteen and is capable of reproducing, and they have learned to hunt. But yes, they will need their *madre*. They will need you to love them, teach them, protect them, and keep them strong."

Kate's head was reeling with this information. How did she even process this? And wet feeders? She'd tackle that one another day.

"Lover...this is all so...different. I've never even seen a vampire child. I guess I just assumed they'd be raised the same. I mean, I understand the need to feed on blood, but the other skills, and the training. I know how close you were to your mother, you mention her often, so I know she had to have an important role in your life. That's what I want. I want to make sure I have an important role in my children's life. I can't just turn my children over to someone else to raise. I don't want to love them from a distance."

"Kate, the boys will be with you when they are small, no different than mortal children. But the boys will go to the camp at age ten. They live at the camp, but you can visit them. The girls are not as likely to be born warrior and will stay at home until they are mated. I can only say I needed my *madre* every moment I could have with her, she was my softness, she read to me, she taught me what it meant to be male, and my responsibility to my female. She held me close to her chest even when I was grown. I would not be the man I am without her loving touch. So, you will have a great place in their lives, *bel,* a great place in their hearts and souls."

"That's comforting to know. I feared they'd be taken away. Who teaches them to gain control over their inner beast? Who teaches them how to survive among mortals without being discovered?"

Shade ran his hand through her hair. "They learn such skills from me, and I would love for you to help me as well. They will also have the best tutors that money can provide. But I learned much from my *padre* the hard way. He had a heavy hand with me. I wish not to be so brutal in my approach with my own children. My *madre* intervened many times. She would come to my rescue when my *padre* had lost patience with me, and comfort me and deal with my *padre* later on her terms, as I am sure will happen with us." He chuckled, "Once you are immortal, *bel*, your beast will be strong and vibrant as well."

Kate leaned her cheek into his hand. "And who will teach me to control my inner beast?"

"I will help you, *mi amore*. Never fear. Do not be afraid of the beast. She is there to protect you so embrace her as she rises inside you."

"If my beast has my temper, and she has to battle with your beasts' stubbornness, then we better have strong furniture."

Roaring with laughter, he pulled her into his arms and kissed her soundly. "Oh *si*, it will never be boring! Anything else you want to ask?"

"Immortality, how does that happen?"

"Do you mean turning you from mortal to immortal?"

"Yes, what do you do, and what will it feel like, and how long does it take, and what do I need to learn before this happens, and when are you planning on making this happen? I mean, you clearly had a plan in your head since you asked me to be your mate?"

Shade shook his head, smiling at her. "Your brain is smoking, *mi amore*, thinking of all these questions, but this is important. It will be the final step in allowing us to live our lives together for eternity. I will take you back to Florence, for it is important that you be turned there, inside Castello. I will feed from you, draining you until right before your last heartbeat. As your heart takes its last beat in this mortal world, I feed you with my blood. You will crave it, want it, and feel me strongly. Your body will go into a death slumber. It will change internally, and that will be painful. I cannot help you during your turning other than to be with you, hold you and try to comfort you. You must fight to come back to me, *bel*. You will hear my voice and you must respond, for I become your maker and master, and I will call you home to me. You must fight the pain, fight the slumber. Once this procedure is complete and you fight through, you will awaken as immortal. You will be starving beyond anything you have ever felt, and you will feed from me and me alone. You will crave no other blood except mine for all eternity."

She gently ran her fingers down his cheek. "I have no fear. I know I'll be pulled back to you. I'll fight through anything to get back to you. Will it change me in other ways? Other than the death slumber and having to avoid the sun, will it change how I feel? Will it change anything for us?"

He smiled down at her. "Oh, *si*. You will have my skills of shadowing, teleporting, you will remain small because you were born mortal, but you will be much stronger. And you will have a gift. What that gift is, I cannot say. I am a dream-walker, Luca a day-walker. We will not know your gift until you are turned. It will make us true eternal mates and you will feel your emotions much deeper, more intensely. Your vision will be enhanced, and your sense of smell will be greater. The bond between us will be so much more intense in every aspect."

"More intense? Lover, I can't imagine more intense. And what is your plan for when this should happen? Does some vampire council have to approve me becoming immortal? What if they say no? Could they keep us apart?"

"This choice is mine, I am a master. I choose to whom I mate and call home to me. No one can stop me."

She laid her head against his chest. "And what do you choose?"

"You are mine. I choose you to be my mate, my immortal lover for all eternity and I choose to be your maker and master."

"And I choose you, lover."

He tilted her face up to his. "I think you should kiss me and seal this deal."

She felt his arms encircle her as they kissed. "You have told me everything except when. Do you have any idea of when?"

"Not yet, but soon. You grow stronger as you continue to feed from me. You will need the strength to survive the turning. Now, I say we lay on this couch and make love all night long in front of this warm fire...hmmmm, what do you say, *mi amore*?"

"I say yes."

46

It didn't take long for Luca to realize he was on his own to complete the installation of the security system when Shade disappeared with Kate. He leaped to the red-tiled rooftop and scanned the property. There was only one roadway into the estate, the two-mile-long private drive. All other footpaths and roads on the land were closed loops or dead ends and were confined to the property. He made sure to position cameras on the front entrance to the house, and the three rear entrances that lead onto a wide patio. He positioned another camera so it was pointed at the staff quarters, and the other was pointed at the winery. He teleported to the staff quarters and placed cameras to monitor both entrances and did the same with the winery.

Once off the roof, he teleported down to the fenced entry off the main road and installed a camera there. The entire property was enclosed with a white rail fence, except for the section that led up the side of the mountains. It was a fence that marked boundaries but wouldn't prevent entry. He noticed the sign near the entrance that read, 'Bel Rosso Vineyards.' As vampires living among mortals, they'd learned over the years the best way to hide was in plain sight. Creating a fortress with a high chain-link fence topped with barbed wire, and lots of No Trespassing signs only made mortals curious about what was going on. This vineyard needed to look like all the other scenic vineyards that dotted the Virginia countryside, and the winery and vineyards remained open for tourists as did all the vineyards. It was a risk they must take.

Luca placed a laser beam motion detector at the entrance to the private road, and another motion detector about two hundred feet in. He knew some people would pull in because they were lost, or checking a map, and had no intention of driving all the way up the driveway. The first detector would alert them that someone had pulled into the drive. The second one would let them know the car didn't turn around and move on. He placed the other motion detectors around the perimeter of the house, staff quarters, and the winery, but far enough out that the staff wouldn't trigger them in their day to day movement around the property.

When he got back inside, he set up the large screen monitor in Shade's office, which would project a small image from each camera onto the screen. He mounted a second monitor in his suite. The system allowed for him to zoom in on any image, and automatically enlarge any image to full screen if a motion detector within that camera's range was triggered. Once everything was wired, he programmed both his and Shade's cell phones to be able to view any camera and to receive a text message if a motion detector was tripped.

It was almost sunrise and he heard Shade and Kate on the stairs as the soft whir of the electronic blinds started to close. Luca stepped out into the hallway to let Shade know everything was installed and functioning. He knew he wouldn't see him again now until sunset.

Luca walked to the staff quarters to see Gi and the rest of the staff and found all of their personal items that were flown over from Florence had arrived. Everyone was busy unpacking and getting moved into their rooms. Luca made several trips back and forth to carry his things. Mostly clothes, books, and art supplies, taking the items back to the suite that would be his living space. He got things put away as best as possible until he had more furniture in the room and then decided he too would sleep. He'd used a lot of energy in the teleport from Italy and then completing the security installation. He'd like to feed, but master hadn't given him the details on the feeders here yet, and he didn't want to hunt when he wasn't familiar with the territory.

The electronic blinds darkened his room as well, and for now, he'd leave them on the same schedule as Shade. He dropped his clothes and stepped into the large shower stall that had multiple shower heads, hitting him at different angles, and let the hot water pour over him, massaging his back as the water pounded and pulsated. In Florence, the warriors all showered in a communal bathroom, with a line of showers and low water pressure. Showers were kept short, so you didn't run out of hot water. He'd never felt a shower like this one, and he took his time. When he stepped out, he grabbed a towel that was thick and fluffy and almost as long as he was tall. He dried off and headed for the big king size bed. In the camp, the warriors slept in bunks, single-width beds that barely fit their large frames. He lay across the large bed, the mattress firm beneath him, and yet, he felt it conform to his shape, cradling him in comfort. The pillows were down-filled, as was the comforter. The sheets were expensive and had a crisp, clean smell. In all his life, he'd never been surrounded by this kind of luxury, living the austere life of a warrior. He didn't usually sleep during the day, but the travel and hard work, the hot shower, and a bed that he'd decided must be the world's most comfortable bed, lured him into sleep. He couldn't believe this was his. He saw the rooms that my lady had prepared in the staff quarters, and he knew she'd make his suite equally luxurious. Hell, he would've come here for the bed alone!

***

Gi and Theresa had finished unpacking when Gi told her they had a job waiting for them in the main house. Theresa was delighted to have been chosen to come to the States. In Florence, she'd been one housemaid among many. But here, she'd serve her master's mate, just as Gi served master. She met my lady briefly during both of her visits to Florence. Gi said she was kind and had a soft heart, like Shade's *madre*. Theresa had been with the Medici family for two generations now, and with any luck, she'd be nanny to her master's children.

She'd watched Shade grow up, losing his parents too soon and taking on the responsibility for the warrior camp, and supporting the coven. His success allowed all of them to be successful as well, and he was a good and fair master who held their loyalty. Theresa had watched him over the years with the women he brought back to Castello. Most of them didn't last long, much to the relief of the house staff. There were two that had lived at Castello for many years that the staff feared would be his choice for a mate. Adriana could be both a regal lady, and a warrior, but she looked down her nose at the staff, feeling her position placed them all so far beneath her. The idea that she'd be their queen was almost unbearable. Theresa knew her master had loved Adriana, but for whatever reason, he never took her as his mate, and when she died, he was inconsolable for many years.

He returned to his bachelorhood ways of courting many women, and then there was Sabine. Sabine could be hard and hateful to the staff, but never in front of master. She made them all wish for Adriana. Sabine's darkness engulfed their master, pulling him down with her, and they watched as he changed before their eyes; sullen, angry, his beast easily roused. And the activities in the underground chamber were only whispered about by the house staff, knowing if Sabine or master heard their gossip they'd be let go. When master finally broke free of her, there was jubilation at Castello among the staff, but of course, they had to hide their joy at Sabine's departure.

And now he was mated. Theresa had heard the talk among the staff that she was mortal, and therefore not suitable for the role of their future queen. But never had Theresa seen her master as happy as he was now. She knew how important this would have been to his mother, to find a mate he loved and would make him happy, mortal or not. Theresa was delighted with his choice. The others would come around once she was turned.

She joined Gi in the great room of the staff quarters, ready to tackle whatever project he threw at her. Gi wanted to go over some instructions first and asked her to sit.

He sat across from her. "Theresa, I wish for you to work in the main house during day hours. Master will be in his death slumber, and my lady tries to match her sleep schedule to his. In the evenings, master frequently leaves the house to work for Master Alec, so my lady is up during the night hours as well. She may or may not need assistance during the night. Perhaps more in the beginning, as she is still working on the house. Master has asked that we give her some space as she is not used to having house staff. Their bedroom can be cleaned at night unless master is home. So, try to keep up with his schedule. Reynaldo has said she is very easy to work for. He says she is chatty and friendly and does not treat him as staff. Today, we need to clean their bedroom, but this is going to be a project."

He stood to lead her to the main house and she followed behind him. "A project? Master Shade was careless with tossing his clothes about, but never left a real mess."

"*Si*. But this is a special circumstance. My lady was home alone, and she was attacked by Sabine. Our master was able to respond in time, and it was a battle to the death. I'm afraid there is little left unbroken in that room. We must clear it out and wash away the blood. Even still, it will require new carpet and repainted walls."

Theresa's mouth was hanging open. Master slayed Sabine! If she wouldn't be reprimanded, she would have danced a jig. "So, that explains the sudden decision for a protector, and probably for all of us to move here as well."

"*Si*. I think once master made the decision to live here, he would have brought some of us over eventually, but this incident just escalated his timeline. Master asked that there be no evidence of Sabine when my lady returns to their room, so we have our work cut out for us."

Theresa smiled to herself. The prospect of washing away Sabine's blood and watching it circle down a drain was bringing her great pleasure. The bitch had it coming.

47

Kate was looking for something to wear in a stack of clothing that had been moved to the guest bedroom. Shade was back at the Dead House for the night, and they'd been sleeping in this guest bedroom since their return from Florence. He'd asked her not to go back in their bedroom until it had been cleared. He'd been going back to their old bedroom and bringing out stacks of clothes for her. She got dressed in a pair of jeans and sweater, and headed down the stairs, joining Reynaldo in the kitchen.

Reynaldo had tried setting a place for her in the dining room, but Kate ate at the kitchen counter, seated on a barstool so she could talk to him. She enjoyed his company, as well as his cooking. As she was wrapping up her breakfast meal, which she ate at an hour most mortals were sitting down to dinner, Theresa entered the kitchen.

"My lady?"

Kate turned to her and smiled. She'd seen very little of Theresa since they'd returned from Florence. Shade was right about the staff being discreet. She never saw them unless she called for them or sought them out, and yet, the house remained immaculate, the laundry done, folded, and put away. Reynaldo's kitchen was clean enough to eat off the floor.

"Theresa, can I help you?"

"No, my lady. Gi has asked that I inform you your bedroom has been cleaned. We worked with the contractor's and they have installed the carpet you had selected for all the second-floor bedrooms, and the walls have been freshly painted. I have laundered the clothing in your closet or had them sent for dry cleaning. The clothing that was in the dressers has also been cleaned. Since the furniture hasn't been replaced, I folded those items and placed them in large laundry baskets. The same for Master Shade. I apologize for the inconvenience, but master was quite clear there was to be…no, uh, evidence."

"You laundered all of my clothing?"

"Yes, my lady, I hope that's all right."

"I…it's fine, Theresa. I was just thinking about how full my closet is!"

"Think nothing of it, my lady. The room is ready for you to furnish." Theresa bowed her head slightly and left the kitchen.

Kate slid off the barstool and climbed the stairs to their bedroom, excited to finish up one of the final rooms in the house. She opened the door and stepped into the empty space. The bedroom was already large, and they'd decided, during all the remodeling, to knock out the wall to an adjoining bedroom to create two large walk-in closets, one for her and one for Shade. Unlike Luca's suite, their bedroom didn't have a separate sitting room, but the space was large enough to accommodate two large armchairs along with the bedroom furniture she'd selected. The adjoining bathroom had a large tub, designed to accommodate two, and a gas-lit fireplace that was open to both the bedroom and the bathroom, enclosed by a glass panel on both sides. There was a long granite vanity with two sinks, and a separate shower stall with a rain forest showerhead. There was a great window in the bedroom that looked out over their property and had a view of the mountains, and a small balcony– too small to accommodate a chair beneath the window. Maybe she'd put some plants out there. She'd loved this room when she saw it. Now she had to make it theirs. She needed to make this their sanctuary. The place he wanted to come home to.

She'd already worked with the designers and the antiquities dealers to purchase the items for this space, so it would take no time to wrap this up.

Gi had an army of workers organized as they brought in the furniture pieces, an old Bombay chest for her, a large armoire for him, the large hand-carved headboard for the king-size bed, flanked by nightstands. Two overstuffed armchairs were positioned near the window. One wall in their bedroom was stone, and the other walls were Venetian plaster. Kate had chosen colors in muted earth tones, with furniture that was heavy and substantial, still keeping a Tuscan feel. She was still looking for art pieces, but she was most excited about the fantastic find of the antique hand-stitched wall tapestry.

As the room came together, she had the workers hang the tapestry over the bed. The colors of the threads were now faded in the ancient tapestry, but the view of a Tuscan estate in the early fall, with rolling hills of green, gold, and brown and the ever-present cypress trees was perfectly proportioned to hang over their bed.

The room looked transformed. This room spoke to her heart, and she hoped it would speak to his. This room held no memories of a battle with Sabine.

With this room completed, she sought out Luca and they met with the designers to plan his suite. She hated that he was living so sparsely and wanted his rooms to be a sanctuary for him as well. She picked out pieces that were heavy and masculine, dark wood tables, and a large leather sofa, a softer upholstered armchair. His room had beautiful large windows and French doors, giving the large space beautiful light and an open feel. All the while, Luca was telling her he needed nothing, and she was doing too much. He feared master wouldn't approve. Kate laughed softly, reassuring him that Shade wouldn't object, and somehow, Luca knew it was true. Shade would deny her nothing and would let her do whatever made her happy. And what made her happy was taking care of others.

Luca looked up to see Theresa standing in the doorway, taking in the flurry of activity. He knew she too was overwhelmed with her good fortune, and the beautiful space she now lived in. Luca had already moved his books onto the bookshelves, but his art supplies were stacked in a corner, along with an easel. Kate worked with the designers to create a small art studio in an alcove by the window that would take advantage of the natural light. She had the designers build custom shelving for him to accommodate storing canvases and drawers for storing paints and brushes.

Luca understood, as did all the staff, that Kate made no class distinction. She cringed when they called her my lady, a title she accepted with reluctance. Her familiarity with them, her casual conversation, made it clear she saw them as an extension of her family here with Shade. And even though a coven was a family, in the vampire world, there had always been a hierarchy within the coven. Luca had seen enough of mortals to know they too had a hierarchy, of the rich and the poor, the haves and the have-nots. But that wasn't Kate's world. She had her own rules, and in her world, everyone was on a level playing field. She was mate to a master, a king, one of the richest vampires in their global community. It was her prerogative to command them at her will, but he saw already she'd rule with a soft hand, and the coven would love her for it.

Being chosen as protector to a royal mate was the highest station a warrior could achieve, but it could also be fraught with turmoil. Luca tried to imagine himself in this role had his master made another choice for a mate, subordinate to the upturned nose of Adriana, or the cruel ministrations of Sabine. He realized his good fortune here meant a life of honor and respect among his peers, as well as a life where he shared in the master's bounty, and my lady's kindness and good graces.

They wrapped up the planning for his room, my lady with a folder full of fabric swatches, paint colors, floor plans for furniture placement, and drawings for the designs of his custom cabinetry. She gave him a smile as she left his suite.

"Just a few days, Luca, and we'll have everything here for you."

"My lady, I'm most thankful. It's more than I deserve."

"I doubt that, Luca. I seriously doubt that. I hope you will be happy here."

Kate headed back upstairs to the newly decorated master bedroom. The electronic blinds were closing as the early light of dawn filtered into the room. *Shade will be home soon.* She marveled at the restrictions on his life. He had this incredible strength and speed, the ability to teleport, to shadow himself in a cloak of invisibility, and yet, the sun dictated his life. She wondered if he envied the life of the day-walkers, who moved about freely day and night, just as she did. She thought about their conversation, about being turned. Would she be like him, and require a death slumber? She'd seen him push against that relentless pull that took him into that deep sleep.

She felt the energy in the room change as he materialized in front of her, dressed in the leathers he wore on the streets at night. She asked little about what he did when he is away, and he volunteered nothing.

He scooped her up in a big hug like they'd been separated for months, not hours. "*Mi amore*, did you miss me?"

She laughed at how happy he was to see her, and how happy she was to have him home. "Lover, I miss you always." He kissed her before she could finish her thought. He set her down on her feet as he turned slowly to take in their bedroom.

"Our room is finished, well, except for some wall art I want to add, but what do you think, Shade?"

He walked around the room, checking the closets, stepping into the large bathroom, and back into the bedroom.

"*Bellissimo*! It is perfect. I would change nothing."

Kate had her hands clasped in front of her, overjoyed with his reaction when he stopped suddenly and stared at the tapestry mounted over their bed.

"You're very quiet. Don't you like it?"

He didn't answer but stood transfixed before the tapestry as he appeared to be lost in thought.

Kate looked at him with concern. "Please, what is it?"

"*Mi amore*, how...how did..."

"You don't like it? We can change anything you don't like."

"Kate, *mi dolce* Kate, my *madre* would sit for hours, hand stitching the tapestry. This is the view of our home, Castello. Do you not recognize it? It was centuries ago, but not much has changed. It brings me such beautiful memories of the love I grew up with. There is such a beautiful story."

Kate looked surprised. "Do you think it's the same tapestry? What are the odds I'd select this very tapestry from all the ones the shopkeeper had to offer? Please tell me the story."

"*Si*." He pulled her onto his lap. "My *madre* hung this tapestry above their bed, just like this one is hung. My *madre* stitched it by hand. My *padre* told the story as one night he came home to find her sitting on the floor of the bedroom in a white dressing gown, by the firelight, her hair long and unbraided. She had toiled meticulously at the tapestry for months on end. He said his beast was insane to have her. She was like an angel to him sitting there. He made passionate love to her on the tapestry that night, and that was the night I was conceived. On the night I was born, she had just finished placing the final stitches on the tapestry, and I was laid upon it. From that night on, it hung above their bed, until the bonfires. On the night of the bonfires the tapestry disappeared, as did many things from Castello. I assumed those stolen things were burned. "

Kate's heart broke to hear the story, and yet, exploded with wonder at having the good fortune to find this piece. "Then I think your mother guided my hand when I was making the choices for our room. She looks over us, she knows the love we have for each other is like what she felt for your father, yes?

"*Si*. They were happy and in love. I cannot believe after all these years, just as *madre* placed you in my path, she placed the tapestry in yours."

Smiling, he pulled her down on the bed with him. "I just want to lay here and look at you, forever."

She laughed at him. "But I know you'll be called away soon tonight."

"No, *mi amore*, I answer no calls this night, tonight belongs to you and me."

Rolling over on top of her, he kept his weight from crushing her as he held himself above her on his forearms, and kissed her softly, nipping and biting at her lips. His kisses softly grazed her skin, little teasing bites, and he felt her respond to him.

He straddled her, sitting on his knees as he began to undress her, opening each button of her blouse. Pulling her blouse from her jeans, he kissed the tops of those tender mounds, licking them before running his tongue over the tops of the lacey edge of her bra, while his hands cupped her breasts. Her hips began to arch into him and he smiled softly.

"Slow down, *mi amore*."

"Slow down, easy for you to say. I'm ready to rip your clothes to shreds as you usually do mine."

Leaning down, he removed her bra and tossed the garment across the room. "So, you want your savage lover?"

She giggled at him. "I love the beast, and I love the gentleman, and I love my master. So, whoever comes out to play will be fine with me. I never know what to expect, which is part of the pleasure."

Sliding his hands under her ass, he lifted her hips to his mouth and buried his face into the crotch of her jeans and growled. Feeling his fangs elongate, he had her out of those jeans before she could even see what happened and found the red lace thong underneath.

"*Cazzo*, I love those!"

She reached up and started to slowly unbutton his shirt, touching his chest with her hands as each button was opened, followed by the lightest kiss, and tiny flick of her tongue. She pulled his shirt free of his jeans and ran both hands from his shoulders down to the waistband of his jeans. She started to remove his shirt, but he grabbed it impatiently and quickly removed it and tossed it to the floor.

"Slow down, lover. Now where did I hear that before? Ah yes, it was you, just a few minutes ago."

"You, minx, are like a drug, never enough."

Standing up beside the bed, he stripped down naked. "Sit up, *bel*."

As she sat up, that red hair screamed at him. He leaned forward and let his cock slide through her hair as he threw back his head, growling.

"*Cazzo!* I could cum in that silk so easily. It makes me so fucking hard."

"Do it, lover, cum in my hair."

He thrusts his hips back and forth, letting his cock become entangled in that swirl of red silk. Reaching into her hair, he gripped fistfuls as his cock slid through that crimson, and he was about to lose his mind. His beast was rocking inside him and urged him on. His breathing was ragged. Everything about her was making him lose control.

Grabbing his cock, he started stroking hard, as her hair tumbled around it like velvet around steel, and then she did something that set his beast free. She grabbed his ass and squeezed hard, and he exploded into the silk. His head was thrown back, his eyes blazing red, his fangs hungry for her essence.

She felt him cum in her hair as she leaned in and gently sucked on his balls, first one, and then the other. She slowly pulled her head back and let her hair gradually fall free, untangling from his cock. Then she took his cock in her mouth and swirled her tongue over him as she sucked away the last of his cum. She looked up at him through her tangled red hair.

"Is that what you needed?"

"You are my walking sin."

Kate lay down, and pulled him into bed next to her, her hand in his hair, held by those piercing blue eyes. "Now close your eyes."

He raised one eyebrow, wondering what she was up to. "Okay, closing my eyes."

She slipped from their bed and walked to the dresser, removing the small gift she had for him before returning to lay next to him.

"You give me so much, and there's nothing I can give that will compare to the lavish gifts you give to me."

She took his hand and opened it palm up and poured the contents of the small drawstring pouch into his hand.

"Open your eyes, lover. I want you to have these rubies that have been faceted into hearts. You can slip them in the pocket of your jeans, or even your leathers, and carry me with you always. Think of me when you reach in your pocket and feel them there."

Shade looked at the stones and holds them in his hand, feeling their smooth edges, so tiny in his hands, and yet, his heart exploded with his love for her. He looked into her dark brown eyes and he had no words. His expression must be so lost on her, for she'd left him speechless. A gift she felt was small but was more precious to him than anything. As he spoke, his voice was soft and cracked with emotion.

"*Bel*, your love is my greatest gift and you have given that freely. But, I have no words."

He reached for her and held her tight against his chest and hugged her, laying his head on her shoulder, snuggling into her neck.

"This is so special to me."

"I hate when you're away from me, Shade. I understand that you must go, and I can't always follow. I wanted to find something small enough you could always carry with you, something that would remind you that you carry my heart."

"You are always with me, *bel*."

48

The work on Luca's suite was almost complete. The furniture was in place, completing his bedroom and sitting room, and the workers were in the process of installing the custom cabinetry for his art studio. Luca seemed thrilled with his new living arrangements and said he couldn't wait to start painting again.

Kate and Shade were checking out the room when Shade turned to Luca, "I will be staying home tonight, so you will have the opportunity to go feed. Be sure to arm yourself." Luca gave him a silent nod as Shade led Kate from his room.

He noticed her pensive mood as he led her up the stairs to their bedroom. With her hand in his, he walked to the overstuffed chair by the window. The moon had begun to stream through the window, and he decided not to turn on any other lights, leaving the room lit only by the moonlight. Sitting down, he pulled her into his lap and they faced the window together. She curled into him as he wrapped his arms around her.

"So, what is on your mind, Kate? Is something troubling you?"

She laid her head against his chest. "I feel awkward asking, like it's none of my business, but you sent Luca out, and I know he's going to feed. He doesn't know anyone here. How will he feed? Will he find a mortal or another vampire? If he finds a mortal, does he have to attack the mortal? You told him to take weapons, so it concerns me. It scares me, actually."

His hands played in her hair, he could feel her concern for Luca and that pleased him, she was attaching herself to him and that was exactly what needed to happen.

"*Mi amore*, listen to me carefully. When a vampire such as Luca feeds, he never attacks a mortal. That is not something I approve of, nor does the vampire culture as a whole. You have been brainwashed from movies and books. *Si*? Do you wish to know more? I would like for you to know what happens."

"Yes, please tell me. And I'm relieved he's not attacking mortals. I was having a hard time envisioning that from Luca. I have no doubt he's a fierce warrior in a battle, but I couldn't see him attacking an innocent."

He chuckled softly, "No attacking innocents. Not how I play. Warriors are born to keep safety within our own ranks. We train to fight other warriors and only battle mortals who attack us. Blood is the mainstay of our life, we need it to live, if we do not feed routinely, our bloodlust overtakes us, and we will attack anything that has blood. It is rather like a heroin addict, we need it and if deprived of it long enough, we go into a state of aggression, and gorge, kill and drain. So, I am quite strict about my warriors feeding regularly. In our culture, we have females we call feeders. They are bred for that purpose, strictly used to feed vampires, male or female. It may sound very unusual to you, but for vampires who are not mated, or feeding from another vampire or mortal, it is a safe way to feed. Their blood is very pure. Mortals may think of them as whores, but that is very wrong. Feeders are highly regarded and respected in our culture. They feed and give strength. Luca had one specifically to whom he liked very much, which is normal. You know that feeding is a bonding of sorts, and before you ask, yes very sexual for them, it is a release in two ways. Do you understand so far?"

"Yes...that part I understand very well."

"Well, now that Luca is here, he can seek out a lair of feeders or he can hunt. When we say hunt, most times it means feed from mortals. Other times, it can mean hunting down bad vampires or a threat. Tonight, and tomorrow, Luca will be hunting someone to feed from, a mortal. But he understands he can go to a club, a bar, any place, and find someone he is interested in, seduce them, get them in a dark corner, outside in an alley, wherever."

He tipped her chin and grinned. "Sometimes your prey will invite you home. He will charm her, then feed from her, and wipe clean her memory, so she will not recollect the event. She may recall meeting him, but the details will be unclear, she may think she had too much to drink or some such. No harm done. As you know, you can easily embrace someone and feed and make it look, from a distance, as if you are cuddling or kissing her neck. It is very erotic for both mortals and immortals, understand?"

"Oh, I understand, lover, believe me. It was why I wanted you to only feed from me. It was most unexpected and took me by surprise the first time you fed from me. But why not just bring the girl who was his feeder here, especially if he was fond of her? Or does he want the thrill of the hunt, and finding someone new?"

He hugged her tight and laughed. "A feeder is not a mate. And a feeder relationship is never exclusive. It is a business relationship. Most have families they support because they are paid well. Luca was attached to her, but his feeder is being taken care of, and she will find another vampire to feed from her soon. It was not love he felt for her. A feeder can never be his mate. But it is not unusual for a warrior living in the barracks to become close to their feeder or prefer one over another, keeping the same feeder for a period of time, if they like her and the sex is good. Luca will find another feeder. There is a lair of feeders just outside of Washington that I have checked out. Luca may go there, or he may hunt. I think Luca was destined to come to the States, like me. Something tells me he will find his mate here, like I did."

Kate stared out the window, a frown on her face. "Wow, that's a lot of information to process. First, I'd love for Luca to find a mate. So that part pleases me. But you went to D.C. to check out feeders for Luca? Couldn't he do that? I'm not particularly thrilled with that idea, Shade."

"Oh, I love when you get jealous, *mi amore*." He laughed, shaking his head. "*Bel*, I checked out the feeder lair to see what it involved, who runs it, how many feeders they have, what they can accommodate. Not to check out the females. I have arranged to pay them. This is a service I provide for Luca, Gi, and Reynaldo, even Theresa, all my staff and warriors. And Luca needs to feed regularly, to protect you. Gi manages the scheduling for the house staff, so they are not all gone at the same time. But Luca must work his feeding schedule around me. He may decline the feeder. That is his option. Or he may decide on some combination of the two, to sometimes use the feeder, sometimes to hunt."

He could see the perplexed look on her face.

"Theresa goes to the feeders?"

"Of course. All vampires must feed."

Kate shook her head. "But you said all feeders were female."

"*Si*. We make no distinction between feeding or sex, although most of us have a gender preference. Theresa may also hunt and seduce a male mortal, or she may find a male vampire who catches her eye. If not, she must also go to a female feeder."

"But it's still sexual...the feelings, if Theresa feeds from a female."

"Oh *si*, that part does not change."

"So, when you said most vampires have a preference, does that mean you have the mortal equivalent of homosexuals?"

"*Si, mi amore*. A male vampire who prefers the company of other males may still need to feed from a female feeder on occasion. But a female vampire who prefers females, I guess she has the best world. She can choose to hunt only other females, as well as use the feeders."

"And did you go to feeders?"

"I am not sure how you manage to always bring this conversation back to me, but *si*, I have gone to feeders. Sometimes it is the most convenient option when we are on unfamiliar grounds. Large cities usually have underground clubs, like the one in San Francisco, where it is easy to meet other vampires looking to feed, or mortals interested in the sex. Or we strike out on our own to hunt. If we go too long without feeding, the beast takes over. The bloodlust must be satisfied, or the beast drains and kills his victim. That kind of behavior puts the whole community at risk of exposure, so for that reason, there is not the same social stigma on our feeding and sexual habits as exists in the mortal world. If a vampire waits too long, we have a last resort to control the beast in a safe house. A safe house is also underground, known only to the vampire community. You will find no mortals there as the beast reigns."

"A safe house? There are feeders there?"

"No, just other vampires who have waited too long to feed. It is savagery on every level. It is the option of last resort. We will not talk of it, *si*? You will never see the inside of a safe house, this I promise you."

He turned his head and looked out the window, his profile outlined in the moonlight, as he remembered his encounters in the safe houses, experiences he'd never share with her.

She looked at him closely. "But you're done with that, right? The feeders? The clubs?"

He turned to look at her. "Kate, you have to ask me that? Have I not made it clear I feed only from you? I take no notice of other females."

"No, lover, but I promise you, the females take notice of you. I trust you implicitly. I want you to know that. But women are drawn to you. I watch them when we're out. If they could mow me down to get to you, they would. So, am I jealous? Yes, I'll always be jealous, but not because of a lack of trust in you. It's the women I mistrust."

He pulled her into his chest, crushing her into him. "I don't want anything to make you feel jealous. My past is past. We have been here so damn long, surviving in the darkness. You are my mate for all eternity. It took me a long time to find you. I am sorry that I bring you any discomfort at all."

He kissed her softly, deepening the kiss, gripping her hair, and letting all his love flow to her. "Let me take you to bed and show you, *mi amore*. Show you how I love you."

49

"Kate, Gi tells me Luca's suite is finished. Have you seen it?"

"I've seen most of it, except for the custom cabinetry for his art studio. Have you been in to see it?"

"No, I have not. Gi says he is quite happy with it. They are all overwhelmed with your generosity with their living quarters. You make me proud, *bel rosso*."

"Lover, I didn't feel like I was being generous. I just wanted them to feel at home."

He smiled at her because her spirit of generosity had no guile, no agenda. "Well, perhaps you would like to accompany me to his suite? I would like to see his rooms as well."

"Of course."

He took her hand as they walked to Luca's suite and knocked lightly on his door. As Luca opened the door and welcomed them in, Shade took in the beauty of the strong, masculine room, and knew no warrior who lived in luxury like this. This level of opulence was reserved for a master, but he approved of *bel*'s choices because it had created a bond between her and the staff he'd brought over from Florence.

In the alcove that had been converted to an art studio, Luca already had an easel displaying a canvas. Shade gasped aloud as he saw it and stopped in his tracks, waiting for her reaction at what she saw before her.

Kate almost bumped into him when he stopped so suddenly. She looked past Luca to a painting on the easel and was dumbfounded. *Me? He's done a painting...of me?*

She walked slowly to the easel, aware that her mouth was open as she gazed in amazement at the portrait. He'd painted her in a three-quarter profile, standing with her bare back and shoulder exposed, as she looked over her shoulder, her hair cascading down her back. She was clearly recognizable in the painting, but there was an abstract quality to the portrait.

"Luca...this is...this is seriously good. I mean, this is museum-quality good. Your technique, with the broad strokes, that's very unique. And you painted me? I've never been an artist's muse before. Wow, I'm really just overcome by it. Lover, look at this. Do you like it?"

Shade stepped up behind her, wrapped his arms around her waist, and put his chin on top of her head. "*Si, mi amore,* I do. I think your protector has captured your spirit." He kissed her cheek softly.

The portrait was spellbinding. "I feel like I shouldn't ask, like I'm taking advantage, but may I have the portrait please?"

"I painted this for you, my lady. It's a housewarming gift from me. This is how I see you when you look at master, your love for him, his blood calling to you. Your demeanor changes when he's near you. There is a light in your eyes, and a softening in your face. It's something I wanted to capture for him as well. I'm so grateful you've given me this honor of protector, given me a home and my own quarters, and I wanted to show my appreciation."

Kate listened to Luca's explanation of his work, what he saw in her when she looked at Shade, and the love that she felt for Shade was visible on the canvas, palpable. She gave Luca a hug knowing that Shade had engineered the situation in Florence to make sure she'd have the best of the best as her protector.

"You honor me, Luca. You honor both of us. I want to hang this in our bedroom. I don't have the words to thank you." Kate planted a small kiss on his cheek before stepping back.

Shade watched as Luca lowered his head. "I am proud of you, Warrior." Shade embraced him, pounding his fist on Luca's back.

As they broke from the hug, Luca asked for permission to leave. "Master, if you'd allow, I'd like to leave again tonight. I can come back tomorrow evening when the painting is completely dry and hang it wherever my lady wishes."

Shade understood the hunger and saw it in his eyes and allowed him to leave. "Go Luca. I will call you if I need you, keep your head about you, new territory, you know the rules."

Taking *bel*'s hand, Shade walked her down the corridor and headed to their part of the house and found it quiet. All the workers were gone, and the staff had cleared out for the night.

"So *mi amore*, what shall we get into?"

"Lover, there's so much to get into."

He laughed as he held her hand, pulling her up the stairs behind him. "Then follow me, there just happens to be this very private bedroom at the top of the stairs."

50

Shade was busy in the Dead House. He'd sent out the list of weapons he needed to Florence and was waiting for delivery. He'd sent the bill to Alec and was re-working some of the grid maps and adjusting the warriors' assignments. He was working with a crew to finalize the installation of the security system they were installing. From his spot in the command center, he could now monitor every room in the Dead House, as well as both exterior entrances. Even with all the activity here, the neighborhood still thought this property was vacant since his crew teleported in, and the high wall around the rear courtyard protected them from view when they stepped outside.

Despite all the busywork and the fact that it was all vital and needed to be done, his mind was restless, as were his hands. He preferred the action on the streets to the activity in the command center. Deciding to take a break and stretch his legs, he headed out on his nightly rounds in his personal grid in G-town. He teleported out, making a few quick checks on the other appointed grids, just to make sure all of the warriors were on point. Everything looked quiet tonight and his warriors looked bored, preferring a little more action themselves. Shade headed into G-town and did a broad sweep, starting at the outside perimeter of the grid, and working his way in, getting closer to the sector that included Alec's house.

As he got closer to the center of the grid, he picked up a scent-vampire. He was only a few miles from the Canton residence and this didn't bode well. He focused his sense of smell and hearing and found them quickly. There were two of them, young street punks, skulking and unaware of the Medici high above them, zeroing in on their heads.

"Stupid punks, you just found yourselves in the hands of the only nightmare you will never escape."

He watched them take a side street on course for Alec's home and with sword in hand, he swooped down on them. One was caught totally unaware, and that was exactly Shade's intention. He hadn't become a warrior of this magnitude by being careless. Before the rogue even saw his face, Shade swung his sword and the rogues' head rolled along the alley as his body dropped lifeless to the street.

Quickly backflipping to face the other rogue, Shade laughed wickedly as the rogue was getting ready to take flight over his head to escape, but Shade had other ideas. The rogue wore a black sweat jacket, the hood pulled over his head, and Shade couldn't make eye contact with him. The rogue leaped over his head and Shade caught the glint of moonlight reflecting off the shuriken the rogue held in his hand. Shade lifted himself higher, hovering in midair, as he grabbed the rogue by the arm, attempting to wrench it from the socket when the rogue broke free. Shade made a grab for him, catching only the hood of the sweatshirt but the rogue swiftly backed away, sliding out of the shirt and escaping into the black night.

Shade's beast roared as he hovered above the ally, looking at the fucking sweatshirt clutched in his hand, the Italian curses flying. He'd had enough of these games! He whipped out his shuriken and with the flick of his wrist, he let it fly with speed and accuracy, aiming it straight into the back of the rogue's shaved head. The shuriken hit its mark and the rogue dropped to the ground like a stone. Shade was there waiting when he landed. The rogue tried to jump to his feet, but it was of no use. Death by the Medici was swift and sure.

Shade immediately called on Tomas telepathically, commanding him to come to this location. He had two rogues down and needed assistance getting their bodies back to the Dead House and into the courtyard for the encroaching morning sun to vaporize them. Shade kicked the dead body at his feet, as the rogue laid on his side. He spotted an emblem on his back and flipped the rogue over, so he was lying face down in the alley. He crouched down to get a closer look and noticed the rogue's back was covered with a tattoo that ran shoulder to shoulder. The black ink wasn't very old, and the design was elaborate and might provide a clue.

As Tomas landed beside him, Shade quickly gave him instructions to gather the other body and the severed head and return to the Dead House. Shade lifted the other dead rogue and teleported straight back himself. He and Tomas landed in the section of the basement that had been cordoned off as a dungeon and holding cell for rogues, though few ever lived long enough to end up here. Shade dumped the rogue's body next to the one Tomas had carried in and instructed Thomas to strip the beheaded rogue of his shirt.

As he did so, they discovered the same tattoo on that rogue's back and Shade knew they had a coven or a master to deal with, and one that was probably on target for Alec. They were no longer dealing with the lone street punks who plagued every city, but something more organized and coordinated. Masters would often tattoo their warriors with the emblem of their coven as a symbol of allegiance or ownership. They felt it created a bond between the warriors, a sense of pride, not unlike a soldier wearing a uniform, or a biker wearing a 'cut'. Shade had never done such. Everyone knew you were a Medici, and no one needed a damn symbol of allegiance to create their bond. Medici warriors were elite and the best in the entire world. Taking out his cell phone, he snapped a few pictures of the rogue's tattoo.

Turning to Tomas, he asked, "What the hell does this mean? I have never seen this tattoo before Tomas, don't recognize the coven. This is going to take some research. The ink looks fresh, so probably new recruits. What the fuck are they doing here? They appeared to be heading in a direct line to Alec's. You ever see this, brother?"

Tomas stood with his arms crossed over his chest. *Stupid fuckers*. He recognized the tattoo all right, and he wondered why Max would want to advertise. This just made his job a lot harder and he'd be sure to let Max know about it too. He kept his mouth shut and plastered a quizzical expression on his face as the Medici inspected the bodies. Tomas thought to himself, Shade could research all he wanted, but he wouldn't find any answers, of that Tomas was quite sure.

Tomas crouched down beside Shade and ran his hand over the inked image and shook his head.

"Never saw anything like that in my travels, brother. Been around a while and I've seen a lot of coven symbols, not familiar with this one, though." Tomas stood back up and waited for his orders, and Shade wasn't long belting them out.

Shaking his head, Shade took several more shots on his camera and told Tomas to haul the bodies to the courtyard. He had a phone call to make.

Tomas quickly did as he was told. He had a phone call to make himself.

Shade climbed the rickety stairs to the upper floor of his makeshift command center and flopped down in his chair, shoving aside the papers that covered the surface of the desk. Looking at the photos on his phone, he was still perplexed at what he was seeing, but he had to call Alec and let him know. Shade knew Alec probably wouldn't have a clue about the tattoo. He had disconnected from the immortals years ago, but he'd need to know of this latest development. He dialed up Alec, and after several rings, he finally answered. Shade filled him in on the details and the locale of the rogues' whereabouts and it was no surprise when Alec informed him to text the images and he'd get to them later and see what he could make of them.

Shade ended the call and ran his hand through his hair. Sliding the phone into his pocket, he heard the warriors as they started rolling into the Dead House, their jobs done for the night. He could almost feel the slow progression of the sun making its way to the dawning, and he was more than ready to head home.

51

Kate was waiting for Shade to return home, it was close to sunrise. Luca had received a shipment of boxes and crates from Florence that were stacked to the ceiling, and lined the long corridor to Shade's office and Luca's suite. She couldn't imagine what it could possibly be. If all this stuff belonged to Luca, it was going to get really crowded in his suite.

"Luca, what's all this stuff?"

"Weapons for the bunker, my lady."

"Weapons? All of this? Are you kidding me? There're enough crates here to outfit an army! Did you order all this stuff?"

"Yes, my lady, I ordered what master requested."

"What he requested? I don't understand. Why would anyone need all this stuff?"

Luca looked at her quizzically. "My lady, master is a warrior, not just any warrior, the Warrior's warrior, the Medici."

Kate held the same questioning expression on her face. "Was that supposed to answer my question?"

Luca could feel the energy shift and knew Shade was teleporting in. Perfect timing. He'd let Shade explain all this. "I think that is a question for master."

Luca broke open the crates and started unloading firearms, swords, blades, bows, and other items Kate couldn't even recognize, just as Shade teleported into the space.

Shade landed softly in the corridor, having received Luca's message earlier that the weapons had arrived for the bunker. He grabbed up Kate and gave her a kiss. "And how is my sweet *bel rosso* this morning?"

"I'm confused by the weapons. We need all of these?"

"*Bel*, do not concern yourself with such. They will be stored in the bunker, *si*?"

He grabbed a crate in each hand and started down the stairs and through the wine cellar to the hidden bunker. Kate followed him and saw Luca had already started mounting some of the weapons on the wall. There were panels that pushed open to reveal large storage spaces behind the wall that held even more weapons. The room had been furnished with a large conference table and surrounded by chairs. The same security monitor that was mounted in his office was mounted on the wall here, along with the console that controlled all the cameras. Shade was walking slowly around the room, admiring the weapons that had been mounted, as well as those behind locked glass cases.

"So, what do you think, *bel*?"

Kate looked around the bunker. "It looks, well, scary actually. You told me once you didn't want me down here, and I don't think you'll have to worry about that. I know you wanted me to learn weapons, but some of these things...I can't even imagine what they'd do to a person. Do we need all this stuff here?"

You have no need to come here. If you need me, and I am down here, you call to me telepathically. You have that gift so use it."

"I understand. If you're here, you expect privacy. But there are enough weapons here for an army. And this large table...It's just you and Luca. I don't understand."

Shade chose his words carefully. He didn't want to alarm her. "*Bel*, I command an army. Did you not see my warriors in Florence? I am working with Alec's mercenaries, but if they cannot get up to speed, I will bring in my own. I may be having meetings here, and my warriors will be in and out. *Bel*, come here."

She walked into his arms and he held her tight. "Listen to me. This is not about requesting privacy. This is about my job, and what I do. The less you know sometimes, the better, *si*? If I am to protect you, and our house, this is a necessity. And if you are not familiar with how these things work, you need not be down here, it is dangerous for you. These weapons are loaded and ready for use. Leave this to me and Luca."

Shade resumed unpacking the crates, laying out weapons on the large table, as Luca carried in more boxes.

Kate looked at the display of weapons. "Are we in danger?"

Shade and Luca exchanged a glance. Shade sighed. "Kate, I am a master, and a warrior. There will always be those who will challenge me. This is just a precaution, *si*?"

Kate picked up a weapon from the table that she'd heard Shade call a shuriken, a large star-shaped wheel containing five razor-sharp finger-like blades. "This looks like Freddie Kruger."

"Who, *bel*? Is he a warrior?"

"Freddie Kruger. He's an evil man in a horror movie. He comes into your dreams and kills you. His hands look like this."

"A dream-walker? They make movies about them now? Fucker sounds right up my alley. Wonder where he hangs out? Might be able to recruit him." He grinned as he teased her.

"I never thought of it in that way, but yes, he is like a dream-walker. Only, when he kills you in your dream, it's not a dream, he can actually kill you. You can't kill people in their dreams, can you?"

"Well, I am warrior. My gift is dream-walking. What do you think?"

Kate stood still and processed this information. He sent her such beautiful dreams. The thought that he could send bad dreams never occurred to her. The thought that he could enter into someone's dreams and do them harm never entered her mind. He was so protective of her, shielded her from so much, and sometimes, what he revealed was unexpected.

"I...I never thought about you sending bad dreams. But yes, why would a warrior need a skill to only send pleasant dreams."

Shivers ran up her spine at the realization he could turn someone's life into a living nightmare, and a skill that brought her only love and comfort could mean death for someone else.

Shade felt her fear and saw her physically shiver. "*Bel*, I am vampire. I am warrior. I cannot hide all that is within me from you forever, but I will admit I have shielded you. I am a dealer of death, but also of peace and protection, as is Luca. Does that make you frightened of me?"

She went to him and slipped her arms around his waist. "I'm never afraid of you. I know you shield me. I've always been aware of that, and there's even a part of me that chooses to be shielded. But I know who you are, and I know what you do. I watched you destroy Sabine in front of me, so trust me when I say, I'm aware of the power you possess. I'm in love with your warrior spirit, even when I sometimes turn a blind eye to what's going on. It was the warrior and the darkness that drew me to you in the first place. So never concern yourself that I'll pull away from you. That will never happen."

Relaxing as he heard her words, he knew she was still his sweet *bel* without fear of him or his beast. "I love you. I love how you love me, and my beast."

"Yes, and how come you aren't jealous of the beast? He loves me, you know."

Smiling, he laid his head on top of hers. "I am the beast, he is the darkness that I hide from you, and I like that you lure him, bring him forth, tame him...because that lets me come back to you, always."

"Lover, I've known that from the beginning. That's why I never had a fear of him. We have an understanding, this beast and me."

He chuckled softly, pulling her into an embrace, crushing her to his chest. "You see me like no other. Now go, let Luca and I get this wrapped up and I will join you upstairs. I can already feel the pull of my death slumber. Wait for me in our bed."

She turned to leave him, casting one last look over her shoulder, as he and Luca focused on unloading this cache of weapons and she was already wrapping herself in denial about this room and its contents.

52

Yesterday, Kate was eating everything is sight, and today, she felt like she had no appetite at all. She wondered if she was coming down with a flu bug. She was feeling a little tired, but she chalked that up to the fact she hadn't slept well. Shade would be in the Dead House again tonight, so she thought this would be a good time to check on the progress of the California house. The designers had informed her that almost all the deliveries had been made, and they had started furniture placement.

She headed for Luca's suite and tapped lightly on his door.

Luca put down his pallet and paint brush and opened the door to her.

"In the mood for a trip?"

"What do you have in mind, my lady?"

She closed her eyes and took a deep breath. The whole 'my lady' thing was getting old real fast. "I was thinking you could take me to the California house, so I can check on things there."

"Of course, my lady. Give me a few minutes to change, and to get the coordinates from master."

"The coordinates?"

"It's like directions. It will allow me to teleport there directly. I haven't been to the California house before."

Kate shrugged. "Okay, well, do whatever it is you do. I'm going to get my notebook and grab a jacket. I'll meet you back here."

She headed back up the stairs when a momentary wave of dizziness hit her. She paused briefly, steadied herself on the railing and then continued up the stairs, sending Shade a message about her plans.

"Lover, I'm going to have Luca take me to the California house. The designers are almost finished, so I need to check on their progress."

"*Si, mi amore*. I am sending Luca coordinates now. Be careful, *bel rosso.* This is the first time you have traveled without me, *ti amo*."

Kate grabbed her notebook and the file that held the photos of the furniture pieces as well as the fabric and paint swatches, pulled on a heavy jacket and returned downstairs to find Luca waiting.

"Just hold on around my shoulders, my lady. And close your eyes. If you aren't used to teleporting, closing your eyes will help with the dizziness."

Great, she was already feeling dizzy. She made a mental note to drink lots of water when they got to California. She was probably just dehydrated. She stepped up to Luca and held on as he slipped one arm around her waist, and before she could even process her next thought, they were in transit. The rush of cold air felt good, clearing her head. Within a matter of minutes, Luca landed them softly in the living room of the California house and released her. As she stepped back from him, she staggered slightly, and he reached out to steady her.

"That is normal, my lady. Most mortals feel dizzy after teleporting. It will pass."

She looked around the living room. The spacious room looked even larger furnished than it did when it was empty. The room was decorated in neutral ivory. The tall floor to ceiling windows opened the space, and the added mirrors and lighting only seemed to open it even more. It was a beautiful room, but very formal as dictated by the rooms architecture. She liked what she saw and it surpassed her imagination, but she still preferred the less formal space in Virginia.

Kate headed through the formal dining room and into the well-appointed, thoroughly modern kitchen. She opened the fridge, taking out bottled water and chugged it down, tossing the bottle in the re-cycle bin, and grabbing another bottle from the fridge to sip on as they toured the house.

Luciano appeared from nowhere, and he and Luca exchanged greetings.

"My lady, is everything all right? I was not notified of your plans to travel here."

"Everything's fine. I hope I'm not upsetting your schedule, but this was a spur of the moment decision. Shade was going to be busy all night, and the designers said the house was almost done. Please, don't let me interrupt. I'm fine here, and I have Luca."

Luciano nodded. "Then if you require nothing further, my lady, I'll take my leave."

Kate completed her inspection of the formal dining room, the library, and the less formal family room, before heading into the space that had been designed for Luca. "These are your California digs. What do you think, Luca?"

Luca looks stunned. "My digs? These are my rooms?"

"Yes, well, I wasn't sure how much we'd use this house, how often we'd come here, so I went ahead and furnished these rooms for you."

The rooms had the same masculine feel as the Virginia house, but the space was larger, and she had included a fully equipped art studio. Luca felt overwhelmed. He never had his own private space before, and now he had two.

"My lady, I love the rooms, but this was not necessary. I can stay anywhere."

"Luca, Shade told me to spend money, so I'm spending money. Enjoy it. Now come on, let's go upstairs and check all the bedrooms we'll never use."

Luca chuckled as he followed her up the wide curved staircase. She paused midway up, and he noticed her clutching the banister rail.

"My lady, are you all right?"

Kate put her hand to her forehead and took a few deep breaths before continuing up the stairs. "It's nothing. Just a wave of dizziness, I'm fine."

"Did you eat today, my lady? Reynaldo said you didn't stop by the kitchen this evening."

"No, I didn't. I'm sure that's it. We should only be here another hour or so, and I can get something when we can get home."

Kate completed the inspection of all the upstairs bedrooms, each with a fireplace, sitting room, and private bath, saving the massive master suite for last. She had made a few notes of things she wanted changed, and a few pieces she wanted to add, including some art installations, and then she let Luca know she was ready to return. Luca noticed she looked paler than when they started this tour of the house and he'd be glad to get her back home.

"My lady, if you don't object, I am going to carry you for the teleport home." He didn't wait for her response but scooped her up and took them both back to Virginia, setting her down in the hallway at the foot of the stairs.

"Thank you, Luca, I was feeling really tired. I think I'm going upstairs and rest."

"My lady...you did not eat."

"Maybe later." Kate started up the stairs to the bedroom when he noticed her unsteadiness again and picked her up to carry her to her bed.

"Luca, this is so unnecessary. I'm fine!"

"Clearly, you are not fine, my lady. I'll have Theresa bring you something to eat, and I am letting master know you are not well." **"Master, we are back from California, but I fear my lady is not well."**

"Oh, for Pete's sake, Luca! I'm perfectly capable of walking."

Luca laid her on the bed as Theresa entered with a tray of hot tea, juice, and toast. Kate was wondering how Theresa got the water to boil that fast for tea, when Shade appeared in their bedroom.

"Kate!" Shade sat on the side of the bed, brushing the hair back from her face. "What's wrong? Are you okay?"

She threw up her hands in exasperation. "Nothing's wrong. I was feeling a little dizzy. I hadn't eaten, and then we teleported to California. I feel tired. Maybe I'm coming down with the flu or something, but nothing to justify all this concern and attention."

Shade sent Luca and Theresa away and then returned his attention to Kate. "Eat and drink what is on the tray and I will get your gown for you, *bel*."

Kate sighed as she propped herself up against the massive headboard and sipped at the hot tea, watching Shade open and close2 drawer after drawer, searching for her nightgowns.

"Bottom drawer, lover."

"Ah, *si*, *mi amore*." He removed a long, soft white nightgown and carried it back to her bed, sitting down next to her.

"Now tell me what happened, *bel*. What caused Luca such concern? I think you brush this off too lightly. Vampires do not get the flu."

"But I'm not vampire."

"*Si*, not yet vampire, but you feed from me, and because of that, you have certain immunities from mortal illness. Talk to me."

"Shade, there's nothing much to share. Yesterday, I was starving. I think I ate everything in the kitchen. I'm sure Reynaldo had to go shopping after I finished. Then, today, I wanted nothing, so I didn't eat. I didn't sleep well, and I felt tired and a little dizzy. I probably shouldn't have gone to California. I probably just overextended myself. That's all."

Shade was watching her closely while she spoke. Her lily-white skin was even paler than usual. He made sure she finished the juice and toast then cleared away the tray, helping her undress and pull the soft gown over her head. He pulled back the covers and tucked her in, kissing her cheek.

"Sleep, *bel rosso*. I will be here the rest of the night if you need anything. You are not to get up, understood?"

Kate would argue that he was being over-protective, that they were all overreacting, but she felt a tiredness that was bone deep, and the pillow beneath her head, and the soft blankets he tucked around her shoulders were already drawing her into a deep sleep. She felt his tender kiss just as she drifted into sleep.

Shade remained seated by her side until he was sure she was sleeping, not sure what to make of her illness. He'd keep a close eye on her over the next few days.

Changing from his leathers, he threw on some sweats and headed down to his office, so he could download those pictures of the rogue's tattoos from his cell phone.

The downstairs was quiet again and it looked like Luca had retreated back to his suite. He entered his office, plopped down in his chair, in front of his desk that faced a large monitor, and started downloading the files. The images were much easier to see this large and provided him with much greater detail. He scrolled through the pictures and chose one of the clearer images to text to Alec.

Shade leaned in close to the screen to try to get a better idea of what the hell he was looking at. It was a symbol of some sort. Both vampires had it in the same place on their back, a clear indication of an allegiance to a coven or master. He didn't know everything in this fucking vampire world, but he'd been here long enough to notice some things and he'd never seen this tattoo anywhere in his travels. It looked like a goat's head of some sort. Working the photo properties on his computer, he turned the image 180 degrees, then 90 degrees. Having no luck with that, he zoomed in on the picture and took a harder look, rolling this image around in his head, trying to think of some connection.

Shade was invested in figuring this out. He knew this was probably not going to be the last time they saw this symbol, and the sooner he figured this out, the better for all of them. He knew Alec would put this on the back burner, and unless something else happened with this rogue coven, it would slip from his memory. But, for Shade, this was top priority. So, what the hell was their purpose and who the hell were they?

Shade heard Luca step up behind him, leaning over his shoulder, staring at the same images on the screen.

Luca pointed at the screen and outlined the shape of the tattoo with his extended finger. "That's the sign for Aries."

"What the hell do you mean Aries? Explain. Have you seen this before?"

Luca responded, "The object in the middle is a ram's head, the astrological sign of Aries. I've never seen this tattoo on a vampire before, but I recognize the astrological sign. The other symbols on each side of the ram's head look to me as if they are shuriken blades...tribal."

Shade rolled this around in his head. "So, would you think this means a coven named Aries, or perhaps the name of the master? They are warriors loyal to this symbol, *si*?"

"I'd say yes, master. That's how it appears, though I've never heard of an Aries coven."

Shade thought this over. "Nor I. No coven or master named Aries that I know of. It could be a new coven. It could be some upstarts who broke away from their master. Or punk rogues banding together. Either way, not good for us." Shade flipped off the monitor and wheeled his chair around. "Now tell me what happened to Kate."

Luca looked confused. "I'm not sure, master. She stumbled a few times when we got to California. I thought, initially, it was just the teleport, but the effects of teleporting a mortal dissipate in minutes. She said she was tired, and she looked pale to me. Other than that, I'm afraid I know nothing."

Shade's emotions were jangled, something was wrong with *bel*, and something was up with these rogue vampires. He hadn't fed, and he couldn't go to her now if she wasn't feeling well. There was nothing he hated more than feeling things were out of his control.

He returned to the bunker with Luca where they finished unpacking and storing the weapons, at least gaining the satisfaction of getting this one project complete when he felt the call of sunrise. Returning to their bedroom, *bel* slept soundly. She looked like she had hardly moved from the position he'd left her in. He slipped from his sweats and climbed in bed bedside her. He heard the soft whir of the electronic blinds. He pulled her close, wrapping his arms around her, kissing her softly as he was pulled into his death slumber.

When he woke at sunset, he fully expected to find her side of the bed empty, but she slept beside him still. He sat up, turning on the bedside lamp, and looked at her closely, her skin deathly pale. He gently shook her awake.

"Kate, you do not look well, are you feeling sick still?"

Feeling him gently shake her awake, she felt groggy and it was hard to focus her thoughts. "I feel so tired. I slept for twelve hours, and I feel like I could sleep twelve more. Just let me sleep. Maybe I have the flu? If I'm not better soon, I'll call for an appointment. I'm sure it's nothing. You're so busy in D.C. now, you're pulled there so often, and I know you have a lot on your mind. I don't want to burden you with this stuff."

He lay his head softly on top of hers. "*Bel*, I am worried about you. You are not yourself, you do not look well and perhaps you are right, perhaps you should see a doctor, but I think it may be wise to call Rissa. You can't see a mortal doctor. Your DNA has been altered. All your blood work will be different. Rissa was mortal once and may be able to guide you to a doctor who can handle mortals in transition."

"Yes, I'll call her. That sounds like a good idea. Could you have Theresa bring me more hot tea and some dry toast? I still don't feel like I can eat anything, but I know I need to drink something."

"Of course, *mi amore*. Whatever you need, tell me, I will have it for you." **"Gi, my lady needs some hot tea, some toast."**

His fingers played with her hair as he lay next to her. "I am sure Rissa will have an answer. She may be able to guide you better."

Kate lay quietly as she felt his fingers in her hair...softly caressing...so relaxing. She loved being curled up next to him. She listened to his voice, so soothing, so comforting, as she felt herself drifting back to sleep. Gi knocked at the door, and Shade told him to enter. Gi laid the tray down on the side table, he excused himself and closed the door behind him. Reaching over for the tea, Shade held it tenderly to *bel*'s lips and lifted her gently.

"Please drink down the tea, take a few sips, it will put something in your stomach."

Kate felt so thirsty, so dehydrated. She tipped the cup to her lips and downed the entire cup, and then picked up the toast and took a few bites. Gi had brought a glass of water on the tray. She picked that up and swallowed it down as well. She dropped back down on the pillow and curled up next to him.

"Better..." Before she even finished the sentence, she felt herself drift away.

Shade watched with concern. Something wasn't right. His blood made her strong and immune to mortal disease.

They were definitely calling Rissa when she awoke. Looking down, he saw she was already asleep. He wanted to feed, but she was too weak. He'd make a quick trip to the Dead House tonight, make sure the warriors had their assignments and were on the streets.

"Ti amo, mi amore."

He dressed in leathers and left the room, stopping in to let Luca know he was out, and to call him home if anything changed with Kate.

53

Kate woke before Shade, but she knew he'd be waking soon. She had slept for hours. She quietly slipped out of bed, so as not to disturb him, and took a quick shower, thinking it would revive her. She still felt tired but thought maybe she could eat something now. She got dressed and tiptoed out of the room, and down the stairs heading for the kitchen where she would see what Reynaldo could fix for her.

As she reached the foot of the stairs and entered the living room, both Reynaldo and Theresa were frantically running about, gathering up all the red roses Shade left for her all over the house. Only the roses were no longer red, they had all turned black. Both Reynaldo and Theresa looked up at her with startled expressions, clearly not expecting to see her.

"What's wrong? What happened to all the roses?"

Reynaldo seemed caught off-guard and reluctant to answer, as he and Theresa exchanged glances.

"I'm not sure, my lady, perhaps you should ask master."

Kate was perplexed by his response. "What? If you know the answer, please tell me? Does Shade know?"

As she was addressing them, she heard footsteps behind her and turned to find Luca. He'd over-heard the conversation and was looking at the black roses Theresa and Reynaldo had gathered and had a concerned look on his face.

"Luca, do you know what this means? Why the roses turned black?"

Luca also looked reluctant to answer, but she gave him a pleading look. "Please don't leave me in the dark. There are already enough things going on in this house I don't understand. If you know something, please tell me!"

Luca sighed. "My lady, when red roses turn black it is a sign of foreboding."

"Foreboding? A foreboding of what, Luca?"

"That I can't tell you, my lady."

"You can't tell me, or won't tell me?"

"My lady, I'm not withholding anything from you. The roses turn black as a warning, but they don't reveal what the warning is about, or who the warning is for."

Kate felt a flash of panic. "Is it Shade? Is he in danger? Will he know the answer? Should I wake him up now? Is the warning imminent? I mean is it something that's supposed to happen now, or in the future?"

Luca ran his hand through his hair. "My lady, whatever it is could not be imminent for I don't feel any danger, and master continues to sleep, so please, relax, and master and I will deal with it as soon as he rises. I assure you, you're in no danger."

Kate wasn't appeased. "But he could be in danger. What if the warning is for him? Or you? What then?"

"My lady, you understand, in our culture, we're always prepared to face adversaries. It's why we train for a lifetime as warriors. We will deal with whatever confronts us."

She sighed and looked at him with exasperation. "Well, now you sound like Shade."

He smiled slightly and bowed his head. "Well, then, I'll take that as a compliment, my lady. Now head off to the kitchen with Reynaldo, and he'll fix you something to eat. This will all be dealt with in due time."

***

Shade woke from his death slumber, realizing he'd slept deeper than normal. Rolling over gently, arm outstretched to gather *bel* in his arms, he found the bed was empty. *"Bel?"*

Taking a deep breath and closing his eyes, he honed in and felt her in the house but fear and concern were taking over her mind. *Fuck! What in the hell happened now?* Pulling on a pair of jeans, he rushed downstairs and followed her scent to the kitchen to find her sitting at the bar talking to Reynaldo. A buffet fit for a queen had been spread before her and she was eating like a starved woman.. Standing with arms crossed over his chest, he leaned against the arched doorway and observed her, tapping into her thoughts, and she was upset about...flowers?

"I see you are hungry again? I like to see you eating, although I prefer you drink from the source of your strength."

Walking up behind her, he wrapped his arms around her, snuggling into her neck and kissed it softly. "What are you doing up so early without me?"

She giggled as he nuzzled into her neck, sending shivers down her spine. "I woke up starving. But, it was the weirdest thing, when I came downstairs, Reynaldo and Theresa were gathering all the roses to throw them away, they'd all turned black. Luca said it was a foreboding? He said not to worry, that you and he would deal with it. Has this happened before? Do you know what it means?"

Shade creased his brow. That explained the strange feeling he got from her about the flowers. The roses turning black was a foreboding of things to come, but he wasn't sure of what. Perhaps it was related to the damn rogues he killed in town and his own turmoil about the Aries tattoo. Sitting down on the stool beside her, he smiled at her and picked up a linen napkin, dabbing at the small crumbs on the side of her lips.

"*Mi amore*, you need not worry, *si*? The roses are a foreboding of something stirring. I would predict it is the rogues I found the other night and that has all been settled, nothing else has happened. So, let me handle this, I have it well in hand. Now, seems as though I need to call the florist and restock. The house will not smell as sweet without your red roses. You seem to be feeling much better, and your appetite has definitely returned."

Kate leaned her head on his shoulder. "See that's what Luca said. So, I'm not going to worry."

As she spoke, she could see Shade and Reynaldo exchange glances over her head. She knew it would do no good to question him further. He'd share what he wanted her to know, and protect her from the rest, and no amount of protest from her would change that. She decided to let this whole flower thing go.

"Do you think we still need to call Rissa? I mean, I do feel better. I'm still a little tired, but that's normal, isn't it? After the flu?"

"Well, I am glad you feel better." He took her hand. "I think we should call Rissa anyway. She may have a doctor who deals with mortal/immortal illness."

Smiling he lifted her hand to his lips, kissing her palm. "So, let us plan to call her, *si*? I think we should put her on the speaker phone, so we can both talk to her."

Helping her off the barstool, they headed to Shade's office to give them privacy, as they made the call. He pulled up a second chair to his desk for her to sit next to him.

Kate pulled out her cell and dialed her up before placing the phone on his desk. After a few rings, Rissa picked up the call. "Kate, I haven't heard from you in a while."

Kate began, not sure where to start. "Rissa, hi. I have you on speaker, I'm here with Shade, he thought it might be a good idea if we all talked about, uh, some things that have been going on."

Shade spoke up, "Basically, we need some direction, so I asked Kate that we both be on the call."

Rissa responded, only half listening to the conversation, "I'm not sure how I can help, but I'll do whatever I can, of course."

Kate continued, "It's nothing serious, but I've been sick, maybe just the flu or something? Shade thought I should call and get the name of a doctor. He said I couldn't go to my regular doctor anymore, that I'd need someone who specializes in transitional mortals."

Rissa perked up at the news Kate had been ill. Mortals who regularly feed from vampires don't get ill. Alec would want to know about this! "Well, first of all, I can tell by the tone of your voice, you're concerned. I have several doctors I can recommend, all specialists, so it depends on your symptoms. Tell me what's going on."

Kate downplayed her symptoms. "Really, it's nothing. Some days, I have no appetite, and can't keep food down, and the next day, I'm starving. I've felt really tired. I sleep for hours on end, like twelve hours at a time and then still feel I need sleep. That's about it, really."

Rissa listened in silence on the other end of the call before responding, "Hmm, does sound a bit off. Are you feeding from Shade?"

"I've not fed from him since I started feeling ill. And, of course, he hasn't fed from me, and that upsets me too."

"Don't let that upset you, Kate. Shade can go a while before he will be forced to feed. He knows how far he can push himself. And if necessary, he can always use a feeder. Shade, I know you well, so forgive my bluntness, but have you fed or been with anyone else lately?"

Shade bristled at her question and Kate's back stiffened at the very mention of a feeder.

"Rissa! For hell's sake, I cannot believe you asked me that. Of course not. I know your line of thinking, and there is no tainted blood in these veins. So, no. Now what other personal business do you need to know?"

Risa answered, sounding contrite, "Okay, I'm sorry, and I can tell this is a touchy subject and you're both worried. But one thing confuses me, as I'm sure it does you. If we have ruled out tainted blood, and you've been feeding on a regular basis from Shade, you shouldn't be getting the flu. You should be well past the stage of getting many mortal diseases." There was a pause before she blurted out, "Oh my god, Kate, are you pregnant?"

Kate answered with a single word, "Pregnant?"

Shade heard the word pregnant and his gut wrenched, but he rejected the idea and lashed out. "Rissa, you have lost your damn mind. No, she isn't pregnant! Now can you email me the doctor's number? I will have Kate let you know how things go with the doctor."

Rissa wrapped up the call. "Done, Shade, I'll get his contact info and send it as soon as I hang up. Remember to mention Alec's or my name when you call the doctor, and you will move to the top of his call list. And please, keep us informed."

Kate looked up at Shade at the end of the call. "Pregnant? I mean, until I met Cory, I assumed it wasn't possible, that you were immortal, and you even said when we had children we'd have to wait until I was immortal."

Shaking his head, he couldn't fathom that *bel* could be pregnant. "Well, I think she was teasing, it is difficult for a vampire to impregnate a mortal, and when you use birth control it becomes a non-issue."

"Lover...I'm not, I mean, I didn't think I needed to be, we never talked about it, I made an assumption, and I never asked you. I'm not on the pill. I'm not on anything."

She started calculating in her head. When was her last period? Six weeks? Eight weeks? "I think I missed my last period. I wasn't paying attention. We've had so much going on. Do you think? No, it has to be something else, don't you think?"

He felt his blood run cold. If she was pregnant, this child might not survive, *she* might not survive. And if the baby survived, he'd be a half-breed. His eyebrows shot up. "You are not on any birth control? Oh fuck, *bel!*" Throwing his hands over his face, he took a deep breath. "When was your last flux? Think hard Kate, think hard."

Her voice shook as she answered, "It's been at least eight weeks, maybe a little longer."

His face turned red. "Two months ago? Two?" Standing up, he started to pace, and his temper was rising. "I need a smoke, I can't think, I need air. Damn it, Kate, how can a woman your age, single and sexually active, not be on birth control?"

Stomping out the patio door into the fresh air, he couldn't think, and he needed to get a grip on this situation. He could see he had hurt her feelings, and he needed to go to her, but he was overcome with the realization he could lose both of them.

Kate felt hurt and confused by his response. He'd raised his voice and turned his back on her, and walked away. She didn't even get time to respond to his question, but how would she have responded? Why didn't she ask him in the beginning when they first started having sex? Why did she just assume it was safe just because he was vampire? The tears started to flow, and she couldn't bear his anger. She dared not chase after him, he needed time to think and cool down. She'd learned there was no use talking to him when he was angry. But she didn't understand. He wanted children. He'd said he wanted lots of children, and she knew he wasn't planning on that now, but why was he so angry?

She left the office and headed for the stairs, encountering Luca in the hallway, and he saw the tears. "My lady, is there anything I can do?"

She couldn't answer him. She shook her head no and ran up the stairs into their bedroom, closing the door behind her. She lay across the bed and cried as the word *stupid, stupid, stupid* echoed in her head.

***

With his back against the house, Shade slid down into a seated position, pulling his knees up and putting his head down, when Luca appeared.

"Master, my lady is very upset. I can see you're upset as well, but she needs you to be strong, be her warrior. If nothing else, you have taught me your mate is above everything, even yourself. Show her that." Luca didn't wait for an answer but turned and left quietly.

Shade knew he was right, and they needed to be together. He carried as much blame as she did. He couldn't lay this at her feet. Sitting there for who knew how long, calming himself, he finally stood and teleported straight into the bedroom and his heart broke. Her face was streaked with tears and she couldn't even look at him. He sat on the bed next to her, pulling her to his chest, cradling her in his arms, rocking her.

"We both made assumptions. This is no one's fault. We will have this *bambino* together, if that is truly what is happening. Let us get the doctor here first, get his opinion and deal with whatever it is. I want a child with you, many children. If the fates have determined now is the time, then it will be the time. I love you, *bel rosso*, and nothing will come between us. We go through it all together."

He tried to convince himself it could be done, and it would be all right. Whatever happened, he'd handle it, but somewhere deep inside his beast growled, knowing this wasn't a good thing, and the warning of the black roses confirmed that.

She wiped the tears from her face. "Yes, let's get the doctor. We may be worried about nothing. We can call for an appointment. Let's get an answer, one way or another, so at least we know what we are dealing with."

"Then let's go back down to the office, and see if Rissa sent the email, and if yes, we can call right away."

He took her hand and they walked back down the stairs to the office. Shade went to the computer and pulled up the email from Rissa with a name and number. He was explaining to her that there were doctors who were themselves vampires, who specialized in dealing with issues related to vampires, as he dialed the number and handed her the phone. She heard a voice answer, "Dr. Cavelli's office."

Kate stumbled over her words. "Oh, uh, I need an appointment, please."

"Are you currently a patient of Dr. Cavelli's?"

"No, I'm new. I was referred by Alec Canton."

"Oh, Mr. Canton, of course. Well, by all means, we'll work you into the doctor's schedule. He can see you next week."

Kate looked up, anxious she'd have to wait that long for answers. "Next week? Do you have anything sooner?"

"Hold on please while I check with the doctor." After a few minutes, she returned to the phone. "Ma'am? Given your referral from Mr. Canton, Dr. Cavelli says he'll work you in tomorrow evening. He said he'd see you around 6:00 p.m. He only sees patient's in their homes. Now if I could just get some information."

They exchanged all the personal information before hanging up. Kate looked at Shade and sighed. "I feel better already, just knowing we've put things in motion."

He gave her a weak smile and hugged her to his chest.

54

Walking back upstairs from the weapons bunker, he joined Kate in the living room and got a nice fire going. He'd tried to keep himself busy while they waited for the doctor's visit. Before he even sat on the couch with her, Gi buzzed through his head. **"Master, will you please come upstairs? The doctor is here to see to my lady. He said he would need to examine her, so I have taken him to wait in your bedroom."** Shade let Gi know he'd heard and they'd be on their way.

"*Mi amore*, the doctor is in the bedroom waiting for us, let us go up and see what is wrong with you and get some answers, *si*?"

Kate seemed surprised. "Our...our bedroom?"

"*Si*, our bedroom, so he can examine you."

He took her hand as they headed up the stairs and saw the bedroom door was closed. Gi stood patiently outside the closed door. Shade took a deep breath, Gi nodded his head and left them. Shade gave *bel* a hug.

"Whatever happens, whatever he tells us, we will get through this." Shade opened the door and they walked in together.

Kate had a grip on his hand like he was her lifeline. She knew this pregnancy, if she was pregnant, was a lot earlier than what they'd planned, but why did he seem so worried? The doctor had taken a seat in their bedroom and was waiting for them.

The doctor stood as they entered. Shade walked to him and shook his hand, introducing Kate. The doctor explained his credentials as a physician to vampires and asked a lot of questions, getting a feel for Kate's symptoms and how long she'd been experiencing them. Then he explained he'd need to examine her and asked if she'd please undress and lay on the bed, pointing to the sheet that he'd placed there for her. The doctor then looked at Shade and said he could wait outside.

"I will not be leaving this room. So, let's get this clear from the get-go. When you are here, I am here." Looking over at *bel*, he could feel her uneasiness. "*Mi amore*, go change, put on a robe, and when you return, I will be here."

Kate followed his instructions and returned in her robe, sitting on the bed next to Shade. "What do you need for me to do, Dr. Cavelli?"

The doctor explained, "I'll examine your abdomen, your heart, and given the symptoms you provided, I'll also conduct a pelvic exam. I can't use blood and urine test developed for mortals because your DNA has been altered. The pelvic exam will tell me what I need to know." He turned his back, so Kate could remove her robe. As she climbed on the bed, Shade covered her with the sheet, then sat beside her, holding her hand. He whispered to her, "Relax, it will be easier. Listen to the song." He willed forth Sixx A.M. singing *Smile*, as he ran his hand through her hair to relax her.

As the doctor finished the exam, he dropped the sheet back in place and told her she could sit up and get dressed. She pulled the robe back on as Shade kissed her forehead and she returned to the bathroom to get dressed.

The doctor put his things away in his bag and began to talk, "Master Medici, I am just a physician to vampires, I don't work with transition mortals. Still, this is an easy diagnosis. Although it is rare..."

Shade held up his hand. "Say nothing more until my mate returns, whatever you tell us, we will hear together." As Kate walked back in, he took her in his arms and he could feel her shaking. "Relax, please. We are ready for the outcome, doctor."

Dr. Cavelli began again, "You are quite healthy madam, in excellent physical condition. The symptoms you have been suffering are no disease, you are with child. My guess would be approximately two months along. I don't handle such situations, as I was saying to Master Medici, pregnancies between mortals and immortals are rare, and have their own special demands. I'd suggest you speak with Mr. Canton again and I'm sure he'll be able to track down a doctor who has experience in handling these types of pregnancies."

Kate seemed relieved. "Thank you, doctor. I guess you confirmed what we already suspected. This is good news, yes? And we need a specialist? Well, I guess we'll call Rissa again."

Shade stepped to the door and called for Gi. "Doctor, Gi will show you to the door, and we thank you."

The doctor and Shade exchanged glances as he parted through the door, the doctor confirming with his expression that Shade understood the consequences of this outcome. His precious *bel* was at grave risk.

55

Working in his study, Shade heard *bel* and Luca come home, and she rushed in to tell him she'd been out shopping and found a few things for the nursery. At first, it shocked him. She was shopping already? He hadn't the heart to tell her this could be a very dangerous pregnancy. She was so happy and her face lit up so much when she even mentioned the baby. As she rushed to head upstairs, he found this the perfect opportunity to call Alec and find out if he could recommend a specialist for her condition. **"Luca, I need you to keep *bel* occupied for a good hour, I must make a business call and I want no interruptions, so keep her out of hearing distance."**

"*Si*, master, not a problem, she has me putting together a crib for the baby."

Picking up his cell, Shade hit Alec on his speed dial and waited for his answer.

"Senator Canton."

"Alec, Shade here. Need a few moments of your time, are you available?"

"Of course, Shade, what's going on?"

Shade ran a hand through his hair as he talked. *Cazzo*, he hadn't thought this out very well, how the hell did he tell him about this situation.

"Alec, I am sure Rissa already told you Kate was sick and she recommended a doctor. The news was not exactly what I expected, and I need your assistance."

Alec was distracted by the document he had open on his laptop and listened with half an ear to Shade's conversation. "Rissa did tell me she sent over her own doctor for Kate. I don't think the two of them have talked, though, since that visit. If they have, Rissa hasn't mentioned it."

Shade took a deep breath and dove in feet first. "Alec, Kate is with child. The doctor Rissa graciously sent to us confirmed this, but he does not handle these high-risk pregnancies as he referred to it and he suggested I contact you for further help. So, I am. She is still mortal, and I have no idea what this involves for either of us, but I need to find out as much as I can."

Alec pushed the laptop aside and sat up straight. "What the fuck, Shade. First, you chose to mate with a mortal and now you get her pregnant? You two sound like a bunch of fucking teenagers. I expected better than this from you!"

As his attitude slammed into him, Shade gripped the phone so damn hard he felt it would melt in his hand. "Things happen, Alec. I love her, she is my mate. And yes, I admit, it was careless. I am asking for another referral, give me some help. I need to know what the hell we are facing here."

"You know exactly what you're facing, old friend. You know damn well. There's nothing good that will come from this. Chances are good this baby won't survive, and the possibility exists that you could lose her too. And if, by some stroke of bad luck, the baby does survive, you'll have a half-breed on your hands. What a fucking mess, Shade. There are doctors who deal with this, specialize in pregnancies between vamps and mortals. I'll have to do some research. I don't have a name off the top of my head. You know you have an opportunity here, to get rid of both of them and start fresh. Let me help you find a more appropriate mate, someone more befitting your station in life. Just say the word and I will take care of it, brother."

The pain rolled through him at the thought of losing his *bel* or the baby and made him want to scream in agony. Cory flashed through his mind. He was a surviving half-breed. He was born weak, not accepted in either world, his life its own special hell. But he and *bel* could protect their child. Shade's beast rolled out of him like he was shot out of a cannon and he stood up and started pacing, growling so loud the house rattled.

"Get rid of them Alec? If she dies, so do I. It is that simple! And I need no help in finding a damn mate, I already found her. I know what I have on my hands, what I have done, and nothing you can say can make me feel any worse about my actions than the hell I am putting myself through. So, I will await your call, senator."

Hanging up the phone, he threw it across the room and watched it smash into a million pieces as he headed outside for a smoke. He wanted that fucking master dead right now!

56

Luca and Kate both felt the house rumble and they stopped the assembly of the crib and looked at each other. Kate started to get up to go downstairs, but Luca grabbed her arm. "My lady, I need to request you remain here. I'll go down to master and see what the problem is."

Kate started to protest, but she was reading something in Luca's eyes, so she deferred to him. "Okay, but I want answers. You'll tell me when you return?"

"Of course, my lady, I'll let you know."

Luca left the room and walked down to the office to find the shattered phone, and the door out onto the patio standing open. He walked outside to see Shade standing with his back to him, smoking a cigarette.

He felt Luca as he walked out onto the patio.

"I take it your business call did not go well, master?"

Shade's mind was in turmoil. He'd put her and the baby in danger. What the hell had he done? Alec's words kept ringing in his ears, but he only knew he didn't want to go on without her. "Is she okay, Luca?"

"*Si*, master, she is fine, I asked her to wait. Tell me what's going on, don't leave me in the dark. I can't protect her if I don't know what's going on, and right now, I can feel the heat rolling from you, you're angry."

He shook his head. "I messed up, bad. I could lose Kate, and I could also lose this *bambino*. I am sick with myself. There is little chance this *bambino* will survive, if it does, we both know the outcome. She is mortal, and the child will be less in all eyes. It will be weak by vampire standards. It will never be accepted by my people. A half-breed will not be able to inherit my dynasty or rule the coven. I don't give a fuck about that. Fuck them all, and their ways! But I need her to never know these things Luca. Ever."

Shade spun around to face him. "Pledge right here, right now, you will breathe none of this to her."

"*Si,* master, I will protect her from all things. She deserves to be happy, but, at some point, don't you think you should warn her?"

"No. She is so...happy. It breaks me in half. I can't take that away from her, not yet. Alec is going to find a specialist who deals with mortal/immortal pregnancy. Once I know more, I will decide what to tell her."

"Shade, you haven't fed in a while, how will you deal with this now? You need to keep your strength, especially now with those rogues, there could be more. What are you going to do? Bring in a feeder?"

As his words hit him, Shade realized he hadn't seriously given this much thought. He hadn't fed in several days because she was ill. But he'd rob the child of nourishment if he fed from her.

"*Cazzo!* I am okay for now, but I know how Kate feels about feeders, she does not understand our world, and it will break her. No way can I touch a feeder. I have made a mess of this Luca. I need to think, to let my beast loose, or I will end up doing even more damage. I want you to stay with her, keep close tabs on her. Just do as I ask, *si*?"

"*Si,* master, I understand. But think on this, you can always feed from me. I will go to her now."

Watching as Luca walked back in the house, Shade headed for the weapons bunker to load up. He needed to find some rogue scum in D.C. to release this beast.

Luca left to go back upstairs and face Kate, and he was torn with emotions. He paused at the foot of the stairs, as he came to grips with his master's pain. *What the fucking hell am I supposed to tell my lady? And how am I supposed to help her keep putting this nursery together for a baby that everyone seems to know will never be.*

He shook off the emotion and started up the stairs. As he entered the nursery, Kate was unpacking small baby clothes, folding them, and putting them in a dresser. She turned expectantly toward Luca as he entered, her face registering her questions. Luca walked into the room, shook his head, and gave her a half smile. "That mate of yours has quite a temper."

She laughed and said, "Tell me about it. What has him riled up this time?"

"He was on the phone with a business partner and clearly, they didn't share the same point of view. There is one very smashed phone in the office."

She looked at him with a frown. "I thought he was calling Alec?"

"Oh yeah, he made that call first, Alec said the specialist would be taken care of. He'll get back to master on that. Then master made the second, not so productive, call. Anyway, he took off for a while, to cool off."

"Wait...he took off? You mean he left the house?"

"My lady, you know him, he just needs some air, and some time to cool off, and he'll be back shortly."

She sighed, she hated when he left like that, but she knew he had his own demons to get under control. She and Luca returned to the crib assembly project.

57

Luca and Kate finished the crib and started putting other things together in the nursery, but she kept thinking this should be Shade. He should be here doing this. She kept checking her watch and it had been hours. She felt exhausted. Between the shopping this evening, and working in the nursery, and the fact she was already tired from this pregnancy, she wanted to wait for him, but she couldn't stay awake. Luca had been watching her carefully all night with a look of concern in his eyes. She knew she looked tired and even more pale than usual, but she wasn't sure that was the reason he had watched her so closely.

"My lady, I think we've done all we can do here tonight, and I think you've been up far too long."

"I know you're right. I was just hoping..."

"My lady, master is fine, if he were in danger, he'd call me. I think you need to go to bed. You know he'll return by morning, at the latest."

She smiled at him. "Is this part of your job as protector? Making sure I get enough sleep?"

He looked at her for a long pause, as if pondering that question, and then responded, "You know, my lady, this is my job, but you and master...you're my family now. This house is my home. My concern for you is genuine. It's not a line in a job description. So yes, my concern goes beyond providing protection against any physical assaults on you or this house."

She returned his look. She remembered thinking when she first met him in Florence that he had coldness in his eyes, but when she looked at him now, she only saw his warmth.

"Well, your loyalty and love for this family are evident. So, if you were going for big scary vampire, you failed miserably."

He chuckled. "So, does that mean you're not going to give me a hard time about getting some sleep?"

"Help me off of this floor, and I'll head to bed right now."

He grabbed her hand and helped her to her feet. As she walked toward the master bedroom, he followed her. When she got to the door, he stood to one side.

"What are you doing, Luca?"

"With master gone, my lady, I'll stand guard here tonight."

"Oh Luca, that's really not necessary. Please go to your own room and be comfortable."

"I wasn't asking permission, my lady. And this isn't a subject I'm going to debate with you."

"Well, now you sound like Shade, and I know better than to argue with him when he hits that wall. Good night, Luca."

"Good night, my lady."

She entered the bedroom, closing the door behind her, slipping into her gown and climbing between the cold sheets. Shade's absence in their bed screamed at her. *Where is he? What upset him so much?* He shielded her from so much, and a part of her sought to live in denial, and he knew that. She pulled his pillow to her chest, buried her face into the soft fabric and inhaled his scent.

"Do you hear me, lover? I wait for you in our bed. I wait here to wrap my arms around you, lay my head on your chest. Come home to me." He didn't respond, so she let that message play like a loop in her head as she drifted off to sleep, alone, holding his pillow close.

***

Teleporting into the house, directly into the weapons bunker, Shade unloaded the weapons. The sun was coming up fast. He'd gone on a rampage, killing every rogue, whether they presented a threat or not. He'd blocked her from his thoughts, and even managed to block Luca, most of the time. But now, it was done and all he felt was empty.

He didn't seek comfort. He wanted no questions, no discussion. He'd come home as late as possible, hoping she'd already be asleep, so he could shower and slip in bed beside her and she'd never know a damn thing. Not wanting to wake her, he teleported into the master bath and dropped his leathers, the material slick with blood. His hair was matted with sweat and blood. His boots caked in the path of his killing. Turning on the water, watching the blood of his victims run down the drain, he wanted the pain he felt to wash away with it.

Closing his eyes, the events of the night were a blur, and the pain and anger overwhelmed him for the position he'd put Kate in. Scrubbing his body clean, letting the hot water sooth sore muscles, a moan escaped his lips as the hunger over took him. He couldn't go to her to feed, and his carelessness kicked his ass.

Finishing up, he walked to the bedroom, slid under the sheets, and laid there. He prayed the death slumber took him quickly when the exotic scent of roses wafted across his nose, and the very nearness of her caused his mouth to water. Closing his eyes, he let it all go.

***

Kate had slept lightly, waking often as she waited for him, and worried about him. She heard the shower running. Had he walked past their bed? She thought for sure she would have heard him. She listened to the water, and he was in the shower for a very long time. When he emerged, she lay quietly. He didn't come to her. He didn't kiss her. He slid into the bed as quietly as possible, making every effort not to disturb her. She lay beside him, waiting. Would he speak? Would he reach out to hold her?

He did none of those things as she felt him slip into his death slumber. Her heart was breaking because she didn't know the source of his pain and he'd blocked her. The bed felt as empty now as it had before he climbed into it. **"Shade, I need you to come back to me."**

She knew he was already asleep, she only hoped her words got through to him, even though he never answered. She laid there for a good hour before rising and walking into the bathroom, only to find his leathers tossed on the floor and covered in blood, bloody boot prints on the tile floor, his boots caked in blood. The blood was so prevalent the stench of it hung in the air.

"Oh my god, lover...what have you done?"

She knew she needed to let him sleep. He'd been gone a long time, and he hadn't fed from her in over a week. Just one more worry in her head.

Kate slipped on her robe and went in search of Luca. He'd stood at her door all night until Shade returned, she hated to disturb him. She walked downstairs to his private quarters to find the door closed. She tapped lightly. She tried to allow him his own space without interference from the rest of the household when he was off duty. He opened the door to her. She could see his hair was slightly damp and he wore only a t-shirt with his jeans, and she felt even guiltier for the intrusion, knowing he'd just showered.

"My lady, is everything all right?"

As soon as she saw him, she wanted to cry but fought back the tears. That's the last thing he needed, some blubbering female at his door after he'd stood guard all night. He opened the door wider for her and indicated with his hand for her to enter. She walked into his space and took a seat on the sofa as he sat across from her.

“Did you talk to him, Luca? When he came in?”

"No, my lady. I knew when he was in the house, and when he was in your room, I left my post. We did not speak."

“He didn't speak to me either. He showered and went immediately into his death slumber. When I got up, I went to the bathroom; his leathers...his boots. There was blood everywhere. I don't think it was his. None of it was his. He didn't appear injured...he is just, shut off. He’s closed off from me.”

Luca shifted his eyes to the floor as she described the blood. Kate could already tell he knew something, and she could tell he wouldn’t share what he knew.

"He just needs some time, my lady, be patient."

With a tremble in her voice, Kate responded, “This has nothing to do with a business call, Luca. This had nothing to do with an upsetting business call.”

Against her best efforts, the tears started to flow down her cheeks. She hated that she was crying, and she could see Luca struggle with how he should respond to those tears.

"My lady, you understand I cannot speak of anything I might know or overhear as it relates to master's business. All I can say to reassure you is his anger isn’t directed at you. He’s not mad at you. Be patient with him, please. He’s fighting his own battles."

So, this was it. This would be the extent of what she knew unless Shade chose to share more later, which she already knew in her heart would be a closed subject. She nodded her head at Luca and stood to leave.

"Trust me, my lady.”

“I do, Luca...I do. It just doesn't make this any easier.”

Kate left his quarters and returned to their bedroom where she removed her robe and climbed in bed beside Shade in his death slumber.

58

Waking very late, Shade lay in bed for a moment getting his bearings. As he awakened fully, everything hit him full force. This wasn't something he could fix. He could feel her in the house, moving downstairs, and he swallowed hard, needing to feed. But he knew a small feeding wouldn't do, he was even weaker now after the rampage of last night. What the fucking hell was he thinking?

The thought of Luca's offer rang through his head and he knew Luca was the only source of survival for him now, and if he didn't feed soon, he could kill her, drain her, and his hunger was progressing. Throwing his legs over the side of the bed, he sat there wondering where the hell his leathers were and then remembered last night.

Walking to the bathroom, he saw the mess and knew she'd probably seen this as well. Sticking his hand in the pocket of his leathers, he grappled around until he found the small red gems she'd given him. Holding the heart shaped rubies in his hand, he rolled them around, staring at them. Her love was right here in his hand. Bringing the biggest gemstone to his lips, he kissed it and grabbed some jeans. Sliding the gems into his pocket, he headed downstairs. The closer he got, the worse the hunger roared, and her scent was like a stab at his gut, his craving ripped through him. He saw her and stopped dead in his tracks, he couldn't breathe, he couldn't swallow as his mouth was so dry. She turned to him and he had to muster every ounce of control to stop from feeding from her.

Kate heard him on the stairs and her heart skipped a beat. After his sudden departure last night, his night-long absence, and the blood-soaked clothes, she had no idea what to anticipate. But she was almost weak with relief that he was up, and home. She walked slowly toward the stairs. Did he want to see her? Luca had said she wasn't the source of his anger, but he'd blocked her from his thoughts and she felt lost from him. As she entered the hallway to the stairs, he was stepping down from the last step and stopped and stared at her. She wanted to run to him, but something was warning her off. She stopped and locked eyes with him.

"Shade, what is it? Please tell me how I can help you."

He held up a hand as if to push her back. "It is not you, *mi amore*." He closed his eyes. "Don't come any closer." His breathing was labored. "I just need Luca, and everything will be all right, I promise. Please don't come after me. I am going to Luca's suite."

Before she could say a word, he rushed to Luca's suite.

Kate felt only confusion. *He is sick?* What could Luca do for him that she couldn't? She wanted to run after him, but the pleading look in his eyes, the raised hand, had kept her planted where she stood as she watched Luca's door close behind him.

Shade stood with his back against the door, trying to remain calm. Luca already knew why he was here. Luca stood before him, bare-chested, in loose drawstring pants that hung low on his hips. As Luca's eyes locked with his, there was something deep in his eyes that spoke to his beast, and it settled Shade. There were no words spoken between them, they both knew what this meant.

Luca locked the door behind him and padded in his bare feet to his bedroom door and looked back at him. Shade could see the vein in his neck pulsing, and his mouth filled with saliva, and his fangs ached. Shade scanned the warrior's body, tight and hardened from years of training.

He followed Luca to his bedroom, stepping up to him, reaching his arm around his broad bare back and pulling Luca hard against his chest. Luca tilted his head back, exposing his neck, inviting his master to feed. As Shade sank his fangs deep, Luca moaned and Shade grabbed his hair and yanked his head back, gulping down his blood.

Luca's young warrior's blood whistled through him. Shade felt his veins pop and crackle, and he drew deeper. His head was spinning, and his body began to respond to the feeding, his cock hard, sliding against Luca's hard abs as Luca's own hot steel was nudging against his balls, teasing. He couldn't stop the desire that came with feeding, but he couldn't do this with him, he couldn't let it go that far, and Shade struggled for control.

He felt Luca's hips begin to grind into him. Shade held him in a tight grip and kept drawing deep. Luca moaned so loud Shade could feel the vibrations in his body. Shade willed the music to play, hoping it would block out the sounds of their mutual pleasure.

The room was filled with the sound of Carol Tatum's *Primitive Kiss*, a seductive, primal beat that drifted out through the house.

The pressure of Luca's hips pressed hard against him, drove Shade like a freight train. He finally unlatched and threw back his head and roared, his body filled with young, sweet warrior blood, but his cock aching now as well. He spun Luca in his arms, so his back was against his chest, and Shade's hand slid slowly up Luca's thigh, over his hip, across his rock-hard abdomen and chest as Shade's lips sought out his neck again, pulling Luca's head back on his shoulder, he whispered huskily into his ear, "Luca, I cannot take release from you, but I will give you release, relax, master will give you pleasure. Close your eyes."

Sliding his hand down Luca's side, he slid it under his hard ass, and squeezed before moving his hand over his hip, around his hard, flat abs and down to his steeled cock. Shade stroked him slowly at first, and then faster, reading Luca's response to set the pace and knowing he would cum soon, but they were both drowning in the sensation. Shade pulled Luca's head back on his shoulder once more and kissed his neck, sinking his fangs in again, drinking deep as he jerked his dick harder and harder until he felt Luca's body tense then shudder before relaxing back into him.

They stood silent and unmoving, still in their embrace as their breathing returned to normal, and their heart rates slowed.

Picking him up, Shade put him on the bed, and drew the blankets around him. Shade had drunk deeply and knew Luca would sleep for a while as his body recovered. Going into the bathroom, Shade washed his hands, splashed cold water on his face and now must face the most difficult part of this whole ordeal...*bel.*

59

As she stood in the hallway outside Luca's living quarters, it didn't take long to figure out Shade had gone there to feed. He wasn't sick. He was starving for blood, the blood she couldn't give to him. Relief flooded through her at the realization he could feed from Luca. But that realization was quickly followed by those intimate sounds she knew so well, the noises that accompanied those sweet erotic sensations that came with feeding, and it felt like more than she could bear. She ran to their room to try and escape the sounds, only to hear music. Her tears started to flow. It wasn't long before she heard him on the stairs. She looked up as he entered their room and sat beside her on the bed, his hand in her hair, pleading with her to listen to his words.

"Kate, I need to talk to you. Give me a chance to explain. I am pleading with all my heart, because I love you and without you...I am nothing."

She looked up at him, placed her hand on his thigh. "Shade, why would you think I wouldn't listen to what you have to say?"

She reached up and pulled him to her, kissing that mouth, those lips, and that tongue. All the pain of the last twenty-four hours, his sudden absence from her bed, the bloody clothes, the feeding with Luca, she'd erase it all. She'd bring him back to her with a single kiss. She felt him respond to her, grab her hair, and hold her in his grip. He returned the kiss with such passion, and she felt his pain flow through her. **"We will fix this, lover. Whatever it is, we will fix this."**

With her lips on his, she was drawing every ounce of pain from him. He needed her more than life, he couldn't breathe without her. His heart took flight knowing she hadn't rejected him. His hands were tangled in her crimson, clinging to her as though he was drowning, and she was the only one who could save him. Breaking the kiss, he pulled her to his chest.

"Kate, I love you. I want a chance to explain to you what I have been through, why I am like this. I can only ask that you try to understand. I can't hold this inside me any longer."

"Lover, come lie next to me, I missed you in our bed last night. Hold me and tell me whatever you need to share. You left me confused and hurt, and I know that's not your intention. So, please, talk to me."

He laid beside her, holding her tight, his nose in her hair. "*Mi amore, mio dolce amore*."

He inhaled her, and it felt like a cleansing of his soul. "It began with the *bambino*, and the doctor. I don't like this, this not knowing. Things could go wrong. I don't know if they will or not, but it tears me apart. I got you pregnant, and my guilt is tearing me apart. I did not feed when you were ill, and I was starving. I'm angry at myself. I was angry at Alec and his ridiculous suggestions for what to do for blood. It pushed me over the edge. I did something last night I have never done. Something a true warrior never does. I killed for no reason. I kill to protect. I kill to defend. I never kill without provocation. I was consumed with guilt. I was in raging need of you, and blood, yet I cannot feed from you now. I could hurt you and take away the precious food our *bambino* needs. I am terrified of having sex with you. Will I hurt our *bambino*? Will my beast emerge? It was all too much. I needed to feed the hunger. There is a solution in my world of which you are aware, a feeder. I know how you feel about it, I know you see it as betrayal, and I won't do that, I owe you that. But I must feed or I die. Luca offered to let me feed. I trust him. I love him, *bel*, as a warrior loves his brother. His blood is clean. He has only fed from feeders. His blood is not tainted with disease. Of all my options, going to Luca seemed like the only path that made sense. I know you heard the sounds, the music...the pleasure that comes with feeding, it comes unbidden."

"Lover, why do we do this? We leave so much unsaid, and we both end up in our own personal hell and torment. I understand you must feed. I've been worrying about that for some time, and I know you were downplaying your need. And given the option between a feeder and Luca, I choose Luca. So, let that go. I'm grateful to him that he offered himself to you, it was just... It was hard to hear, knowing the intimacy it brings, but I can deal with that. What happened that pushed you that far?"

He held her to his chest. "I felt guilt, *mi amore*. I wanted a *bambino*, but after a time, after you were immortal, once you were strong. But you are mortal, and our *bambino* will only be part vampire, like Cory. I don't know what could go wrong. What if something happens and I can't save the *bambino*? So many things I can't control, I can't fix, and that tears me apart. I carried guilt for getting you this way. This is my fault. I should have known to make sure it was safe to make love to you and I didn't. Now I carry that with me. My anger consumed me, and I had to let the beast go, I couldn't let him go around you, I could hurt you.

"And now, Luca. I don't know what I would have done without him. You asked I not feed from another, and I told you I would not. I thought we would have more time for you to understand my world. That you would be immortal and understand the bloodlust, and that I would need to go elsewhere to feed whenever you were with child. I was not prepared for this now. I did not seek out a feeder, even though their blood is pure. Please, understand."

"Lover, you can't feel guilt over this baby. That judgment lies as much with me as it does with you. In fact, in my eyes, it lies more with me. But we can't change that. It happened, and we'll deal with it together. It's not within your power to control the outcome for this baby, nor is it in mine. We'll just do what the doctor directs us to do. We'll be fine, all three of us."

She took his hand and placed it on her abdomen. "All three of us. In the meantime, I need you. Please, don't leave me like last night with no answers, Shade."

"I didn't want to leave you. I had to protect you from me."

He kissed her tummy, laying his head on her, sighing as he closed his eyes. "I love you both so much, so damn much. I am so tired *mi amore*, so tired. I just want to lay here with you. I want the world to go away and leave us alone."

She lay on her back, his head resting on her belly, as she ran her hand through his hair. "Hmmm, I, too, want the world to go away. It seems to just dump problems at our door. But I know you. Your warrior spirit would be quickly bored. But tonight, we'll shut out the rest of the world."

Shifting his position on the bed, he situated them comfortably, taking her in his arms, her head on his chest, her hair surrounding them both as he held her.

"Deal. Now we both need to rest, no more talk. I just want to be here, with you."

60

As Alec entered the house, she heard him call out to her, "Rissa, are you home?"

She quickly rushed from her home office to the stairs. "Yes, Alec, coming!"

Walking into the study, she could already sense his aggravation and took a seat. "Something is wrong, what do you need me to do?"

He was pacing the floor of the study. "I just talked to Shade on the phone. Are you aware of this situation with his mate?"

She watched as his agitation increased. "Well, I'm aware she was sick, but when last I talked to them, she wasn't sure what was wrong. I sent over my doctor. I jokingly blurted out that perhaps Kate was pregnant. Tell me she isn't pregnant?"

He sat down across from her, lit a cigarette, and took a long drag before passing it to her. "I'd love to tell you she isn't pregnant, but that's not the case. You know how this goes, don't you? You know this can't possibly have a good outcome. And in the meantime, I'll have one fucked up warrior. Your doctor confirmed the pregnancy, but then said it was out of his league since she was a mortal, so they need a specialist, and I have just the specialist in mind, my devious darling."

She put the cigarette to her mouth and inhaled deeply. "Alec, I know it means this thing, whatever it is inside her, probably won't survive, and if it does, it has to go. No one wants a half-breed. Shade will be preoccupied with her and this thing. He's already showing signs of neglect to you. What an irresponsible and selfish act!"

As a wicked grin spreads across her lips, she looked him in the eyes and saw he was already making plans. Her heart raced, knowing he'd give her a task and when she executed it perfectly, she'd get her reward.

"Tell me the plan, Alec. What are you thinking?"

"What I want, Rissa..." He took the cigarette back from her and took a drag, leaning his head back and slowly exhaling the smoke into the air. "What I want...is for you to find one of your actor friends, who can successfully pull off the role of doctor. That's who will make the next house call. And our *doctor* will proceed to prescribe a nutritional supplement. You may need to make these, my darling. Just empty out some over-the-counter gel capsules and fill them with crushed white snake root. Have our 'doctor' prescribe them for her three times a day. They'll make her sick, he needs to tell her that, but she'll need to take them anyway, and this ridiculous mortal will do as she's told. In about a week or so, our problems will be over, at least, as far as that baby is concerned. Oh, and he must inform Shade under no circumstances is he to feed from her. I doubt he would, but the last thing I need is to poison my own warrior." He handed the cigarette back to her. "Can you do that for me, my darling?"

As she listened to his plan, her heart was pounding, the sound of his voice made her moist between the legs. She loved when he was scheming, and needed her help to implement his plan.

"Of course, I can do this. I have all the resources at hand, and I already have someone in mind. He's currently playing a doctor in a stage production, and he's a vampire of course."

She laid her hand on his knee, letting it slide slowly up his thigh, looking deep into his eyes and smiling, lowering her eyelids seductively. "And you know, my wicked vampire, we could always get a feeder in to help him along with his hunger."

He smiled that wicked, crooked grin. "My darling Rissa, great minds think alike. That was the second part of my plan. I offered, tonight, to help Shade get rid of both of his problems, the baby, and the mortal, but he has some silly notion of being in love with her. She's so beneath him. I want you to make a house call yourself, Rissa, the day after the doctor's call. I want you to find the hottest, horniest most sought-after feeder. Bring her here from Europe if you have to and take her with you. Shade has always been a player. All he needs is some strong temptation. And he probably hasn't fed from the mortal since learning of her pregnancy, so he has to be getting weak. That will make the temptation even harder to resist. There is more than one way to get that mortal out of his life. Let Shade get a taste of what sex is like with his own kind again. And make sure that little mortal is aware that being with a feeder involves sex. Be very graphic. Use that naughty imagination to paint her a picture she'll never get out of her head. Be sure she knows that every time she gets pregnant in the future, he'll have a multitude of feeders to satisfy his every need. Let's see how eager she is to stick around then. Mortals, and their ridiculous ideas about fidelity and romantic love." He shook his head. "Now, be a good girl and bring daddy a glass of Midnight."

Standing up, her body was screaming for him. His compliments made her high. Leaning in slightly, she slid her long red nail along his jaw. "Daddy always gets what he wants."

He reached up and gripped her wrist firmly, squeezing to the point of pain, as she winced. "And don't ever forget it, my darling."

"I never forget that, Alec. So, I think, perhaps I will find him a red-haired beauty, fully endowed with a touch of something in her blood that will scream to him, make him unable to resist his hunger. How wonderfully devious does that sound? I almost feel sorry for Shade...almost." She laughed softly.

He tipped back the glass of Midnight and emptied the contents into his throat, licking his lips and then locking eyes with her. "We are two of a kind, my darling. Pull this off, and you'll get what you're hungry for."

Her hunger spiked with his words, and the anticipation of what was to come. She had to rein it in and concentrate on everything he had laid at her feet.

"Have I ever failed you, Alec? Leave this to me. It's a simple enough plan to accomplish. Everything will fall neatly into place with no sign of either of us being involved. " Smiling softly, she stood, running her hand down the sides of her thighs. "Is there anything else you wish for tonight?"

"That will be all, my darling. I think it's enough, don't you?"

She left the room, with a sway in her hips and could feel his eyes were still on her. He knew he could count on her to implement this plan.

61

Sitting in her home office, Rissa twirled her cell phone around in her hand. The time had come to get this plan in motion. She'd already hired her actor friend, and she'd made the gel capsules filled with white snake root. Now she was ready to find the feeder, and she had one already in her sights. She was just waiting for a few return calls. Running through her phone list, she found Kate's number and grinned like a Cheshire cat. *Your immortal dream is about to come crashing down, you naive little bitch!* Dialing Kate's number, she cleared her throat and prepared to be the most concerned best friend in the world.

Kate had finished dressing and heard her cell phone ring. She made a mad grab for it, so as not to disturb Shade. She rushed out of the bedroom, closing the door behind her, as she read the caller ID and answered the call. "Rissa, I'm so glad you called."

"Kate, congratulations! Alec told me the news. We're so happy for you both. I know you must be so excited. And Shade, I can't imagine how proud he must be to have a child who'll finally inherit the Medici legacy. How are you feeling, my friend?"

Kate was a little surprised at her response, but welcomed Rissa's enthusiasm. "Thank you. And thank you for sending your doctor. Shade and I are both appreciative of your support. I know Shade called Alec last night. I guess I need a specialist now?"

"Yes, but don't worry one moment. Alec and I want the very best for you and Shade. So, I have made some contacts, and I couldn't get the specialist immediately. Believe it or not, he's in Switzerland at the moment, treating a royal over there. I told you, only the best for you. He promised me he'd be available next Thursday evening, and I must insist Shade be with you. Now, you just relax, Kate. Alec and I have this taken care of. Let us get you the help you need, and we'll be at your side for anything that comes up."

"Of course, next Thursday will work. Shade is asleep now, but I know how important this is to him. He'll make any changes to his calendar he needs to. You don't need to worry, he won't miss this appointment. Rissa, I can't thank you enough. I had no idea this pregnancy would be so complicated. You know this wasn't planned, right? I have to admit, as excited as I am, it has been very stressful. I don't know what I would have done without your help."

Rissa grinned to herself at pulling off her charade. "And I'll make absolutely sure Alec won't need him next Thursday. The stress will end once you see my specialist and he'll help you through the pregnancy. I'm always willing to help. I'll go now and let you get your rest, but keep me informed, sweetie. I want to know everything that happens, so I can be there for you, no matter what. Take care, sweet friend."

As she hung up, Rissa threw back her head and laughed wickedly. *You stupid bitch, this child will disappear, and then you'll lose your Shade. If you think you'll win him back, I can make sure you disappear as well.*

62

Alec took a deep breath. He had so little quiet time. He'd take advantage of it and maybe get caught up on some reading. He knew Rissa would be back soon and wondered if she'd made any progress on their plan. He poured himself another glass of Midnight and browsed through the *Washington Post*.

It was late when he heard her walk in the front door. He heard her rush upstairs to change before joining him in the study. He looked up to see her standing in the doorway, dressed in red lingerie.

"And exactly who are you trying to tempt with that outfit, my wicked little demon? Have you had a drink? Come in and fill me in."

She smiled slyly. "I'm dying for a drink." She poured herself a glass of Midnight, as she ran her hand along the back of his shoulders.

"Would you like another?" Not waiting for a response, she refilled his empty glass and leaned against the edge of his desk, sipping at the wine.

"I called Kate earlier, she's so ridiculously happy and in love, it's sickening. The fake doctor will arrive on Thursday. I made sure Shade would be there, I stressed that, and she assured me he wouldn't miss it."

"Yes, well, hopefully your conversation with Kate went more smoothly than mine did with Shade. The ending was rather abrupt, and knowing Shade, I can pretty much guarantee that's one fucked phone. I'm not concerned about him missing that appointment. He's such a simpering puppy at her feet. I told him he was pussy-whipped. He's an old school vampire, how he could allow himself to become ensnared in this mess is beyond me. You know her—this Kate—please explain to me the attraction?"

Lifting the lid of the cigarette box, she pulled one out, lit it, and took a long drag. She smiled as she passed him the cigarette.

"When we travelled together in college, she was always such a romantic. The arts, museums, live theater. She didn't want to go to clubs, just those sappy romantic things. I always thought she was a bit naïve. Mortals are attracted to that deep, dark, mysterious soul, I suppose. It attracted me to you. Perhaps she thinks she can tame him. I don't understand his attraction to her myself."

"Ah...and that's the problem, Rissa. She has tamed him. At least, she's tamed him from the Shade I've always known. He was a much nastier warrior when he had nothing to lose and was wallowing in his own loneliness. A warrior with a broken soul is a very dangerous warrior, indeed. Now, he's more cautious, and he worries about her. She's a distraction. My life was much easier before this mortal nymph came into the picture. You know I hold you partially responsible?"

"How so, my wicked love? I didn't push either of them into each other's arms. I can't be held responsible for where Shade puts his cock. And as I recall, you were the one who insisted Shade attend all those events when he first came here to the States."

He drew on the cigarette, and slowly exhaled the cloud of smoke before he handed the cigarette back to her, making sure to touch her hand as he did. He could feel her respond immediately to his touch. *Don't be too eager, my darling. You know I'll only prolong your suffering.*

"True, and believe me, that's one cock that has made the rounds, which is another reason this sudden undying loyalty has me scratching my head. I can't wrap my head around a domesticated Shade. Which brings me to my next question, darling. The feeder, I hope you have found someone that can wreak havoc in this little love nest."

"Everything's in place, ready for attack. It's all arranged." Throwing back her blonde hair as she sat on the edge of his desk, she laughed an evil laugh. "Oh, my wicked love, I've found the gem of all gems to tempt your Shade. She's a redhead. He seems to crave them, apparently. But her body..." Leaning forward, she was face to face with him. "...voluptuous, built to handle a warrior and his beast. Not skin and bones like that snippet of a mortal. Her breasts are heaving, and she smells delicious beyond belief. She was bred to fire his soul and ride him like a wild bitch in heat. He won't be able to resist her, of that I'm sure."

He grinned back at her. "Hmm...this feeder, maybe I should take her for a test drive? I can't remember the last time I rode a redhead. Who better to determine her skills to lure Shade away from that mortal?"

Her eyes locked with his. "Better yet, perhaps she could join both of us?" Her voice had become husky and alluring.

He threw his head back and laughed. “Oh, you are my devious darling, aren't you? But then, that’s what I love about you. Well played, Rissa, well played.”

She smiled at him. “Now, I have some phone calls to catch up on and I’m sure you’re much too busy at the moment to deal with feeders, a domesticated warrior and me.” Pouring him another glass of Midnight and lighting another cigarette, she handed it to him. “I’ll be in my office, taking care of some dirty deeds.”

Spinning on her heels, her hips rocked as she walked to the door and untied her robe, letting it slide down her shoulders as she stopped at the open door. Slipping one arm out of the robe, she let the robe drape to the floor, dragging it behind her.

He watched her grand exit from the room. No one had more confidence than Rissa. No one. She made the game a challenging one, he’d give her that.

63

Kate lay in his arms and reflected on his words. Sleep wouldn't come because her mind was filled with questions about his world. He wanted them to be in his world. But that was the problem. She wasn't of his world. She'd fallen in love with an immortal, and he shielded her still from so much of his world. She knew his heart, but not his life. Or did she only think she knew his heart? They lived in a world where he kept her in a bubble, to keep her safe. But the bubble was fragile, and his world seeped in through the cracks. She tried to understand. She wanted to understand. But she was wondering if that was even possible, especially when he sheltered her from so much. She only saw pieces of the puzzle. Protection, he called it. But was it?

They stayed in this cycle of passionate loving, followed by tormented misunderstanding. Would it eventually rip them apart? Would he tire of this drama that constantly played out between them and seek one of his own kind? She was drawn to his darkness, she wanted to dive into that darkness and heal his pain. But she watched his torment, and so much of it seemed to be caused by her, by them, and their cycle of miscommunication, or cryptic non-communication.

And this baby! There was still much left unsaid about this baby. She knew every parent worried about a new baby, but not like this. Not this level of worry and anguish. *What secrets do you keep from me still?*

She wanted this life with him so desperately, and yet, she couldn't even define this life because he hid it from her. After everything, did he still fear she'd run? Did she appear that fragile to him that she'd crumble under the truth of his world? *I couldn't love you more if I tried, my savage lover, but you leave me filled with doubt*.

She curled into him, the feel of his arms as they cradled her, and she could only hope he remembered his promise. *Don't break my heart, lover. Please don't break my heart*. Eventually, she drifted into a troubled sleep.

Shade was startled awake and felt her in his arms, asleep. *What the hell?* He lay still, watching her sleep. As he stared at her face, there was a slight frown, a subtle shake of her head, and he felt something was bothering her. It would be easy for him to enter her dreams, wipe away whatever troubled her. Before he lifted his hand to her forehead to enter her dreams, she moaned softly, and nuzzled into his neck, as if she were trying to feed. She hadn't fed from him since she first felt ill. The baby was hungry, gnawing at her in her sleep. He could feel her hunger, and her need for his blood. Gently moving from under her as she lay with her head on his shoulder, he held still, making sure he didn't wake her. Sliding down her body and between her legs, he began kissing her with soft wet kisses on the inside of her beautiful soft thighs.

He could feel her awaken to his touch, but he knew she was still in dream-land. His tongue caressed her sex, and he inhaled the scent of her sweet honey, as he flicked his tongue inside her, tasting her as she wiggled her hips. Increasing her sexual desire would heighten her hunger and she'd feed deeply, which is what he needed her to do. He'd held back making love to her since they learned of the pregnancy. He felt unsure, but his need for her is great. Sliding his hands up her inner thighs, he buried his face between her legs, sliding his tongue softly up and down her sex, flicking and sucking her clit, she was so wet and sweet it was driving him wild. This woman took him to levels of need he'd never felt, and he was never letting her go.

From deep in her sleep, she felt herself in the midst of an erotic dream. Her hands gripped the sheets beneath her, as a moan escaped her lips. She felt herself rising slowly from sleep, but the delicious sensations were becoming more intense, not less. As she surfaced into wakefulness and realized it was Shade who lay between her legs, very much alive and in the flesh. Not a dream.

She reached down and ran her fingers through his tangled curls as she felt his tongue probing. The heat, the ache, the desire to have him overwhelmed her. "Lover," she whispered to him. He'd not been with her for days, and she knew his worry, but her body screamed out for him. "Lover, please."

"I wish to please, *si*? What is it you wish for?"

"To feel you deep inside me. To have you cum inside me while I cling to you, legs wrapped around you. That is what I wish for."

Sliding up on his knees, he ran his hands up both sides of her body, as he slowly pushed his cock inside her, and felt her hips lift to take him deeper.

He kissed her hard and passionately, and moving his hips slowly, bringing pleasure to them both. Cupping the back of her head, he pulled her to his neck and whispered to her.

"Give it up to me and feed."

His mouth covered hers, and she inhaled him. She'd missed him so. She hadn't fed from him in more than a week, and her body had been calling out for his blood for days, but they'd been at such odds.

Feeling his neck against her lips brought a desire that was beyond any resistance, and she bit into his skin, and drew hard, pulling his blood into her mouth. As soon as his blood touched her tongue, she felt that explosion of heat between her legs as she locked her legs around him, pulling him to her. She moaned into his neck as she felt his body respond, felt his cock throbbing inside of her. Her hips thrust at him, her sex pulled at him. More, more blood, and she felt the orgasm wash over her, like a forest fire burning out of control. Despite her desire to drink more, her lips broke away from him and her head was thrown back as she cried out with the intensity of the pleasure his body brought to hers.

His mouth covered hers once again as she felt him explode inside her, and his own cries of pleasure drowned out hers. She buried her face in his neck once again, and drank slowly now, as her heartbeat returned to normal, and his ragged breathing slowed.

He gently pulled away from her and rolled to his back, drawing her to his chest. He hands trailing down her back, comforting her.

"*Bel*, are you all right? The *bambino*?"

"Of course I'm all right. You worry far too much. Pregnant women have sex all the time. In fact, I think I read they're even hornier, so you better get used to it." She giggled at him.

"You are making that up." He chuckled softly.

Rolling her over on her back, he lay on top of her, keeping his weight on his elbows, taking her face in his hands, he looked in her eyes. "*Ti amo, mi amore*. Tell me we're going to be okay, all of us."

"Of course we'll be okay. We'll all be okay."

Kissing her gently, his hands slide into her hair, as he intensified the kiss, rolling his tongue inside her warm mouth. He wants her blood. This will kill him, surely. He wanted all of her, not just some of her and he didn't know how long he could handle feeding from Luca, when all he wanted was her. Clearing his mind of those thoughts, he moaned against her lips. He could kiss her forever, and still, it would never be enough. "Did I happen to mention that I love you?"

"I think you may have mentioned it, once or twice, but tell me again. Tell me every day, because I never get tired of hearing it, *si*?"

He smiled at her. "You know I love when you mimic me. And you, my minx, I never get tired of that mouth. It brings me such pleasure." Laughing wickedly, he kissed her again. "We must get up soon. I do have some things to attend to. What are your plans?"

"My plans? Oh, well, I guess my plans are spoiled, because I had planned to keep you busy in bed, but if you must get up, then I guess I'll finish up in the nursery."

He threw back his head laughing. "Keeping me in bed, *si*? Now you know," smacking her ass lightly. "I would rather cancel what I have to do and stick to your plan, but I have things to attend to. But show me the nursery, please? I want to see what you have done."

She climbed out of bed and slipped back into her clothes. "Lover, I guess this means...for the next several months, it's Luca you will seek out to feed from? I know why it has to be. But maybe you could have a schedule, so I don't have to be here."

Lowering his head, he closed his eyes and took a deep breath. "I have no choice, *mi amore*, I need blood. My alternative is a feeder, and I will not do that. It will have to be Luca. I push out my feedings as long as possible, and I will be discreet. I know you don't want details, but you must know, because I want you to understand. This is not something I wish to do, but I would be lost without Luca. He offered, it was not a command. I had not actually thought of it, but without him, you would have a female feeder living with us throughout, to feed me at my command."

"Shade, no. I'm not judging. I understand your need, and I appreciate Luca's offer because, quite frankly, if your only option was to have a female feeder, there'd be no babies. I can't even bear the thought of it. I chose Luca, you know I chose Luca. But that doesn't mean it's easy when I can hear the sounds of pleasure from both of you, sharing something so intimate that was meant for us. There will be no female feeders in this house. Not now, not ever! And those are my rules."

Getting down on one knee, he lowered his head in honor to her. "My queen has spoken, and I shall abide by her ruling. But as a subject of my lady, may I have one small request?"

She bit her lip to keep from smiling. "You know, my loyal subject, your queen can deny you nothing, unless it's for a feeder, in which case, you better get off your knees and start running."

He threw back his head. "Damn, you are a little firecracker when you get jealous, and I like it, *si*!" Reaching up, he pulled her onto his knee, and got serious. "*Mi amore*, please do not judge, nor take this out on Luca. Treat him no different, he will feel bad enough. Be kind to him, he does us both a great service. I love you. No other. Luca has been raised as was I, to be in a brotherhood, to take care of our own. In our culture, this arrangement is not odd or unusual, but creates a stronger bond between us. He adores you, do not ruin that by looking at him any differently, I ask this of you please."

"I don't judge him at all. I appreciate his willingness to do this. I wouldn't dream of treating him differently. His decision to offer himself to you has spared me the agony of you being with a feeder. And for that, I'll be forever grateful. Because..." She shook her head. "If a feeder ever walked into this house, my reaction to her would put your beast to shame, and that's a promise."

He kissed her cheek and smiled. "What did I ever do to deserve such a beautiful heart? Now get your ass up and show me this nursery. I have things to do, woman!"

"Come with me then. The room isn't finished, but I've done a lot with Luca's help. You'll get the general idea. I'm thinking, since you said Theresa was also trained as a nanny, I'd make a place for her to sleep in that room as well, at least while he's still a baby."

She led him to the room, decorated in red and white checks, and a nanny's bed in an alcove. He admired the work she'd done, as he took her by the hand. There was more she needed to know now, about when the baby is born.

"Kate. Sit here beside me." He took a seat on the nanny's bed and held his hand out to her. "There are things to discuss about this *bambino*."

She sat beside him. His tone was serious and she looked at him with a creased brow. "Is everything all right?"

"*Si*, everything is as it should be. Had you been immortal when our baby was born, I would understand clearly our baby's needs. But this baby, half-mortal, half-vampire. There are things I do not know. An immortal pregnancy is only six months. I don't know if that still holds true for you. The specialist will know. He will drink blood. But like Cory, he will consume human food. We may not know the answers to all the questions until he is here. But as part vampire, he will need blood. Initially, he feeds from you, but his body grows fast, *si*? Like all babies, and his needs are great. I feed from you as well, and your body will not sustain both of us. Infant vampires feed from their nannies. So, there will come a point, very quickly, that Theresa will feed our child."

Kate stood up and paced the room. She loved Theresa, and she had no reservations about Theresa feeding her child. But she envisioned feeding her own children. She understood what he was saying, that he must feed from her as well. She comprehended the logic of it. She was just wrestling with the emotions of it.

He watched her response, and gauged when he could tell her the rest. "You understand, *mi amore*?"

"I understand, lover."

"*Si*. There is more." He took both of her hands and held them firmly. "Theresa can only sustain him for so long. The *bambino* will feed for a lifetime. Unlike an adult vampire, the *bambino* will not feel a sexual bond to his feeder. That does not happen until the *bambino* grows to be a young man or woman, around eighteen to twenty years. Until then, the feeding is just feeding, you understand, *si*?"

Kate was trying to pull her hands free, but he held her in a firm grip.

"You must listen, Kate. Listen with an open heart. There are feeders that are bred for this purpose and this purpose alone. They are assigned to an infant at birth and remain until the vampire reaches his or her puberty at eighteen or twenty. They are pure of blood and serve that one *bambino* only. They are young themselves, virginal, and remain so through the duration of their service. They are called wet-feeders, like a wet-nurse in your mortal world. Once their ward reaches puberty, they can choose to remain as a wet-feeder, or they can be freed from this servitude and pursue another station in life. Each child will have their own wet-feeder. Kate, hear me please, if we have more than one child, you could not feed them all, Theresa could not feed them all, do you understand? It also helps the vampire to develop independence. To be able to survive should something happen to either of us. It insures the survival of our species."

She broke the hold of his hands gripping hers and pulled away from him. She needed to process, she felt betrayed, angry.

"Kate, you have only one experience of feeding. I ask that you talk to Theresa. She has fed *bambinos* before. She can explain to you, from a woman's perspective, the difference. Do not judge the wet-feeders yet. Talk to Theresa. And your *bambinos*, they will still come to you. Even with their own wet-feeder, they will still seek you out, seek out your blood. They will need to reaffirm their bond to you, feel their connection to you. They will do that until they reach puberty and become adult vampires. *Bel*, tell me you understand. Tell me you can do this."

She stood with her back to him, looking out the window at the rolling hills, the vineyards in the distance. Oddly enough, she did understand. But it still broke her heart. She knew how much Shade fed from her. She knew she couldn't sustain feeding both of them. And if they had more children, and they all fed until they were twenty...*Welcome to the world of vampires, Kate*.

"I can do this, lover."

64

Heading down to the bunker, Shade saw Luca was already busy. Closing and locking the door behind him, Luca looked up to see the confused look on his face.

"I wasn't expecting to see you here, master. Is something wrong with my lady?"

Shade frowned at him. "No, why would anything be wrong with *bel*? I just needed to come down and clean up some, uh, weapons I used the other night. Everything is fine."

Luca watched him, and he wasn't fooled. Everything may be fine between them, but something was still bothering Shade, or he wouldn't be down here with him when he could be with her.

"The feeding, she understands I only wanted to help the situation, right?"

"Luca, what you did last night was good. Sometimes, mortals get this image inside their heads, when they don't know the facts, or how things operate in our world. *Bel* is worse, I think." He smiled and gave Luca a slap on the back.

"I know I'm still new here, master, and this is new to her. I know no other life, no other reality, so it's hard to understand a mortal's jealousy, but I try to see it through her eyes."

Shade grabbed the knife sharpener and started sharpening his blades. As he rolled things over in his head, he got lost in his thoughts and kept grinding away at the blade.

Luca kept watching him work. He definitely had his mind on something and he could only assume it was my lady and the baby. He didn't appear angry, but damn, he'd have no blade left if he kept up this pace.

"Master, you expect to have any blade left on that knife? At this pace, it will be useless."

Shade paused and looked down at the knife and sighed. "I have a lot on my mind, Luca. Something I want to ask you."

Luca stopped cleaning the weapon in his hand and gave Shade his full attention. "I'm all ears, master. I'll do what I can to answer."

"That is good Luca, because I need to talk to another warrior. When you were in the training camp, did you ever hear of an immortal impregnating a mortal female? Knew of anyone at any time?"

Luca looked at him and almost laughed. "Master, we didn't fool with mortals in camp, you would have sliced off our balls and fed them to us. But to be honest, I've heard of it before. I knew it must happen, but until I met Cory, I'd never met a half-breed. I've seen enough to know mortal women seem drawn to immortals. Is something wrong with my lady?"

"Not exactly. But Alec made hints that I should know what the outcome will be, that the *bambino* might not survive, and there is the possibility *bel* won't survive." Shade threw the knife across the room, watching it hit and stick in the wall straight and true. "I am worried. I cannot lose her. I cannot lose the *bambino*. Everything is out of my control. I have no idea what to do. I never thought this would happen. I want *bambinos* with *bel*. But Alec also reminded me that if the *bambino* survives, it will be a half-breed, not fully vampire, and not accepted in our community. The Council will never accept him, and he could never be a warrior. He could not be king."

Luca watched his struggle. He knew this was going to be rough. If she lost the baby, she'd be devastated, and he'd lose his mind. And if he lost her, Luca couldn't even process that thought.

"Master, do you not have someone special to help with this? I know the doctor was here. I know he is sending you elsewhere for help. That has to mean something?"

Shade looked at Luca and sighed. "I hope so, Luca. Perhaps the specialist that is coming will know something. Perhaps he will have answers. It is the only hope I can cling to at the moment. It tears me up inside."

Luca stared at him and could see the worry in his eyes. Luca knew Shade would give his own life if he could save my lady and their child. He didn't say anything. Shade wouldn't have heard him anyway. His mind was in a twisted battle, trying to work it out. Standing up, Luca clapped him on the back and walked to the door. Turning to see him staring into space, Luca hoped this turned out okay for all of them. He'd have his hands full with both of them if anything should happen to this baby.

65

Rissa made use of her time before Alec got home by catching up on a few phone calls. She'd finally met with the feeder and she was perfect to destroy the happy little home of Kate and Shade. Rissa couldn't wait to see this little show play out. Before she'd left the feeder compound, she'd asked the feeder to pose for her, and Rissa was thrilled with the picture. She wanted Alec to have a good look at the hot sex goddess she planned to land in Shade's lap. Perhaps it would spark his interest and she could tease him as well. She was desperate for his attention.

She wanted Alec fucking her hard, taking her and giving her what she wanted. His teasing and holding out was driving her out of her mind. She printed out the photo of the feeder from her phone, and laid it near the bottle of Midnight and cigarette box. She knew he'd find it when he arrived home. Writing a small note, she laid it beside the photo.

> My Wicked Vampire....
> I think she will tempt your warrior and ruin a
> mortal's naive thoughts of happiness in our immortal
> world.
> Always,
> Your Devious Darling

Grabbing her bag, she left for the gym with a swing in her hips and a wicked smile on her face.

***

Alec got home late, and headed for the family room to fix a drink. He saw a photo propped against the bottle of Midnight along with her note. He read the note then picked up the photograph. He had to chuckle in spite of himself. She was all tits and ass. Even her curves had curves as he looked at her breast spilling over the top of her dress. Her mass of red hair tumbled down around her shoulders. She looked tall, like all natural-born vampire females and equal to handling whatever the male beast could dish out.

Alec wanted to make sure she understood what he wanted her to do. Shade must be delirious by now if he hadn't fed from that mortal since he learned she was pregnant. The very scent of a feeder's blood would push him over the edge. Alec wanted her to push him balls to the wall the minute she walked in the door. Alec summoned his manservant, Santos. He'd been with him for four hundred years, and they had an understanding. Alec didn't want to see or hear him; however he was to make sure everything he wanted was where he wanted it when he wanted it and to show up only when he was summoned.

Santos appeared in the doorway. "Yes, master?"

Alec held up the picture of the feeder. "This feeder Rissa hired, find her and bring her here, now."

Santos nodded. "Yes, master, I will take care of it."

Alec passed the time returning phone calls and had moved on to checking a few things on his laptop when he heard Santos at the door. He looked up to see him standing there with the feeder. Her red hair hung in a mass of loose curls down to her shoulders, her full lips painted glossy red, her tits strained against the fabric of her barely there dress and bulged over the top of her low-cut neckline. She was all curves; tits, hips, and ass. Rissa had outdone herself.

"And your name is?"

"Desire, master. My name is Desire."

He laughed out loud. "Of course it is, and a well-deserved name, I'm sure. You can go now, Santos. And you, Desire...you need to come in and take a seat. We have much to discuss." His body responded unbidden to the pheromones the feeder released, and he had to fight his own desire to take her where she stood, pushing back the beast.

She moved into the room with the gracefulness of a jungle cat, a slow walk that allowed her to roll her ample hips. She was wearing at least a 4" stiletto shoe that was all straps and accentuated the narrowness of her ankle and the curve of her calf, in a dress that stopped high on her thighs. She sat across from him and crossed her legs, making sure he noticed she wasn't wearing panties.

With his eyes locked on the sensuous movements of the feeder crossing her legs, as if in slow motion, he felt his cock grow hard. "I assume Rissa has filled you in on your assignment?"

"I know a little, master," she practically purred when she spoke in her soft, breathy voice. "I know I've been asked to service a vampire whose mate is pregnant."

"Yes, well, that is the case, but I want much more from you than that, Desire. This vamp is a warrior. He's my best warrior, and much to my dismay, he has mated with a mortal. I find he's much too distracted by all the drama this mortal has created in his life, and your assignment will be to break up that union. This mortal doesn't understand the ways of our world. She won't be happy to learn her newly found mate must spend the next four or five months feeding from another woman, and certainly won't be happy to learn her mate will be enjoying all the pleasures your ample body has to offer him while she lies alone in her bed, listening to the sounds of his pleasure you so expertly provide."

"Of course, master, it's what I was bred for."

"Yes, well, it may not be as easy as you may think. This warrior, he has some romantic idea that he can somehow get around his need to feed. I know he hasn't fed from his mate since they learned she was pregnant, so from that perspective, he'll be easy prey, but he may try to resist you. Your job is to make sure he can't.

"When Rissa takes you to their home, I want you to zero in on him immediately, lock eyes with him, go straight to him, touch him, rub up against him, make sure he picks up your scent. I want you to masturbate yourself in the car on the way over, take yourself to the brink of orgasm, but do not cum. I want you to smell like sex when you walk in the door and I want that scent to hit him like a cannonball fired at his chest, and I want your own need to be felt by him. I want you to radiate so much sex that any male vamp within a hundred yards of you that night will have an immediate erection. Are you up for the task, Desire?"

"This may be my most fun assignment yet, master, and I assure you, I'm up for the task."

He chuckled to himself, almost feeling sorry for the torment Shade was about to endure, but Shade would thank him later, after he sampled the delights of what was clearly the most delectable feeder Alec had ever seen.

"Desire, I'll grant your wish for anything you want, and believe me, I have the means to provide it, if you can push him to the point where he takes you right there on the floor with that mousy mortal mate looking on."

"Not a problem, master, ask and you shall receive. Now, what can I do for you?"

***

Rissa arrived home later than she planned and kicked off her gym shoes as soon as she came in the door. She'd seen Alec's car outside, so she knew he was home. She headed for the family room, sure she'd find him there having a drink and unwinding, and she was eager to find out what he thought of the feeder she'd selected. As she approached the hallway, she heard voices, and picked up the scent of another female. When she entered the family room, she saw Alec on the sofa, his suit jacket tossed to the side, his white dress shirt still on but unbuttoned, his tie hanging loosely from his neck. Both arms were spread across the back of the sofa, as his head was laid back, eyes closed, lips slightly parted. Her eyes traveled down his body and saw the mass of red curls bobbing between his legs, her body almost obstructed from Rissa's view by the table that sat in front of the sofa. She paused briefly as she took in the scene and tried to process what she was seeing. As she did so, Alec raised his head and looked at her, smiled, and held out his hand to her, and said, "Come join us, darling."

She moved to sit next to him on the sofa, cradling her head on his shoulder as he dropped his arm around her, placing his hand at her waist, and slowly moving it up her back. As his hand reached her neck, he grasped a handful of her hair as he bent his head to her up-turned face and kissed her, gently, lips barely touching. Then he kissed the corners of her mouth, before he drew her bottom lip into his mouth and gently tugged.

She raised her hand and placed it on his cheek, allowing her fingers to toy with their joined lips. He tilted his head to bite as one of her fingers slide into his mouth. He teased her finger with his tongue, and she responded in kind, and their kisses deepened and Desire continued to work her magic on his cock.

His hand was still tangled in Rissa's golden locks as Desire brought him to orgasm, and he clinched both fists as he came, pulling hard on Rissa's hair until he heard her cry out. He pulled her head back, exposing her neck and bit into that soft succulent skin, and sucked hard to draw her blood into his mouth, increasing the intensity of his own orgasm as he felt his cock unload into the feeder's throat. Rissa's body responded to the bite, going rigid as her hand dropped to his chest, and he listened to her moans mingling with his own. As her body went limp and relaxed into his, he looked down at Desire. Her eyes were locked on his as she used her tongue to lick away the last bits of cum from her lips.

"Will there be anything else, master?"

"I think you've done quite enough for one evening, Desire. Just remember everything I told you, and Rissa will be in contact when she's ready to take you to my warrior's house. Santos will show you out."

The feeder stood and smiled at Rissa and made the same slow, hip rolling exit from the room.

Rissa lay quietly with her head on his shoulder and her hand on his bare chest.

"You know I love you, Rissa, in my own way, as much as I'm capable. We are kindred spirits, you and me. We take too much pleasure in hurting others. If you're looking for love sonnets and roses and other ridiculous displays of romantic mortal love, well, you won't find it here. But I do love you, my beauty. I love how other men look at you and envy me. I love reading the nasty thoughts in their heads as they try to conjure up an image of all the dirty deeds we perform between the sheets. You are my most prized possession."

Rissa soaked in his praise, and his declaration of love. Both of them were too self-absorbed to care much about anything but themselves, and they both know it. She smiled to herself, lucky to have found him.

66

Shade was pacing outside the house, chain-smoking one cigarette after another as he waited. The doctor would be here any moment. Trying to get control of his nervousness, he had left *bel* taking a shower, so he could take a smoke break and try to wrap his head around this situation. She seemed calm, but then she would, not knowing what might be coming. Hell, he wished he didn't know. As he stubbed out his cigarette, Gi showed up to announce the doctor had arrived and was waiting in the living room. Gi told him he'd informed my lady of the same. Shade teleported into the bedroom where Kate came to him, still wrapped in a towel and hugged him tight.

"Shade, Gi said the doctor was here? Rissa said he wouldn't need to examine me again since Dr. Cavelli had already done that, so let me just slip on a robe and we can go downstairs."

"*Si*, get your robe and we will see him in the living room. Now, come along, let us get this over with."

Kate returned in her robe and took his hands. He looked shaken, worried. "Okay, my territorial warrior, let's go downstairs and get this over with."

He walked with her hand in hand down the stairs and into the living room where the doctor stood as they entered.

"Master Medici, Miss Reese, my name is Dr. Loggia. I was contacted by Senator Canton and told of your special circumstances. I specialize in immortal/mortal pregnancies. We seem to be seeing more and more of them and they do present some unique issues."

Shade laid his hand on the small of Kate's back, directing her to the couch where they sat side by side. "Please continue. Let us know what to expect, and what these unique issues are."

The 'doctor' remained standing. He'd researched the topic and rehearsed his role carefully, knowing there'd be a big payout if the Canton's were pleased. "Well, certainly you're both aware that mortal/immortal pregnancies are not recommended. The mortal mother is usually not strong enough to support the demands the growing baby is going to put on her body. That is why we so strongly suggest pregnancies should be delayed until the mother is immortal.

It's not impossible to carry the child to term, but it will be extremely important you take these nutritional supplements. It's a special formulation, designed to make up for the deficiencies in what her body won't be able to provide the growing infant. Without these supplements, well, there's almost no chance for the baby to survive. He, or she, won't be able to draw enough nutrients from the mother and the baby dies in the womb."

Kate felt her heart skip a beat, and she looked at Shade, but his face showed no emotion, and she knew he was trying to be strong for her. She looked at the doctor.

"But if I take the supplements...it will be all right?"

"Well, Miss Reese, we can't guarantee anything, but yes, your odds of carrying this baby to term improve dramatically with the supplements. But I must emphasize, you have to take them according to directions, without fail."

"Of course, of course, I'll take them."

The doctor continued, "The supplements must be taken three times a day, and I have to warn you, they'll make you ill. The supplements are for the nutritional needs of the immortal infant, but will fight with your own DNA. Your body will reject them. But regardless of how you feel, you must continue to take them."

Kate could feel Shade's hand tighten at her waist, as she felt the sweat in her palm against his other hand.

"That...that's not important. If it will help the baby, we'll do whatever we need to do, right lover?"

She turned to look at him and he gave her a weak smile, but it didn't cover the hurt in his eyes. The doctor turned his attention to Shade and addressed him directly.

"As for you, Master Medici, it will be extremely important you not feed from her at all. Immortal pregnancies are shorter, and as a rule, we've found the mortals pregnant with half-breeds also have shorter pregnancies. The infants grow faster, and therefore demand more from the mother. She'll need everything she has, and more, to support the growth of the baby, so you'll need to make arrangements for a feeder. I have many contacts for feeders and I've provided a list to Miss Benneteau, so I'm sure she'll be able to help you with that."

Shade stiffened next to her. "Not necessary, it has been taken care of."

The doctor pushed once more. “Master Medici, I can't emphasize the importance of this feeding issue enough.”

Shade's temper built as he said in a booming voice, "I said it has been taken care of, I understand your instructions, doctor!"

The doctor's face reddened as he backed down from Shade. “Well then, I don't need to examine you today since Dr. Cavelli was just here. I’ll leave you a month's worth of supplements, and I’ll be back for a follow-up visit next month and will bring your next supply at that time. You should start taking them as soon as possible." He placed the bottles of capsules on the table. "If you have no other questions for me, then, I guess I’ll take my leave.”

Gi appeared from nowhere and escorted the doctor to the door. Kate sat numb beside Shade, trying to absorb the information the doctor had just delivered. She turned to Shade.

“I won't let this baby die, Shade. I won't.”

He closed his eyes and leaned his forehead to hers, and whispered, “*Bel rosso*.”

Once the doctor had left the house and they were alone, he turned to her. “*Bel*, I want you to be okay, if you can’t go through with this, you need to tell me. Whatever you decide, this is your choice, it is your body, and this sickness will be horrible for you. Please tell me what you wish.”

She clung to him. “I’m frightened. It was foolish of me to let this happen, but now that it has, I can't let our baby die. Many women feel sick through their pregnancy. I’ll be fine. Unless...unless this is not what you want?”

His hand slid down her face, softly touching her lips, then kissing her on the forehead and crushing her to his chest. “Kate, there is nothing I want more than to have *bambinos* with you, but I am worried about this sickness. The pills worry me. If you were immortal, we would not have these problems. This is not your fault, we fell in love and that is that.”

Kate stroked his back, soothing him. “Let's try not to second guess everything. Neither of us knows the future. Can we just take it a day at a time? I don't know any other alternative. Let's just follow instructions and hope for the best, okay? I know that worrying about it won't be good for the baby, so I’ll just hope for the best.”

“*Si*. We will take it one day at a time. I will make sure Alec knows my schedule will need to be flexible. That’s all there is to it! Now, as a special treat, I think before you start all this pill taking, I owe you something, and I am going to pay my debt."

He looked down at her and smiled wickedly.

"You have a debt? To me?"

"Oh *si*, to you, *bel*," kissing her softly. "I recall a rooftop in Paris, a gorgeous woman with strawberries, roses, and champagne, and not finishing something I started. I promised this woman I would repay that debt. I wonder if she will be free."

"When? Now? You want to take me to Paris now? I hope I can change out of this robe first."

"*Si*, there is my *bel rosso*! Now, we will leave around 3:00 a.m., and we will take my private plane, so run along and pack your things so they can be loaded on the plane. We will have time to get to the hangar before sunrise and we will sleep on the plane. And do not pack so damn much, *bel*!"

"I thought you were just going to zip me over there again like last time."

"I can teleport you, but taking your luggage is another thing, so we will take my plane this time. Now, run along, I have to find Luca, and give him some instructions. I will meet you in the bedroom when I am done. You lift nothing! You call Gi or Theresa to help you pack. Gi will get all the bags when you are done and get them to the plane."

67

Rissa was to meet Alec at their regular hangout, Old Ebbitt Grill, the place to see and be seen by everyone in D.C. politics. She was immediately escorted to their table. Usually, they arrived together, but tonight, they couldn't coordinate their busy schedules. Getting out of the cab, she knew she was a little overdressed, but she was coming from a semi-formal event and didn't have time to change. She hoped Alec wouldn't be too upset with this dress with its low cut back.

She was just getting settled at the table when her cell went off and she was sure it was Alec, but found, instead, it was the actor friend she'd sent to Kate's to play 'doctor'. Answering quickly, he gave her the rundown of how things had gone with Kate and Shade, and Rissa was ecstatic. Things were going just as planned, and she was well on her way to making a success of breaking up this little happy home.

Alec was greeted as soon as he entered the restaurant and escorted to their table. He bent down to kiss her when he reached the table and slid his hand down her back, noticing the ravishing red dress was backless. He wasn't amused. As they finished the kiss, he leaned to her ear and whispered.

"That dress suits you, my darling, but probably shows more skin than is proper for a Senator's fiancé."

He took his seat across from her and nodded at several acquaintances and colleagues around the room. He reached across the table and took her hand. Alec would never show his displeasure with her in public, where prying eyes were always on the lookout for some bit of gossip that would show up in the next day's newspaper, something about a 'little incident' in a local eatery between 'a certain handsome, single Senator and his blonde girlfriend.'

"I hope you have some good news for me. I haven't had the best of days on the Senate floor."

Rissa beamed at him. "I have some excellent news. Everything went well with the doctor visit. Kate was adamant that she'd take the supplements no matter how ill she became. And we haven't even introduced the wonderful kicker for Shade."

Alec flagged down their waiter and he practically stumbled over his own feet trying to get to the table fast enough.

"Yes sir, my name is Roger and I'll be your server tonight."

"Well Roger, I have some wine here that's held exclusively for me..." Before Alec could finish speaking, Roger acknowledged him.

"Yes sir, Senator, The Medici Midnight. The manager makes sure we never run out, and emphasizes it's only available to you. Would you like me to bring over a bottle now, sir?"

"Please, Roger. And have the chef prepare us that sushi platter, he knows what I like. That will be all."

Turning his attention back to Rissa, he responded, "That's excellent news. If she starts taking her pills right away, we should have part of this problem behind us within a week. I couldn't be more pleased, my darling. And the wonderful kicker for Shade?"

"Well, apparently Shade was quite angry when our doctor mentioned a feeder. He's clearly agitated with not feeding. I do believe, between Desire and his hunger, he'll take to Desire quite well. I do hope that has made a better ending to your day?"

Alec laughed out loud, loud enough to draw the attention of other people seated nearby as they turned to look in his direction. He lifted Rissa's hand to his lips and kissed her palm, letting his tongue gently tease. With a genuine smile on his face, he responded. "My darling, you have no idea. I almost feel sorry for my old friend Shade. Now, what about you? What about your day?"

"I do apologize for the dress Alec, sincerely. I was held up longer than anticipated. I had the big charity event for the Polo set this afternoon and had no time to return home and change. But the event went off without a hitch, of course."

The waiter returned with the wine and food. The sushi platter was placed in the middle of the table for both of them, and he poured the wine into their glasses before he scurried off once more. Alec lifted his glass to Rissa, and she responded by lifting her glass to his.

"May we get everything in this world we so richly deserve, and may we do it together. I love you, Rissa." He clinked his glass to hers and watched her face closely.

Rissa was momentarily taken aback. It wasn't that she'd never heard those words before, but normally, they were only spoken in private. It was rare for him to speak of love in public. Licking her lips softly, she looked down, not sure how to respond and brought the glass to her lips and lifted her eyes to him. Taking a small sip, she twirled the glass in her hand, her eyes still locked with his.

"As I love you, Alec. Did something happen today? Anything I can do to help?"

Alec had watched her face as he delivered those words, and she seemed surprised, unsure. He smirked to himself, withholding from Rissa and keeping her off balance was what he did best.

"You've changed the subject, my darling, and here I was trying to talk about love. But no, unless you can get fifty-two Democrats to vote on my bill, then I don't think you can help me with this problem, but then, that's what my money and the lobbyists are for. And do you love me, Rissa? You know we'll never be conventional, but that doesn't mean I don't see what you do for me, or that I don't see how you care for me. I'm a selfish man, and I make no apologies for it. I want what I want, and I'll always find a way to get it. But I'm not blind, my darling."

Reaching across the table, she slid her fingers up and down the lapel of his jacket and smiled softly, moist between her legs from just his words and the power he had to make her so.

"I love you, Alec. I've always loved you. You keep me on my toes, to say the least. You give me so much, and I want to give that back tenfold. I want us to rise above them all, together. No one else can do that with you, I know that, and I intend to keep your attention and your love."

He placed his hand over hers. "Rissa, no man in power, mortal or immortal, gets there without climbing over the backs of others. I've made many enemies, and I'll make many more. What I have in you is a partner I can trust to keep my secrets, who won't make judgments about moral or immoral decisions. As I said, I'll always get what I want. I don't take that lightly, my darling. I can't promise fidelity, but I will promise love, and I'll be honest with you. I won't hide things from you. Like I said, we'll never be conventional."

Rissa smiled wickedly at him. "I've always understood your terms Alec, and I can live with them quite easily. I have your love, and that's all that's important to me."

She bit her bottom lip, shifting slightly in her seat, wet and aching for him, crossing her legs under the table, letting her shoe drop to the floor as her toes slid softly up his leg.

He drained the glass of wine and pushed the sushi around on the platter, so it appeared to have been picked at. He listened to her response, feeling her foot sliding up his leg.

"Why don't you put your dainty foot in my crotch? I think you'll find a surprise waiting for you, and this tablecloth should give you adequate privacy."

Laughing softly, her foot snaked up between his legs. She felt his cock straining huge and hard against his dress slacks and her foot slid up and down his hard cock, watching his face mask any response.

Without emotion, he responded, "Too bad there's not more privacy. You've sparked my appetite, I fear."

Alec reached under the table and cupped her foot in his hand. "If you're finished here, darling, I can call for my driver."

She was completely finished here, but hoped he was just getting started for a longer night. "Please do call for the driver."

He pulled out his cell phone and had Alto bring the car around. Alec threw some money on the table, stood, and offered his arm to Rissa who quickly slipped back into her shoe, before they walked out together. Alec knew every man in the room was watching her ass in that backless dress.

As they got outside, the car pulled over to the curb and Alto got out, opening the back door for them. They climbed in together and Alto got back in the driver's seat. Alec spoke to his driver. "The privacy screen Alto?"

Alto immediately raised the black glass screen that separated the front seat from the back.

"Now, my darling, where were we? I believe you were attending to my cock, if I remember correctly."

He was unzipping his fly and releasing the massive hard-on he'd had since entering the restaurant. "Why don't you straddle this for daddy?"

Pulling her dress over her hips, she exposed her flawless skin. She was waxed completely bare, smooth as silk, just as he liked it. Her sex was already swollen with anticipation of that hard cock and feeling it deep inside her.

Straddling him, her hand on his shoulders, she softly nuzzled into his neck, her blonde hair falling across his face, as she whispered in a soft growl. "I love riding your cock, daddy."

Sitting upright as she slid down on his cock, she was wet and tight. She threw back her hair and looked him straight in the eyes as she sat down hard, driving him to the hilt.

He slid his hips forward on the seat so she could ride the full length of his cock, as he laid his head back against the seat. She was riding him hard and he could feel his cock throb inside her. He grabbed her bare ass with both hands and gripped her hard. He squeezed past the point of pain, as he pushed her hips down even harder onto his cock. He delivered a loud slap that left his red handprint on her bare ass, and then repeated the action on the other cheek.

"Now fuck me harder, baby girl. Show daddy just how hard you can ride that cock."

Throwing her head back, she reached up and grabbed his tie, pulling his face to hers so they were eye to eye. She yanked hard on his tie and began to undo it while her tongue slid along his vein. She was never to feed without permission.

"Please, daddy... I need you, don't deny me."

She had him on the brink of exploding, but he resisted the urge to cum to prolong the pleasure. He reached up and tugged the tie free and grabbed the shirt at the collar and gave a quick yank, which had buttons popping free. He laid his head back on the seat and turned to one side, giving her free access and permission to feed. "Take it now, baby girl, and make sure you cum with me."

Her body was shaking with want for him as she sank her fangs deep. She heard him moan as his blood filled her mouth. She felt his overwhelming power flowing inside her. Her body was tense, and she felt her orgasm building, coming fast and violent. She felt his body go rigid, and she drew deep as they both exploded in unison. His hands were on her hips, squeezing tight. She unlatched and collapsed on his shoulder as his entire body shuddered. He was magnificent, and belonged to her, and she dared not say a word. She lay still, not moving until he gave her some signal of what he wished. He wasn't one to be romantic after sex, no matter how soft or rough.

His breathing was ragged and rapid, and he waited for his heartbeat to return to normal. He raised one hand and placed it on the back of her head, tangling that golden hair in his fingers, and lifted her face to his. He kissed her hard, bruising her lips as he tasted his own blood in her mouth.

"Good job, baby girl. Just what daddy needed."

68

Walking into the bunker, Shade saw Luca unloading some new weapons and he smiled. "Just came looking for you, need to grab a gun. Listen, I know you heard what the doctor told us. So, before *bel* takes these damn pills and starts to feel sick, I am taking her on a short trip to Paris. We will take the jet. I don't want to teleport her in her condition. You are in charge of this house Luca. Keep your wits about you, and get your ass out there and feed. Stick with a feeder so your blood is not tainted. I will need to feed like a mongrel by the time I get back."

He found the handgun he was searching for, a Desert Eagle .50 Caliber Mark XIX pistol, and slid it into his shoulder harness.

"No problem, master, I'm glad that, perhaps, my lady will have a chance with the baby. I know it makes you feel better. First time I've seen you smile in days. But, you can feed from me before you leave if you wish."

Shade nodded. "*Grazie,* Luca, but I am fine. When I get back will be a different story. *Bel* has a tendency to wear me out." He winked at Luca.

***

Kate had rushed upstairs to start packing for their impromptu trip to Paris. As excited as she was about the trip, the news the doctor delivered was in her head. She needed to try to put that aside so they could enjoy this time together. She packed bags for both her and Shade, not knowing their full agenda.

She called down to him, "Shade, could you help me, please?" He bounded up the steps, helping her to finish packing their bags.

Gi entered with a tray filled with breakfast food for Kate.

"Master, it is close to 3:00, Reynaldo thought my lady should eat before you leave. She is with child now and her appetite will be ravenous. The car awaits you outside whenever you are ready. Dante says you must lift off by 4:00 if you want to arrive just after sunset. And, on behalf of all the staff, may I take this opportunity to say how excited we are for the arrival of the little one, and we wish you both a safe and romantic trip abroad."

"Thank you Gi, I cannot do any of this without all of you, so I am very appreciative of your help. We will be down shortly."

Gi nodded, leaving the bedroom, and closing the door behind him.

Kate had finished dressing and had stuck a few magazines and some ear buds into a tote bag when she smelled the rich fragrant coffee on the tray Gi delivered.

"Oh my gosh, I'm starving! Reynaldo has outdone himself, as usual. Our staff pampers me so." She leaned over to kiss him before diving into the food.

"I am happy to see you have an appetite. This is a good sign, *si*? Finish up, *mi amore*, we need to get to the plane, they are waiting on us in the hangar. You can change on the plane if you want, for we will sleep during the flight."

Shade finished getting dressed, putting his gun in the waistband at the back of his jeans. He stopped and turned to her, standing with his arms crossed over his chest, a smile on his face as he watched her eat while she continued to pack.

She finished up the last of the food on the tray and slid off the bed. Walking to him, she wrapped her arms around his waist and laid her head on his chest. "I'm so excited! There's so much I want to share with you in Paris. It's a city for lovers, and I can't wait to be there with you."

He lifted her face to his and kissed her softly, looking deep into those dark brown eyes. "I love you, *bel*, this city was made for us, *si*?"

Picking her up in his arms, he carried her downstairs and headed out the front door to the car, buckling her in, and waiting while the staff loaded the luggage into the trunk before driving to the private hangar.

He glanced over at her as he drove at his usual break-neck speed and chuckled as she gripped the door handle. He winked at her as they pulled up to a small private airport, which housed a large hangar. Someone rushed out to open a garage door entrance and Shade drove into the hangar and right up to his private jet. Kate's mouth was hanging open.

"This is yours?"

He leapt out of the driver's side door and rushed around to open her door, extending his hand and helping her out of the car.

"*Si*, this is one of my planes. I have several jets, but this one is my favorite."

As they climbed up the steps, Shade saw their pilot Dante was ready to take off and began introductions to the flight crew who'd attend them on this flight; the pilot, a co-pilot, and the very tall statuesque blonde female vampire, who looked like she stepped off a Victoria Secret runway.

"*Bel*, our pilot Dante, he has been with me for many years, has also been my driver and sometimes bodyguard. This is our co-pilot, Ciro, and our flight attendant, Isabella."

Kate nodded to each of them, shaking the hands of the pilot and co-pilot. She turned to see Isabella giving Shade a huge smile as she stepped in close to give him an intimate hug.

Isabella's eyes didn't leave him as he boarded the plane. It had been a long time since she'd been allowed to 'be of service', and she was hoping his mortal female companion wouldn't put a damper on things. As they stepped on board, Isabella picked up her scent. *Mated! Well who knows, not all masters are faithful to their mates. There may still be opportunity for a little in-flight entertainment.* Stepping past Kate, she gave Shade a most unprofessional hug that implied a history of intimacy. "Welcome aboard Master Shade, everything is ready for your flight. I'm pleased to accommodate your every need on this trip."

Shade gave Isabella a stern look. "*Bel*, this is Isabella." Shade admonished the flight attendant under his breath to behave before he broke away to stand beside Kate.

"Issa, this is my beautiful mate Katherine. Will you give her a quick tour while I talk to Dante about the flight?"

He turned to Kate, kissing her and taking her into his arms. "Issa will show you around. Get comfortable, I won't be long, and if you need anything, Issa is your girl." He pulled her closer and spoke in a whisper, "And stop looking at me with that jealous hell in your eyes!"

Kate tried to swallow her jealousy as he turned her over to Issa. *Oh, I bet Issa would be more than happy to help him with anything.* As Shade turned his attention to Dante, Kate redirected her attention to Isabella.

"Isabella, could you show me where they put our luggage? Shade dragged me out of the house so quickly, but he said the luggage would be on board."

Isabella laughed. "That sounds just like Master Shade."

Kate fumed. *Really*? She felt her anger flair. *And what would you know about being dragged out of the house by Master Shade?* Kate took a deep breath and tried to rein in her emotions. She couldn't react to every female he'd had ever known in his lifetime, but it was a struggle.

Isabella took her to the private bedroom on the plane where their luggage had been stored. Issa was sizing up her competition, wondering how far she could push this situation and not anger Shade. She sat down on the bed and ran her hand across the spread.

"Would you like a tour of this bedroom? I'm very familiar with it."

Kate gave her a look that would melt steel and in a hard voice responded, "Of that, I have no doubt, but I can manage everything from here. You can go now."

Isabella stood and left the room as Kate went through her luggage and pulled out a nightgown, laying it across the bed. The sun would rise soon, and he'd retreat here to this windowless room for his death slumber. She unpacked some toiletry items and returned to the main cabin to find Shade, with Isabella leaning over him, sharing the view of her ample cleavage.

Shade looked up as Kate entered the main cabin. He smiled and held out his hand to her, drawing her to the seat beside him, pulling her in close to his chest. "*Mi amore,* it is a long flight, we will sleep, *si*? And before you know it, we will be in Paris. I have booked us at the Ritz, does that please you?"

As he waited for Kate's answer, Isabella asked if there was anything else he'd require. "*Bel*, do you want anything?"

Kate pointedly directed her answer at him and ignored Isabella, "I'm fine, lover, and there's nothing else we require."

Shade could feel the tension between these two she-cats. He turned to Isabella, dismissing her. "We are fine now Issa, I will call if we need anything, thank you."

He was aware of the cold stare he received from Isabella as she nodded and headed for the front of the plane. Quite frankly, he'd completely forgotten about their little tryst. There had been so many women. He couldn't be expected to recall them all, but no need to parade them in front of Kate. He sent a message telepathically to Dante to switch out Issa on future flights with a flight attendant he had not had sex with.

Dante responded, **"Of course, master. And which of the flight attendants might that be?"**

Shade ran through the list of candidates through his head, trying to remember if there was one he hadn't fucked, and sighed. **"Dante, just start from scratch, brother."**

Shade could hear Dante's chuckle in his head as he responded, **"No problem, master. Consider it done."**

He snuggled Kate as she flipped through travel brochures on Paris, planning out their schedule. Shade took her hand as she put the brochures away, and led her to the private bedroom, watching as Issa closed all the shades over the windows in the main cabin, avoiding eye contact with him.

He stripped down nude as Kate slipped on the gown she'd laid out on the bed, climbing into the round bed next to him. He held her close, falling into his death slumber. When they were about an hour out from Paris, he heard a light tap on the door and Issa opened the door slightly to inform him they were almost ready to land, her attitude decidedly cool as she delivered her message.

"Master Shade, we're almost ready to land, we're arriving in Paris soon. Please prepare my lady for landing. A car will be waiting, and the ground crew will unload your luggage into the car and get you on your way. I hope you enjoy your stay."

Shade thanked her as Kate woke and saw Issa standing in the door. The two women exchanged a cold look. Oh yeah, he definitely needed to make a change before the flight back home. Issa turned on her heels and flipped her blond hair as she walked back toward the front of the cabin to prepare for landing.

Shade turned to Kate. "Hey beautiful, wake up and get dressed. You will need to be in your seat with the seat belt buckled for landing. We will land in about an hour."

Kate threw on a casual outfit and some flat shoes and got to their seat and buckled in just in time to feel the soft bump of the smooth landing. The shades were still drawn over the window, but Dante had announced it was 6:00 p.m local time, so she slowly lifted the shade, making sure there was no sunlight before pushing it open. She looked out the window to see the plane taxi into another hangar, with another car waiting. *Jeez...who travels like this*? She looked up at him, placing her hands on either side of his face and kissed him.

"Thank you for this. I think we needed a break from our own drama."

They departed the plane with Dante and all three of them climbed into yet another car, Dante driving, and headed off in the early evening traffic to The Ritz. As the car pulled up in front of the hotel, a bellhop rushed to open the doors, while another started removing the luggage and the doorman snapped to attention at the door.

"*Bon soir, Monsieur* Medici. We are so happy to have you back with us."

Shade nodded and tipped the bellhop and doorman lavishly as he took Kate's arm and walked them into the main lobby, where the staff immediately responded to his presence.

"Your suite is waiting and ready, *Monsieur* Medici. If you will just follow the bellman."

They walked with the bellman down the plush corridor to the bank of elevators where they were whisked to the top floor and the Coco Chanel Suite. Kate had read about this suite. *$50,000 a night! Are you kidding me?*

The bellman unlocked the door and passed the key to Shade, who discreetly placed a number of large bills into the bellman's hand.

"*Merci monsieur*, and if there's anything you need, just use the call button in the room, you are familiar, *oui*?"

Kate walked into the massive suite. As Shade closed the door behind him, she made a running jump into his arms and wrapped her legs around his waist, her arms around his neck and covered him in kisses.

"Whoa, *mi amore*, what is all this about? We are happy, *si*?"

She leaned back slightly, supported by his arms, and looked into those eyes.

"Lover, we are so happy. I know I teased you about our interrupted trip, but this is really my most favorite city in the world. I love Paris, but not as much as I love you."

She released her legs from around his hips and dropped down to stand in front of him, holding his hand.

"You've stayed here before? Everyone seems to know you. I want to look around please? Come with me?"

"*Bel*, your happiness makes my life complete, and *si*, I have stayed here before, many times. I have never really seen much of the city. To be honest, whenever I have been here, it was about work and I did not take the time to explore."

She pulled at his hand as she dragged him off to explore the rest of the suite. "Oh my god, look at the bedroom. That bed is so lavish!

He had to laugh at her enthusiasm as she continued to lead him through the suite. "Where are you taking me now, *bel*?"

"The bathroom, I heard the Ritz has gold fixtures. The faucets look like swans. I want to see!"

He followed her into the opulent bathroom and she squealed with delight as she saw the gold fixtures, shaped like swans that pour water from their open mouths.

"Damn, it is just running water, *bel*. But it is beautiful, *si*?"

Kate walked through the large bathroom, admiring the tub big enough for two before turning to explore more of the suite. He chuckled. "Go, go, I know you are dying to be let loose."

"Lover, I can't believe I'm going to say this, but I'm hungry again. Can we unpack and order room service? It must be the pregnancy, I'm never this hungry. But I'll need my energy for all the things I want to share with you. I made a list of places to show you. I hope you aren't going to be bored."

He laughed to himself, glad to see her appetite returned. "Order whatever you wish from room service, and you could also order some Medici Midnight for me. I know they have it stocked here for me. And once you are done eating, we shall head out for our tour."

The bellman delivered their room service, and Shade sipped at the wine, allowing it to tame his hunger for her while Kate devoured the light dinner and the hot, rich coffee.

***

Back in Virginia, Rissa had only a few appointments for the day as she wrapped up her schedule with a meeting for a catering service. Thinking about the plan for Shade and Kate, she decided to give Kate a call on her cell, making sure she was taking those pills and to make arrangements to come meet her at their house. It was time to introduce her to Desire.

After several calls to Kate's cell, she was getting nothing but her voicemail. Rissa began to wonder what exactly was going on over there. She didn't like her calls to go unanswered. Finally getting to the car, she decided to call Shade's cell and see if she could get someone on the damn horn. The phone only rang twice when she heard the voice of an elderly gentleman with a thick Italian accent. It must be Shade's manservant. Rissa couldn't remember his name, Fee, Fi, Fo, Fum, some damn ridiculous name.

Asking for Kate, he politely advised her that the master and my lady were in Paris and would not be returning for several days. Thanking him, Rissa hung up, her blood already boiling. *In Paris? What in the hell are they up too? Damn it, you foolish bitch, you should be taking the pills by now.*

Slamming her hand down on the steering wheel, her temperature was rising. This may only hold up her plans for a few days, but a few days were like months to Alec. *Damn you Kate, you will pay for this!*

69

Shocking him with her appetite, Kate finished eating. She was so petite, and yet, she had wolfed down that food as if she hadn't eaten in days. Shade sat back sipping his Midnight, watching her eat. "So, if your tummy is now full, are you ready to start this tour?"

She knew they only had a few short hours of darkness to tour the city, but this was the City of Lights, and Paris was as beautiful at night as it was during the day.

"I am ready, lover, whenever you are."

He smiled and kissed her softly. "Come, let us leave now, for we have much to see. Where shall we go first? It is your choice. This city lies at your feet, yours for the taking."

"I'd thought originally of just walking, but there's so much to see, your driver said he'd take us from place to place, so we'll drive some, and walk some, and kiss under the stars some, *oui*?"

"*Oui!* Lead the way, minx."

They walked together down to the lobby, and Kate watched as the hotel staff nodded and deferred to him. Dante had the car waiting outside the hotel entrance. The doorman rushed to open the hotel entrance door, while Dante held the car door open for them, and they headed off into the Paris night. Kate asked the driver to take them down the Champs Elysees.

Kate was giddy with excitement to be back in her favorite city. "This is the widest street in Paris. There are seven roads that lead to the Arch de Triumph. If we were here during the day, this street would be teeming with people. Even now, you can see how many people are still walking about."

Kate turned to address Dante, "Please take us to the Pont Royal Bridge on the left bank, and let us out there, Dante."

"Yes, my lady." Dante expertly navigated the Paris traffic, heavy at all hours. He pulled up to one of the many bridges that cross the Seine and stopped the car, exited, and opened the door for them. As they climbed out of the car, she put her arm in his and asked him to walk with her across this bridge.

"This is one of many bridges in this city, all beautiful and each with its own rich history. Walk with me across the bridge. "

He let her take the lead, guiding him across the bridge. "*Bel*, which bridge is your favorite?"

"Pont Alexandre is my favorite. I just love the beauty of that bridge. I love all the architecture of Paris. The architects and craftsmen weren't content to build something that was just functional, but to create a piece of art, and it has stood through the centuries. Napoleon crossed this bridge. Marie Antoinette crossed this bridge. It has seen such history! And speaking of art and history, this bridge leads to the Louvre, one of the largest art museums in the world. It used to be a royal palace. Your mortal ancestor, Catherine de Medici, lived there briefly. She played a big role in the architectural development of this city during the French Renaissance after she married into the Valois family. She brought the best of both French and Italian design. You could spend weeks inside the Louvre and never see everything. Isn't it magnificent? It takes up two city blocks." They crossed the busy street and walked into the courtyard behind the Louvre.

He relished in her joy in being alive and it made his heart explode with happiness to share this time with her. He looked at her, the lights of the city reflected on her face.

"Nothing in this city can compare to the beauty of you." Bending down, his hand slid along her cheek, and then he kissed her.

She was engulfed in his arms as they stood inside the courtyard of the Louvre, in the glow of the light from the glass pyramid. After all, Paris wasn't just the city of lights, but the city of love. "Lover, we'll never finish this tour by sunrise if we get too distracted. Can you do that thing you do, and summon Dante to meet us outside the Louvre, please?"

Shade took a deep bow. "As you wish." **"Dante, hustle your ass man, my beauty needs a lift, pronto, outside the Louvre!"**

Dante pulled the car up to the curb and they climbed into the back seat once more. "Dante, could you go back across the bridge and take us to Notre Dame, please."

As Dante crossed yet another bridge, he took them to the Ile de la Cite, the island in the middle of the Seine where the cathedral was built. "Look at it Shade. This cathedral was built in the Fourteenth Century. I mean, look at the majesty of this building. They didn't have heavy equipment, it was all manpower. Look at the artistry of the stonework. I doubt it could even be replicated today. To think a man would dedicate his life to creating this building, knowing he'd never live to see the completed project and would have to rely on a second and third generation of stonemasons. I'm just in awe of it!"

They walked through the cathedral, speaking in whispers, as solitary worshippers were scattered throughout the great cathedral, kneeling in prayer, while others offered up prayers as they lit a candle. She took his hand and led him outside into the night, and back to the car.

Kate leaned forward to Dante and whispered, "Eiffel Tower please, and we'll get out for a while."

Dante continued to drive along the road that ran parallel to the Seine. As he pulled up near the iconic image so many associate with the city of Paris, the plaza was lit and the Eiffel Tower glowed with lights.

"Lover, this tower was built for the World's Fair in the Eighteenth Century, and the city hated it. They wanted it torn down as soon as the World's Fair was over. But it has remained and is now the image most people associate with the city."

Dante opened the door for them and they exited onto the plaza, surrounded by other lovers enjoying this night in Paris. Shade opened the door and took her hand.

"Come please, I wish to enjoy this night with you in my arms."

He led her away from the crowd and into a secluded side street where no one could see them.

"Where are we going?"

"Close your eyes, *bel*."

As she did so, he teleported them up into the clear night sky of Paris and landed atop a beautiful old building. Still holding her in his arms, he said, "Open your eyes."

She opened her eyes, her arms still around his neck and glanced at the tower.

"*Si*, you are not dreaming. You have an unobstructed view from the rooftops of Paris. And for me, all I ever wanted is within my arms. I want you to remember this night. Now, kiss your vampire as you should under the moonlit sky in Paris."

She held him tighter and closed her lips over his, tasting him, inhaling him, and felt his hands with their firm grip on her rear.

"Shade, I'll remember this night for all eternity."

He teleported them unnoticed back into the crowd and set her down as they walked around the plaza, taking the elevator to the top of the tower and looking out across this beautiful city, feeling the cold crisp night air, and the clear skies above them. He slipped his sports coat around her shoulders and pulled her closer to keep her warm. In time, they returned to the car, and climbed into the back seat.

Kate asked Dante to drive into Montmartre. They left the tower and crossed the river again, heading to the outskirts of downtown.

"This section of Paris can be rather shabby to some, but I love it! This is where the artists throughout history lived and worked, and they still do today. Renoir, Picasso, Van Gogh, Matisse, and so many others, they lived here and their art was inspired by their surroundings, not unlike how the artists were drawn to Florence during the Renaissance. During the day, there's always a huge artist colony here displaying their work. On the hill, that white cathedral, that is La Sacre Cour, or The Sacred Heart. Isn't it beautiful?"

"It is beautiful in the night lights, *bel*".

Kate asked Dante to let them out of the car, so they could walk down the steps in Montmartre. As they exited the car and he took her hand, she led him to the steps that ran beside the great cathedral.

"Come with me down the steps, aren't they beautiful? Down here, at the base of the steps is where the artists set up during the day, hundreds of them. You can find anything to your taste."

She held his hand as she tried to drag him down the steps of Montmartre. "Follow me, and have Dante follow us in the car. I'm going to take you to the underbelly of Paris now, down some dark alleys to the Moulin Rouge. Come on, we're going inside."

The music was blaring as they entered the infamous Moulin Rouge, and even today, it drew an eclectic crowd from the Paris underground. They were seated at a table near the stage of the famous cabaret performers. As the elaborately costumed dancers performed, the audience drank freely. She felt such exhilaration at the loud music and the energy of the crowd. She wished she had him all to herself like this all the time.

The celebration lasted long into the night, and Shade could feel the pull of the sun. "Come, *mi amore,* we must move. We have little time before sunrise."

He took her hand as they left the famous club and found Dante in the car on the narrow street outside. They slipped into the back seat and Kate leaned forward and whispered to Dante the instructions for their last stop. As he drove the car through the streets of Paris in the hours just before sunrise, he took them to the famous Pont des Arts, which had become known as 'The Lover's Bridge.' He stopped the car to allow them to exit.

"Look, Shade. The bridge is literally covered in padlocks. This is called The Lover's Bridge, and people come here from all over the world to place a lock on the bridge to ensure they will be bound together for all time."

She extended her hand and showed him a heart-shaped lock she had brought with her, and together, they walked to the bridge and placed their own lock among the thousands. As the lock clicked into place, they stood, and she tossed the key off the bridge and into the river Seine. She turned to him and he enfolded her in his arms for a kiss.

On cue, Dante went to the trunk of the car and released the red heart-shaped balloons into the early morning sky, which was turning pink on the horizon from the rising sun. They watched together as the balloons floated skyward and across the city of Paris.

She took his hand in hers and kissed the back of his hand. "I have one more thing, a ring for you, made of titanium, strong like my warrior, and unbreakable like our love."

As he looked down, she placed the ring on his finger. Her words took his breath away. He took her hand inside both of his and kissed it.

He didn't want this night to end, but he cringed a bit as he felt the heat from the rising sun burn his skin, warning him to take cover and his heart ached. He wanted to stay here forever with her, walk the streets in daylight, and never leave.

"Kate, I love you so much, this means so much to me, but I have no... Damn it, we need to go, the sun, *mi amore*."

Shade told Dante to drive back to the hotel, they were teleporting, and he'd run out of time. Cuddling her in his arms, he whispered softly, "It is okay. I am not hurt, but we have to go now."

As they teleported directly into their hotel suite, he sat her down on the bed as his hands slowly stroked her face before sliding through her hair.

"Thank you for this night. I love you so damn much."

70

Shade had her safely back in their hotel suite at the Ritz, the heavy black-out drapes pulled against the sun. He'd fight the pull of his death slumber to stay with her longer. "Are you hungry? Tell me what you need."

"I want you, lover. I want to make love to you. Put that 'Do Not Disturb' sign on the door, and climb into this bed with me, that's how I want this adventure to end."

He smiled wickedly as he walked toward her. He began to strip, sending his shoes and socks in one direction, and dropping his shirt to the floor in the darkened room

He knew this would be the last time he'd allow himself to feed from her during this pregnancy. His hands at his waistband, he hastily removed his jeans.

He moved to the foot of the bed and grabbed her ankles, pulling her to him. He removed the delicate shoes from her feet, tossing them carelessly aside.

Her rose scent surrounded him, making him ache to have her, to take her here and now. He crawled onto the bed beside her.

His hunger screamed and he could barely breathe. Helping her to sit upright, he removed her dress with shaking hands. She was the only female to ever make him quiver with desire. He flung her dress to the floor, his head nuzzled into her neck, licking her vein and feeling her pulse beating strong and fast. Pushing her slowly back down on the bed, he ran his hand the length of her legs, starting at her ankles. His hands were roughened from being a warrior, and her skin was soft as silk, smooth as satin, and white as snow. He looked at her face as she lay across the pillows, her crimson spread out in a fan beneath her. Her moans were barely a whisper and yet, so erotic in how they communicated her need.

He pulled a rose from the vase by the bed, and slid the petals over the lacey edge of her silken panties and watched as she arched her hips in need. Dragging the rose along her tummy, he made circles around where the baby grew inside her. He leaned down, kissing her there. He slid the red rose up to her breasts as they protruded over her bra, noticing her beautiful white skin in contrast to the deep red petals. Laying the rose between her breasts, he growled, "Mine!"

He knelt between her legs. His growl was primal. Her body lay open to him, like a rose opening its petals to the sun. He nuzzled his nose into her panties, licking across them, sucking the panties and the soft petals of her sex into his mouth, tasting her honey and it drove him out of his mind. He felt his fangs punch through as he slid them beneath the narrow band of her panties, and with a single bite, cut through the delicate silk. Tossing the panties aside, he slid his hands under her ass and squeezed tight, lifting her to his mouth and sliding his tongue along that sweet heaven to her clit and sucking hard, feeling her body scream with need and passion. He felt her hands grip his curls and pull at him, trying to pull him closer. Driving his tongue deep into her, he stroked her with his tongue as she rode his mouth, and he gripped her hips, pulling her tighter against his lips. "Cum, give me your honey, cum!"

She arched her back as her moan turned to a strangled whisper. She gasped for air and was reduced to a long-extended moan as the orgasm gradually faded.

He nipped softly at her inner thigh, and felt her body tremble with the sensation. In a single motion he turned her over on her tummy, giving her no rest.

His tongue glided along the curve of her back, starting at her hips and making his way up to her neck. He lifted her body upward until she was on all fours, just where he wanted her.

Sliding his cock along her sweet sex, he teased her with his hardened steel. Holding his erection in his hand, he circled around her sex, inserting the head of his dick and pulling back out again. He nuzzled into her crimson hair, nipping at her neck, her ears. Sliding one hand under her tummy to steady her, he leaned back and slapped her ass cheeks, creating that sweet sting, as the beast growled deep in his throat. He wanted to cum inside her. He wanted to take her blood.

The beast wanted control, but Shade was still mindful of her condition. Pushing her head down to the pillows, her ass high in the air, he used his knees to push her knees further apart. He massaged her back, as he slowly slid his hands from her shoulders, back to her hips, before he started to explore between her legs, teasing and coating his fingers in the sweet honey. With his free hand he gripped a handful of her hair, and lifted her head up as he laid his body over hers, and kissed her hard on the mouth. Kneeling upright behind her, he guided his cock home as he responded to her moans. He moved slowly, seductively, as he felt her passion build.

He felt her hand between her legs, stroking her sex, and teasing his cock, cupping his balls, as his body began to shake and he threw back his head and growled. Leaning over her, he sank his fangs deep into the soft flesh of her neck as he thrust even deeper and came like a volcano inside her, feeling the spasms around his prick being squeezed tight as he felt her cum again. His mouth drew hard, drinking deep and loving the taste of her, as she took him to another place.

Their bodies collapsed on the bed and his beast retreated, as Shade tried to catch his breath. He had released the beast with his beauty and the beast had been protective of her. He pulled her close, snuggling into her hair.

He kissed her, as they lay side by side. "Feed, *mi amore*, feed our *bambino*, you need to be strong. I want you strong for all of us." Stroking her hair softly, he felt her dull teeth bite into him.

She drew the blood into her mouth and felt the heat between her legs, despite all the things he'd already done to tempt and tease her body. She thrust her hips against him as she felt his cock harden. She reached down and grasped it in her hand, as she continued to drink. She listened to the moans, not sure which were hers and which were his, as she drank deep from him and slid her hand up and down the full length of his erection, feeling it throb in her hand. She savored the hot, salty, metallic taste of his blood and realized her craving was much stronger with each feeding. She grinded her hips against him, as she stroked him harder and felt him throw his head back as he came once again, spilling that hot, sticky sweet cum over her hand, and across her abdomen. She removed her lips from his neck, and licked at him gently, knowing her tongue didn't have the power to heal yet, but someday, lover, someday.

Nothing gave him more pleasure than to have her feeding from him. It was sexual and intimate and belonged to just the two of them. Her feeding was longer and deeper now, and he knew this was the baby taking his share. **"Grow strong my young warrior. You are so wanted and loved already."**

Kissing her softly, laying with her in his arms, he whispered hoarsely, "*Mi amore*...death slumber is taking, me. I have been awake so long, rest. We leave as night falls. I will hold you as I sleep."

He felt the unwanted slumber taking him, but he didn't want to go, he wanted to stay here with her, to never sleep again.

She caressed his face and ran her fingers through his hair. "Sleep, and I'll sleep beside you, as it should be. We have all eternity, my savage lover."

71

Waking, Shade moaned softly, his body feeling strong and energized. Looking down at *bel*, she was sleeping soundly on his chest and he made up his mind, then and there, they would teleport back to the States. Flying took too damn long. He hated to do this, leave this city without her knowledge, but there was nothing more important than getting her home safe and making sure she began her regimen of pills.

Their memories here would last a lifetime, and he knew this wouldn't be their last visit to Paris. He telepathically let Dante know they were heading straight out from the hotel room back home, and he needed Dante to arrange for their luggage to be loaded up and flown back. Dante informed him it was as good as done. Lifting her softly in his arms, not waking her, he cuddled her tight to his chest, wrapping a blanket from the bed around them to shield her from the cold. Kissing the top of her head he closed his eyes. **"Hang on little warrior, welcome to flight our way!"**

They landed softly inside their home. Gi greeted him and welcomed him back. Shade took the stairs, and carried her to their bedroom, laying her down gently, her body shifting slightly in her sleep. Crawling in bed beside her, he snuggled her close and waited for her to wake. She slept much more now, and he was happy he'd decided to teleport her home.

He let Luca know they'd arrived. **"Luca, we are home, but I am not leaving this bed until *bel* wakes. I do not want her to be startled when she fell asleep in Paris and wakes up in Virginia."**

"Good to have you home, master. Nothing to report here, I've got you and my lady covered. Rest easy."

Smiling, Shade snuggled his face into those fiery crimson locks and knew it would be a long road ahead for them both from this moment on.

Kate felt herself slowly surfacing from a deep sleep, with him lying next to her. She nuzzled in to him and felt him stir slightly. She smiled to herself as the memories of their Paris adventure came flooding back, and she stretched out in the bed, putting her hands above her head, and pointing her toes into a long, slow stretch as she heard him chuckle next to her.

She opened her eyes to see his beautiful blue eyes looking back at her, and she could see past him into their bedroom. She raised herself up on one elbow and looked around their bedroom, confused.

"Shade? A dream? Was Paris just a dream?"

"No, *mi amore*, no dream. But I did not want to put you through the flight, so I teleported us home while you slept, easiest way. How are you feeling?" He kissed her softly.

She leaned her head against his as her arm slid over his shoulder. "I feel like the most loved woman in the world. That trip was a lifetime of memories in one night."

She took his hand that now bore the titanium ring, and kissed the back of his roughened hand, kissing the ring that bonded them, turned his hand over in hers and kissed the palm of his hand.

"No matter what I do to show you my love, it never feels like enough. I need an eternity just to show you. And now, my favorite city has so many more reasons to be my favorite. Thank you." She kissed him gently on the lips.

"*Bel*, I think we should return to Paris often, *si*?" He kissed her nose. "I think you should rest, take a nice hot bath and climb back in bed. We need to get you started on those pills in the morning before the death slumber takes me. I want to be here to help you once darkness falls, they probably won't affect you right away. I need to get down to Luca, make some calls, check on some things, then I will be back to check on you. Rest."

"You pamper me too much. I don't need to sleep, but I'll take it easy. And I'll take you up on your offer to go to Paris again. There's so much more to see!"

She slid out of bed and got ready to head for the shower, when she heard her cell phone ringing in her purse. It reminded her she'd never taken it out to charge it, and she made a grab for it. It was Rissa.

"Hello. Hi Rissa. Yes, Paris. We just got back. Of course, that would be great. I can tell you all the details. Okay, see you later then, bye."

She looked over her shoulder at Shade, as she made her way to the bathroom. "That was Rissa, she called while we were gone, heard we were in Paris, she's going to stop by later."

A sarcastic thought flashed through his head. *Rissa? Oh, Great! Just what I wanted to hear.* "That's fine, girl time I suppose. Will you need me around? I can make myself disappear."

She laughed at him from the bathroom. "Yes, we wouldn't want to bore you with our girl talk. By all means, you can disappear."

"*Grazie*, you won't see me until her prancing ass leaves then."

"You should at least say hello. She helped us find a doctor. Now go, you and Luca go play with your toys, and I'll see you later."

She blew him a kiss from the bathroom door before climbing in the shower and letting the hot water wash over her, reliving the events of the last twenty-four hours. She washed her hair and used her rose scented bath gel before rinsing off and climbing out. Drying her hair, she put on some make-up and thought she still looked a little more pale than usual. She covered her damp skin in the rose scented body lotion before she slipped into jeans and a soft, off the shoulder cashmere sweater, and sprayed the rose scented perfume at her neck and wrists. There...just what he liked.

72

Rissa ended the call after talking to Kate. They were all set for tonight and Rissa's blood was rushing with anticipation. In a few days, that warrior would belong to Alec one hundred percent and the doormat would be out on her sorry ass, back in the mortal world where she belonged. With the cell still in her hand, Rissa dialed up Desire, sex goddess of the feeder world, and heard her answer within a few rings.

"Desire, this is Rissa. I'll be picking you up at the compound at 7:00 p.m., don't make me wait. I don't do waiting. My time is precious, and we have a long drive. Have yourself prepared as you were instructed."

Hanging up the phone, Rissa almost screamed with glee. Her plan was coming together, and Alec would be so pleased when everything returned to normal. Rushing to get ready, she bathed and fixed her hair and make-up, looking stunning as usual, feeling her energy rise in anticipation of watching the warrior fall.

She took one last look in the mirror and headed out to the study where she could feel Alec. She was damn sure he could feel her excitement and anticipation. Strolling past his study, she saw him sitting on the sofa with papers spread everywhere, laptop balanced on his thigh, as he was intensely working on something.

"Alec? I'm getting ready to leave for the evening."

He looked up from his work, taking her in as a wicked smile spread across his face, looking at her dressed in leather from head to toe. "And where are you off to, my darling?"

Strutting slowly over to the sofa, she smiled down at him. "Your devious darling is on her way to pick up the feeder and head to the warrior's stomping grounds, to drive out this mousy doormat of a mortal that is pestering you."

He laughed. "If it wouldn't risk spoiling this ploy, I'd consider going along, just to enjoy the show."

He slid his hand up her smooth leather clad leg. "Please, remember every detail, because I'll want a play by play report of Shade's response to this feeder. I told her she could have anything she desires if she could push him to the point of fucking her right there on the floor."

He threw his head back and laughed. "Oh, what I wouldn't do to see that, and watch the mortal's puritanical response to the two of them fucking like wild beasts right in front of her. Give your daddy a kiss before you go."

Straddling his lap, she leaned against his chest and whispered softly, "Will daddy be awake for his baby girl when she gets home?"

"Oh, you can count on me being awake. I wouldn't miss this for anything." He slid both hands across that leather clad ass before giving her a hard slap. "Now kiss me and be on your way, the sooner you leave, the sooner we'll be done with this mortal."

Growling, she kissed him hard on the lips, pulling his bottom lip into her mouth and then letting go, quickly kissing his neck. Standing up, she turned to walk away.

Her ass was poured into those leathers and she stopped without turning, flicked her hair back hard and threw up her hand.

"Tah, tah, my wicked vampire, I'm off to work."

She knew his eyes were glued to her as she exited the room. She heard him speak to her in her head. **"I see it, baby girl, and trust me, that ass is mine when you get back here tonight."**

As she walked away, he reached between his legs and stroked his cock which was already straining against the fabric of his jeans.

Strutting out of the room, she stopped and pulled the Glock from the drawer of the curio cabinet just inside the front door and stuck the gun in her purse. A vampire could never take chances dealing with other vampires, especially some lovesick warrior who thought he was in love with a weak mortal.

Sliding into the Bugatti, she could feel Alec, feel his pleasure and it riled her. Laying her head back on the leather seat, she moaned, her sex aching for release. **"Damn it Alec, you know exactly how to fire me up!"**

Sliding the Glock between her legs, the cold steel excited her and she slid it fast and hard against her sex. She could feel his body respond as he stroked himself, and she kept the same pace, sitting in the driveway, masturbating herself against the hard steel of the Glock, her body ready to release. She felt him cum, and she came as well. Growling loudly, it felt so good, took the edge off her nerves and he knew it. Throwing the Glock back into her purse, she fired up the engine and pulled out the driveway, squealing tires.

"Thank you, daddy."

"You're welcome, baby girl."

Pulling her black Bugatti into the gated community that held the feeder compound on the outskirts of D.C., Rissa's mood had already turned, and she was cursing under her breath. She had to pick up the feeder and take her to the warrior's estate in Virginia. She hated making that drive, and with a feeder no less. There was no way that bitch was sitting up front with her.

Rissa pulled up to the huge locked gates and lowered her driver's side window to see the guard at the gate. No one got into a feeder community that wasn't vamp. The guard looked her over, picking up her scent as Rissa spoke to him.

"Good evening. I have an appointment. Larissa Benneteau. I'm here to pick up Desire and then we'll be on our way. I'll have her back later this evening."

Smiling sweetly, Rissa flicked her hair. Normally, feeders weren't taken off the compound, but Alec had pulled some strings.

The guard responded, as he opened the gate, "Miss Benneteau, go right in, she's waiting. Enjoy your evening!"

"Oh, I plan to, I most assuredly plan to!"

As the gate opened, she drove up to the front door of the compound and sat there. She'd be damned if she was getting out of this warm car for some feeder. Rissa watched as Desire came out of the house and was looking like a piece of candy made for a starving vampire. As she reached for the passenger door and peered in, Rissa made it clear she was setting the rules.

Giving her a stern look, Rissa snapped at her, "Get in the back seat, and remember your instructions."

Desire was barely inside the car before Rissa was slamming the Bugatti into gear, and heading out onto the highway, hitting the fast lane, and catching a rare break in D.C. traffic as she drove south to Charlottesville. Rissa looked in the rearview mirror and sneered at the feeder. Desire looked back at her with some trepidation. Rissa was responding to the pheromones released by the feeder, and it only made her more agitated.

Reaching over, Rissa hit the satellite radio and the gas pedal at the same time and laid her head back on the seat, trying to ignore the feeder and the rising heat between her own legs on her long drive.

Rissa let the feeder know when they were about twenty minutes out from Shade's estate, so the feeder could masturbate herself to enhance her scent. Feeders were bred to naturally have pheromones that enticed and excited the male vampires, making the feeder irresistible to them, and designed to enhance both the feeding and sexual experience. A feeder that was in a sexually excited state only increased that effect. Desire nodded, slid down in the seat and lifted her skirt to do her dirty little deeds as Alec had requested of her.

Rissa's irritation was even greater as she felt her body's unbidden respond to the pheromones released by the feeder, and she had to fight the burning need between her legs. She fought to keep her fangs from punching through. If the feeder's scent impacted her this strongly, she could only imagine the ten-fold impact on a male. She squirmed in her seat, glad she'd taken the edge off with the Glock earlier. Still, her mouth salivated in response to the feeder's pheromones. Looking over her shoulder, she barked at her, "There are towels on the seat, don't even think you are going to fuck yourself in my car and leave your stench. Do as you're told, you're being paid a handsome sum for this job, and I expect you to deliver on everything you've been paid for, if not more."

73

Gi tapped at her bedroom door. "My lady, the luggage has arrived from Paris, may I bring it inside?"

"Of course, Gi, bring it in."

He carried in the luggage that had come back on the plane, and she asked him to place the luggage on the bed. She thanked him as he left and started opening and unpacking both Shade's and her bags, sorting through what to put away and what to toss for laundry. She heard the doorbell downstairs and hoped Gi had enough time to get there.

***

Working in the bunker with Luca, Shade needed a break, and besides, he wanted to check on *bel*.

"Come on Luca, let's go upstairs and grab some Midnight, we both could use a break!"

They headed up the winding stairs from the basement. Entering the corridor that led to the living room, he was going for the Midnight when the doorbell rang. **"*Bel*, Rissa is here, come on down!"**

Shade didn't see Gi downstairs, so he headed for the door and swung it open. He was hit with the power of a fucking freight train. *Feeder! Aroused feeder. Cazzo!* Before he could think, the feeder stepped around Rissa and was all over him. His mouth dropped and his fangs punched through. She was built like a brick shit house, made to ride hard. Her sex was smoking and instantly fired his cock, turning it to steel. She was climbing his body, her hands in his hair, and he couldn't fucking think. Her neck brushed against his lips, and his mouth salivated to feed.

He balled his hands into fists and held his arms tightly to his side. His eyes turned to bright red and her blood sang to him, as he tried backing away, but she clung to him. His body was instantly aching to take her where she stood. She was made for this, made to be taken and fucked for his pleasure, and he shook his head back and forth, growling and fighting the compulsion to respond to an impulse that was coded into his very DNA, the impulse that was designed to insure his very survival.

"My name is Desire, Master Shade, and I am here to accommodate you. Let me pleasure you, master."

Her lips were so fucking close to his, and her body was sliding against him. Every time he took a step back, she followed with her hands in his hair.

"No...No! Step the fuck back, now!"

Rissa fought her own body's response, as she gripped the doorjamb, closing her eyes tight, trying to block out the power of the feeder.

As Kate continued to unpack, she could hear Shade speak to her in her head, letting her know Rissa was here, and she started for the stairs. She felt a powerful wave of emotion from Shade wash over her. It almost staggered her with its power. Her first reaction was fear, that there was danger, and then she felt his arousal, his overwhelming sexual desire, and...a struggle? *What the fuck?* She hurried down the remaining steps and into the living room to see Rissa standing in the doorway, gripping the door frame, as if some invincible force was trying to pull her into the room. Luca was approaching with a look of shock on his face. She looked at Shade, and there was a woman in his arms. No, not in his arms, she clung to him, climbing him and yet, Shade's arms remained rigid at his side. The woman's eyes glowed red as did his, and his fangs were elongated as his head was thrown back, and the saliva dripped from his fangs. The woman moved her body against him, undulating her hips, teasing, seducing, luring. Kate watched in horror as Shade was clearly aroused by her, and yet, struggling to resist.

Rissa smirked as she slowly opened her eyes to see the show taking place in front of her, and Kate standing in shock.

"Oh Kate, there you are! I brought along a feeder for Shade. Her name is Desire. Isn't she perfect? I thought, perhaps, you'd need her. I know it will be such a struggle not letting him feed from you while you're pregnant. But please don't worry. I've heard she's the best. She comes highly recommended. I can assure you Shade will want for nothing and will be well fed and pleasured during your pregnancy. I have her things in the car, she can move in tonight."

Smiling sweetly at Kate, she continued to maintain her grip on the doorframe, keeping her distance from the feeder. Rissa was putting on the act of her life when she heard a thud and looked over to see Luca on his knees beside Shade, as he too fought his body's response to the feeder. *Oh my, two for one. How lucky is this girl tonight?*

"Oh dear...well, that was unexpected."

Shade's body was trembling, trying to get control, and his beast was on the surface, riled up and wanting to take this feeder. The beast was pushing him beyond his limits of control. **"Fuck, Luca!"** Shade was aware of Luca dropping to the floor beside him when he stepped in to help, only to succumb to power of the feeder. **"Luca, fight! Fuck, help me!"**

Luca heard Shade's plea for help, but the scent of the feeder's sex overcame him, and he was helpless to respond. A feeder's scent was designed to excite the male beast, to make the feeder irresistible, but he'd experienced nothing like this before. She was on top of master before he could even focus. His fangs punched and his eyes turned, and the growl instantly rolled out of him. Luca couldn't move and all he wanted was to mount her, and gorge himself on her blood.

Shade continued his struggle, every muscle tensed. His breathing was ragged, and his body trembled with want. He'd never had to resist the pull of a feeder before, and this one arrived ready to service him. His body fought the beast, but the beast was winning this battle, when he screamed out for her, *"Bel!"*

Kate looked at Rissa, trying to process Rissa's words. *She brought this bitch into my house? She brought him a feeder?*

Kate looked back at the redheaded feeder. She was like an enhanced version of her. More hair, more tits, more ass, and she was glued to Shade as Kate watched him stepping backward to escape her. The feeder matched him step for step, her breasts pressed against his chest, her hips pressed to his and she could hear Shade's words in her head, and his plea to Luca, as she watched Luca drop to his knees. *What the fuck is going on? Luca is under her spell as well?*

Her heart was pounding as her blood began to boil. *How dare she? How dare this bitch?* Kate launched herself at the feeder and grabbed a handful of those curled red locks and yanked at her with all her strength, screaming at her, "Get off him, you fucking bitch!"

The feeder was momentarily pulled back, as she turned her head to Kate and bared her fangs and delivered a long hiss. The feeder broke away from Kate and clung to Shade even tighter, climbing his body, wrapping her legs around him as she used her tongue to lick at his neck, his lips. Kate grabbed her by the hair again and pulled with all her strength and reached around her to try to pull her away, clawing at her face, pummeling her hard.

The feeder hissed and growled at her, snapping at her with her teeth, but was refusing to release her grip on Shade. Kate was no match for the feeder's physical strength, but she refused to let her have him. Kate reached behind Shade to the blade he kept sheathed in his waistband and removed the knife. This was not a fight she intended to lose. She swung the blade across the feeder's face, leaving a diagonal gash, and the blood started to pour. The feeder released her grip on Shade as she threw her hands over her face. Kate grabbed her hair again and yanked with all her strength as the feeder let go of the tight grip of her legs around his hips and dropped back to the floor. Kate raised the knife once again, prepared to cut her throat, remove her head if she needed to.

Shade shouted, "*Bel*, no!"

His beast responded, moving faster than the mortal eye could see, and grabbed Kate into his arms, the blade still in her hand held high in the air. She was kicking and screaming in his arms like a wild cat.

"Kate, Stop!"

He kept one hand tight around Kate's waist as he held her back against his chest. He reached up and grabbed her hand that held the knife.

"Kate, stop fighting! I am okay. The spell is broken. I am free of her. Luca, get up!"

He heard a growl from Rissa, and although he wanted nothing more than her head mounted on a wall, he warned off Luca as he rose into a crouch, ready to attack her. Alec would seek the ultimate revenge if they harmed her.

"No, Luca, she belongs to Alec, listen to your master. Stay on guard!"

Shade heard the clanging of metal on the floor and knew the knife was down and felt Kate turn toward his chest, and he knew she was okay. He snuggled into her neck, never taking his eyes off the scene before him.

"Shh *mi amore*, I have you, nothing is going to hurt you."

He turned toward Rissa, and his growl was loud and vibrated through Kate. "Get...the...fuck...out...of...my...house! Take that bitch with you."

His voice was low and lethal, and Rissa retracted her fangs. Luca moved closer, ready to escort them both out. Rissa stood glaring at him, but she knew she was out of her league against two warriors.

Shade had no idea what the fucking hell she'd been thinking bringing that bitch into his house. He watched as she started to speak, and Luca growled low.

"Hold, Luca. Say your piece Rissa, make it quick and get the hell out of my house!"

Rissa was stunned as things unraveled so quickly and could only watch as all her well laid plans fell apart before her eyes.

Desire lay on the floor bleeding, holding her face like some whimpering child and Rissa wanted to kick her. *Useless bitch! I will take care of you later,* thoughts were rolling through her head, why weren't either of these fucking warriors jumping to lap her blood, and suck her dry? Something was not adding up here. Even Rissa's blood was singing sweetly to taste her.

"I'm sorry. I was trying to be a good friend to Kate by providing you with the best feeder I could find. I thought it would ease her mind to know you were well cared for. I wanted to help you both, make this easier for you. I came to help, not to harm. Let us leave you in peace."

Rissa looked directly at Kate and cried her false tears, as if she'd waste a second of hell caring about her. "Kate, I'm so, so sorry, please understand." Shaking her head as the tears streamed down her face. "I only wanted to make your pregnancy easier for you. Remove any worries."

Rissa reached down and took Desire's hand and helped her to stand upright. Desire continued to hold one hand over her face. Luca held the door open wide as Shade stared back at her hard, and Rissa guided Desire from the house. Luca followed her to the car. Rissa acted as though she was upset about this whole incident with Desire. She put the feeder in the back seat and picked up the towels and rammed them into her hands and as she leaned down close to her ear so only she could hear her. "Shut the fuck up with the tears and don't get blood on my seat, you stupid bitch."

Closing the car door, she climbed in, revved up the Bugatti and rolled out. *Oh, you will pay for this...all of you!*

Driving back in the direction of D.C. to dump the bitch back at the feeder compound, it was a long silent ride as Rissa was fuming and her blood ran cold with dread. Alec was not going to be pleased with her failure and she took small comfort in knowing the pills would do away with the unwanted half-breed. Driving like a bat out of hell down the highway, she heard the feeder sniveling in the backseat and it disgusted her. "Shut the fuck up! You'll heal. There won't be any scars. You're pathetic, you've failed at your assignment, and master won't be pleased. You're a feeder! How hard could it be to fuck a vampire, especially one who hasn't fed?"

Rissa laughed when she heard the feeder sobbing. Getting close to the compound, Rissa barked her commands at the feeder, "Slide behind me in the seat. Keep that damn towel to your face. The tinted windows will hide your face when the guard lets us back in. Do it now!"

Watching in the rearview mirror, she could see Desire slide over and compose herself. Rissa pulled up to the gate and rolled down her window, smiling at the guard. He recognized her from the earlier pickup, opened the gate, waved, and smiled. Pulling up in front of the compound that housed the coven of feeders, Rissa turned to her. "Get the hell out! Speak of this to no one. Go!"

As Desire climbed from the car, she ran into the house, eager to get away from Rissa. Driving back to the gate, Rissa stopped at the security shack and once again, put her window down. Reaching into her purse, she pulled out the thick, crisp stack of one-hundred-dollar bills, held together by a band and waved them at the guard. As he smiled and reached his dirty hand out.

"Take care of it. I don't want to ever see her again."

The guard grinned an evil grin. He'd been given permission from a master's mate to be true to his nature, and to get paid for it. "It will be my pleasure, Miss Benneteau."

Slamming the gas pedal down, she headed for home, knowing, at least, the fucking bitch would never touch her vampire again.

74

Standing in the foyer, blood on the floor, Shade's head was spinning, as he held *bel* in his arms. He felt her body begin to shake as the release of adrenaline hit her. Cuddling her into his chest, he stood there rocking her.

Luca walked in, shaking his head. "They're gone, master. Rissa drove off with her."

"Luca, thank you. I am sorry you had to fight through that hell as well. I am taking her upstairs, and I want you to watch this damn house like a hawk, anything moves, you call me!"

Luca shook his head in acknowledgement, as Shade turned and took the steps two at a time with Kate in his arms. He took her into their bathroom, turned on the taps and ran a hot bath. Stripping them both down, he slid them deep into the hot, steaming water to soak her muscles. He pulled her into his chest, her back relaxing against him.

"*Cazzo,* what the hell just happened? You are a hell cat!"

Kate was letting the hot water sooth her. "I protect what is mine, lover."

"*Si*, you most certainly do. Please do not be angry with me, I fought her as best I could. And tonight, my *bel rosso* saved her savage lover. Damn, never saw that coming."

"I'm not angry with you. I could see your struggle. I didn't understand the power the feeders have to seduce. But it's not a mistake I'll make twice."

"I never asked for her, Kate. What in the living hell was Rissa thinking? I told that damn doctor I had it taken care of. Did she tell you when she called she was bringing a feeder into this house?"

"No, she never mentioned a feeder. Do you think I'd have agreed? You know how I feel about you having a feeder. I had no idea. I felt your turmoil as I came down the stairs."

"She was no ordinary feeder. She was pure heroin to a vampire. She was irresistible to the beast. I never want to feel that again. *Cazzo* ."

Kate rested her head back against his chest. "I watched as even Luca collapsed to his knees. It took me a second to figure out what was going on. When I came down the stairs and I saw her clinging to you. We won't see another feeder near this house. Like I said, I'll protect what is mine."

He began to softly shampoo her hair, massaging her scalp. "Damn, you were something. I was lucky I had just fed from you, and that gave me strength to resist. The next time I feed from Luca, I want no complaints about the sounds. You now have a first-hand experience of the alternative."

She leaned back as his hands worked their magic in her hair, massaging her neck and shoulders.

"Lover, I hope that didn't sound like a complaint. I do understand your need to feed, and you know how much I hated the idea of you feeding from another woman. I have such gratitude for Luca, and for you. I know you could brush away my concerns and feed as you want. It's part of your culture, and I'd just have to bear it. So, you'll hear no complaints from me."

"That's my *bel rosso*! We both have our own battles to fight for the birth of our son."

Gi communicated to him telepathically that he was attending to the mess in the foyer, and all were concerned for the welfare of my lady, inquiring as to whether she'd like a meal or something. They were all awaiting her command. Chuckling, it amused Shade and also made him proud that she had the staff wrapped around her little finger already.

"*Mi amore*, Gi would like you to know they are very concerned for you, and they wish to be at your beck and call. Is there some something you wish from the kitchen at this time?"

"I'm starving! Again. Please just have Reynaldo fix me something, he knows what I like. And tell them all thank you. They're all dear to me."

"Gi, my lady would like a meal, Reynaldo will know what to fix and damn man, bring me a bottle of Midnight, I fucking need it this night!"

Gi responded, **"*Si*, master. We are most pleased to find both you and her ladyship well."**

"Now, my little crimson headed minx, let's get you out of this tub, and into something comfortable and back in the damn bed."

75

Alec was sitting in the study, reading through several bills that were up for vote this coming week. He was passing time until Rissa returned with news of Shade and the feeder when he felt her anger roll through him. He stopped reading and honed his senses, waiting to see if she reached out to him for help, but she wasn't beckoning him. There was no fear, he didn't feel any sense of danger from her, but her anger and turmoil were clear. Anger at whom or what wasn't clear. It might not even be related to the feeder. He was thinking to himself, how could that plan go wrong? There was no way Shade was able to resist that feeder, no fucking way. He'd had instructions from the doctor not to feed once his precious mortal took those pills, and Alec felt certain he'd been holding back for some time. His ability to resist the feeder would be zero. Hell, even if he'd just fed yesterday, the Shade he knew wouldn't resist her. But for now, he'd have to wait until Rissa arrived to see what had her so fired up.

Pulling into the drive of their Georgetown home, Rissa turned off the engine and saw a few lights on inside the house. Alec was waiting. Taking a deep breath, she got out of the car, grabbed her bag, and walked inside. The house was so still. Leaning against the wall, she stood there a minute and breathed, trying to get her thoughts together. He was going to drill her like Chinese water torture for every damn detail, and she'd tell him blow by blow. *The mortal is still there, going strong, and the feeder didn't work. He'll blow up, and you Rissa, you will be denied, once again, of his touch and his attention.*

Looking down, Rissa stared at the floor. Well, at least the pills would take care of the half-breed, and with some careful planning, the mortal may go down as well. Quietly, she made her way to the bar and poured a crystal tumbler full of Midnight and downed it in one shot. She slammed the glass on the counter. It was time to face her vampire.

He'd heard her enter and could feel her hesitancy to face him. This could only mean bad news. He braced himself for whatever it was she was about to share. He called out to her, "Rissa?"

She walked in to face him. "Alec..."

He could read the look in her eyes. “Okay, well, let's hear it. Clearly, it didn't go as planned. The feeder? Did she perform as directed?”

“She performed to the letter, Alec, perfectly. And Shade responded as well, all was going as planned. Shade fought a good battle, she was all over him and he wanted her. She did exactly what we asked her to do. She almost had him on the floor, fucking and feeding, until...” walking to the table, she lit a smoke and inhaled deeply.

Alec answered her in an irritated tone. This wasn’t the time for a smoke break. “Until, Rissa? What happened that destroyed our plan?”

Looking annoyed, she spoke through gritted teeth, “Don’t raise your voice to me, Alec.”

He lowered his head as he locked eyes with her, and a low growl built deep in his chest as his eyes turned a deep shade of red. “Don't fuck with me, Rissa. I'm running short of patience here. I asked a simple fucking question, I think I deserve an answer, don't you? Now, what the fuck happened?”

She could feel his beast and knew she better give him what he wanted.

“Kate walked in, and the fun began. Desire was climbing all over Shade. Kate went lunatic. She didn’t think twice. She attacked the feeder, pulled a knife from Shade and slashed her across the face. Kate was ready to take the feeder’s head off, but Shade's beast took Kate in hand, got her under control.”

Alec roared, “The mortal? The mortal foiled our plan? Are you fucking kidding me?”

He threw his glass across the room, watching it smash into a million pieces as it hit the fireplace and the Midnight ran down the wall. He paced back and forth, hands fisted. He kicked the table in front of him as it splintered into pieces.

“The mortal, Rissa?”

He ran both hands through his hair. *How could I have misjudged? Shade resisting pussy? When did that ever happen? And the fucking mortal? That sniveling, weak, clinging mortal?* “Well, this is just fucking great! If Shade was enamored with her before, I can only imagine what he’ll feel now that she’s come to his fucking rescue. What a fucking nightmare!”

"Alec, please listen. We still have the pills. It will take care of the main problem, the half-breed."

Rissa tried hard to redirect his attention to the rest of the plan, reminding him of their ultimate goal. Grabbing the opened bottle of Midnight, she filled two glasses and walked to him.

"It's not over, Alec. This can still work. We'll just redirect our focus on the pills. You know she'll lose the baby, at the very least, and the stress that puts on their relationship, you never know; it could still pull them apart."

Offering him the drink, she wondered if he'd heard a word she said.

Alec could hear her talking, but only a few of her words got through. *The pills, yes, we still have the pills. At least Shade won't be distracted by the idea of "fatherhood" much longer. What the fuck is he thinking? How did this fucking plan fail?*

"We're not done here, Rissa, not by a long shot. I can't have my best warrior distracted. You make sure she takes those fucking pills. Even if it means you have to shove them down her throat yourself. In the meantime, I'll think about what I want to do next. I underestimated this mortal once. I won't let it happen again."

Rissa sighed with relief. At least she was able to keep his anger directed away from her, and his mind was already planning the next move. "Yes, Alec, of course I will. I'll stay on top of it. I'll leave you now. I know you have much to occupying your mind." Turning, she headed for the door.

He looked up as she left the room. "Rissa, we'll come out on top, my darling, we'll always come out on top."

Without turning around, she smiled to herself. "I have no doubt about that, none whatsoever."

Walking out the door, she pulled it closed behind her and went upstairs to her dressing room. She needed a hot bath. She could still smell the stench of that bitch, Desire.

76

Kate was trying to get back into their routine, knowing this baby growing inside her would change everything soon, and wanting to put the whole feeder incident behind them. Shade had asked her not to start the pills right away after the feeder incident. He felt the stress of it might be too much, so she had waited another day. It was a few hours before sunrise when Shade teleported in from the Dead House, wearing his leathers.

"*Mi amore*?"

Kate was stretched across the bed, watching him. "Yes, lover?"

"How are you? How are you feeling?"

"I'm good." She smiled up at him. "And you?"

That slow smile spread across his face as he looked down at her, running his hand through his hair.

She laughed softly. "You push every button, and you know that, don't you?"

He answered innocently, "Me?"

"Yes, you. You're killing me here."

He pulled his black t-shirt over his head and tossed it aside, stretched his arms above his head and leaned his head back, stretching out his back, before he walked across the room towards her. "You don't look dead, *mi amore*."

He propped his foot in a chair, bent over as he unlaced his boots and turned his head to look at her through his black curls.

Kate put the pillow over her face. "Killing me softly, lover..."

He took the pillow from her and tossed it aside, then walked barefoot to his dresser, pulled the gun from his waistband, and removed the clip, before laying it down on the dresser.

"I am warrior, my walking sin. I know how to kill hard and soft as well."

She watched as he stripped from the soft leather pants, and stood naked before her, leaving her speechless.

He walked toward the bed, never taking his eyes off her, his curls tousled and hanging low over his face. "*Bel*, you are one hot mess."

Kate giggled. "Oh, you have no idea."

He crawled from the foot of the bed, straddling her on all fours. He leaned down, nudging into her neck, and whispered in a low, deep voice. "*Ti amo*."

"And I love you. Do you have any idea what you do to me? "

Smiling down into her eyes, his hands sliding into her hair, he took a fist-full of that red crimson and moaned. "You have any idea what you do to me, *mio bel rosso*?"

She bit her lip as she looked up at him. "Kill you softly?"

He rolled over on his back, moaning and clutching his chest. "Already dead and gone, so fucking gone!"

She rolled on top of him, kissing his sweet mouth. "Not too gone. I need you here with me."

He slid his hands over her ass, cupping her softly and closed his eyes as her hair cascaded over his face, the scent of roses making his cock throb.

"Never leaving you. Have you started the pills yet? I think it is time. That's an order, minx." He slapped her ass softly and grinned.

She wiggled her ass after receiving the light slap, which allowed her to rub against his bulging erection. "I haven't yet, but I'll start tonight. First thing, or maybe the second thing?"

He growled, nipping her chin, sliding his tongue down her neck, and over her shoulder. "Mmm, yeah, later."

His hand moved slowly up her body and into her hair, cupping her head as his hips rose up to tease. Pulling her into his neck, he turned his head slightly, inviting her to feed.

She nuzzled into his neck and inhaled his scent. It never failed to excite, and she licked his neck along the pulsing vein and listened to the low moan escape his throat. It was a sound that resonated deep inside of her, drew her to him. She bit hard into him and felt his body respond immediately. As she drew the first mouthful of blood into her mouth, her own body responded, starting with that deep-seated heat that burned between her legs.

Her feeding from him brought forth so many emotions. She was his to feed and protect, his *bel rosso*. He closed his eyes, lost in the sensations of her feeding. He ran his hand down her back, letting his fingers brush softly across her smooth skin, sliding them under her silken panties. His fingers played in the honey that flowed from her, gently rubbing and teasing her, he felt her body respond. Her moans vibrated against his neck as he slid his fingers inside her, probing that velvety sweetness that belonged to him.

As her body succumbed to the involuntary response of feeding, she drew more blood from him, trying to quench a hunger that now felt bottomless. She swallowed mouthful after mouthful, and felt his fingers probing as she moved her hips against him. They found their own rhythm as she rocked against his fingers.

She felt his cock replace his fingers and her body shivered. She wanted all of him, his blood, and his dick. Her hips rocked against him, riding the full length of his erection, first slowly, taunting in the deliberate slowness. Her own need for him drove her to increase the pace, to ride him harder, his hands gripping at her hips. She could feel his shaft throbbing inside her, as she pushed them both to the abyss. She wanted to feel him cum inside her, fill her.

He roared loudly as he came with her, and his fangs punched through, dripping and aching. His eyes opened and bathed the room in bright red light, as he laid still and heard her moaning as she lay on top of him. He licked her lips, kissing her deeply, tasting his own blood inside her mouth.

Kate could feel she had all of him, and it satisfied her soul. She was woman to his man, and she felt their connection, their bond, more than body, more than heart, even more than blood. They were one. She was still breathing hard, her heart pounding, and his blood coursing through her veins. She felt his strength in her for the first time. She licked his fangs, slowly, deliberately, one at a time, to bring him the ultimate pleasure.

His body jerked with intense pleasure as he felt her tongue on his fangs. His head was thrown back onto the pillows and his eyes closed. His cock rose like a sword, hard and straight, and he moaned with passion as his body shook once, then twice as she licked his fangs again, sucking the sharp tips into her mouth, making him come again as she lay on top of him. He grabbed her by the hair and burrowed into her neck, laying his head against her shoulder, his breathing raspy, his body released of everything.

Kate rolled off of him, a smile on her face, knowing she'd left her vampire drained, in the non-traditional sense. Her head on his shoulder, her arm across his chest, and her leg thrown over his, she purred into his ear. "Was it good for you, lover?"

Shade only grunted in response.

"More? Do you need more?"

He moaned louder, as if in pain.

"Is that a yes? Because I can give you more." She reached for his cock and cupped it in her hand.

"Fuck!" He moaned loudly as he writhed on the bed and his fucking beast took over.

Kate teased him. "I'd never want this weak mortal girl to leave you wanting. I understand your appetite, your need. It must be so much greater than my own."

She crawled back on top of him, sliding down his body, licking and nipping at his chest, his hips, letting her tongue glide across his abdomen as she slid her hands under his hips.

He felt her hair across his cock and his hands gripped the bedding, his body trembled.

She sat upright and straddled him, both of her hands on his hips as she slid her hands slowly up his hard, muscled chest. As she reached his shoulders, she pushed his arms upwards, above his head and held them there, gripping his wrist. Her breasts were an inch from his face as she gave him instructions.

"Grab the headboard, lover, and don't let go."

He gripped the headboard with both hands, and she pulled the belt from his leathers and bound his wrists. He started to protest, but she lowered her mouth to his and kissed him deeply, and whispered the word, "Trust," into his mouth. She took her silky gown that lay on the bed and tied it around his eyes and leaned into him again and whispered into his ear, "Trust." She laid her body against him and slid down the length of him, knowing he couldn't return her touch and he couldn't see her next move. He must focus only on the sensations she created.

She straddled him once more and took an ice cube from one of the food trays Gi was constantly delivering to their bedroom, and touched the ice cube to his throat, slowly drawing it down his chest, his abdomen, and listened to him take a sharp intake of air. She held the ice cube above his belly and allowed for the slow drip of the cold water. She watched the drops of water hit his skin and run down his side.

Her lips were all over him. Her plea for trust did little to soothe Shade, but he tried to relax. He was the dominant one, and it was unsettling to play the submissive. Memories of his past kept trying to break through and he pushed them back down. Once blindfolded, his whole body went into warrior mode. His senses heightened beyond normal, his hearing crystal clear. He heard the clinking of ice against the glass then felt the cold against his throat and he pulled hard on the strap, but not hard enough to break it.

The cold made a path across his abdomen. The sensations rocked him deep, and the memories began to roll in. He tried to shut them down, but images like photographs captured in time flashed through his head. The chamber, he saw the chamber, the rack, the whip, every nature of sexual pleasure and pain, the cult, the cult. He felt the water, heard it coming. It bounced slightly on his hardened abs and ran down his side, and he roared out of control. He wasn't the tormented, but the tormentor. He wouldn't be caged. He wouldn't be controlled. He inflicted pain. He didn't receive it, except for the pain and fear of what he felt through his victims. The memory gates were opened wide, and he was flooded with the images of Sabine and the sex cult.

Kate was shocked by his roar. It wasn't a roar of pleasure. She dropped the ice cube to the floor and folded her body over his. She licked at the rivulets of water that she had dripped on his body. She slid her hands up his chest and followed with her body until her lips were on his lips, she kissed him gently. "Shh, lover. Tell me to stop and I'll stop. Tell me to release you and I'll release you. I only bring you pleasure."

She felt him settle as she slid her body back down the length of him, teasing him with her tongue as she went. She ran her hands along his inner thighs, teasing with her nails, gently scratching the surface of his skin.

Kate's words failed to calm him, and he tried to get back to her, reminding himself where he was in time and space. *Not the chamber, not the chamber.* He struggled, pulling on the restraints when his beast emerged, enraged. He yanked the belt free of the headboard. His fangs punched through as he ripped through the belt with his teeth, releasing his hands and tearing the blindfold from his eyes. He glared at her, his beast wanting to attack. He was breathing hard and ragged, fighting to get control, gasping for air.

He swung his feet to the floor as she fell off of him, and he stood and paced. He knew he was scaring the fuck out of her. "Don't ever do that again! I can't, I..." Growling loud. "Fuck!"

Anger consumed him for doing this to her, ruining a night of passion, and his hand swiped across the dresser and knocked everything to the floor, as he teleported out instantly, angry with himself and the memories that consumed him.

Kate sat on the bed and stared after him, confused, hurt, abandoned, and afraid. His anger had never been directed at her before. She sobbed for him. Tears rained down her face and she realized he was gone. Was it something she did, or something she triggered? She shut down, retreating into herself. She curled in a ball in the middle of the bed, head to her knees, and face hidden, no longer sobbing, just dead quiet. She laid there for minutes…or was it hours… She had no concept of time as she waited for his return.

She climbed out of bed, loosely pulling on her robe, and left the bedroom, as she headed down the stairs and outdoors into the frigid night air, hoping to find him. She looked to see if she could find that glow from his cigarette. Luca appeared behind her, took her by the shoulders, turned her around and walked her back toward the house. The night air was cold and the thin silk robe did little to protect her, as he removed his shirt and put it over her shoulders. He was preparing to lead her upstairs when they heard his voice.

Shade stood naked in the doorway. "She is mine, Luca, give her to me."

"Yes, master, I only brought her in from outside."

Shade took her in his arms. "Leave us."

"Yes, master, if you need me–"

Shade interrupted him, his voice deadly, "Leave us!"

Luca backed away without speaking, bowing his head to his master.

Shade picked her up and carried her upstairs to their bedroom and sat with her in his lap in the chair at the window, cradling her to his chest.

"I can't...talk about this. Not right now, *bel*. This is not about you. It has nothing to do with you. This is about me. You can listen to me or not, but give me a sign you hear me. It's all I am asking for."

Kate opened her eyes and looked at him, but she didn't speak.

His eyes absorbed her pain. Taking her hand, he held it over his heart. "I will sit here until the sun rises, holding you. You can't hurt me any more than I have hurt myself."

She spoke to him in her head. **"Do I tell you what's in my heart? Because I never feared you before, and I never feared the beast.**

When you warned me, I pushed ahead, I was drawn to your darkness. You know that. But tonight, I felt fear."

Pain screamed through him and he laid his head back and gritted his teeth from the hell ripping through him at her words. **"Your actions brought memories, *bel*. A past I thought I had buried but cannot seem to get out of my head. My past haunts me. You are where my comfort lies, *mi amore*. You are where my barriers fall. You are my strength and my weakness rolled into one. I have never travelled here before."**

She reached her hand to his cheek. **"I feel your pain as I feel my own, and we're both tortured and tormented. You by a past that is hidden from me, and me from feeling your rejection during our most intimate time together. Ripping free of that belt, tossing me aside to escape our bed, destroying things in the room, it was anger that felt directed toward me, and I hear your words. I know something I did evoked a memory. And now I feel paralyzed. What else? What else will evoke a memory? Must I walk on eggshells? I don't know your past and you share little. How do I avoid the landmines when I don't know where they're buried? How do I know when I've crossed the line, when I can't see the line? You underestimate my love for you. Let me heal you, open yourself to me, and let me heal you."**

***"Mi amore*, I don't know what will evoke it. I don't know how to tell you to avoid these things, I do not know myself. I have never loved this deeply. I cannot see this line either, can you please try to believe me and understand this? And I do not underestimate your love. Walk into my heart please, *bel*, I can't take what I have done to you. Look at me, and tell me I am still loved. I left because I, too, feared myself. I did not know if I could control the beast. I saw your fear and felt it and it mixed with my own. It was sudden and unexpected, I was stunned and needed control and there was none inside me. If I talk of these things, of my past, will they leave me? Will they never return? I do not know the answers to this."**

She looked at his pain-filled eyes and spoke to him out loud as she slowly stroked his face. "Then know this, I'll never leave you. I'll never stop loving you. To have you leave me, even for this brief time, I feel gutted. It's a pain I cannot bear. You are mine, body, and soul, for all eternity. And whatever torment you carry, I'll also carry. There is no life without you."

She pulled his face to hers, and locked eyes with him. "Do you hear me, lover? There is no life without you."

Her words ran singing through his blood and he let go and felt her healing the hellish caverns he had inside. He'd fallen into the deepest holes of hell and fought to climb out, her love filled them, and made him whole. Her touch brought light into the darkest places. He kissed her like his life depended on it. It had always been about her, every breath and move he made was for her and he felt renewed in her love.

"I will never love another. You are mine, and I take responsibility for what I have done to you. I am sorry. I left so as not to hurt you. My word is my honor. I will always come back. I will always love you. Nothing can take you from me."

"I never doubted you'd return, Shade. Our bond is too strong to be broken. But I feel such pain when the bond is stretched, and I feel I've lost you for even that break in time. Now carry me to our bed please and lay with me."

"Put a leash on me, *mi amore*, because sometimes...I lose myself."

Standing up, he felt her curl into his arms, her head on his chest, and a soft sob escaped him. He was still her warrior, her savage lover, her vampire. Kissing the top of her head, he slowly walked over to their bed as he left behind the pain with each step.

77

He was aware that it was a long time before his *bel* slept, her mind still troubled by the trauma of his memories, and his sudden exit from their bed. It wasn't her fault, her actions dredged up memories of events he thought he'd buried, events where he was the tormenter, and not the tormented. Memories he was afraid to share with her, even now. But those experiences, part of a torrid tortured past, molded him. They showed him more about who he wasn't than who he was, but they held him in their grip, like a sick addiction for far too many years. The sex cult, the women, the chamber at Castello. It was a time when the beast ruled the man, at Sabine's urging, and the man followed willingly. A time when he succumbed to the deepest, darkest part of who he could be if he gave up his humanity. Sabine fed that in him, and it took every fiber of his being to break away from the twisted, deviant lifestyle that had nothing to do with love. It was a part of his past he hoped to hide from her.

His *bel* was all goodness and light. Her love was pure, and unconditional. Her love was healing. And despite their passion together, there was innocence in her he hoped she never lost. He tamped those memories down again, in the deepest recesses of his mind, and hoped the day would never come that he had to explain them to her. He was aware of just how much he hid from her about the true nature of his world.

His hunger was raging, and he looked down at her soft heartbeat as it pulsed in her neck and his body screamed for her. He couldn't feed from her now. Luca was his only solution throughout this pregnancy. Sighing, he knew these past few nights had brought to her eyes a whole different view of vampire life. That incident between Rissa and the damn feeder, her over-hearing his feeding from Luca, and then his sudden departure from their bed, as his beast took control and those memories haunted him. His beast would never rule him like that again. He no longer feared the beast would take her the way others were taken, but he still had to remain on guard. He was grateful she stayed with him, loved him through it all.

He'd go to Luca, so he could survive and protect what was his. Shade climbed quietly from the bed, grabbed some jeans, sliding them over his hips, not bothering to button them, and headed to Luca's quarters.As he approached Luca's suite, the door was slightly ajar, enough for him to see inside. He could hear Luca moving around, so Shade stepped into the doorway and peered in. Luca stood with his back to the door, shirtless and in jeans, before a large canvas. Shade quietly watched him paint, holding the palette of colors in one hand, and his other hand moving the brush deftly across the canvas.

Luca became aware of his presence and spun quickly to see Shade at his door.

"I need you. I am losing strength. *Bel* feeds deep and heavily now, with the *bambino* growing inside her."

"Consume what you need, master, it is yours for the taking."

Luca set aside the palette and the brush, wiping his hands on his jeans and exposed his neck to him fully, but Shade took his wrist instead and locked eyes with him.

"Not this time, Luca, I cannot feed from you in the traditional way tonight, just your wrist for now, I cannot offer you...release. She has been through too much and I cannot risk hurting her more. I will starve before I do that. She needs some time."

Luca offered up his wrist. "It's fine, master, I have someone I can go to for release. I don't wish to make this more difficult for you or my lady."

Before the words were out of his mouth, Shade sank his fangs deep and the intensity of his power railed through Luca's body. It wasn't the same level of eroticism as feeding from his neck, but it was master, and Luca would die for him.

As Shade's hunger abated, he could feel his body rushing with this young warrior blood, it was so fresh, like sun ripened fruit, the taste bursting on his tongue. He drew only what he needed, not wanting to push Luca too far. Shade had enough on his plate and didn't need to deal with Luca's sexual appetites this night, nor his own. He just needed to take the fucking edge off and get back to *bel*. Licking Luca's wrist as he unlatched, he turned to leave. "Luca, forgive me, please. I must return to her. You will be fine, si?""

Luca sighed as Shade fed much too quickly and it almost hurt when he extracted his fangs from him. His cock was hard and aching.

"Yes, master, I'll be leaving for a while. If you need me, call for me, I will return immediately."

"Be careful," Shade warned, "take a weapon. And let me know when you have returned, I will hear you in my death slumber. Now go." Spinning on his heels to leave, Kate stood at Luca's doorway, looking in.

She had slept little, sleeping then waking, as the events of last night kept replaying in her head. *What torments you, lover? What wounds your soul?* She felt him as he lay beside her throughout the day, restless in his death slumber, and knew it played on his mind as well. She had finally drifted into a fitful sleep, and when she awoke in the darkened room of early evening, she discovered he'd slipped from their bed. She wondered if perhaps he'd left early for the Dead House.

Gi had already delivered the breakfast tray, loaded with food, and the two pills. So tonight was the night. She had such a huge appetite, and she knew it was the baby's demands. She ate everything he'd brought for her, and swallowed down the pills. **"There you go, little one. Special nutrients to make you strong, like your father."**

She dressed and prepared to go downstairs when the memory of Luca, gently guiding her back into the house last night, came rushing back to her. What had she been thinking? The drama they had tossed him into. She must thank him. She must apologize. She walked to his suite and found the door was slightly open, and stepped inside and saw them. Shade, feeding from Luca's wrist, and Luca lost in the throes of a sensation she knew only too well. She put her hand on her belly, feeling the slight swell of it. **"For you my little warrior, he does this for you."**

She regretted that she had interrupted this intimate moment. She turned to slip away unnoticed when Shade saw her.

"I'm sorry...I didn't mean to intrude. I thought you'd left for the Dead House. The door was open. Forgive me, please."

Smiling, Shade went to her, enfolded her in his arms. "No apologies, *mi amore*. I needed to feed, to keep you and our *bambino* strong. I tried to wait, but we have been through so much lately, it has drained me. You feed heavily now, and I am grateful for that."

Turning with her in his arms, he looked back at Luca, standing near the easel, looking unsure of her presence.

Kate addressed him hesitantly, "If this isn't a good time..." She stepped tentatively into his space. "I only wanted to thank you, Luca, and to apologize. I feel so foolish for my actions last night..." She tucked her head, hating that he was a witness to so much of their drama.

"My lady, please, it's nothing. You don't need to feel shame around me. My job is to protect you, even if that protection is sometimes from yourself. No apologies necessary."

She felt Shade as he stepped behind her, and wrapped her in his arms, pulling her to his chest, kissing her on the top of her head.

He took her hand and led her back to their room. "Come, my walking sin, we need to give Luca his privacy." He knew they'd always face challenges, but they'd remain as one, and he'd fight to make sure nothing ever came between them.

78

Kate was one full day into taking the pills. She took two pills, three times a day, and she could already feel their impact. Her bones ached, her head ached, and she felt weakened. She steeled herself to the idea she had four more months of this, because she would do whatever she needed to bring this baby into the world. She took comfort in learning pregnancy for the vampire was an escalated process.

Her appetite didn't feel as strong, but she wasn't nauseated, so she'd continue to eat as before. She dared not stop eating, or change her pattern, as she didn't want to worry Shade. He had enough on his mind already. And if she slept more, well, that was normal. Pregnant women tired easily. **"Whatever it takes, my little warrior. You will gaze upon your father's face, I promise you."**

Shade was already up and moving about the room, getting ready to go downstairs when he glanced at her with concern.

She smiled at him and shook her head. "You aren't going to worry over me this whole pregnancy, are you? It will be a long four months if you do. I'm just feeling tired. I think I need to sleep more, so just kiss me please, and go about your night. I'm fine."

There was a tap on the door, and it was Gi with another tray, and more pills. She ate as if she was hungry, so he'd think she had an appetite, and she swallowed down more pills.

He gave her a concerned look. "But you will rest, *si*?"

"Shade, the staff already waits on me hand and foot. I can't think of anything else they could do. You'll have them carrying me around soon. But yes, I'll rest. I promise."

That was an easy promise to keep. She could barely stay awake to talk to him. She just wanted to lie down and sleep.

He looked at how pale she was, and it worried him. He pulled the duvet up around her and kissed her softly. "Sleep, Kate. Please let the staff take care of you. If you need me, I can be here in seconds. Don't try..." As he looked down, she was already sound asleep. He kissed her cheek before leaving.

Closing the door softly as he left the room, he headed down to his office, trying not to stay so focused on her, to discover Alec had left a message on his phone. He had to see what the fuck he wanted, and he needed to pull himself together.

***

Gi brought up the lunch tray and had to wake Kate. He propped the pillows behind her as he said, "Master has instructed you to stay in bed tonight, my lady."

She thanked him as she took the pills he held out for her and let him know she'd be fine as she watched him leave. She had forced herself to eat breakfast while Shade had been there, but she had even less appetite now and couldn't bear to look at all the food on the tray. She slipped from the bed and dumped the contents in the toilet and flushed it away, putting the empty plate back on the tray, arranging the silverware so it looked used.

That minimal effort exhausted her, and she climbed back into the bed, head pounding, joints aching, and so tired. She fell back asleep until she heard Gi enter once more with the dinner tray and more pills. He left the dinner tray as he cleared away the lunch tray, and as soon as he was out of the room, she repeated the process of flushing the food down the toilet. Her body felt weaker by the hour, but the doctor said she'd be sick. This was the price she must pay, and she'd pay it. But getting back to the bed was a challenge. She needed to be careful that Shade didn't see her struggle, besides, she was sure her body would adjust, it just needed time.

79

Alec dressed for a morning in Congress, plus an early afternoon interview. Appearance was everything. Mortals were like sheep, and he would lead them, like lambs to slaughter. Rissa was in her dressing room, getting ready for her own day. He walked to her door and watched her as she dressed. Her fashion sense was flawless, and it started with her lingerie and the matching bra and panties, the garter belt, the silk stockings. She kept her beauty on display, carefully crafting her image.

"Rissa, before I leave, remember to call that mortal. After this situation with the feeder, you need to make sure she takes those fucking pills. Stay on top of it, will you, darling? And if she gives you any indication she's not taking them, let me know, so I can formulate a Plan B. The last thing I need is a warrior reading bedtime stories. Shade has mentioned some rival coven has moved into the D.C. area. I haven't had much time to look into it, but I certainly can't afford a rogue coven to expose my cover. And right now, I'm not sure Shade has his head in the game. This is critical, Rissa. Please tell me you have this under control."

"I'm always on top of things. And I'll inform you immediately if there are any glitches with this pill process. Alec...what do you mean there's a rival coven in D.C.? You never mentioned this. When were you planning to inform me?"

As she walked over to him, swinging her hips, she lightly brushed invisible lint from the shoulders of his immaculate jacket, and straightened his impeccably tied necktie.

He creased his brow. "I didn't share the information about the coven because, quite frankly, I don't have all the details. I need to sit down with Shade and see what he's found. I know there were a few rogues he killed, and something about a tattoo made him think this may be a coven. Like I said, I don't have all the details at this point. That's his job, to stay on top of this stuff, and that's why I need him focused. And why I need you to see to this...baby issue."

He reached around her, cupping her ass in his hand and gave her a hard squeeze. “Behave yourself today, my darling.” Smiling wickedly. “Or not.”

She got the exact response she wanted with that smile. He belonged to her and she threw back her head and laughed with loving wicked intent. “Oh, daddy, there’s only one man I want to misbehave with, and only one hard, steeled cock I desire!”

“Fix this problem and I'll show you steeled cock.” He slapped her ass hard as he turned to leave and meet his driver.

As he walked out the door, she rubbed the spot still stinging from his slap. *Damn Alec, you will torture me to the point of begging soon.* Brimming over with happiness, she went to find her cell phone. *You may have screwed up my plan once, doormat, but I will be damned if you will do it twice!*

80

Dialing up Kate, Rissa didn't look at the time and didn't really care, Kate would take her call, and she'd get answers. If she didn't, Rissa would be making a house call, like it or not. Shade wouldn't keep her out of that house, no matter what he tried. Nor will that fucking puppet he brought in as Kate's protector. The phone rang several times, and Rissa started pacing. "Damn you, answer!"

Kate awoke to the sound of the phone and groggily grabbed for it on the bedside table. She checked the caller ID to see it was Rissa. "Hello? Rissa?"

"Kate, yes, my heavens, I didn't even realize the time. I hope I didn't awaken you, sweetie?"

Kate shook the sleep from her head. "Oh...no matter. I seem to sleep a lot lately. But Rissa, I have to ask, what were you thinking? The feeder? Why didn't you call me and check?"

"Oh, Kate, I wasn't thinking, I just wanted to do everything I could to help. Having a feeder is such a normal occurrence for male vampires when their mate is pregnant. I just assumed you would need one, and that you certainly would want Shade to be taken care of. I had no idea it would upset you. I'm sorry. I forget sometimes, you're still mortal, and not accustomed to our ways. I've been devastated since it happened. Please forgive me, won't you? I want to be there every step of the way to help with your pregnancy, Alec insists, and I so agree with him."

Rissa sniffled as she pulled out all the stops for her little performance.

"No, I understand. I'm still struggling with the whole concept of feeders. I understand you were trying to help. But God, what a nightmare that was, she attacked him."

Rissa acted contrite. "Yes, I had no idea she'd act so inappropriately, or I'd never have brought her. I mean, can you believe the audacity of her? Most feeders are very demure and discreet. This one was acting way above her station, if you ask me, and I don't blame you one second, for how you responded. If she'd acted that way with Alec, I'd have done the same.

"But I did check in with the doctor I sent, and he told me he gave you supplements and informed Shade he'd need a feeder. I just thought I'd help any way I could and arrange to set up the feeder for you. But Shade was able to resist her, and that does concern me. Please tell me, sweetie, he's not feeding from you as you take the supplements, I'm told they make you so sick."

"Of course not. Shade knew even before the doctor said anything, he'd have to stop feeding from me. Neither of us is going to do anything that puts this baby in any more jeopardy than it already is."

"Oh, I'm so glad to hear that. So, did he hire a feeder on his own? How is he feeding?"

"He...he made some arrangements. He knew it was upsetting to me, so it's something he takes care of away from the house. I wish it didn't bother me. I understand in your culture it's common. He's explained all that to me. I have one foot in the mortal world and one in the immortal, and I'm still grappling with some aspects of his life. I'm sure you went through the same struggles and look at you. I'll get there with time."

Rissa almost laughed out loud. *You will never be like me, and you have no idea of the struggles I went through.* "Well, if anything happens and you need assistance with another feeder, I promise I can help, and do much better. You should try and find out where he goes to feed. If Desire was upsetting to you, then you'll want to see who he's feeding from. Each feeder coven caters to specific needs and tastes. And then you have to make sure they don't have tainted blood."

Rissa grinned wickedly. *Stick that in your romantic dream and deal with it!* "Are you sick with the pills already? Tell me everything, I want to know."

"Shade understands bloodlines, and tainted blood. I'm sure he's been very careful in his selection. I wouldn't dare inquire about his choice. He's already made adjustments to accommodate me. And the pills, yes, I started them, two days now. Shade wanted us to have the Paris trip, so I delayed a few days. I'd like to say I feel fine, but quite honestly, they do make me feel bad. Not unbearable, although, today has been worse than yesterday. Just aching all over, headache, and no appetite, but I'm able to eat, so I've been forcing myself. I'm sure my body will adjust to it. But don't worry, Shade and Gi are both making sure I take them, they watch over me like a hawk. Not that I wouldn't take them. I'll do whatever we have to do to keep this baby safe."

Taking a deep breath, Rissa composed herself. "Oh, Kate, it sounds horrible. I'm sure Shade is busy, so if you need me to come by, I'd love to sit with you or bring you anything you might need. And I'm sure you'll take the pills. I know I'd do anything to protect my child. Maybe you should think of taking more, just to be on the safe side. They certainly can't hurt, and can only help the baby. I'm so excited for you and can't wait until the baby arrives. I'd love to give you a baby shower. Wouldn't that be so much fun?"

"A shower sounds wonderful, Rissa. I'm really more excited about this baby than my voice conveys, I'm just so tired, and I sleep so much."

"Oh sweetie, I can totally understand. Look, perhaps I'll stop by later in the week for a visit, and we can discuss some shower ideas and make some plans. I'll call you before I come over. I don't have my schedule book with me at the moment. Now get some rest, and don't forget those pills. If you need anything, my sweet friend, I'm but a phone call away. I must dash, I have an appointment and if I'm late, it makes me late the entire day, working girl, you know."

"That would be great, Rissa, I look forward to seeing you."

Kate ended the call and laid on the bed thinking. Since she'd been with Shade, she'd really cut herself off from her mortal family and friends, making only brief contact by phone, making excuses for why she couldn't see them. She did miss having girlfriends, she really missed Shannon, and seeing Rissa would be good for her. Kate's experience with female vamps had not been the greatest. First, Sabine tried to kill her, and then this feeder was climbing Shade like a demon from hell. Rissa had been her only immortal girlfriend, and they were never that close during college. And the pills, Rissa said take more. Kate wondered if she should take more. She tried to calculate how long the supply would last before the next doctor visit, but she was so tired she drifted back into a deep sleep, the cell phone still in her hand.

Rissa finished up her hair and got dressed, and all she could do was smile. *Oh, this is going to be so much fun to watch naive Kate, and her poor dead baby. You can bet your mousey ass I will be there this week. Your 'dearest friend' will come calling, bearing gifts, and more pills. And I'll convince you to sneak extra pills because you'll want to save that thing inside you, but you won't be successful, and daddy will be rewarding his baby girl soon.*

***

Alec had a few minutes between bills being read on the floor, so he slipped out to the corridor to give Shade a call. It was a late-night session in Congress. He'd been pre-occupied with work lately, but he really needed to understand what was going on, if there was a rival coven moving into D.C. The phone rang several times and went to voicemail.

Are you fucking kidding me? He left his angry message on Shade's phone. "Shade, let me make one thing clear. When I call, you answer. I don't ever want to hear a fucking voicemail message again. Now call me back, so we can set up some time to discuss this coven."

He ended the call and missed the days of handheld phones when he could slam down the receiver. He was ready to put his fist through a wall, but there were too many mortals around him, so he swallowed his anger, for now.

81

Kate laid in this bed yet another day. Gi brought meal trays, watched her take the pills and then left the tray behind. She picked at the food, eating what she could, but continued to throw most of it in the toilet. She slept a deep dreamless sleep, and then she slept some more. In the evening, she heard Shade enter the room. She felt him, felt his love and concern and the light touch of his hand. His voice was sweet music to her ears. *"Ti amo, mi amore*." Did she answer? She's sure she answered, but she was already falling back asleep. She awakened hours later to see a single red rose on the white sheets beside her, and his simple note. *'Ti amo.' Lover...pull me out of this black hole, I'm not sure I can climb out on my own.*

Shade walked to the closed bedroom door and stood outside, listening. He could hear nothing but dead silence. He hated that sound. She was inside, and he missed his bubbly, chatty *bel*. Slowly opening the door, he saw her lying in the bed. He could tell she hadn't moved since the last time he checked on her, and she looked weak. Walking closer, he could barely take the pain that went through him. She looked even paler than before. Gently lifting her hand, she didn't move and for one second, he felt panic race through him, and then she turned her head slightly toward him.

"Kate, wake up please. I am worried. You look very...not yourself. What can I do to help?"

"I don't need anything, Gi has been most attentive. And I did as you asked. I've been in bed all day."

She started to sit up. She needed to show him she was okay. She knew how much he worried.

He watched her sit up and could tell she was trying to hide her pain. Reaching out, he helped her and fluffed up some pillows behind her back.

"Well, you look very pale and weak to me. Did you eat, take your pills?"

"I ate everything. Gi brings my meals, and my pills. You can ask him. I cleaned my plate."

He tried not to show his concern. "Well, that is good you are eating. You don't need to lose any weight. You should be gaining now."

"I talked to Rissa on the phone, she was sorry about the whole thing with the feeder, and just wanted to check on me. She said she might stop by this week. So, be nice, lover, please?"

He smirked at the mention of Rissa. "Rissa, huh? Well, not sure I want her ass back in this house so soon, but I understand if you want some company. Her mate is my boss, so be cautious what you discuss. He already mentioned Rissa informed him of the incident, she is his mate, and she will not hide anything from him. Keep that in mind, please."

"I never discuss our lives with her. She's trying to figure out who your feeder is. I promise you, what happens between us remains private."

Shade growled low. "Nosy is what she is! Never discuss Luca with her. You need to protect him as much as he protects you. She need not know a damn thing about him. Not just the feeding but anything."

Sighing, he held her in his arms. "*Bel*, I don't want to seem unreasonable. I don't want to come off like a hard ass to you."

She relished the feel of his arms around her. She had felt so bad today, the pleasure of his arms supporting her felt so delicious, she allowed herself to melt against him. "Luca is my family too. I'd never discuss the personal issues of our family. She wants to plan a baby shower. And I never see you as mean. You're my protective warrior."

"Then lay here in your protective warrior's arms and fall asleep. I won't be going out tonight, I promise you, and if you wake, I will be right here."

He lay down next to her, cuddling her onto his chest. He felt her relax into him and fall asleep. "That's it, rest. I'm right here with you."

He waited until she was sleeping soundly, then slid her off his chest and onto the bed, pulling the blankets around her. Getting down to his office, he saw his phone blinking and already knew he had to deal with Alec or all hell would break loose. Dialing into his voicemail, the message Alec left was abrupt, and his tone was...deadly.

Shaking his head, his anger rose up. So, Alec was finally worried about a coven after all this time, and now he wanted to talk? *Right! Let me get right on that.* Slamming his fist down on the desk, he grabbed his smokes and walked out onto the patio and paced, lighting up a cigarette. He needed to get his anger under control before he returned the call, knowing he couldn't let his anger out on Alec or he'd pay the price. He finally calmed down and walked back in to return his call.

82

Alec wrapped up his interview with the press under the impressive dome of the Capital, and then headed back to his office, checking his cell to see if Shade returned his call. The whole day had passed, and he was ready to get out of there for the night. *Fuck! Nothing! Who the fuck does he think he is?* As soon as he got in his office and closed the door, he dialed his cell again, angrily pacing.

Shade heard the phone just as he was returning from outside and grabbed the cell off the desk as his ass hit his chair. He didn't have to look to see who it was, Alec was one impatient fucker, and everything happened on his schedule. "Shade, here."

Alec could barely repress his anger. "First of all, when I call, I expect an immediate pickup, so keep your phone on you at all times, and I mean all times. Don't take a fucking piss without your phone, got it? And second of all, if, by some stroke of dumb luck, you happen to miss a call and I leave a voicemail, I expect an immediate response. Is anything about that message unclear?"

Shade propped his feet on the desk and let him ramble. "Well, let me see if I have this straight. Rissa marches in to my house, bringing the feeder from fucking hell. I've got a pregnant mate, who doesn't need that kind of aggravation and is sick as a fucking dog from those pills. But I'll drop everything for your fucking problems."

Suppressing his annoyance, Alec responded, "Curb that attitude with me, warrior. You know Rissa was just trying to help, and it's not my fucking problem you got a mortal pregnant, so I don't want to hear about any fucking issues with your mate. What have you found out about the rogues? Do we have another coven moving in? Or was this an isolated incident? What do your instincts tell you?"

Shade leaned his head back on the chair. It was just as he thought. Alec didn't give a fucking thought to anything until it might actually threaten his ass.

"This looks like some new coven, possibly called Aries. The two rogues I found concern me. What the hell are they after? How many more are there? I have had your warriors scouting every night, and I personally keep close tabs in your immediate area. My instincts tell me this won't be good. I have no other leads, I have never heard of this damn Aries coven before. What the hell do you know about them?"

"Aries...never heard of them. I'll put out some feelers, see if anyone has heard anything. Do you have a feel for the size of this coven?" He paced the floor of his office. This could be nothing.

Shade scoffed. "No, not at this point, but I've got warriors in every hot spot in town. They keep a lid on everything, and we have begun to sniff out some strange blood, but no trouble. If they have tattoos, it's a fucking serious problem, it means they are organized, which is why I can't understand why I never heard of them before. The rogues I found were damn young, perhaps they are recruiting, and you know as well as I do, young rogue vampires are one dangerous breed."

Alec continued pacing the floor. "I'm well aware, warrior, well aware. If they blow my cover, expose me...it's over for all of us. I can't emphasize enough how important it is you get a handle on this. And listen, I know you have some shit going on. Rissa has kept me informed, but you have to stay in the game here. You can't allow yourself to be distracted. If I go down, we all go down."

Sighing loudly, Shade slid his hand through his hair. "None of us can be exposed, and you don't have to remind me. I have one hell of a lot to lose as well. I got this. I will take their lowlife asses out, one by one, and it won't be pretty. But here is what I will lay on the table. You have a few good warriors, all mercenaries. Most of them know their shit but they lack discipline. If this situation escalates beyond what your boys can handle, I'm bringing in my own warriors and you can bet your ass, this city will rock to its core when I let them loose. We don't play games. We are true warriors, you want death, you came to the dealer, brother."

Alec stopped pacing as he shoved his hand in his pocket. "Let me be clear. I want this coven gone at all costs! Whatever it takes, and the bloodier the better. That sends a message, if you know what I mean. Keep me informed. I want to know what you see, what you hear. Don't think any detail is too small. There's too much at risk here. Okay, well I have a heavy calendar, and I was on my way home for the night so, I need to run. Talk again soon."

"Keep me in the loop as well, Alec. Respect me. You need me to take this fucking coven out of here."

Hanging up, Shade closed his eyes. *Fuck, he will drive me mad!* He had enough to worry about, but war and warriors was like breathing to him and until something happened, Alec's ass could sit and wait. Getting up, he headed back upstairs to check on *bel*, this damn house was so quiet lately, he couldn't stand it.

83

Rissa teleported to the Bel Rosso estate, and before walking to the door, she took the pills out of her coat pocket and slid them into her purse. That damn manservant would take her coat and she wanted these pills handy. And just as she predicted, he took her coat and asked her to sit and wait for the master.

Shade was getting ready to go back upstairs and check on *bel*, when he picked up her scent. Gi appeared and announced he had left Miss Benneteau in the living room, waiting to see Kate. Taking a deep breath, he walked into the living room to see her sitting like a damn queen on her throne, with a basket of baby things. Maybe this was a good idea, perhaps it would cheer up Kate.

"Welcome back, Rissa."

Rissa looked up as he entered, thinking he looked ravaged, like he hadn't fed or rested in months. *Wait until Alec hears this.* She stood and smiled timidly. *It's show time, Rissa!*

"Shade, thank you. I know this is awkward, but I come with good intentions. I wanted to visit with Kate. I know she isn't feeling well, but I brought her a small gift, hoping to cheer her up." She smiled sweetly. "And of course, I insist on giving her a proper baby shower, so I hope planning that will lighten her mood." While she was speaking, she heard Alec in her head, and he knew she was at Bel Rosso.

"My devious darling, I'm so happy you decided to speed along this process. It's quite possible the only person in this world more devious than me, is you. I can't tell you how happy that makes me. You are a woman after my own heart."

Rissa responded to him, **"Alec, you should see your warrior. He looks a bit worse for wear, but I have the pills, and am about to see the mortal."**

Alec huffed. **"I don't need a warrior who's looking 'worse for wear' my darling, so get this fucking thing over with, quickly."**

"Your wish is my command. There's nothing I want more than for this to be over. I'll fill you in when I return home, my wicked vampire."

Shade was watching her closely. He thought she was being uncharacteristically sweet, or maybe he was just too damn tired. "Rissa, let's get one thing clear. She is not well, she does nothing but sleep. I want no trouble. I want her to stay in that bed. If you are clear on that, I will take you up to her."

As Rissa agreed, he led her upstairs and gently opened the door. "*Mi amore*, you have some company, are you up for that?"

Kate heard his voice, and it pulled her up from the darkness. She sat up in bed as he entered. "Company? Oh, Rissa. Yes, I remember you said you were coming. Yes, come in."

Walking in with Rissa trailing behind him, he leaned down and kissed her softly, whispering in her ear, "*Ti amo, mi amore*, I'll be close by if you need me. Don't overdo it, please."

Helping her sit upright, he fluffed the pillows behind her and tucked a stray strand of crimson behind her ear. "Not too much fun, *bel*. You need your rest."

He closed the door behind him and returned to his office, keeping his senses tuned to Kate. He would feel if she was becoming upset.

Rissa could see things were worse than she thought, and it could not have made her happier. It wouldn't be long now. She watched the warrior mooning over Kate, and it only convinced her that the thing growing inside her had to go, and fast. She took a good look at Kate and knew it wouldn't be long. She looked like death warmed over and Rissa had to bite her lip to keep from laughing. "Oh, my dear Kate, you look so ill. Good heavens, I had no idea it was this serious with you."

Sitting on the edge of the bed, Rissa softly rubbed Kate's arm as she plastered a look of concern on her face.

"Rissa, I'm glad you stopped by. I'm afraid I won't be much company though, I feel even weaker since our phone call. All I do is sleep, if you can call it sleep. I'm really not eating much. I have downplayed that with Shade, he's already so worried."

"Oh Kate, he loves you so much, he's so caring and loving. You are lucky to have such a strong, caring mate. And you should keep downplaying your sickness. No need to make him worry needlessly. I mean just look at him, already in such a state of concern for you and the baby, but don't you worry, sweetheart."

Sliding her hand down Kate's cheek, Rissa felt how cold her face was, how sunken her eyes appeared, and it almost made her grin thinking about what was to come, once that dead thing flushed from her. Rissa lowered her voice to a whisper. "I brought you more pills."

She put her finger to her pursed lips. "Shh, he'll hear your thoughts, don't think about it."

Slipping her hand into her purse, she quickly pressed the bottle of extra pills into Kate's hand. "Hide them, and make sure you take them in between your current dosage. We want that baby strong, just like his daddy."

Kate seemed surprised when Rissa pushed the bottle into her hand. "Rissa, do you think I should? This whole pregnancy, I just don't know what to expect. But if you think it will help. If it will help the baby then by all means, I'll take them. Put them in the drawer of the nightstand please, and I'll take them in between meals when no one is here. They can't hurt, right? I mean, they're only supplements. I'm already sleeping most of the time anyway."

Rissa reassured her as she laid her hand across Kate's stomach. "Oh they're only supplements, nothing harmful for you or the baby. You must take them. You have such a strong warrior inside you."

As her hand lay there, Rissa could feel the baby's dying energy, its small body ravaged from the drug. There was very little heartbeat and she knew, within a few days, this would all be over.

Taking the pills from her, Rissa opened the bottle and removed two capsules, grabbing a small carafe of juice from the nightstand. She poured a glass and held the pills out to her.

"Now come, take them, and besides, you should be sleeping more. We don't want you to do anything strenuous in these critical stages of your pregnancy. " *Yes, you stupid naive mouse, take more, so Alec can have his warrior back, and I can have my Alec.*

Kate swallowed down the pills. "Thank you, Rissa, for the pills, and the doctor, and the baby gifts. It is a boy. I haven't had a scan, but I have felt all along it's a boy. I could feel the male energy. No question."

Rissa softly stroked her hair as she smiled at her. *Ah, that's what you think. Dead boy!* "Oh Kate, I'm sure you can tell. I wish Alec would want children, I can only hope. So jealous of you! Now lie back, you look so exhausted. I won't stay longer, I can tell you're tired, and I don't want to keep you up. I'll leave the gift basket, and I've put together a portfolio of ideas for a baby shower. Look them over when you feel up to it, my sweet girl. I'll call in a few days, and if you're not up to seeing me, then we can just talk on the phone, and besides, with the extra dosage, you should be feeling better very soon."

Rissa left the folder on the nightstand and leaned in, kissing her cheek. "Rest Kate, I'll see myself out. Alec and I are supporting you both 100%, now sleep."

Picking up her purse, she quietly left the room, smiling as she descended the stairs. Shade met her at the bottom, escorting her back to the front door. She had to control herself from skipping with joy, as she left the house and teleported back to G-town.

Shade had returned back upstairs to check on Kate, and re-adjust her pillows so she could lie down. Within minutes, she felt herself falling back to sleep. She had no concept of time passing, no sense of day or night. The only breaks in her sleep came when Gi entered to bring her food. Either he or Theresa was now staying to watch her eat, so she was no longer able to discard the food. No one mentioned anything about discovering her rouse, but somehow, she thought they'd figured it out. There was no way to eat all that they brought, so she picked at it, and ate what little she could. As soon as they took the tray away, she took the extra pills from Rissa.

She could always feel when Shade entered the room. Sometimes he spoke to her, sometimes he just touched her cheek, and other times she felt him lay down beside her. He was her only comfort in this darkness.

***

Rissa quickly arrived at her home office and kicked off her heels. She had a few hours of work to catch up on since she'd spent so much of the evening in Virginia. She felt the anger roll through Alec. *Hell! Someone is not having a good night.* She never paid much attention to his mood swings when he worked, there was always something that got him riled up at least once a day, but this felt more intense.

Checking the clock, not sure of his evening appointments, she thought, perhaps, her wicked vampire needed a bit of good news. Sliding out of her business dress, she snuggled onto the chaise lounge in her dressing room and decided to let him know how her visit went. She wished she could lure him home for a sweet snack. She was feeling her hunger rise rapidly and she ached to taste him. She needed him, and he knew it. He always made the wait such sweet torture, something she'd come to expect, but still struggled to manage. **"My**

wicked vampire is not having a good night, but his devious darling has some wonderful news about that pesky mortal. Busy?"

Alec had a rough day, and the evening wasn't going any better when he heard her speak to him in his head. He stood still and listened, then responded, **"I'm never too busy for you, my devious darling, especially if you have something to brighten my day. What's up?"**

Rissa smiled, glad to have his attention. **"I called on the mortal. Good news. The pills have begun the process. She is quite ill. It won't be long, but there's more!"**

Alec chuckled wickedly, as much at Rissa and the joy she was taking in this plan as this news itself. **"What do you have up your sleeve, my darling?"**

"I came bearing gifts and more pills. I've already convinced her she should sneak in more pills between the doses they give her. That thing inside her is already dying and dragging her down with it."

Alec grinned. **"What a brilliant idea! Do whatever is necessary to speed up the process. I had a talk with Shade today. He seems on top of this rival coven, but I can't afford for him to get off track, so the sooner the better. Maybe this warrior will tire of all the drama of sick mates and dead babies and get back to doing what he does best. Push her, Rissa, push hard. I know I can count on you."**

Rissa lounged seductively on the chaise lounge, hoping he got the visual. **"Have I ever let you down? I inquired again about the feeder. Apparently, he already has one. I couldn't get her to tell me who, but I'll work on it. Not that it matters. She did clarify he's not feeding from her. Will you be home later this evening? Your baby girl misses you."**

Alec looked at his watch. **"I have a few things to wrap up here, but I should be home before too long. Have a drink and cigarette waiting, and you, of course, my darling. We'll be celebrating soon, it sounds like."**

"I'm already waiting, wet and hungry, and all yours."

Alec laughed. "**Rissa, when are you not waiting, wet and hungry?"**

She laughed wickedly. "**Just get that sweet ass home to me and who knows...I may be involved in my own fun activities when you arrive."**

Alec shook his head. **"Of that, my darling, I have no doubt. Now let me get back to work. I'll see you when I get home."**

84

It had been almost a week since Kate started taking the pills and Shade kept checking on her, as she just laid there like the dead. She ate little, took pills and slept, and this house felt like a morgue. He could barely take it any longer. As he left their bedroom, he closed the door softly behind him. Despite their blood bond, she didn't respond to him. As he made his way downstairs, he knew he must look a mess. This was taking a toll on him as well, with Alec and the rogues, and these fucking pills and his *bel* sleeping like the dead, he was beside himself with worry.

He flopped down on the couch and sat staring, wondering what the hell he would do. He could feel her slipping away, but the doctor said she'd be ill. Before he could finish his thought, Gi appeared before him, looking a bit nervous.

"Master, I know it is not my place to come between matters of you and your lady, but I feel there is something you should know."

Shade looked up at him. He had a feeling in his gut this wasn't going to be good news. "Go on, Gi."

"Master, Theresa has been cleaning my lady's room every day, keeping everything as clean as possible. She has noticed that there are food bits floating in the toilet. I do not wish in any way to tell on her ladyship, for we love her dearly, but I fear something is amiss with these findings."

"Gi, has she been sick? Throwing up? Perhaps that is what Theresa is seeing?"

"Oh no, master, these are un-eaten food pieces, as though she is..." He cleared his throat. "...depositing the plates of food down the toilet. So, we started staying while she eats. For a few days, she picked at her food, but now she is not eating anything. The trays remain untouched, but she continues taking the pills on a regular basis. I speak openly, master, but she has become quite peaked and weak very quickly."

Shade absorbed everything Gi reported to him, and he knew suddenly, deep in his soul, that these pills were not helping her. They would kill her long before they helped the baby and he stood and paced. His heart was at a crossroads, and he felt he must choose between his *bel*, or the baby.

In a quiet voice, he spoke to Gi,d "I have to make a decision, and I am torn beyond words. This may be devious, but I can't let her go on like this. I can't risk losing her, and that is my fear. There will be other *bambinos*, once I turn her. What can I do, Gi? I don't want her to suffer any longer and I don't want her to think it is her fault if she loses the *bambino* because I demanded she stop taking the pills."

He felt Gi's hand on his shoulder. "Master Shade, in life, we must sometimes make decisions that alter our course. We have all lost our *bel rosso*. You must help her. And we will help you if you need us."

Shade's heart felt as though it would break, but he made the choice for her. It was selfish of him, but he could not lose her. "Gi, take the pills, remove the medicine within them, fill them with something else, powdered sugar or something, and keep giving them to her. Perhaps we will see some change. I have no damn choice!"

"Master Shade, it will be done, we will see then how it works. Do not riddle your soul with guilt. You are saving her master, for all of us."

***

Kate didn't know how many extra pills Rissa had brought, or how many days had passed, but she had taken all of Rissa's pills now, so the only pills she took were those brought to her by Gi.

As she moved into the second day of just taking the original dosage, she started to sleep a little less, and to actually feel hungry again. Not enough to eat everything that was brought, but at least she was craving food, and Shade's blood, and that had to be a good sign. She felt relieved that her body was adjusting, and hoped Rissa's pills had given her the jump start her body needed after all.

***

Gi reported to Shade, "Master, we have been giving my lady the placebo pills for three days now. The first day, I didn't see any difference, but on the second day, she was eating a little, and now today, she was already awake when we took in her food tray, and she is regaining her appetite, eating a little more. It is still small, but I can tell she wants the food she is eating and is not picking at it because she is being supervised. I think your decision to switch out the pills was a wise one. I think you will have my lady back as soon as this medicine is flushed from her system. Theresa and I will continue to watch her closely, and if there is any change, we will let you know immediately."

"That is good news, very good news!"

He needed to see her. Pushing past Gi, he rushed up the stairs and burst in through the door of the bedroom and stopped dead in his tracks. She was sitting up, her color was back, but there were still dark circles under her eyes and she still looked weak as hell. But he could tell Theresa had helped her bathe, and her hair was brushed, which meant she was moving about.

He had been riddled with guilt from his decision, but he kept telling himself he did this for *bel*, not for him, but he was kidding no one. He was selfish, he would not lose her. Walking to the bed, he got a weak smile from her and he lay down beside her, taking her into his arms and holding her.

"*Bel*, you look better. How are you feeling?"

"Lover...I felt like I was away somewhere, lost...and I couldn't find my way back. But now I'm home, and with you. How I've missed you. I know you were here, I could sense it, but it felt far away. It feels so good to be held. I'm much better."

"*Cazzo*, Kate, you scared the living hell out of me, I never felt so damn lost, and I thought I would lose my mind. I was so scared and helpless. I am so grateful you came back to me. I wanted you to fight, I could tell you were trying, but just couldn't make it. I was here the whole time. Every second I could find, I was here. I wish you would feed. It would make me feel better. Would you do that for me, can you manage it?"

"Yes. I was starting to crave your blood today, for the first time in...I can't even remember how many days. That's a good sign, don't you think?"

He smiled softly. "*Si*, very good sign indeed. Now, hold still."

Getting out of the bed, he took off his black tee. Leaning down, he carefully picked her up in his arms, and cradled her close to his chest. Grabbing a blanket, he wrapped it around her and walked to the large arm chair by the window. He looked into her eyes, absorbing all of her.

"I have missed looking at you, holding you, talking to you, feeling you make me feel alive. This house is so quiet. *Mio bel* was gone. Perhaps, we are past the worst and things will get much better, now come and feed. Take all you need."

Pulling her up to his neck, he cupped her head and supported her back. "I love you so damn much, *bel*."

Her lips grazed his neck, and she loved the feel of him, the scent of him. She bit into his skin, but she didn't bite hard enough. She didn't draw blood.

"*Mi amore*, you must try harder. Drink."

She bit him a second time, harder, breaking through his skin and feeling his warm blood seep into her mouth. She drew his blood into her mouth, and as she swallowed, she could feel his energy healing her from the inside out. This was what her body needed. She continued to drink from him, slowly; small swallows, but each swallow bringing more healing, and peace. Such comfort, her eyes felt heavy as her body felt restored and she felt sleepy, but this was a natural sleepiness, not that dark hole that held her captive for so long. She drank her fill, and with the last swallow, she felt herself drift back into a deep natural sleep.

Shade was distraught when her first attempt to feed showed him just how weak she had become. He fought back the panic, hoping she wouldn't fall back into that abyss, but finally, she fed. He knew she was taking enough to sustain her and held her close. After some time, he felt her body relax into a sleep, her head against his shoulder. He sat staring at her body, looking rail thin, but with so much fight. He felt the trickle of his own blood run down his neck from her unfinished feeding, as the blood tears ran down his cheeks.

"I won't let you go, *bel*, I won't. Forgive me, *mi amore*."

Standing, he cradled her gently as she slept soundly, and carried her back to their bed. He laid her down and then stripped naked. He kissed her gently, getting in bed beside her, pulling her to his chest and he knew, he'd do all in his power to save her, and this journey wasn't over.

85

Shade laid there as she slept. She seemed to be in a much better place now, sleeping more peacefully. Slipping quietly from their bed, his mind was so tormented, he went outside for a smoke and found all he could do was pace and worry.

Luca could feel his master's turmoil, and looked outside to see him pacing, and watched as he finally sat down. He seemed defeated, something Luca had never seen in him before. His head hung down, the cigarette dangling from his mouth, and Luca wondered if either of them would be able to make it for the duration of this pregnancy. Both of them were so lost without the other, in pain each in their own way. My lady had been so ill, she seemed completely unaware of her surroundings, and sometimes even unaware of master, and it broke him. This child had become something that could easily take one or both of them out. Luca didn't like it, he didn't want to lose either of them, and if anything happened to my lady, Shade would surely follow her into that blackness. If something happened to the child, they would both suffer greatly, and Luca was stuck on how to comfort either of them. Walking outside, Luca joined him, feeling, perhaps, he just needed to talk. "Master, got a smoke?"

Shade's head snapped up, he hadn't even heard Luca come out. "Sure, help yourself." Shade threw him the pack of cigarettes and the lighter.

Luca caught the pack and lit up. "My lady seemed a bit better today, up and moving some. How is she tonight?"

Shade looked at him and shook his head. "Luca, she had a better day, but I fear it is only a small reprieve. She fed from me tonight and was not strong enough to break my skin. It wasn't normal, she fell asleep feeding. Fuck! It is hell without her, the pain and worry are eating me alive. I did this to her! I got her in this situation, put her in jeopardy, and watching her suffer through this illness almost kills me. She seems a little better. I told her this was probably the worst of it, but I have no idea what lies ahead."

"Master, there is only so much you can do."

"*Si*, Luca. And in that, lies the hardest part of all, I can do nothing to help her, I cannot fix this, make it right for her, make this pain go away. And that pains my heart to the core." *If he only knew the things I have selfishly done to save her. There is hope, she is eating now, and I can only hang onto the smallest of hope that every day she will get better. Those damn pills almost took her away from me, and if I have to lose the bambino to keep her, then that is what I will continue to do. But that deception will die with Gi and me, for I will never confess to her or anyone that I have chosen that path for us.*

"Master, you need something to take your mind off of this, let's walk out to the garage, maybe we should fire up the bikes and take a spin? Work off some pent-up energy. We both could use it."

"I love the idea Luca, but I am not leaving here. I am sticking close to this house in case she needs me. But hell, let's walk down to the garage and take a look, maybe give them a good detailing and if *bel* feels better soon, we can take a short spin one night."

They walked down to the garage. Shade felt better when he could at least keep his hands busy. As they got inside, he saw his custom Harley and sat astride the machine and lit up a smoke. *Yeah, this feels good. Real damn good!*

86

Kate was feeling much better, still a little tired and Shade was insisting she remain in bed. At least she was awake, sitting upright, reading a book, and her appetite was back. She wasn't ravenous for food like she'd been before she got sick, but she at least had her normal appetite back. Gi still brought her food and pills, and she was grateful her body had adjusted to those pills. The darkness, the black hole they kept her in, she wasn't sure she could have endured that much longer.

Kate had to laugh, as Theresa found excuses to "clean" in the bedroom all throughout the day, as if she didn't know the real reason she kept coming in the room was to check on her. Kate put her hand on the slight rise of her belly. **"Little one, I know your daddy wants a big, bad warrior, but I think you will be so spoiled by everyone in this family."**

Gi and Theresa had hovered over her, and if that was any indication of how they'd respond to this baby, this infant might never know a crib. Even Luca would be so protective. *And Shade, you are my warrior with the heart of a lion, but you have such passion and love. This baby will know he's loved by so many. This baby, will he be mortal? Or vamp? Or something in between, like Cory? I can't think of that now.*

She laid her book aside and leaned back against the pillows, her hand resting lightly on her belly as she imagined him, when she felt a stirring. *Did he move? Did the baby move?* She started to sit upright when she was hit with a cramping sensation, and she froze in position. *What is that?* Then it was followed by another severe cramp...and another. *No! No! Not now! Not after all we have been through... Please!*

The cramps became intense and rapid, and then she felt the hot, wet flow of blood between her legs.

"Shade! Oh god, I am losing him. Shade!"

***

Luca and Shade spent another evening in the garage, working on the bikes, laughing and joking, and it felt good to relax and get his mind off things. Suddenly, he was struck with a small pain inside his soul.

Something was wrong with *bel* and her scream assailed his ears like she was dying. "*Bel!* Luca, now!"

Instantly teleporting inside, Shade landed in their bedroom and heard Luca right behind him. Gi and Theresa ran up the stairs and stopped at the open door. Shade looked at her. There was fear in her eyes and her body was shaking. He scanned the room, looking for any sign of an intruder. Then she cried out again, doubling over in pain and he quickly moved to her side of the bed. It was then he saw the bloody sheets between her legs. He fell to his knees beside the bed, feeling such horrendous pain seer through him. The baby was gone. He'd done this to her, to him, to them. He laid his head on the bed and gripped the sheets in his fists. *This is not happening to us. No, not my bambino, no!*

Kate folded her body over top of his. She heard his howls of pain, and they mirrored what her heart felt. She clung to him as her tears flowed.

"I'm so sorry, lover. I've lost our baby. I did everything, I was so careful."

How could she console him when her own heart felt ripped from her? And yet, she felt the depth of his pain, compounding her own. She saw Luca move slowly toward Shade and place his hand on his shoulder. She heard Gi giving Theresa some instructions and Theresa ran from the room. But Shade was inconsolable, as was Kate. What could possibly ever take this pain away?

Shade felt someone touch his shoulder, and without conscious thought, his beast arose, for he'd let nothing harm either of them, especially his *bel*. He instantly swung his arm back, striking whoever was behind him and could hear whoever it was sail through the air and slam back against the wall.

He felt his *bel* move from him and he lifted his head, his eyes red and he looked around the room to see Luca against the wall, staring him down and Gi held up his hand.

"Master Shade, you must relax, calm yourself, you will frighten her."

Shade looked at *bel* and took her in his arms, holding her as they sat on this death bed together. Suddenly, the world had all gone wrong. "*Bel*, my *bel*. Oh my sweet Kate, I..." His tears fell and he fought hard to be the strength she needed, and held her close, rocking her in his arms. He felt Gi approaching them.

"No! No one touches her, no one. Leave us alone. Get the fuck out, now!"

Kate watched as Luca stood and joined Gi and Theresa, as they reluctantly backed out of the room and closed the door. "Lover, I tried so hard...I'm so sorry. The baby...our baby."

His face was covered in his blood tears and she knew his pain was as great as her own. Gi returned to the door.

"Master, I have a medication. It will stop the bleeding, it is important my lady take this now."

Kate saw Shade nod at him, giving him permission to re-enter the room, and Gi handed her more pills, different pills, and a glass of juice to swallow them down. As soon as she'd taken them, Gi left as quietly as he entered. Kate started to pull back the top sheet. She needed to find him. She needed to see him, this tiny life that had grown for such a short while inside her.

Shade saw *bel* pulling at the sheets and it dawned on him she was looking for the baby. "No! *Bel*, no. Stop it!"

He saw her frantically trying to find the fetus and it broke him in two and he had to stop this now. Picking her up in his arms, he carried her out of the room while she cried, fighting to get out of his arms, wanting to see the baby.

Grabbing her chin hard, he went nose to nose with her. "*Bel!* Stop! Look at me! I will not let you do this to yourself. I know you feel pain, so do I, but we will go through this together."

She stopped struggling and curled into his shoulder and sobbed, deep agonizing sobs as he carried her to the bath. Seeing it was already filled, he knew Gi was thinking ahead to help them manage this event in their lives. Stripping down, he got naked and then slipped off her bloody gown and tossed her soiled clothes outside the door. Holding her, he sank deep into the steaming hot water.

"Now listen to me. The pills will stop the bleeding, they will heal you physically, and together, we will heal, as best we can, our hearts and souls. But we have to be together, let our pain enjoin, to help each other."

His voice cracked, the emotional challenge of taking charge harder than he could ever have imagined and he knew they need to just get the fuck out of here and be alone together this night. **"Gi, clean that damn room. I want nothing there when I return that reminds her of this night. Sheets, blankets, everything, replace them. Have a blanket**

and gown ready when we emerge from the bath. We are going to the California house for the night. We have to leave here, or we will both go insane with pain."

As Gi answered and told him he'd take care of it all, Shade gently washed *bel*, letting his touch try to calm her, heal her somehow. Lifting her from the tub, he dried her and opened the door to find the things he'd asked for lying on the freshly stripped bed.

"*Mi amore*, let's get this nightgown on you, we are going to California for the night, teleporting there."

"No, lover...the baby. I have to find the baby..." But they were already gone, he was teleporting them away from this nightmare.

Landing in the California house, into the master bedroom, Shade felt he needed to pull them both out of the situation, put some distance between them and the pain, as if that was even possible. He needed this time to be alone with her, just the two of them. Laying her gently on the bed, she reached for him, as if afraid he'd leave her, and he laid down beside her, pulling her into his arms.

"Shh, *mi amore*, I am right here. Cry, scream, do whatever you have to, but know I love you."

She looked into his eyes, and a tear ran down her cheek. He kissed it away and felt his own tears begin to fall. She curled onto his chest, and he couldn't hold her close enough. Softly caressing her hair and back, he felt her retreat into a deep sleep, and his tears still came.

"*Madre*, why? Protect her, help me. This pain I cannot bear. I can bear what I have done and the choice I made, but I need her more than my own life. I just want her back, please!"

He closed his eyes, exhausted, emotionally spent, and whispered softly, "*Ti amo, mi amore, per sempre*."

87

Gi moved about the house, checking and double checking, making sure everything was in order. He knew master would summon him when he was ready to return, but he had no idea when that might be. The house was as quiet as a tomb. Even Luca had remained in his suite. Theresa had cleaned and checked the master bedroom so many times, she was wearing a path to the door. Reynaldo had cleaned the kitchen until there was no surface left to shine. No one spoke, and the silence alone said all there was to say. They grieved with master and my lady over the loss of this tiny baby they all secretly hoped, against all odds, would survive. It would be a long road to recovery, and master would expect much from them.

***

Rissa was pacing her home office, anxious beyond words to know if Kate had lost that damn thing yet. It was so close to being over she could taste it. Grabbing her cell, she thought to herself, *I don't care if I wake up that whole damn household, I'm calling!*

Dialing the house, it rang a few times, and that was unusual. What the hell was going on over there? Finally, the old one answered.

"This is Larissa Benneteau, I was calling deeply concerned for my dearest friend, Kate. I was just there, and she was so ill, I was wondering if I might speak with her?"

Gi responded, "Yes, Miss Benneteau, I am afraid my lady is not home at the moment."

What? Not home? What the hell has gone wrong now, I will kill that bitch myself! "Oh, not home? I'm sorry, but I'm having a great deal of difficulty comprehending this news. I was just there a few days ago and she was so ill, and now she's not home? Please, I'm a very close friend, is she all right?"

Gi heard her fake sincerity but knew not to challenge a master's mate. "I am sorry madam, but I regret to inform you that my lady lost the baby, and master has decided to take her away. I do not know when they will return, but I will be happy to deliver any message you may have for her."

Rissa gasped loudly. "Oh, I'm so very sorry. Oh dear, what terrible news. Please, I just...oh, this saddens me so. Please, will you just relay our love and support, and deepest sympathy from Senator Canton and me? I'm so overwrought with this loss for her. Thank you for informing me."

Hanging up, she threw back her head and spun around and around in her office chair, laughing with glee. "Oh, my wicked sweet Alec, it is done!"

88

Teleporting back to Virginia, the house was still quiet, the house staff was moving about their business, not really looking or addressing him or *bel*, trying to give them space. He didn't blame them. He wasn't much in the mood for conversation, or anything else at the moment.

The death of their child had taken its toll on both of them, in more ways than one. He made sure *bel* was settled inside the house. She seemed lost, torn, and he knew she'd be this way for a while. But if she didn't snap out of it, he had no idea in hell what he'd do. He was struggling, himself. It had been the hardest torture of his life, and he didn't think he'd ever completely get over it.

He hated to leave her, but it must be done. He'd try to stay home this night, but he was feeling caged in and aching to be let loose, or he'd lose control on those who didn't deserve his wrath, over something only he felt responsible for.

"*Bel*, I need to check in with Luca, make sure things are fine here. I don't plan on leaving, but if I have to, I will tell you, and Luca will always be here with you."

He watched her look back at him with dead eyes, emotionless, and he took a deep breath. *Come on bel, work through it.* "Make sure you try to eat something, build your strength back up, take it easy, your body has been through a lot."

Walking to her, he still got nothing from her. He kissed her head softly, as his hands slid down her arms. "I love you, Kate. I will always love and protect you."

Turning, he headed for his office and Luca's quarters to find something to occupy his mind.

Shade had shielded her, protected her, taking her out of this room where they'd lost their baby, to the California house where he held her while she slept, waited on her when she was awake. Now they were back home, and she wanted so desperately to talk to him, but she knew if she started to talk, the tears would start again, and once they started, she felt they'd never stop. He was in his own pain, and she knew her retreat into herself was only adding to his personal misery, and her tears brought him such agony as well. She must find a way to push through this, for both of them.

Walking into the bunker, Shade ran his hands over some of the weapons, and fought the damn ache to gut something, take something out hard. His emotional state was on edge and he needed to get out of this house and release some of it, but he knew he should stay close to her. Picking up one of his favorite shuriken's, he twirled it in his hand, watching the sharp-edged blades catch the light. Running his fingertips over the razor-thin edges, he knew it was sharp and ready for war. He wished he was in a war, something that would give him an outlet for this pain and anger. He realized that, unfortunately, he *was* in a war, but not the type he was used to.

Grasping the shuriken in his fingers, he should go outside and practice. It had been a while, although he knew he needed no practice with any weapon in this room. He felt his cell phone buzz on his hip. With a flick of his wrist, he sent the shuriken spinning across the room and watched as it stuck deep into the wall. He glanced at his phone...Alec.

"Shade. Alec here. Rissa told me about the baby. Can't say I'm surprised. I hope you understood that going in and didn't get too attached because I need your head in the game here. I got a call from Tomas while you were in California. Seems this coven not only likes to strike mortals but leave them exposed for others to find. Both careless and stupid, and we can't afford this right now. You need to get on top of this. Tell me this isn't going to be a problem."

Shade listened to Alec's matter-of-fact voice and the complete lack of emotion. He was a heartless fucking bastard, black to the damn bone, and sitting all high and mighty. He was probably one of the most powerful master's Shade knew, but damn his heart was cold and ruthless. Shade was in the fucking mood to show him he wasn't the only one who was deadly, as he looked for a way to let go of this shit boiling inside him.

"Well, I never expected hearts and flowers from you Alec, so let it go, don't ever fucking mention it again, it's done. What the fucking hell do you mean leaving bodies? Where? Never mind, I'm heading out now. I'll see Tomas at the Dead House and will roll out from there. Leave it to me. This is what I do best. Go play with your political chess pieces, the only fucking warrior you can rely on will be there before you hang up the phone."

Alec knew all of Shade's anger over his loss would be channeled into his work. "That's all I need to hear, Shade."

Shade ended the call, loaded up on weapons and was ready to teleport. *Fuck! Bel. Damn it Shade, stop running out without telling her where the hell you are going.* "Luca!"

Luca instantly appeared in the bunker.

"I am going out, trouble in D.C., don't know when I will be back. Stay as fucking close as you can to her, she is fragile and let me know if anything happens."

Luca watched him load his weapons and knew this was no ordinary situation, he was a walking arsenal, and on the edge. Luca could feel his blood rushing and his adrenaline pumping. "As you wish, master, I'll take care of her, you need not worry."

Shade nodded at him. "I don't worry when you are here Luca, just do your job." **"*Bel*? Answer me."**

"Yes, lover..."

"I need to go into D.C. I will be gone for a while, Luca is here. He'll be with you. If you need me, you call or let Luca know, and I will return immediately. Tell me, *mi amore*...say it, I need to hear you say it before I leave, I need to know that no matter what happens..."

"Go...I'll be fine. Be safe, please." Her heart broke to let him go, but she couldn't keep him trapped here with her in this darkness.

He sighed. He needed to hear her say she loved him, and she couldn't say it. Grabbing his latest prized weapon, he twirled it in his fingers, his blood screaming to get moving. This was just what he needed, a good hunt and a few dead rogues oozing through his fingers. Teleporting straight into the Dead House, the league of warriors under his command were already gathered and it felt fucking good to have a mission, and his mind immediately went into warrior mode and he forgot everything before this moment.

89

Kate felt his absence as he teleported from the house. It felt like more than she could bear, and yet, she knew this was how he'd deal with his own pain. He was a warrior, and heaven help anything in his path. But where did she put all of her pain? She couldn't lay it at his feet, she couldn't. She curled up on their bed, and drifted into a light sleep when she was awakened by the sound of a baby's cry. She sat upright and slipped from their bed, walking into the nursery. The crib was empty. She ran her hand across the sheets as the tears fell. *Oh, my little warrior...I'm so sorry...I failed you.*

She walked through the room, touching the things that were to have been his; his bed, his dresser, his toys, his books, his clothes. She felt her soul shattering into a million pieces, and she wondered if she could put it all back together again. She walked to the nanny's bed and lay down, letting the tears flow, as she clutched a soft teddy bear to her chest.

Luca could hear my lady moving about upstairs. She hadn't come downstairs since master brought her back from California. He walked up the stairs to check on her. The bedroom door was open, and he stepped lightly into the room, but she wasn't there. He turned to walk down the hall when he caught a glimpse of her in the nursery. He stood in the doorway and watched as she lay on the small twin bed she had set up for Theresa, clutching a stuffed toy as silent tears fell down her cheeks. He took a deep breath and wondered if he should even interrupt her. He was much better equipped to deal with Shade's anger than my lady's sorrow. She seemed completely unaware of his presence. He stepped into the room and she turned her head toward him, and he was confronted with her pain filled eyes. He walked to the chair by the bed and sat next to her.

"My lady, is there anything I can do for you?"

Kate heard the gentle concern in his voice and she knew she could talk to him, but not this night. Her own pain was too great to let it free yet. She reached her hand out to him and he took it in his. "Luca, I just need to be alone. But thank you for checking." She squeezed his hand to let him know she was okay, and that he could leave.

He looked at her small hand in his, so white against his dark skin, so fragile, and he felt why master was so protective of her. He released her hand as he stood to leave.

"I'll leave you then, but please, if there's anything you need..."

He started to leave the room when she spoke. "There is one thing, Luca...one thing I need."

"Yes, my lady, anything."

"When we're in this room, when we're alone, I need you to call me Kate."

He dropped his head and closed his eyes. He could already feel master's wrath if he ever heard him address her as such. He knew this was a line he shouldn't cross, but he couldn't deny her request. He raised his head and looked at her and spoke her name aloud for the first time, "Kate."

She felt his inner turmoil as he struggled with the request, but then he said her name. She mouthed the words "thank you" and then turned her back on him, curling herself into a ball, clinging to the stuffed bear.

He left the room, wishing he knew how to fix her, and Shade, and how to get the life back in this house.

***

For Shade, it was a very different night. As dawn approached, he was getting ready to head for home. The night had been long, but there was still an intense edginess inside him. There were not enough rogues for him to let loose on, but they were popping up in the strangest places, no rhyme or reason, and he kept running it through his mind. He stayed close to his grid in G-town, in case they moved their activity closer to Alec, but the rogues stayed on the outskirts of the city, slaughtering, draining, and leaving their victims lay in the open. It made no fucking sense to him.

If they wanted to draw a lot of attention, why not come into the heavily populated areas with a lot of nightlife? He was trying to keep one step ahead of their next strike and it kept his mind in a tangle. He had no fear. They would get them all, the bastards, each one branded with the same Aries tat. This wasn't a few random rogue attacks that were unrelated, as they earlier thought. This was a well-planned and organized strike and was much bigger than they originally perceived.

Wrapping up for the night, he swung by the Dead House, got a kill count, and sent them all home. He wasn't too badly messed up, but he needed a shower and there was blood all over his boots. He teleported home, landing outside the French doors that led into Luca's suite. He tapped lightly on the door and entered. Luca was awake as usual and painting at his easel and looked up as he entered.

Shade nodded. "Anything happen here?"

Luca looked him over. He seemed a bit more relaxed, but there were still underlying signs of his master's frustration. Luca wouldn't tell him much, he wouldn't speak of the worry he held for my lady. He felt sure she'd soon emerge from the nursery and not spend her time locked away in that room. No need to add to his master's burden. Plus he'd keep my lady's secrets.

"Nothing happened here, master, everything's fine. Quiet. Looks like you had some success by your appearance, but I don't think it would be a great idea to go to your mate looking like that."

Shade looked down at himself and decided he was right. "Damn Luca, let me use your shower, that way *bel* won't see the clothes or boots, and Gi can get them before she notices, *si*?"

Luca nodded. "Whatever you need, master."

As Luca shrugged, Shade stripped the bloodied leathers from his body, stepping into the shower stall and allowing the hot water to wash off the night.

***

Kate felt, as much as heard him when he entered the house, and she jumped up from the small bed in the nursery and ran to their bedroom, pulling back the sheets and climbing in. She kicked at the blankets to make the bed look tumbled and slept in. She never wanted him to see her hiding in the nursery. It was where she went to feel the pain, and he had enough of his own pain to carry around.

Quietly making his way to their bedroom, he felt better, the hell of the night washed away, his hair still wet. Shade walked in and found her asleep. She looked better, but he didn't feel any better about her condition. Already naked, he dropped the towel and climbed in beside her. It was impossible to slip unnoticed into any bed at his size, he was no small vampire and the bed always sank when he climbed in, but he had come to like it. It always made her roll toward him. He pulled her into him, as his hands caressed those crimson locks he adored and closed his eyes. "I am home, *mi amore*, right here with you."

She kissed his chest as she nuzzled into him. "Lover...I missed you," she whispered to him.

Smiling softly, his heart took a small leap that she was recovering. At least she was talking to him, and just feeling her closeness to him made him feel better. He needed this so desperately, to have her in his arms, feel her, and protect her. "I missed you too, but things are beginning to stir in D.C. and I needed to be out there, it is my job. But as I have promised, I will always come home to you, my *bel rosso*."

She listened to his voice with her head on his chest, felt the vibrations of his deep tone, and it struck right to her heart. She loved him with every cell of her being. "I understand. I hate when you're away, and I worry...but I understand."

She reached up and stroked his cheek with her hand. "I love you, Shade. I feel like I haven't said that enough lately. So much...too much..." She couldn't finish the sentence, she wasn't ready to talk to him about all that had happened, and she wouldn't burden him further. "Lover, just know what's in my heart."

As her hand stroked his cheek, he wanted to curl inside her, fill her void, make her whole again, but he couldn't do that. He couldn't fix all the hell she was going through, and it broke him all over again.

"I know what is in your heart, because I hold it within my own, and nothing will tear me from you or you from me. Just remember, this love is for eternity, and I never take that lightly. *Bel*..."

He wanted to tell her there would be more babies, but he knew however many children they had, they couldn't replace one child with another. "I love you, and if you can possibly say it to me before I walk out that door each night, it gives me a thousand times more strength, because I fight to return to you."

It broke her heart that she hadn't said those words to him last night. She raised herself up and looked into his eyes. "Lover, you'll never leave this house again without hearing those words. I'm so sorry. I've felt so broken, and you've protected me from it all. I've felt so disconnected when I was sick, lost in the darkness...and afterwards."

She felt her eyes burn with tears that wanted to fall, but she wouldn't let him see her cry again. She closed her eyes and kissed his sweet mouth, before tucking her head into his neck. "I love you more than life."

"It is okay, I know you hurt, it will pass with time. But this was my *bambino* as well. We must push through it. We will fight this together, if we do not, we each lose the other and by fucking hell, I will never lose you! Now sleep, I am tired, I am here, I love you, nothing will touch you, and when I come home tomorrow night, you will feed. It will make you feel better. We will fight, we will win, and in the end, our love will conquer."

She clung to him as she heard his words. She wouldn't drag him down. And she couldn't lose him. Losing the baby was her worst hell, but losing Shade, it was unthinkable. A pain she could never bear.

"Yes, lover…sleep." Her head on his chest, cradled in his arms, she felt him slip into his death slumber.

90

Kate felt his absence as he teleported from the house. It felt like more than she could bear, and yet, she knew this was how he'd deal with his own pain. He was a warrior, and heaven help anything in his path. But where did she put all of her pain? She couldn't lay it at his feet, she couldn't. She curled up on their bed, and drifted into a light sleep when she was awakened by the sound of a baby's cry. She sat upright and slipped from their bed, walking into the nursery. The crib was empty. She ran her hand across the sheets as the tears fell. *Oh, my little warrior...I'm so sorry...I failed you.*

She walked through the room, touching the things that were to have been his; his bed, his dresser, his toys, his books, his clothes. She felt her soul shattering into a million pieces, and she wondered if she could put it all back together again. She walked to the nanny's bed and lay down, letting the tears flow, as she clutched a soft teddy bear to her chest.

Luca could hear my lady moving about upstairs. She hadn't come downstairs since master brought her back from California. He walked up the stairs to check on her. The bedroom door was open, and he stepped lightly into the room, but she wasn't there. He turned to walk down the hall when he caught a glimpse of her in the nursery. He stood in the doorway and watched as she lay on the small twin bed she had set up for Theresa, clutching a stuffed toy as silent tears fell down her cheeks. He took a deep breath and wondered if he should even interrupt her. He was much better equipped to deal with Shade's anger than my lady's sorrow. She seemed completely unaware of his presence. He stepped into the room and she turned her head toward him, and he was confronted with her pain filled eyes. He walked to the chair by the bed and sat next to her.

"My lady, is there anything I can do for you?"

Kate heard the gentle concern in his voice and she knew she could talk to him, but not this night. Her own pain was too great to let it free yet. She reached her hand out to him and he took it in his. "Luca, I just need to be alone. But thank you for checking." She squeezed his hand to let him know she was okay, and that he could leave.

He looked at her small hand in his, so white against his dark skin, so fragile, and he felt why master was so protective of her. He released her hand as he stood to leave.

"I'll leave you then, but please, if there's anything you need..." He started to leave the room when she spoke.

"There is one thing, Luca....One thing I need."

"Yes, my lady, anything."

"When we're in this room, when we're alone, I need you to call me Kate."

He dropped his head and closed his eyes. He could already feel master's wrath if he ever heard him address her as such. He knew this was a line he shouldn't cross, but he couldn't deny her request. He raised his head and looked at her and spoke her name aloud for the first time. "Kate."

She felt his inner turmoil as he struggled with the request, but then he said her name. She mouthed the words "thank you" and then turned her back on him, curling herself into a ball, clinging to the stuffed bear.

He left the room, wishing he knew how to fix her, and Shade, and how to get the life back in this house.

***

For Shade, it was a very different night. As dawn approached, he was getting ready to head for home. The night had been long, but there was still an intense edginess inside him. There were not enough rogues for him to let loose on, but they were popping up in the strangest places, no rhyme or reason, and he kept running it through his mind. He stayed close to his grid in G-town, in case they moved their activity closer to Alec, but the rogues stayed on the outskirts of the city, slaughtering, draining, and leaving their victims lay in the open. It made no fucking sense to him.

If they wanted to draw a lot of attention, why not come into the heavily populated areas with a lot of nightlife? He was trying to keep one step ahead of their next strike and it kept his mind in a tangle. He had no fear. They would get them all, the bastards, each one branded with the same Aries tat. This wasn't a few random rogue attacks that were unrelated as they had earlier thought. This was a well-planned and organized strike and was much bigger than they originally perceived.

Wrapping up for the night, he swung by the Dead House, got a kill count, and sent them all home. He wasn't too badly messed up, but he needed a shower and there was blood all over his boots. He teleported home, landing outside the French doors that led into Luca's suite. He tapped lightly on the door and entered. Luca was awake as usual and painting at his easel and looked up as he entered.

Shade nodded. "Anything happen here?"

Luca looked him over. He seemed a bit more relaxed, but there were still underlying signs of his master's frustration. Luca wouldn't tell him much, he wouldn't speak of the worry he held for my lady. He felt sure she'd soon emerge from the nursery and not spend her time locked away in that room. No need to add to his master's burden. Plus he'd keep my lady's secrets.

"Nothing happened here, master, everything's fine. Quiet. Looks like you had some success by your appearance, but I don't think it would be a great idea to go to your mate looking like that."

Shade looked down at himself and decided he was right. "Damn Luca, let me use your shower, that way *bel* won't see the clothes or boots, and Gi can get them before she notices, *si*?"

Luca nodded. "Whatever you need, master."

As Luca shrugged, Shade stripped the bloodied leathers from his body, stepping into the shower stall and allowing the hot water to wash off the night.

***

Kate felt, as much as heard, him when he entered the house, and she jumped up from the small bed in the nursery and ran to their bedroom, pulling back the sheets and climbing in. She kicked at the blankets to make the bed look tumbled and slept in. She never wanted him to see her hiding in the nursery. It was where she went to feel the pain, and he had enough of his own pain to carry around.

Quietly making his way to their bedroom, he felt better, the hell of the night washed away, his hair still wet. Shade walked in and found her asleep. She looked better, but he didn't feel any better about her condition. Already naked, he dropped the towel and climbed in beside her. It was impossible to slip unnoticed into any bed at his size, he was no small vampire and the bed always sank when he climbed in, but he had come to like it as it always made her roll toward him. He pulled her into him, as his hands caressed those crimson locks he adored and closed his eyes.

"I am home, *mi amore*, right here with you."

She kissed his chest as she nuzzled into him. "Lover... I missed you," she whispers to him.

Smiling softly, his heart took a small leap that she was recovering. At least she was talking to him, and just feeling her closeness to him made him feel better. He needed this so desperately, to have her in his arms, feel her, and protect her.

"I missed you too, but things are beginning to stir in D.C. and I needed to be out there, it is my job. But as I have promised, I will always come home to you, my *bel rosso*."

She listened to his voice with her head on his chest, felt the vibrations of his deep tone, and it struck right to her heart. She loved him with every cell of her being. "I understand. I hate when you're away, and I worry...but I understand."

She reached up and stroked his cheek with her hand. "I love you, Shade. I feel like I haven't said that enough lately...So much...Too much..." She couldn't finish the sentence, she wasn't ready to talk to him about all that had happened, and she wouldn't burden him further. "Lover, just know what's in my heart."

As her hand stroked his cheek, he wanted to curl inside her, fill her void, make her whole again, but he couldn't do that. He couldn't fix all the hell she was going through, and it broke him all over again.

"I know what is in your heart, because I hold it within my own, and nothing will tear me from you or you from me. Just remember this love is for eternity, and I never take that lightly. *Bel*..."

He wanted to tell her there would be more babies, but he knew however many children they had, they couldn't replace one child with another. "I love you, and if you can possibly say it to me before I walk out that door each night, it gives me a thousand times more strength, because I fight to return to you."

It broke her heart that she hadn't said those words to him last night. She raised herself up and looked into his eyes. "Lover, you'll never leave this house again without hearing those words. I'm so sorry. I've felt so broken, and you've protected me from it all. I've felt so disconnected when I was sick, lost in the darkness...and afterwards."

She felt her eyes burn with tears that wanted to fall, but she wouldn't let him see her cry again. She closed her eyes and kissed his sweet mouth, before tucking her head into his neck. "I love you more than life."

"It is okay, I know you hurt, it will pass with time. But this was my *bambino* as well. We must push through it. We will fight this together, if we do not, we each lose the other and by fucking hell, I will never lose you! Now sleep, I am tired, I am here, I love you, nothing will touch you, and when I come home tomorrow night, you will feed. It will make you feel better. We will fight, we will win, and in the end, our love will conquer."

She clung to him as she heard his words. She wouldn't drag him down. And she couldn't lose him. Losing the baby was her worst hell, but losing Shade, it was unthinkable. A pain she could never bear.

"Yes, lover... sleep." Her head on his chest, cradled in his arms, she felt him slip into his death slumber.

91

Rissa kept looking over her shoulder. She was used to the photographers, although they seemed to cling to Alec more than her. Tonight, as she did her socializing without him, they were following her. Her gut was telling her something wasn't right, and she had learned to trust her instincts. She was used to their celebrity status in this town. They worked hard to craft their reputation, and it was a part of who they were. She and Alec were the darling couple of Washington politics, and many eyes were always upon them, so she tended to not pay much attention to the cameras and phones pointed in their direction. Hell, she worked it to their advantage, always doing the right thing, wearing the right thing, and saying the right thing. Her vampire ran this damn town and before long, the whole world would know his name, and hers.

As the night wore down, she began to notice the paparazzi thinning out. There was nothing unusual about that since Alec wasn't with her. But there was one guy she'd never seen before, and he looked out of place. He wore a ball cap low over his eyes, sunglasses, and dark clothing. She tried to concentrate on him, but he'd appear and disappear so quickly in the crowd, she could never get a good look at him.

Making her last stop of the night, she needed to run into the fashionable night spot and make an appearance for a friend. Rissa entered the club, and the music pounded her. She took a drink from a passing waiter and held it in her hand, chatting with her friend, making sure the crowd saw her. There was no Midnight available, so she pretended to sip at her drink. She didn't want to seem in a hurry, this party was an important gig, and Rissa needed to make some contacts. She stayed for about an hour, making the rounds then making her excuses, always explaining that Alec was waiting for her, and of course, they understood. Hell, most of the women turned green with envy at the mention of his name and she loved it. He belonged to her and there was no way in hell they'd ever have him, but she knew there were plenty of women who saw Rissa as a way to get to him. *Stupid bitches, not a chance in hell.*

Exiting the night spot, the suspicious photographer appeared out of nowhere, clicking away, close to her, blinding her, and she stopped dead in her tracks, lifting her arms in a defensive manner against anything that might attack. He was vampire, and suddenly, all her instincts went into overdrive. It happened in a flash and then he was gone, no trace of him. Was he after photos, or something else? Rissa brushed it off, and filed it away, reminding herself to be on guard.

She teleported home and decided not to mention this to Alec. It was, after all, nothing. And she didn't want any restrictions placed on her schedule.

The next day, Rissa ran from one appointment to the next, her day went by fast, but she was constantly on alert, her senses tuned for anything suspicious. The night before had her unnerved, wondering what the hell that vampire was doing so close to her. As the work day came to an end, she headed for the gym. Working out was her way of relaxing, releasing some energy while building her body and keeping strong for most anything, but especially for sexual activities with Alec. He liked her sleek and firm, and she had to be able to handle his sometimes-unusual sexual appetite. He wasn't one to take anything easy, much preferring to push the limits of what she could endure, and she loved it.

Kickboxing was one of her favorite exercises. It was fun, and it worked out her whole body, made her sharp and above all, gave her time to think. Wrapping her hands, she went after the bag next; punching, kicking, taking out her anger and stress on that bag. She was strong, stronger than a mortal, but not as strong as those who were born vampire. Still, she had to be careful not to draw the attention of mortals.

Next, she did a one-hour spin class, pushing her body. Getting ready to cool down, she glanced at the clock and realized it was past 10:00 p.m. and she'd been here for hours. She felt like she could go longer, wanted to go longer, but knew she'd better get home soon. Alec would wonder what the hell she was up to. Not bothering to hit the showers, she gathered her things and headed home.

Alec could sense Rissa was ill at ease. She wasn't angry or afraid, but something was bothering her. He tuned in to her, reached out to see where she was, picking up an image of her working out at the gym. He could feel something definitely had her worried. The gym was her outlet. He needed to talk to her when she got home. After the conversation with Shade, this coven seemed much larger, much more organized than they had originally thought. They didn't seem to care if their activities were exposed to mortals, and there was nothing more dangerous than a vamp who liked to flaunt his prowess in front of mortals. Rissa needed to be on guard. Hell, they both needed to be on guard.

92

Waking from his death slumber, the sun had not yet set. Shade got up, dressed, ready to get back to the streets. Before heading down to the bunker, he stood beside the bed and looked at *bel*. She was the most beautiful woman he'd ever seen, and he knew he needed to wake her and tell her he was leaving. Softly kissing her cheek, he slid his hand over her breast and whispered in her ear, "*Mi amore*, I need to go, I won't be back early. Luca is here, *bel*. Call if you need me. *Ti amo*."

Kate was pulled from her sleep as she heard him whisper his goodbyes. "Then be careful, please, come back to me. I love you, Shade. I need you."

Her response irritated him, and he knew he was over reacting, but the words were out of his mouth before he could think. "Have faith in your damn warrior."

Walking out of the room, it ruffled him that she thought he'd get hurt or not come back. Fuck, he would drag his body home to be with her. Slamming into the bunker, he loaded up with weapons and yelled at Luca, "I'm out. Get your ass to my mate!"

Teleporting out to the Dead House, he was more than ready to rip the fuck out of something this night.

As Shade left her, she felt his anger. Kate knew it wasn't directed toward her. She knew he suffered in his own way. This bed, where they had shared such passion, felt so cold to her now. He didn't touch her in the same way. He held her like a fragile china doll. She slipped from beneath the sheets where, only seconds ago, he laid beside her, and she returned to the nursery.

This room was meant to hold such joy but seemed to be the only place she could let go of her pain. Someone had made the nanny's bed where she'd spent the previous night. Most likely it was Theresa, which meant the staff knew she came here to grieve. Kate climbed atop the twin bed, drew her knees up to her chest and laid her head on her knees, letting the pent up tears flow. She wept for the loss of their baby, and she wept for the loss of Shade, for the loss of them as a couple, as they used to be.

Luca walked up the stairs and headed for their bedroom again, only to find the room empty. He didn't need to look for her tonight. He knew exactly where to find her. He walked to the nursery and saw her on the bed and heard her soft sobs. Master would never have left her like this. She was hiding her grief from him, as he hid his from her. He stepped inside the room and she looked up at him. They locked eyes, and she put her hand on the chair by the bed, indicating she wanted him to sit with her. He walked over and sat in the chair, facing her, waiting in silence for her to speak.

"I feel like I'm drowning and everyone around me is just watching me sink, helpless to save me. He can't save me. I have to save myself. I'll either pull him under with me or he'll have to break free of me to save himself. Am I losing him, Luca? I tried so hard to mask my pain while he was here, but he barely stayed through the daylight. A few minutes of his time before his death slumber, and then he wakes before sunset and leaves me."

"My lady...Kate...he grieves in his own way. I assure you, you aren't losing him. I have known him my whole life. You know our history. There is no one I respect more, love more. In all of my life, I've never seen him as happy, as devoted, as he is with you. He finds his strength in you."

"But not now. He finds no strength in me now. I'm lost in the darkness and I can't find my way back. I want to go back. I want to get back to us, and a time when I could smile and laugh, and it didn't take everything in me to do it."

"That comes with time, Kate. This is all so fresh. You both need time to heal."

"But in the healing...there's so much pain in the healing, and I get so afraid we'll never get back to where we were. I bear so much of the blame."

"There's no blame, Kate. You can't carry that around. This is no one's fault. You lost your baby. You had no control over that."

"But it is my fault. It's my fault I was even pregnant in the first place. I wasn't doing anything to prevent a pregnancy. I assumed, since he was immortal...I don't know, I assumed nothing could happen. He was angry when I told him. This wasn't what he planned for us. And then, I learn once I'm pregnant a mortal/immortal pregnancy is high risk, so even from the beginning our baby..." Tears streamed down her face. "Stupid, stupid decisions. I put us in this place. I lost our baby, and

I put Shade in this place. Tell me how that isn't my fault. Tell me how he won't see it as my fault."

"I watch him with you. I know him, and I can tell you, he's carrying this entire burden on his own shoulders. His need to protect you overrides everything else. I watch him when he's angry or frustrated with you, and it dissipates in minutes. He can't even hold onto that. His love for you consumes him. Be patient with him. You both just need time."

"I can be patient with him. I can wait a lifetime for him if I have to. I fear he'll get tired of waiting for me. Get tired of the drama. I try to fit into his world, but he still shields me from so much. I think his life was much simpler before I came along."

Luca smiled slightly. "Simpler, maybe, but much lonelier. I assure you, Kate, he'll always choose a life with you in it, regardless of the drama. You can never appreciate the isolation and loneliness of a warrior."

"Are you lonely, Luca?"

He held up both hands and laughed. "Oh no, you aren't going to make this about me."

She giggled at his response. "I'm going to find you a girlfriend, Luca."

He stood up and started backing out of the room. "And on that note, my lady, I'm leaving. Call me if you need anything."

She watched as he left the room, and realized she had a smile on her face. It slowly faded as the pain crept back in and gripped her heart. She lay down on the bed, holding the bear, and let the hours pass.

93

The warriors spanned out, taking their assigned quadrants and providing cover for the city. It was the easiest way to monitor activity against the fucking rogues who just popped up with complete unpredictability, then killed and left their drained victims on display. Shade stayed in the Dead House, monitoring his crew and directing their movements for hours, and he was getting more edgy by the minute. None of this made any fucking sense to him. Who the fuck were they? And why the hell didn't Alec know them?

Shade had well over twenty warriors on the streets, and not a damn one of them could get a strike. It was so fucking random, and whoever these Aries rogues were, they were keeping well-disguised. It was cold here. It was snowing hard and everyone was bundled up like fucking Eskimos. He had whipped Alec's crew into good warriors, not like his, not exceptional, but decent and they should be able to smell out a vampire five miles off, but they couldn't.

He sent them out in teams of three. Two to hunt, one to bring back the dead left behind. If even one body was found by the mortals, Alec would have his head, not to mention, they all risked being exposed. The longer he was shackled up inside the Dead House, the worse his attitude got until he bolted out alone. Nothing was going to fuck with him tonight. He was ripped, emotionally ragged, and ready to take them all on, if he could find them.

He scanned for miles and began to think this would be another wasted night for him, when he decided to hang out on the edges of Georgetown. Nothing seemed to be happening in this grid closest to Alec, and that also had him confused. Shade personally went down there every night to check it out for a few hours before sunrise. He was determined to figure these bastards out, if it was the last thing he ever did.

As he lit up a smoke, he dropped down to street level, walking among all the pretty people who had more fucking money than sense in this damn town. He hated it here. D.C. was not Florence, and he wouldn't have stayed if it hadn't been for *bel*. She was the only damn thing keeping him here, and he wasn't sure he could even hang onto her anymore. She was in a place he couldn't reach, lost in pain he could not fix. Then his eyes caught something, stragglers who looked out of place here. They weren't blending in, and he knew in his gut they were rogues.

Instinctively, Shade called for backup to surround this area, but he wasn't waiting for anyone to get there, these rogues belonged to him. There were four of them wearing sweats and hoodies, looking like wanna-be gangsters and totally out of place in this upscale neighborhood. They were clearly hunting when they got a whiff of him, and the battle began.

He drew them into an alley, away from the crowds. Things moved fast, and the rogues were quickly all over him. He relished in the adrenaline rush of battle, the speed, the alert and focused mind, and his skill with weapons. He took two of the rogues out, removing their heads with a single swing of his sword. The other two played cat and mouse, stayed with him, trying to circle him. *You fucking little pups, you will not wear me down.* Then he felt the sudden pain as a shuriken sliced into his arm. Shade didn't stop or even look down. He let his anger and pain fuel his fight, as he nailed the rogue through the heart. Suddenly, his own warriors were surrounding them, and there was only one lone rogue left. "You are mine, you scum sucking piece of shit!"

Shade's warriors made a seething, hissing circle enclosing them, as the rogue stood speechless.

"Full of fight until you are confronted by real warriors, is that it? Talk and you will come out alive. Keep fucking with me and you will die like your *compadres*."

The rogue came at Shade at a blistering speed, invisible to the mortal eye, and yanked on the shuriken sticking out of his arm. Shade screamed from the pain, and tried to grab the rogue's neck, but the rogue maneuvered out of his grasp. Shade did a backflip and slammed his fist straight into the rogue's chest cavity, ripping out his heart and squeezing it in his hand until it oozed through his fingers. The rogue stared back with a look of surprise, as Shade held his beating heart in front of his face, in that split second before the rogue dropped dead to the street.

Shade ripped the clothes off the rogues back to discover the Aries tattoo. "Get these bodies off the street and take their asses back to the Dead House. I need to get home. Call in the rest of the warriors for the night, the sun will be up soon, so we are done here. I need to rest, as do all of you. We will have the same schedule for tomorrow night. This is how we hunt where I am from. So, take heed and get it done!"

Teleporting home, his arm was damn near useless until he could extract this fucking shuriken. Shade stumbled in through Luca's entrance from the patio, to see him waiting and pacing. Luca had felt that something had gone wrong. As he made it inside, Shade just looked at him. "Need your help. Shuriken lodged in my arm. Fuck!"

Shade slid down to the floor. He felt like shit and the adrenaline was wearing off.

Luca knew he had to be in pain and he'd lost some blood. Luca cut away the jacket around the shuriken lodged deep into his bicep. He shook his head, looking at the jagged saw-tooth teeth of the shuriken lodged deep in the tissue. "This is going to fucking hurt."

"Yeah, just do it, Luca. I need to get to *bel*, I need to clean up. I need to sleep."

Shade laid his head back and braced himself for the pain, but Luca appeared to be stalling. "What are you waiting for? Just fucking do it!"

Luca winced. "Shade, you've already started to heal around the blades. I'll have to rip it free, one stroke, then bind it up quickly until you heal."

"Do it!"

Shade felt Luca's hand around the blade as his other hand was pushed hard against his shoulder, bracing him for the pain. The pain screamed up his arm and into his neck as Luca ripped the shuriken free. It tore through the muscle, making Shade's head spin.

"Master, let me help you up, you need to bathe before I can bind it, come on."

Luca hoisted him to his feet. He knew his master would heal before the next sunset. Luca helped him to shower; standing close by and letting Shade clean himself off, helping him as much as he could. He could tell Shade was feeling better just washing away the grime and blood from his body.

Shade left the shower and toweled off as Luca immediately wrapped his wound. The bleeding had stopped, and he tried not to think about how fucking lucky he was to still have his damn arm.

Luca finished wrapping the wound. "Master, do you need to feed? Are you feeding at all?"

"I am fine, I only feed from *bel* now, and I haven't lost enough to make a difference. The wound has already sealed over. Anything happen tonight?"

Luca shook his head. "No, my lady is fine, quiet night. She...sleeps."

Shade left his bloody and torn clothing behind as he left Luca's suite. "Good, heading up to her now. Fuck, I am tired, Luca."

Heading up the stairs, the towel wrapped around his waist, he felt so tired and lost, and he hoped *bel* was asleep and didn't notice the binding around his arm.

Kate heard him come in downstairs again and knew he'd go to Luca's suite and shower like before, so she rushed from the nursery and ran to their bedroom. She ripped down the blankets and tossed the pillows around before climbing under the sheets. She could hear the shower running, and then the water stopped. She waited for him, but still, he didn't come to her. Her already broken heart felt the pain. She knew he was avoiding her. He was fighting his own pain and couldn't carry hers as well. Luca said she wasn't losing him, but she felt him slipping away from her, and she didn't know how to stop it.

Shade entered their bedroom quietly and slid into the bed beside her. He pulled her onto his chest. She stirred and he could tell she was awake. "I am home, *bel*."

Kate draped her arm across his chest, her leg across his legs. His skin and hair were still damp, and she was aware of the fresh bandage on his arm. She knew he fought. She knew all his anger was taken out in battle, but she wouldn't make the same mistake as this morning. Her worry over his safety only angered him.

"Lover, I've missed you."

Shade nuzzled his face into her crimson locks. "Not as much as I have missed you. I want you to feed. I need to know you are strong. I worry about that. Will you please, for me?" He tilted up her chin, looking deep into her eyes. "I love you. I want you to be strong for me."

Kate fought back her tears. She hungered for his touch and he'd felt so far away from her, if he only knew how desperately she had craved him, and yet, she didn't feel wanted or welcomed in his embrace. She felt like his obligation, not his mate. Looking into his eyes with his dark damp hair falling around his face, she kissed his forehead, and his nose and then his lips, hoping she wouldn't feel rejection.

He returned her kiss, grasping the back of her head, fisting her soft silky hair and moaned. "Please *mi amore*, take from me, I need to feel you, know you still love me, need me."

His touch was the touch she needed to feel, his words were the words she needed to heal, and she slid her lips across his cheek and his strong jaw, down to his neck where she licked at his vein and kissed his neck before she bit hard and felt the rush of his blood into her mouth. She moaned with the pleasure it brought. She felt him arch his neck as his head was thrown back on the pillow and a low moan escaped his lips. She couldn't remember when she last fed from him, it seemed so long ago, so much pain ago. But he would heal her, and she'd heal him. She felt his cock grow hard as steel against her leg, and she slid her leg against him as she drew deeply from his neck, the heat between her own legs building. **"I know you battle, I feel your anger and your pain, but I'm in a battle too, and I won't lose you. I'm fighting my way back to you. Please don't give up on me."**

"Never, *bel*, I will never give up."

She gripped his shoulder with her hand as she drank from him with an unquenchable thirst. Her need for him overcame her pain, her hurt, her loss, and right now, she only wanted him, only needed him. She broke away from his neck and covered his mouth with hers, her tongue probing at his, her hand sliding down his chest, across his hard abdomen and into that tight mass of curls before wrapping her hand around his cock.

"Now take me, lover, and feed from me. Heal us...heal us both."

She lowered her head beside his, her neck at his lips, she could feel his breath on her, and she needed to feel the sharp bite of his fangs. She needed to feel his hands with their strong firm grip as they explored her body. She needed to feel him inside her.

Shade felt her desire and his own need overpowered him. She was his and no one else would ever fill the void she filled in him. Sliding his hands slowly down her body, he gripped her hips gently and eased inside her. His moan was deep and low. Sinking his fangs into her neck, he drew deep and groaned with pleasure, drawing softly, taking it easy on her as he felt her body move into a slow, sweet glide on his erection and he rubbed her back, encouraging her to set her own pace. It was *bel rosso* and her savage lover, joined in their love for each other.

Kate had missed him so much. Her love for him overwhelmed and she felt the tears fall. She buried her face because she didn't want him to misunderstand her tears. They were tears of love, not grief. Her hips glided slowly up and down as she rode his shaft, and she felt him respond to her, matching the rhythm. When he fed from her, she felt it was a turning point, a small one, but she felt him open up to her. Her own body responded as he bit and drank again, and it was like an electric current that ran through her. She thrust harder against him, feeling his cock throbbing deep inside of her, and it sent shivers down her spine. He drank slowly from her, still cautious, but each swallow he took increased the heat between her legs. As he unlatched and broke away from her neck, she sat upright on him, taking all of him, letting him fill her. She rode him hard, because she knew it was what he needed, what they both needed, to find their way back to each other. She watched as he threw back his head and she heard the growl that rumbled up from deep in his chest, mouth open and fangs bared. His dick throbbed and released. She felt her body respond to his when that delicious wave of ecstasy flowed over both of them, again and again, before she collapsed onto his chest, breath ragged, heart pounding. She placed her hands on either side of his face and kissed him, and with her lips still against his, she repeated to him, "I love you, I love you, I love you."

“I love you so fucking much! Please tell me you are coming back to me. I cannot bear much more without you.” He wrapped himself tightly around her and buried his head into her neck. “Don’t leave me, *bel*, I need you. I need to come home to you. You are all to me, everything. And without you, I am nothing.”

Holding her, he felt the pull of the coming dawn, the wear and tear on his body, the sweet release of emotions and the words they both had left unsaid for far too long, as he was being pulled deep into his slumber.

Kate heard the pain and anguish in his words. She knew he was hurting as much as she was, and the separation between them had to end. She couldn’t bear his absence in her life. This emotional barrier they had built between them had to go, and they would tear it down. Tonight, they removed a few bricks from that wall, but she knew they both had to break through it, if they were going to come out on the other side together.

“I could never leave you, Shade.”

She stroked his face as she slid off him, lying beside him, head on his chest, and hand to his cheek, her leg tossed across his. She felt his arms around her. Felt his body relax and she knew he would slip into his death slumber soon.

"Sleep my savage lover, and your *bel rosso* sleeps next to you."

She fell asleep next to him, a calm sleep, not tormented by the sound of the baby crying. It was the first time she'd slept since losing the baby that she hadn't heard that sound. The day passed too quickly, and as the sun set, she felt him stir and quietly slip from their bed, dressing himself all in leather. She watched him as he dressed, knowing he prepared himself for another night of battle when he suddenly looked up at her.

"I did not wish to wake you, you were sleeping so soundly."

"Lover, I'd be upset if you didn't wake me. I hope you never leave our bed without waking me."

He walked to their bed and sat down next to her, running his hand through her hair and bent to kiss her. *"Ti amo*."

She remembered his reaction to her request of yesterday to be careful, and she had noticed the bandage around his arm. She would never stop worrying about him, but she knew it wasn't what he wanted to hear. It wasn't what he needed to hear. "Fight well tonight, my savage warrior." She ran her hand across his cheek. "And never forget how much I love you."

94

Kate could hear him downstairs in the bunker, and she felt when he left. Almost immediately, the darkness gripped at her, tried to pull her down. She slipped from their bed and moved to the bathroom, stepping into the shower, letting the hot water pour over her. She stood still and let her tears flow, masked by the water. She could cry here, and no one would hear her. All of the memories of Shade rushed back at her, the memories of them together, and she wanted him back, full time.

She had made herself numb to try to block the pain, but she had realized she couldn't numb herself to the painful loss of their baby, without numbing herself to all the other emotions as well. She couldn't selectively numb, so when she numbed the pain, she also numbed the joy, and gratitude, and happiness, and most importantly, the love. She had lost this baby, and she couldn't lose Shade. She had to find the strength to pull herself out of this maze of grief. She finished her shower, stepped out and toweled off, and made some effort to put herself together, to reclaim her routine. She dressed and headed downstairs to a startled Gi.

"My lady, is there anything I can get for you?"

"Nothing now, thank you, I'm just going to the kitchen, see if Reynaldo can fix me something."

Reynaldo wanted to fix a huge breakfast, but she begged off with coffee, juice, and toast. After eating, she headed upstairs to return to their bedroom, but as she walked past the nursery, she felt the pull. It was like a hand reaching out, grabbing at her, pulling her in, and she gave in and entered the room.

She walked over to the nanny's bed, which had once again been made. She said a silent prayer, thanking the house staff for keeping her secret from Shade. Perhaps the staff knew they were both bearing as much burden as they could carry right now. She sat on the bed, her back against the pillows, and she could feel him, their baby. She couldn't remember what it felt like to not be broken, and she could feel the darkness pulling at her. She saw a shadow across the door and looked up to see Luca. She gave him a sad smile. "Guess you knew where to find me."

He sighed and just stared at her. "Kate, it's not my place, but you know this has to end."

She motioned for him to join her, and he walked over and sat in the chair by the bed.

"I know. I'll be okay, just not today. Have you told him? About this?"

Luca shook his head. "Of course not, and I won't unless...unless I think you can't find your way back. You're both working through your grief, in your own way. But you've placed me in the middle here."

She reached out and took his hand. "I know that. I understand your loyalty to him, and please believe me when I say, I understand the position I've placed you in. I can't thank you enough, for being here, for listening. He was hurt last night, wasn't he?"

He paused before answering, deciding how much he could share. "Yes, but it was a small wound, delivered by a poorly delivered shuriken."

She creased her brow. "A what?"

"Oh...uh...I think you call them 'those shiny star-shaped thingies.'" He tried to suppress a smile. "But you don't need to worry about master. Like me, he has trained all his life to be a warrior."

"Trained...I have news for you, Luca. Warriors aren't trained. Speed and strength are developed through training. Knowledge of weapons is developed through training. But a warrior is one who chooses to stand between their enemy and all that he loves and holds sacred. That's in the heart. You can't teach that. You are born with it. Shade was born with it. You were born with it. Warriors are born. The training just improves their skills."

He looked at her a second before responding, "I have underestimated you, Kate. But you know, you have a warrior's heart as well. I watched you attack the feeder. Stupid move by the way, but you attacked with your heart, and not your head."

"I know it was stupid, but I'd do it again. And I have to fight for him again now. Fight through this pain we're both trapped in. But there's something I need to know."

"What? Whatever it is, if I have the answer...if it will help you...I'll tell you."

She looked him in the eyes. "I need to know where the baby is."

He sat upright, pulled his hand from hers, and paused a moment. “Stay here, I'll be right back.”

He left the room and went downstairs to find Gi, and together, they returned to the nursery.

They walked into the room together, and she looked from one to the other. Her eyes finally settling on Gi and she pleaded to him. "I need to know."

Gi nodded his head. “Yes, my lady, I knew the time would come. You understand we could not report this birth...this miscarriage. There could be no autopsy, no examination. We could not allow a mortal doctor to discover this baby was...different. But we loved the baby too, and I found a place for the baby, in the garden. When you were in California with master...I, all of us, we buried the baby. Do you wish to see him, my lady?"

She threw her hands over her face as the tears poured from her and she heard her own sobs. “Please...take me to him...”

Luca went to her and helped her off of the bed, and led her from the room, Gi walking ahead of them. As they reached the bottom of the stairs, Theresa was there, and she grasped Kate's hands. Kate saw the blood tears Theresa shed for the baby she never got to hold as well. As they all walked past the kitchen toward the back patio, Reynaldo joined them, and they walked outside. With Gi leading the way, they walked down the garden path.

“This way, my lady." Gi led them to the garden bench he’d made and placed there for her, surrounded by fresh plantings of lavender which wouldn’t bloom until spring, knowing this would not be her last visit to this spot. As they reached the bench, Luca directed her to sit. She looked at him with questioning eyes and he just nodded at her. “Sit please, Kate.”

Kate sat on the bench, still holding Luca's hand, surrounded by these people she loved when Gi spoke to her once again, "You understand, my lady, we can't have a traditional marker, nothing that would draw the attention of other mortals. But the baby is here, and I have marked the place with this garden statue of the cherub. We do not believe in angels, but I know in your culture...I hope this brings you peace."

The wave of grief and gratitude washed over her, and she didn’t block the pain. She knew, now, the only cure for the pain was through the pain, as she cried out loud to the heavens for her lost baby. She dropped from the bench to her knees as her body was wracked with sobs, and she felt Luca drop to the ground beside her. She leaned her head on his shoulder and cried until there were no tears left to cry. When she finally looked up, Gi, Theresa and Reynaldo were all still there. She felt their love, and their strength, and she couldn't begin to find the words to thank them for what they had done.

She started to stand and felt Luca's strong grip supporting her, so much like Shade's. She walked to the tiny cherub and laid a kiss on his head. **"Sleep, my tiny warrior. Sleep knowing how hard I fought for you. Sleep knowing how much your father loved you, how much all of these people loved you."**

She turned and looked at all of them, this was her family now. "Thank you. Thank you for this, for understanding I couldn't let him go. Thank you for understanding that, in my heart, I saw him growing up to be a man, and following in his father's footsteps, and that wasn't something to be thrown away. I'm ready to go back to the house now."

They all walked back to the house, but only Luca followed her upstairs. As she walked to their bedroom, they passed the nursery and she paused, the room pulling at her, calling to her.

Luca reached inside and grabbed the door knob, pulling the door closed. "No more, Kate, no more."

95

The night was long, but Shade remained inside the Dead House, managing things from the command center. The attacks were less frequent tonight, and that worried him even more. Was Aries hunkering down for a bigger, more aggressive attack to come? He spent some time giving the warriors a few tips on shuriken's and sword battle. He wanted them to be at the top of their game.

Heading home, he strolled in through Luca's entrance. He had no need to shower here tonight. He was fine and showed no telltale signs of a battle. Luca looked up from his easel and nodded, telling him all was well, another quiet night. Shade headed to the bedroom and quietly opened the door, hoping if she was asleep he didn't wake her, but always inside his heart, he hoped she was awake and waiting for him. At least, tonight, he was a bit early. The sun was still a good hour from rising, so, perhaps, that would make her a bit happier.

When he entered, he saw the bed was made and she was dressed, and he got a smile. "*Mi amore*...I am home."

She walked to him, sliding her arms around his waist, and laid her head against his chest. "I was waiting for you. You're home early. Did you have a good night?"

"*Si*. I stayed in the Dead House managing things mostly, boring stuff. I like when my *bel* is up and waiting for me, makes me feel good."

Bending down, he tipped up her chin and kissed her on the lips. "Mmm, and what was my minx up to this night?"

"Keeping busy. Missing you, mostly." She slid her arms from his waist and dropped them to his hands, holding both of his hands in hers as she looked up at him.

"I know I've been in a dark place that felt closed off from you, and I can't live like that. I've been fighting to get back to you, just as you fight every night. And I know how you spend your nights, even though you take great measures to protect me from it. I've felt your pain as I've felt my own. But I have something to show you...to share with you...if you think you're ready."

His brows furrowed. "Something to show me?"

Kate didn't know what his reaction would be. Would he find the same healing she'd found? Or would this bring more pain and heartbreak? She was torn with her decision. She took his hand and led him from their bedroom and down the stairs. "The sun isn't up yet...we have time."

They walked through the house, and out through the back-patio door into the early light of dawn. A light fog hung close to the ground and she turned and looked at him, and wondered again if she was doing the right thing?

"*Bel*, where the hell are you taking me, the sun will be up soon."

She could feel his turmoil, the questioning, and a part of her wanted to turn back, but something compelled her to move forward. Their baby called to her. "The garden, please walk with me to the garden, down this path and here to this bench."

She sat down, still holding his hand and pulled at him to sit next to her. She could see he was bewildered.

"Kate, please, what is it? I can feel your emotions rolling."

She gripped his hands in hers. "Our baby, lover. Our baby is here. Gi, Luca, Theresa, and Reynaldo...all of them. They buried our baby here, where he'll be with us forever. He's there. The angel marks his grave." Silent tears ran down her cheeks as she clung to his hands.

"The baby is...what?"

His looked at the garden statue, and realized this was the place where her heart came to heal, and provided an outlet for her emotional pain. He let go of her hands and knelt in front of the statue. Closing his eyes, he spoke to his son, **"I am so sorry, my *figlio*. I sacrificed your life, so I could keep her. Forgive your *padre*."** Laying his hand on top of the statue, he whispered in a tone filled with the pain and sorrow he had stored inside him, "Sleeping warrior."

Kate dropped to her knees beside him, put her arms around him as she leaned her head against his shoulder, and let the healing tears flow. It was the first time she'd felt okay to show him her pain, because she was no longer in the dark.

Shade felt her let go of the pain inside, and knew she was going to be all right now. This was what he'd been waiting for, that break in the dam. He knew she'd been holding it all inside, and now he can help her. Pulling her into his lap, he laid his head on top of hers as they sat in the middle of this garden, facing the one thing they both had forgotten, they were a family forever, including this little one.

"Kate, I know this is something we will never completely get over. But we move forward, for our sleeping warrior. He would not want either of us to be in so much pain. He was part of both of us. We have a place now, to come and visit him, and I promise, as the months go by, the pain will ease. And when you hold our next *bambino* in your arms, he too, will know his brother rests with him inside his heart, as he does yours and mine. I love you. We will be fine, *mi amore*, it is normal for us to grieve."

Kate clung to him like a drowning woman as his words washed over her, and her tears fell like rain, healing her...healing them. They'd be okay. She felt all the broken pieces coming back together, slipping into place. She felt whole again, but more importantly, they felt whole again. The sun was starting to rise as the sky turned pink and the fog began to lift, and she knew they must leave here for now, but grateful, so grateful, for this family, and for him.

Rising with her in his arms, Shade willed forth a rose. "It is just a bud, almost bloomed, like our sleeping warrior. The morning dew will settle upon the petals, as if it weeps. Let the rose weep for us now, *mi amore*. Let it weep and let us be done with our tears of grief. Let us lay it here for him, our sleeping warrior, so he knows we will miss him always. And when the time comes, we will plant red roses, and we will watch, as the years pass, how they grow, *si*?"

Grasping the rose in their hands, together they lay it on his grave marker. He picked her up in his arms and carried her back to the house. It was a new start, a better start for *bel rosso* and her savage lover. Eternity waited.

96

As Shade arrived with her back inside the house, he carried her upstairs to their bedroom. The sun was breaking through and they heard the whir of the electronic blinds as they lowered to block the light, leaving the room in darkness. Kate heard him strip the leathers from his skin. She dropped her own clothes to the floor, and they both climbed into their bed. She slid against him and felt his arms embrace her, as she laid her head on his chest. She felt his kiss on the top of her head, as he whispered, "*Ti amo.*" She felt his hands gently caress her hair. She was at peace, and she felt his calm. This was how it should be. His words replayed in her head, and yes, she knew there would be other babies to hold, to love. She felt the rhythm of his breathing change as he slipped into his death slumber, and she fell asleep beside him.

The day passed into night, and she felt him stirring beside her as he awoke and headed for the shower. She turned on the light by the bed and propped her pillows against the headboard and watched him as he returned to the room wearing only a towel, his hair hanging loose and wet around his face. *My beautiful vampire.*

He dropped the towel and started to put on fresh leathers. "I can feel you watching me, *mi amore*."

"Can you, lover? And can you also hear what I'm thinking?"

"*Si*. And you are too much of a distraction right now."

He walked to the bed and sat down next to her, wearing the leather pants, feet, and chest still bare, and leaned in to kiss her. "I must go, so no tempting me, please."

She reached her hand up and ran it through his damp hair, and let her fingers caress his neck, before leaning in and licking him in the middle of his chest, running her tongue up to his chin. "And what fun would that be? Not tempting you?"

She watched as he dropped his head back and moaned, before shouting, "*Cazzo!*" Standing quickly, stepping back from the bed with a chuckle. "It looks like my little minx is back."

"Oh, she's back...and she'll be waiting for you." She watched him as he finished dressing.

"*Si*. I have no doubt. Now behave yourself and kiss your savage lover goodbye."

She kissed him, and watched as he left the room, pausing briefly at the door, their eyes locked on each other. "I love you, Shade."

"*Ti amo, bel*."

She heard him head down the stairs and into the bunker. She could feel him as he left. She slid from the bed and got dressed. Leaving their bedroom to go downstairs, feeling hungry. She passed the closed door of the nursery and stopped and stared at the door. Her brain was screaming, *Don't go in*. But her heart...it was pulling at her once more. She reached for the door knob, gripped it tightly in her hand and leaned her head against the door.

She could feel the pull of the darkness, like a hand reaching out, slipping beneath the door, pulling, inviting, and calling to her. Did she hear the baby cry? She was startled by the firm touch of hands on her shoulders, and she gasped as she looked up to see Luca standing behind her.

Luca gently pulled her from the door. "Don't, Kate. Let go of the door. Come downstairs."

She let go of the doorknob and stepped back, but she knew this was a battle she'd fight every day as long as the nursery remained.

"Luca, I can't walk past this room every day. I can't look at it and not have all the emotions come back, and the dreams of him growing up in this room. It has to go. It all has to go!"

He responded, "Don't worry about that. I'll have Gi take care of it. He can have everything returned. It's not a problem."

Kate felt her agitation grow. "No! No, I can't have another baby use his things. These were *his* things." The tears started to flow again. "Don't you understand? That is *his* crib. His!"

Her raised voice drew the attention of Gi and Theresa, and she looked up to see them both coming up the stairs.

"No...I have to...it has to all be destroyed. It has to be burned, Luca. All of it."

Luca knew this was her last hurdle. They watched her healing at the baby's grave yesterday, and they saw her take Shade to visit the baby as soon as he got in. If burning it all to the ground was what it took, then he'd make it happen. He looked at Gi and nodded. "Are you sure, Kate? Is there anything you want to keep?"

In a trembling voice, she answered, "The bear...I want the bear. Burn everything else."

Luca opened the door and she stepped inside, looking around the room one last time and then picked up the stuffed bear that she had clung to on the bed.

"Now leave the room, Kate. Go with Theresa. Theresa, send up Reynaldo. We'll empty everything into the back lot, and when it's empty, we'll come get you."

Kate felt Theresa take her hand. She led Kate down the stairs, away from the nursery. She sent Reynaldo upstairs, and continued to lead her out of the house and into her private quarters. Theresa headed back to the main house and returned with a tray of hot tea and buttered toast.

"Eat, my lady, you need to eat something. They will let us know when they are ready."

Kate thought it would be hours, but in a short period of time, Luca was standing at the door, his hand extended, letting her know they were ready. She stood and took his hand and let him lead her to an obscure section of their property, where they had stacked everything; furniture, toys, books, and clothes, into a huge pile.

Luca watched her face as he led her to the pile of belongings, looking for any signs of remorse, any sign that she wanted to turn back, but he saw nothing but determination in her eyes. They all approached the huge pile as he continued to hold her hand. "Are you sure, Kate? Are you sure this is what you want?"

She nodded her head once, and softly said the word, "Yes."

He nodded at Gi, who poured gasoline onto the items, and then Luca pulled a lighter from his pocket. He held the lighter out to her and asked, "You or me?"

Kate looked down at his hand and saw the lighter, and answered him, "Me."

She took the lighter from his hand and walked to the pile. She could smell the gasoline. She stuck the lighter and held it to a pile of books and watched as the flames immediately ignited in a whoosh and spread quickly across the path of the gasoline. She stepped back from the flames, feeling the heat on her face as Luca slipped his arm around her. It was the same protective way that Shade put his arm around her shoulder.

They stood together, Gi, Reynaldo, Theresa, Luca, and Kate, as they watched the flames lick high into the sky, watching the burning embers catch the wind and float away, heard the hiss and crackle of the flames, and the pile of everything that was to be her baby's slowly disappeared. There were no tears. She felt the burden being lifted from her, the weight of all that pain being carried away in the flames. They stood together until the pile was reduced to nothing but ash and glowing embers. As they turned to walk back to the house, she walked slowly, holding onto Luca's hand, allowing the others to walk ahead.

"I need one more thing, Luca."

He stopped walking and turned to face her. "Whatever you need, Kate."

She swallowed hard. She knew she was asking too much. She knew she was putting him in a position where if he gave her what she asked for, he would be going against Shade's instruction. But she knew this was what she needed.

"I want you to teach me to fight, like a warrior."

He dropped her hand and took one step back from her. He hadn't seen this coming. But there were images flashing through his head, of master, unleashing his own anger on the rogues over the loss of this baby, and he knew she must feel some of that same anger. He saw her as she threw herself at the feeder, with no thought of her own safety. And he heard her words, *Warriors are born, not trained.*

He knew Shade would be angry, hell, more than angry, if... No, not *if, when* he found out. He looked down at his feet and shook his head, because he couldn't believe the words that were about to come out of his mouth. He took her hand again and started walking back toward the house as he answered her, "I will teach you to fight."

Sample of Book 2

The Turning

Book Two in the Medici Warrior Series

Rissa has made an appointment to meet with a competitor at noon. They occasionally worked together on large projects, although technically, she was a rival to her business, taking more middle-class clientele than Rissa did. She had called and wanted to speak with Rissa about a specific florist she used on a regular basis. Rissa didn't normally share information on her business, but she knows the client and knows they could not possibly afford her services, so she thinks she will throw her competitor a bone. Besides, she is feeling generous. She is still basking in the glow of Alec's approval of the role she played in Shade and Kate's loss of that half-breed thing she was carrying around.

Rissa doesn't deal with the middle-class if she can help it. She is above that now. Her business has grown leaps and bounds, and she is determined to keep it there as the event planner for the elite. One false move in this town could wreak havoc with her reputation and put her on the blacklist, so every client is screened and chosen to meet her select criteria. Driving up to her friend's business, she feels a little nervous, the Capital Hill district has some great attractions, like the Eastern Market, but it is not the upscale neighborhood of G-town.

As the meeting progresses, her rival is most appreciative, but then everyone is when they need her. All in all, it is entertaining to see how she operates and to intimidate her as much as she can. Rissa wraps up the meeting as soon as possible. She has a huge gala for the foundation tonight, and she wants to get home and relax before the event. It is a huge event she and Alec attend every year, and all the right people will be there.

Excusing herself to use the restroom before leaving, she freshens her make-up, says her goodbyes and leaves. Eager to get back on familiar turf, she hurries to her car, throws her designer tote bag on the seat next to her and notices a scrolled note lying on the passenger seat. *What in the hell is this?* Picking up the note, she unrolls it and begins to read...

'Rissie,
My angel, I let you go once.

It is not a mistake I will
make twice.

Max'

"Max." His name is out of her mouth before she can think. Suddenly, her head is spinning, her heart is racing, and her blood begins to pound in her head. She throws her head back on the seat and takes some deep breaths. If Alec ever knew! She has to control this, Alec will feel her, feel her turmoil. *What is Max's purpose? And why now?*

Firing up the engine and putting her foot to the pedal, she speeds out as her thoughts churn in her head, the memories of her and Max, how he smelled, how she felt in his arms, his kiss. *Stop it, Rissa! Stop it!*

Slamming on the breaks, she rips the note to shreds and flings it out the window. *Max! Why, why, why?*

Taking the longest route home, she stews about this unexpected intrusion and tries to get him out of her head before returning home to Alec. *If Alec ever knew...*

End of Sample

About the Author

Emily Bex is an avid life-long reader, and a first time writer of the epic six book Medici Warrior Series. As she says, "Why start small?"

She worked for over twenty years in marketing, developing ad campaigns, catalogs, product launches and promotional literature. She figured if she could write creatively about products, then surely she could write something about these characters that were rattling around inside her brain.

She currently lives in Virginia, but has used her extensive love of travel, both foreign and domestic, to create the backdrop for her characters to play out their story.

Be Sure to Stay Caught Up with the Series Now Available from Foundations Book Publishing!

Book Two: The Turning

Immortality beckons.

Unable to escape crushing grief, Kate needs an outlet to channel her anguish. Turning to Luca, she pleads to be trained to fight like a warrior, but such a thing is in direct violation of Shade's commands.
If she can get Luca to agree, her training must be done in secret.

Unfortunately, any training is too little too late. Intent on crushing Shade, the Aries coven is pressing in on him from all sides. Shade's only weakness is Kate, who becomes their perfect bait.

While Kate has been made stronger, as long as she's mortal, her life is in peril. But going through the turning to become immortal would be a big gamble to her survival.

So many decisions, too many obstacles. This second installment in a vampire saga will draw you in from the first page to the spellbinding end.

Book Three: The Medici Queen

The sexy, powerful King Shade Medici, intends to increase his coven and territories to include the U.S. The new Medici Queen proves she can hold her own beside her king. She carries rare abilities believed extinct by the vampire community. She also possesses something never seen in the vampire world. What will it mean to their kind?

A male heir must be produced to carry on the Medici line.The royal couple has many new plans in business to advance their hold in the States. Not everyone is happy about it. The sprawling Medici estate is a threat to its neighboring coven, controlled by Max. Their lifestyle is Rissa's greatest envy. Secrets will be revealed, old scores will be settled, and many will fall.

View the Medici Warrior Series Here:

https://www.emilybex.com/books/

Make sure to stalk me!

Instagram:
https://bit.ly/3dAaO5k

Facebook:
http://bit.ly/3k5GHUC

Goodreads:
http://bit.ly/3ukYcVU

Twitter:
https://bit.ly/3s6m3GG

Bookbub:
http://bit.ly/2ZBJ9ZM

Website:
https://www.emilybex.com/

Printed in the USA
CPSIA information can be obtained
at www.ICGtesting.com
LVHW061730270824
789448LV00020B/138